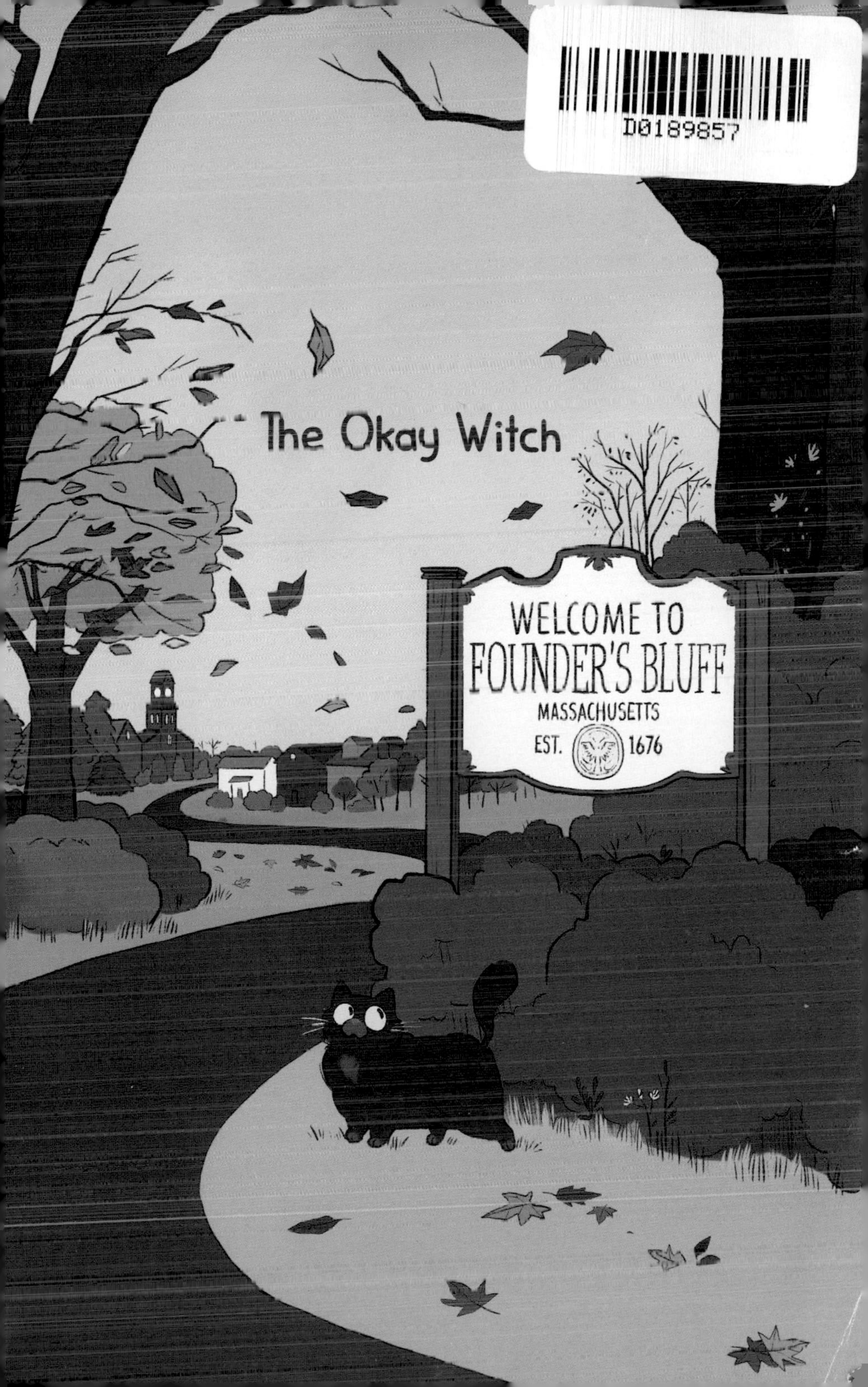
The Okay Witch
WELCOME TO
FOUNDER'S BLUFF
MASSACHUSETTS
EST. 1676

For Team Steinkellner.

I love this family of ours.

ALADDIN | An imprint of Simon & Schuster Children's Publishing Division | 1230 Avenue of the Americas, New York, New York 10020 | First Aladdin edition September 2019 | Copyright © 2019 by Emma Steinkellner | All rights reserved, including the right of reproduction in whole or in part in any form. | ALADDIN and related logo are registered trademarks of Simon & Schuster, Inc. | For information about special discounts for bulk purchases, please contact Simon & Schuster Special Sales at 1-866-506-1949 or business@simonandschuster.com. | The Simon & Schuster Speakers Bureau can bring authors to your live event. For more information or to book an event contact the Simon & Schuster Speakers Bureau at 1-866-248-3049 or visit our website at www.simonspeakers.com. | Designed by Karin Paprocki and Emma Steinkellner | The illustrations for this book were rendered digitally. | The text of this book was set in Minou Regular. | Manufactured in China 0420 SCP | 10 9 8 7 6 5 | Library of Congress Control Number 2018960169 | ISBN 9781534431461 (hc) | ISBN 9781534431454 (pbk) | ISBN 9781534431478 (eBook)

THE OKAY WITCH

By Emma Steinkellner

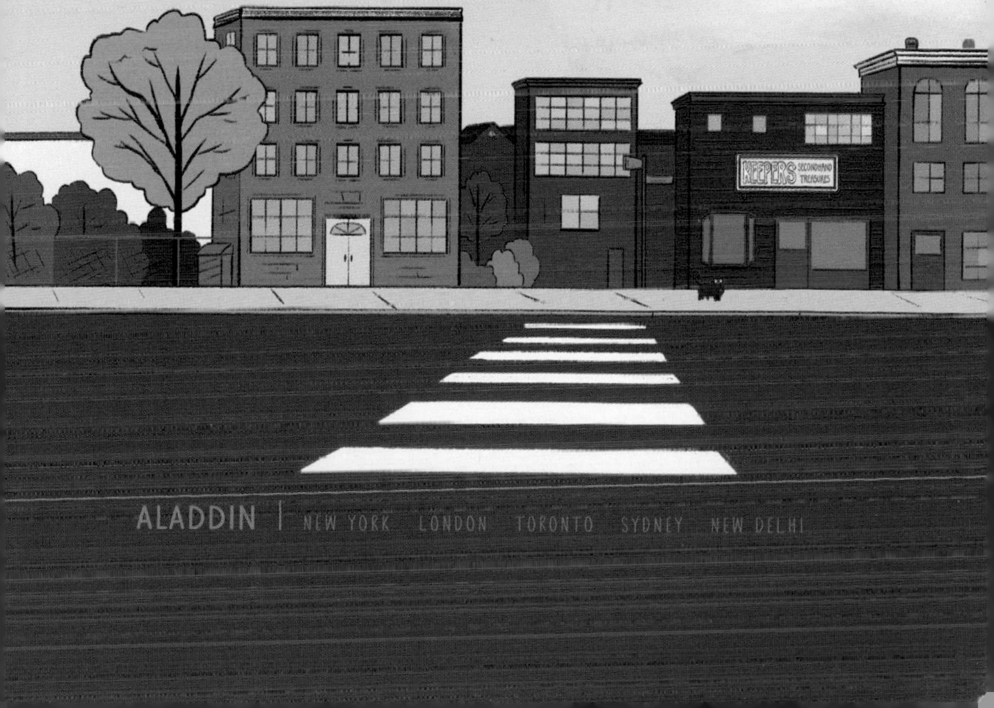
KEEPERS SECONDHAND TREASURES

ALADDIN | NEW YORK LONDON TORONTO SYDNEY NEW DELHI

CHAPTER 1

Something Wicked This Way Comes

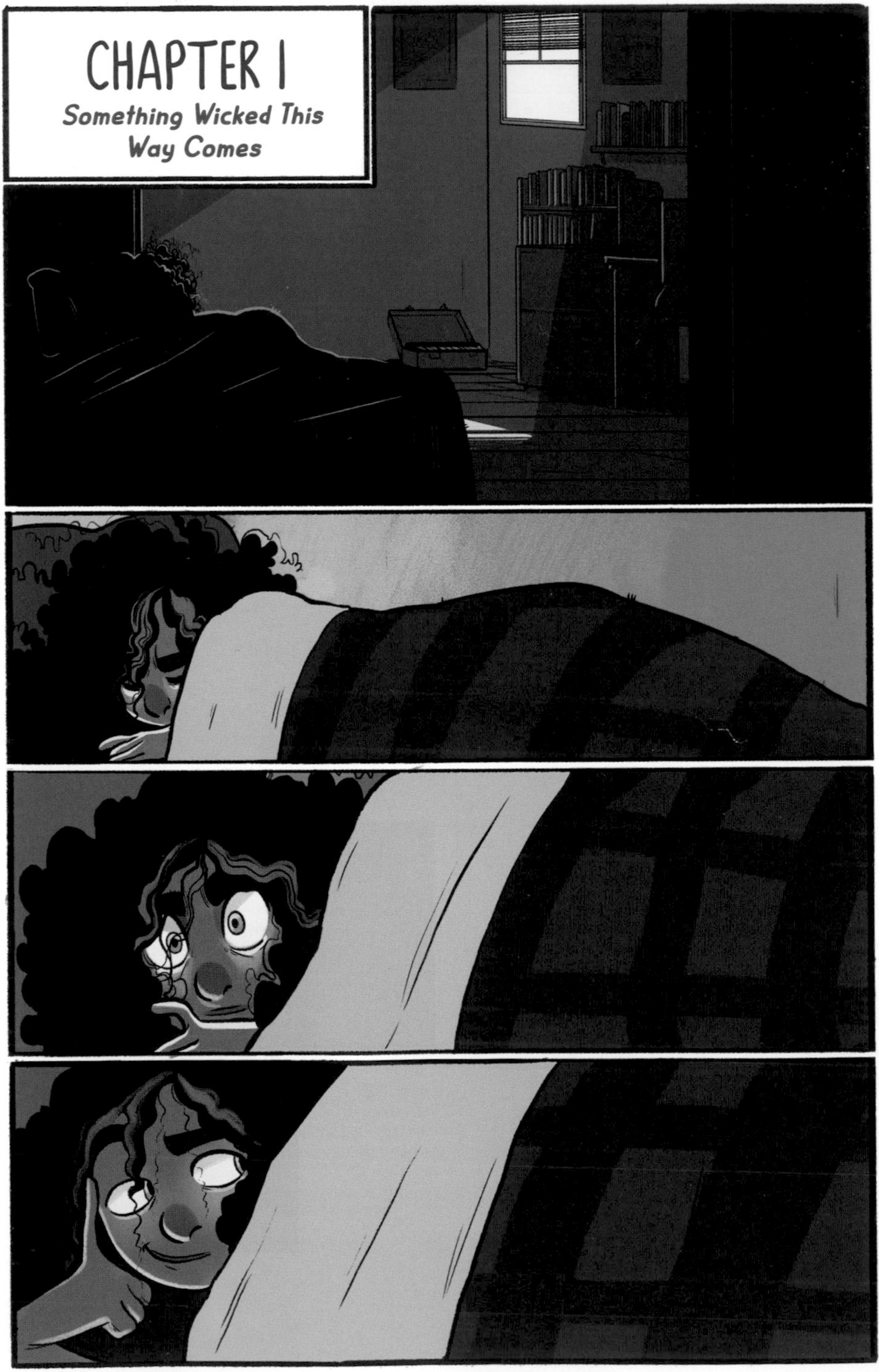

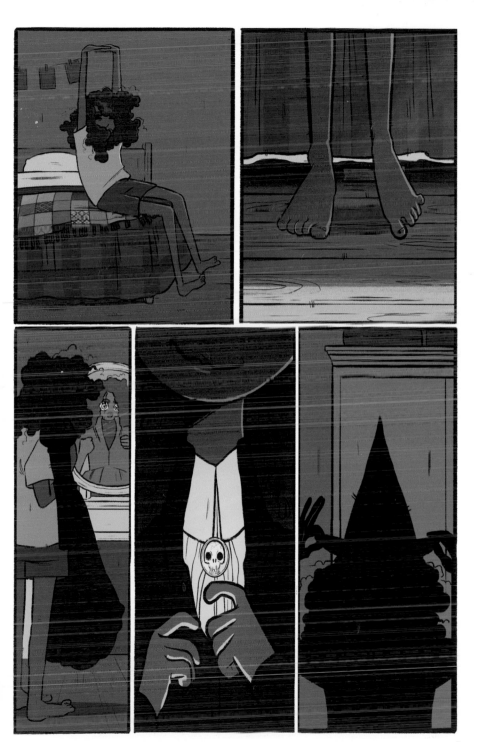

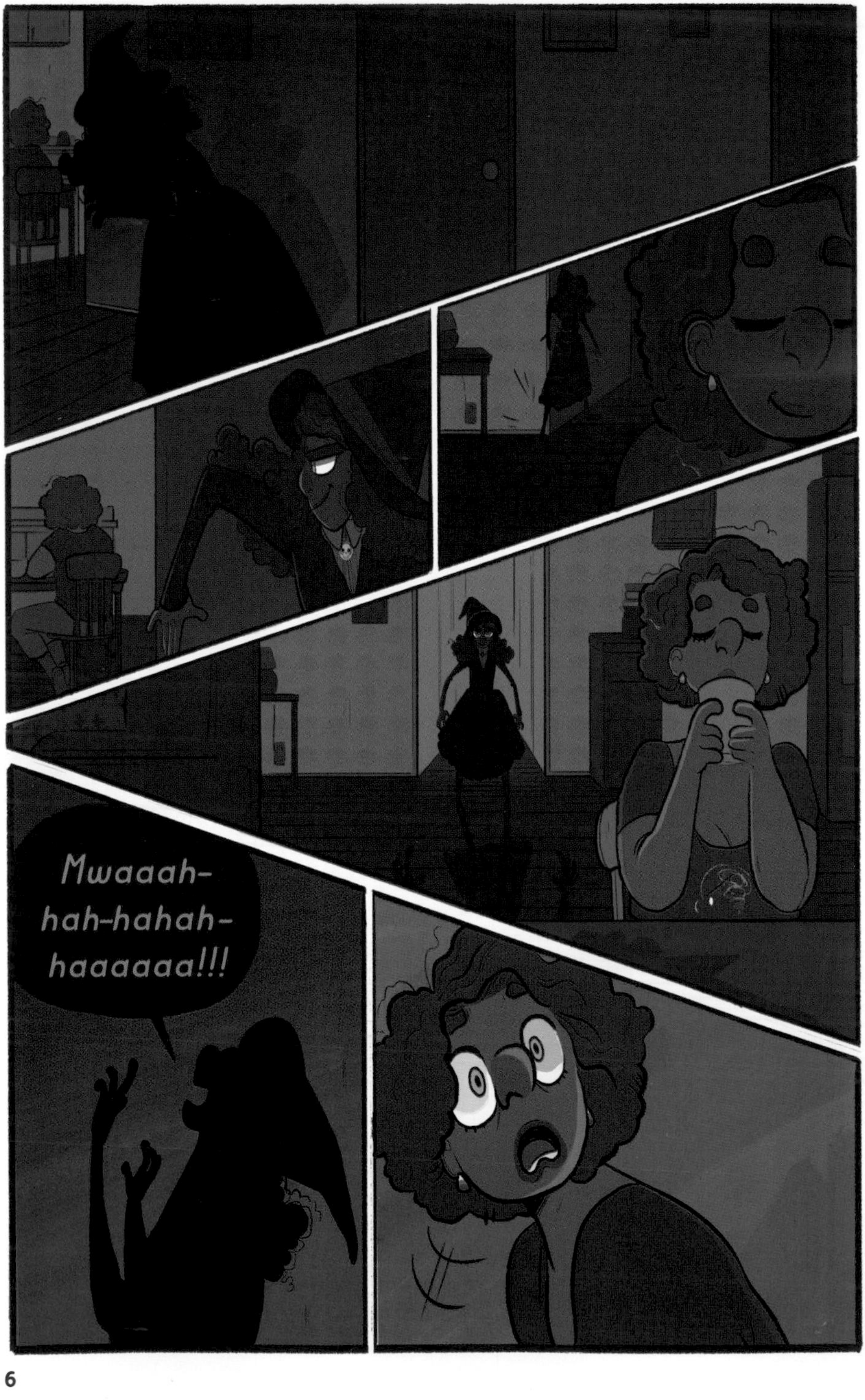
Mwaaah-
hah-hahah-
haaaaaa!!!

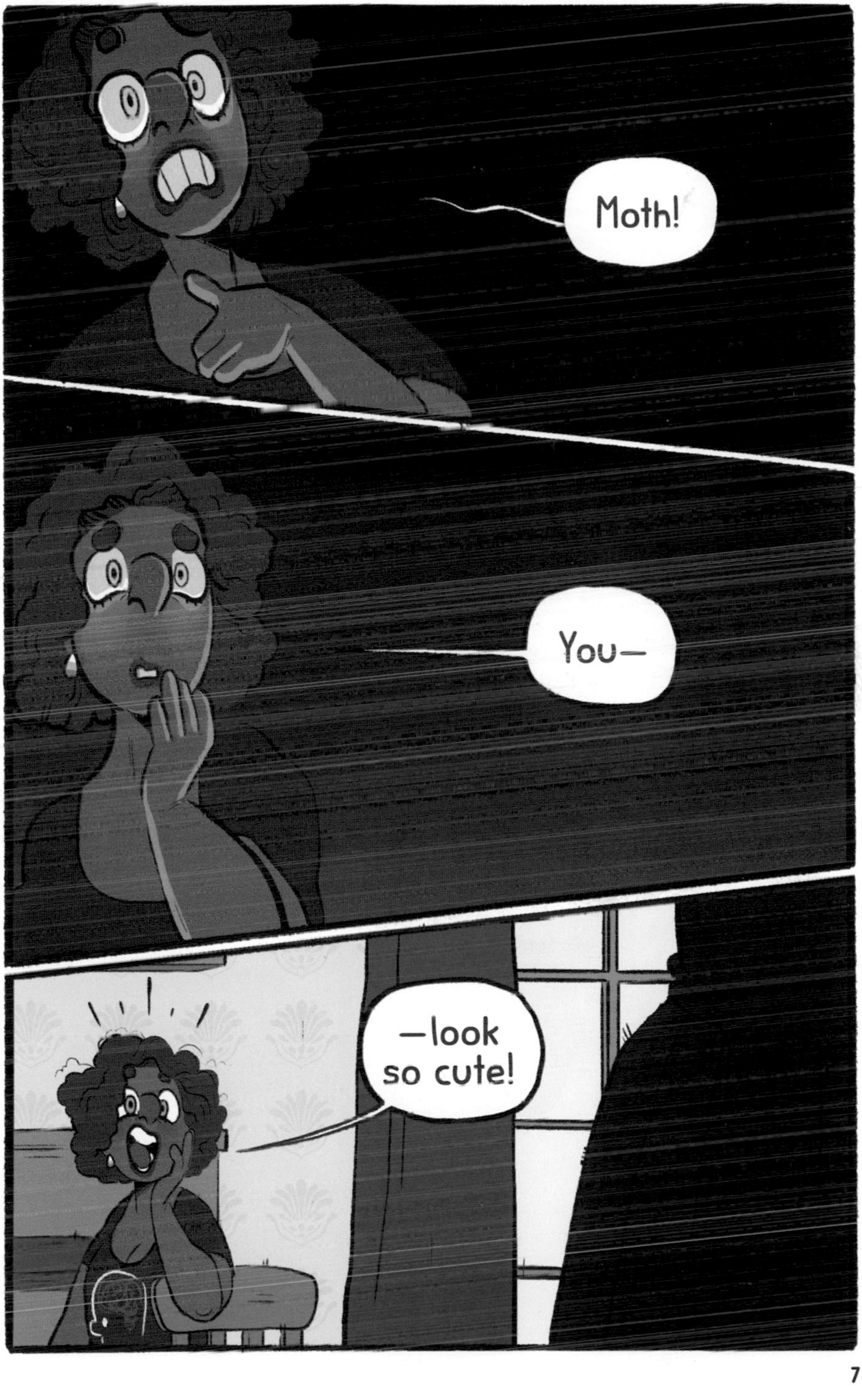
Moth!
You—
—look so cute!

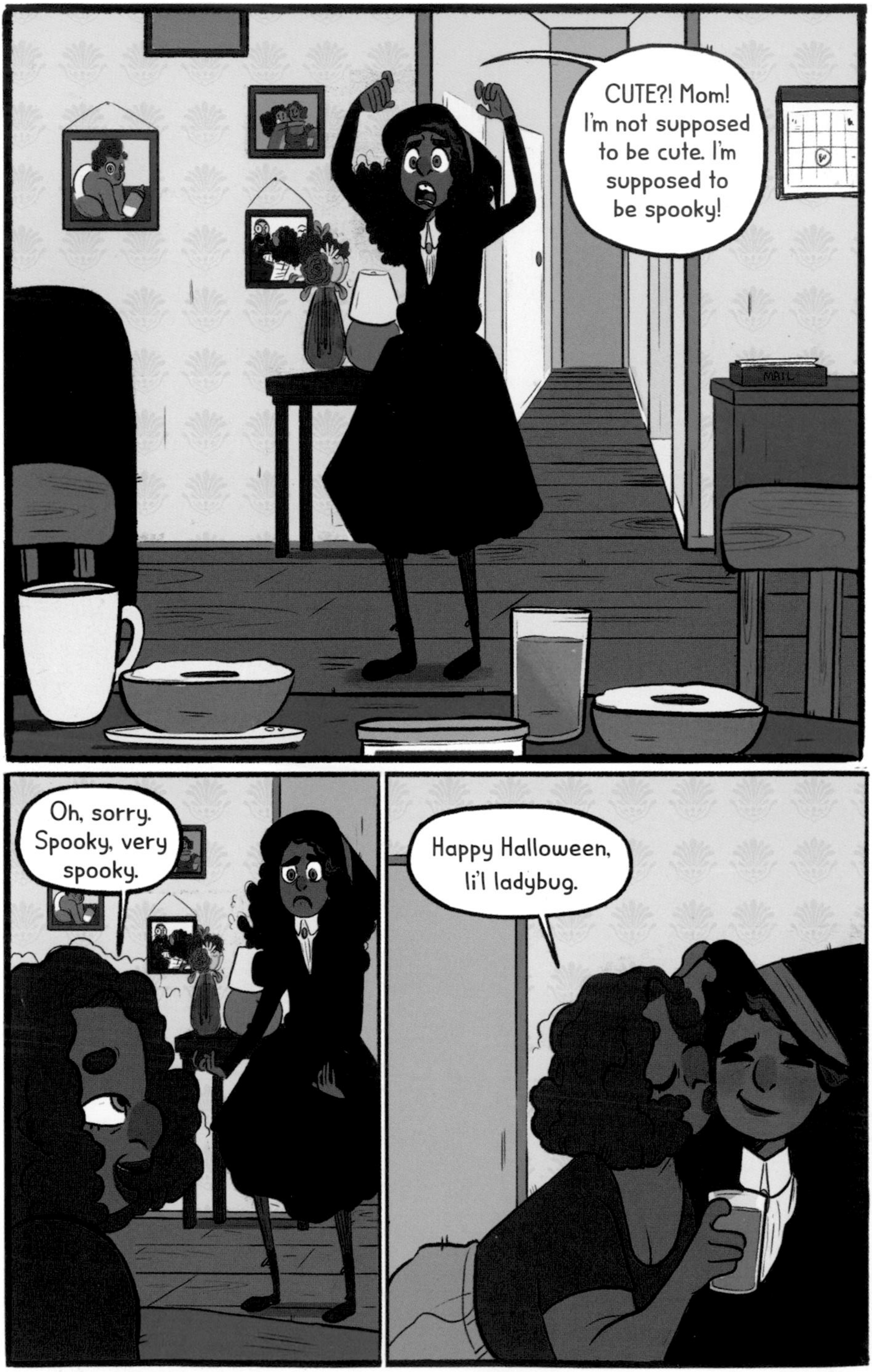
CUTE?! Mom! I'm not supposed to be cute. I'm supposed to be spooky!
MAIL
Oh, sorry. Spooky, very spooky.
Happy Halloween, li'l ladybug.

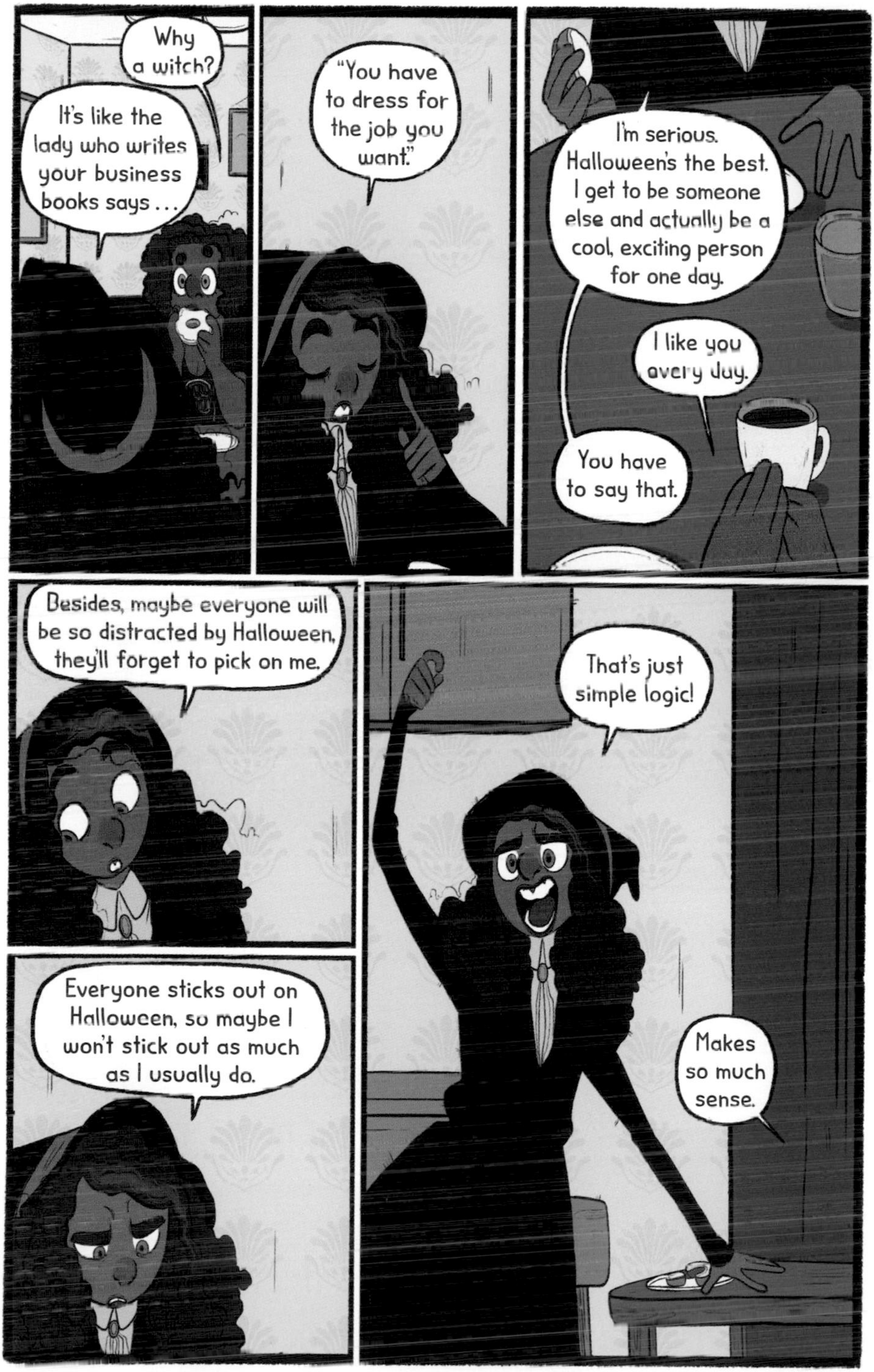
Why a witch?
It's like the lady who writes your business books says . . .
"You have to dress for the job you want."
I'm serious. Halloween's the best. I get to be someone else and actually be a cool, exciting person for one day.
I like you every day.
You have to say that.
Besides, maybe everyone will be so distracted by Halloween, they'll forget to pick on me.
Everyone sticks out on Halloween, so maybe I won't stick out as much as I usually do.
That's just simple logic!
Makes so much sense.

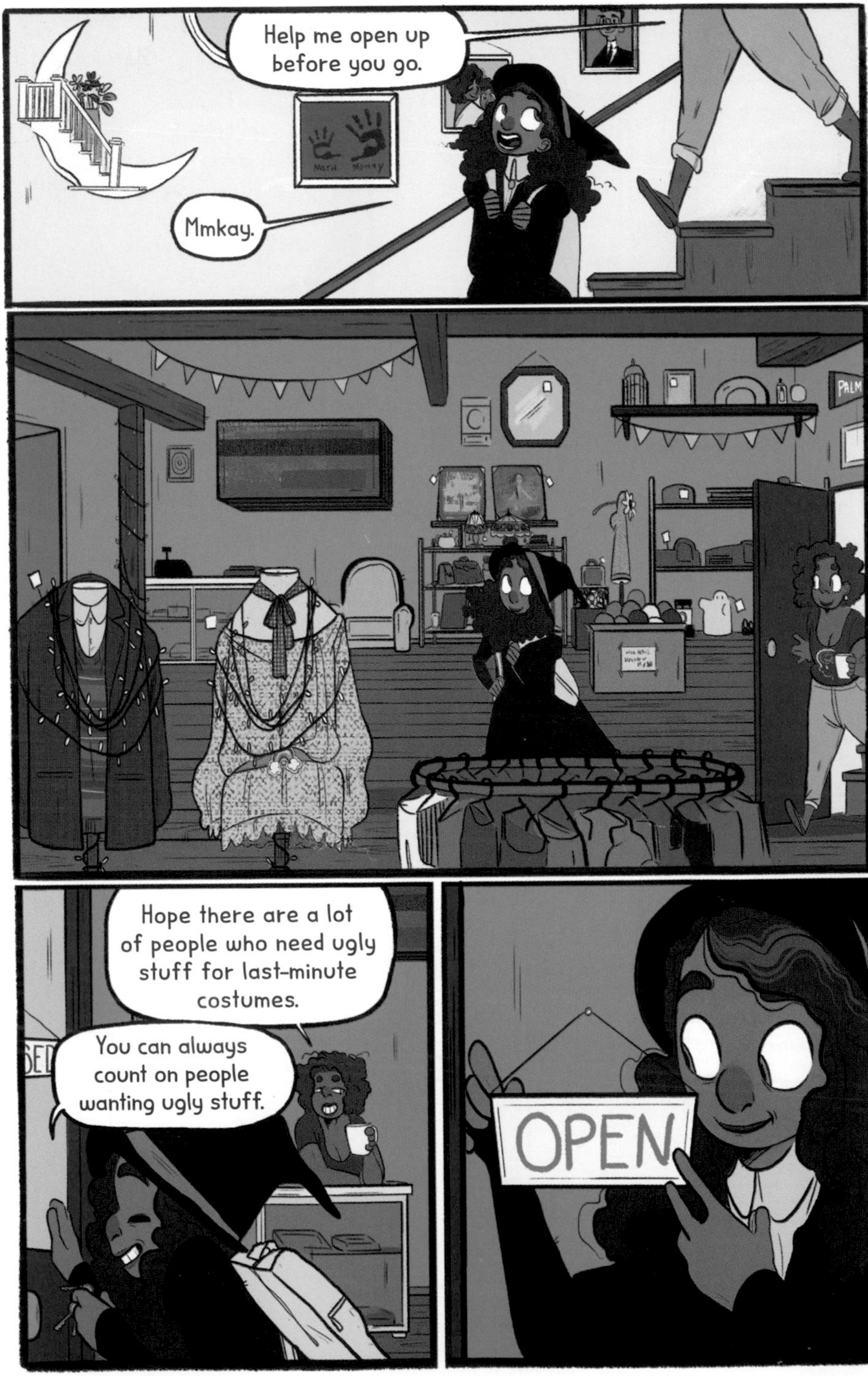
Help me open up before you go.
MOTH
MOMMY
Mmkay.
PALM
Hope there are a lot of people who need ugly stuff for last-minute costumes.
You can always count on people wanting ugly stuff.
OPEN

Happy Halloween, Mr. Laszlo!

In Loving Memory of Joe Laszlo
1932 – 2012
First owner of Keepers Secondhand Treasures

In Loving Memory of Joe Laszlo
1932 – 2012
First owner of Keepers Secondhand Treasures

If you leave without giving your mother a hug, Halloween is canceled.

Bye, Momma, love you.

Have a good one, bubba.

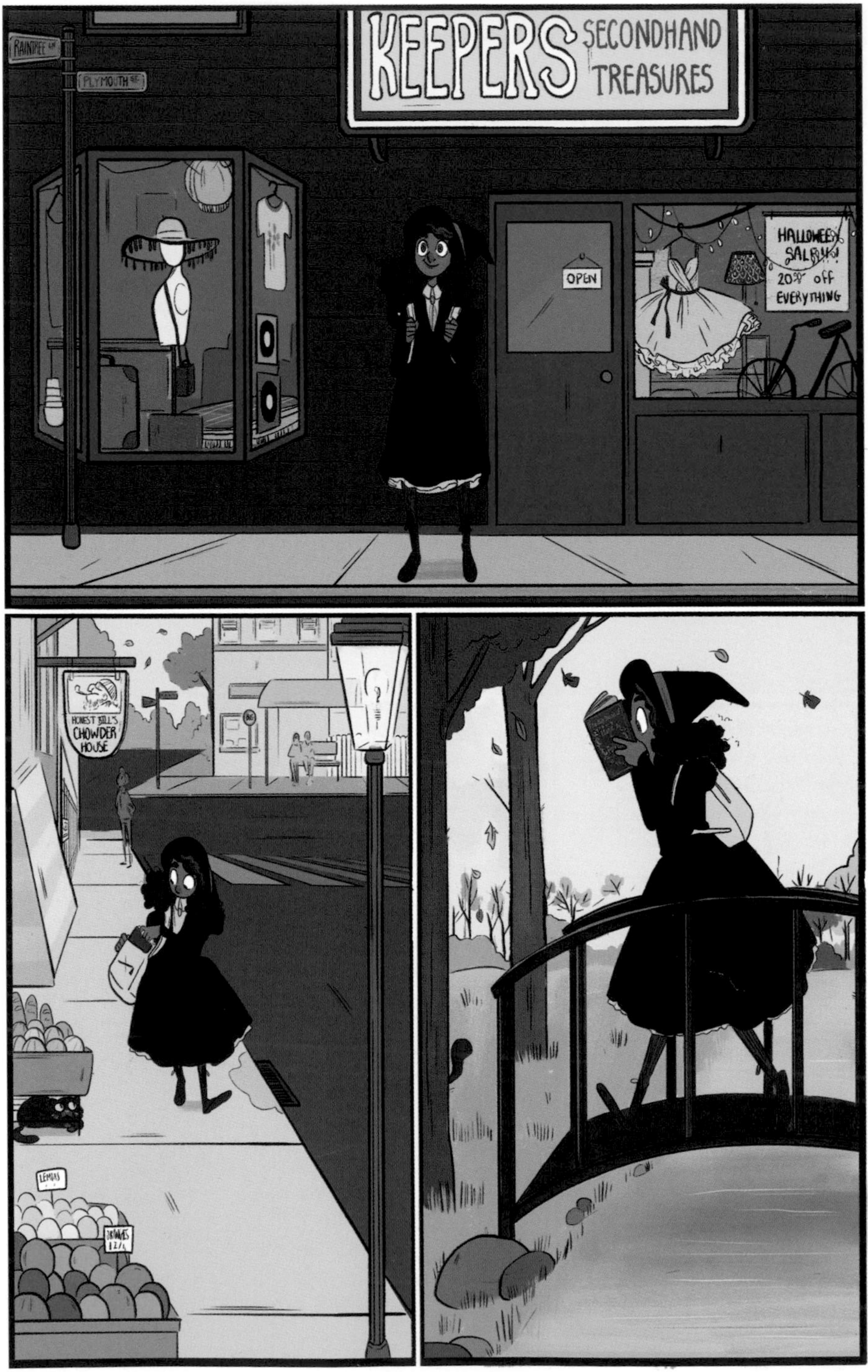
PLYMOUTH ST
KEEPERS
SECONDHAND TREASURES
OPEN
20% off
EVERYTHING
HONEST BILL'S
CHOWDER HOUSE
LEMONS

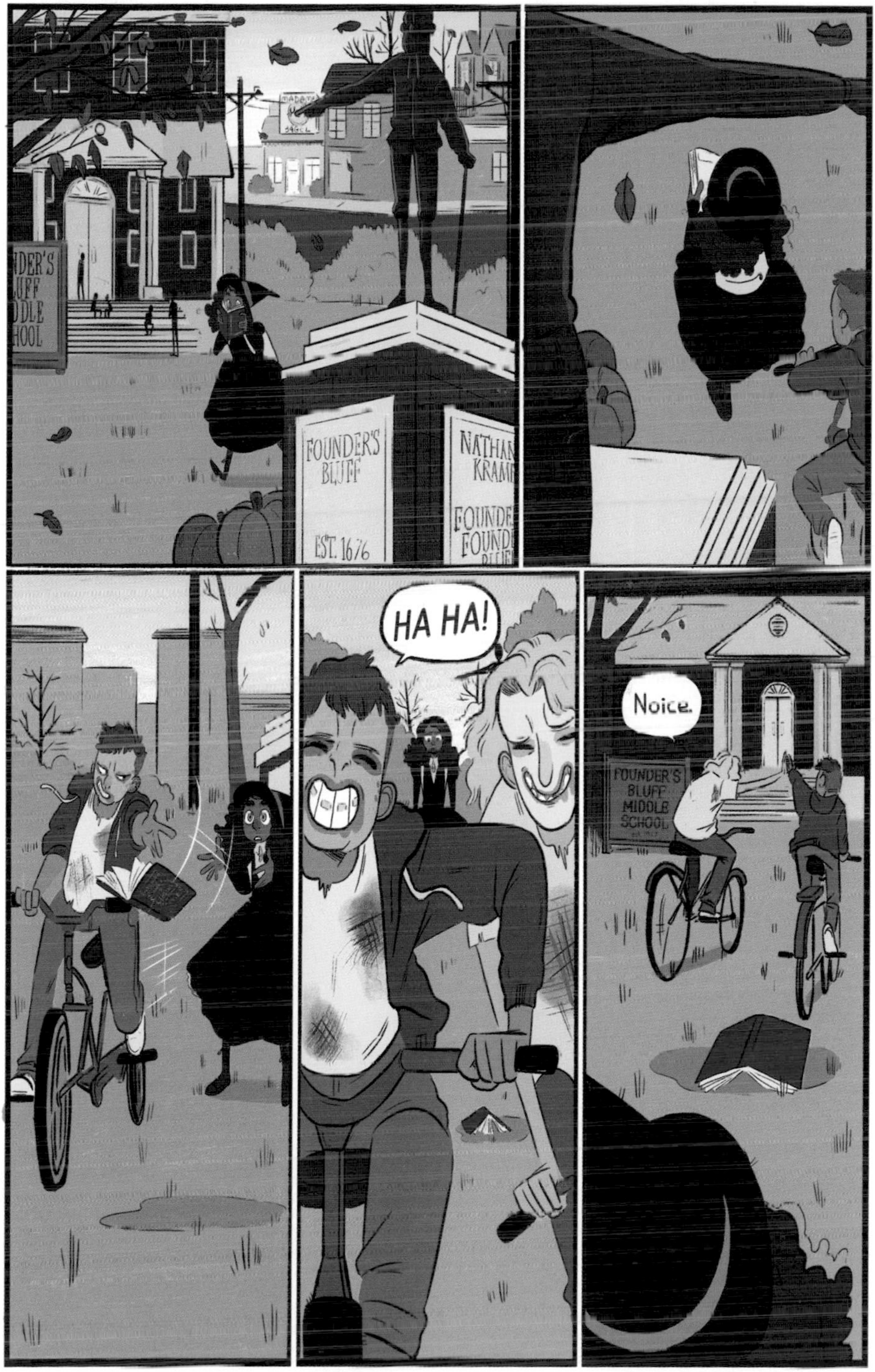
FOUNDER'S BLUFF
EST. 1676
HA HA!
Noice.
FOUNDER'S BLUFF MIDDLE SCHOOL

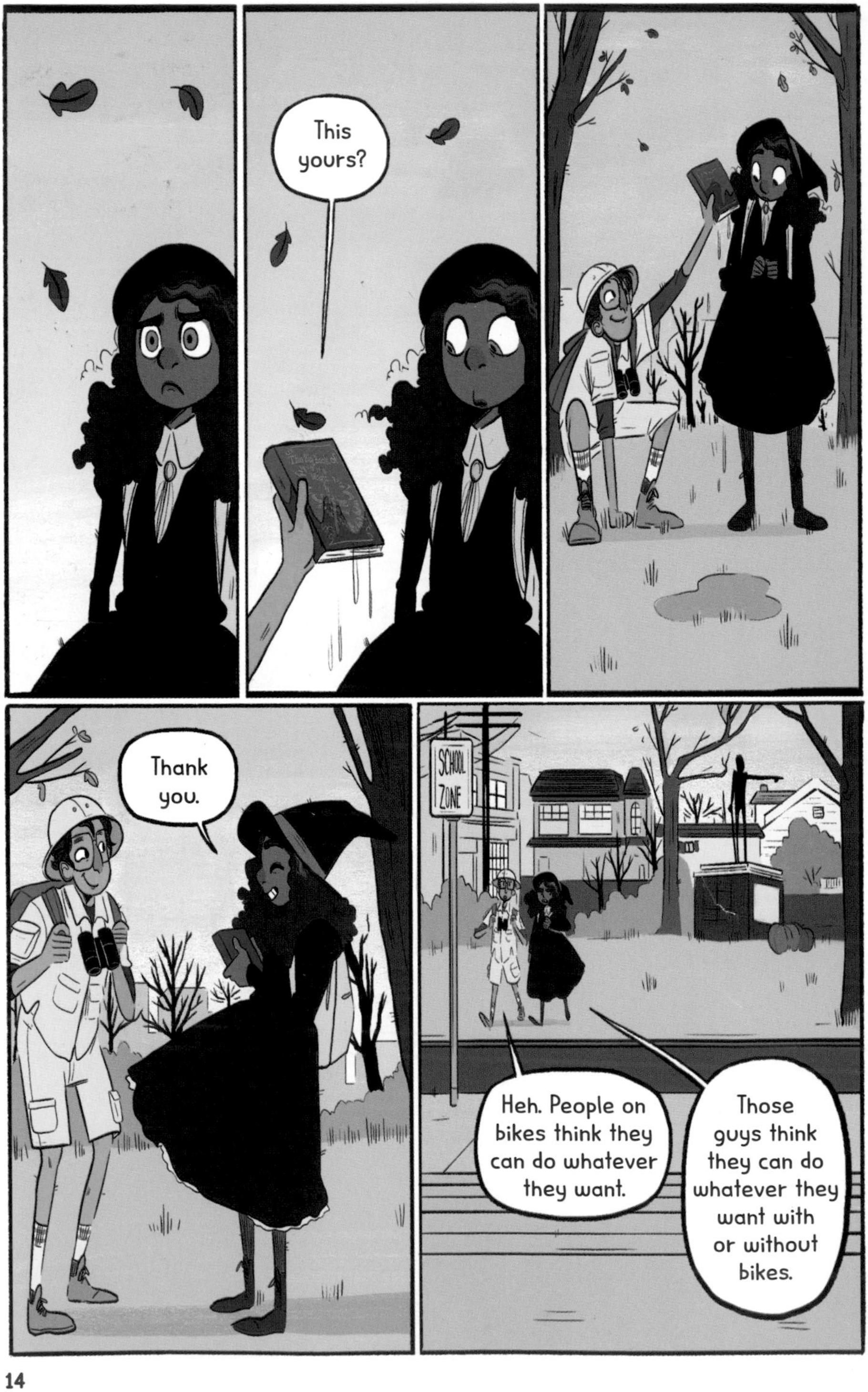
This yours?
Thank you.
SCHOOL ZONE
Heh. People on bikes think they can do whatever they want.
Those guys think they can do whatever they want with or without bikes.

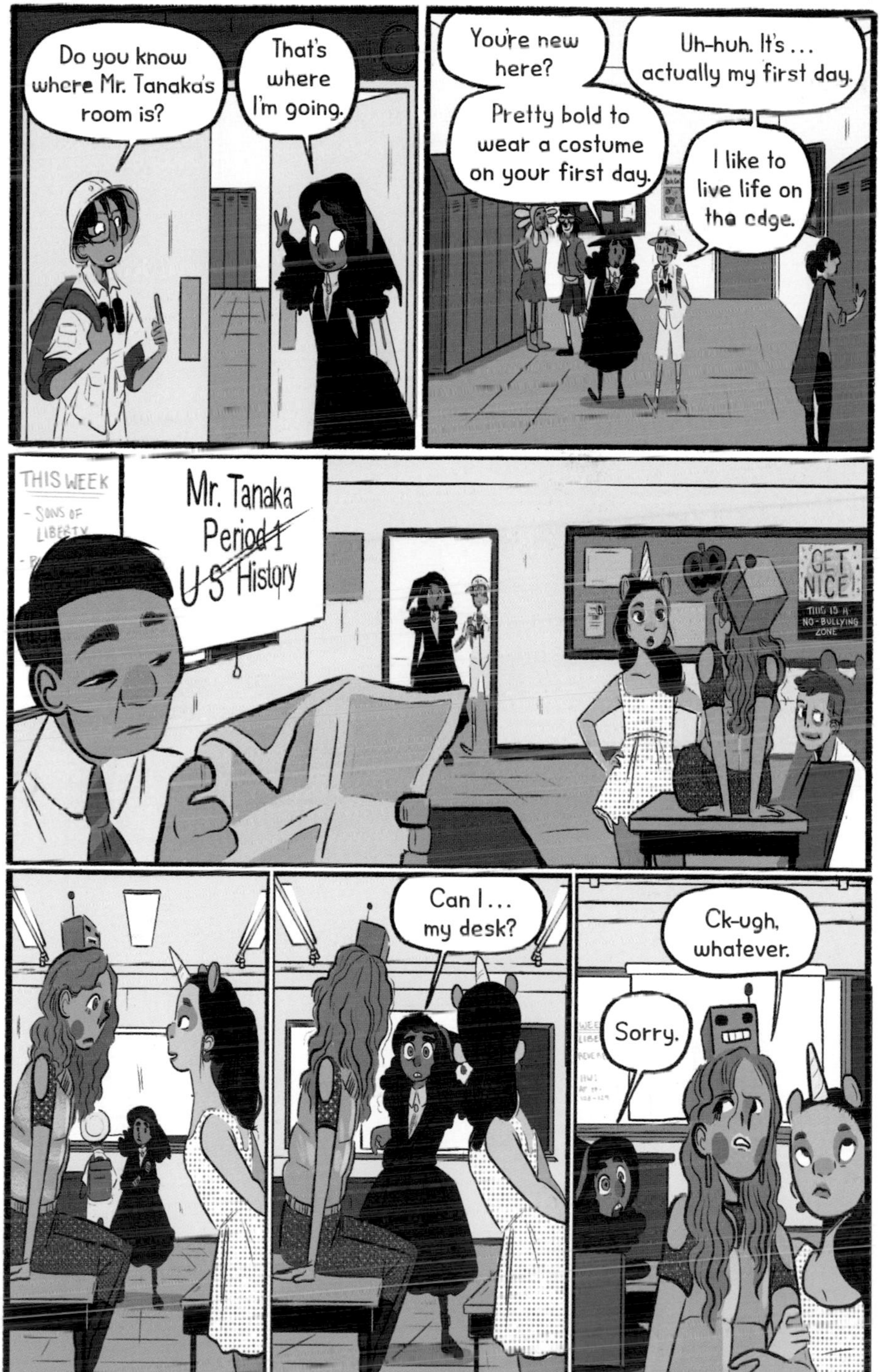

Do you know where Mr. Tanaka's room is?
That's where I'm going.
You're new here?
Uh-huh. It's . . . actually my first day.
Pretty bold to wear a costume on your first day.
I like to live life on the edge.
THIS WEEK
- SONS OF LIBERTY
Mr. Tanaka
Period 1
US History
GET NICE!
THIS IS A NO-BULLYING ZONE
Can I . . . my desk?
Ck-ugh, whatever.
Sorry.

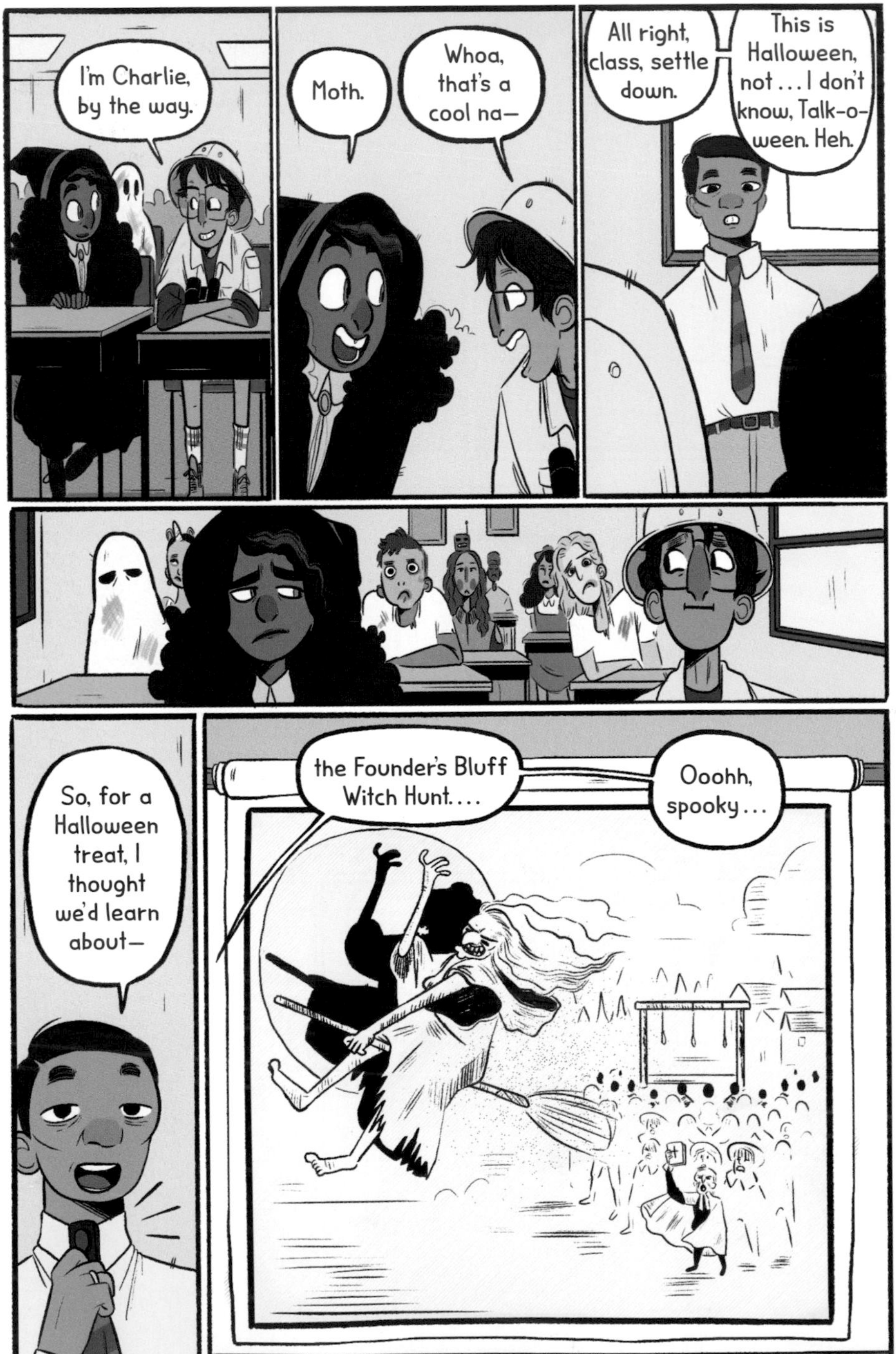
I'm Charlie,
by the way.
Moth.
Whoa,
that's a
cool na—
All right,
class, settle
down.
This is
Halloween,
not . . . I don't
know, Talk-o-
ween. Heh.
So, for a
Halloween
treat, I
thought
we'd learn
about—
the Founder's Bluff
Witch Hunt. . . .
Ooohh,
spooky . . .

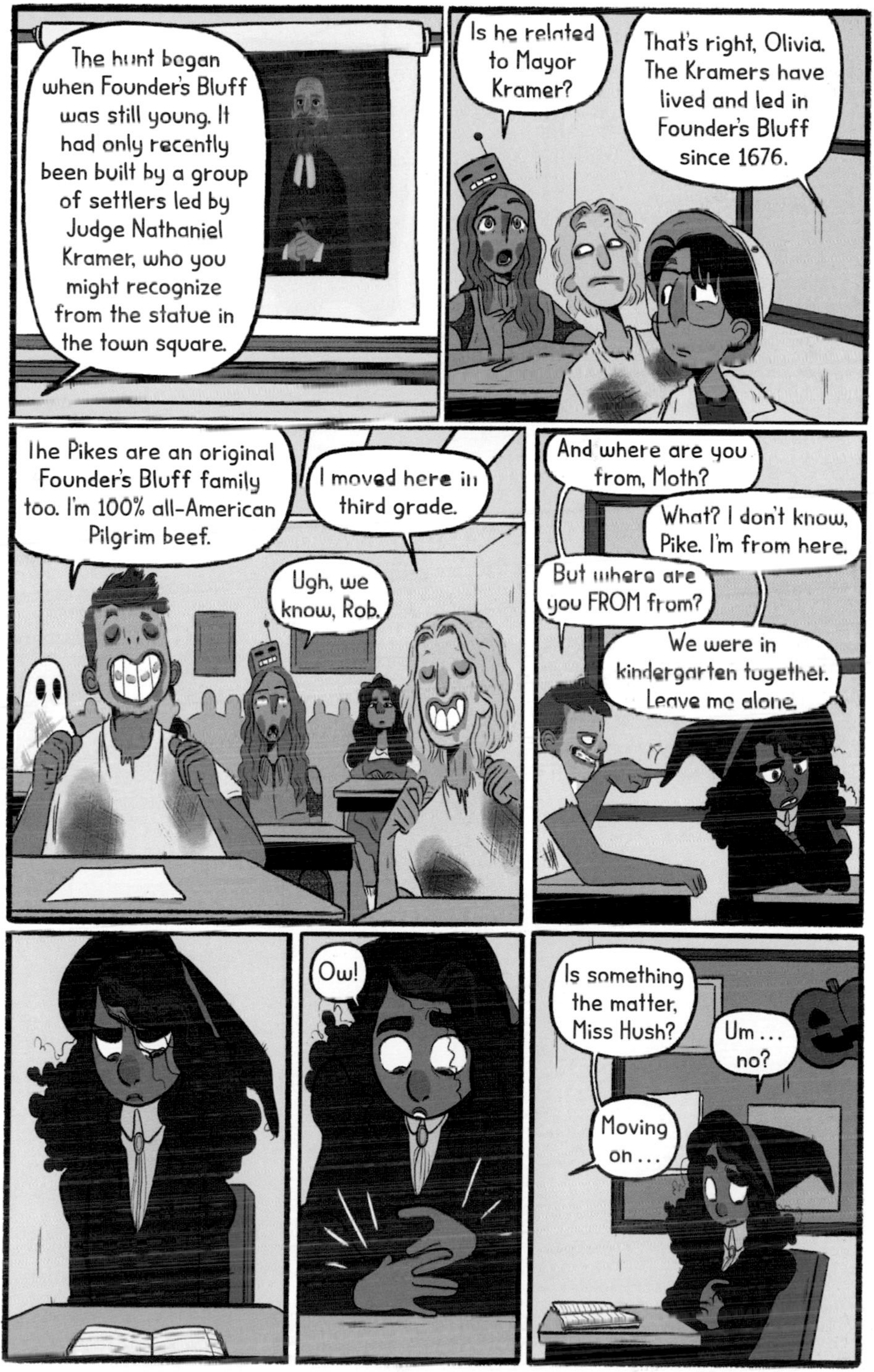
The hunt began when Founder's Bluff was still young. It had only recently been built by a group of settlers led by Judge Nathaniel Kramer, who you might recognize from the statue in the town square.
Is he related to Mayor Kramer?
That's right, Olivia. The Kramers have lived and led in Founder's Bluff since 1676.
The Pikes are an original Founder's Bluff family too. I'm 100% all-American Pilgrim beef.
I moved here in third grade.
Ugh, we know, Rob.
And where are you from, Moth?
What? I don't know, Pike. I'm from here.
But where are you FROM from?
We were in kindergarten together. Leave me alone.
Ow!
Is something the matter, Miss Hush?
Um ... no?
Moving on ...

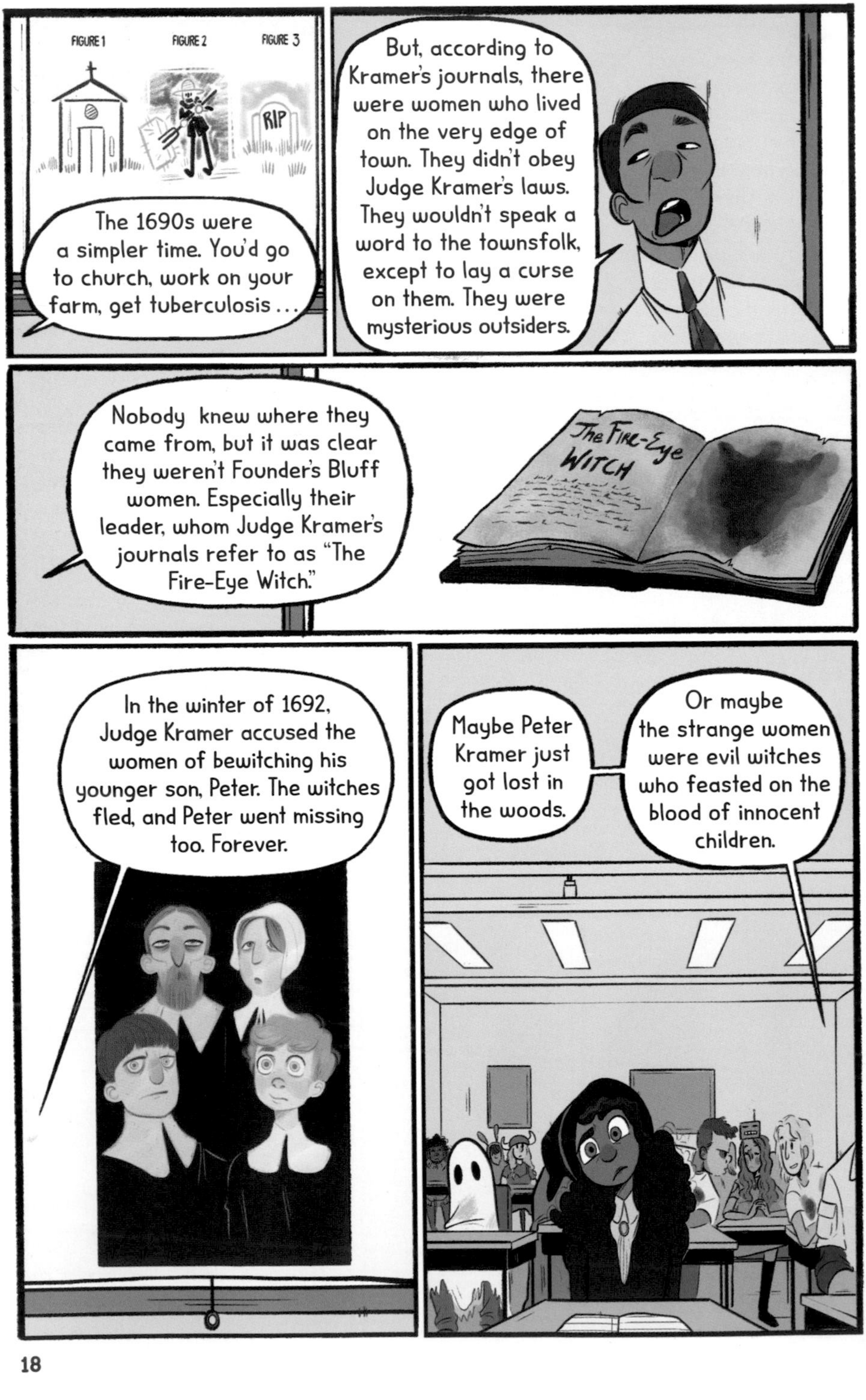
FIGURE 1
FIGURE 2
FIGURE 3
RIP
The 1690s were a simpler time. You'd go to church, work on your farm, get tuberculosis . . .
But, according to Kramer's journals, there were women who lived on the very edge of town. They didn't obey Judge Kramer's laws. They wouldn't speak a word to the townsfolk, except to lay a curse on them. They were mysterious outsiders.
Nobody knew where they came from, but it was clear they weren't Founder's Bluff women. Especially their leader, whom Judge Kramer's journals refer to as "The Fire-Eye Witch."
The Fire-Eye WITCH
In the winter of 1692, Judge Kramer accused the women of bewitching his younger son, Peter. The witches fled, and Peter went missing too. Forever.
Maybe Peter Kramer just got lost in the woods.
Or maybe the strange women were evil witches who feasted on the blood of innocent children.

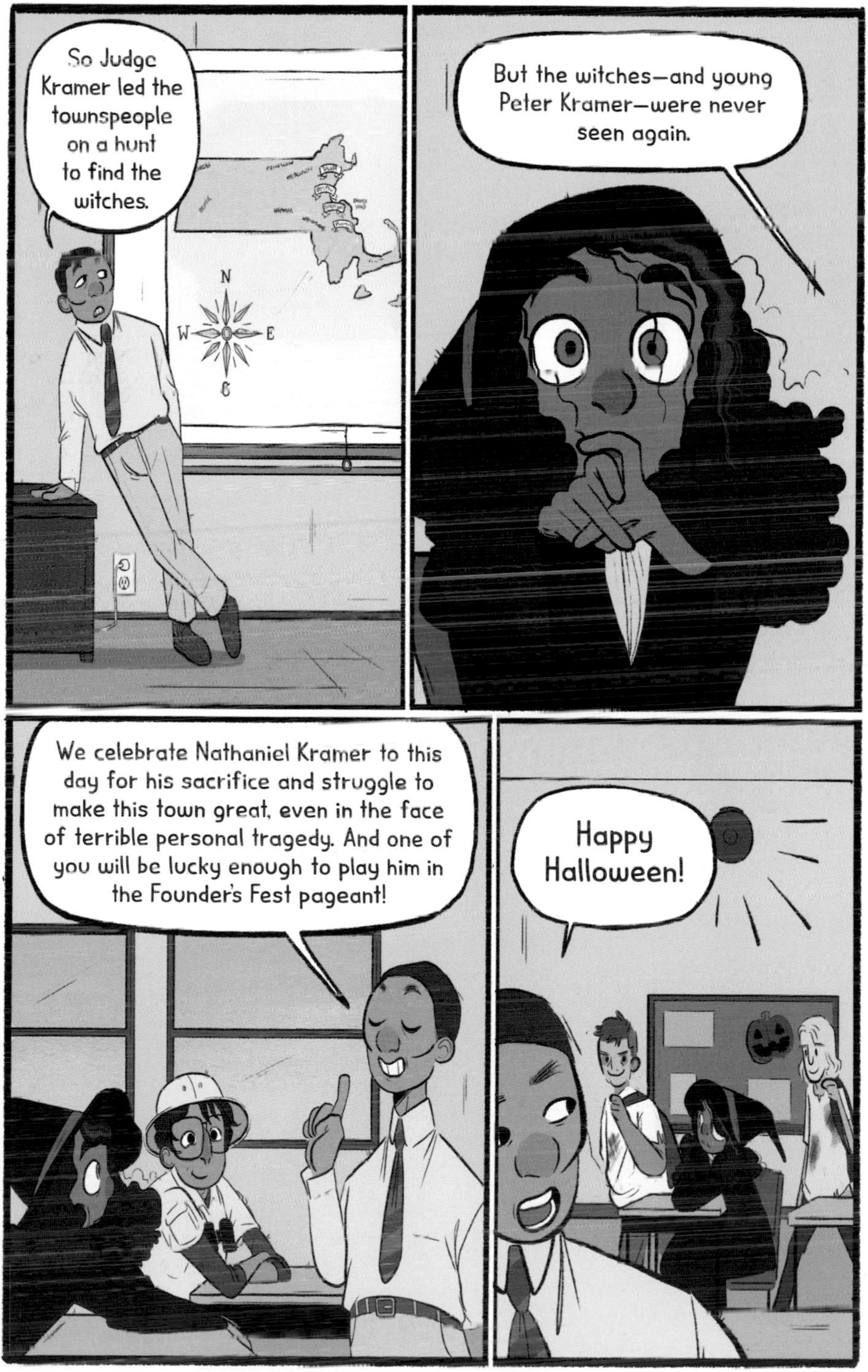
So Judge Kramer led the townspeople on a hunt to find the witches.
But the witches—and young Peter Kramer—were never seen again.
We celebrate Nathaniel Kramer to this day for his sacrifice and struggle to make this town great, even in the face of terrible personal tragedy. And one of you will be lucky enough to play him in the Founder's Fest pageant!
Happy Halloween!

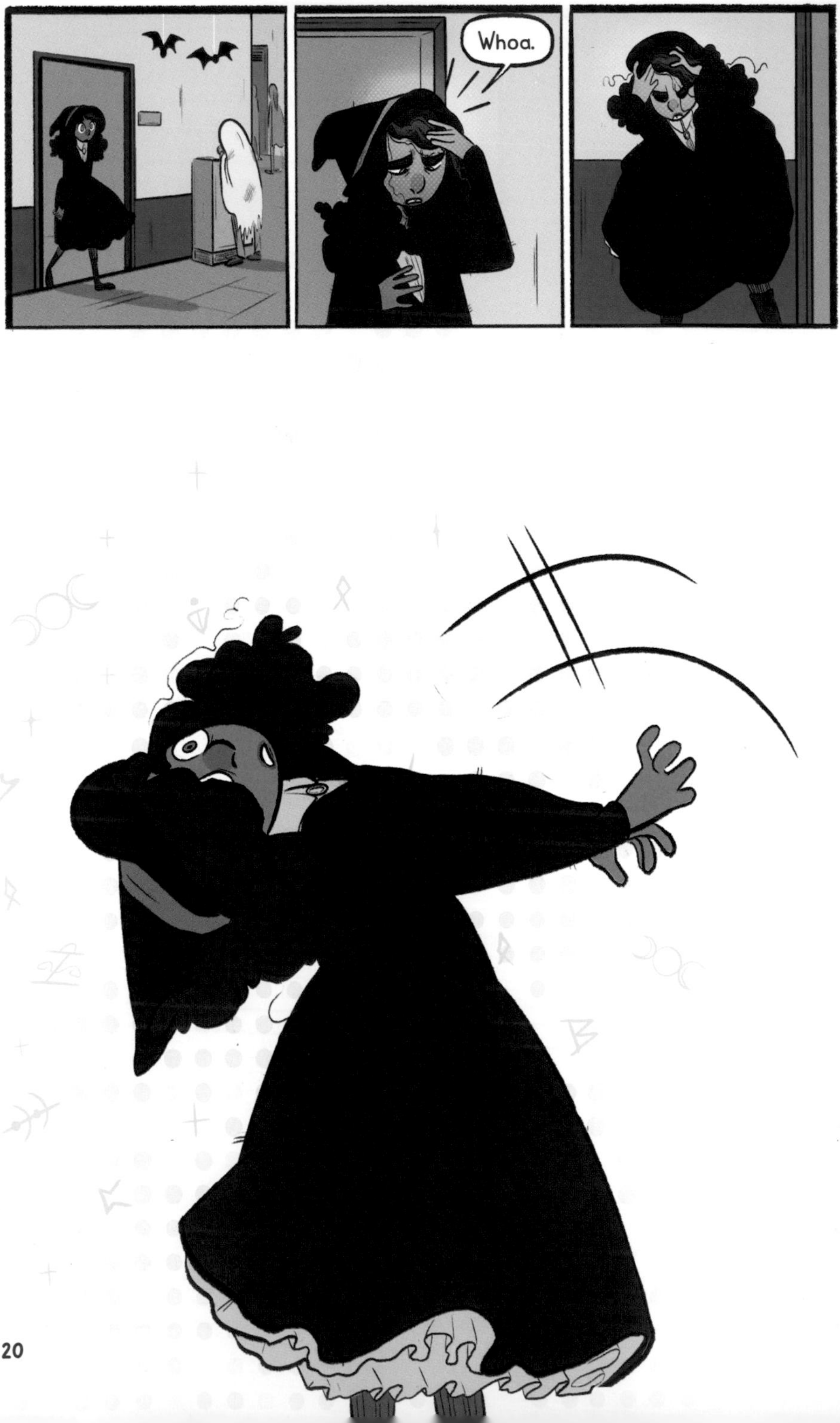
Whoa.

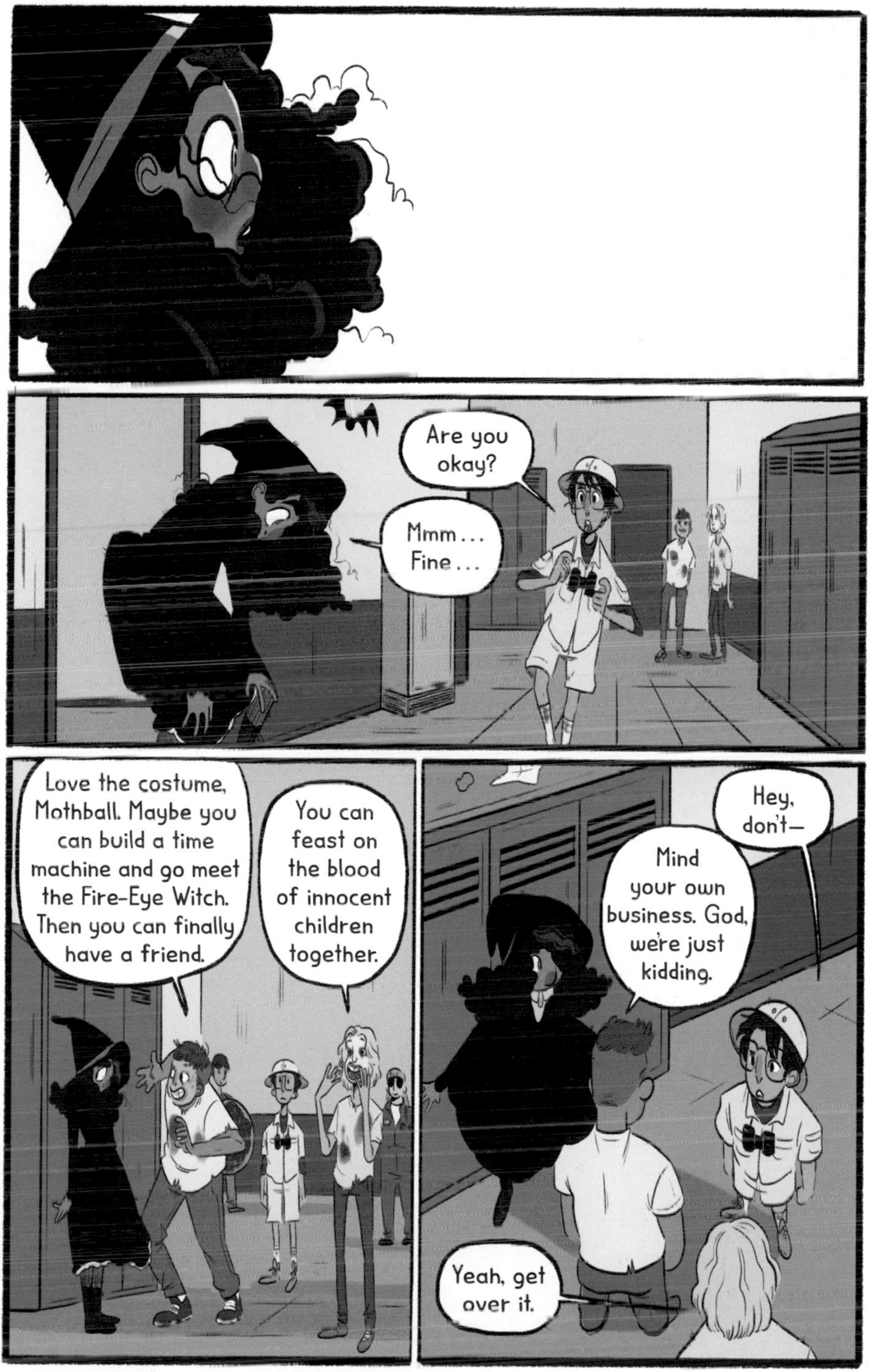
Are you okay?
Mmm... Fine...
Love the costume, Mothball. Maybe you can build a time machine and go meet the Fire-Eye Witch. Then you can finally have a friend.
You can feast on the blood of innocent children together.
Hey, don't—
Mind your own business. God, we're just kidding.
Yeah, get over it.

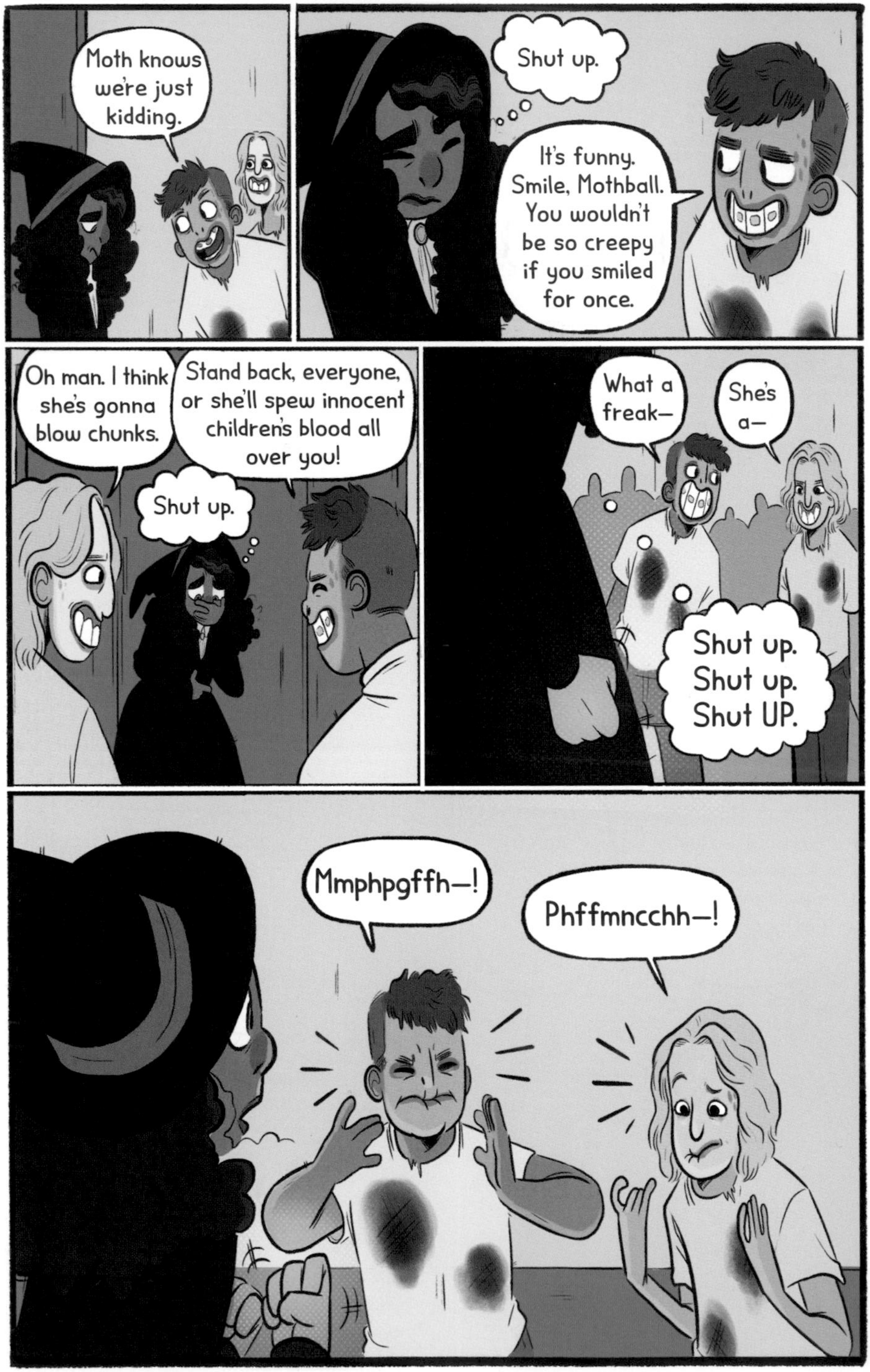
Moth knows we're just kidding.
Shut up.
It's funny. Smile, Mothball. You wouldn't be so creepy if you smiled for once.
Oh man. I think she's gonna blow chunks.
Stand back, everyone, or she'll spew innocent children's blood all over you!
Shut up.
What a freak—
She's a—
Shut up. Shut up. Shut UP.
Mmphpgffh—!
Phffmncchh—!

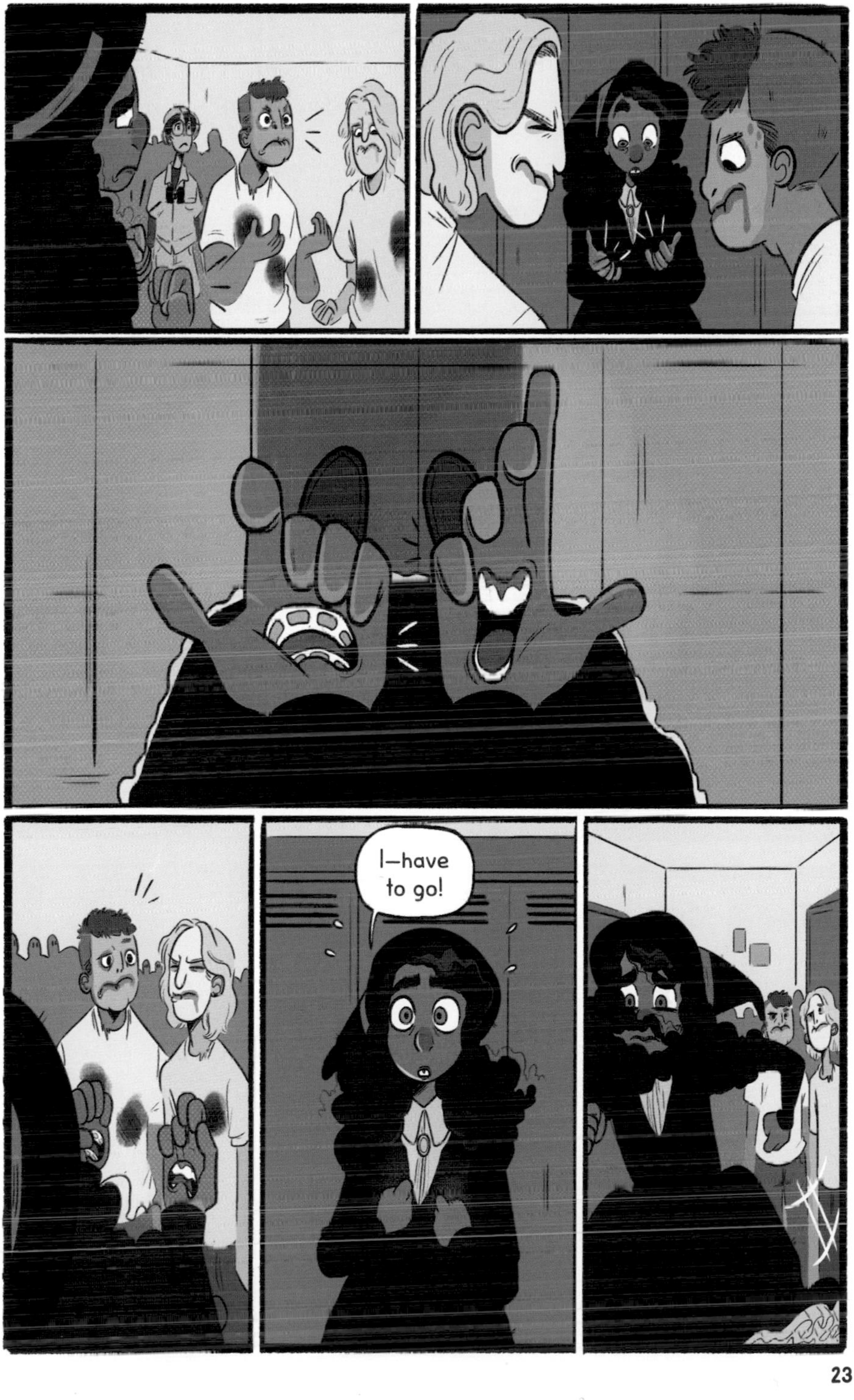
I—have to go!

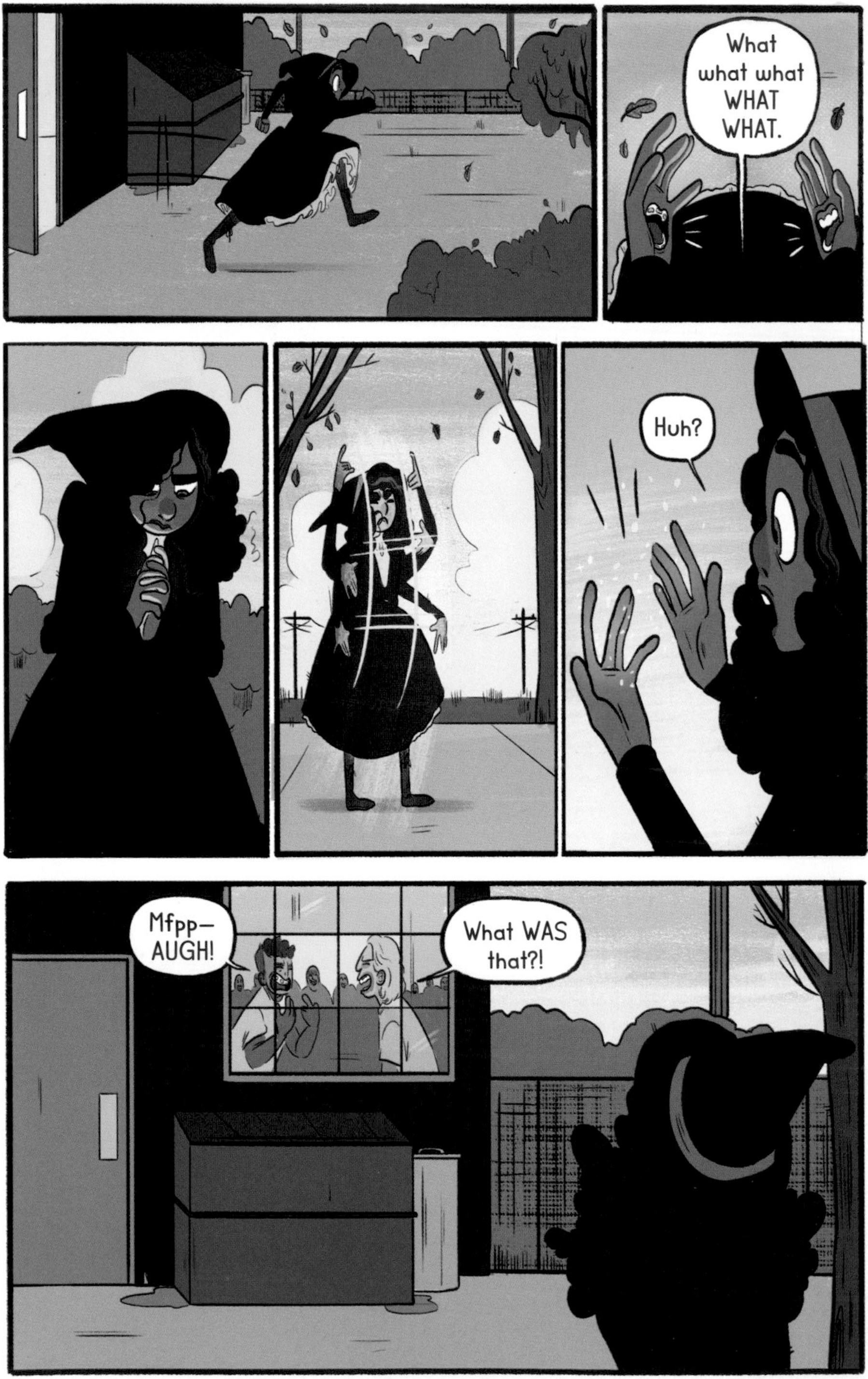
What what what WHAT WHAT.
Huh?
Mfpp—AUGH!
What WAS that?!

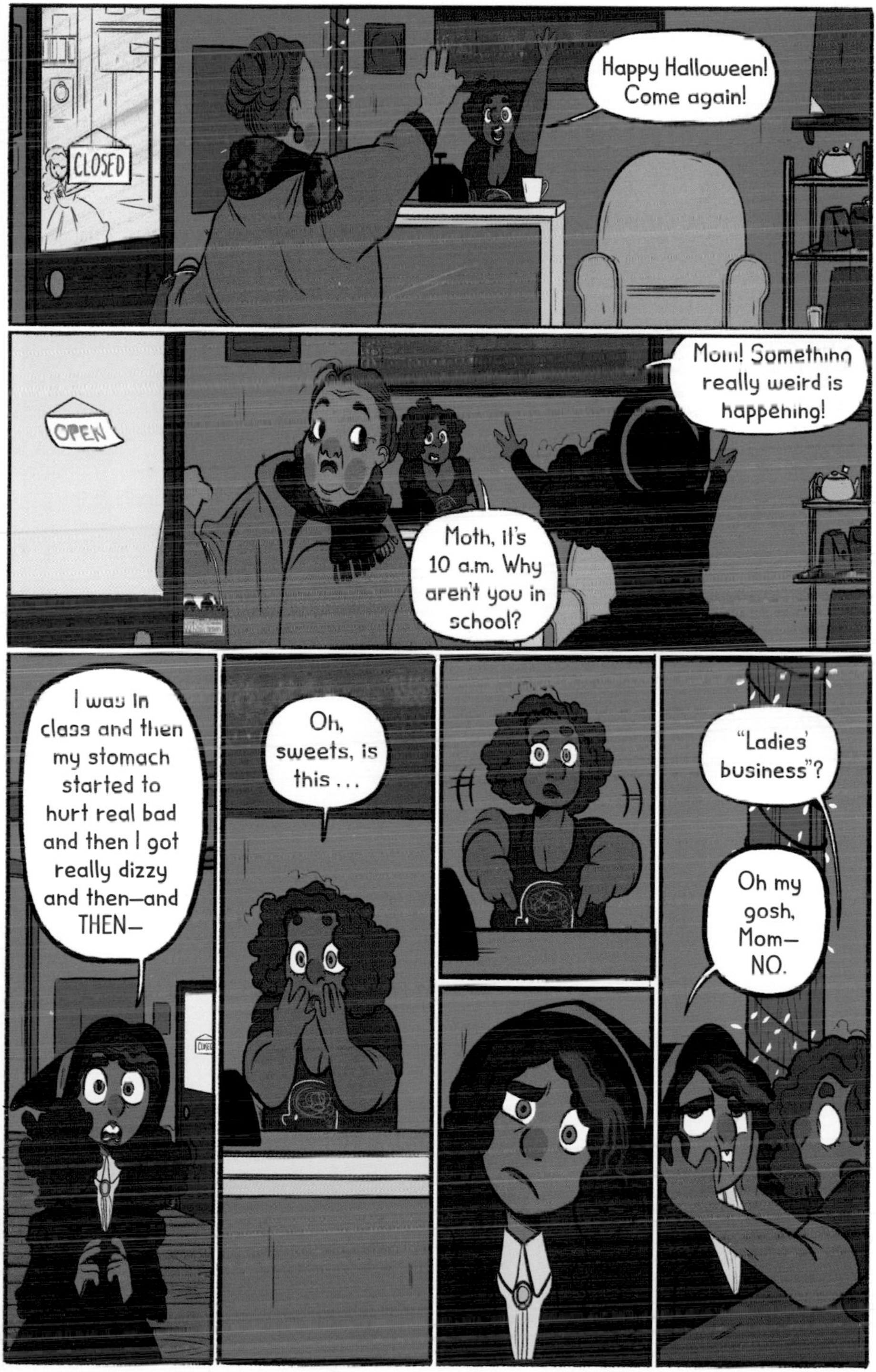

CLOSED
Happy Halloween! Come again!
OPEN
Mom! Something really weird is happening!
Moth, it's 10 a.m. Why aren't you in school?
I was in class and then my stomach started to hurt real bad and then I got really dizzy and then—and THEN—
Oh, sweets, is this . . .
"Ladies' business"?
Oh my gosh, Mom—NO.

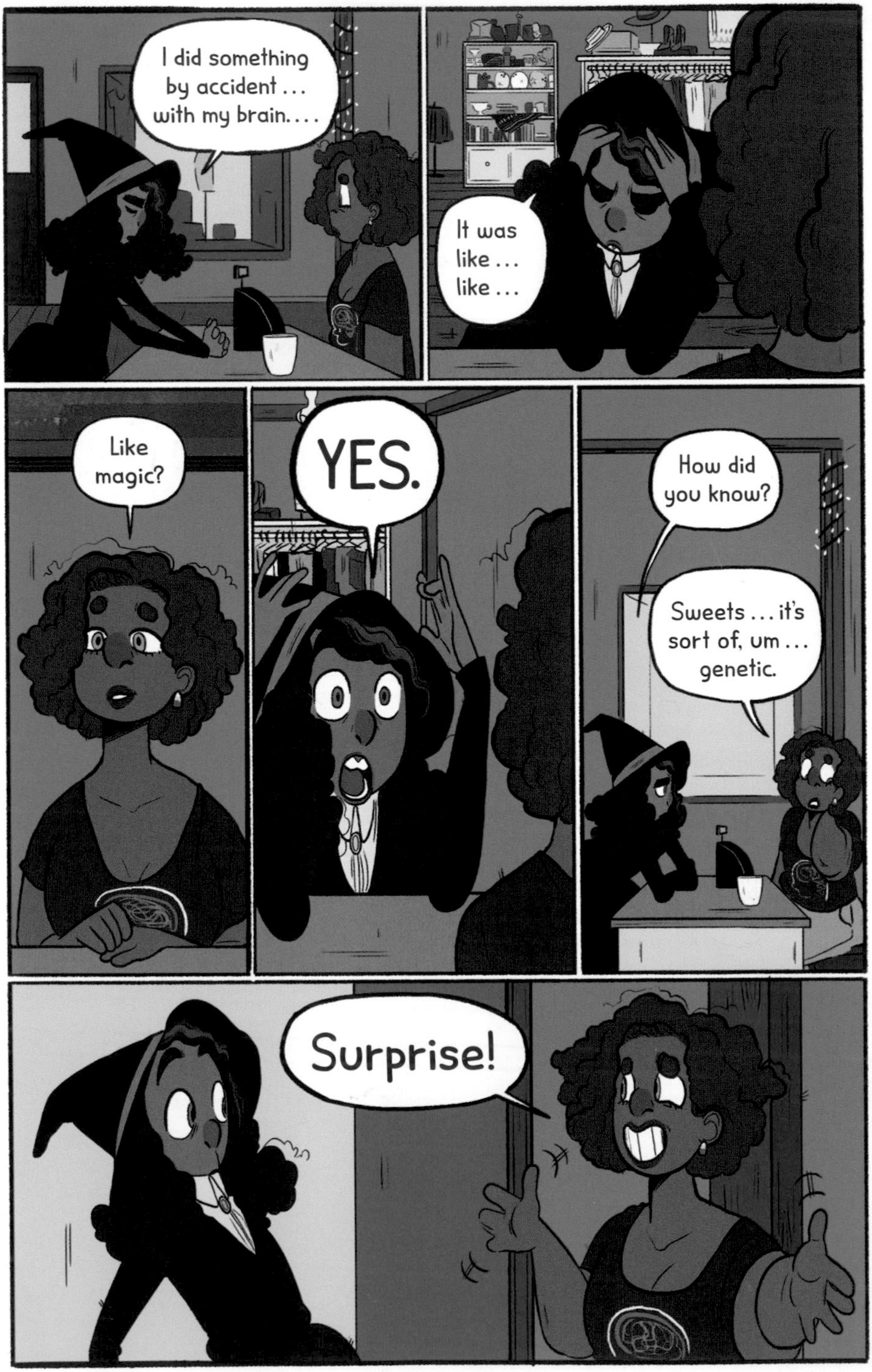
I did something by accident . . . with my brain. . . .
It was like . . . like . . .
Like magic?
YES.
How did you know?
Sweets . . . it's sort of, um . . . genetic.
Surprise!

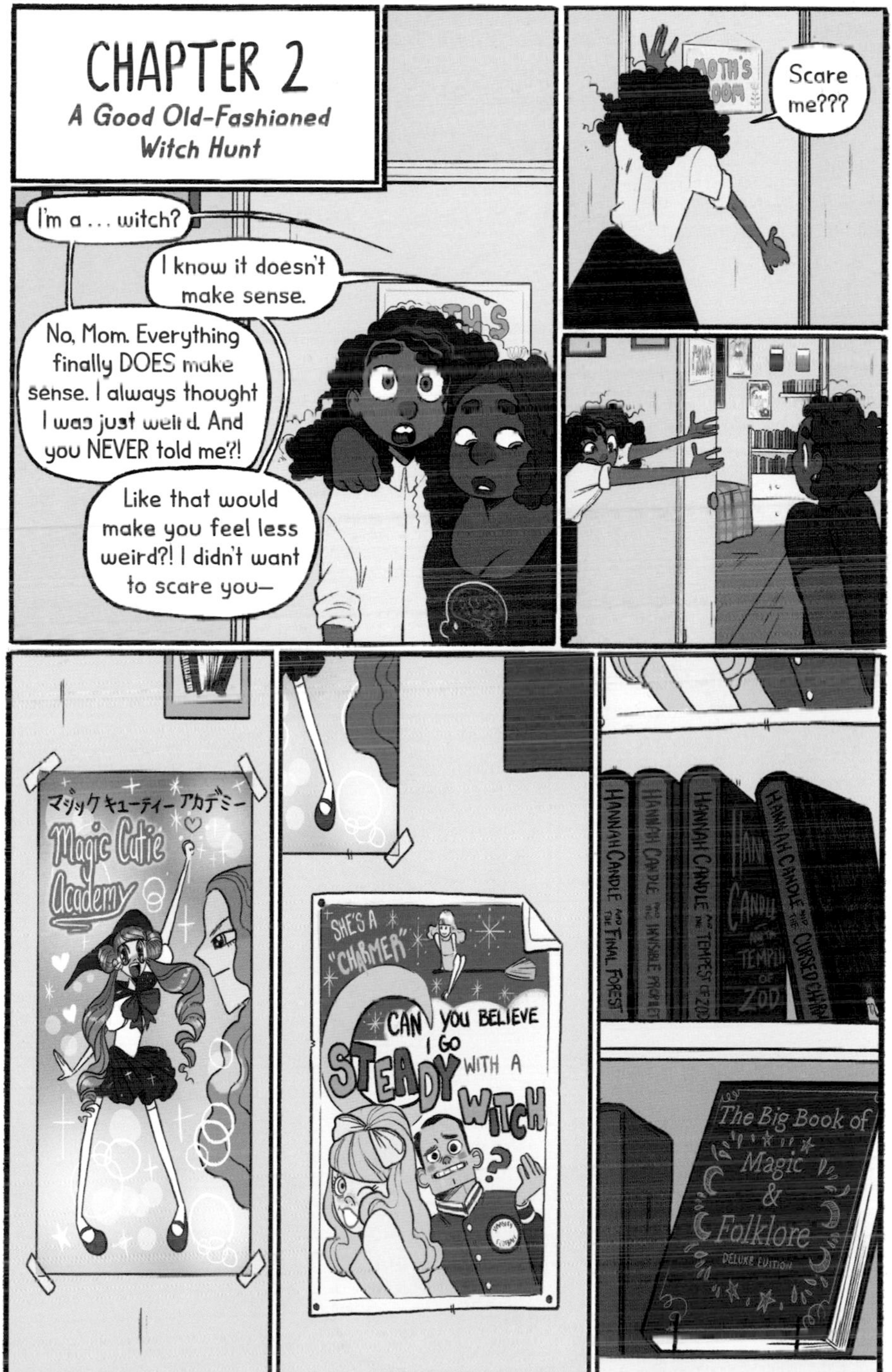
CHAPTER 2
A Good Old-Fashioned Witch Hunt
Scare me???
I'm a . . . witch?
I know it doesn't make sense.
No, Mom. Everything finally DOES make sense. I always thought I was just weird. And you NEVER told me?!
Like that would make you feel less weird?! I didn't want to scare you—
マジックキューティーアカデミー
Magic Cutie Academy
SHE'S A "CHARMER"
CAN YOU BELIEVE I GO STEADY WITH A WITCH?
HANNAH CANDLE AND THE FINAL FOREST
HANNAH CANDLE AND THE INVISIBLE PROPHET
HANNAH CANDLE AND THE TEMPEST OF ZOD
HANNAH CANDLE AND THE TEMPEST OF ZOD
HANNAH CANDLE AND THE CURSED CHAIN
The Big Book of Magic & Folklore
DELUXE EDITION

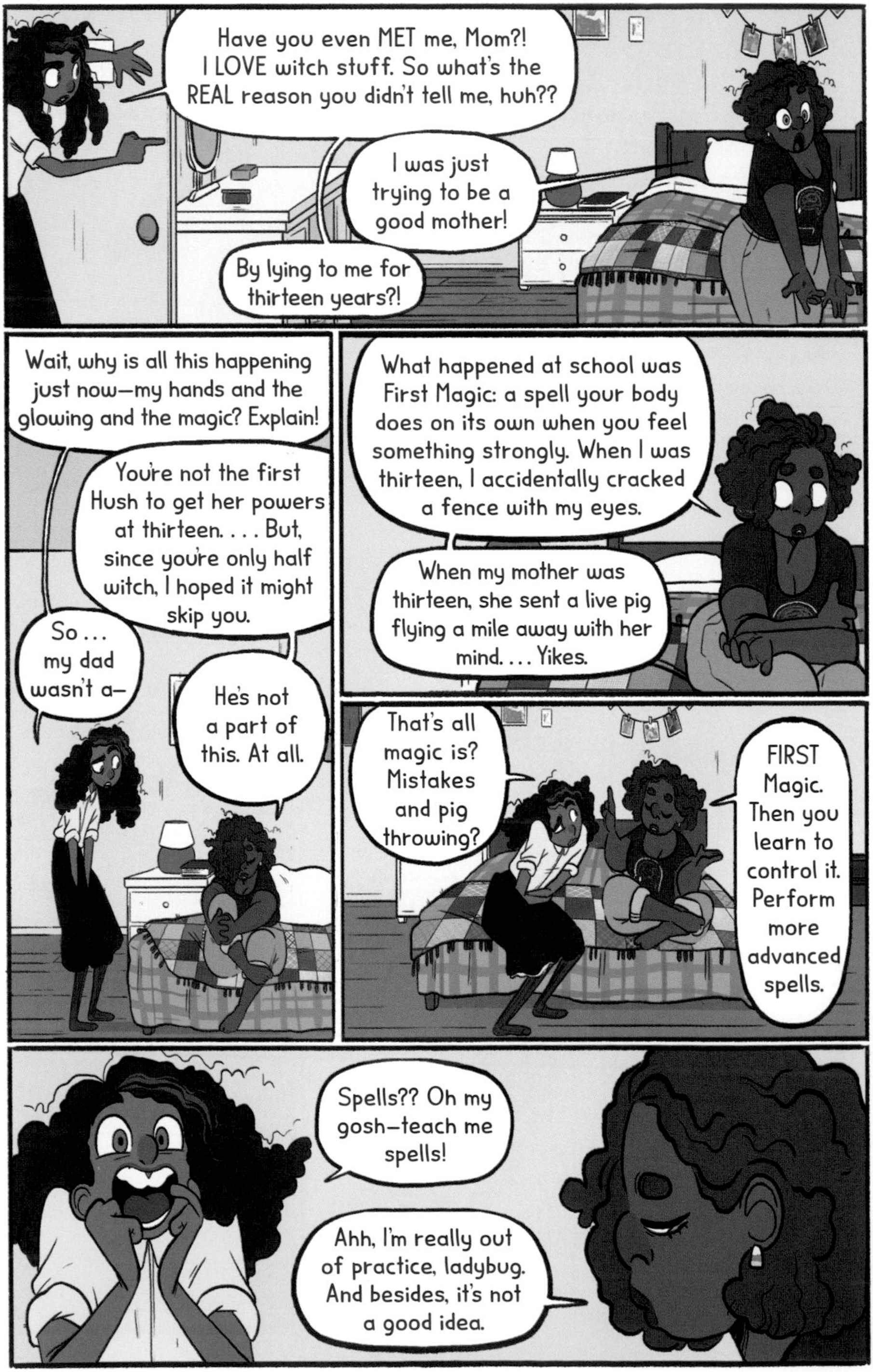
Have you even MET me, Mom?! I LOVE witch stuff. So what's the REAL reason you didn't tell me, huh??
I was just trying to be a good mother!
By lying to me for thirteen years?!
Wait, why is all this happening just now—my hands and the glowing and the magic? Explain!
You're not the first Hush to get her powers at thirteen. . . . But, since you're only half witch, I hoped it might skip you.
So . . . my dad wasn't a—
He's not a part of this. At all.
What happened at school was First Magic: a spell your body does on its own when you feel something strongly. When I was thirteen, I accidentally cracked a fence with my eyes.
When my mother was thirteen, she sent a live pig flying a mile away with her mind. . . . Yikes.
That's all magic is? Mistakes and pig throwing?
FIRST Magic. Then you learn to control it. Perform more advanced spells.
Spells?? Oh my gosh—teach me spells!
Ahh, I'm really out of practice, ladybug. And besides, it's not a good idea.

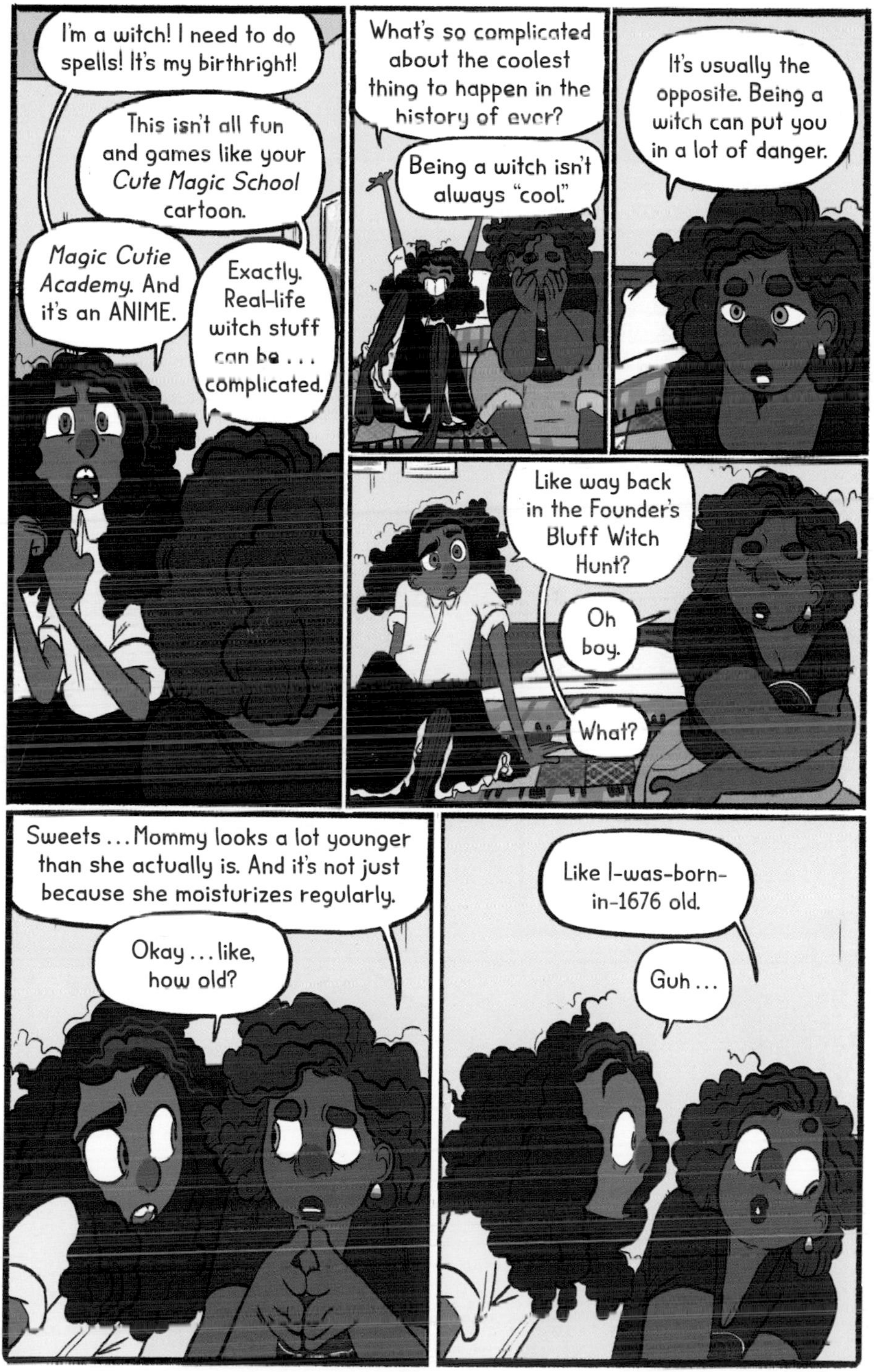

I'm a witch! I need to do spells! It's my birthright!
This isn't all fun and games like your *Cute Magic School* cartoon.
Magic Cutie Academy. And it's an ANIME.
Exactly. Real-life witch stuff can be . . . complicated.
What's so complicated about the coolest thing to happen in the history of ever?
Being a witch isn't always "cool."
It's usually the opposite. Being a witch can put you in a lot of danger.
Like way back in the Founder's Bluff Witch Hunt?
Oh boy.
What?
Sweets . . . Mommy looks a lot younger than she actually is. And it's not just because she moisturizes regularly.
Okay . . . like, how old?
Like I-was-born-in-1676 old.
Guh . . .

THE REAL STORY OF THE
Founder's Bluff Witch Hunt

My mother, Sarah Hush, was part of an order of witches from an island city in the Bay of Biscay.

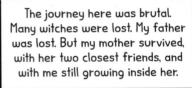

In the final gasps of the witch trials in Europe, their home was attacked. Sarah and her order had to escape across the sea.

The journey here was brutal. Many witches were lost. My father was lost. But my mother survived, with her two closest friends, and with me still growing inside her.

She always survives.

They did not know what to expect when they came ashore. Would the people here want them dead? Would they be welcoming? Would they at least leave them alone?

Jenny

Sarah

Adelais

They hoped they might find peace in this new land, but they were wrong. My whole childhood, we were never welcome in Founder's Bluff.

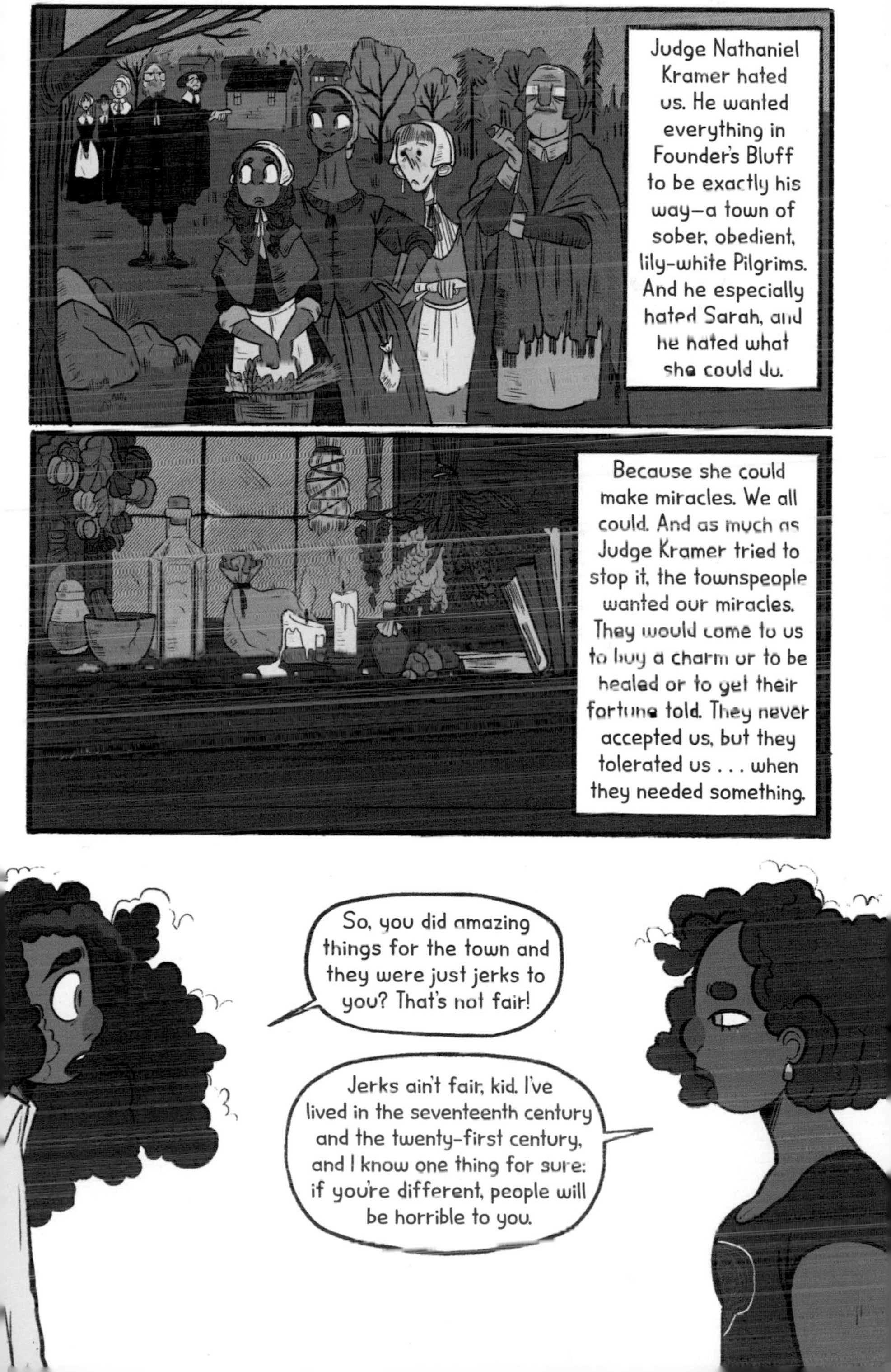
Judge Nathaniel Kramer hated us. He wanted everything in Founder's Bluff to be exactly his way—a town of sober, obedient, lily-white Pilgrims. And he especially hated Sarah, and he hated what she could do.
Because she could make miracles. We all could. And as much as Judge Kramer tried to stop it, the townspeople wanted our miracles. They would come to us to buy a charm or to be healed or to get their fortune told. They never accepted us, but they tolerated us . . . when they needed something.
So, you did amazing things for the town and they were just jerks to you? That's not fair!
Jerks ain't fair, kid. I've lived in the seventeenth century and the twenty-first century, and I know one thing for sure: if you're different, people will be horrible to you.

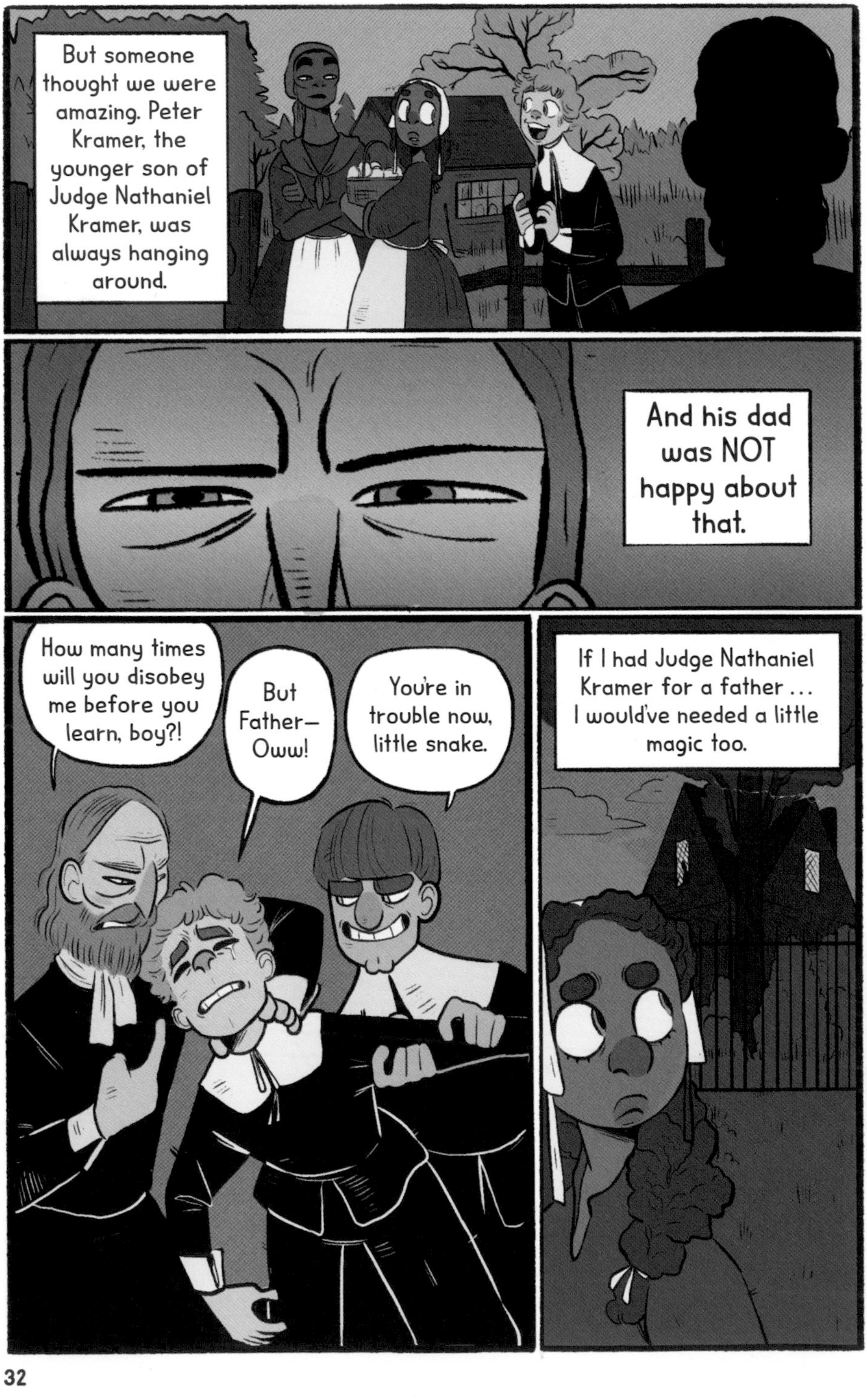
But someone thought we were amazing. Peter Kramer, the younger son of Judge Nathaniel Kramer, was always hanging around.
And his dad was NOT happy about that.
How many times will you disobey me before you learn, boy?!
But Father— Oww!
You're in trouble now, little snake.
If I had Judge Nathaniel Kramer for a father . . . I would've needed a little magic too.

Judge Kramer always hated us, but when he couldn't control his own son, he kicked the hate up a notch.

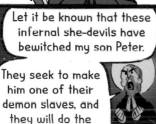

Let it be known that these infernal she-devils have bewitched my son Peter.

They seek to make him one of their demon slaves, and they will do the same to ALL your children if we don't destroy them first!

Sarah Hush!

You and your heathen bunch are charged with witchcraft! Come out and face the law!

The witches have disappeared!

Impossible!

The hunt had only begun.

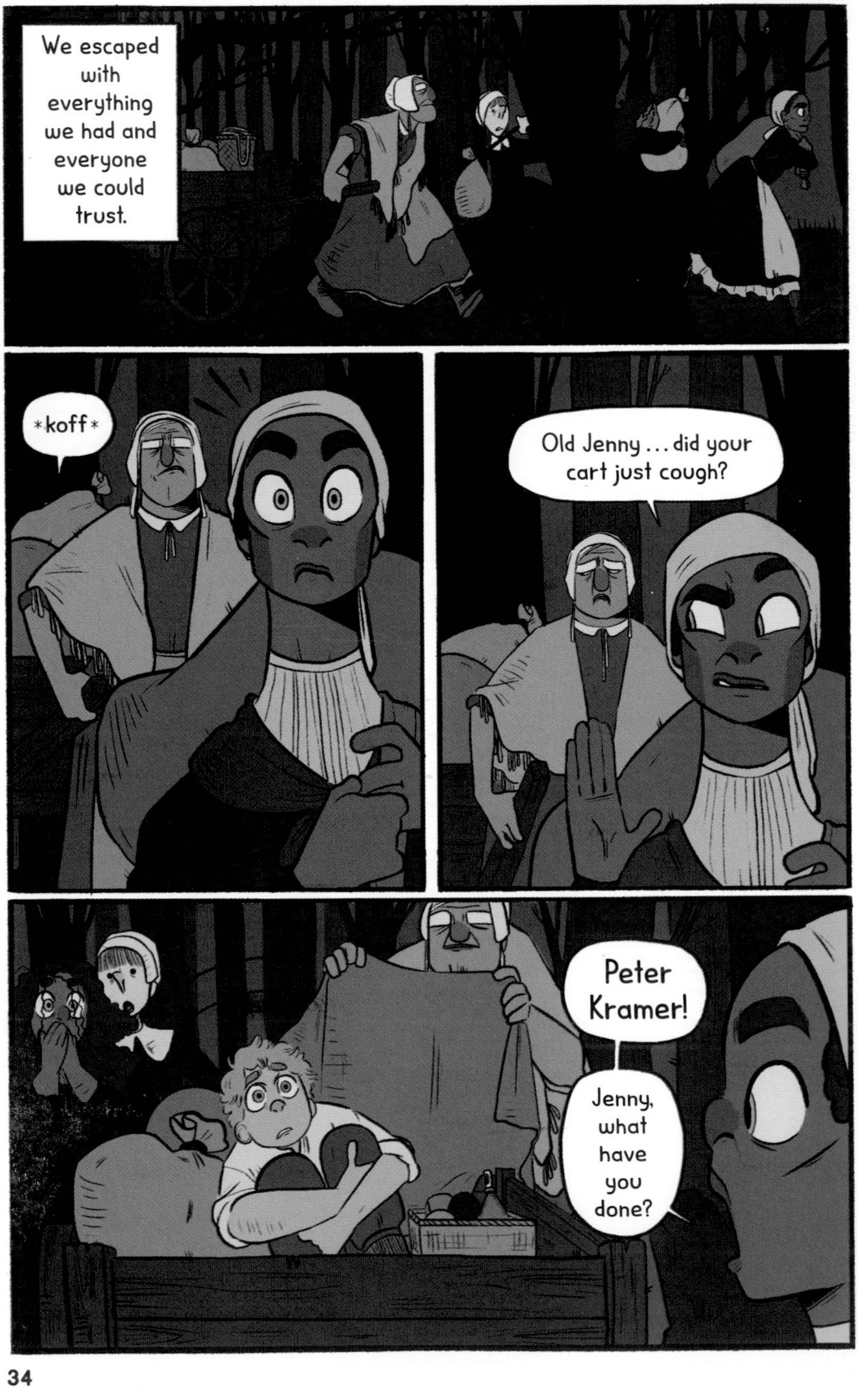
We escaped with everything we had and everyone we could trust.
koff
Old Jenny . . . did your cart just cough?
Peter Kramer!
Jenny, what have you done?

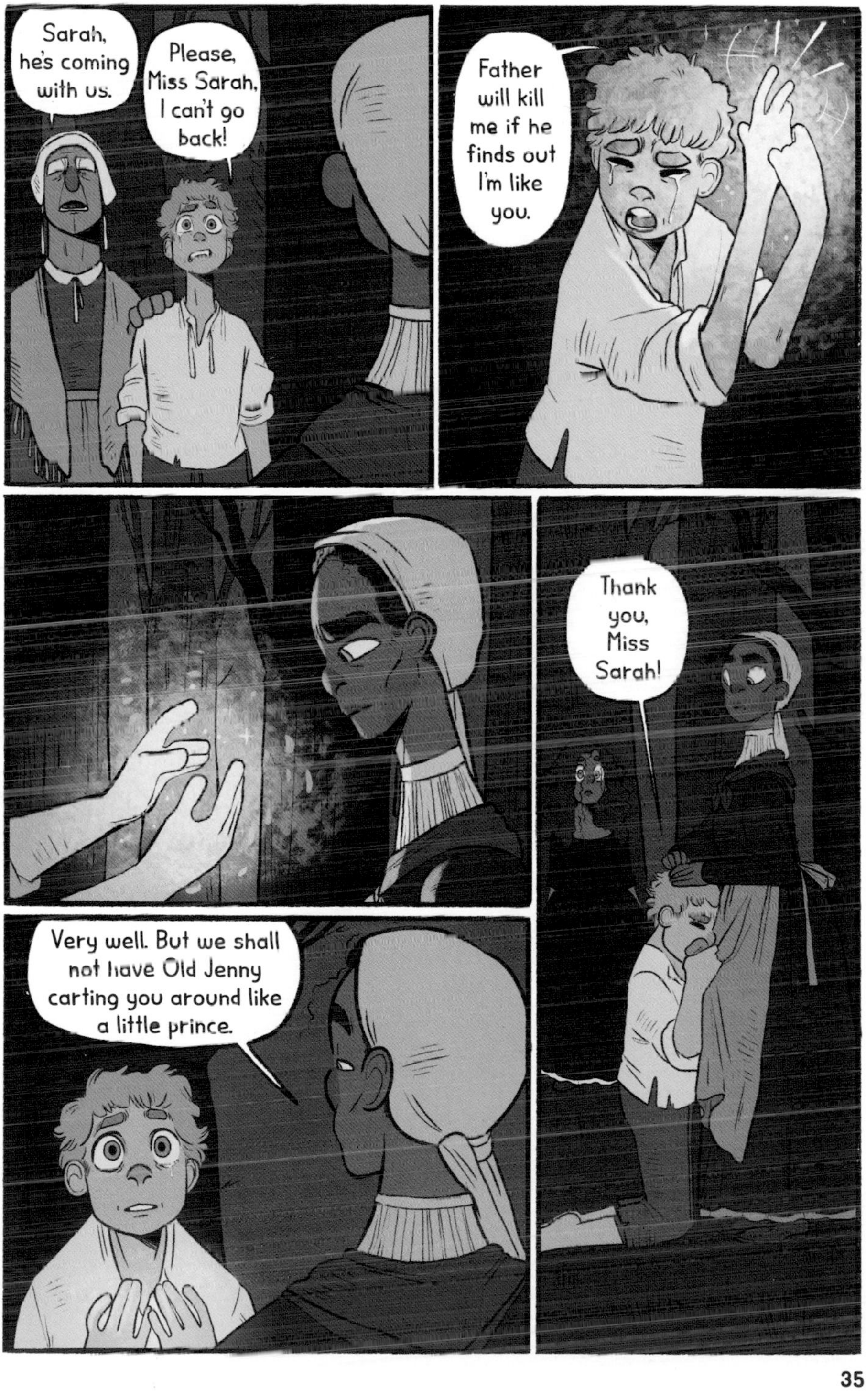
Sarah, he's coming with us.
Please, Miss Sarah, I can't go back!
Father will kill me if he finds out I'm like you.
Very well. But we shall not have Old Jenny carting you around like a little prince.
Thank you, Miss Sarah!

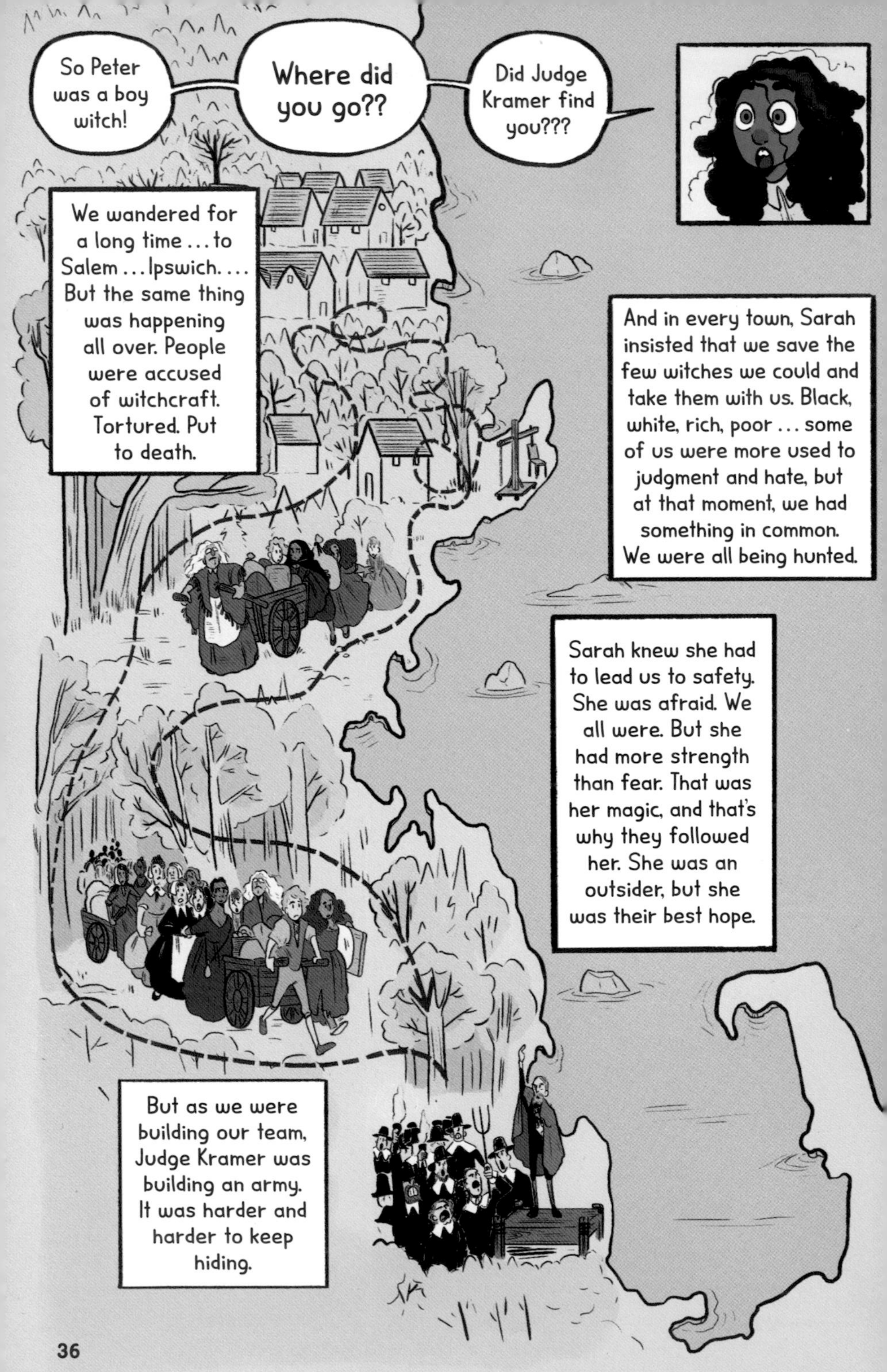

So Peter was a boy witch!
Where did you go??
Did Judge Kramer find you???
We wandered for a long time . . . to Salem . . . Ipswich. . . . But the same thing was happening all over. People were accused of witchcraft. Tortured. Put to death.
And in every town, Sarah insisted that we save the few witches we could and take them with us. Black, white, rich, poor . . . some of us were more used to judgment and hate, but at that moment, we had something in common. We were all being hunted.
Sarah knew she had to lead us to safety. She was afraid. We all were. But she had more strength than fear. That was her magic, and that's why they followed her. She was an outsider, but she was their best hope.
But as we were building our team, Judge Kramer was building an army. It was harder and harder to keep hiding.

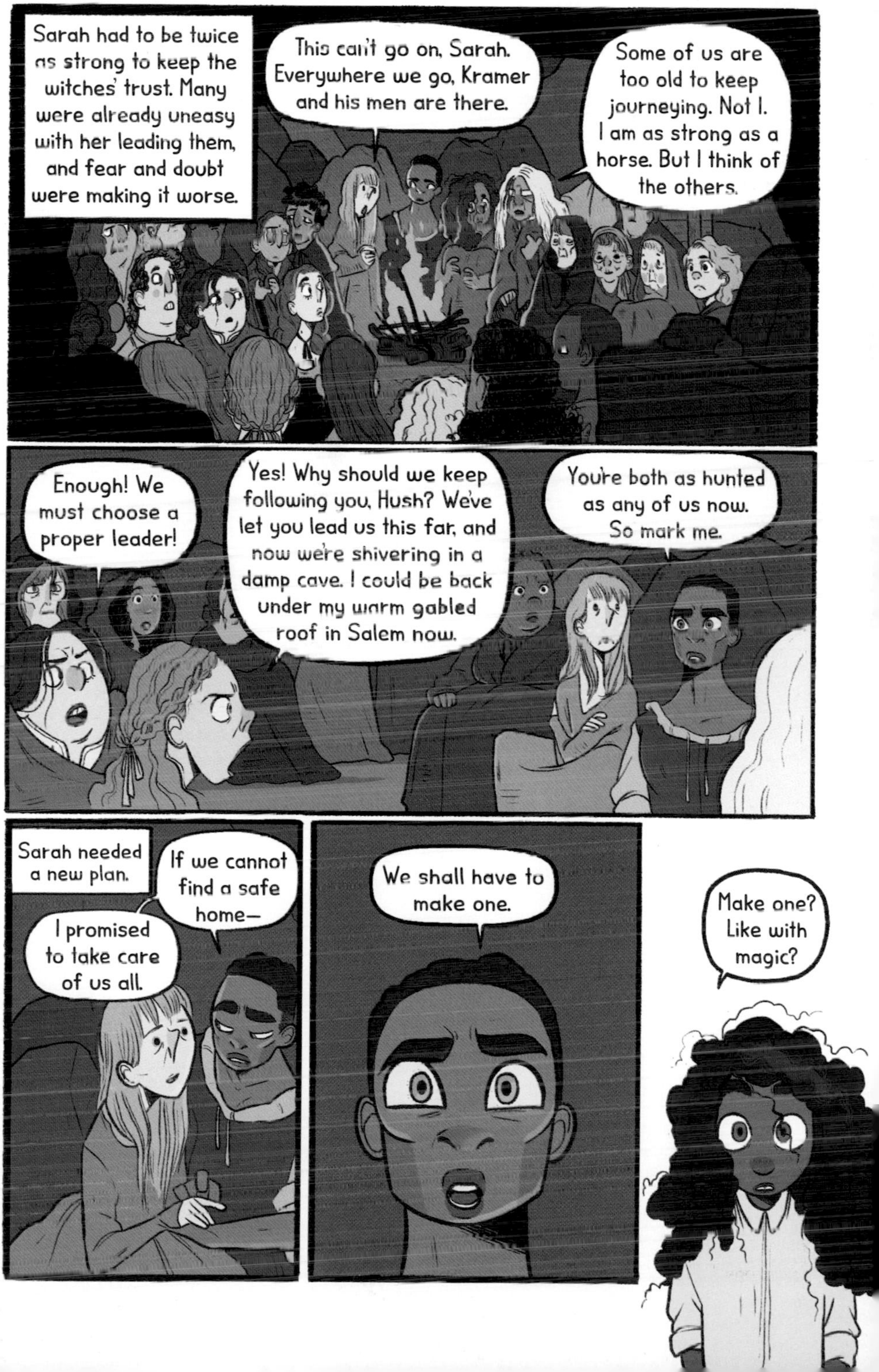
Sarah had to be twice as strong to keep the witches' trust. Many were already uneasy with her leading them, and fear and doubt were making it worse.
This can't go on, Sarah. Everywhere we go, Kramer and his men are there.
Some of us are too old to keep journeying. Not I. I am as strong as a horse. But I think of the others.
Enough! We must choose a proper leader!
Yes! Why should we keep following you, Hush? We've let you lead us this far, and now we're shivering in a damp cave. I could be back under my warm gabled roof in Salem now.
You're both as hunted as any of us now. So mark me.
Sarah needed a new plan.
I promised to take care of us all.
If we cannot find a safe home—
We shall have to make one.
Make one? Like with magic?

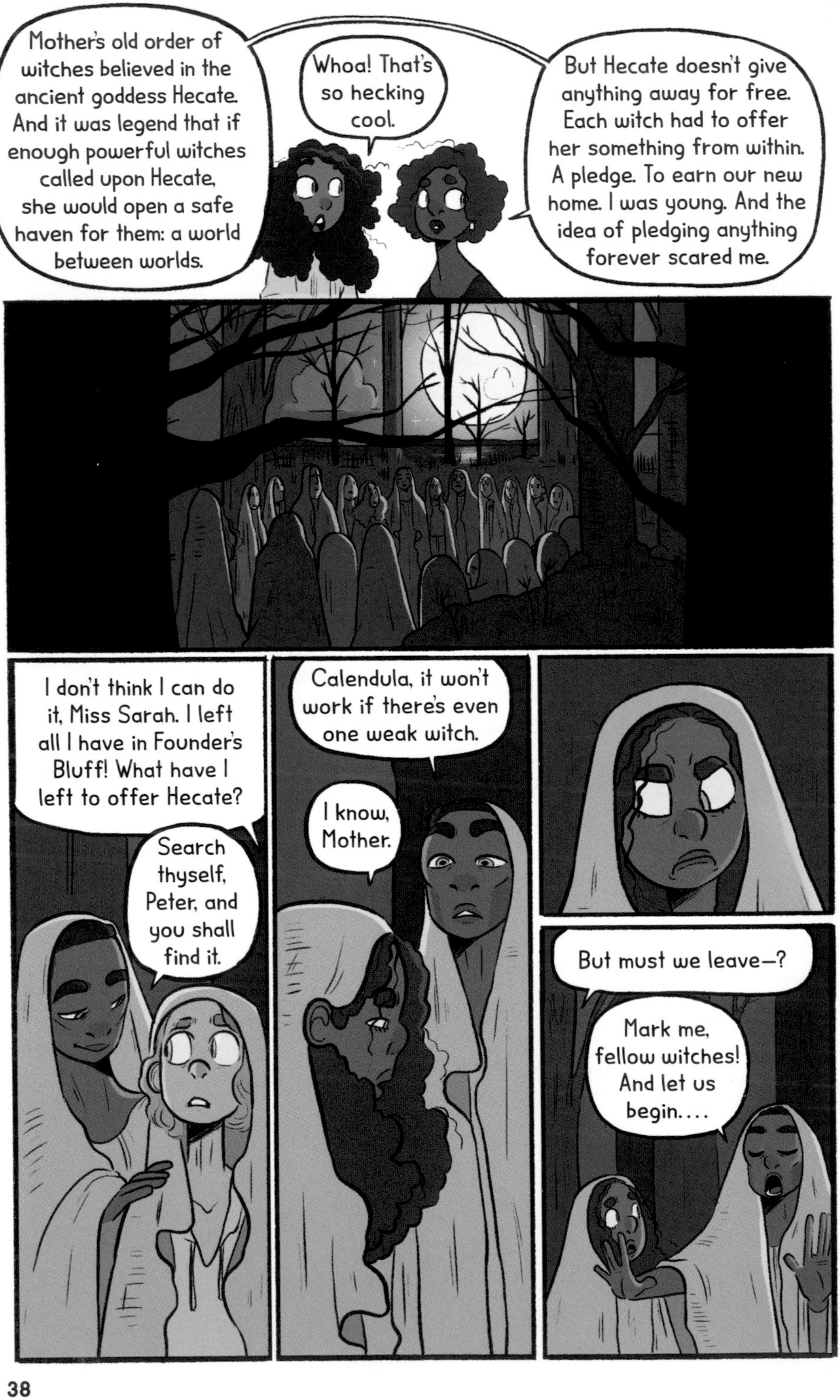
Mother's old order of witches believed in the ancient goddess Hecate. And it was legend that if enough powerful witches called upon Hecate, she would open a safe haven for them: a world between worlds.
Whoa! That's so hecking cool.
But Hecate doesn't give anything away for free. Each witch had to offer her something from within. A pledge. To earn our new home. I was young. And the idea of pledging anything forever scared me.
I don't think I can do it, Miss Sarah. I left all I have in Founder's Bluff! What have I left to offer Hecate?
Search thyself, Peter, and you shall find it.
Calendula, it won't work if there's even one weak witch.
I know, Mother.
But must we leave—?
Mark me, fellow witches! And let us begin. . . .

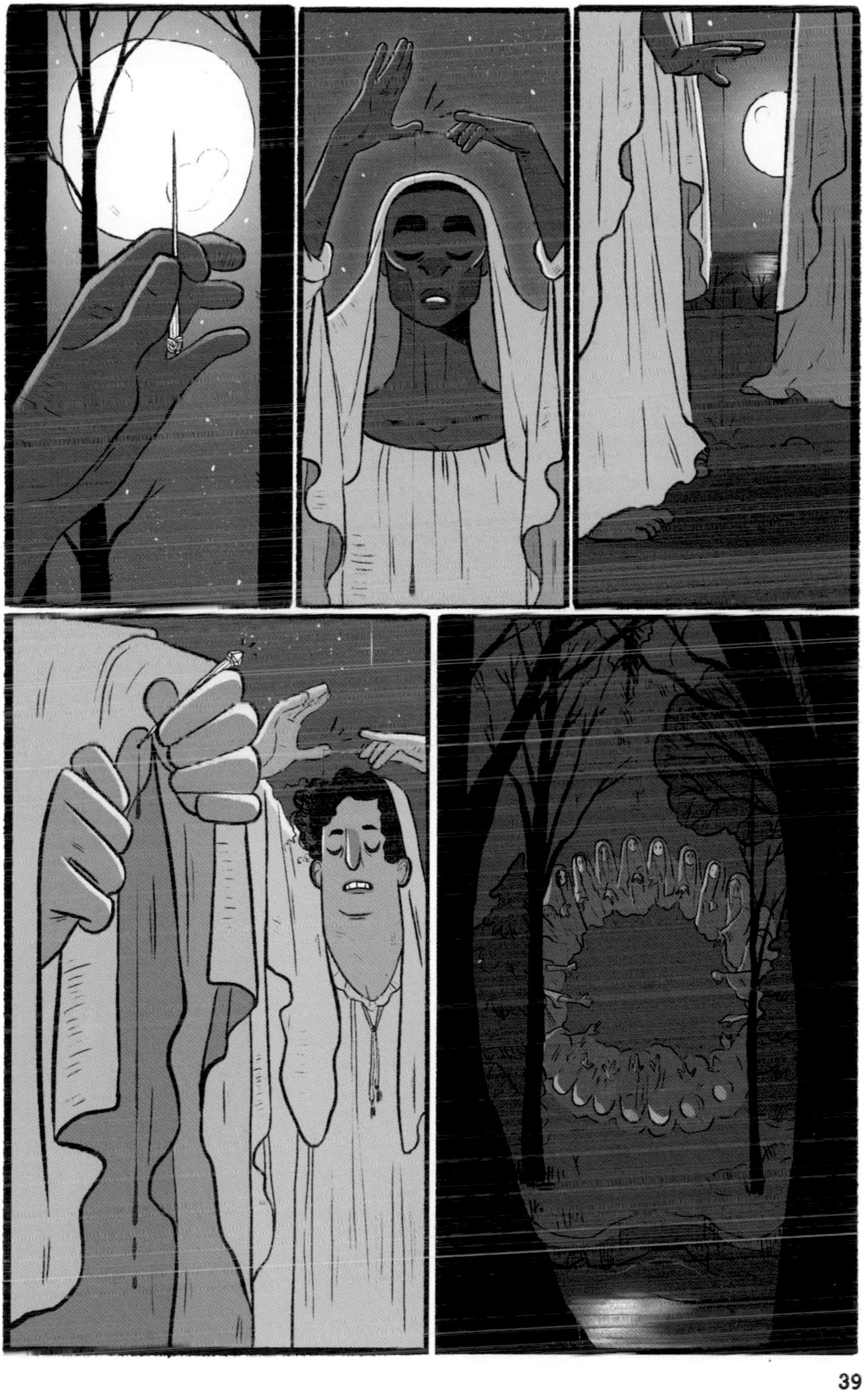

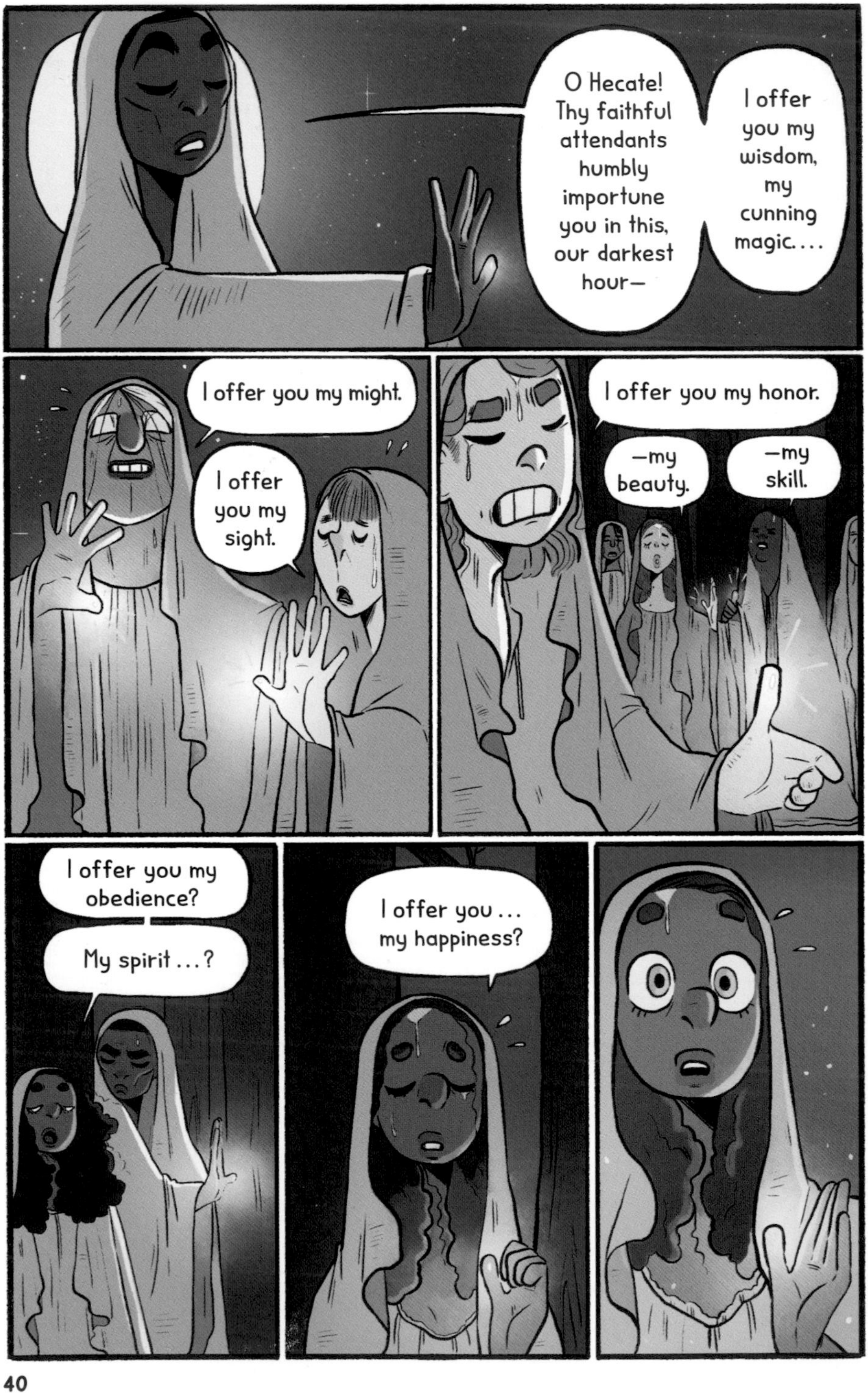
O Hecate! Thy faithful attendants humbly importune you in this, our darkest hour—
I offer you my wisdom, my cunning magic. . . .
I offer you my might.
I offer you my sight.
I offer you my honor.
—my beauty.
—my skill.
I offer you my obedience?
My spirit . . . ?
I offer you . . . my happiness?

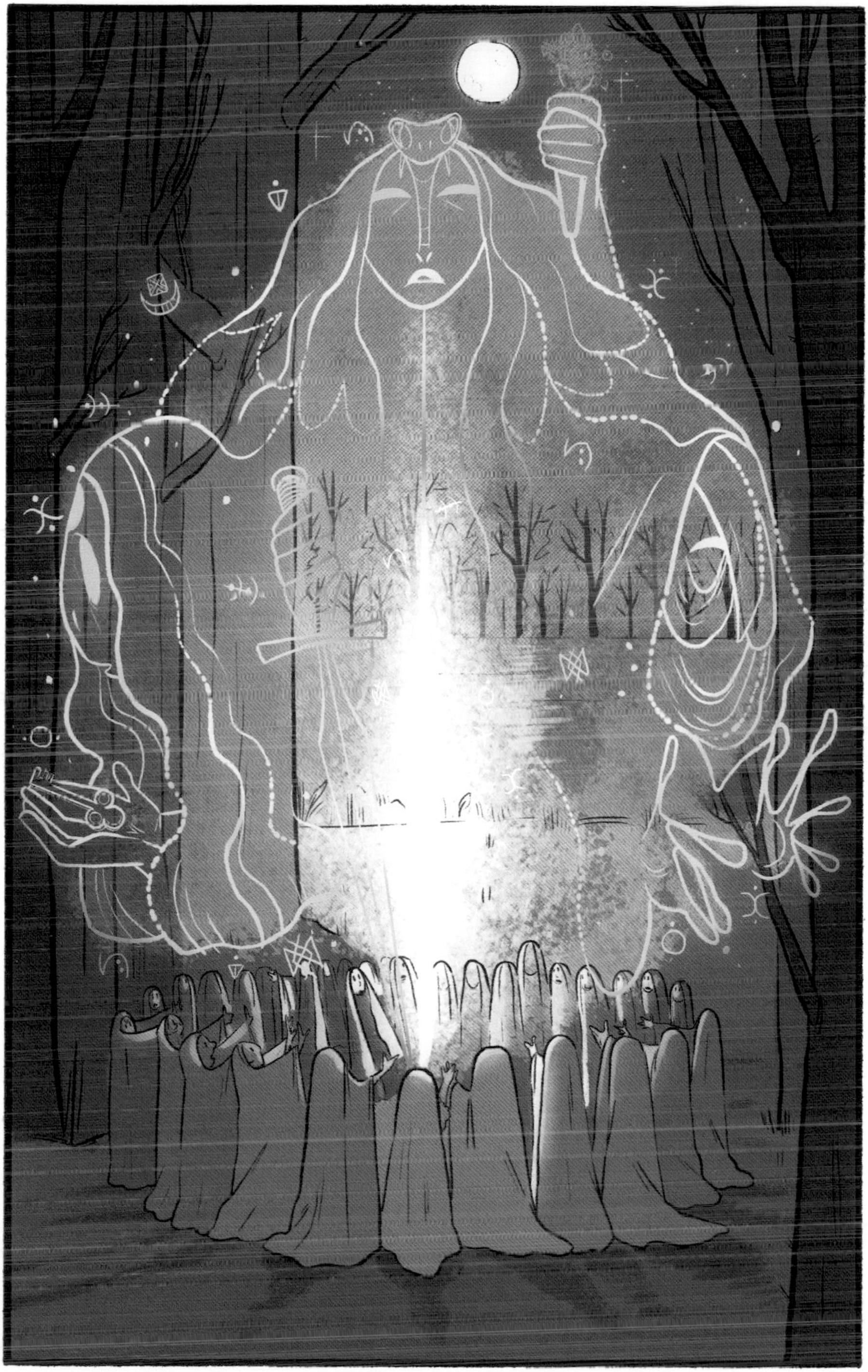

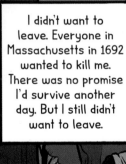

Calendula, come!

I didn't want to leave. Everyone in Massachusetts in 1692 wanted to kill me. There was no promise I'd survive another day. But I still didn't want to leave.

Calendula!

But I did.

And there, in Hecate, we were finally safe.

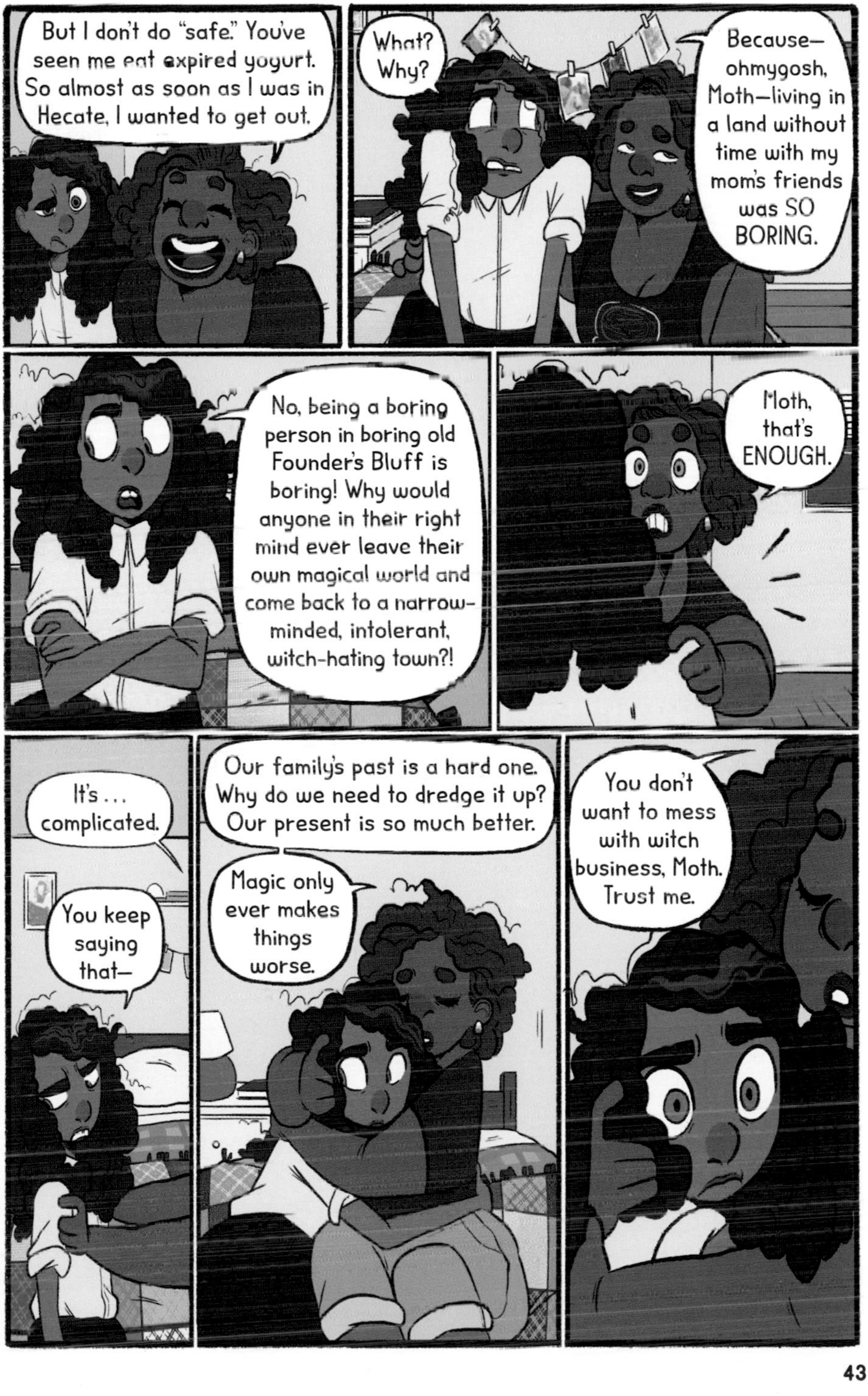
But I don't do "safe." You've seen me eat expired yogurt. So almost as soon as I was in Hecate, I wanted to get out.
What? Why?
Because—ohmygosh, Moth—living in a land without time with my mom's friends was SO BORING.
No, being a boring person in boring old Founder's Bluff is boring! Why would anyone in their right mind ever leave their own magical world and come back to a narrow-minded, intolerant, witch-hating town?!
Moth, that's ENOUGH.
It's . . . complicated.
You keep saying that—
Our family's past is a hard one. Why do we need to dredge it up? Our present is so much better.
Magic only ever makes things worse.
You don't want to mess with witch business, Moth. Trust me.

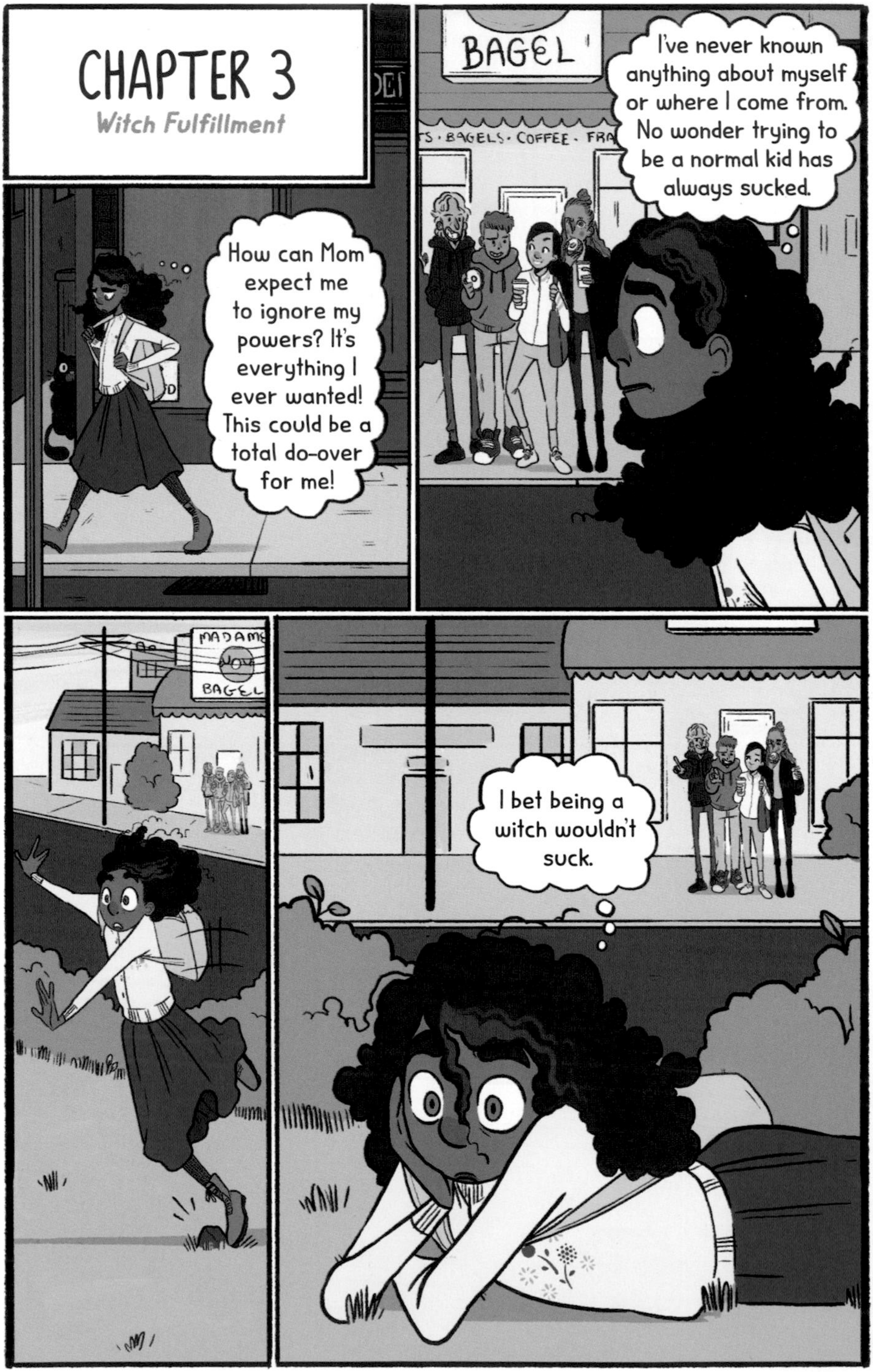

CHAPTER 3
Witch Fulfillment
How can Mom expect me to ignore my powers? It's everything I ever wanted! This could be a total do-over for me!
BAGEL
BAGELS · COFFEE
I've never known anything about myself or where I come from. No wonder trying to be a normal kid has always sucked.
BAGEL
I bet being a witch wouldn't suck.

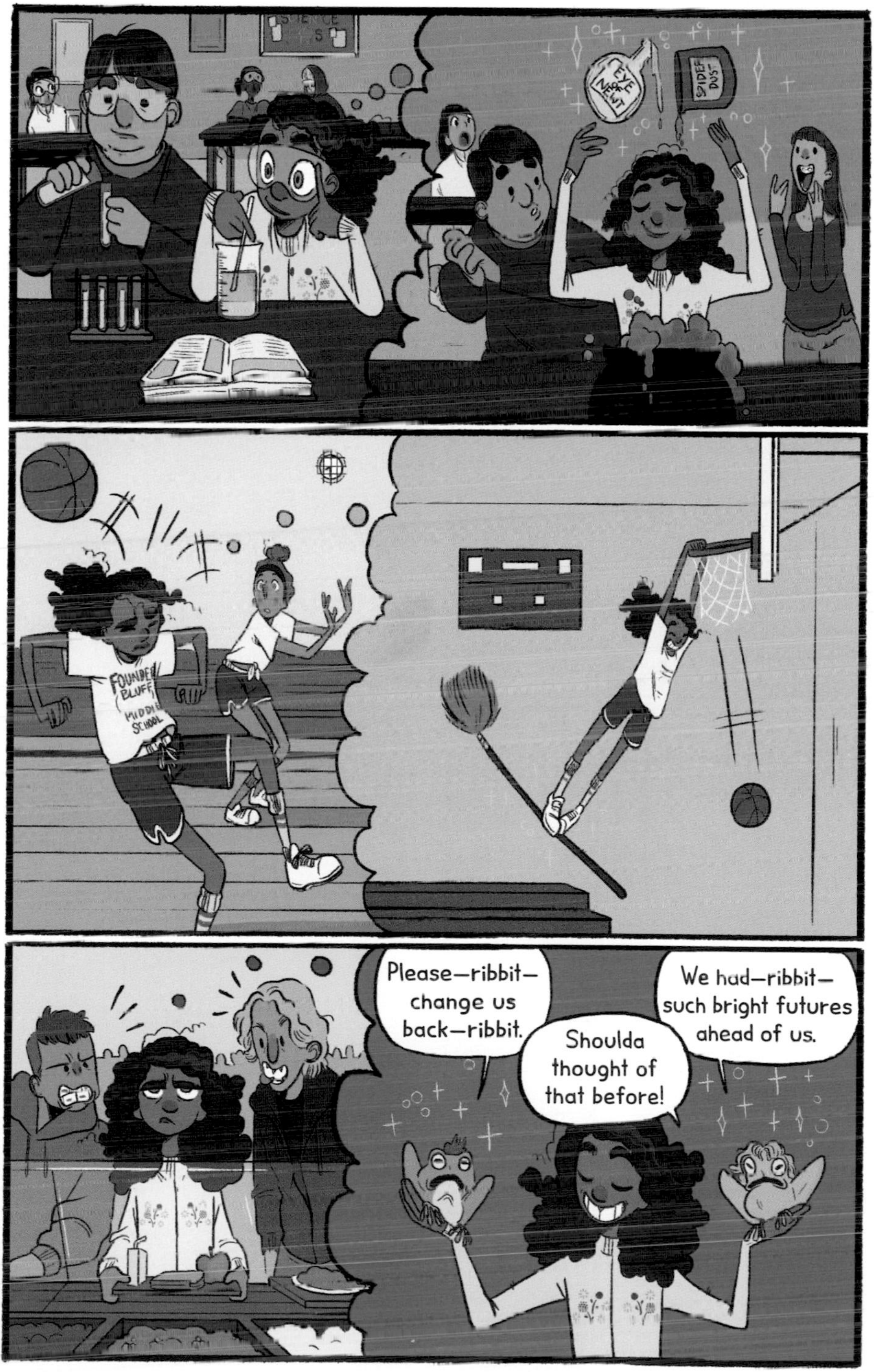
SCIENCE
EYE OF NEWT
SPIDER DUST
FOUNDERS BLUFF MIDDLE SCHOOL
Please—ribbit—change us back—ribbit.
Shoulda thought of that before!
We had—ribbit—such bright futures ahead of us.

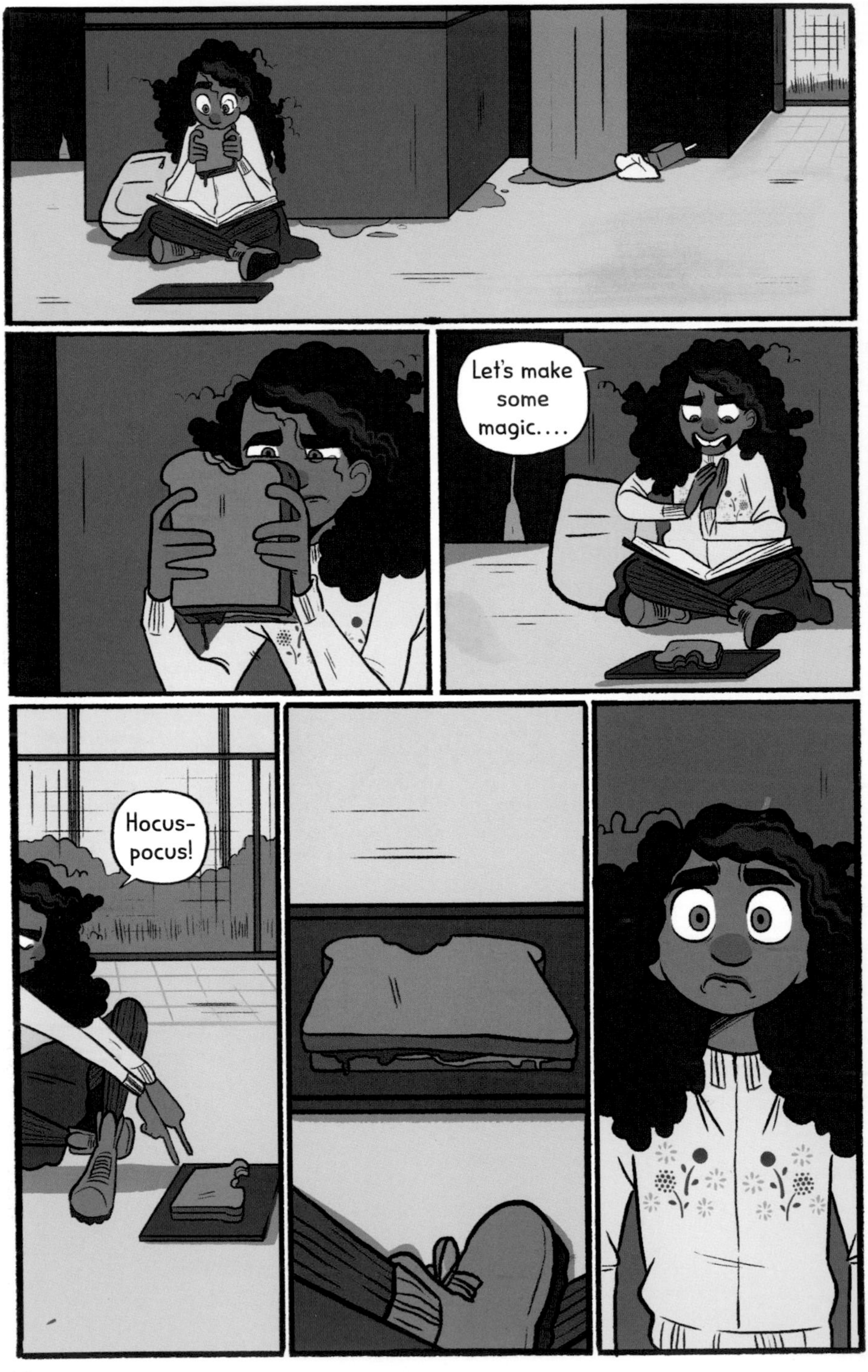
Let's make some magic....
Hocus-pocus!

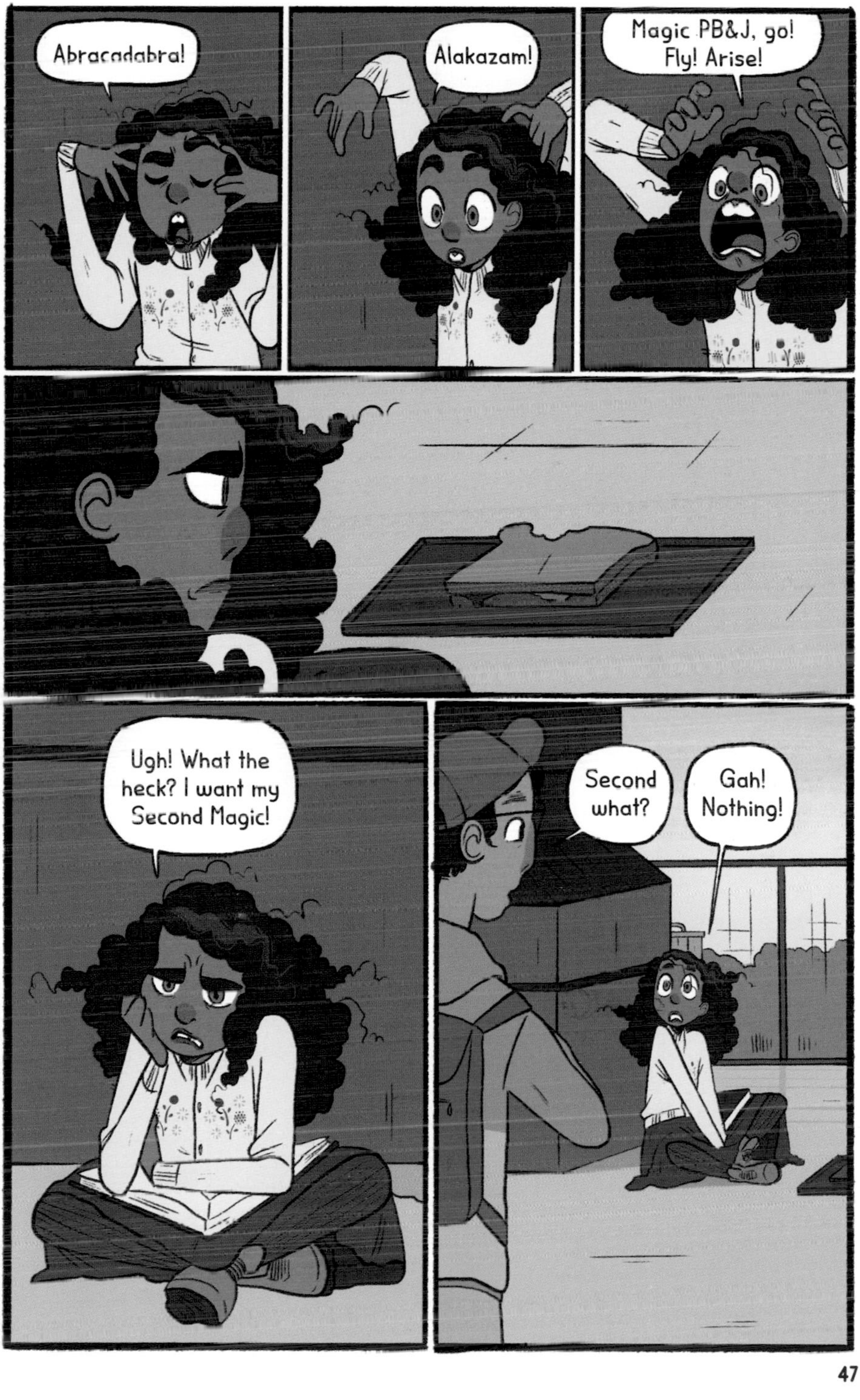
Abracadabra!
Alakazam!
Magic PB&J, go! Fly! Arise!
Ugh! What the heck? I want my Second Magic!
Second what?
Gah! Nothing!

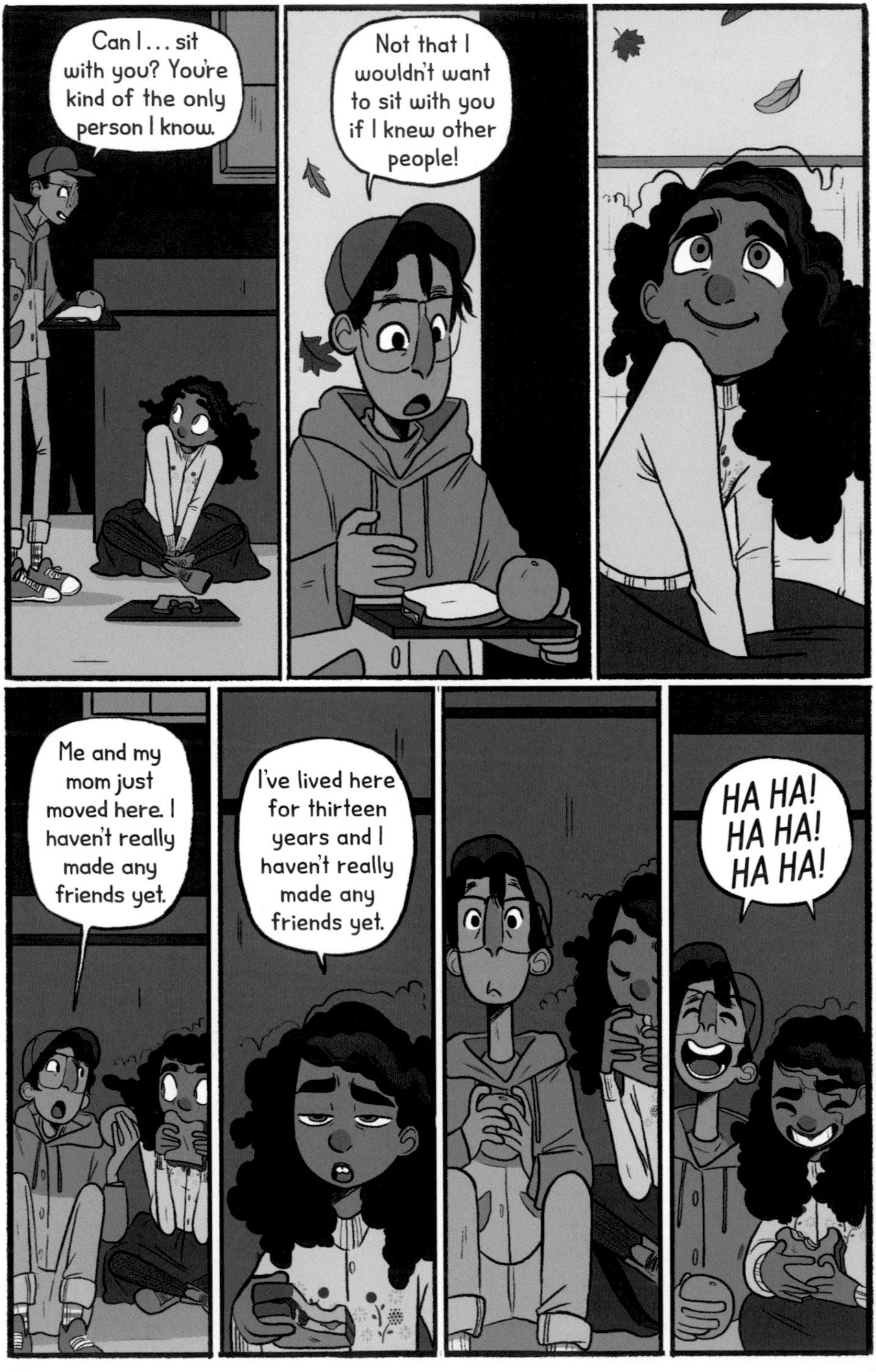
Can I... sit with you? You're kind of the only person I know.
Not that I wouldn't want to sit with you if I knew other people!
Me and my mom just moved here. I haven't really made any friends yet.
I've lived here for thirteen years and I haven't really made any friends yet.
HA HA! HA HA! HA HA!

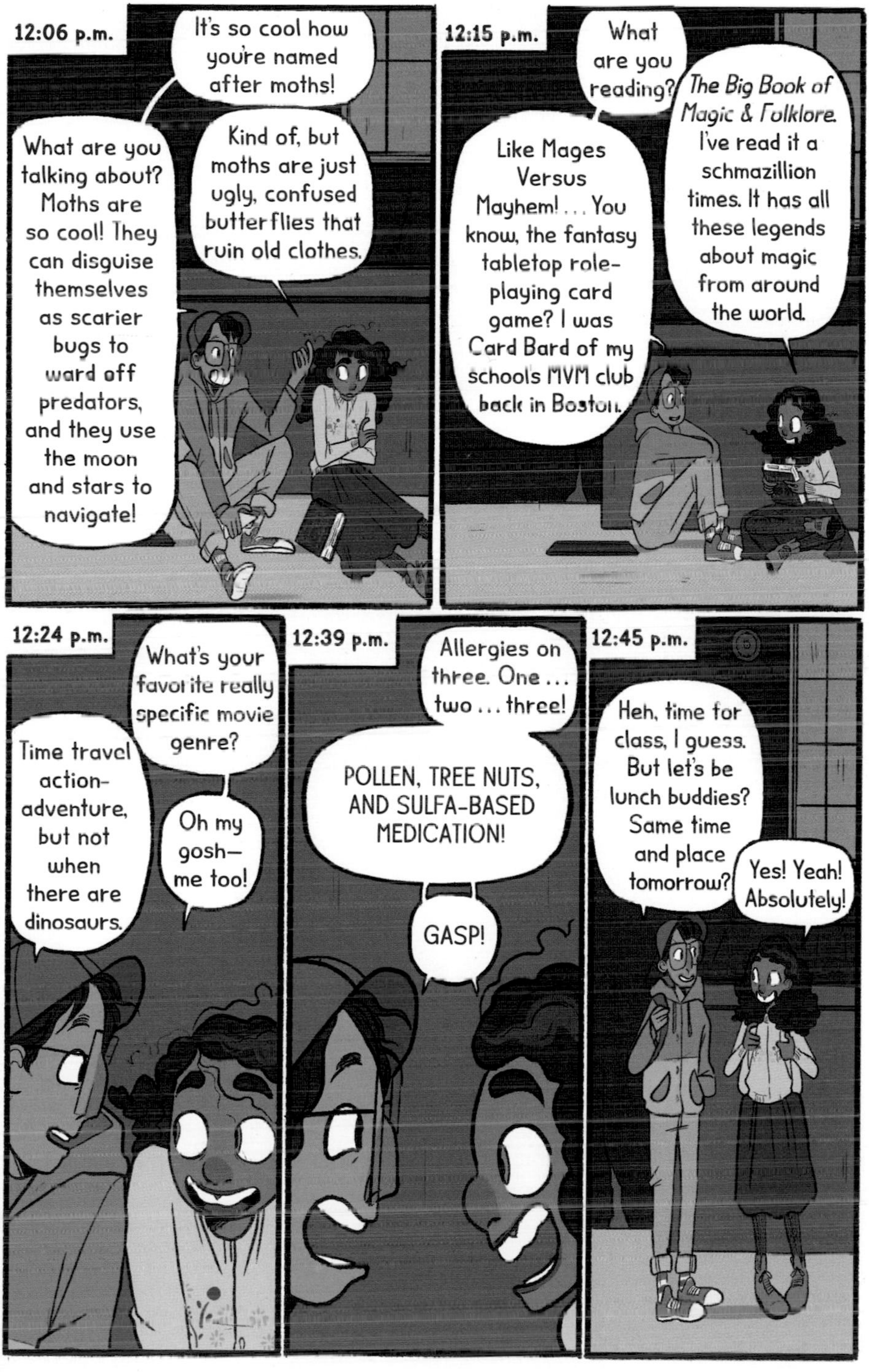
12:06 p.m.
It's so cool how you're named after moths!
What are you talking about? Moths are so cool! They can disguise themselves as scarier bugs to ward off predators, and they use the moon and stars to navigate!
Kind of, but moths are just ugly, confused butterflies that ruin old clothes.
12:15 p.m.
What are you reading?
Like Mages Versus Mayhem! . . . You know, the fantasy tabletop role-playing card game? I was Card Bard of my schools MVM club back in Boston.
The Big Book of Magic & Folklore. I've read it a schmazillion times. It has all these legends about magic from around the world.
12:24 p.m.
What's your favorite really specific movie genre?
Time travel action-adventure, but not when there are dinosaurs.
Oh my gosh— me too!
12:39 p.m.
Allergies on three. One . . . two . . . three!
POLLEN, TREE NUTS, AND SULFA-BASED MEDICATION!
GASP!
12:45 p.m.
Heh, time for class, I guess. But let's be lunch buddies? Same time and place tomorrow?
Yes! Yeah! Absolutely!

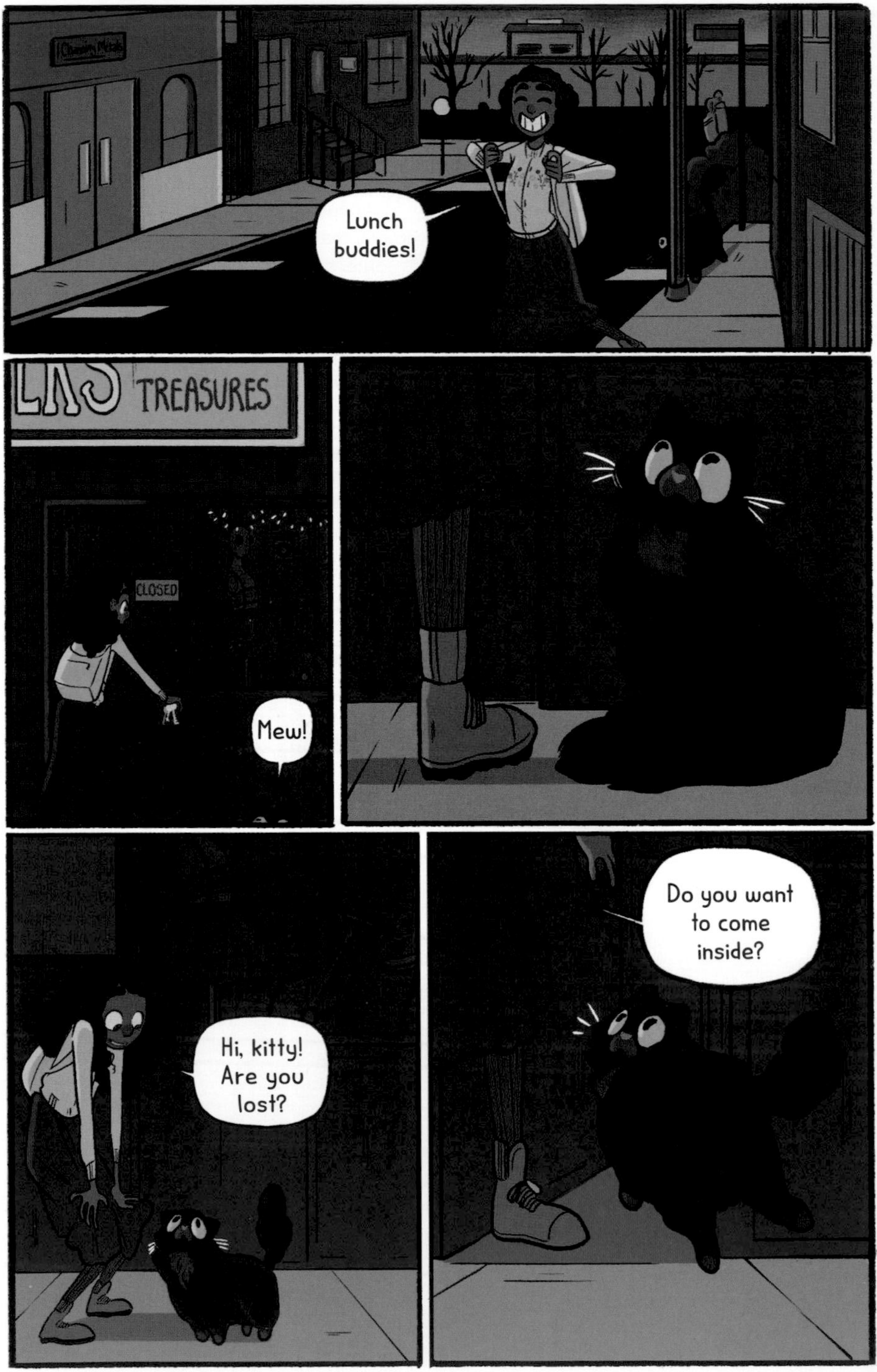
Lunch buddies!
TREASURES
CLOSED
Mew!
Hi, kitty! Are you lost?
Do you want to come inside?

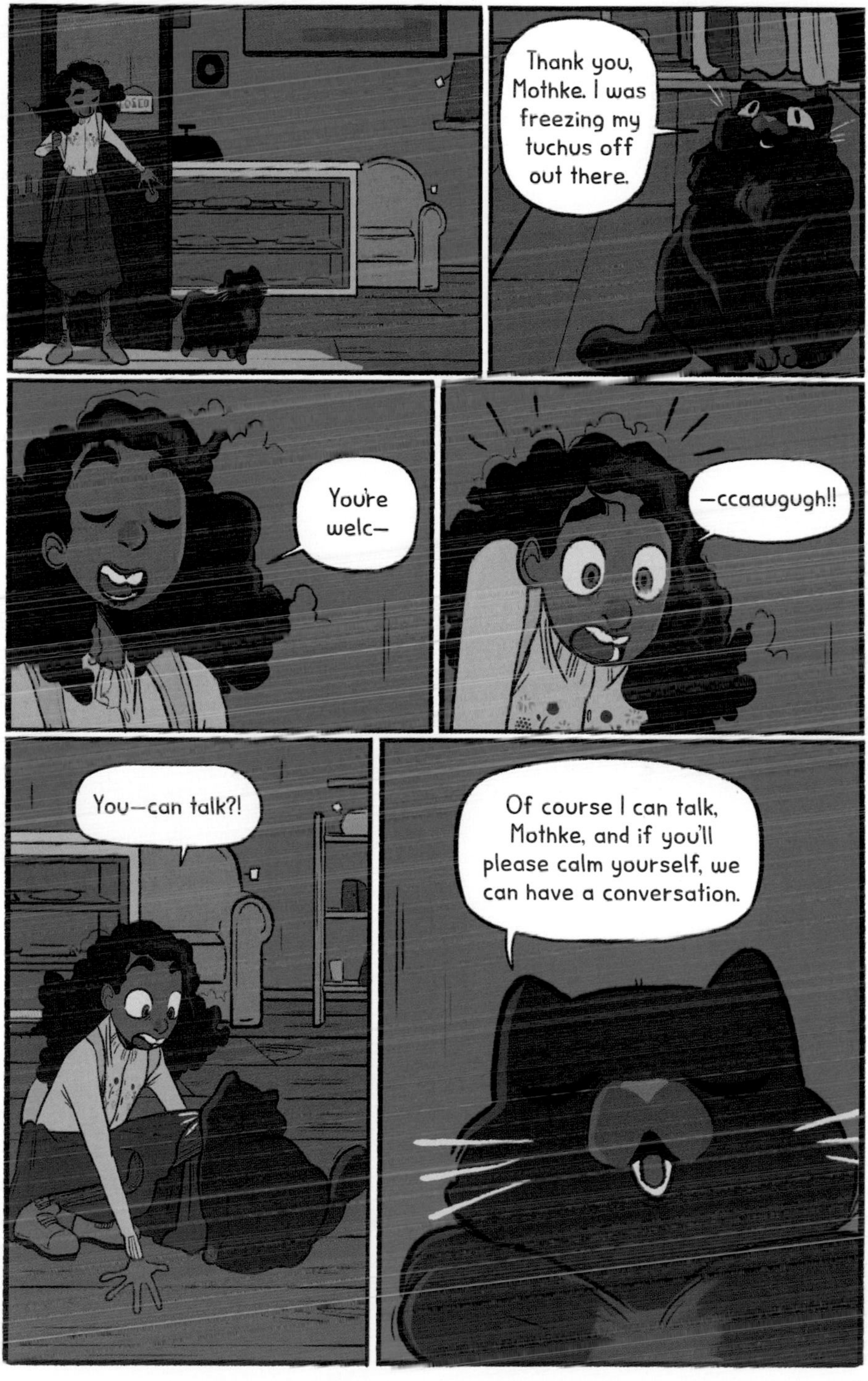
Thank you, Mothke. I was freezing my tuchus off out there.
You're welc—
—ccaaugugh!!
You—can talk?!
Of course I can talk, Mothke, and if you'll please calm yourself, we can have a conversation.

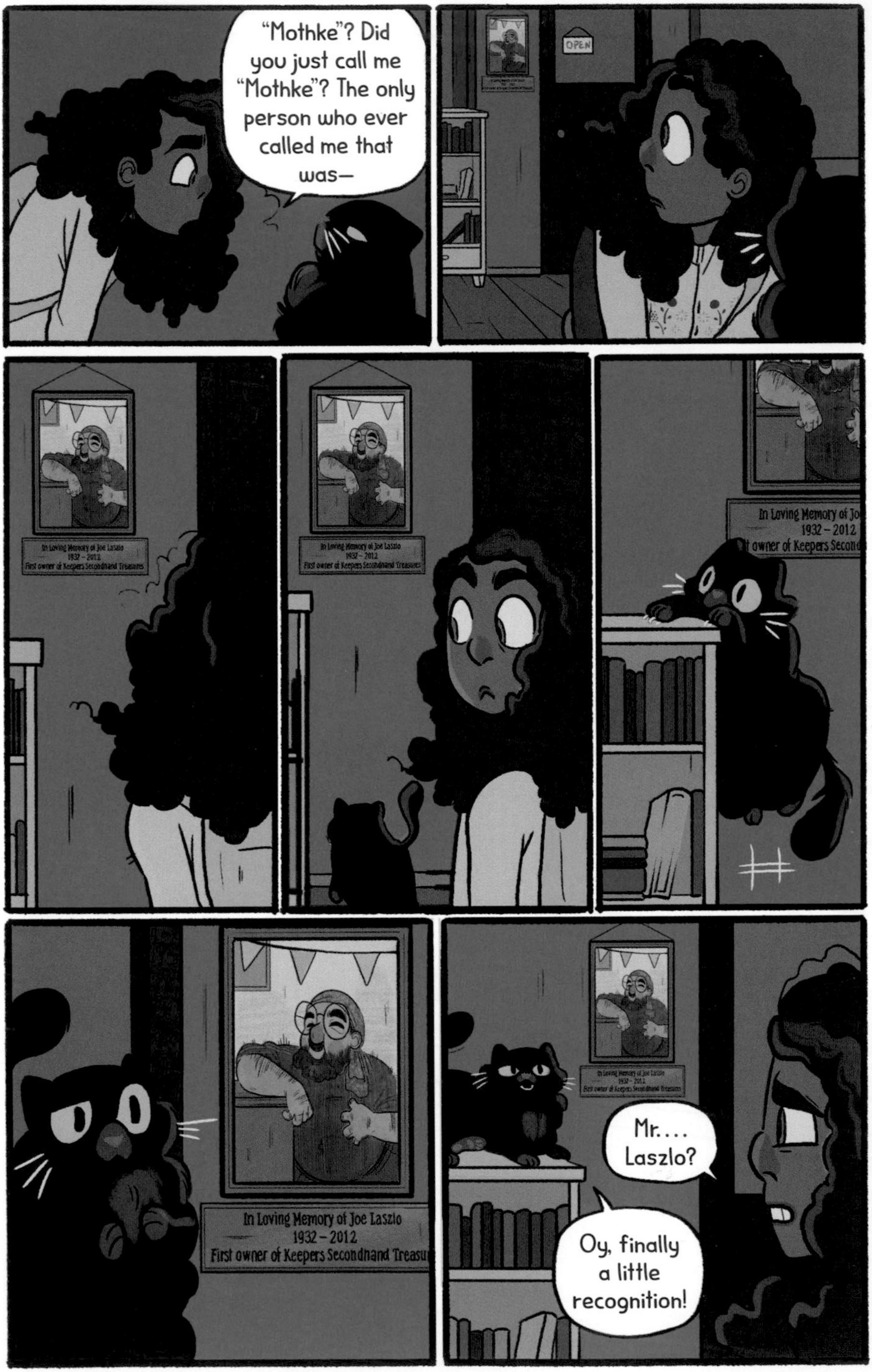
"Mothke"? Did you just call me "Mothke"? The only person who ever called me that was—
OPEN
In Loving Memory of Joe Laszlo
1932 – 2012
First owner of Keepers Secondhand Treasu
Mr.... Laszlo?
Oy, finally a little recognition!

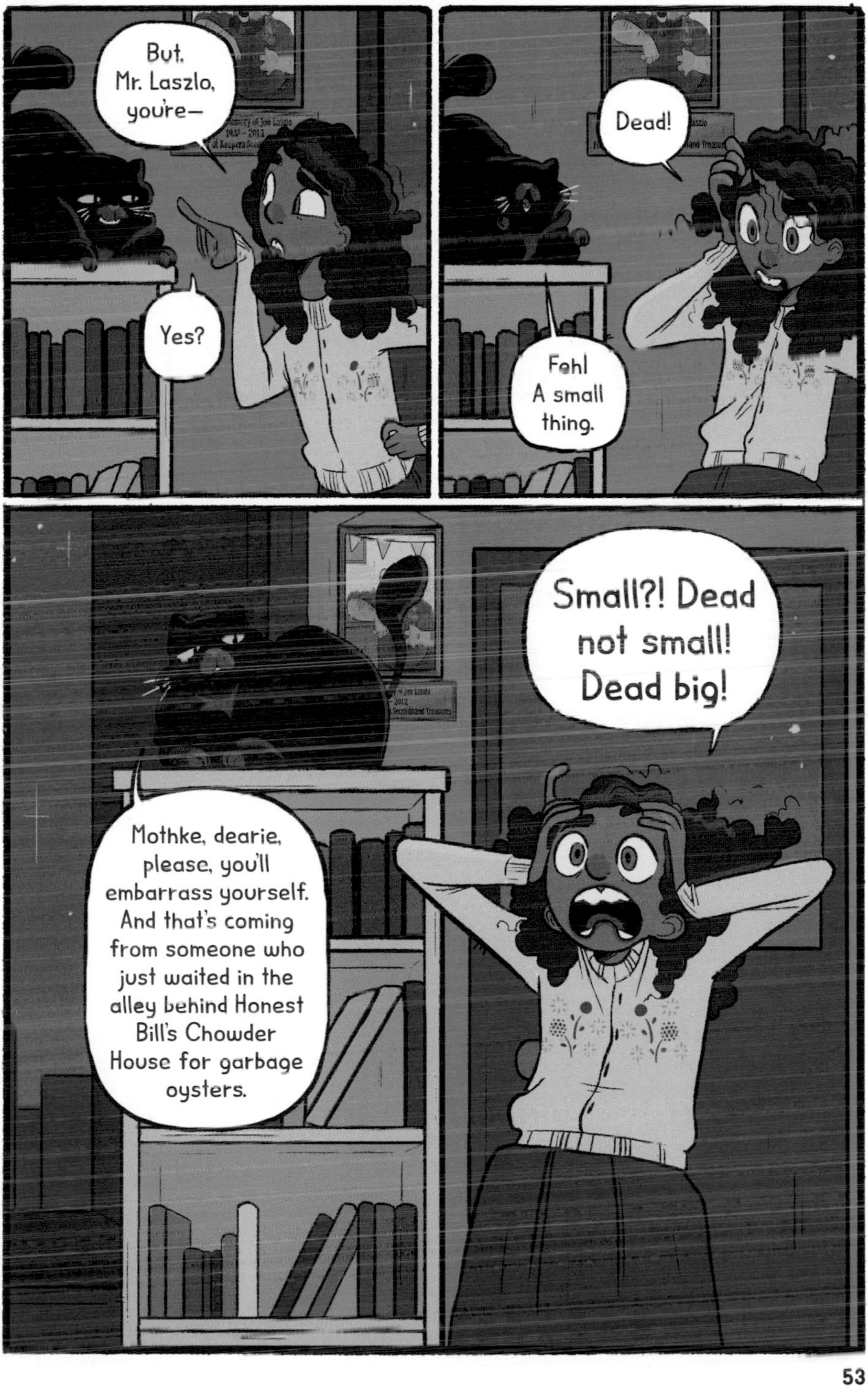
But. Mr. Laszlo, you're—
Yes?
Dead!
Feh! A small thing.
Small?! Dead not small! Dead big!
Mothke, dearie, please, you'll embarrass yourself. And that's coming from someone who just waited in the alley behind Honest Bill's Chowder House for garbage oysters.

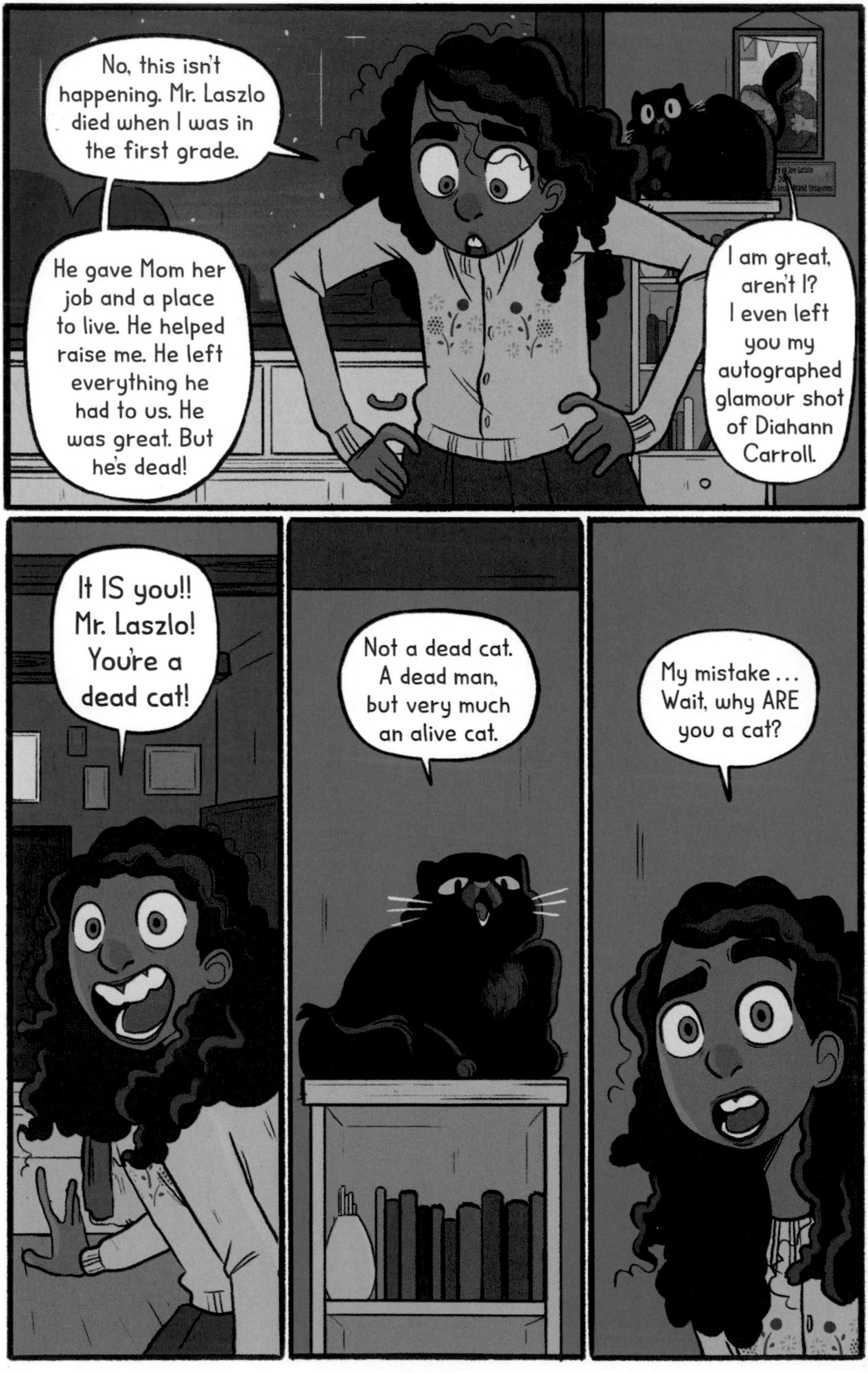
No, this isn't happening. Mr. Laszlo died when I was in the first grade.
He gave Mom her job and a place to live. He helped raise me. He left everything he had to us. He was great. But he's dead!
I am great, aren't I? I even left you my autographed glamour shot of Diahann Carroll.
It IS you!! Mr. Laszlo! You're a dead cat!
Not a dead cat. A dead man, but very much an alive cat.
My mistake . . . Wait, why ARE you a cat?

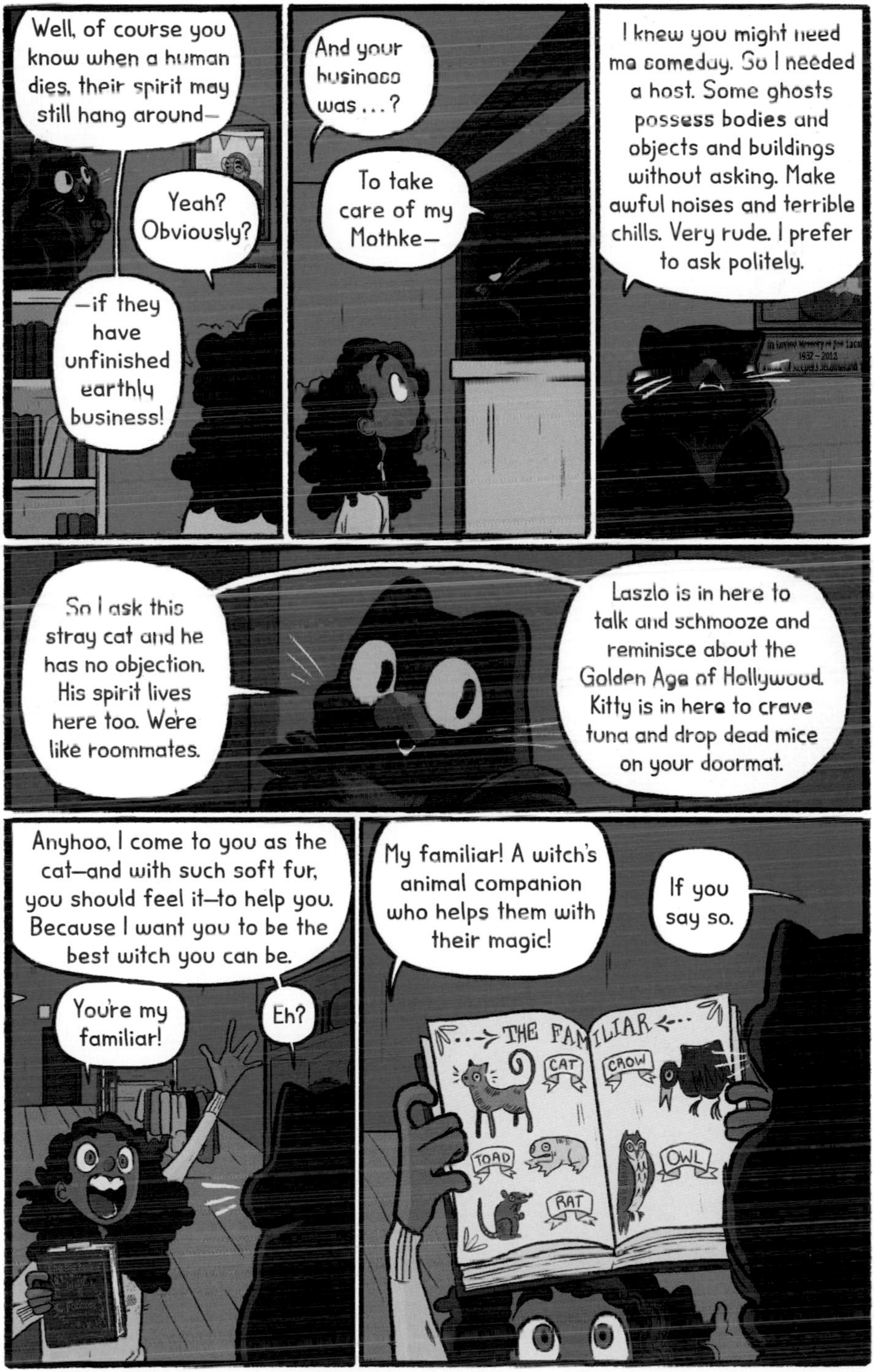

Well, of course you know when a human dies, their spirit may still hang around—
Yeah? Obviously?
—if they have unfinished earthly business!
And your business was . . . ?
To take care of my Mothke—
I knew you might need me someday. So I needed a host. Some ghosts possess bodies and objects and buildings without asking. Make awful noises and terrible chills. Very rude. I prefer to ask politely.
So I ask this stray cat and he has no objection. His spirit lives here too. We're like roommates.
Laszlo is in here to talk and schmooze and reminisce about the Golden Age of Hollywood. Kitty is in here to crave tuna and drop dead mice on your doormat.
Anyhoo, I come to you as the cat—and with such soft fur, you should feel it—to help you. Because I want you to be the best witch you can be.
You're my familiar!
Eh?
My familiar! A witch's animal companion who helps them with their magic!
If you say so.
THE FAMILIAR
CAT
CROW
TOAD
OWL
RAT

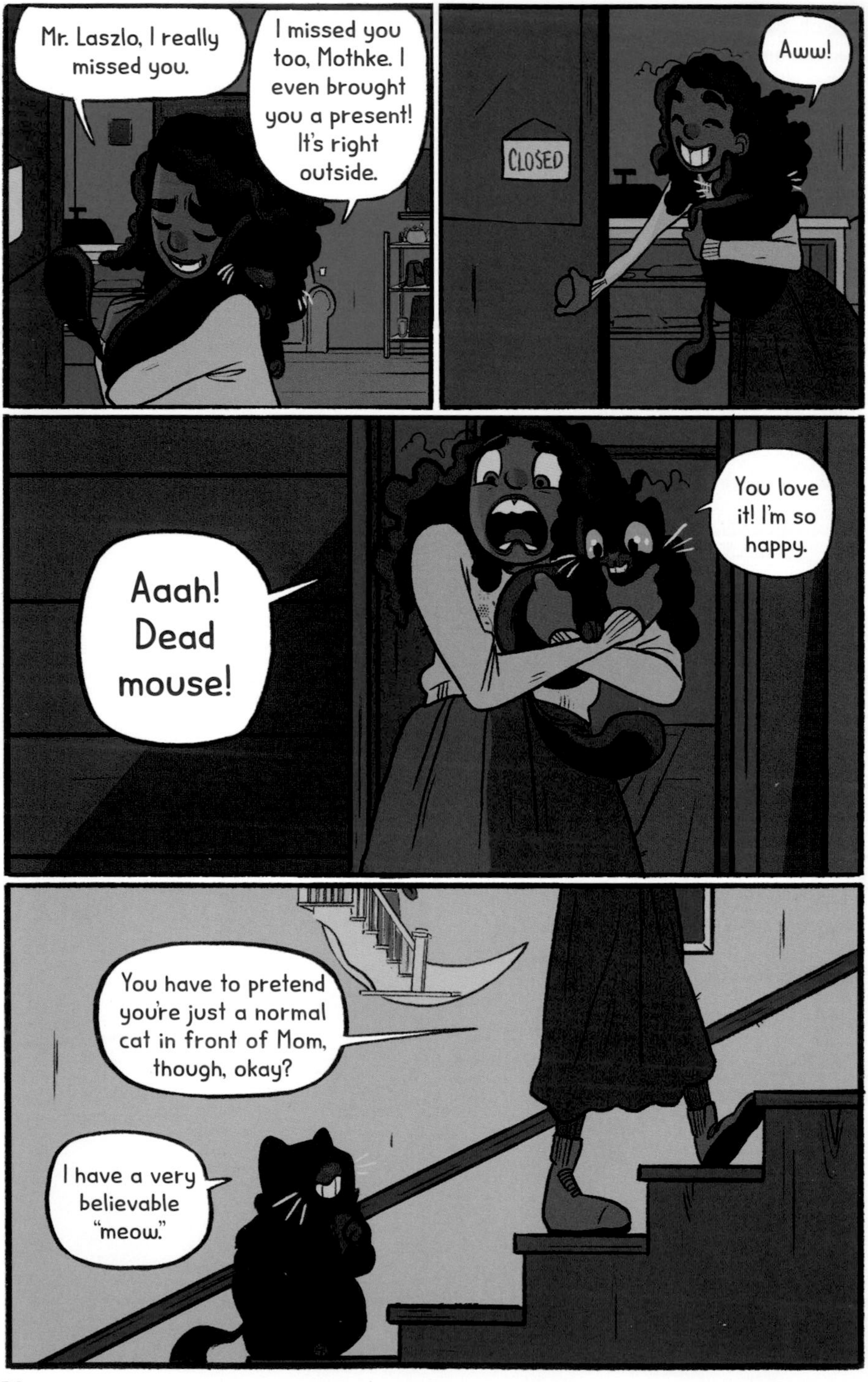
Mr. Laszlo, I really missed you.
I missed you too, Mothke. I even brought you a present! It's right outside.
CLOSED
Aww!
Aaah! Dead mouse!
You love it! I'm so happy.
You have to pretend you're just a normal cat in front of Mom, though, okay?
I have a very believable "meow."

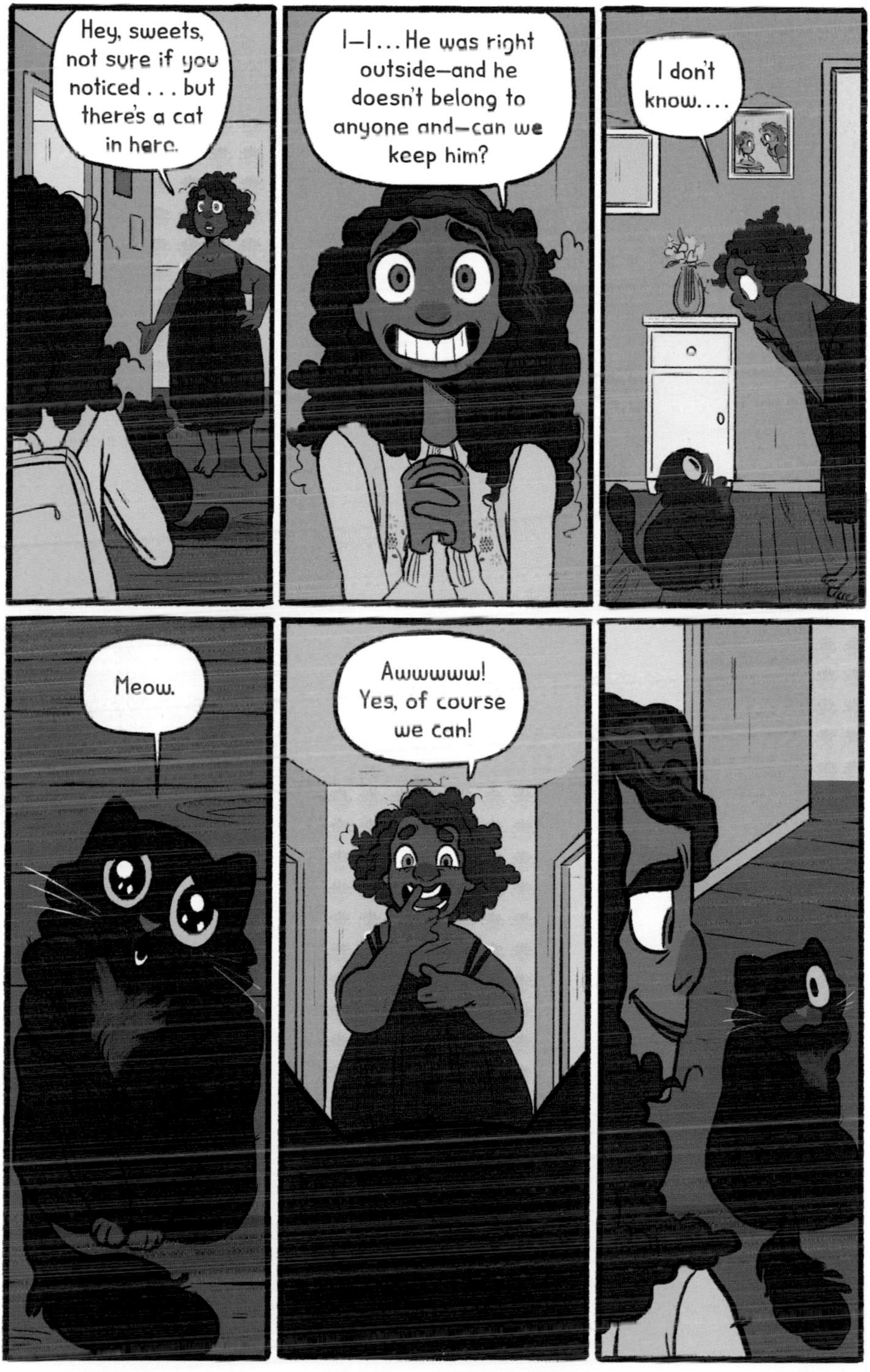
Hey, sweets, not sure if you noticed . . . but there's a cat in here.
I—I . . . He was right outside—and he doesn't belong to anyone and—can we keep him?
I don't know. . . .
Meow.
Awwwww! Yes, of course we can!

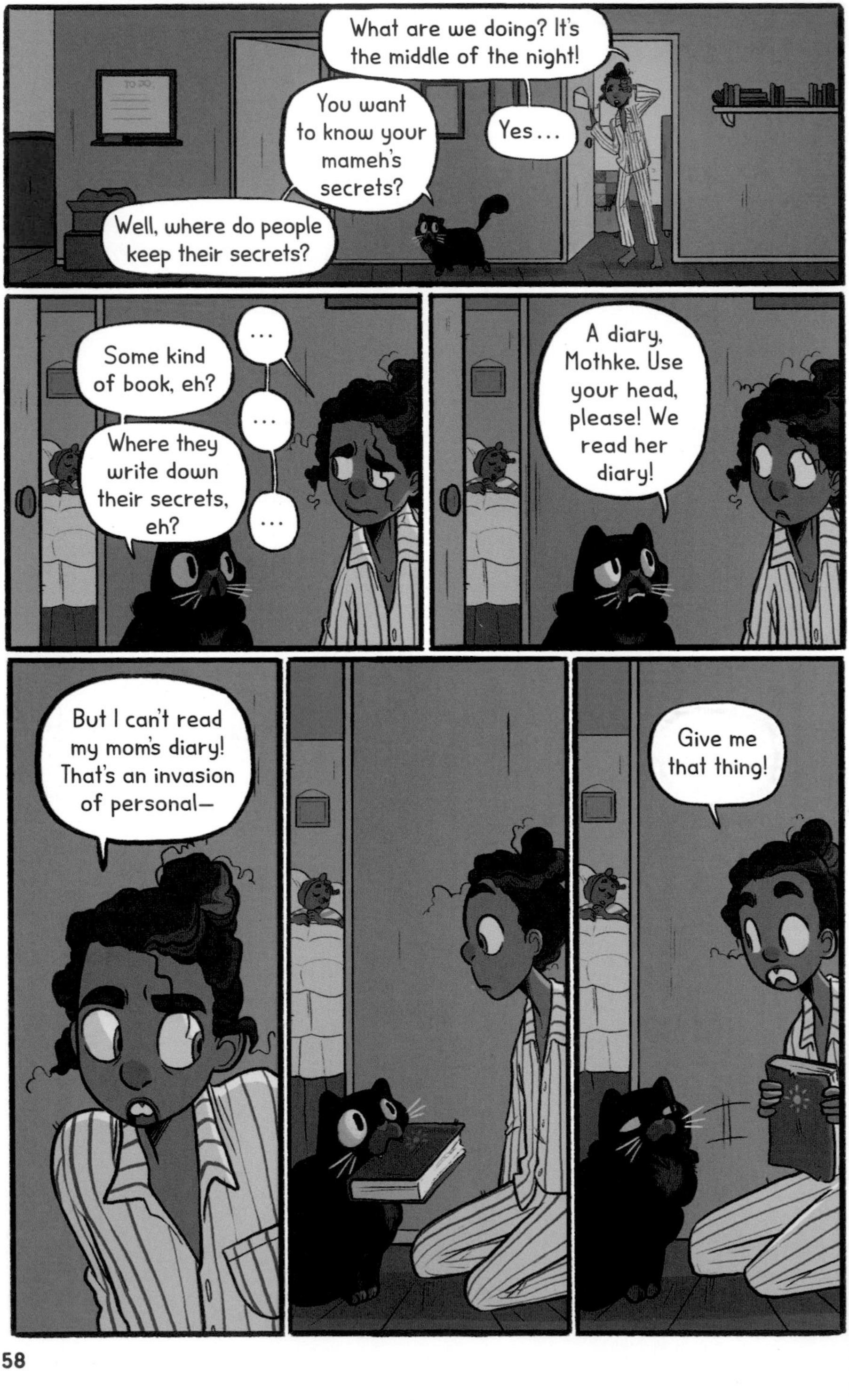
What are we doing? It's the middle of the night!
You want to know your mameh's secrets?
Yes...
Well, where do people keep their secrets?
Some kind of book, eh?
Where they write down their secrets, eh?
...
...
...
A diary, Mothke. Use your head, please! We read her diary!
But I can't read my mom's diary! That's an invasion of personal—
Give me that thing!

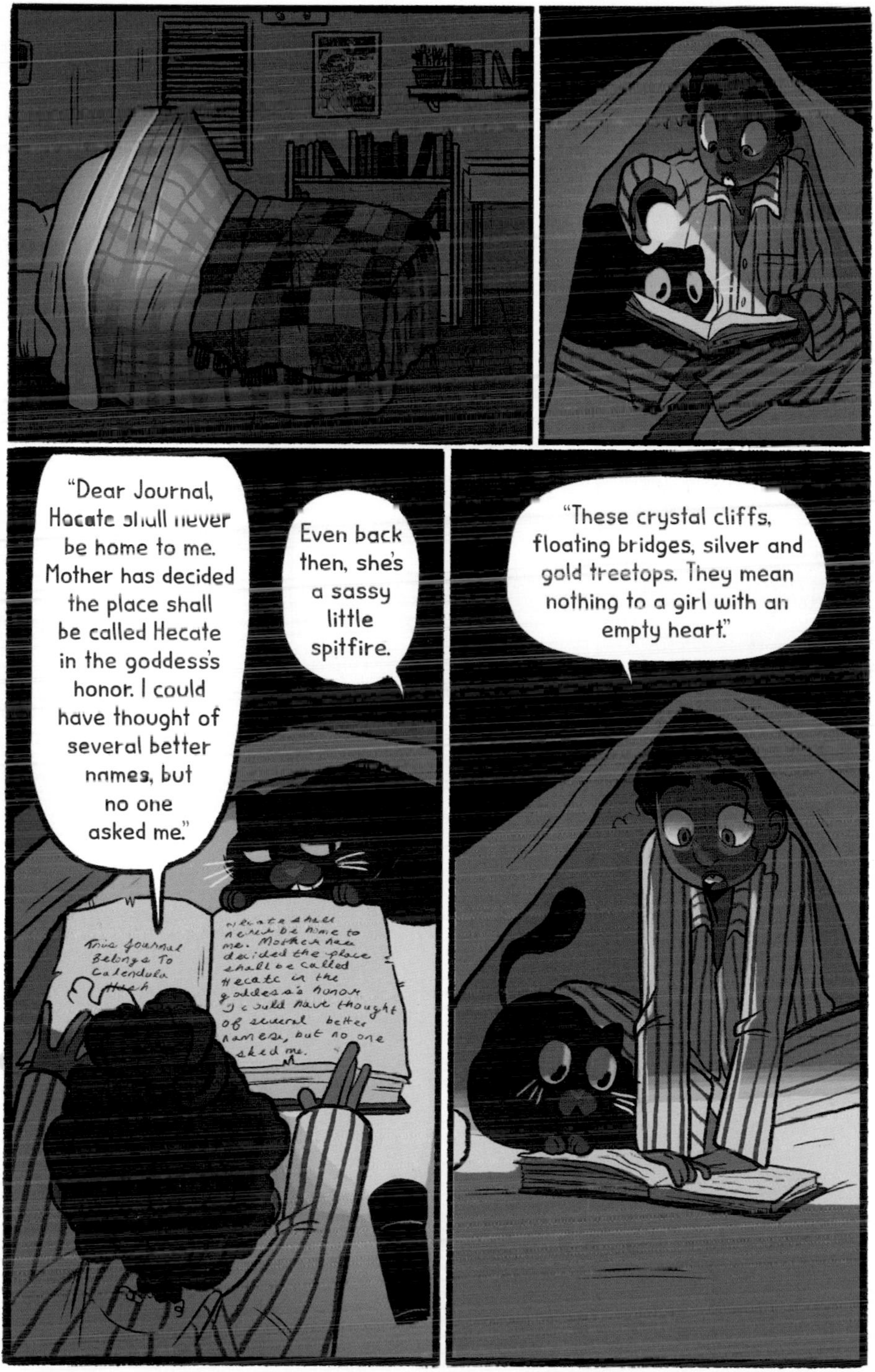
"Dear Journal, Hecate shall never be home to me. Mother has decided the place shall be called Hecate in the goddess's honor. I could have thought of several better names, but no one asked me."
Even back then, she's a sassy little spitfire.
"These crystal cliffs, floating bridges, silver and gold treetops. They mean nothing to a girl with an empty heart."

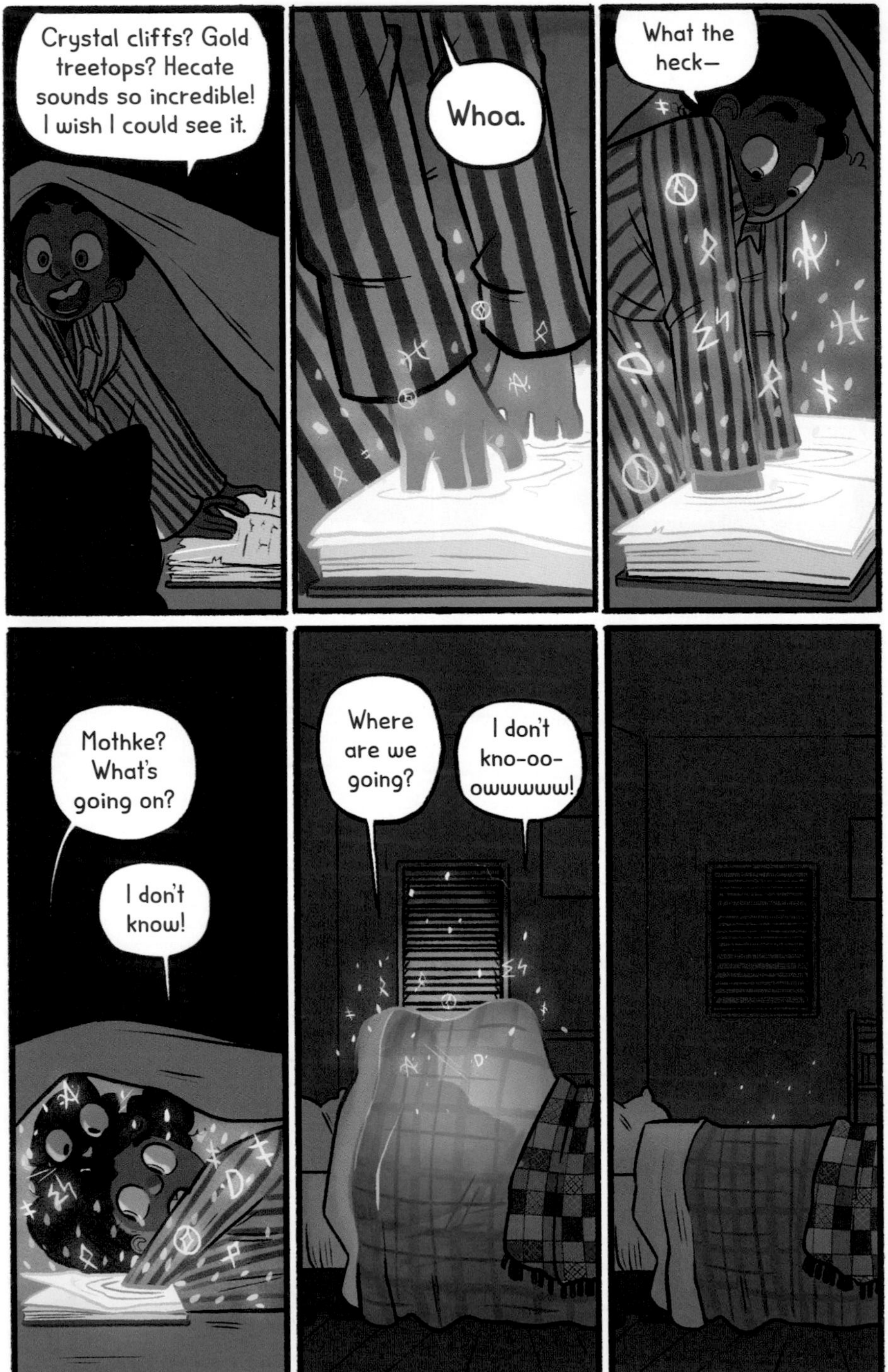
Crystal cliffs? Gold treetops? Hecate sounds so incredible! I wish I could see it.
Whoa.
What the heck—
Mothke? What's going on?
I don't know!
Where are we going?
I don't kno-oo-owwwww!

CHAPTER 4
Dear Diary

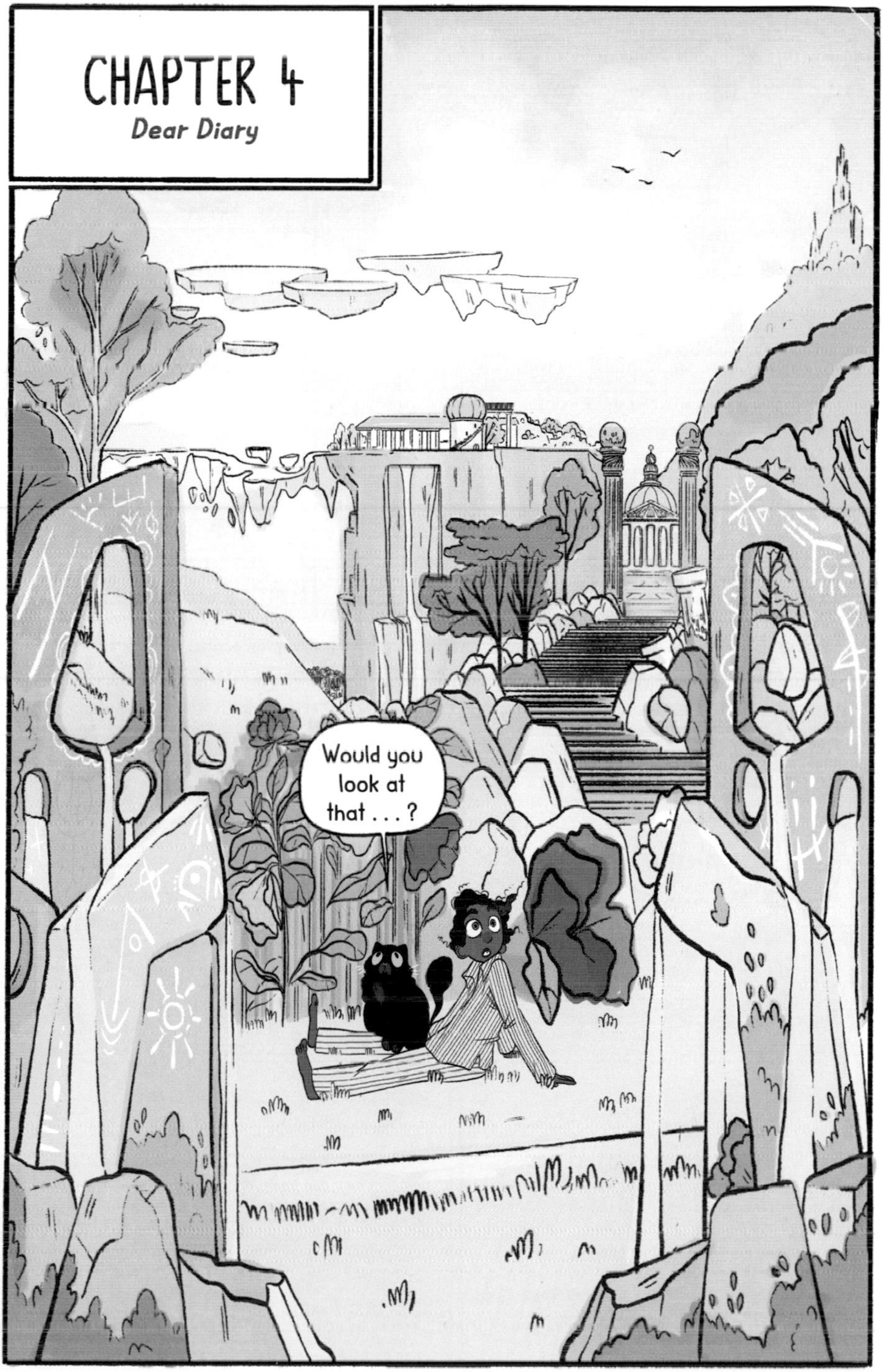
Would you look at that . . . ?

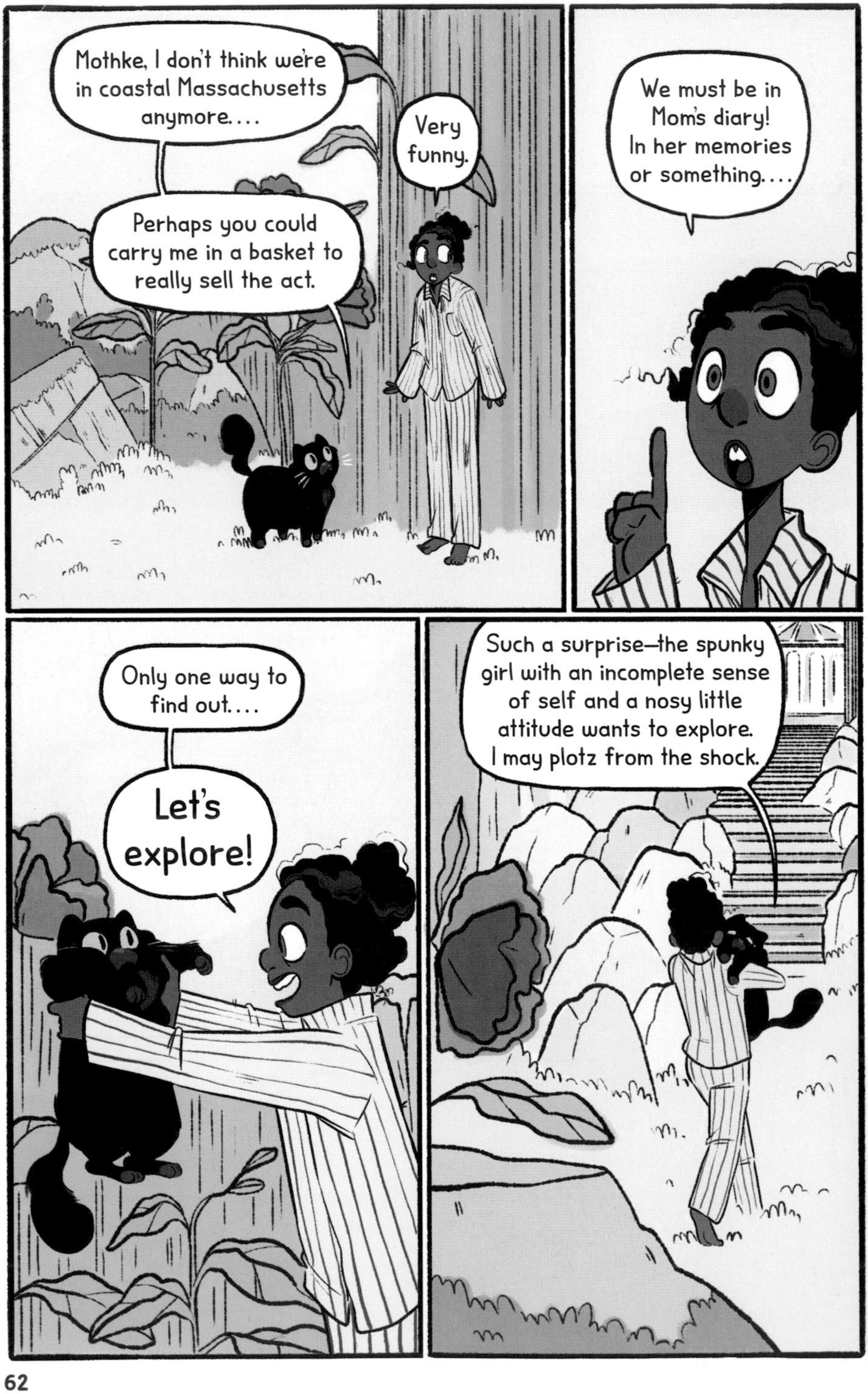
Mothke, I don't think we're in coastal Massachusetts anymore. . . .
Very funny.
Perhaps you could carry me in a basket to really sell the act.
We must be in Mom's diary! In her memories or something. . . .
Only one way to find out. . . .
Let's explore!
Such a surprise—the spunky girl with an incomplete sense of self and a nosy little attitude wants to explore. I may plotz from the shock.

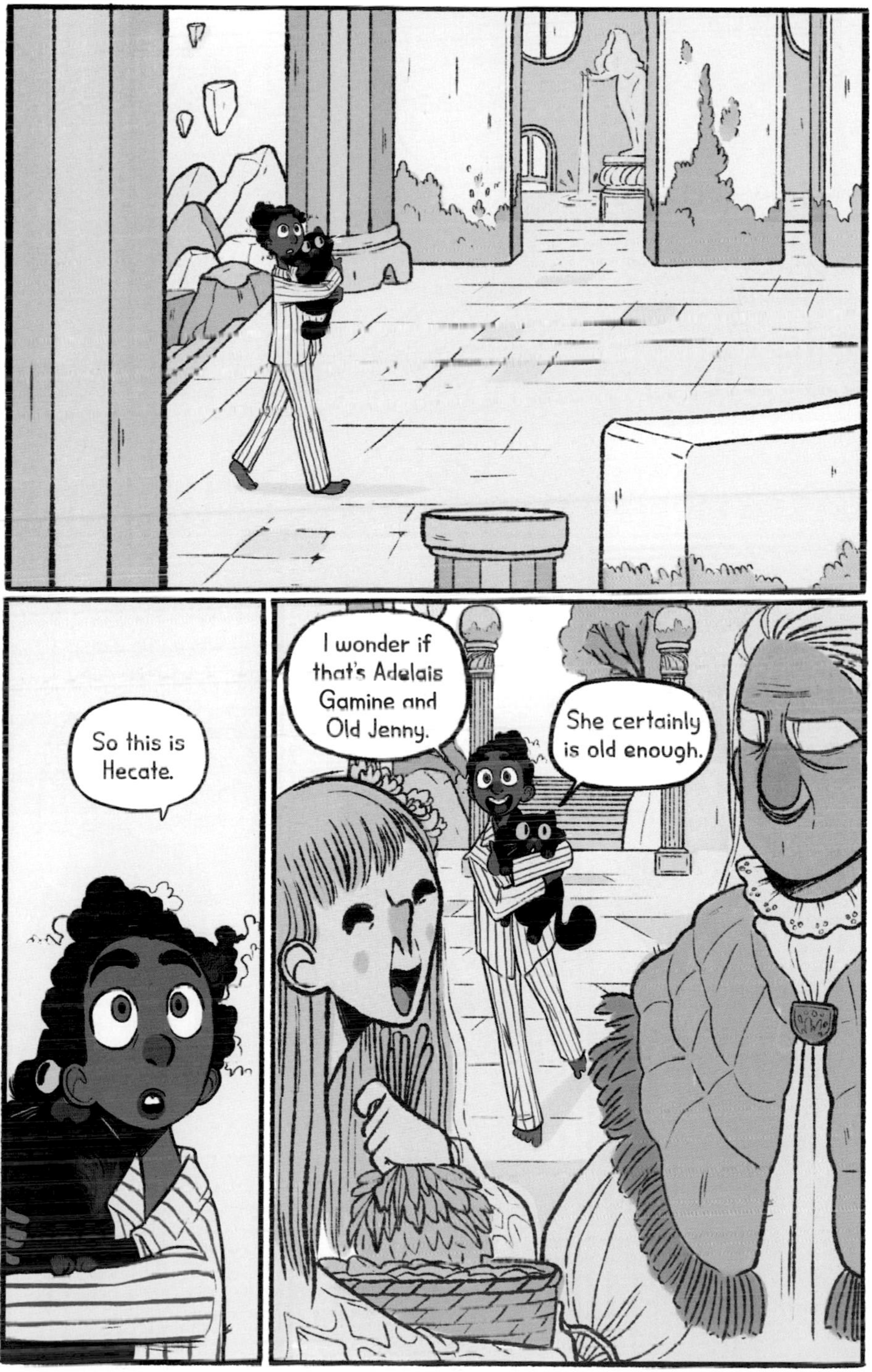

So this is Hecate.
I wonder if that's Adelais Gamine and Old Jenny.
She certainly is old enough.

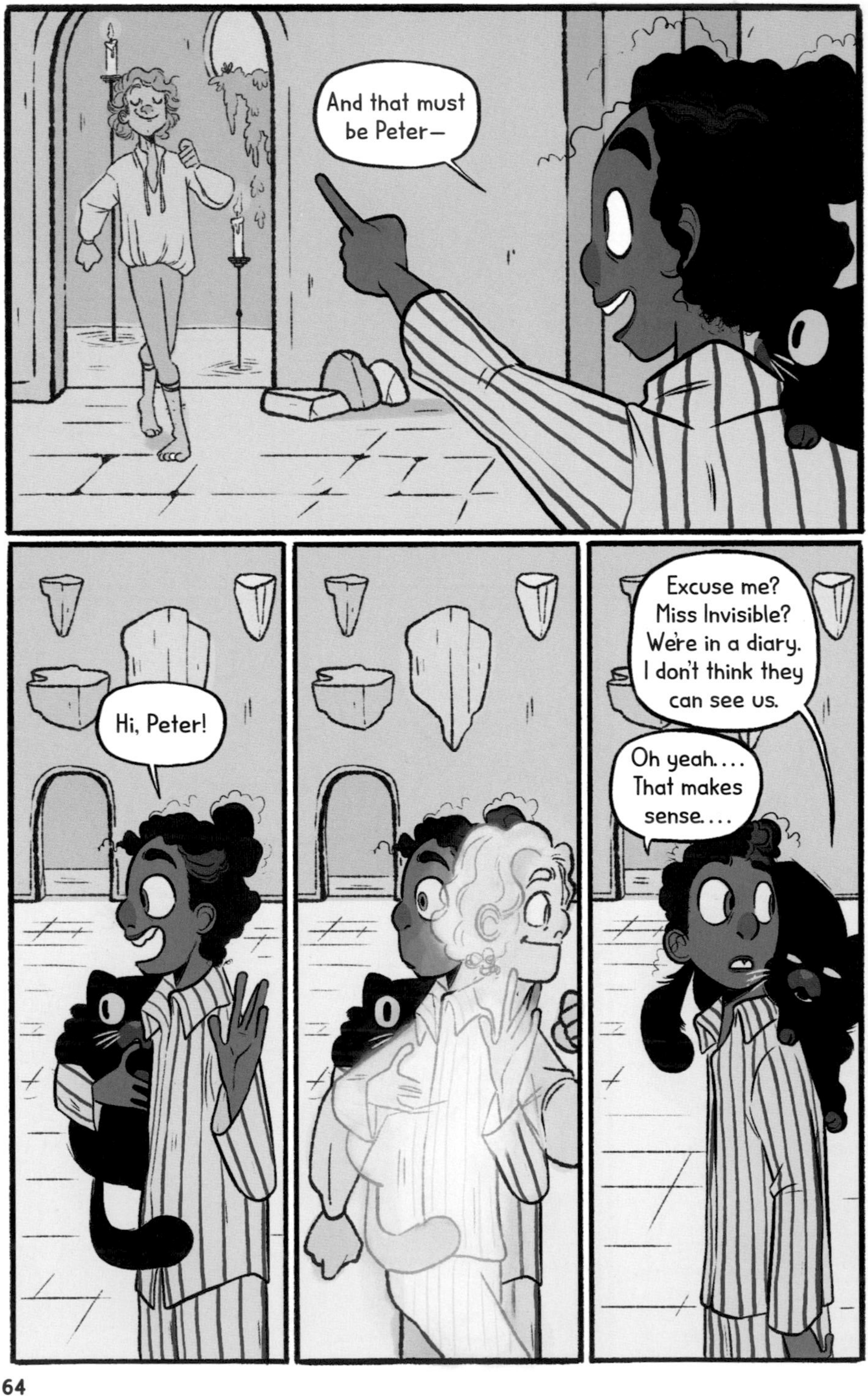
And that must be Peter—
Hi, Peter!
Excuse me? Miss Invisible? We're in a diary. I don't think they can see us.
Oh yeah.... That makes sense....

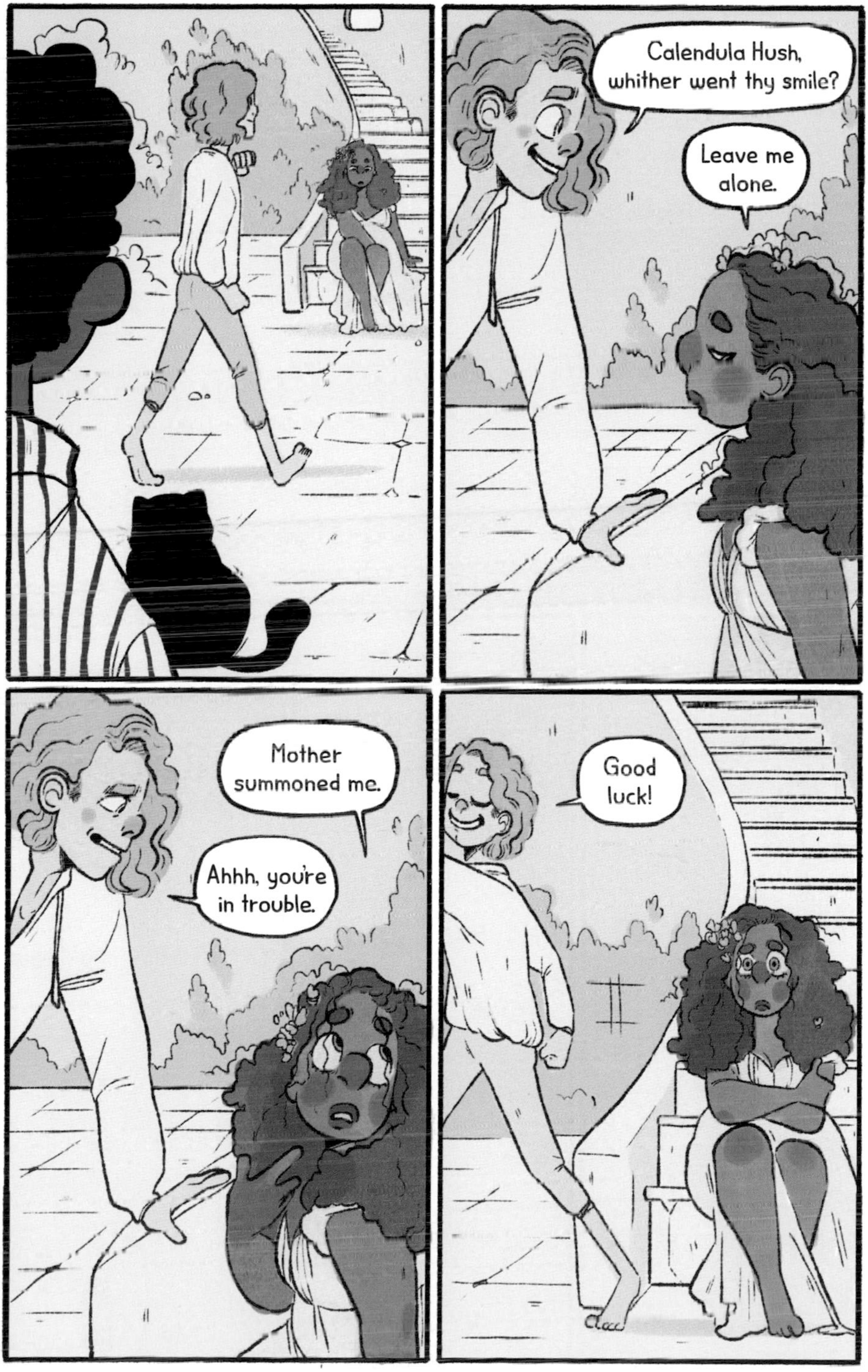
Calendula Hush, whither went thy smile?
Leave me alone.
Mother summoned me.
Ahhh, you're in trouble.
Good luck!

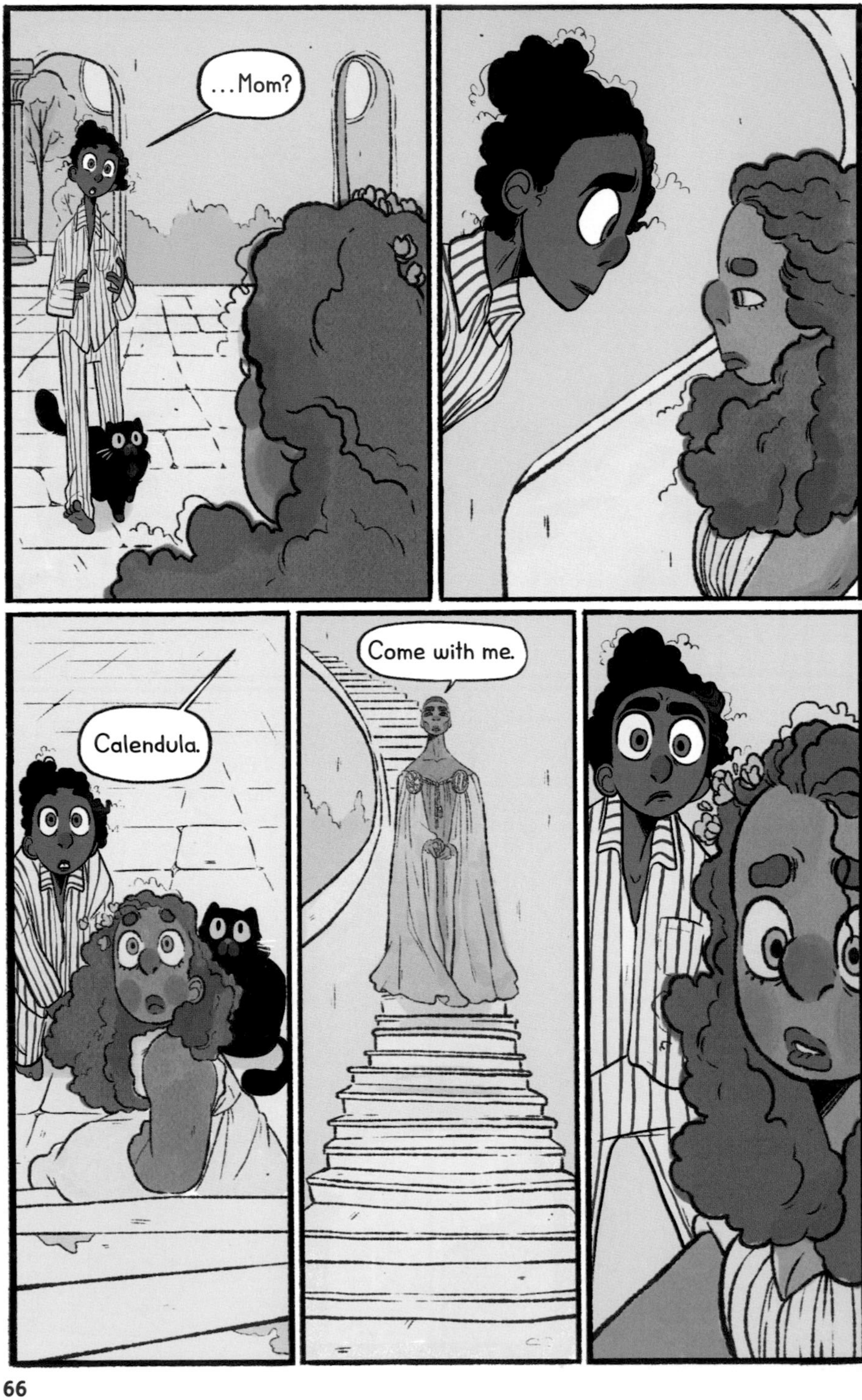
...Mom?
Calendula.
Come with me.

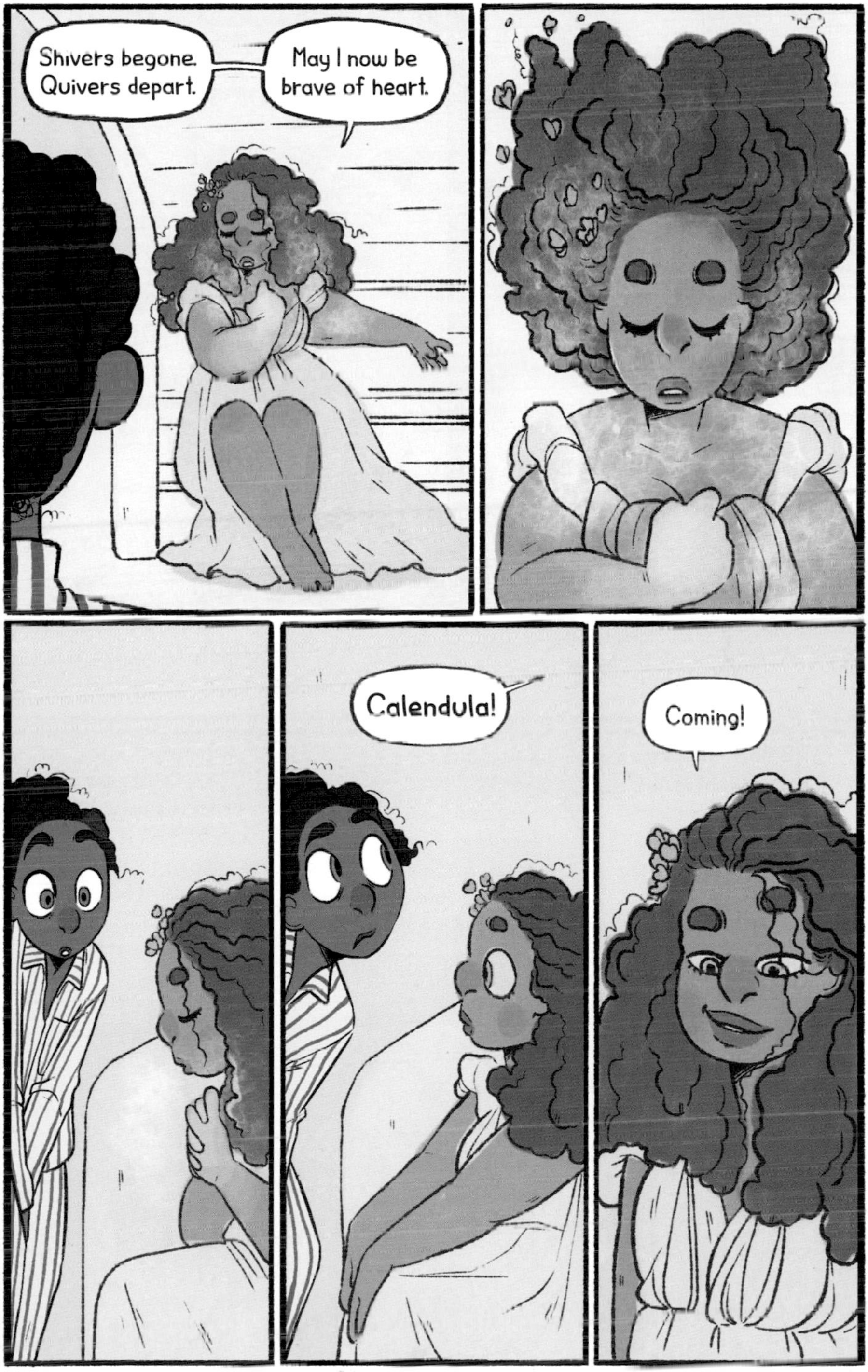
Shivers begone. Quivers depart.
May I now be brave of heart.
Calendula!
Coming!

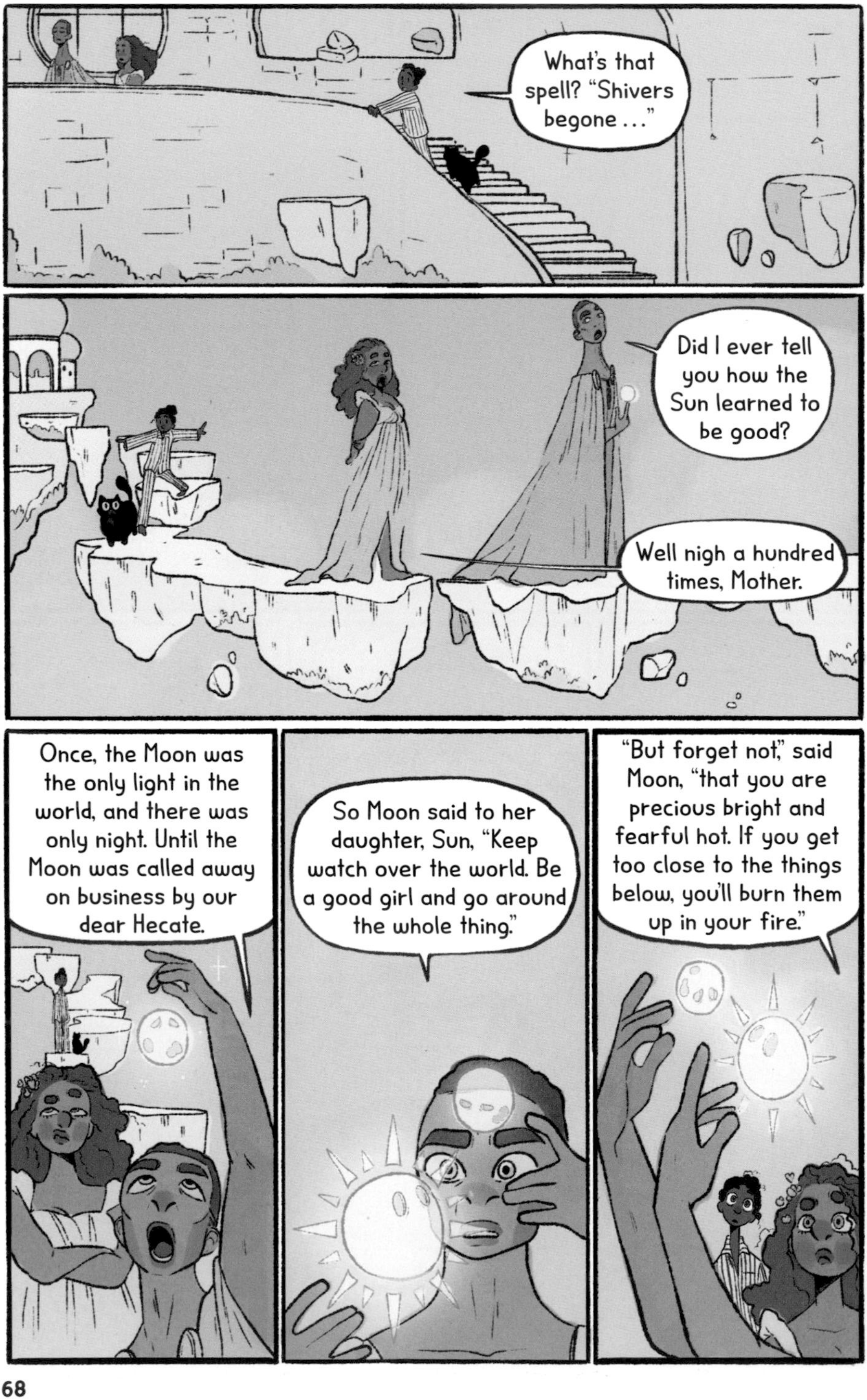
What's that spell? "Shivers begone . . ."
Did I ever tell you how the Sun learned to be good?
Well nigh a hundred times, Mother.
Once, the Moon was the only light in the world, and there was only night. Until the Moon was called away on business by our dear Hecate.
So Moon said to her daughter, Sun, "Keep watch over the world. Be a good girl and go around the whole thing."
"But forget not," said Moon, "that you are precious bright and fearful hot. If you get too close to the things below, you'll burn them up in your fire."

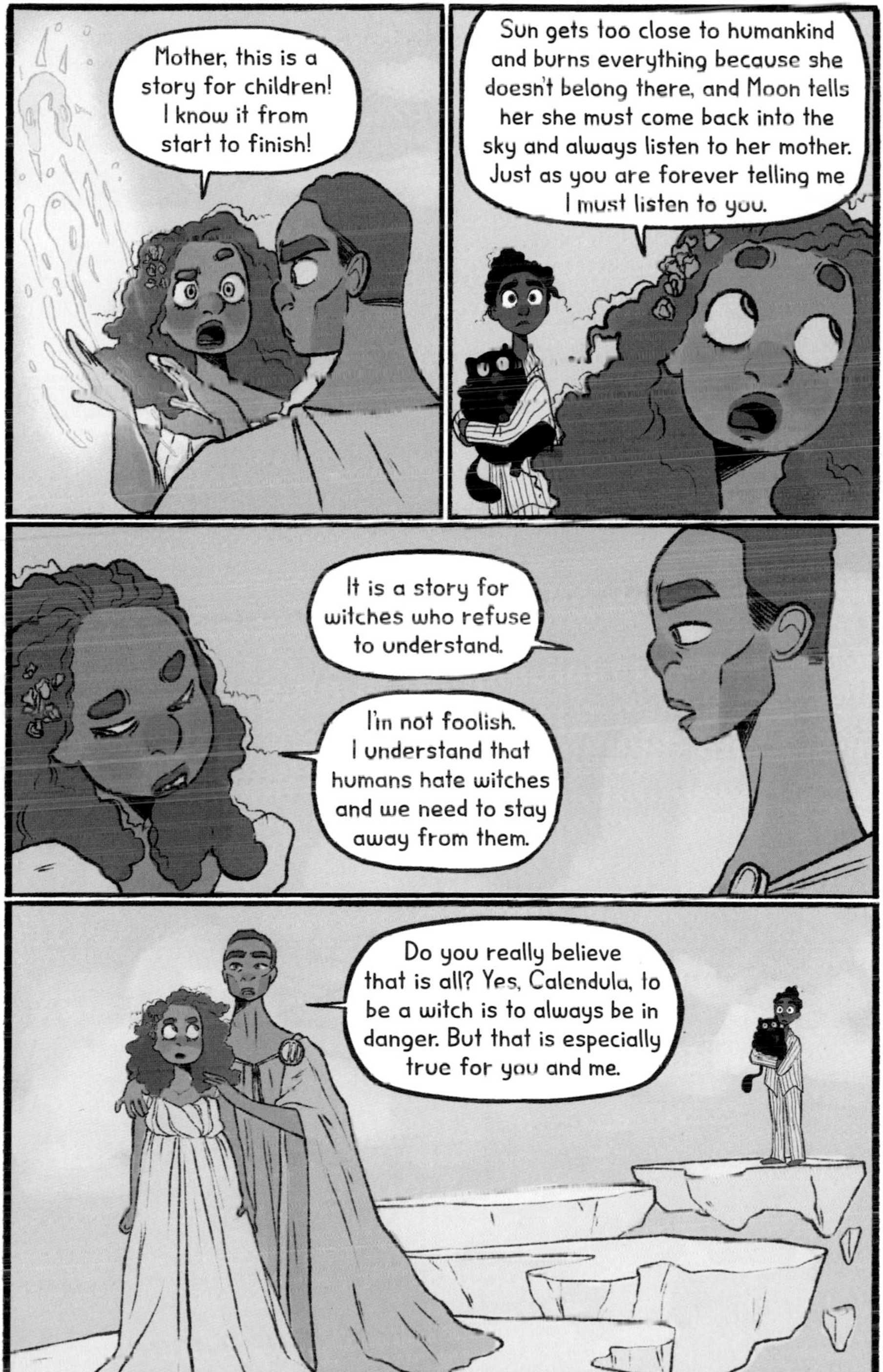
Mother, this is a story for children! I know it from start to finish!
Sun gets too close to humankind and burns everything because she doesn't belong there, and Moon tells her she must come back into the sky and always listen to her mother. Just as you are forever telling me I must listen to you.
It is a story for witches who refuse to understand.
I'm not foolish. I understand that humans hate witches and we need to stay away from them.
Do you really believe that is all? Yes, Calendula, to be a witch is to always be in danger. But that is especially true for you and me.

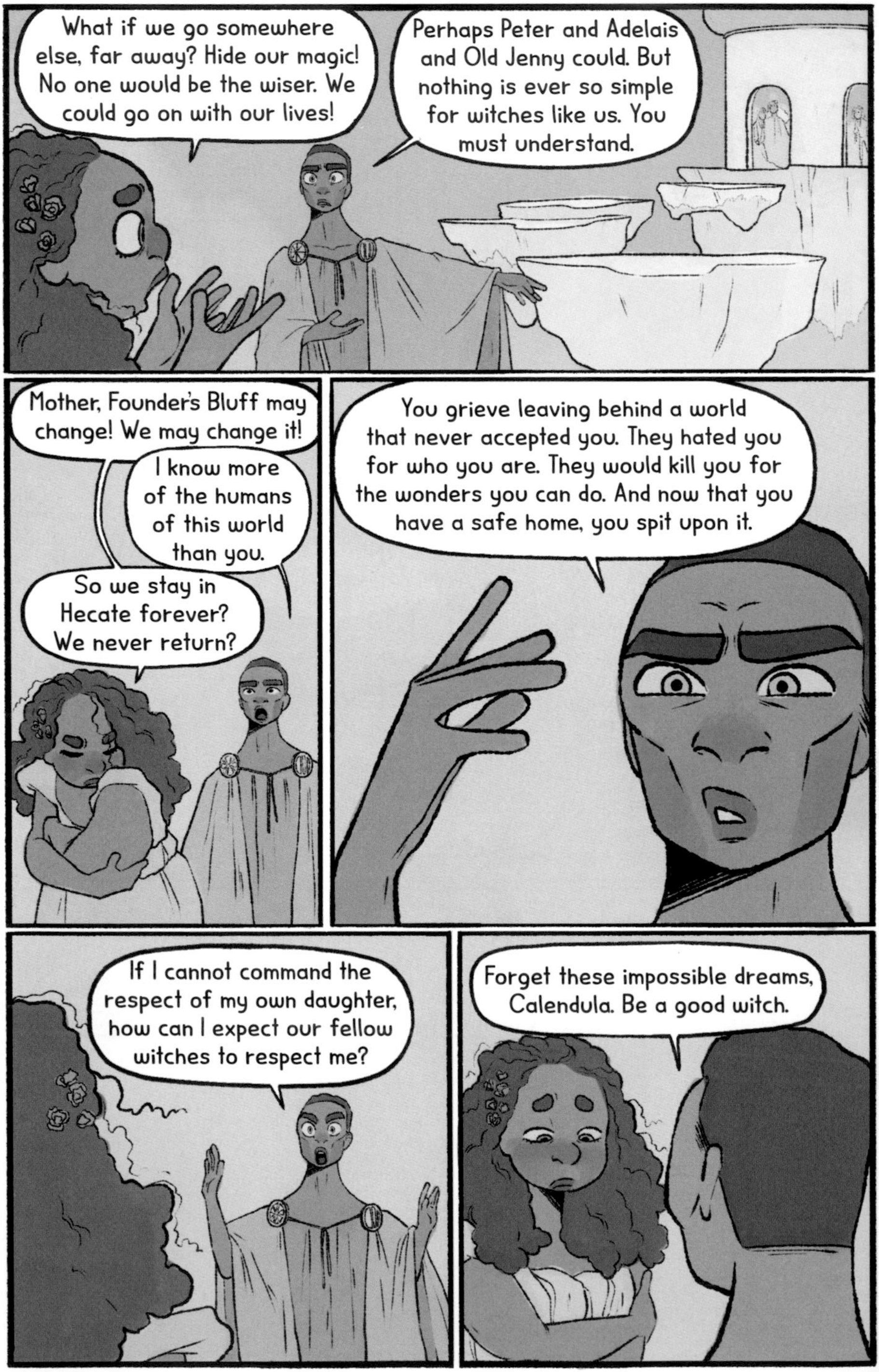
What if we go somewhere else, far away? Hide our magic! No one would be the wiser. We could go on with our lives!
Perhaps Peter and Adelais and Old Jenny could. But nothing is ever so simple for witches like us. You must understand.
Mother, Founder's Bluff may change! We may change it!
I know more of the humans of this world than you.
So we stay in Hecate forever? We never return?
You grieve leaving behind a world that never accepted you. They hated you for who you are. They would kill you for the wonders you can do. And now that you have a safe home, you spit upon it.
If I cannot command the respect of my own daughter, how can I expect our fellow witches to respect me?
Forget these impossible dreams, Calendula. Be a good witch.

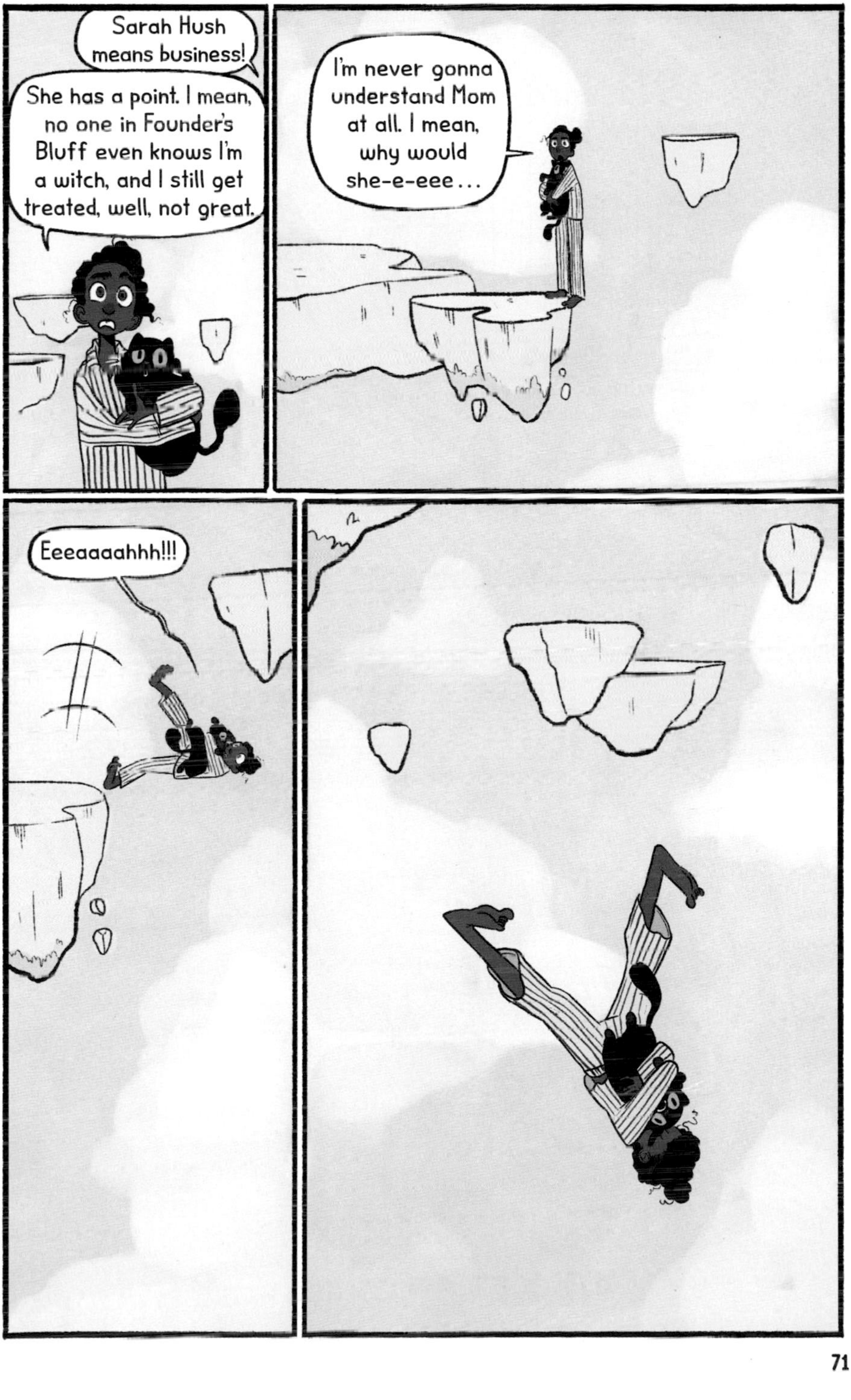
Sarah Hush means business!
She has a point. I mean, no one in Founder's Bluff even knows I'm a witch, and I still get treated, well, not great.
I'm never gonna understand Mom at all. I mean, why would she-e-eee . . .
Eeeaaaahhh!!!

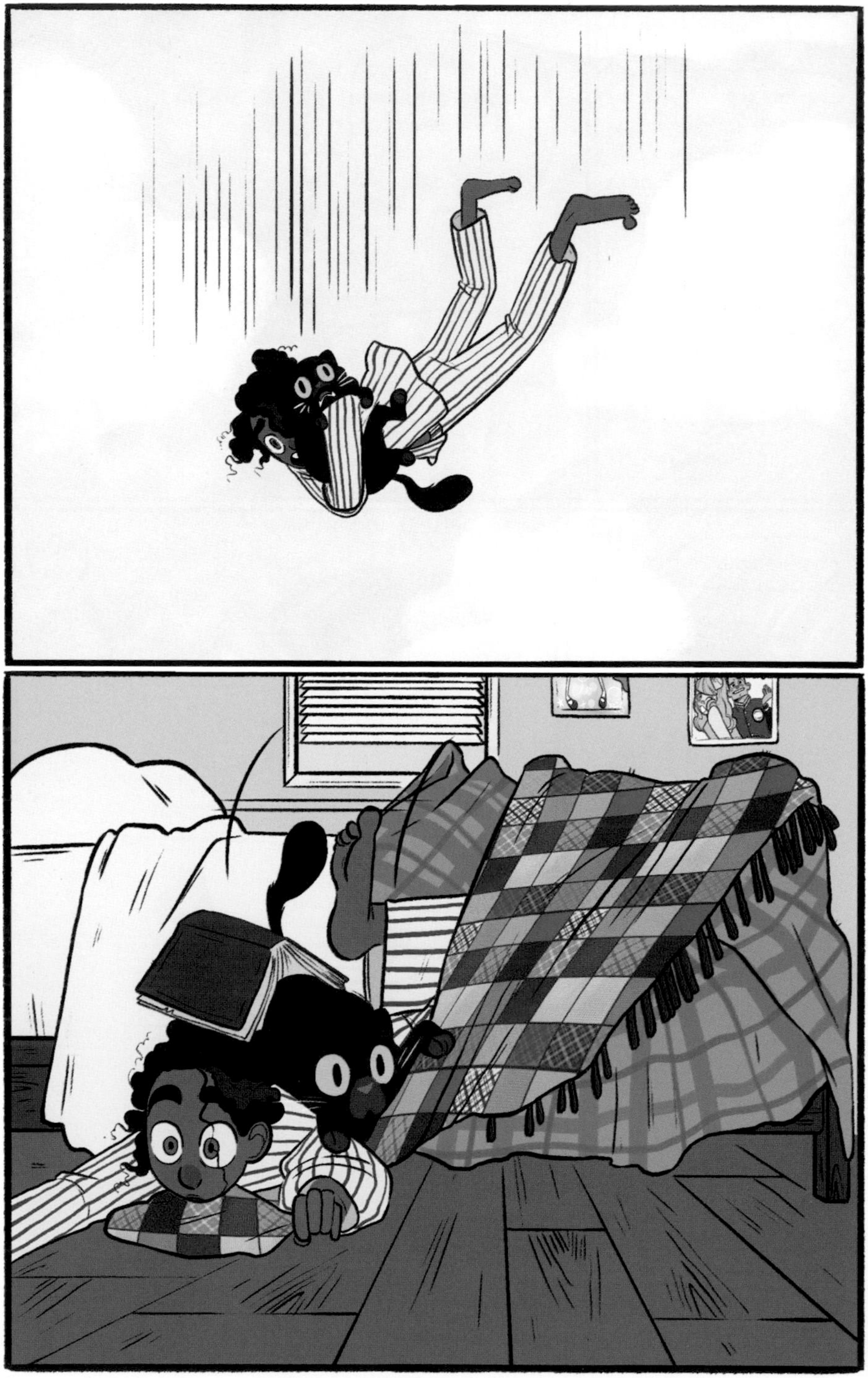

CHAPTER 5
Sympathetic Magic

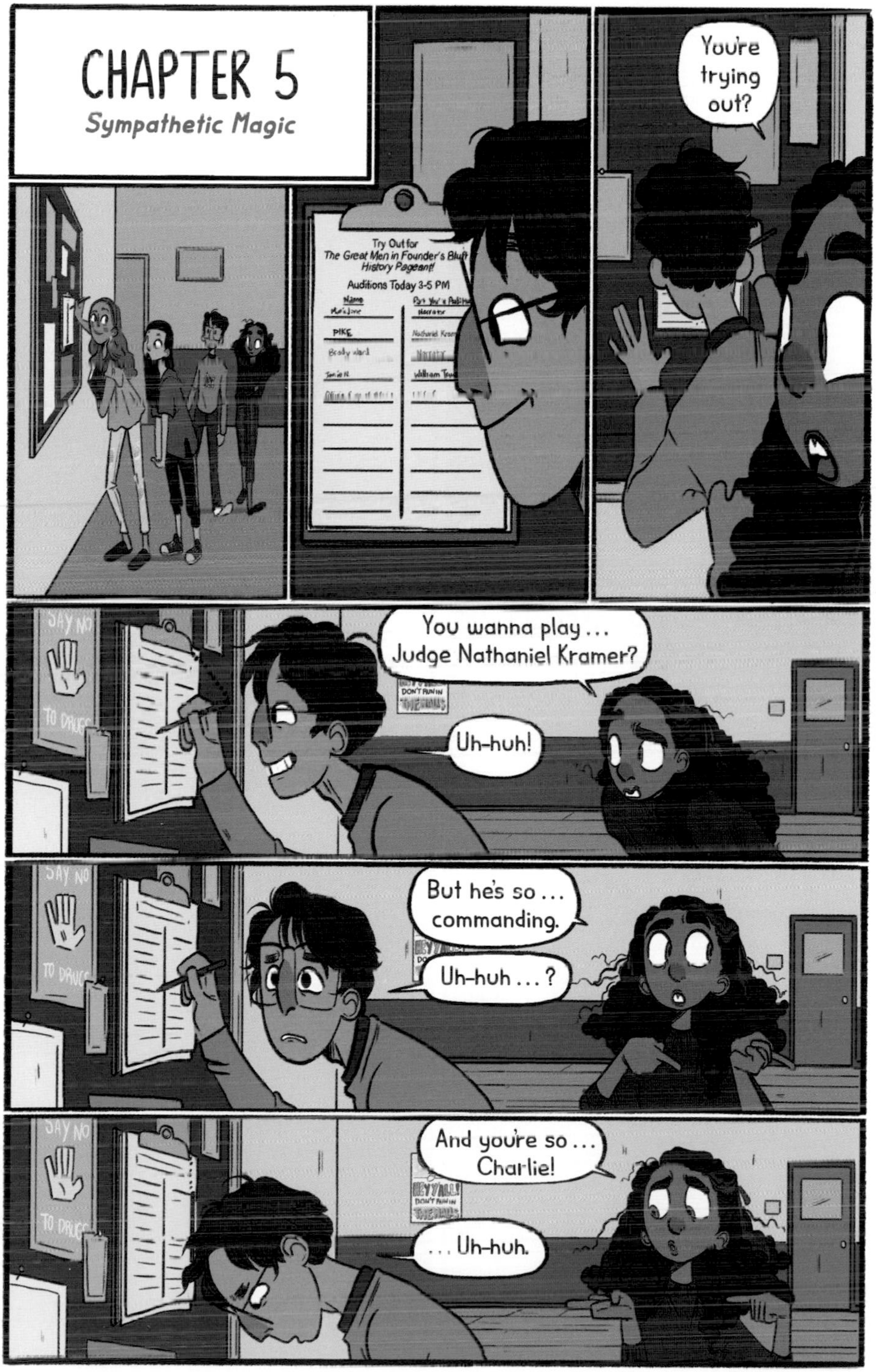

Try Out for
The Great Men in Founder's Bluff History Pageant!
Auditions Today 3-5 PM
You're trying out?
You wanna play . . . Judge Nathaniel Kramer?
Uh-huh!
But he's so . . . commanding.
Uh-huh . . . ?
And you're so . . . Charlie!
. . . Uh-huh.

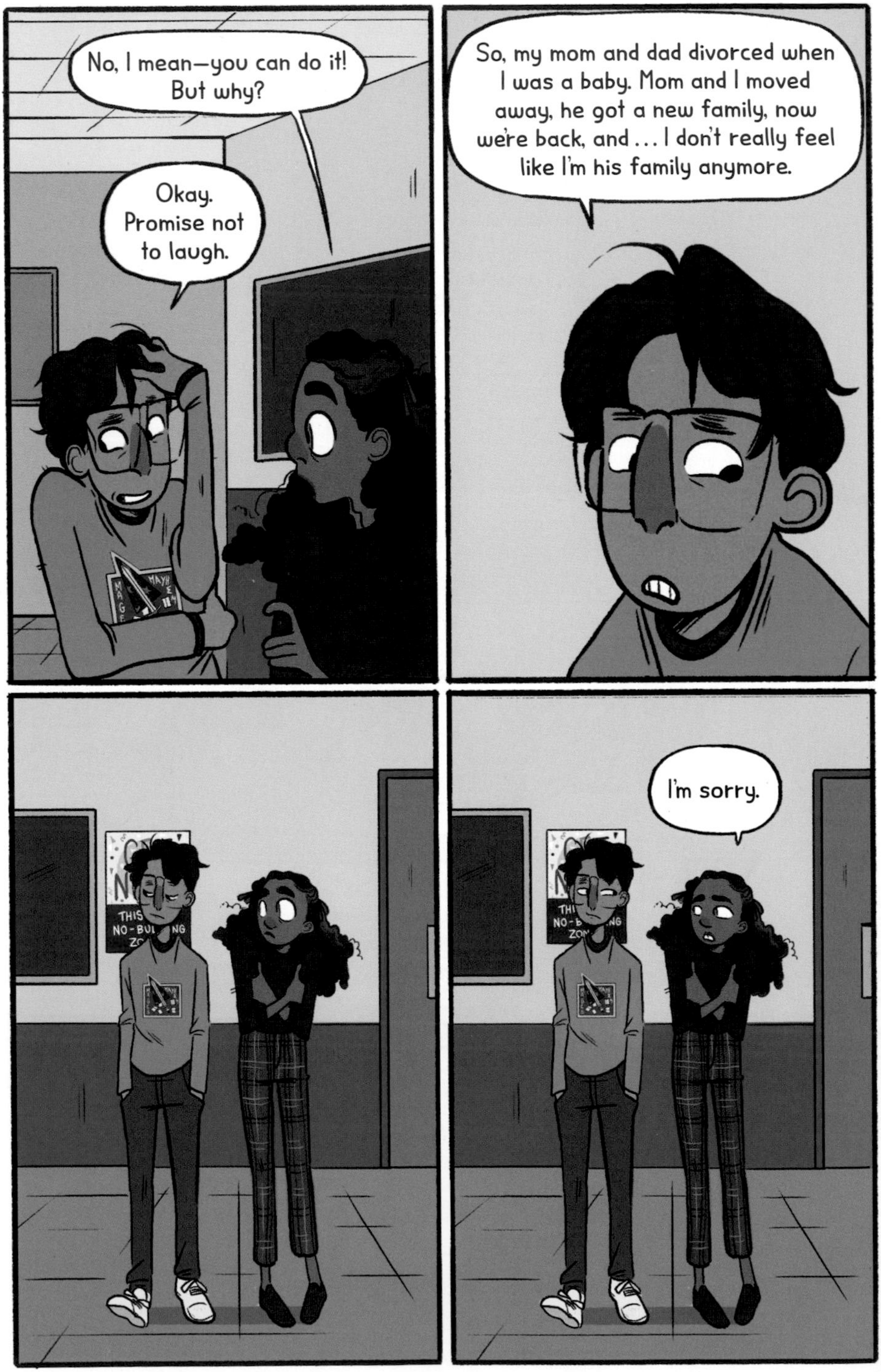
No, I mean—you can do it! But why?
Okay. Promise not to laugh.
MAYHEM MAGE
So, my mom and dad divorced when I was a baby. Mom and I moved away, he got a new family, now we're back, and . . . I don't really feel like I'm his family anymore.
I'm sorry.

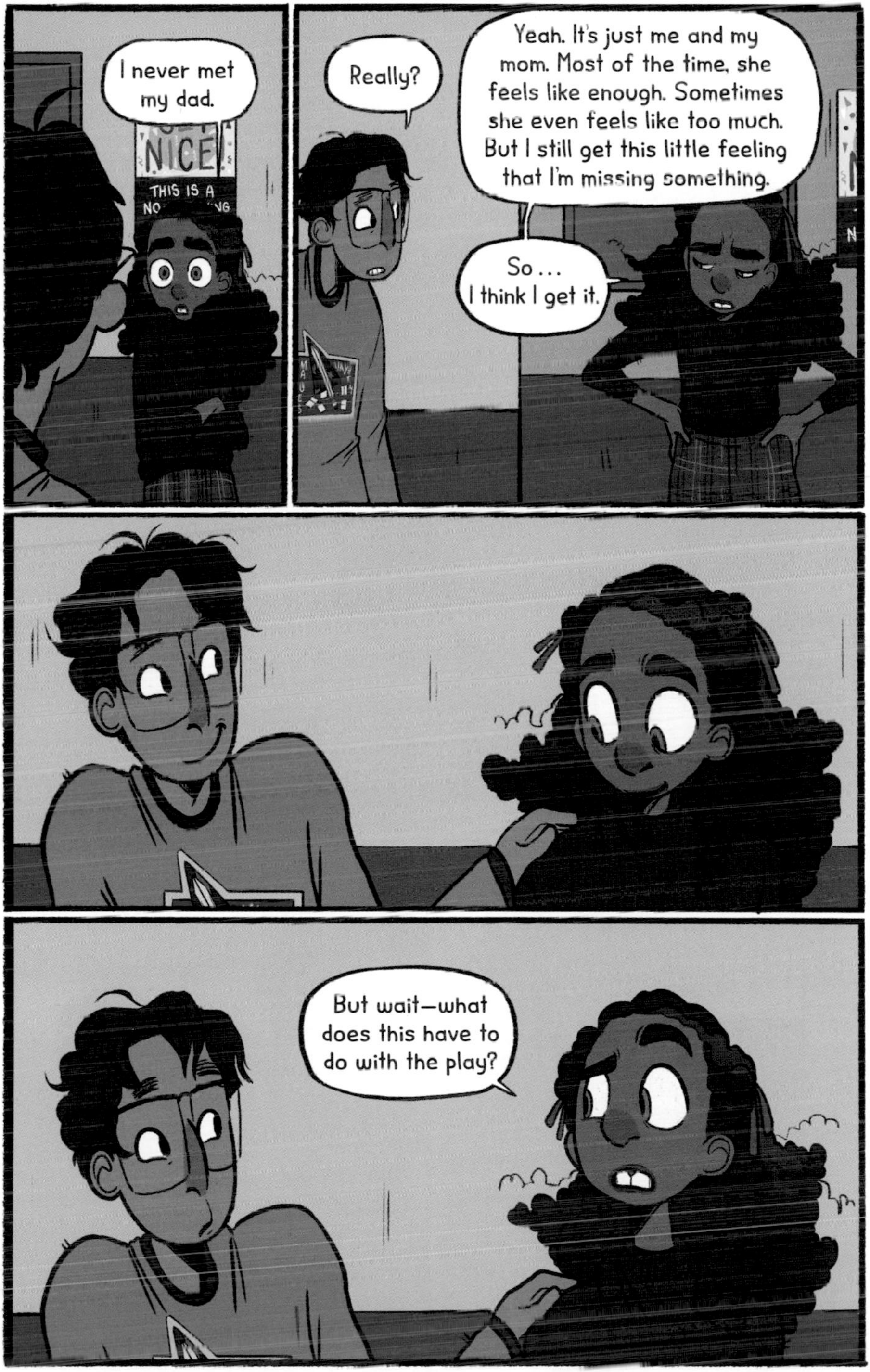
I never met my dad.
NICE
THIS IS A
Really?
Yeah. It's just me and my mom. Most of the time, she feels like enough. Sometimes she even feels like too much. But I still get this little feeling that I'm missing something.
So . . . I think I get it.
But wait—what does this have to do with the play?

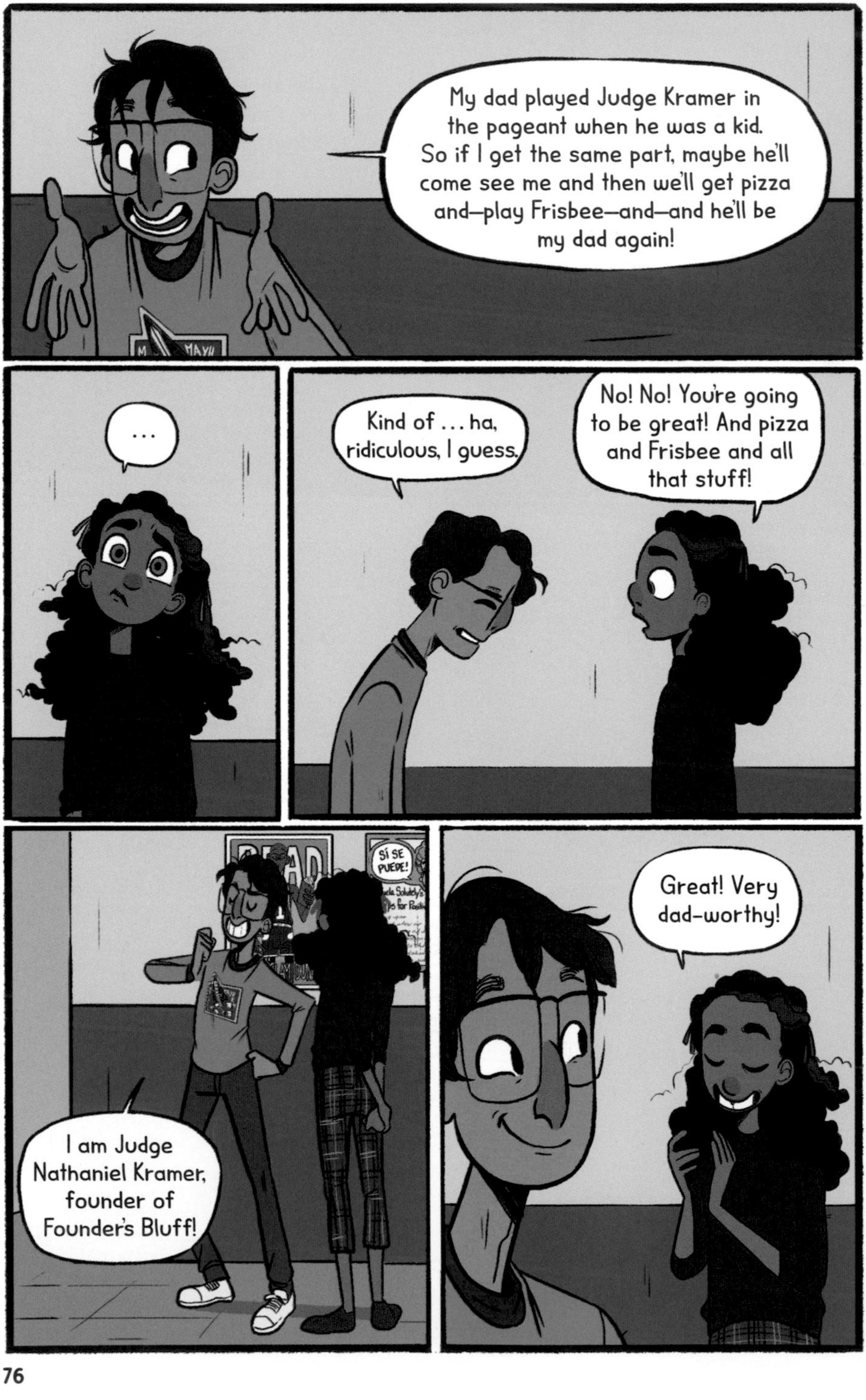
My dad played Judge Kramer in the pageant when he was a kid. So if I get the same part, maybe he'll come see me and then we'll get pizza and—play Frisbee—and—and he'll be my dad again!
...
Kind of . . . ha, ridiculous, I guess.
No! No! You're going to be great! And pizza and Frisbee and all that stuff!
SÍ SE PUEDE!
I am Judge Nathaniel Kramer, founder of Founder's Bluff!
Great! Very dad-worthy!

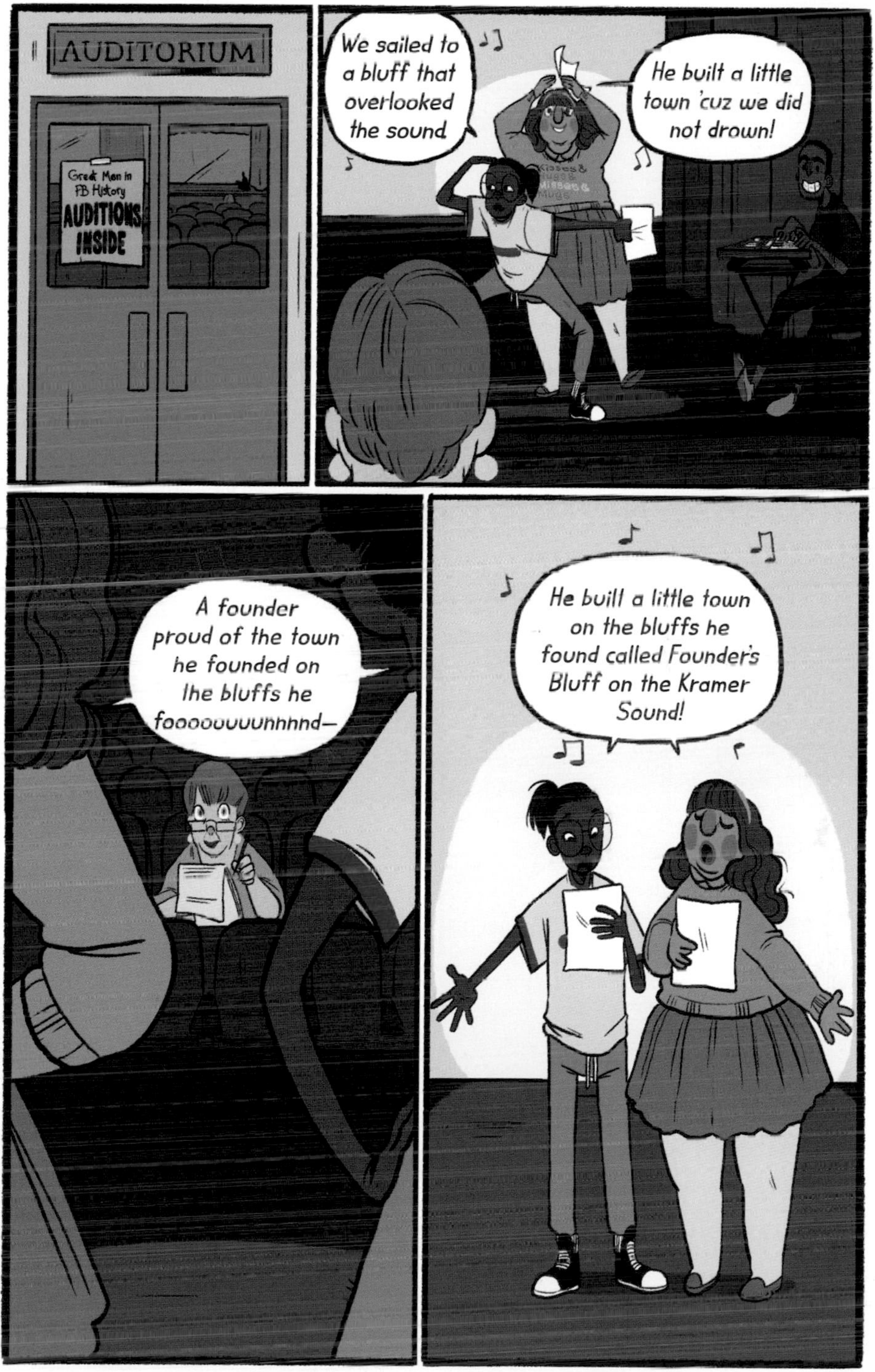
AUDITORIUM
Great Men in FB History
AUDITIONS INSIDE
We sailed to a bluff that overlooked the sound
He built a little town 'cuz we did not drown!
Kisses & Hugs & Kisses & Hugs
A founder proud of the town he founded on the bluffs he fooooouuuunhhnd—
He built a little town on the bluffs he found called Founder's Bluff on the Kramer Sound!

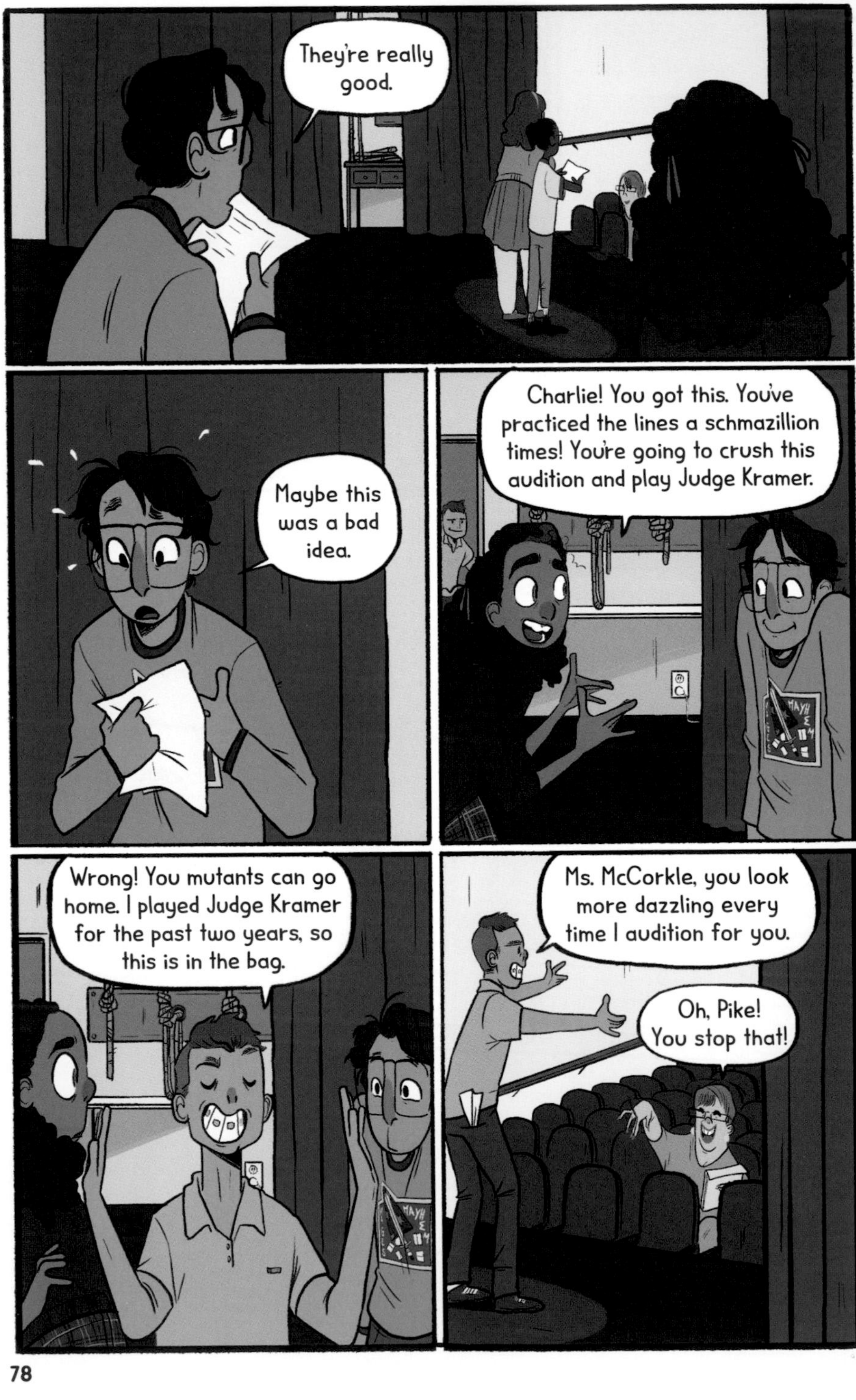
They're really good.
Maybe this was a bad idea.
Charlie! You got this. You've practiced the lines a schmazillion times! You're going to crush this audition and play Judge Kramer.
MAYHEM
Wrong! You mutants can go home. I played Judge Kramer for the past two years, so this is in the bag.
Ms. McCorkle, you look more dazzling every time I audition for you.
Oh, Pike! You stop that!

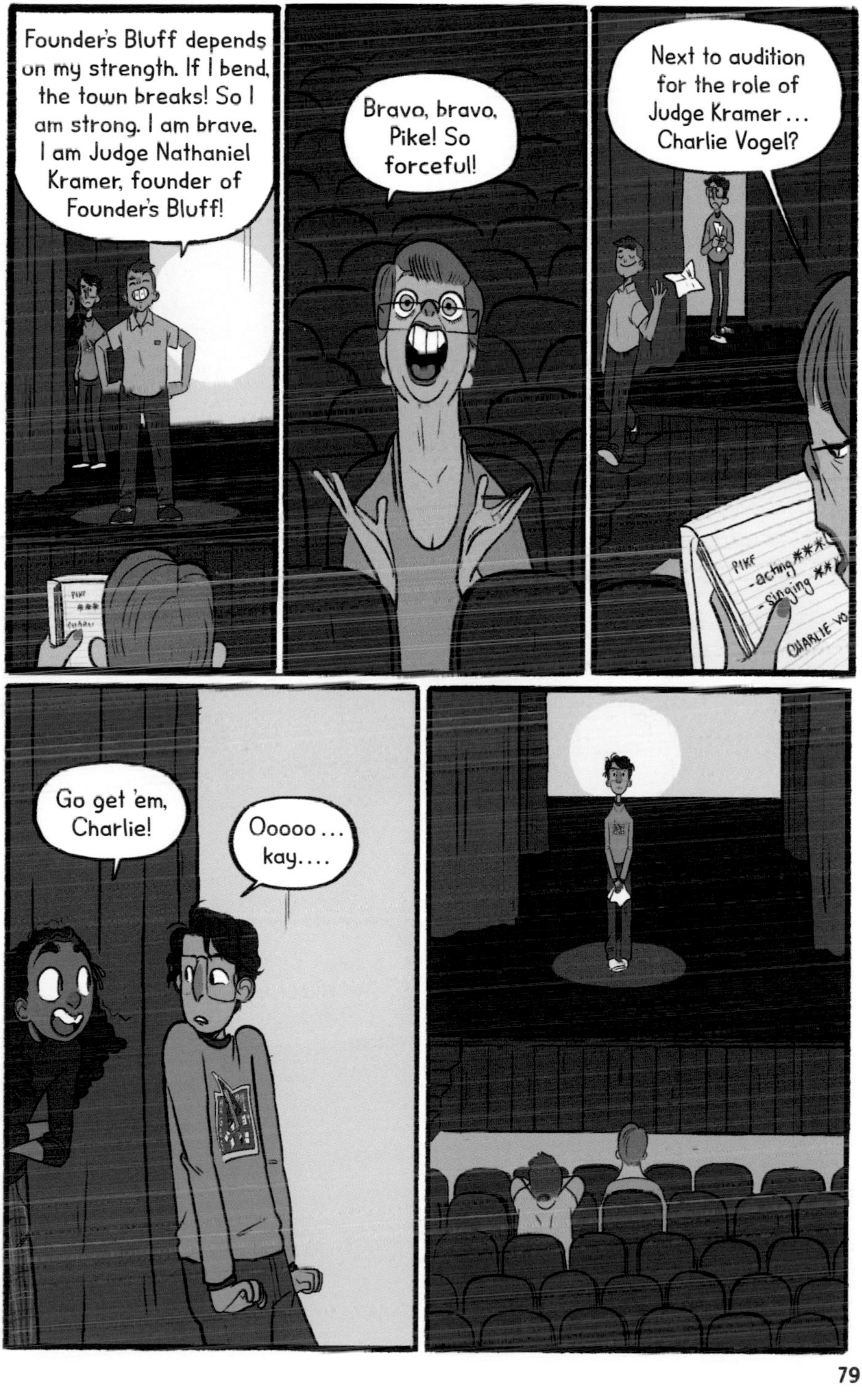
Founder's Bluff depends on my strength. If I bend, the town breaks! So I am strong. I am brave. I am Judge Nathaniel Kramer, founder of Founder's Bluff!
Bravo, bravo, Pike! So forceful!
Next to audition for the role of Judge Kramer... Charlie Vogel?
PIKE
-acting ***
-singing **
Go get 'em, Charlie!
Ooooo... kay....

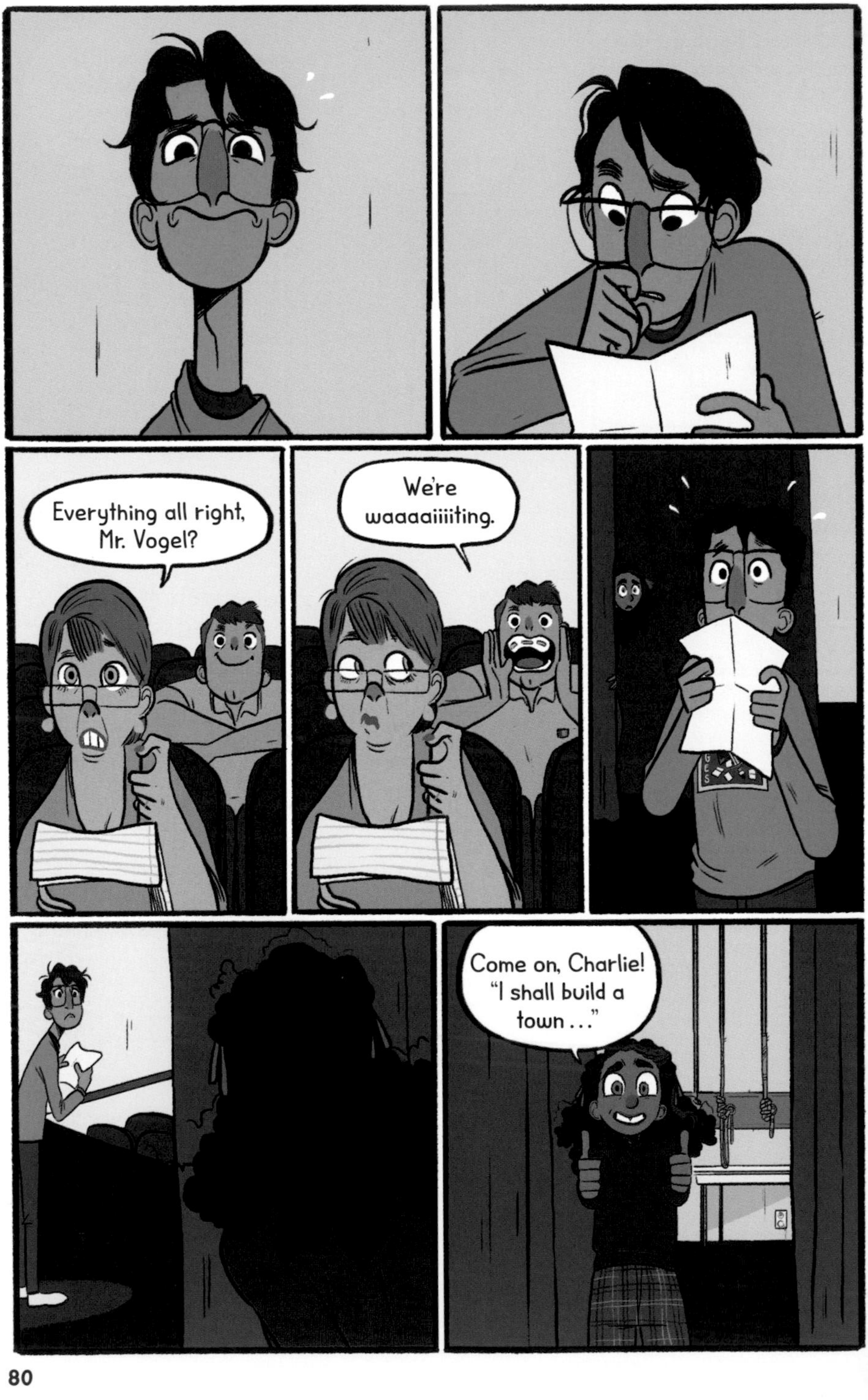
Everything all right, Mr. Vogel?
We're waaaaiiiiiting.
Come on, Charlie! "I shall build a town . . ."

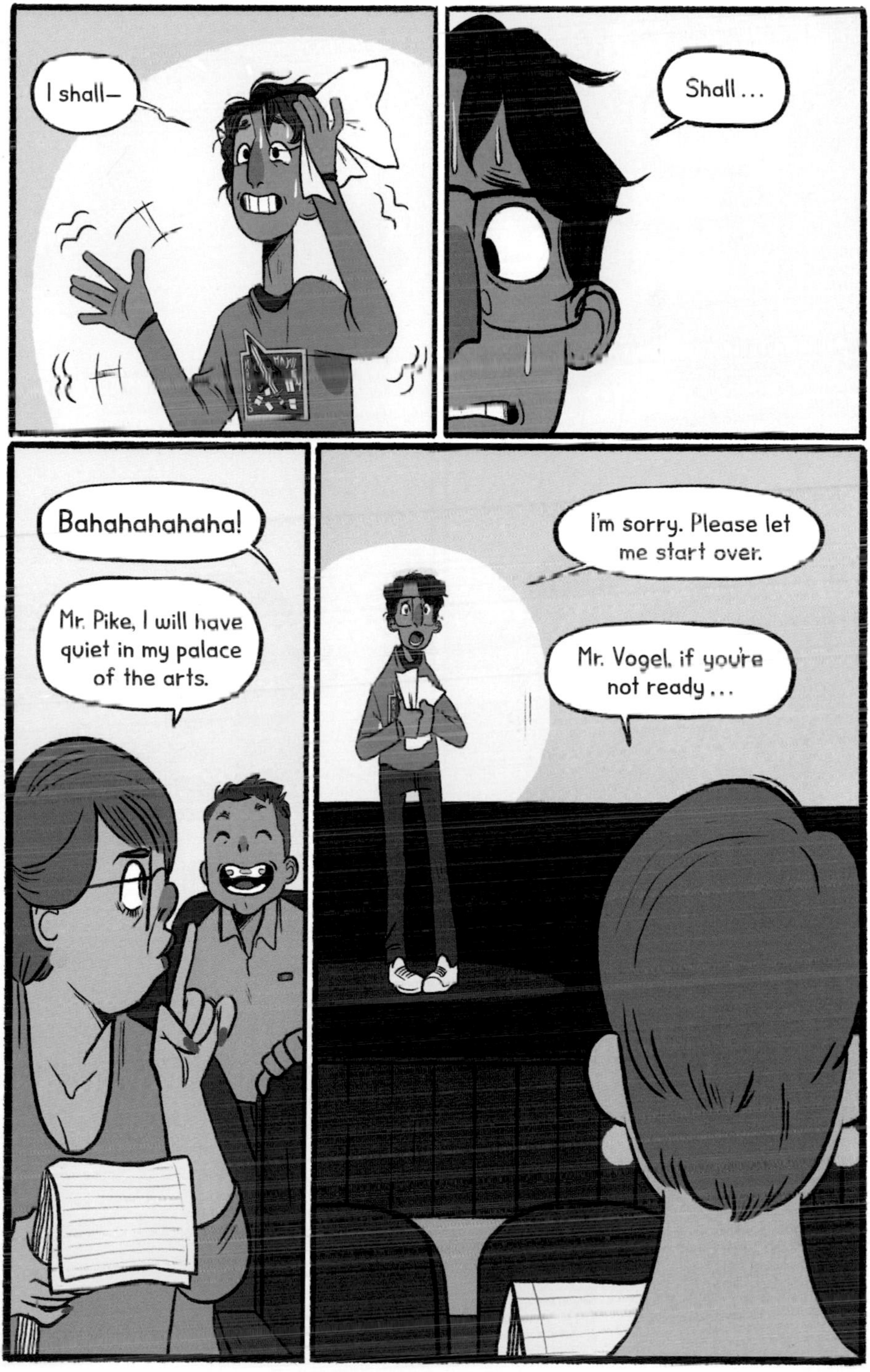
I shall—
Shall . . .
Bahahahahaha!
Mr. Pike, I will have quiet in my palace of the arts.
I'm sorry. Please let me start over.
Mr. Vogel, if you're not ready . . .

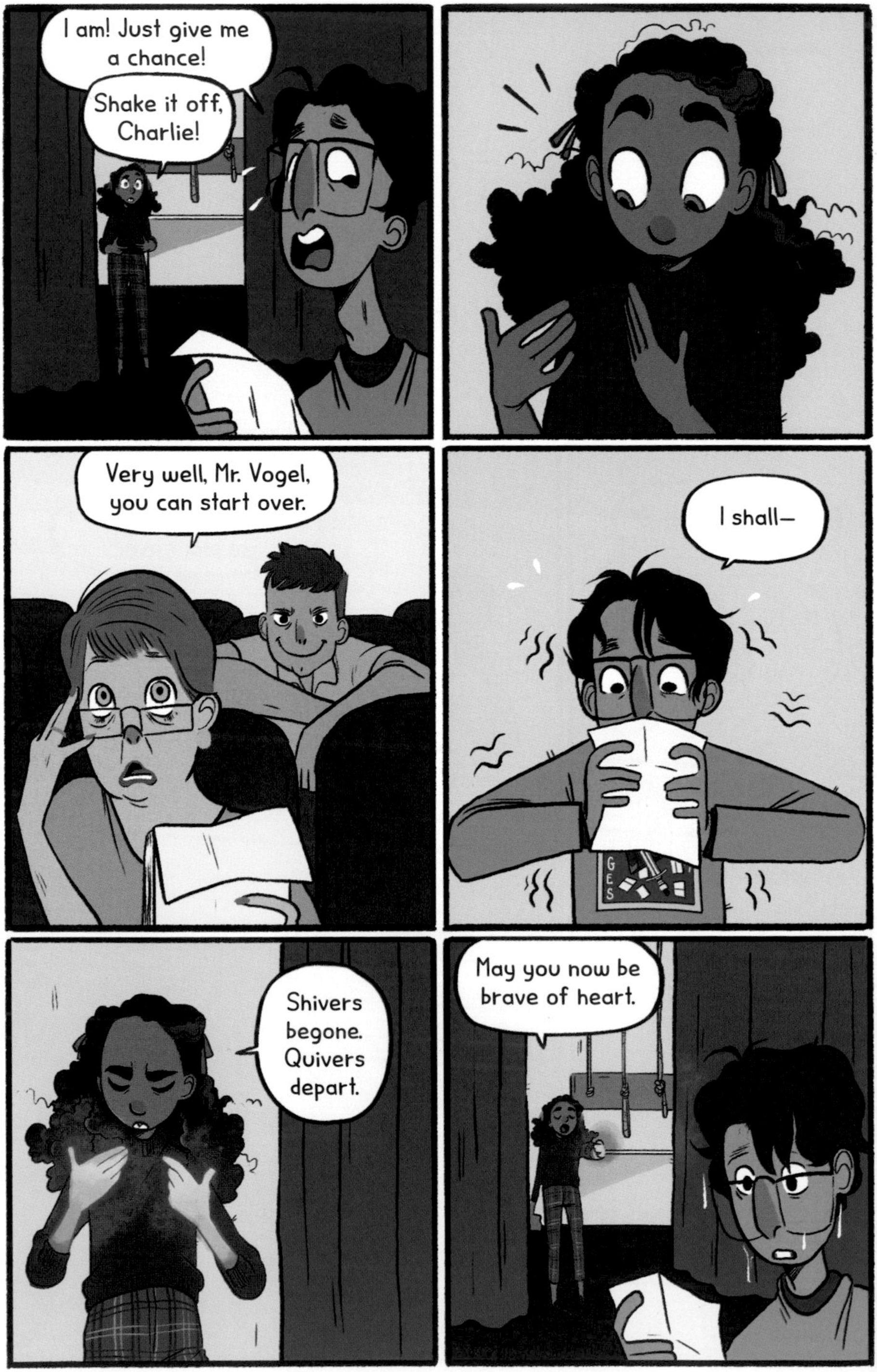
I am! Just give me a chance!
Shake it off, Charlie!
Very well, Mr. Vogel, you can start over.
I shall—
Shivers begone. Quivers depart.
May you now be brave of heart.

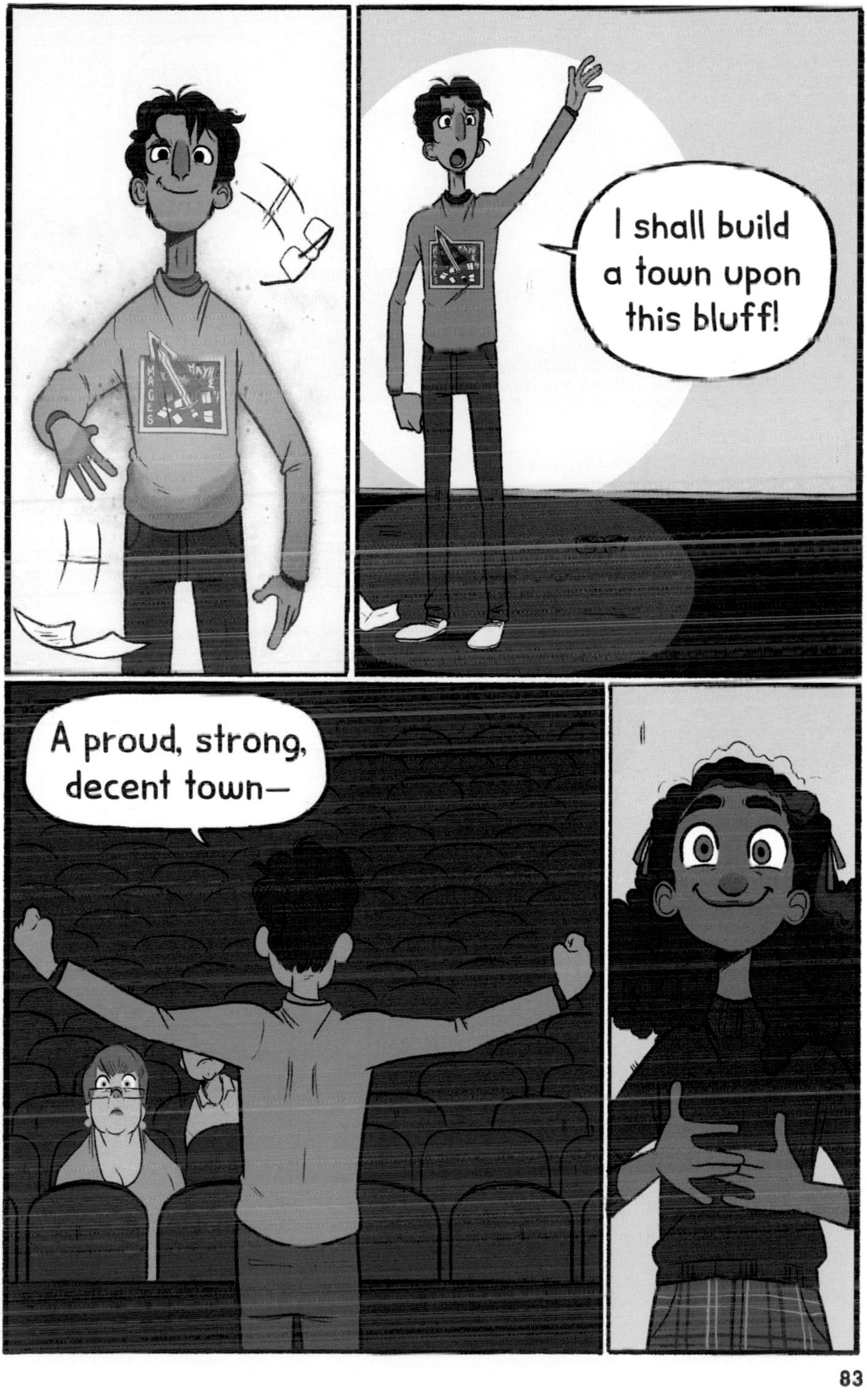
I shall build a town upon this bluff!
A proud, strong, decent town—

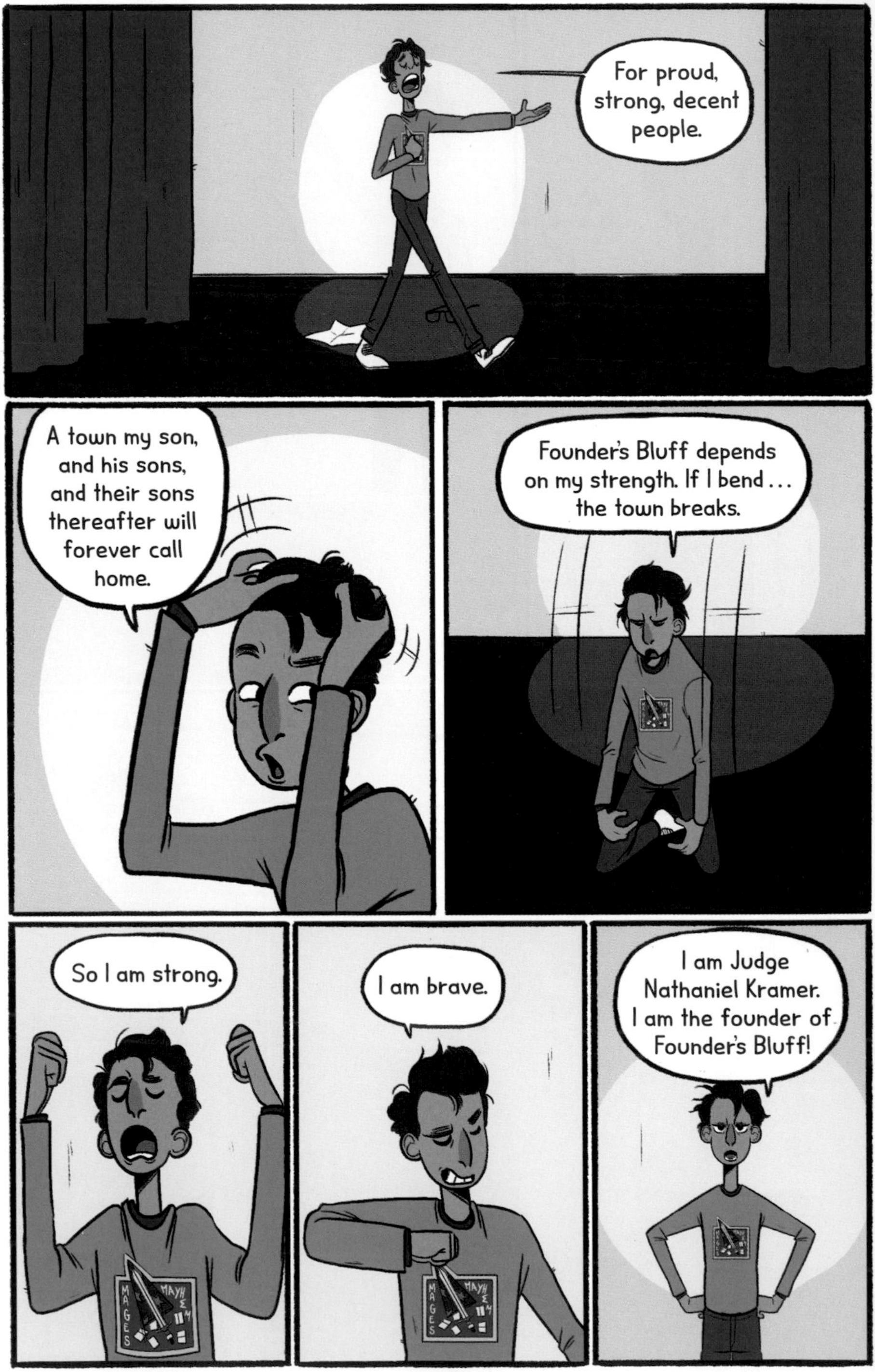
For proud, strong, decent people.
A town my son, and his sons, and their sons thereafter will forever call home.
Founder's Bluff depends on my strength. If I bend . . . the town breaks.
So I am strong.
I am brave.
I am Judge Nathaniel Kramer. I am the founder of Founder's Bluff!
MAGES MAYHEM

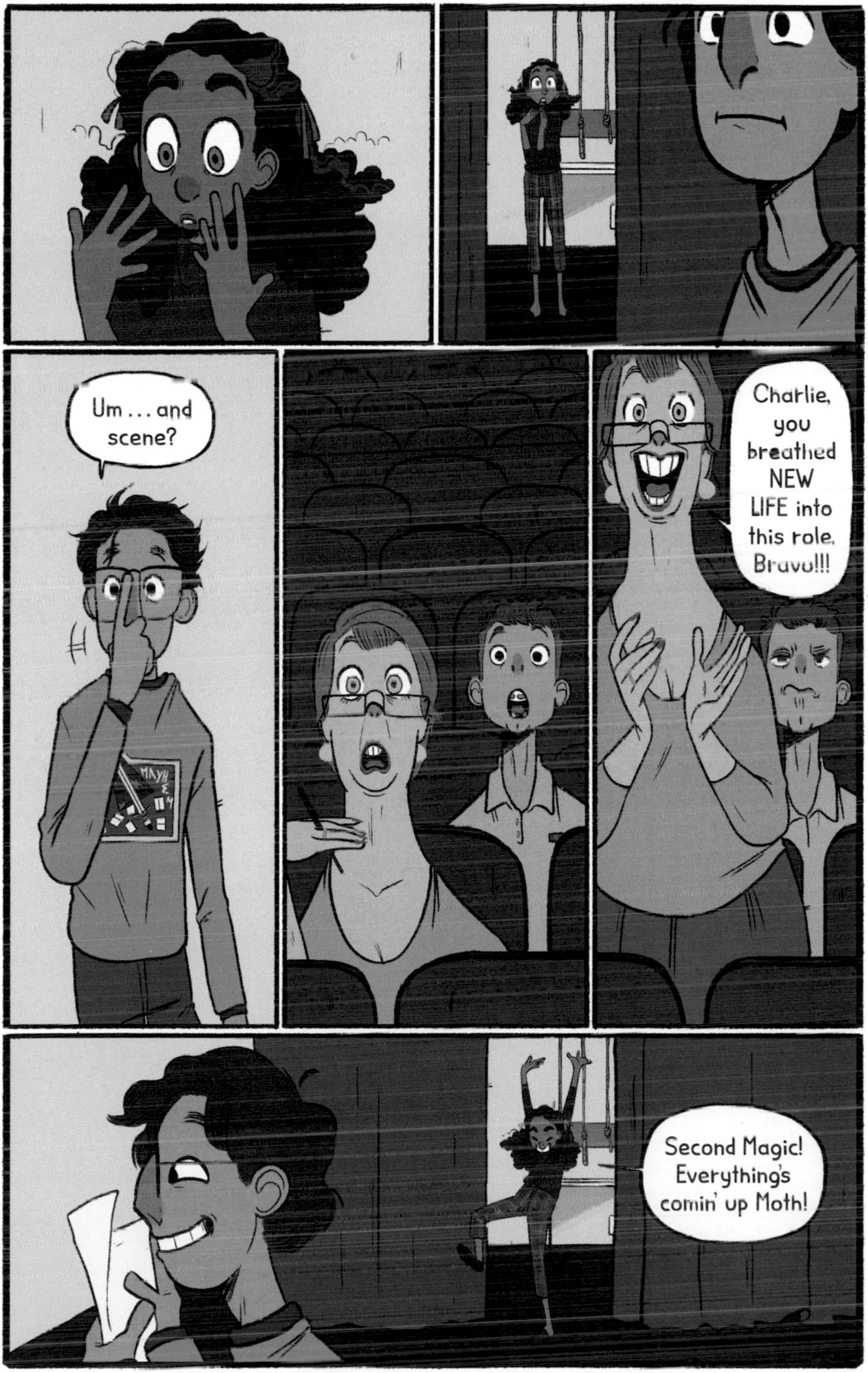
Um . . . and scene?
Charlie, you breathed NEW LIFE into this role. Bravo!!!
Second Magic! Everything's comin' up Moth!

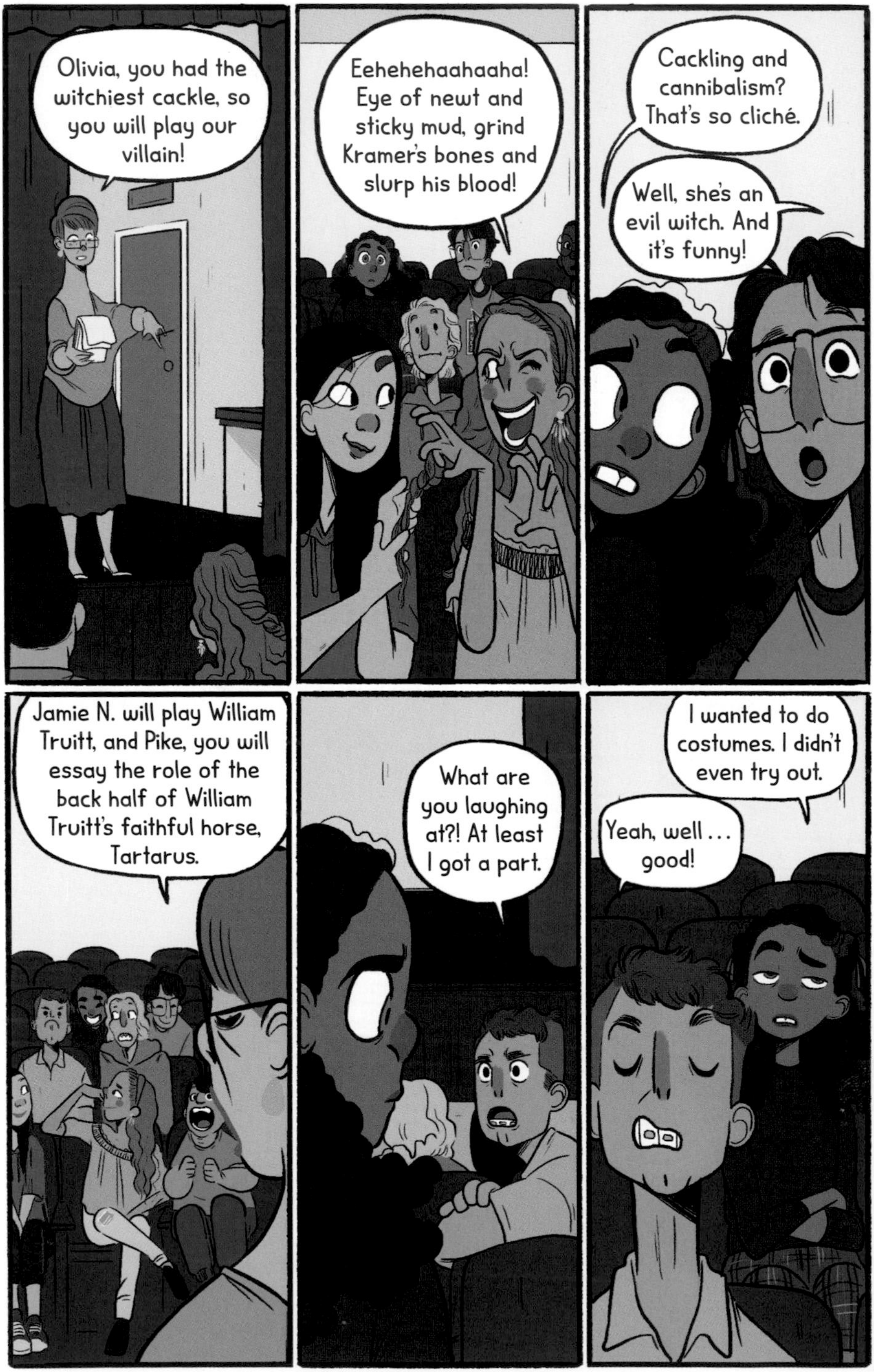
Olivia, you had the witchiest cackle, so you will play our villain!
Eehehehaahaaha! Eye of newt and sticky mud, grind Kramer's bones and slurp his blood!
Cackling and cannibalism? That's so cliché.
Well, she's an evil witch. And it's funny!
Jamie N. will play William Truitt, and Pike, you will essay the role of the back half of William Truitt's faithful horse, Tartarus.
What are you laughing at?! At least I got a part.
I wanted to do costumes. I didn't even try out.
Yeah, well . . . good!

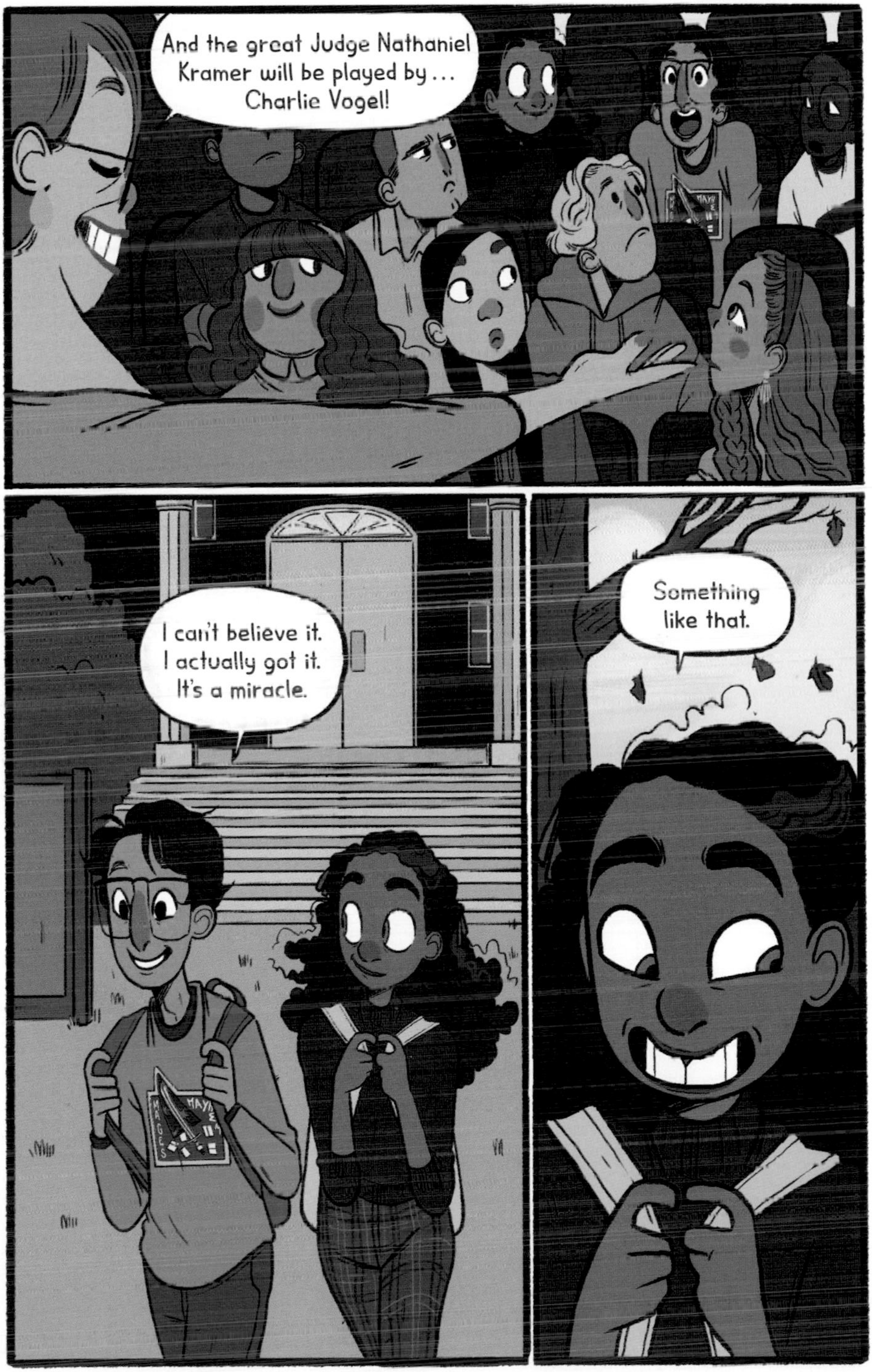
And the great Judge Nathaniel Kramer will be played by . . . Charlie Vogel!
I can't believe it. I actually got it. It's a miracle.
Something like that.

CHAPTER 6

Spells, Spells, Spells

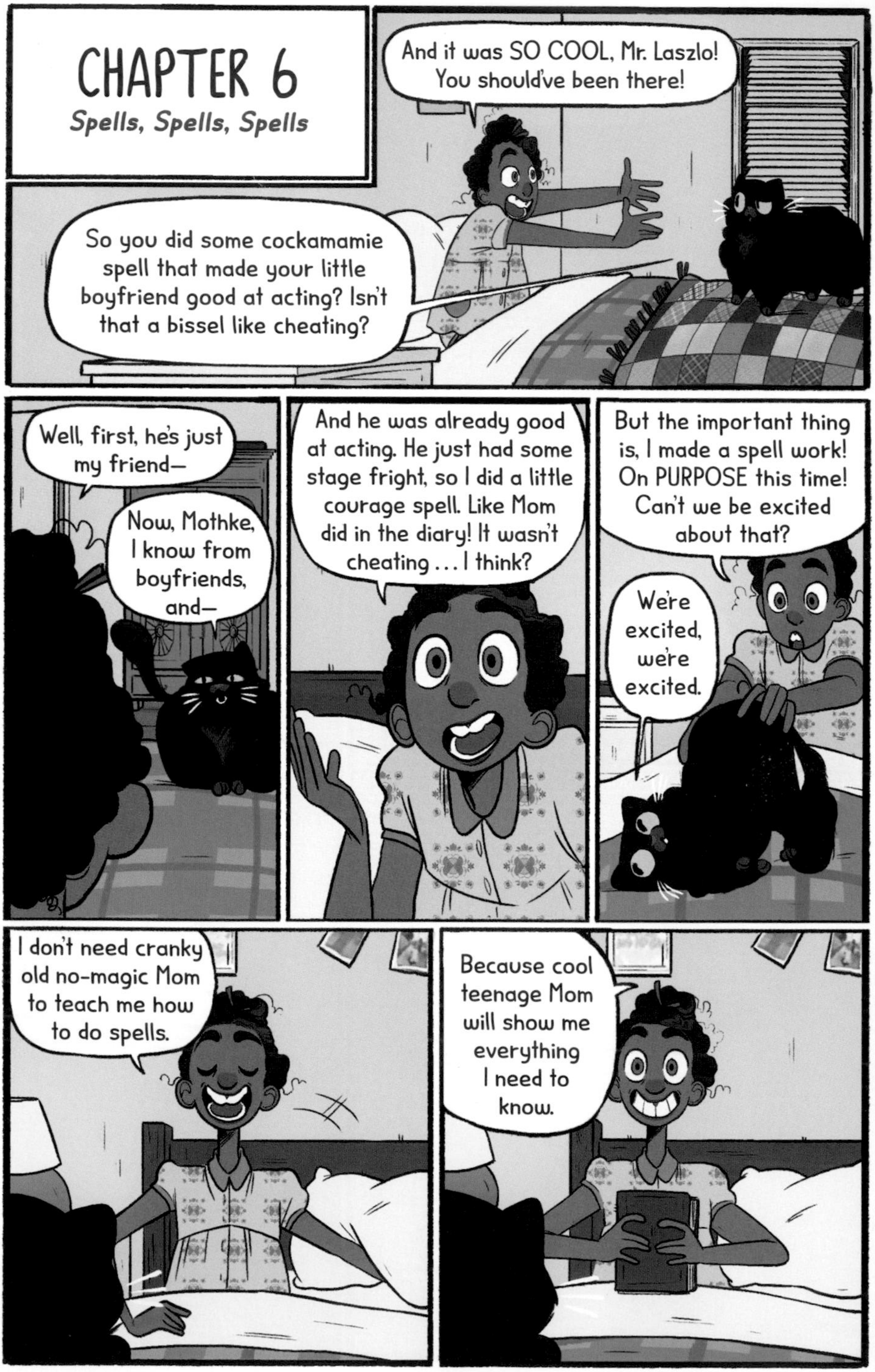
And it was SO COOL, Mr. Laszlo! You should've been there!
So you did some cockamamie spell that made your little boyfriend good at acting? Isn't that a bissel like cheating?
Well, first, he's just my friend—
Now, Mothke, I know from boyfriends, and—
And he was already good at acting. He just had some stage fright, so I did a little courage spell. Like Mom did in the diary! It wasn't cheating . . . I think?
But the important thing is, I made a spell work! On PURPOSE this time! Can't we be excited about that?
We're excited, we're excited.
I don't need cranky old no-magic Mom to teach me how to do spells.
Because cool teenage Mom will show me everything I need to know.

Simple Transitive Levitation Incantation (Make Stuff Float)

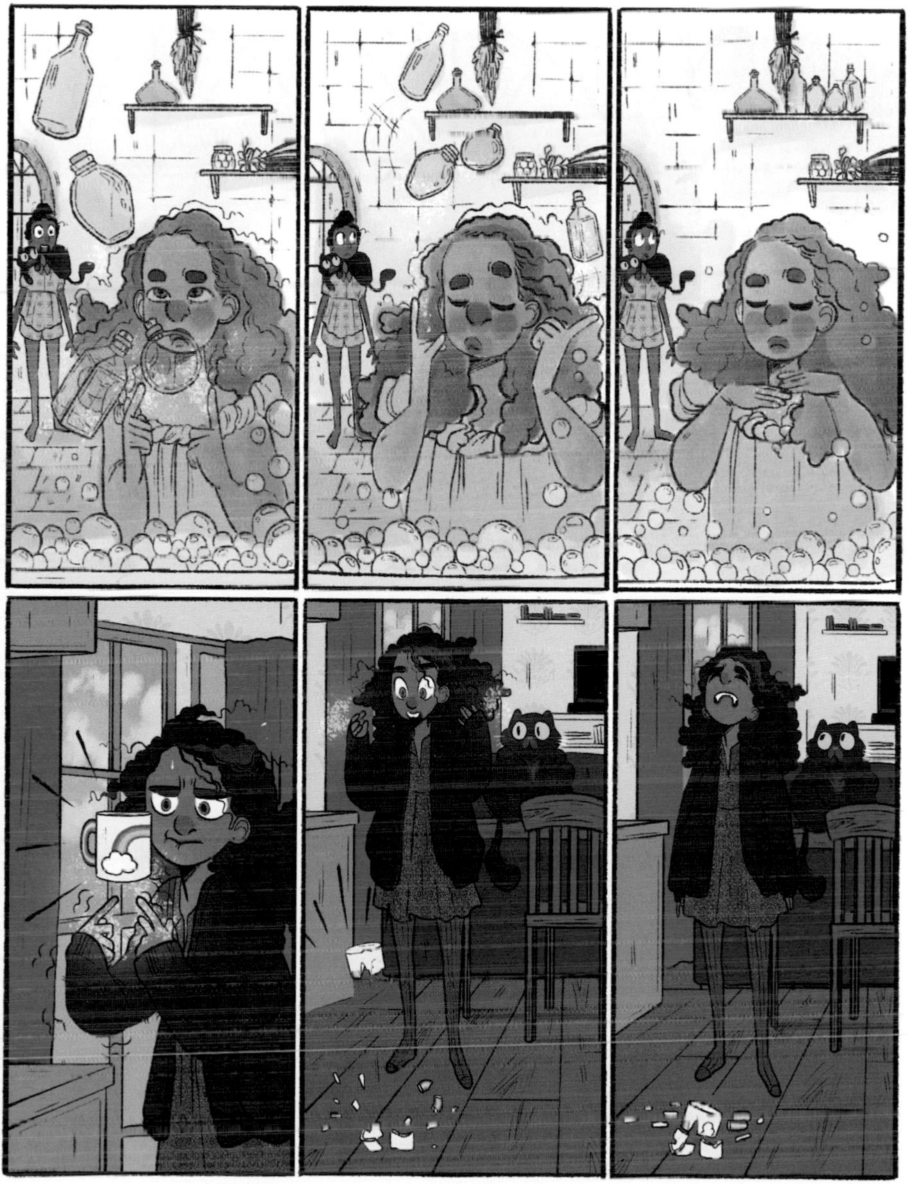

Abundance Charm
(Got Stuff? Make More of It)

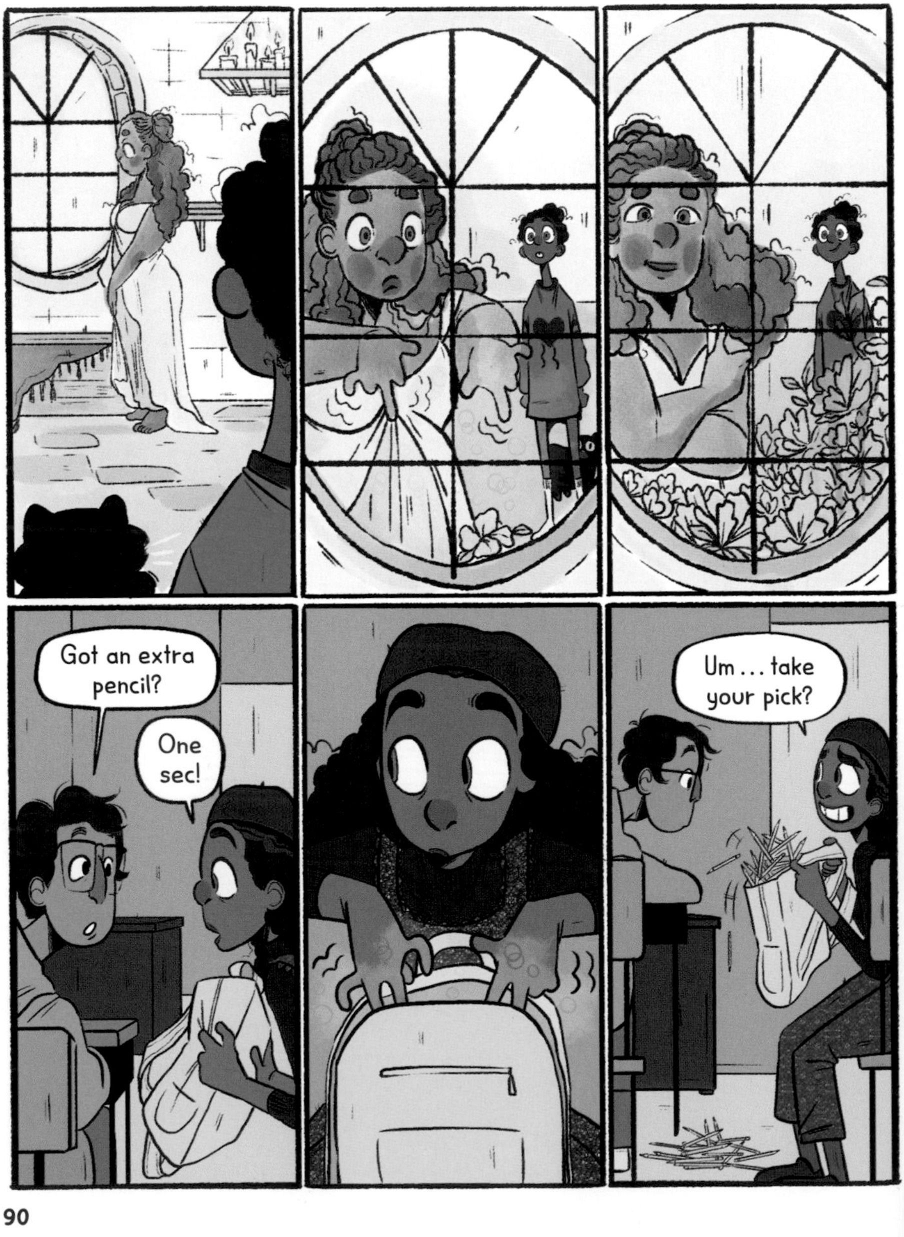
Got an extra pencil?
One sec!
Um ... take your pick?

Highland Agricultural Detangling Spell (Make Large Mammals Look Not Gross)

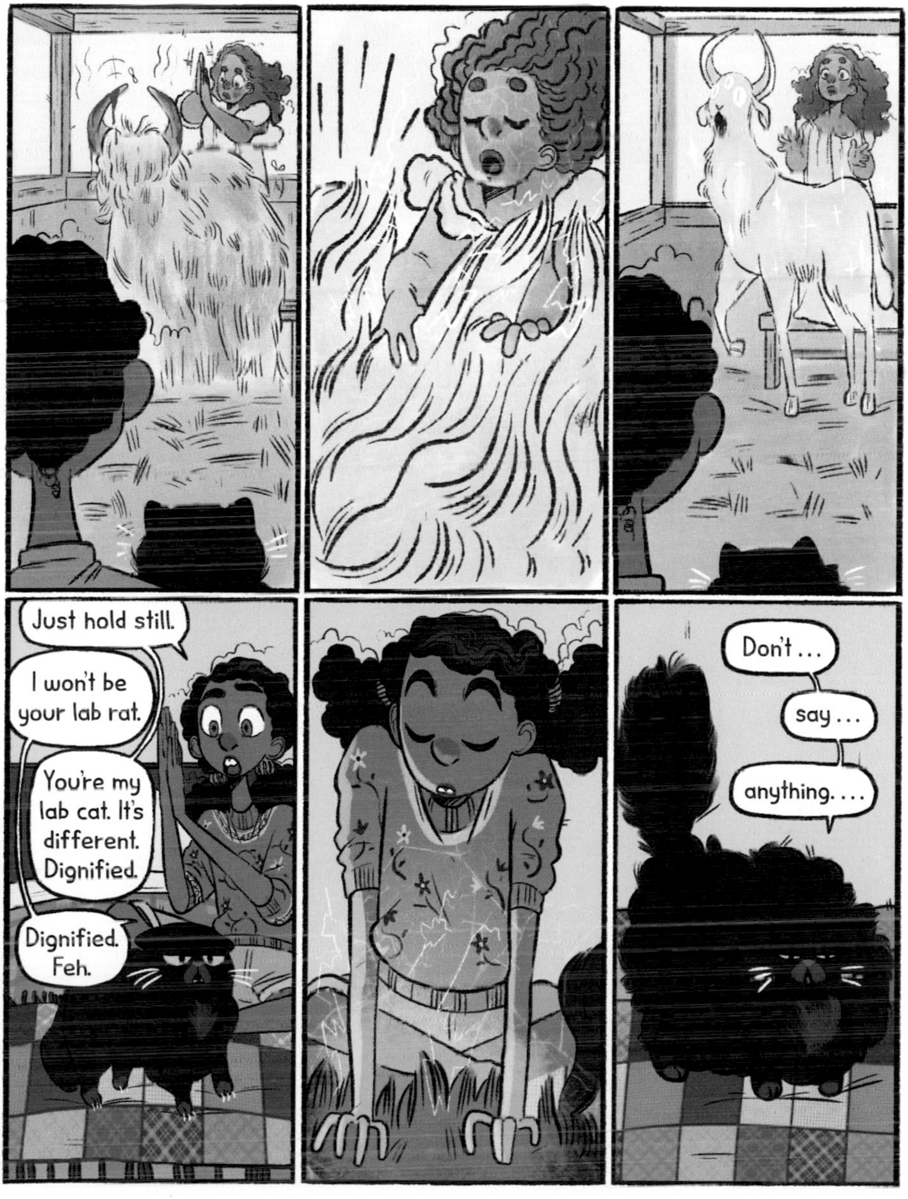
Just hold still.
I won't be your lab rat.
You're my lab cat. It's different. Dignified.
Dignified. Feh.
Don't . . .
say . . .
anything. . . .

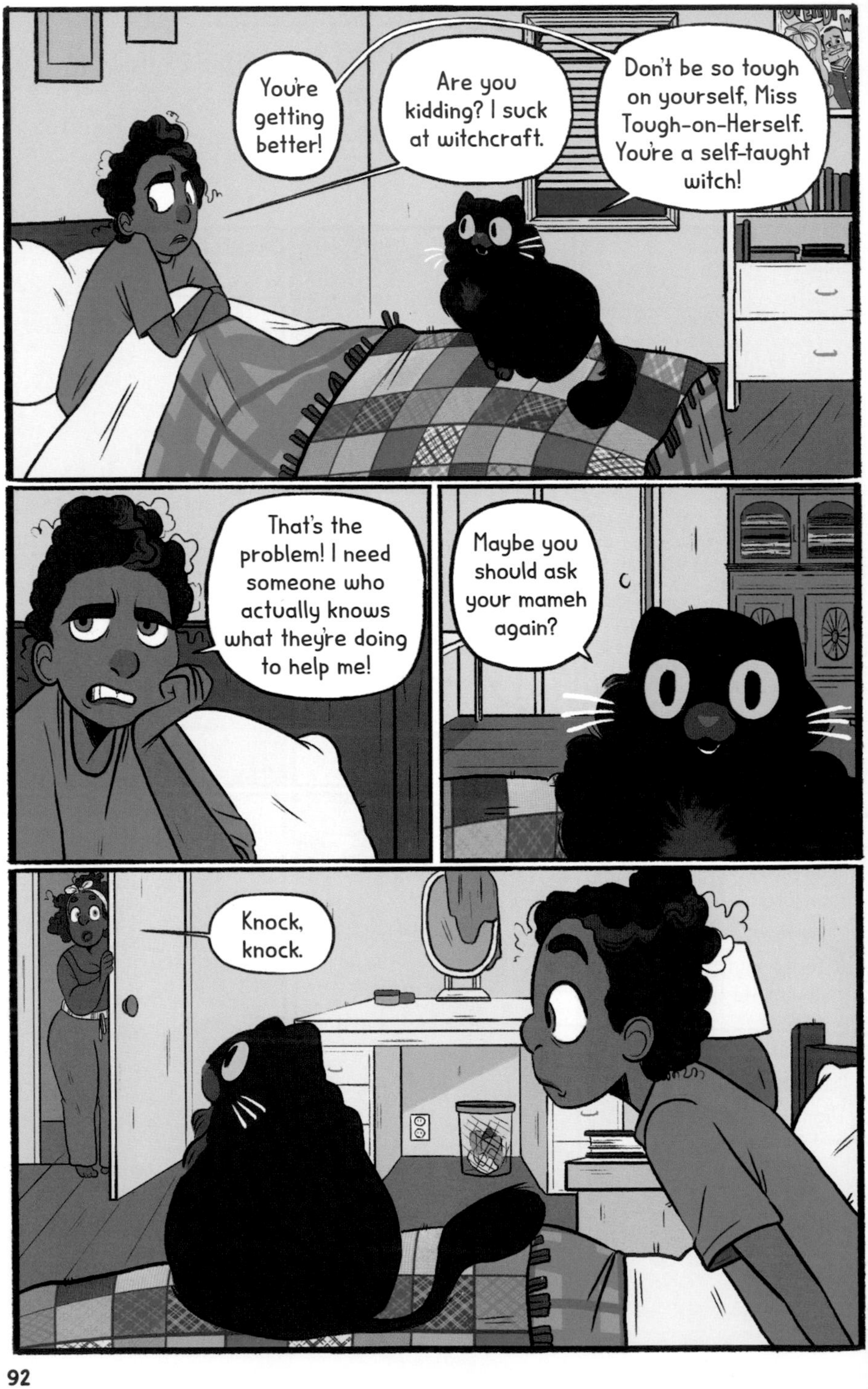
You're getting better!
Are you kidding? I suck at witchcraft.
Don't be so tough on yourself, Miss Tough-on-Herself. You're a self-taught witch!
That's the problem! I need someone who actually knows what they're doing to help me!
Maybe you should ask your mameh again?
Knock, knock.

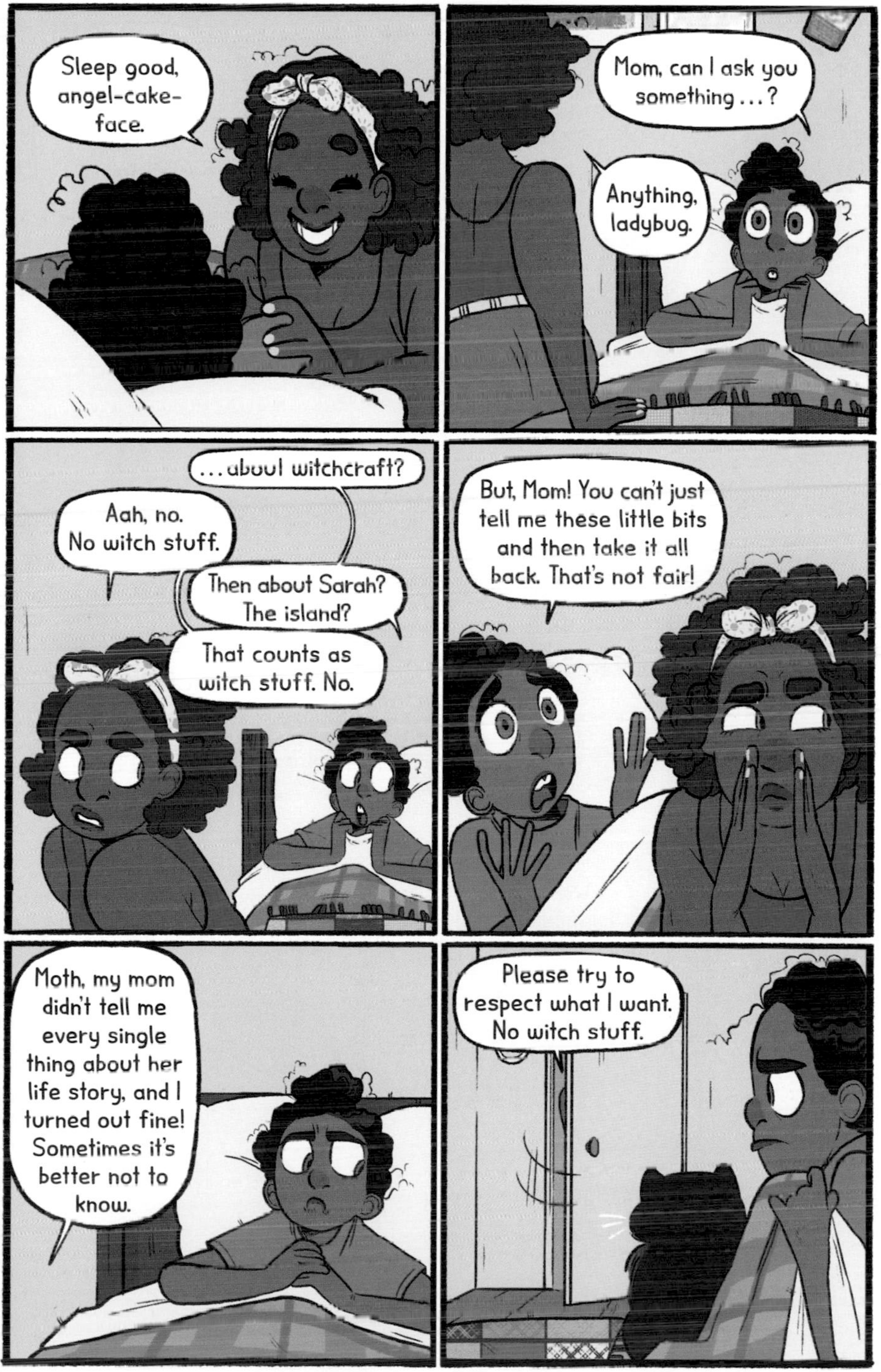
Sleep good, angel-cake-face.
Mom, can I ask you something . . . ?
Anything, ladybug.
. . . about witchcraft?
Aah, no. No witch stuff.
Then about Sarah? The island?
That counts as witch stuff. No.
But, Mom! You can't just tell me these little bits and then take it all back. That's not fair!
Moth, my mom didn't tell me every single thing about her life story, and I turned out fine! Sometimes it's better not to know.
Please try to respect what I want. No witch stuff.

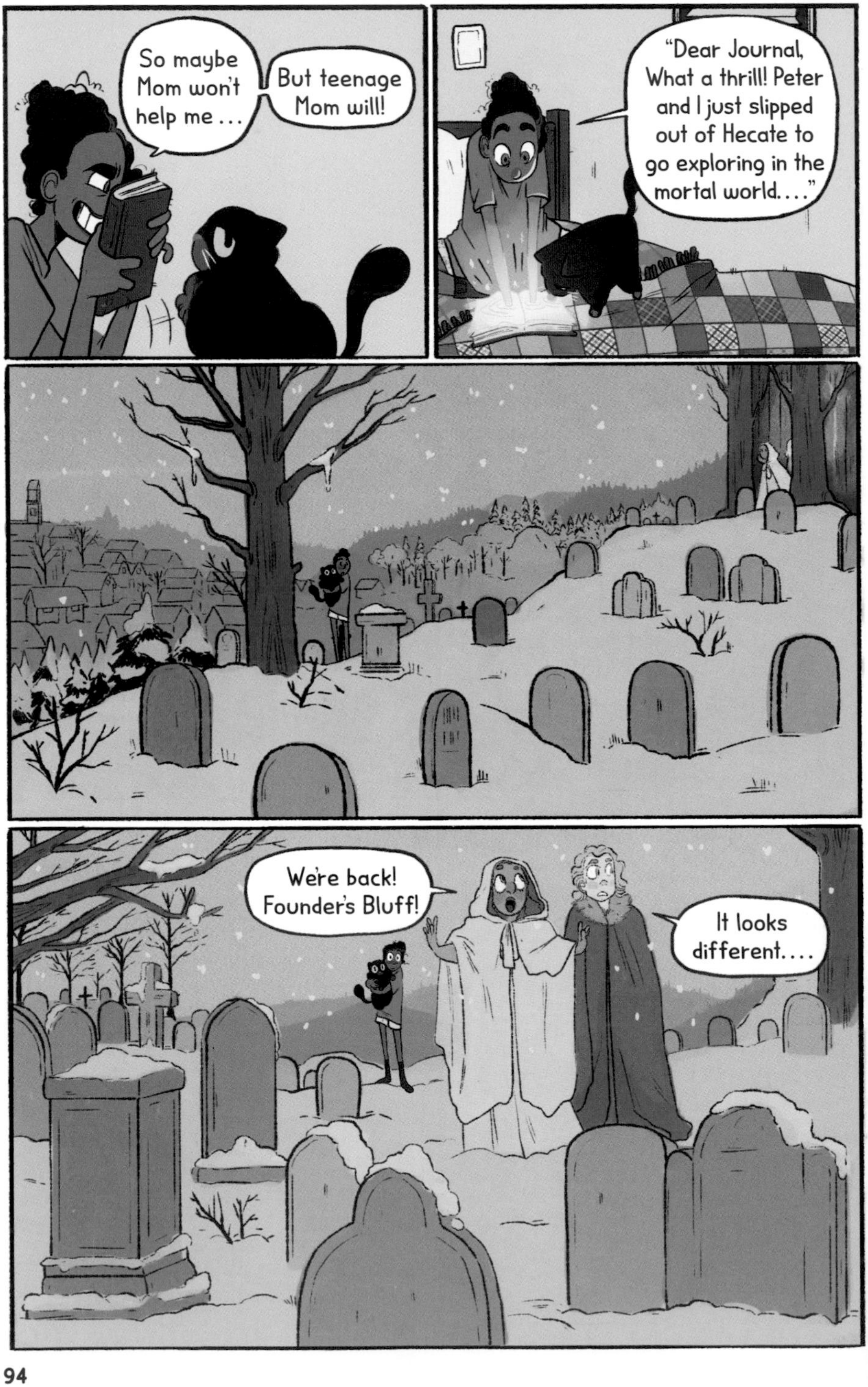
So maybe Mom won't help me . . .
But teenage Mom will!
"Dear Journal, What a thrill! Peter and I just slipped out of Hecate to go exploring in the mortal world. . . ."
We're back! Founder's Bluff!
It looks different. . . .

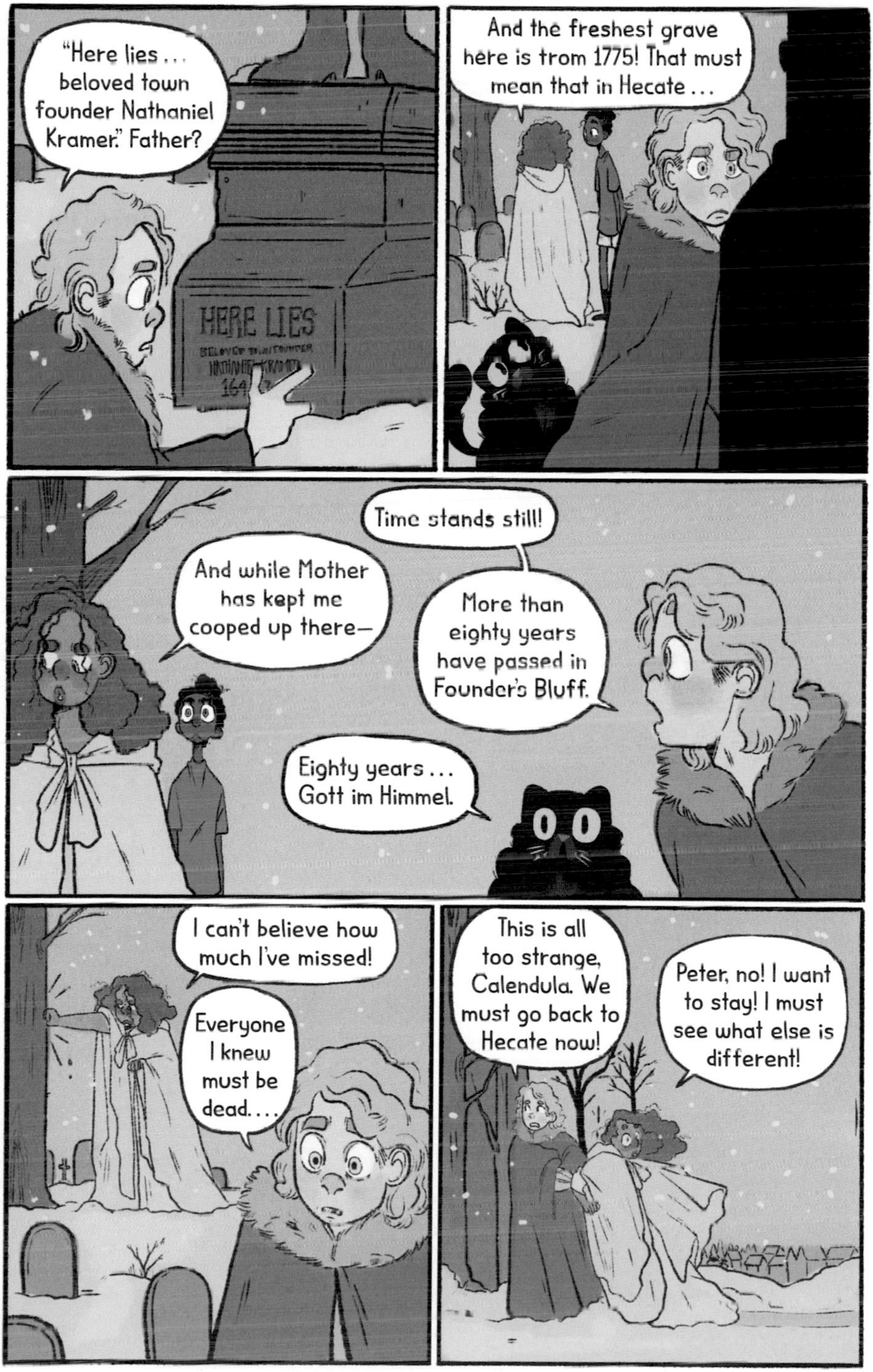
"Here lies . . . beloved town founder Nathaniel Kramer." Father?
HERE LIES
And the freshest grave here is trom 1775! That must mean that in Hecate . . .
And while Mother has kept me cooped up there—
Time stands still!
More than eighty years have passed in Founder's Bluff.
Eighty years . . . Gott im Himmel.
I can't believe how much I've missed!
Everyone I knew must be dead. . . .
This is all too strange, Calendula. We must go back to Hecate now!
Peter, no! I want to stay! I must see what else is different!

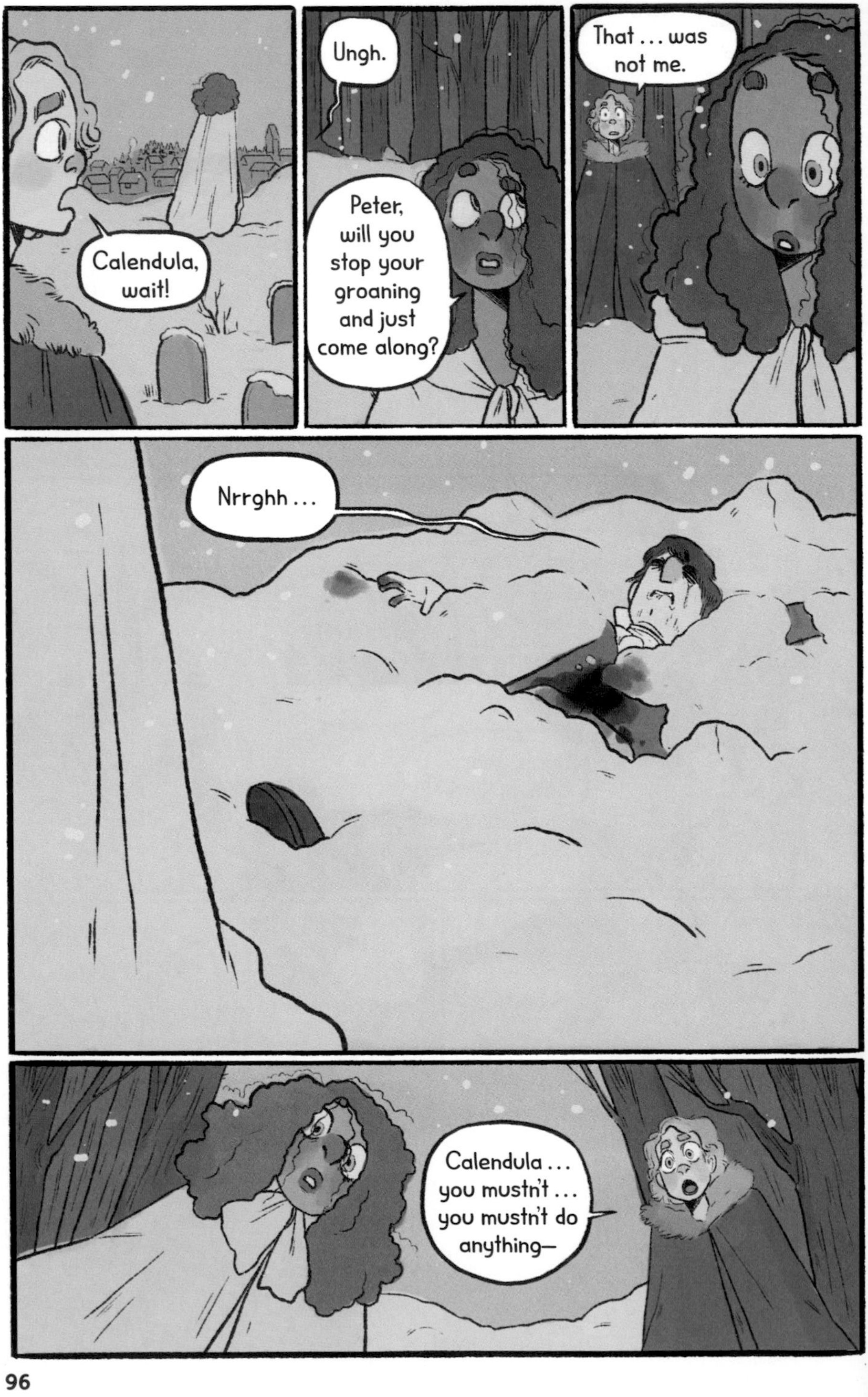
Calendula, wait!
Ungh.
Peter, will you stop your groaning and just come along?
That . . . was not me.
Nrrghh . . .
Calendula . . . you mustn't . . . you mustn't do anything—

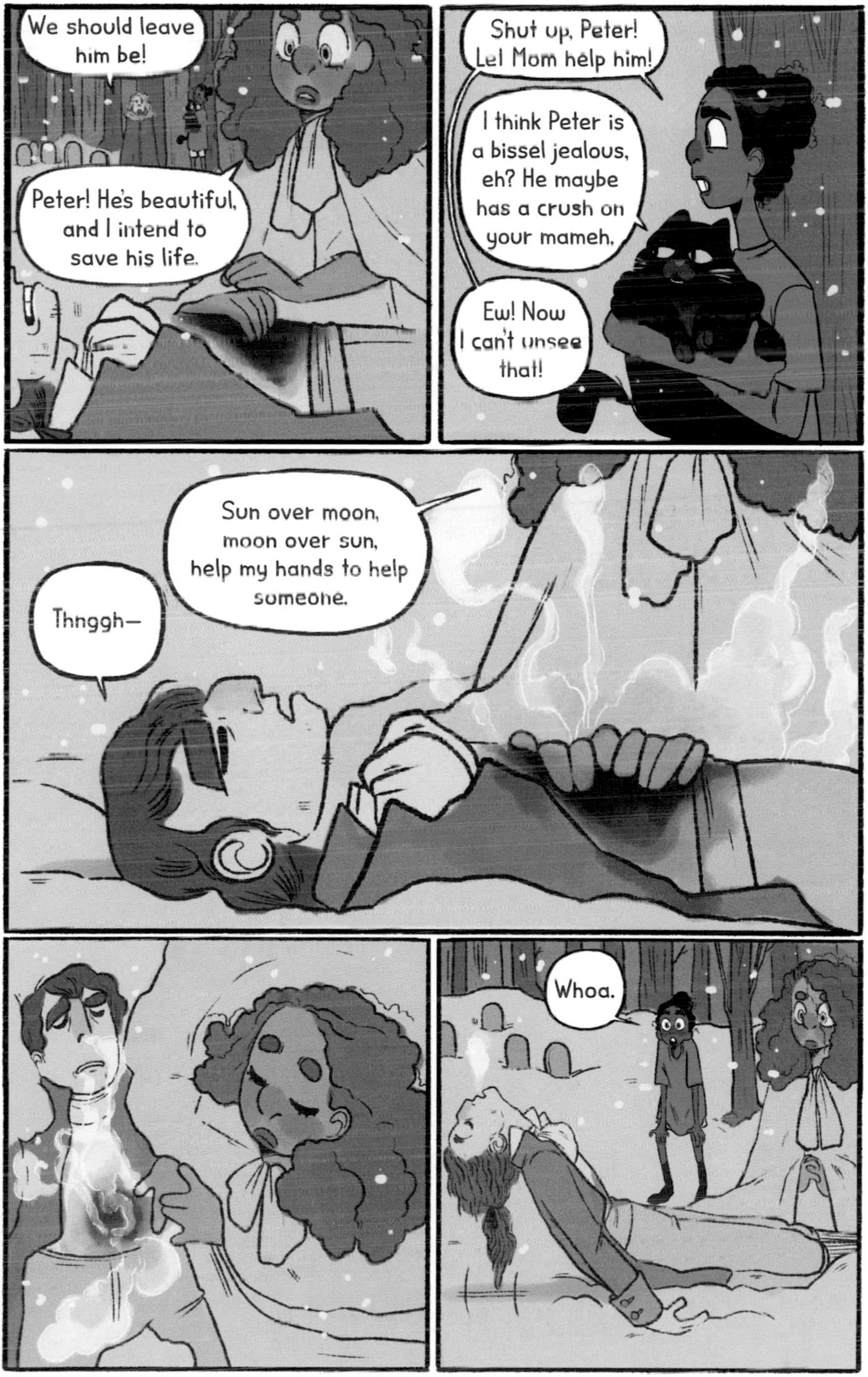
We should leave him be!
Peter! He's beautiful, and I intend to save his life.
Shut up, Peter! Let Mom help him!
I think Peter is a bissel jealous, eh? He maybe has a crush on your mameh.
Ew! Now I can't unsee that!
Sun over moon, moon over sun, help my hands to help someone.
Thnggh—
Whoa.

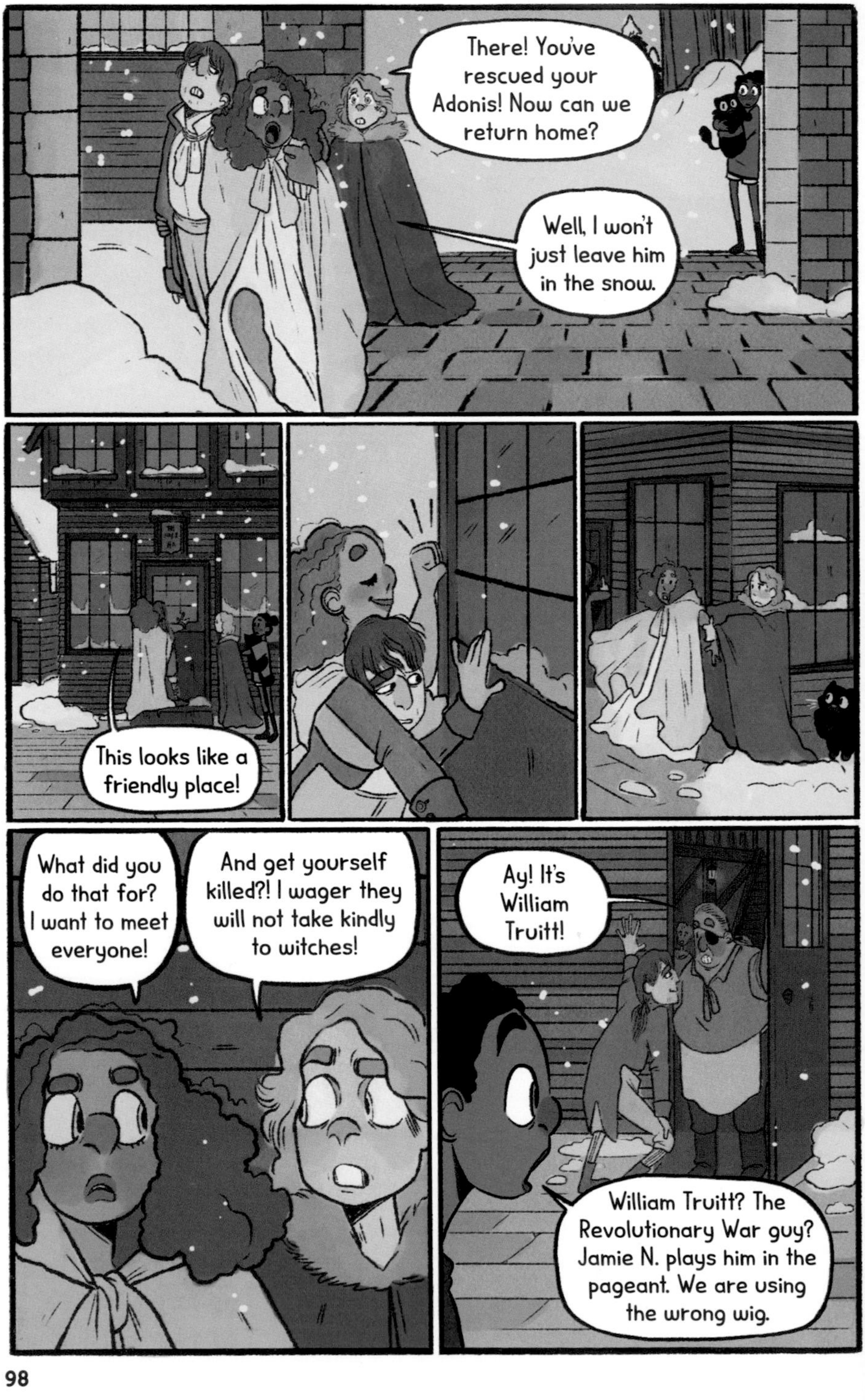
There! You've rescued your Adonis! Now can we return home?
Well, I won't just leave him in the snow.
This looks like a friendly place!
What did you do that for? I want to meet everyone!
And get yourself killed?! I wager they will not take kindly to witches!
Ay! It's William Truitt!
William Truitt? The Revolutionary War guy? Jamie N. plays him in the pageant. We are using the wrong wig.

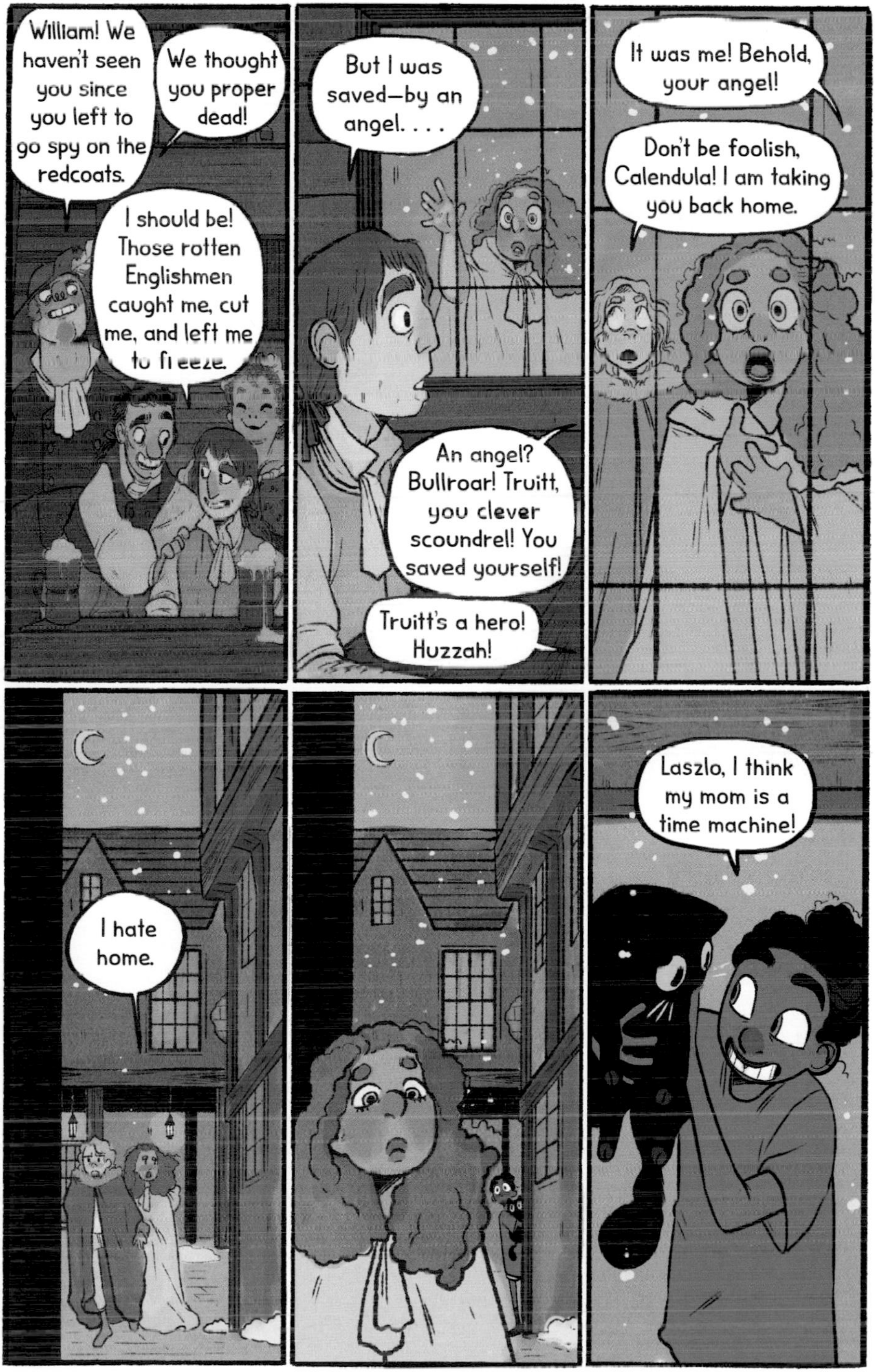
William! We haven't seen you since you left to go spy on the redcoats.
We thought you proper dead!
I should be! Those rotten Englishmen caught me, cut me, and left me to freeze.
But I was saved—by an angel. . . .
An angel? Bullroar! Truitt, you clever scoundrel! You saved yourself!
Truitt's a hero! Huzzah!
It was me! Behold, your angel!
Don't be foolish, Calendula! I am taking you back home.
I hate home.
Laszlo, I think my mom is a time machine!

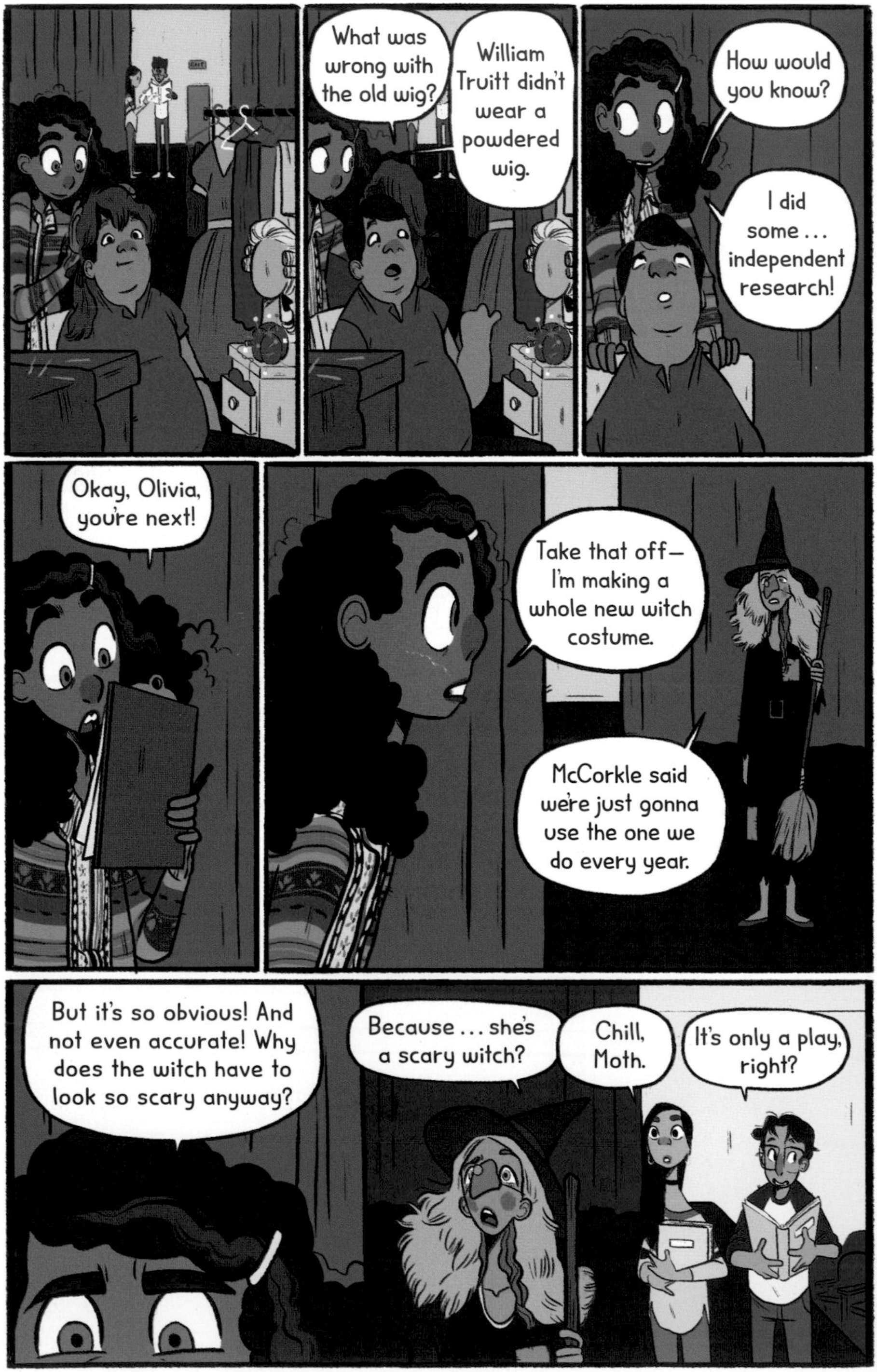
What was wrong with the old wig?
William Truitt didn't wear a powdered wig.
How would you know?
I did some . . . independent research!
Okay, Olivia, you're next!
Take that off— I'm making a whole new witch costume.
McCorkle said we're just gonna use the one we do every year.
But it's so obvious! And not even accurate! Why does the witch have to look so scary anyway?
Because . . . she's a scary witch?
Chill, Moth.
It's only a play, right?

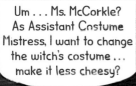

Um . . . Ms. McCorkle? As Assistant Costume Mistress, I want to change the witch's costume . . . make it less cheesy?

Cheesy? What DO you mean?

Well, weren't the women accused of witchcraft people too? Why do we have to make them into monsters?

Hmm. Miss Hush, I'm impressed by your passion.

Our play should be about the real history of the town, not just the story we've been comfortable telling every single year—

One thing at a time, darling.

Moth has drawn my attention to a very serious issue. You are playing actual, historical, flesh-and-blood PEOPLE.

And to do them justice, you will need to learn more about them.

And horses.

Instead of having the day off, there will be a mandatory extra rehearsal at the Founder's Bluff History Museum tomorrow morning. Thank you, Moth.

But—!

Saturday morning rehearsal. Gosh, you're the best, Moth.

Yeah, thanks a lot, Moth.

. . . That went well.

CHAPTER 7
A Secret History of Founder's Bluff

MUSEUM HOURS
TUES-SAT
10 AM-5 PM
SUNDAYS
NOON-4 PM

If we are to embody history on the stage, we must first experience history. Let history feed your mind, let history touch your heart. . . .

Haw haw haw!

I'm letting history pick my nose!

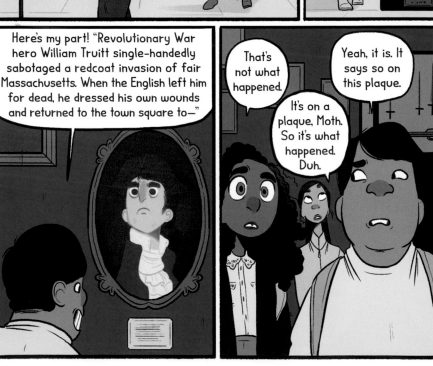

Here's my part! "Revolutionary War hero William Truitt single-handedly sabotaged a redcoat invasion of fair Massachusetts. When the English left him for dead, he dressed his own wounds and returned to the town square to—"

That's not what happened.

Yeah, it is. It says so on this plaque.

It's on a plaque, Moth. So it's what happened. Duh.

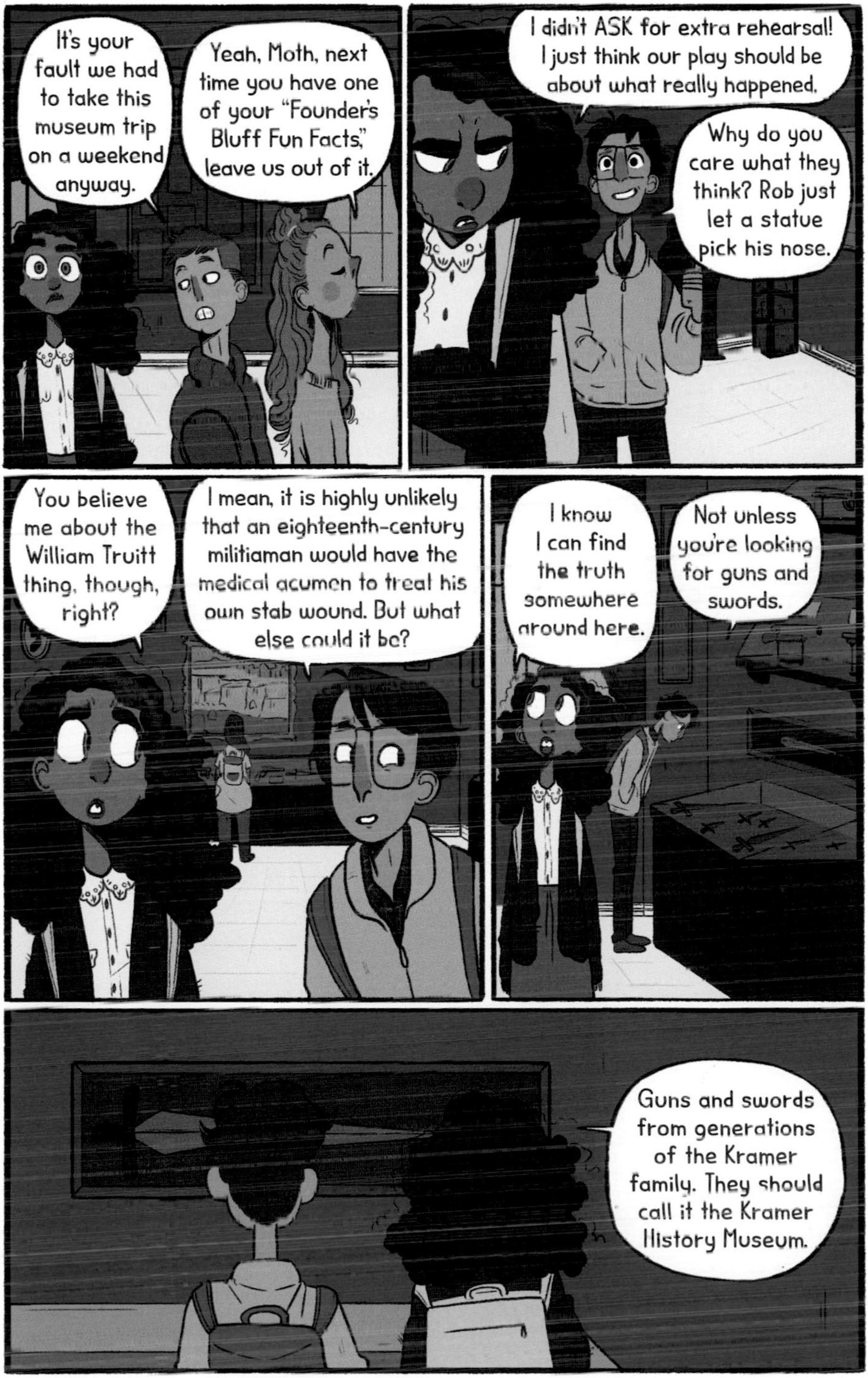

It's your fault we had to take this museum trip on a weekend anyway.
Yeah, Moth, next time you have one of your "Founder's Bluff Fun Facts," leave us out of it.
I didn't ASK for extra rehearsal! I just think our play should be about what really happened.
Why do you care what they think? Rob just let a statue pick his nose.
You believe me about the William Truitt thing, though, right?
I mean, it is highly unlikely that an eighteenth-century militiaman would have the medical acumen to treat his own stab wound. But what else could it be?
I know I can find the truth somewhere around here.
Not unless you're looking for guns and swords.
Guns and swords from generations of the Kramer family. They should call it the Kramer History Museum.

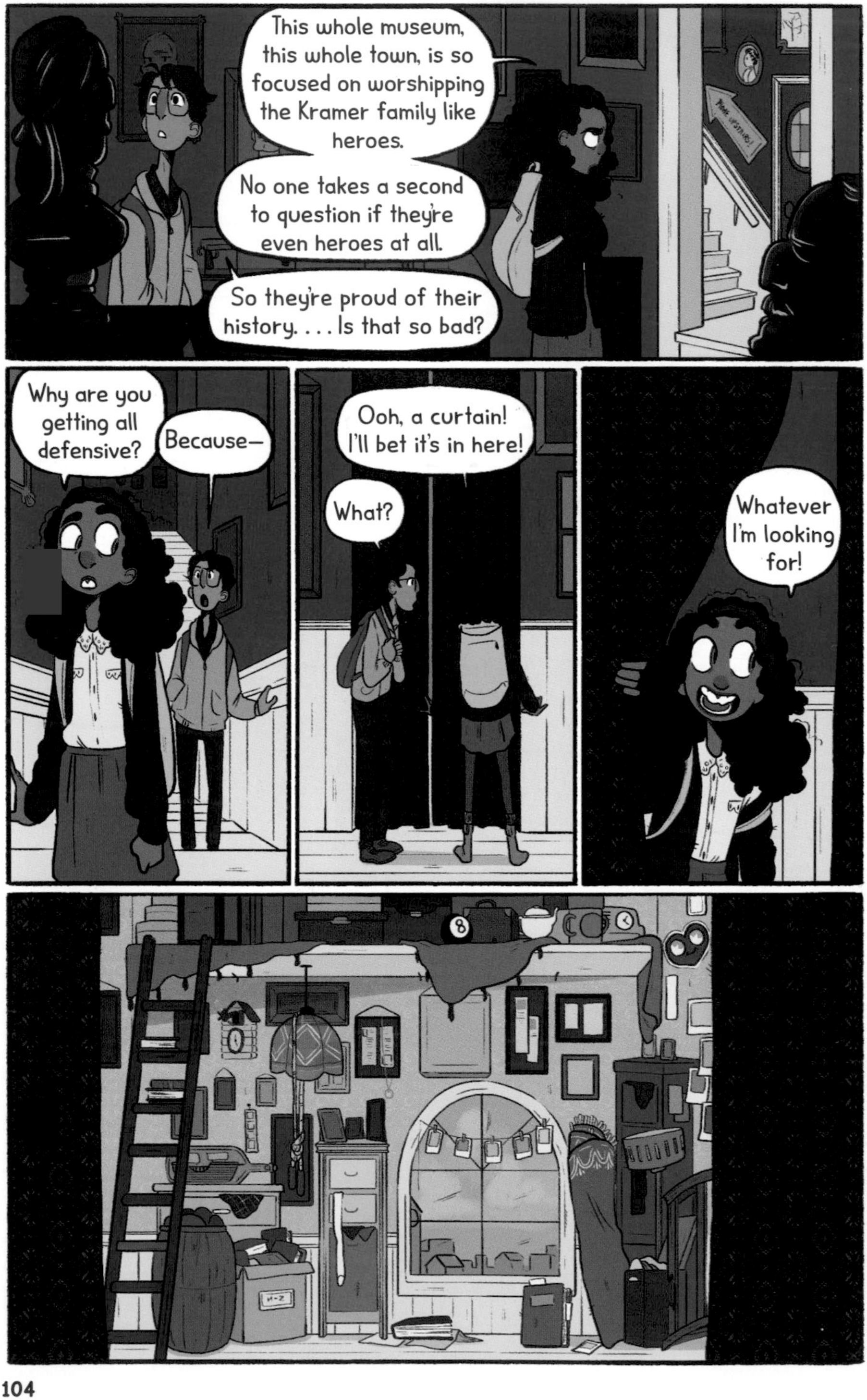
This whole museum, this whole town, is so focused on worshipping the Kramer family like heroes.
No one takes a second to question if they're even heroes at all.
So they're proud of their history. . . . Is that so bad?
Why are you getting all defensive?
Because—
Ooh, a curtain! I'll bet it's in here!
What?
Whatever I'm looking for!

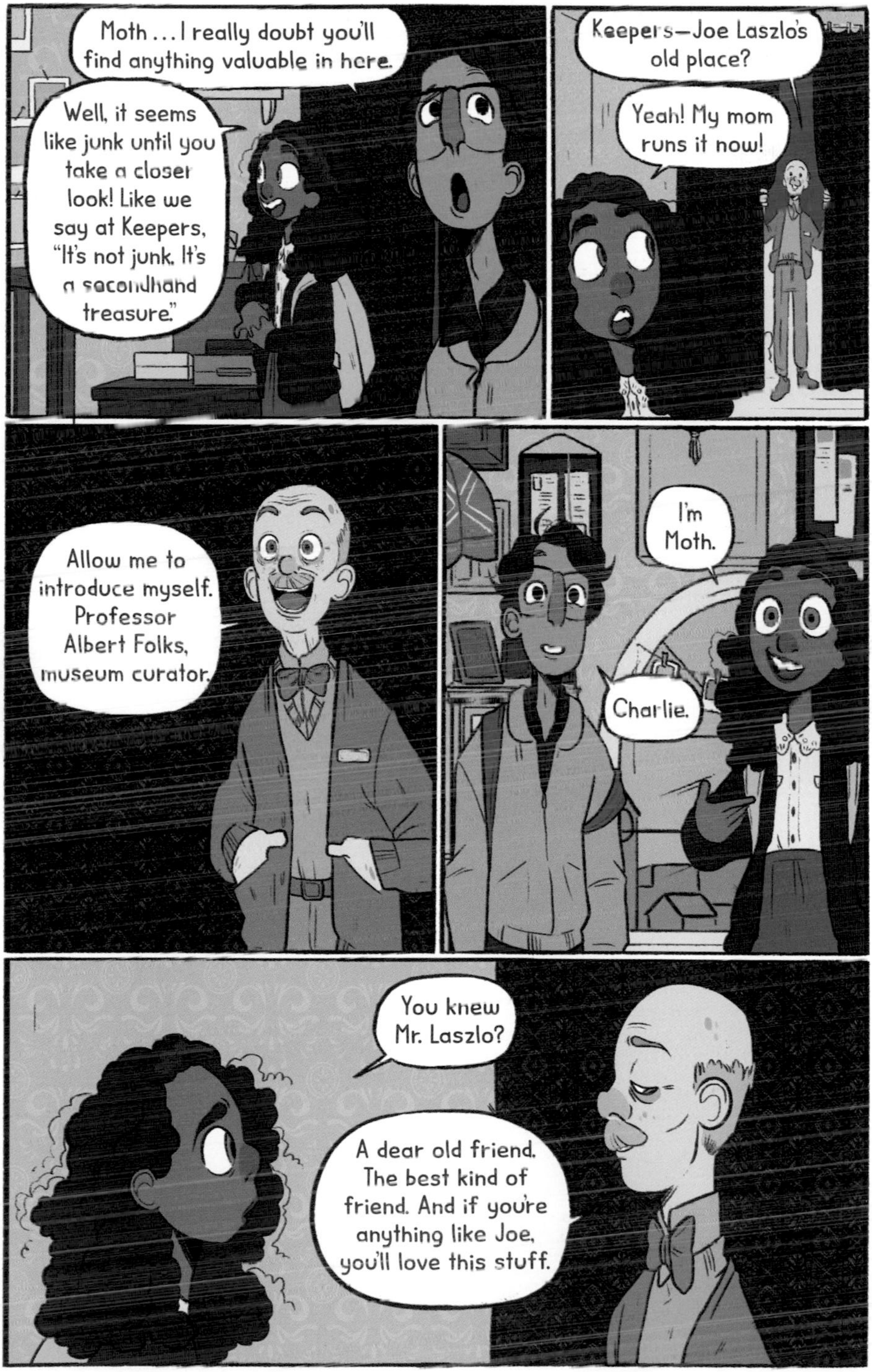
Moth . . . I really doubt you'll find anything valuable in here.
Well, it seems like junk until you take a closer look! Like we say at Keepers, "It's not junk. It's a secondhand treasure."
Keepers—Joe Laszlo's old place?
Yeah! My mom runs it now!
Allow me to introduce myself. Professor Albert Folks, museum curator.
I'm Moth.
Charlie.
You knew Mr. Laszlo?
A dear old friend. The best kind of friend. And if you're anything like Joe, you'll love this stuff.

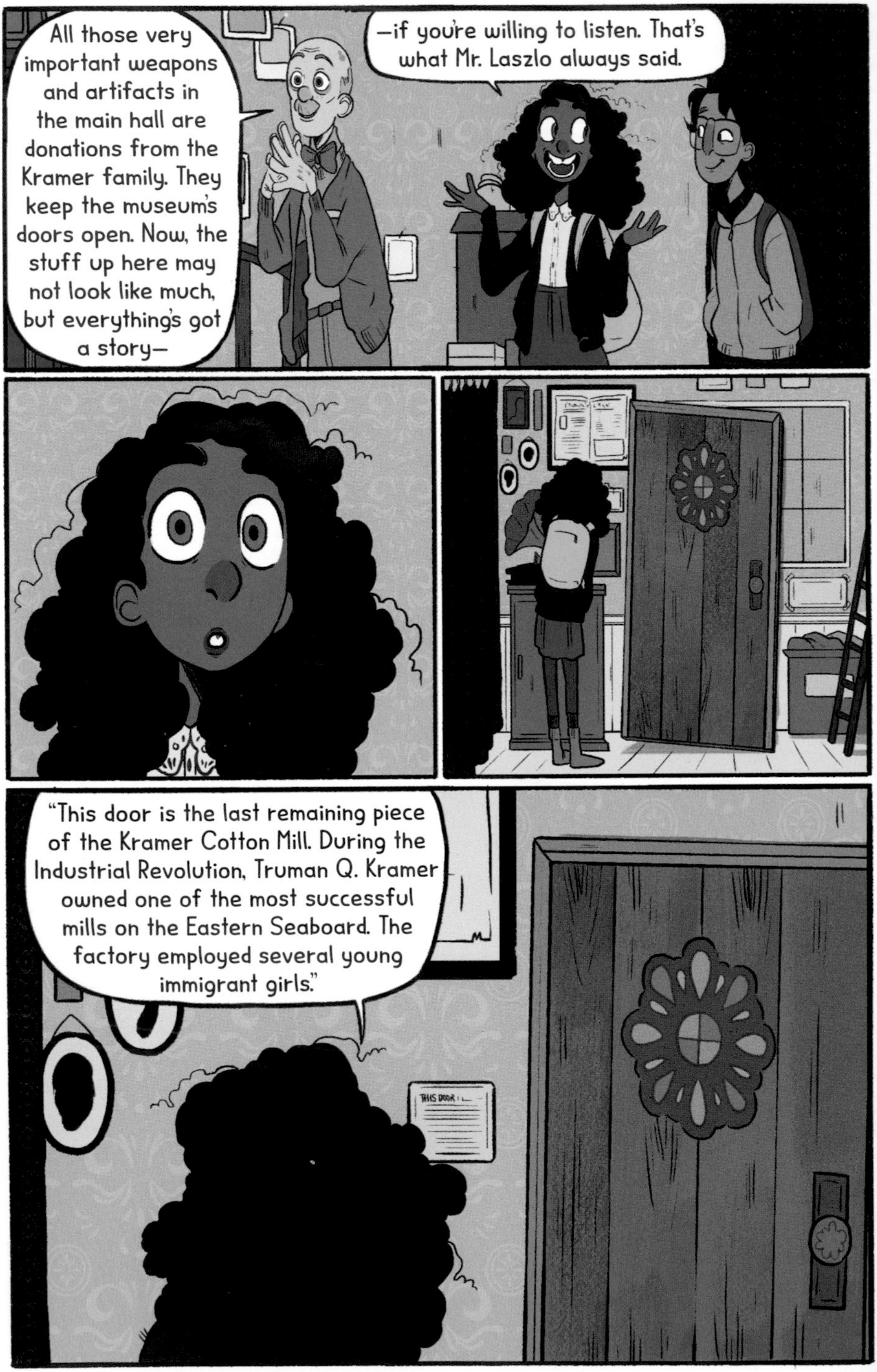
All those very important weapons and artifacts in the main hall are donations from the Kramer family. They keep the museum's doors open. Now, the stuff up here may not look like much, but everything's got a story—
—if you're willing to listen. That's what Mr. Laszlo always said.
"This door is the last remaining piece of the Kramer Cotton Mill. During the Industrial Revolution, Truman Q. Kramer owned one of the most successful mills on the Eastern Seaboard. The factory employed several young immigrant girls."
THIS DOOR

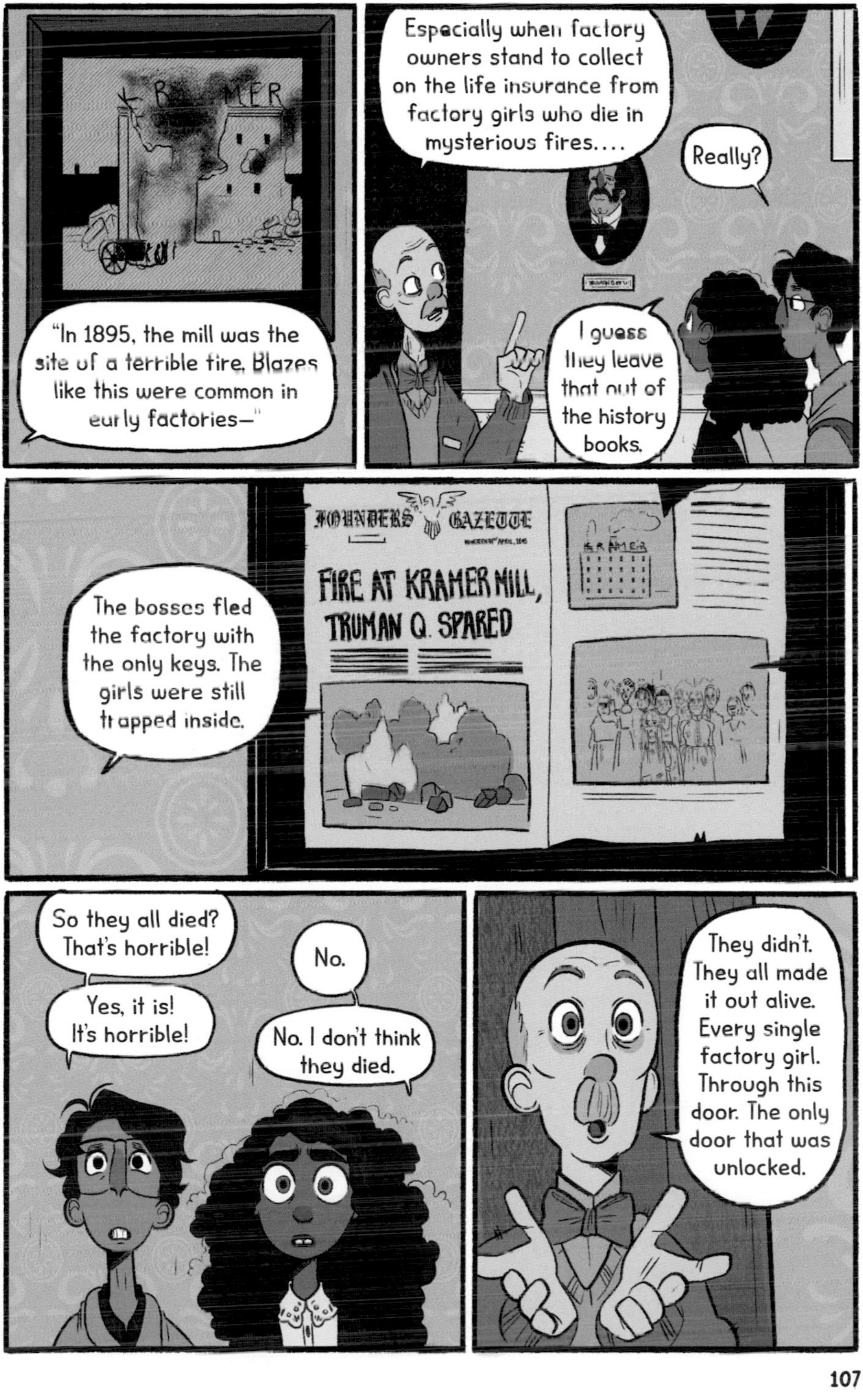
KRAMER
"In 1895, the mill was the site of a terrible fire. Blazes like this were common in early factories—"
Especially when factory owners stand to collect on the life insurance from factory girls who die in mysterious fires....
Really?
I guess they leave that out of the history books.
FOUNDERS GAZETTE
FIRE AT KRAMER MILL, TRUMAN Q. SPARED
The bosses fled the factory with the only keys. The girls were still trapped inside.
So they all died? That's horrible!
Yes, it is! It's horrible!
No.
No. I don't think they died.
They didn't. They all made it out alive. Every single factory girl. Through this door. The only door that was unlocked.

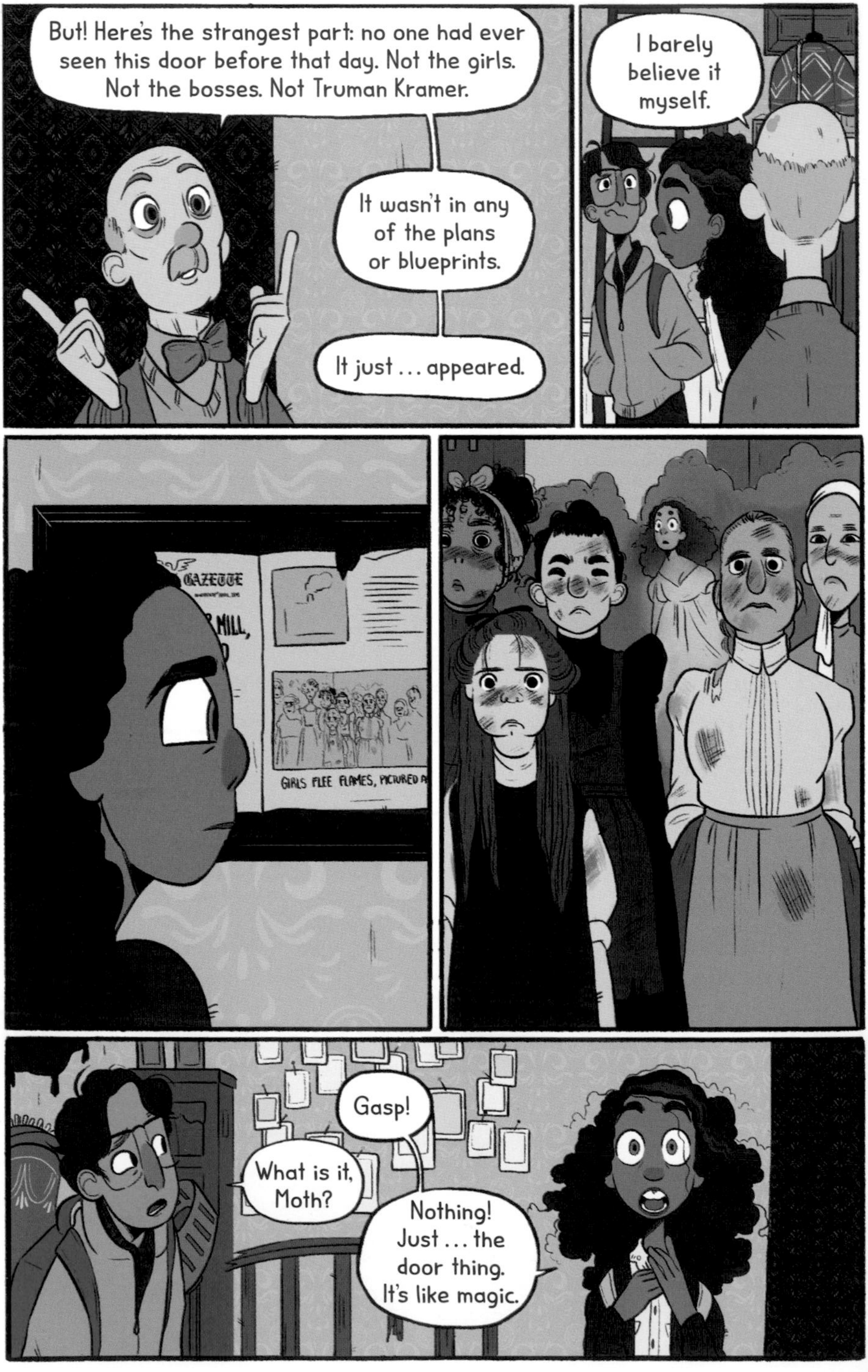
But! Here's the strangest part: no one had ever seen this door before that day. Not the girls. Not the bosses. Not Truman Kramer.
It wasn't in any of the plans or blueprints.
It just ... appeared.
I barely believe it myself.
GAZETTE
MILL,
GIRLS FLEE FLAMES, PICTURED
Gasp!
What is it, Moth?
Nothing! Just ... the door thing. It's like magic.

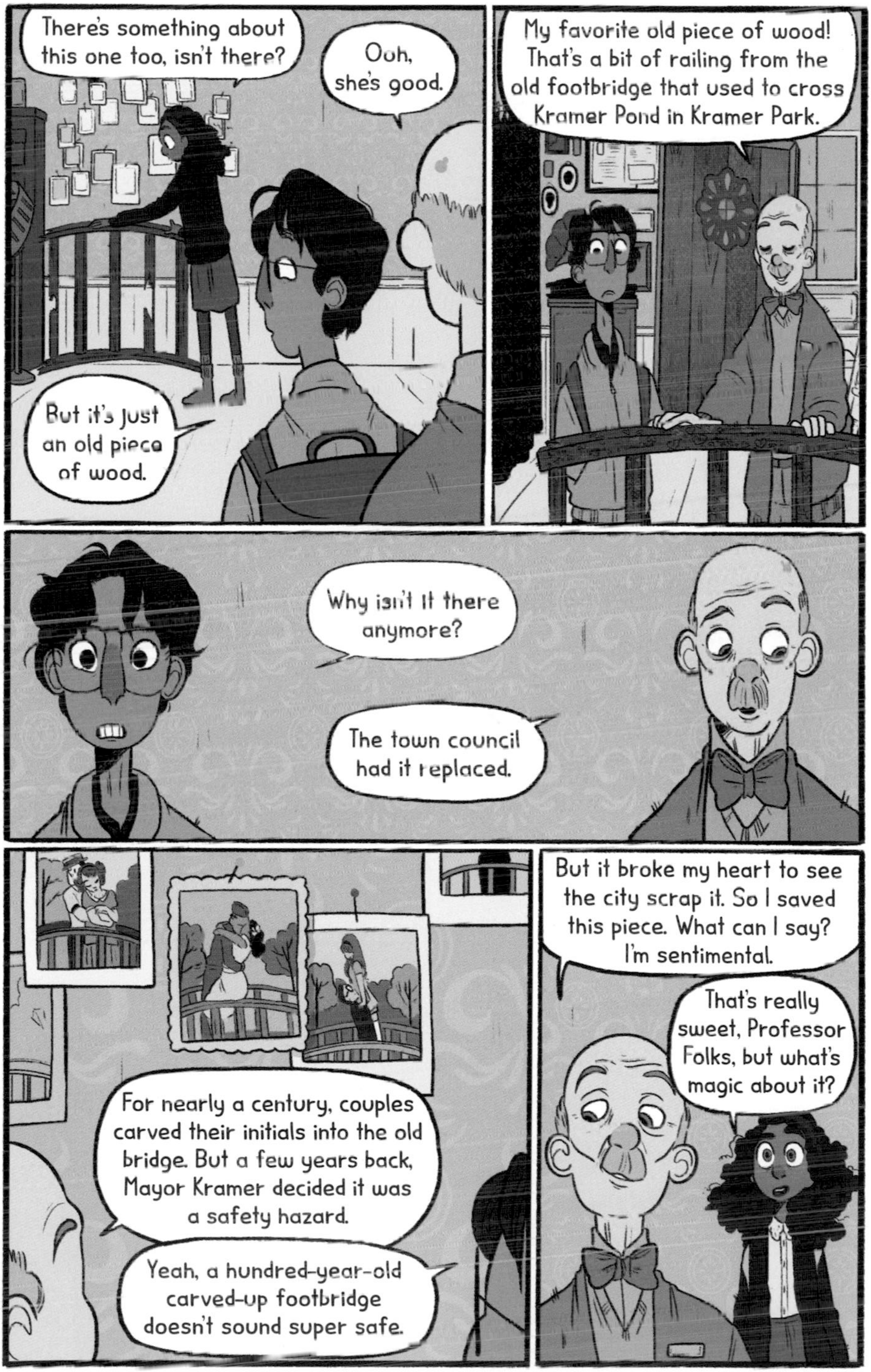
There's something about this one too, isn't there?
Ooh, she's good.
But it's just an old piece of wood.
My favorite old piece of wood! That's a bit of railing from the old footbridge that used to cross Kramer Pond in Kramer Park.
Why isn't it there anymore?
The town council had it replaced.
For nearly a century, couples carved their initials into the old bridge. But a few years back, Mayor Kramer decided it was a safety hazard.
Yeah, a hundred-year-old carved-up footbridge doesn't sound super safe.
But it broke my heart to see the city scrap it. So I saved this piece. What can I say? I'm sentimental.
That's really sweet, Professor Folks, but what's magic about it?

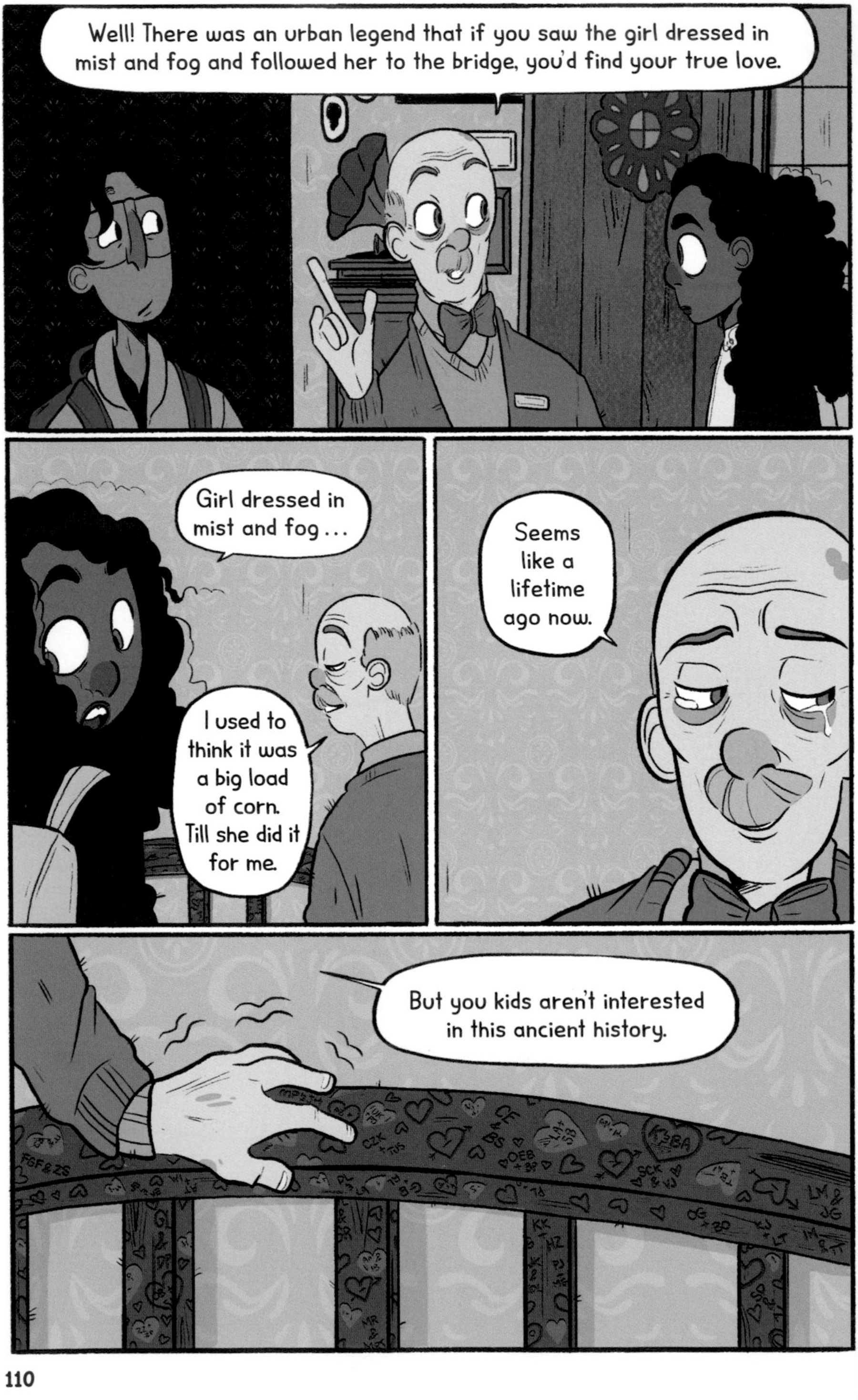
Well! There was an urban legend that if you saw the girl dressed in mist and fog and followed her to the bridge, you'd find your true love.
Girl dressed in mist and fog . . .
I used to think it was a big load of corn. Till she did it for me.
Seems like a lifetime ago now.
But you kids aren't interested in this ancient history.

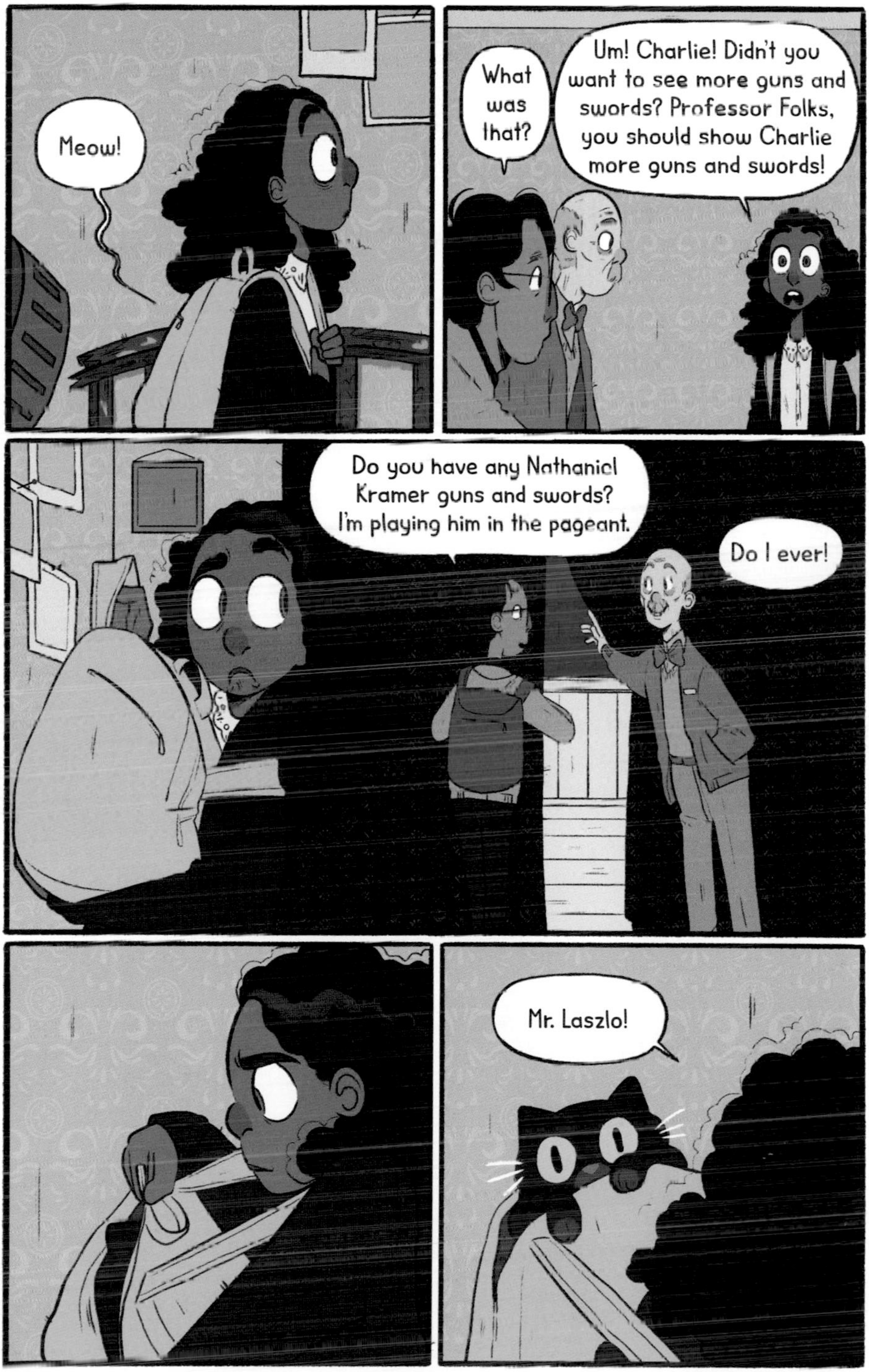
Meow!
What was that?
Um! Charlie! Didn't you want to see more guns and swords? Professor Folks, you should show Charlie more guns and swords!
Do you have any Nathaniel Kramer guns and swords? I'm playing him in the pageant.
Do I ever!
Mr. Laszlo!

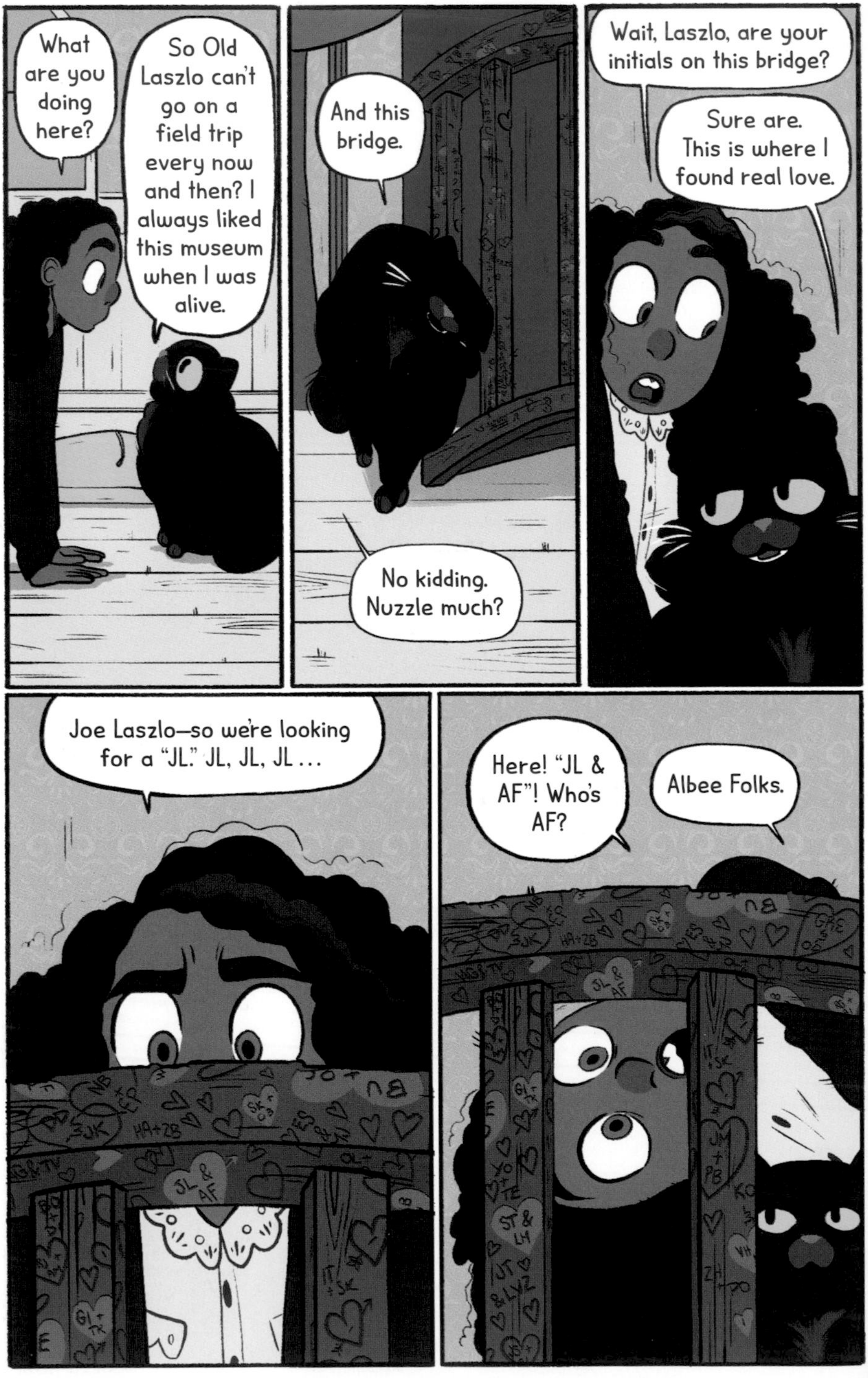

What are you doing here?
So Old Laszlo can't go on a field trip every now and then? I always liked this museum when I was alive.
And this bridge.
No kidding. Nuzzle much?
Wait, Laszlo, are your initials on this bridge?
Sure are. This is where I found real love.
Joe Laszlo—so we're looking for a "JL." JL, JL, JL . . .
Here! "JL & AF"! Who's AF?
Albee Folks.

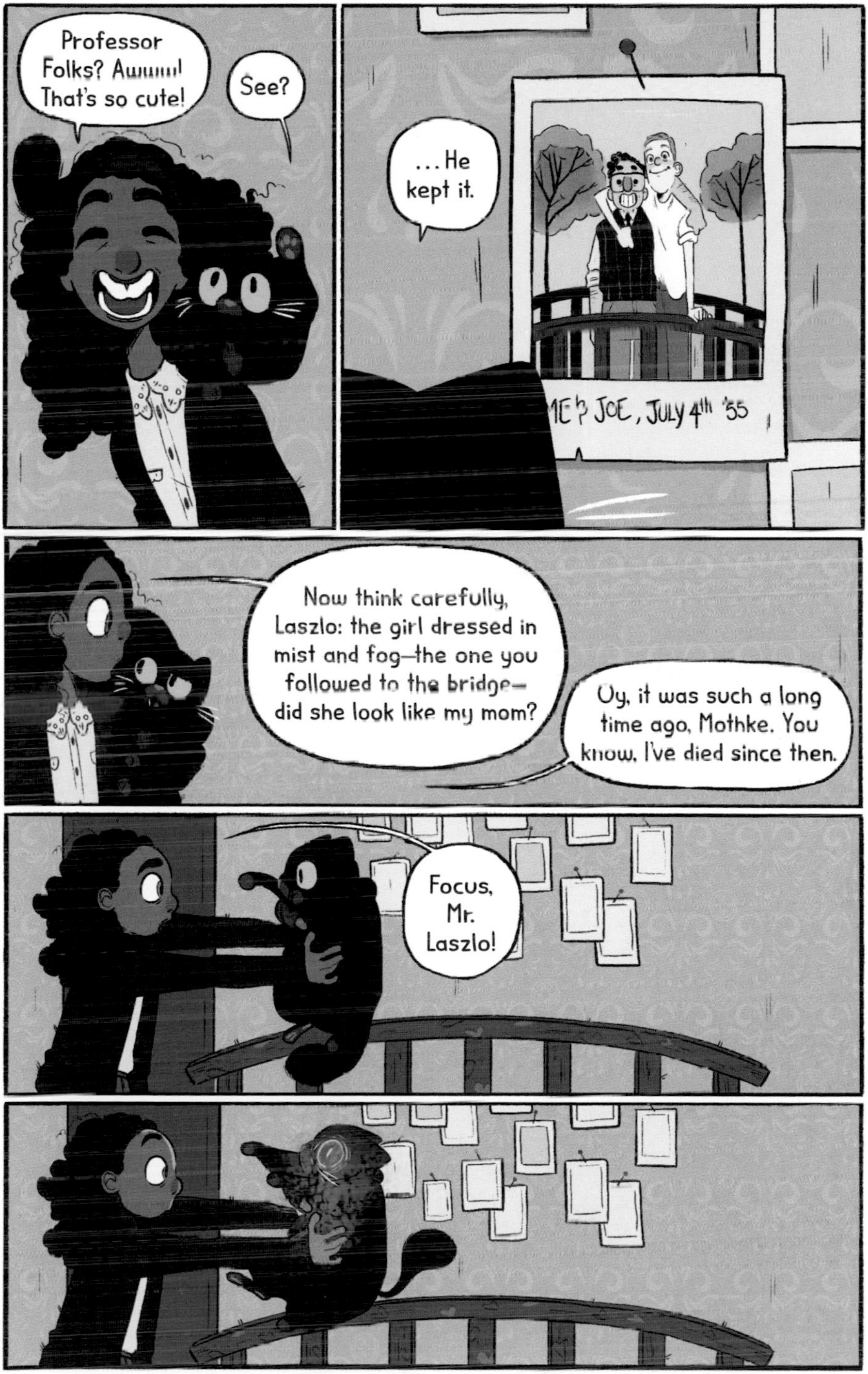

Professor Folks? Awwww! That's so cute!
See?
...He kept it.
ME & JOE, JULY 4th '55
Now think carefully, Laszlo: the girl dressed in mist and fog—the one you followed to the bridge—did she look like my mom?
Oy, it was such a long time ago, Mothke. You know, I've died since then.
Focus, Mr. Laszlo!

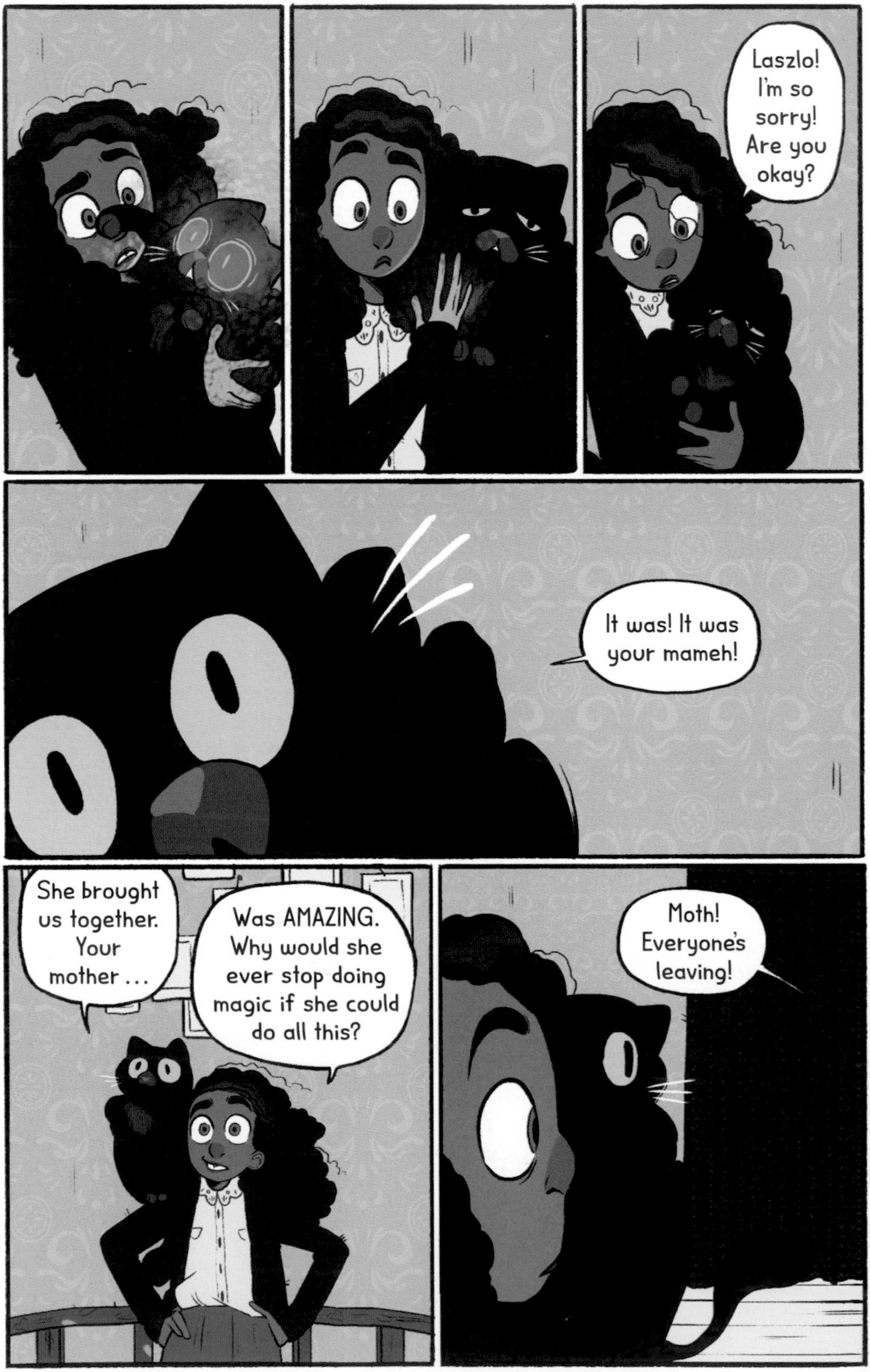
Laszlo! I'm so sorry! Are you okay?
It was! It was your mameh!
She brought us together. Your mother . . .
Was AMAZING. Why would she ever stop doing magic if she could do all this?
Moth! Everyone's leaving!

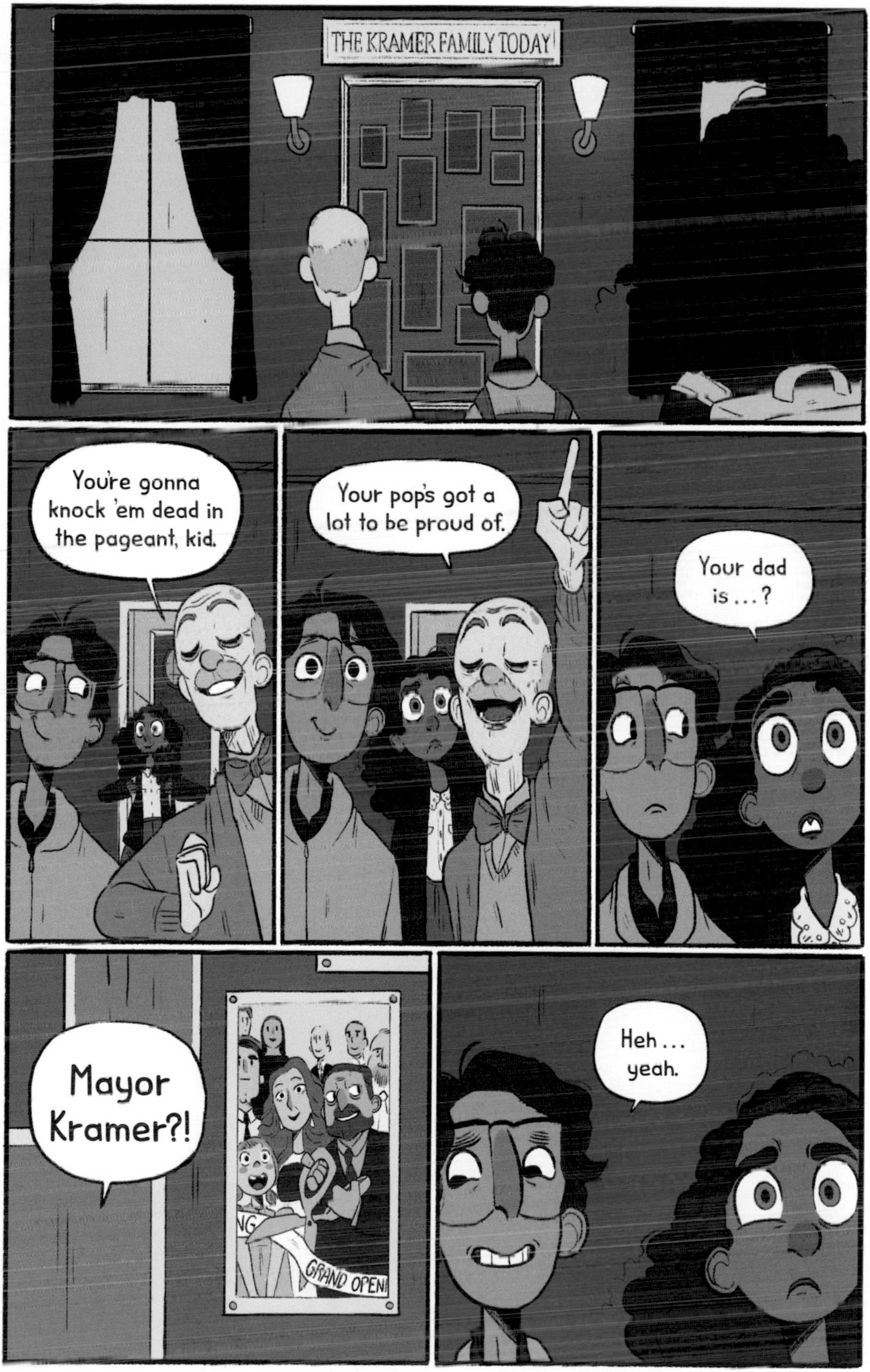
THE KRAMER FAMILY TODAY
You're gonna knock 'em dead in the pageant, kid.
Your pop's got a lot to be proud of.
Your dad is . . . ?
Mayor Kramer?!
GRAND OPEN
Heh . . . yeah.

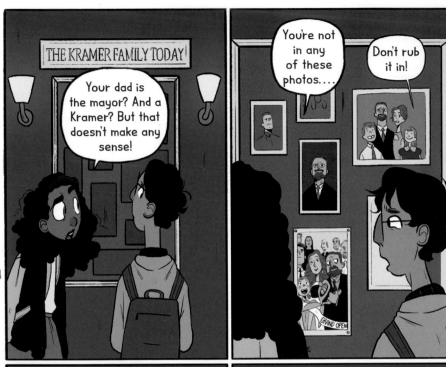

THE KRAMER FAMILY TODAY

Your dad is the mayor? And a Kramer? But that doesn't make any sense!

You're not in any of these photos....

Don't rub it in!

I told you. I'm from my dad's first marriage. We never really got to know each other.

No, I know, but I didn't know your DAD was Mayor Bruce KRAMER.

THE KRAMER FAMILY TODAY

I wish you didn't know. Apparently, you hate all Kramers.

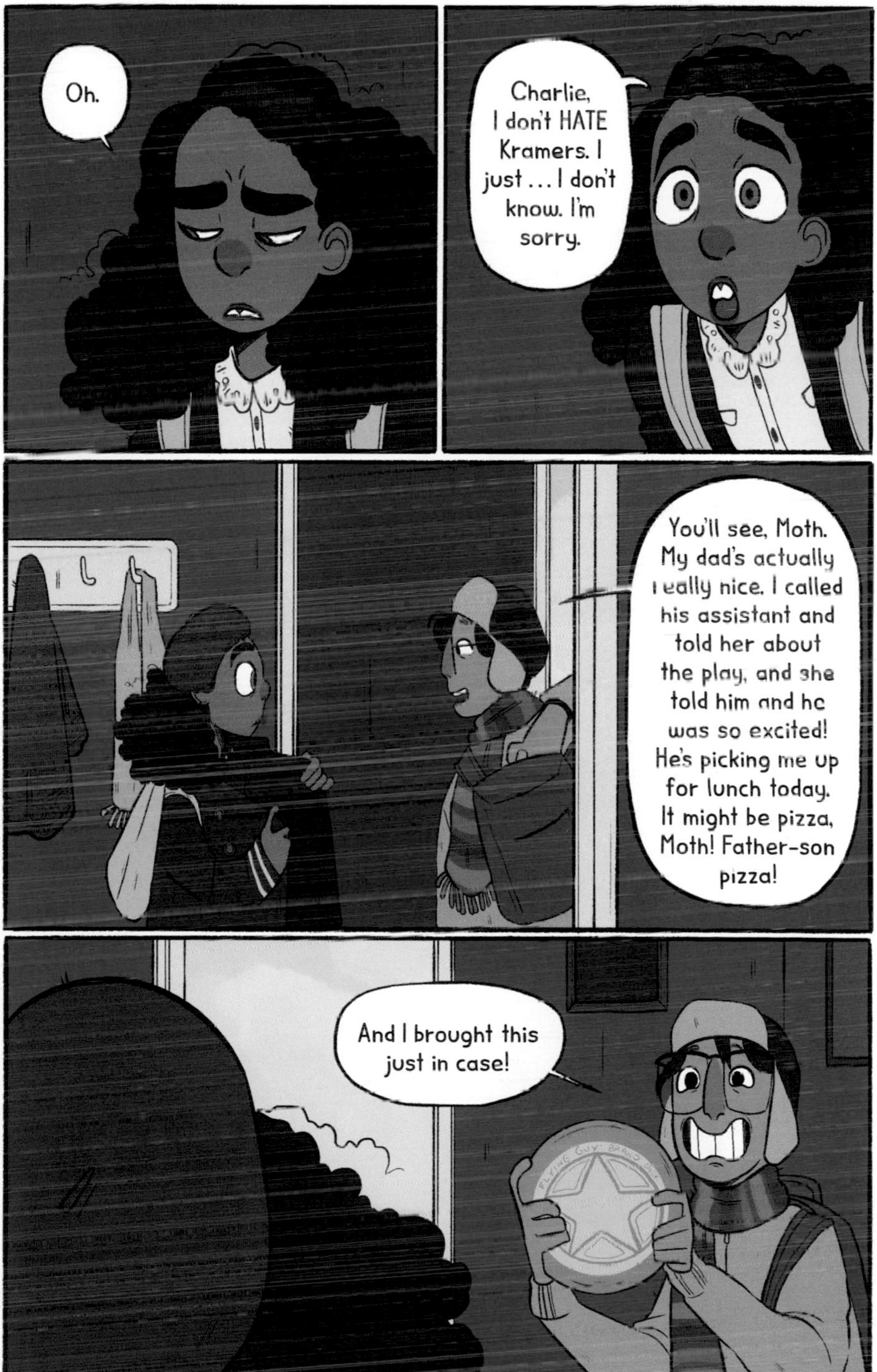
Oh.
Charlie, I don't HATE Kramers. I just . . . I don't know. I'm sorry.
You'll see, Moth. My dad's actually really nice. I called his assistant and told her about the play, and she told him and he was so excited! He's picking me up for lunch today. It might be pizza, Moth! Father-son pizza!
And I brought this just in case!

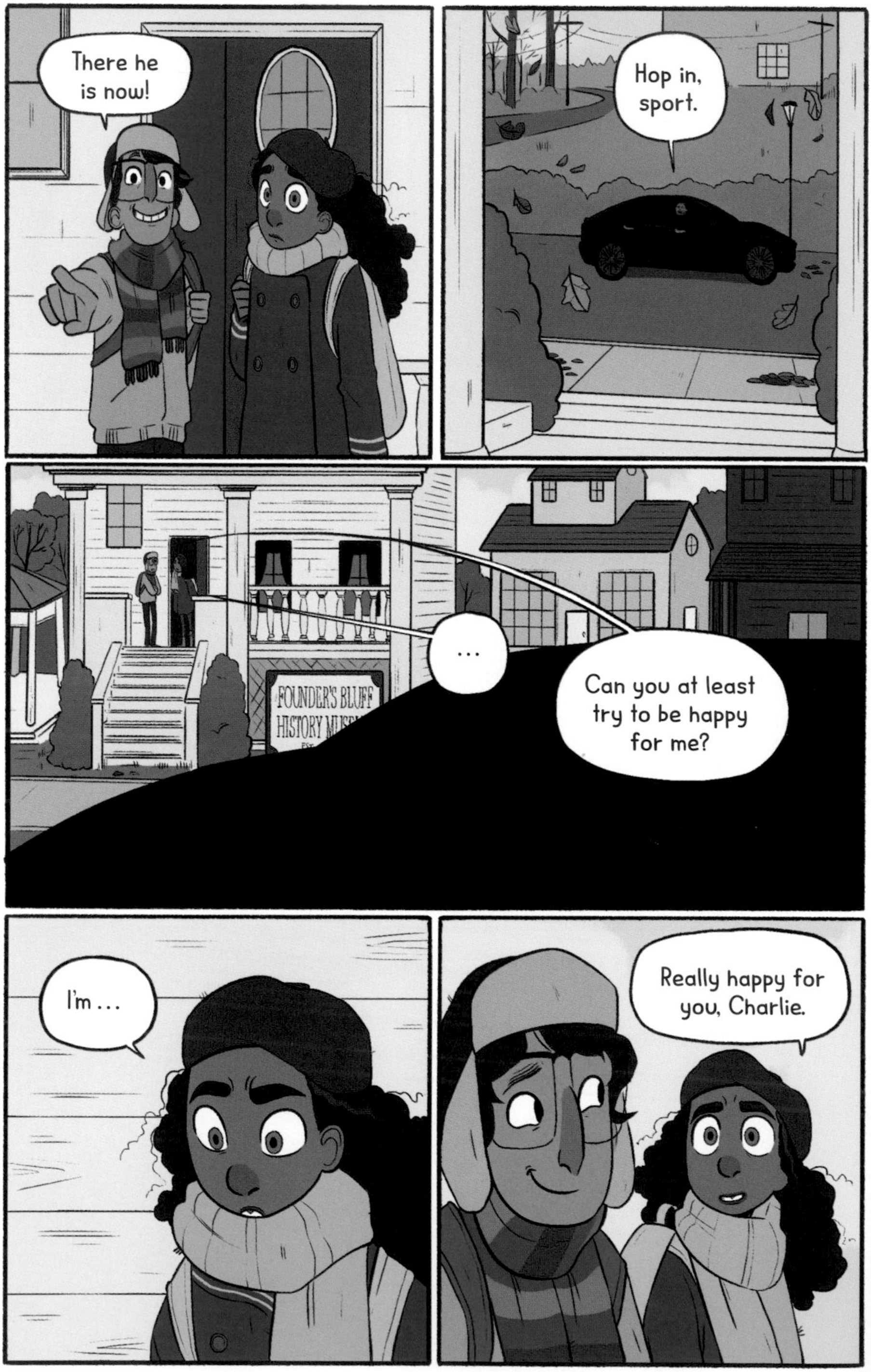
There he is now!
Hop in, sport.
...
Can you at least try to be happy for me?
FOUNDER'S BLUFF HISTORY MUSE
I'm...
Really happy for you, Charlie.

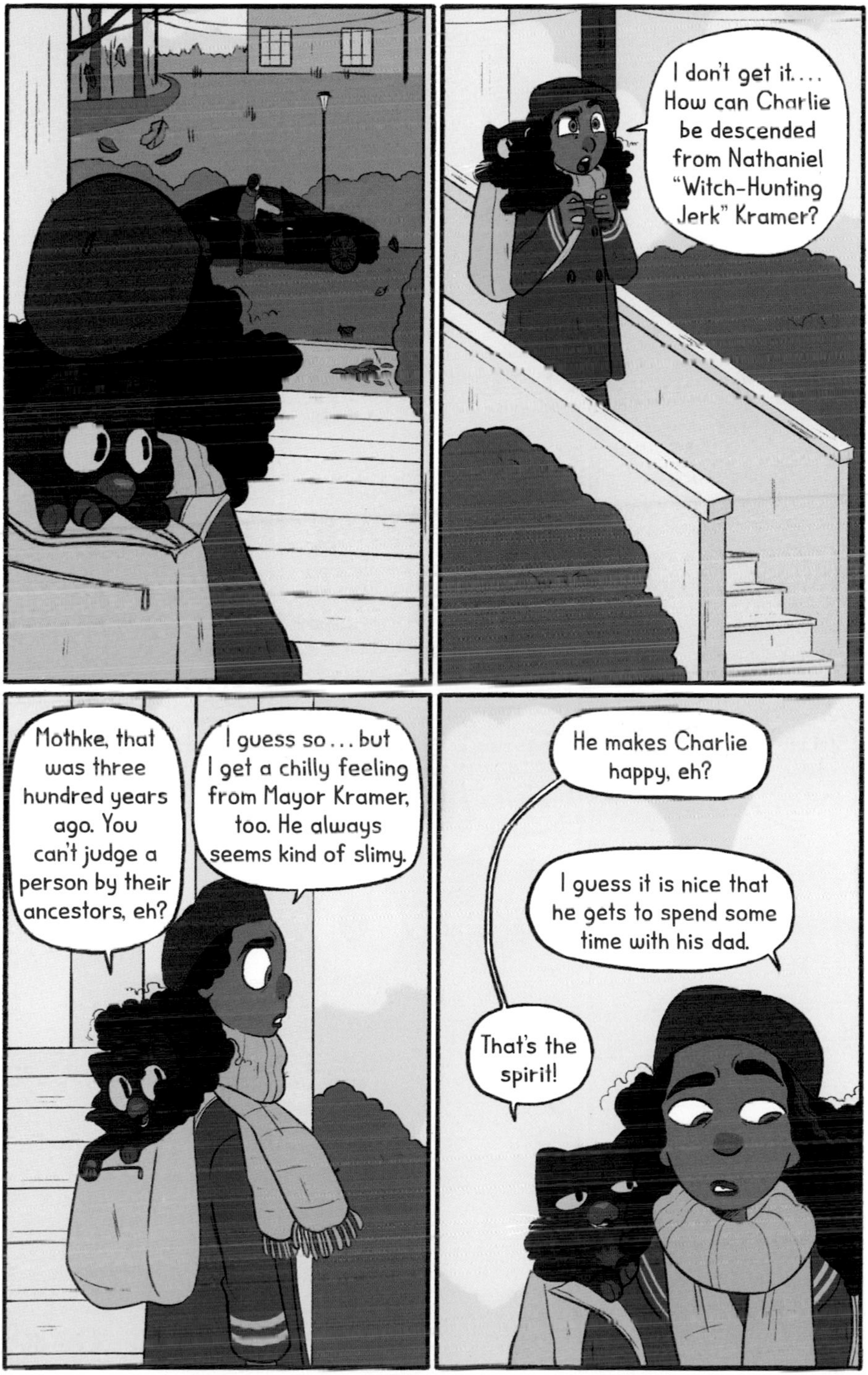
I don't get it.... How can Charlie be descended from Nathaniel "Witch-Hunting Jerk" Kramer?
Mothke, that was three hundred years ago. You can't judge a person by their ancestors, eh?
I guess so... but I get a chilly feeling from Mayor Kramer, too. He always seems kind of slimy.
He makes Charlie happy, eh?
I guess it is nice that he gets to spend some time with his dad.
That's the spirit!

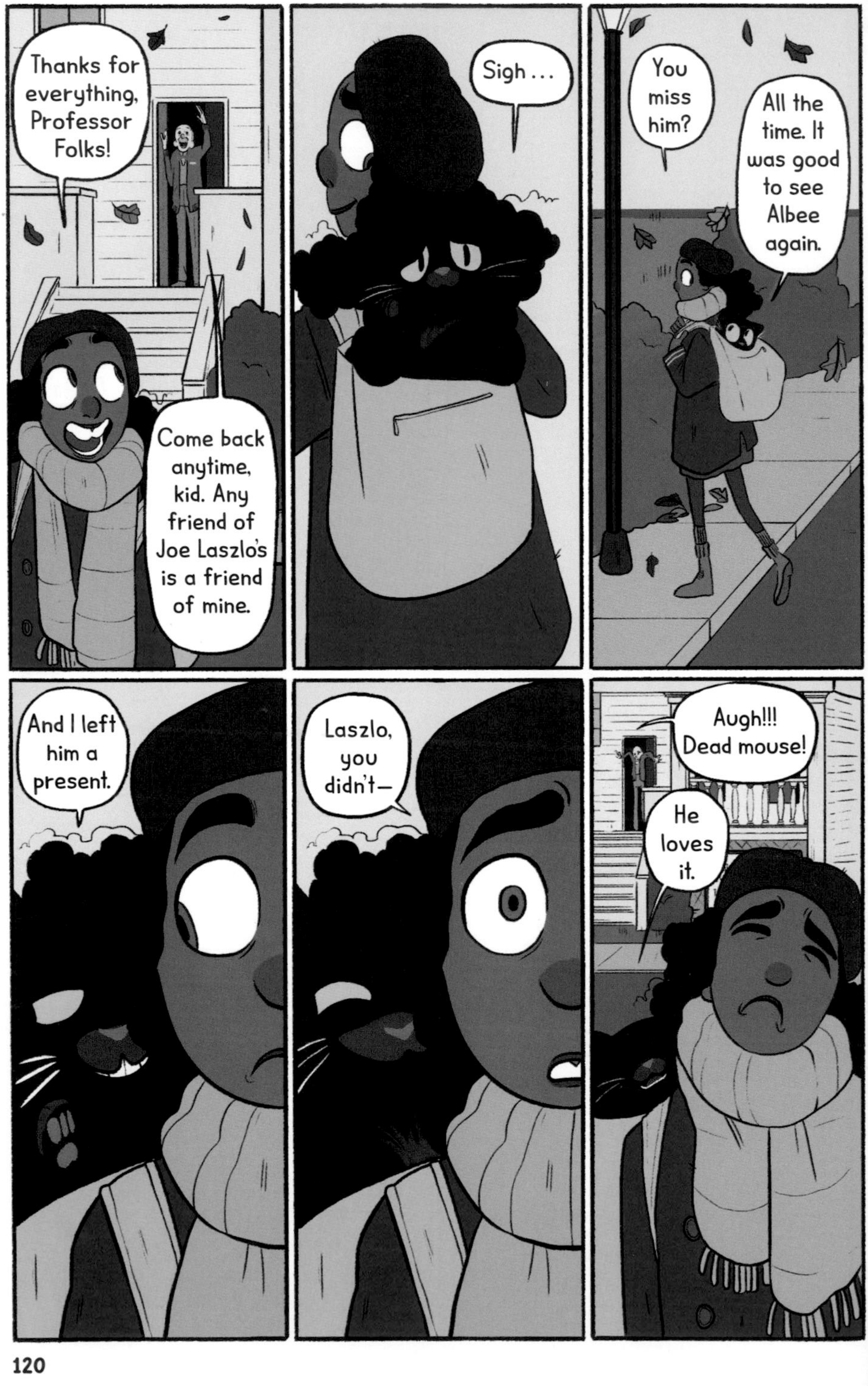
Thanks for everything, Professor Folks!
Come back anytime, kid. Any friend of Joe Laszlo's is a friend of mine.
Sigh . . .
You miss him?
All the time. It was good to see Albee again.
And I left him a present.
Laszlo, you didn't—
Augh!!! Dead mouse!
He loves it.

CHAPTER 8
Ex-Witch

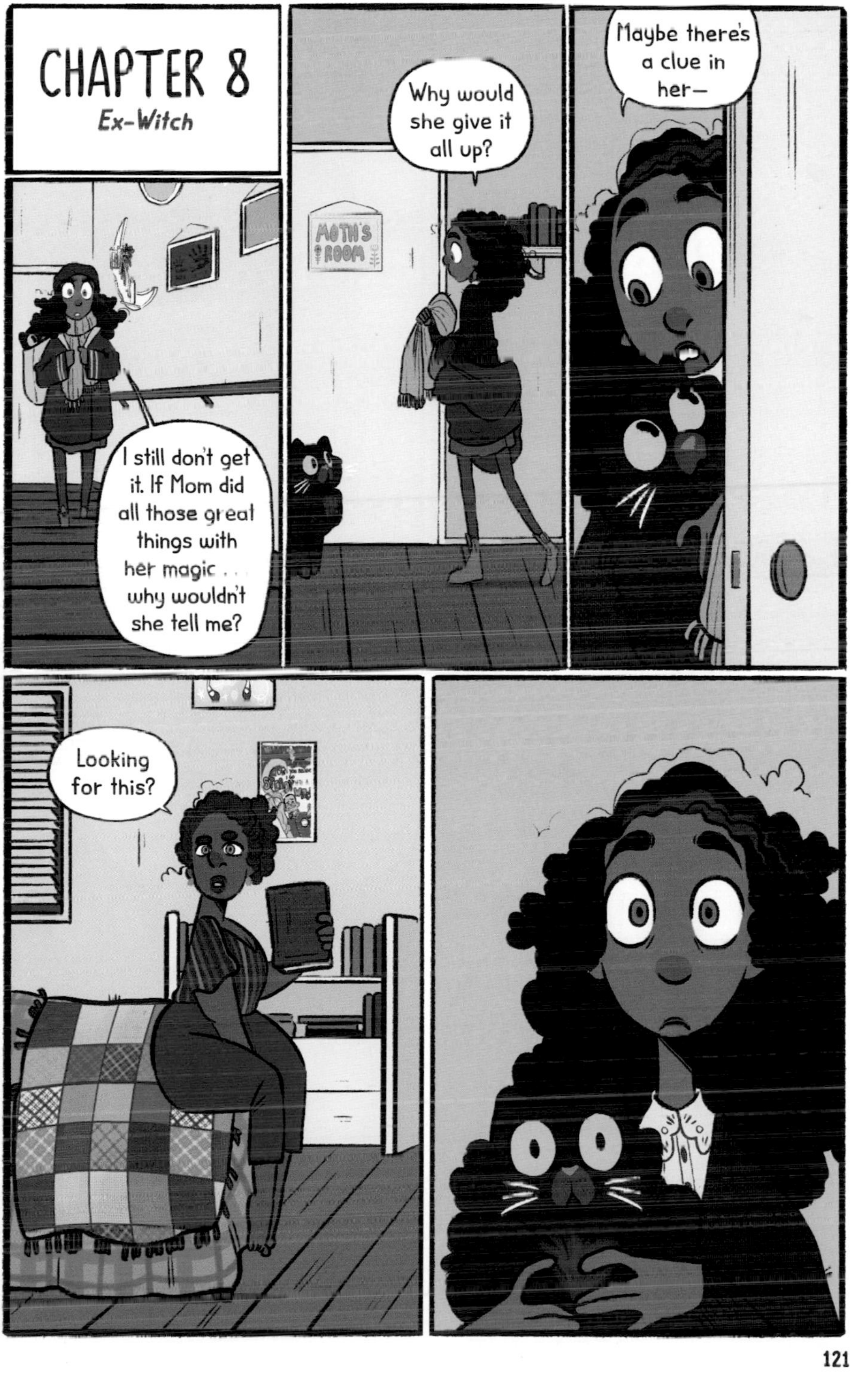
I still don't get it. If Mom did all those great things with her magic . . . why wouldn't she tell me?
MOTH'S ROOM
Why would she give it all up?
Maybe there's a clue in her—
Looking for this?

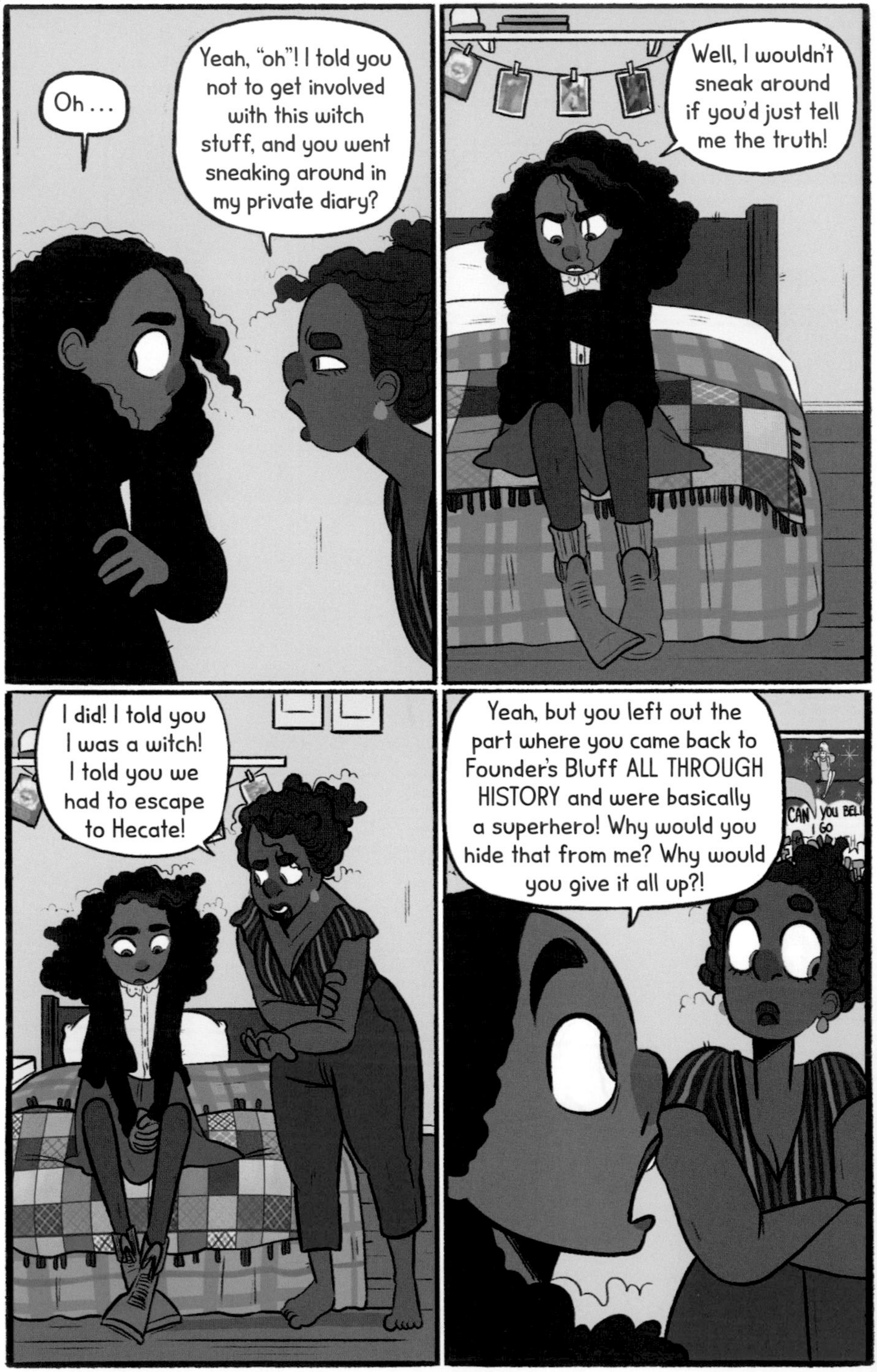
Oh . . .
Yeah, "oh"! I told you not to get involved with this witch stuff, and you went sneaking around in my private diary?
Well, I wouldn't sneak around if you'd just tell me the truth!
I did! I told you I was a witch! I told you we had to escape to Hecate!
Yeah, but you left out the part where you came back to Founder's Bluff ALL THROUGH HISTORY and were basically a superhero! Why would you hide that from me? Why would you give it all up?!

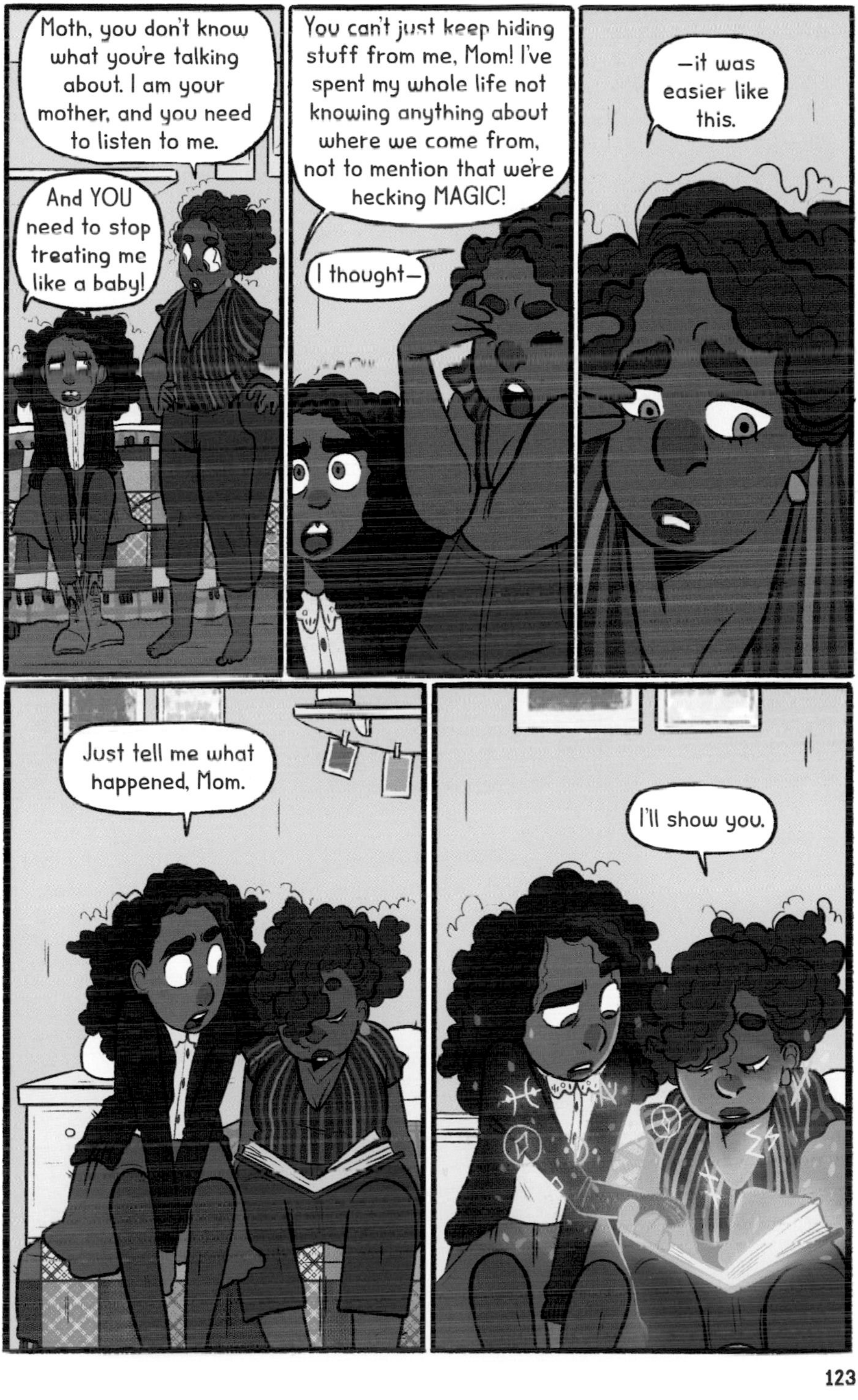
Moth, you don't know what you're talking about. I am your mother, and you need to listen to me.
And YOU need to stop treating me like a baby!
You can't just keep hiding stuff from me, Mom! I've spent my whole life not knowing anything about where we come from, not to mention that we're hecking MAGIC!
I thought—
—it was easier like this.
Just tell me what happened, Mom.
I'll show you.

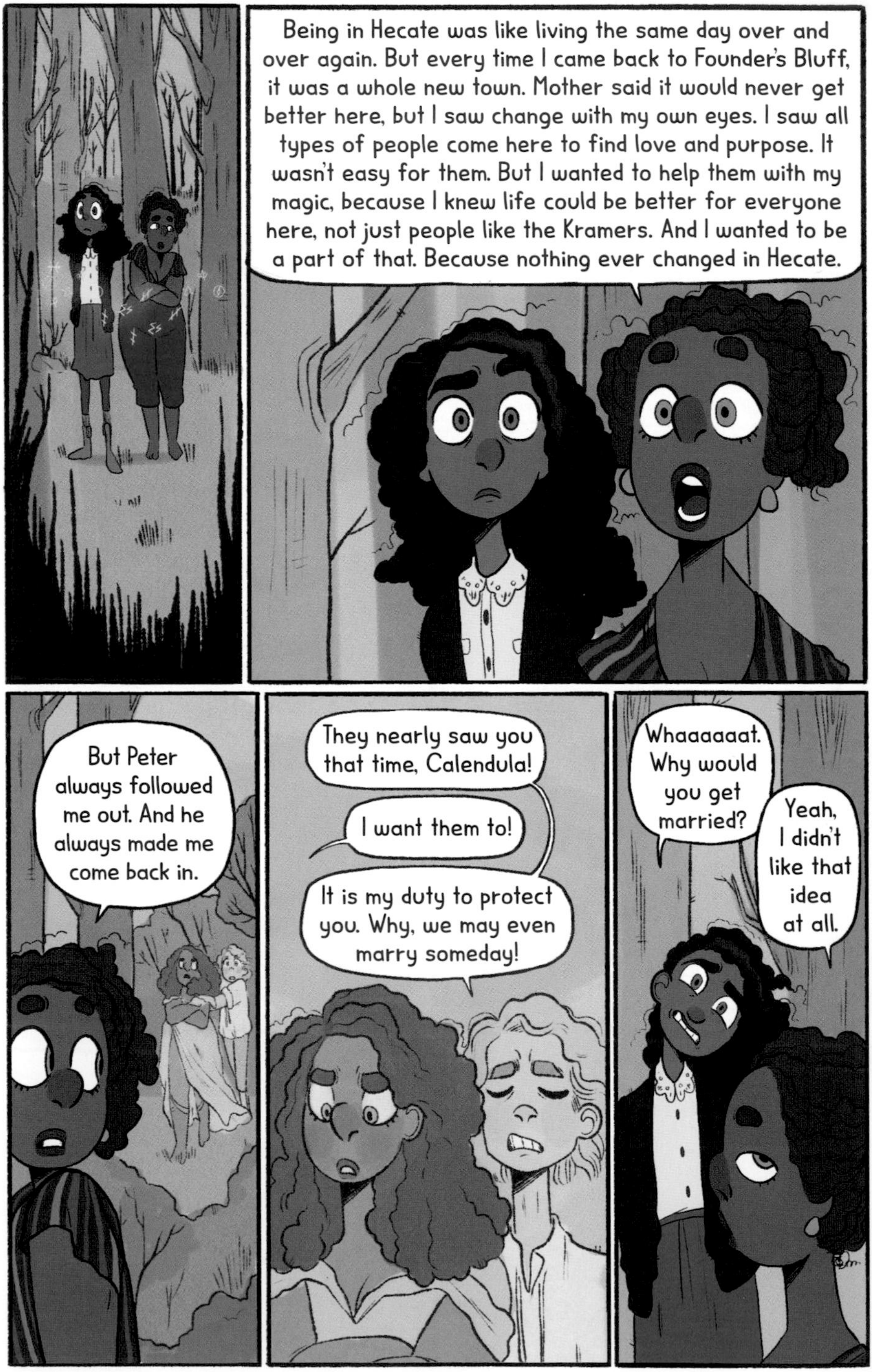
Being in Hecate was like living the same day over and over again. But every time I came back to Founder's Bluff, it was a whole new town. Mother said it would never get better here, but I saw change with my own eyes. I saw all types of people come here to find love and purpose. It wasn't easy for them. But I wanted to help them with my magic, because I knew life could be better for everyone here, not just people like the Kramers. And I wanted to be a part of that. Because nothing ever changed in Hecate.
But Peter always followed me out. And he always made me come back in.
They nearly saw you that time, Calendula!
I want them to!
It is my duty to protect you. Why, we may even marry someday!
Whaaaaaat. Why would you get married?
Yeah, I didn't like that idea at all.

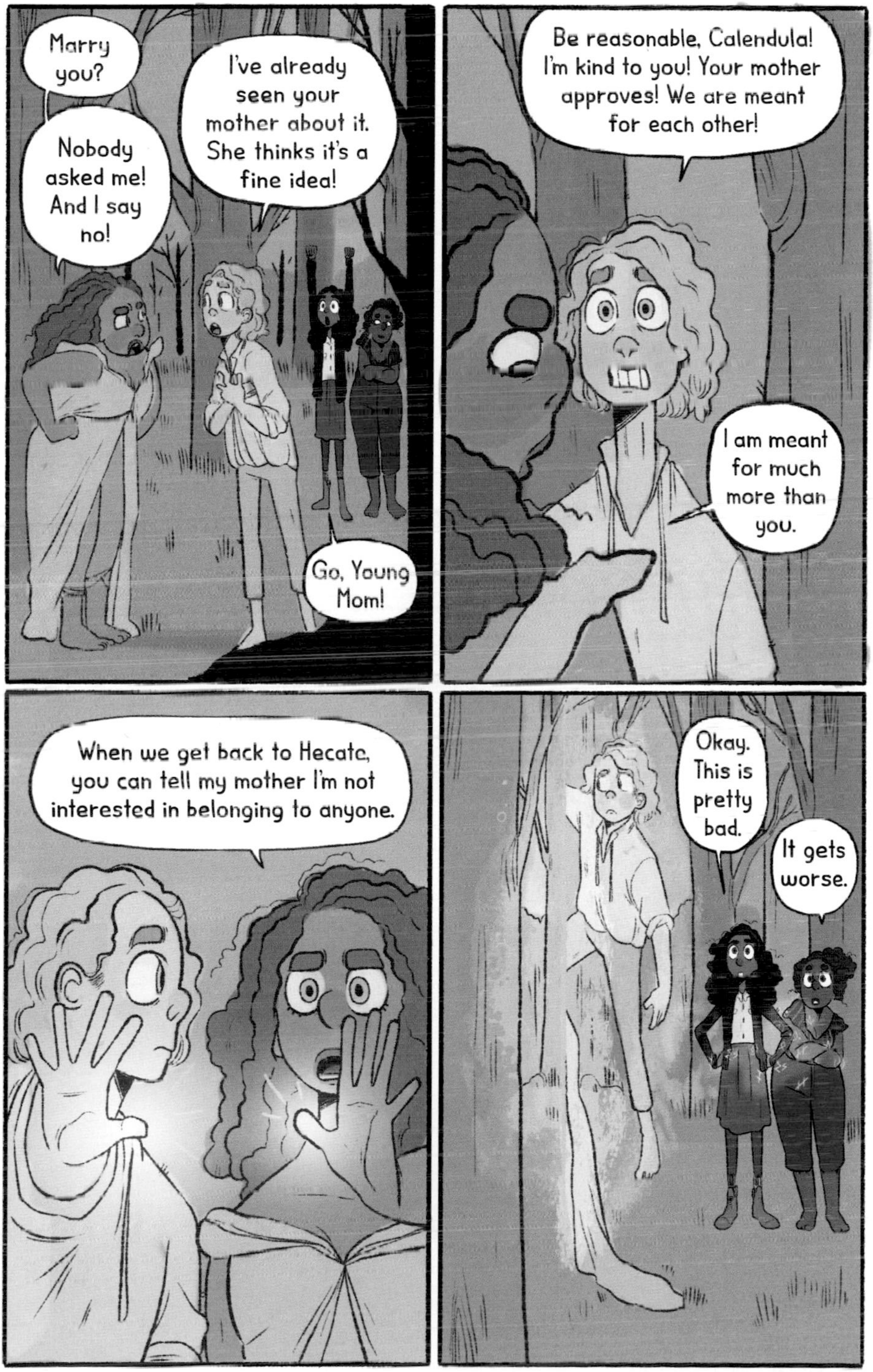
Marry you?
Nobody asked me! And I say no!
I've already seen your mother about it. She thinks it's a fine idea!
Go, Young Mom!
Be reasonable, Calendula! I'm kind to you! Your mother approves! We are meant for each other!
I am meant for much more than you.
When we get back to Hecate, you can tell my mother I'm not interested in belonging to anyone.
Okay. This is pretty bad.
It gets worse.

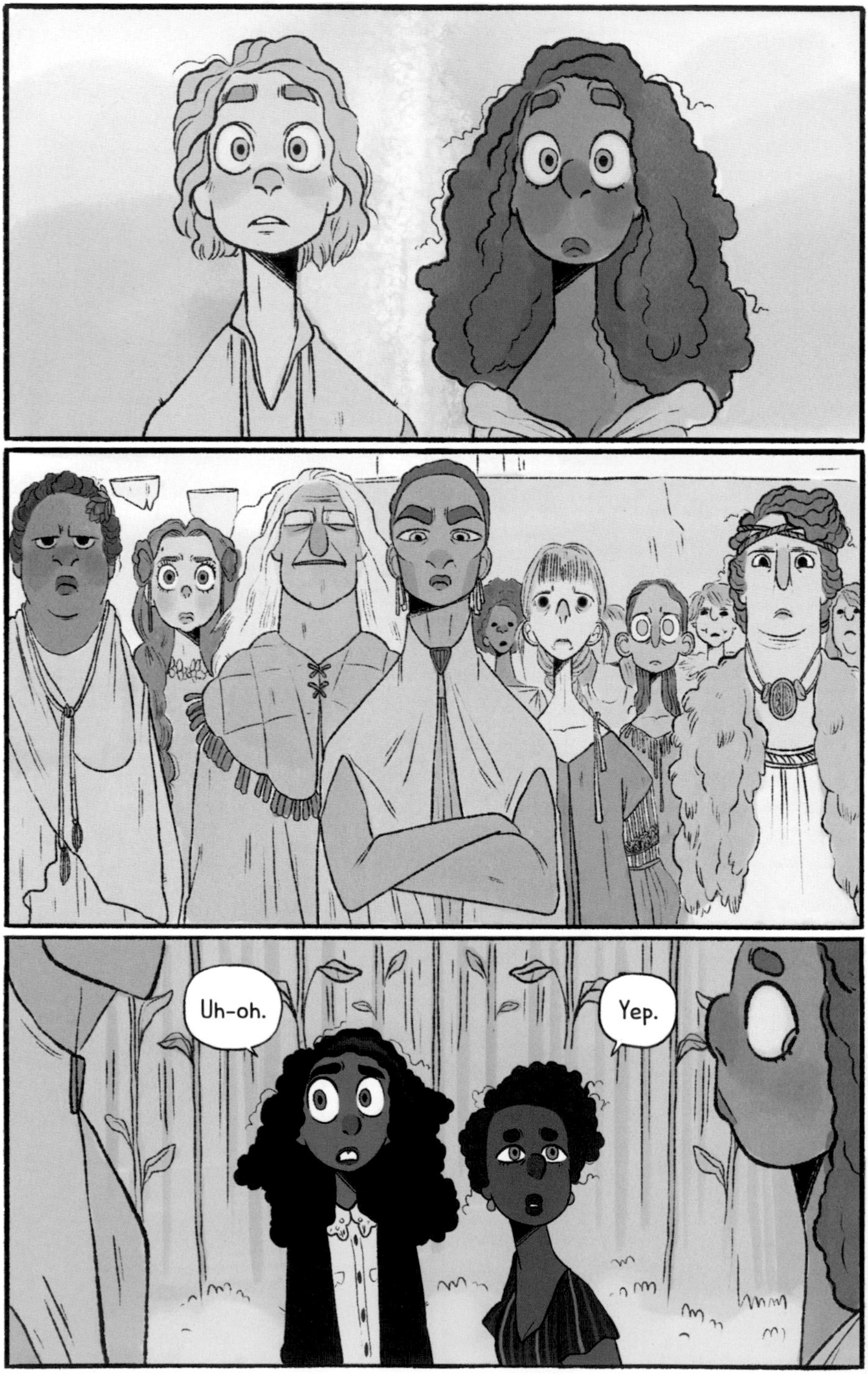
Uh-oh.
Yep.

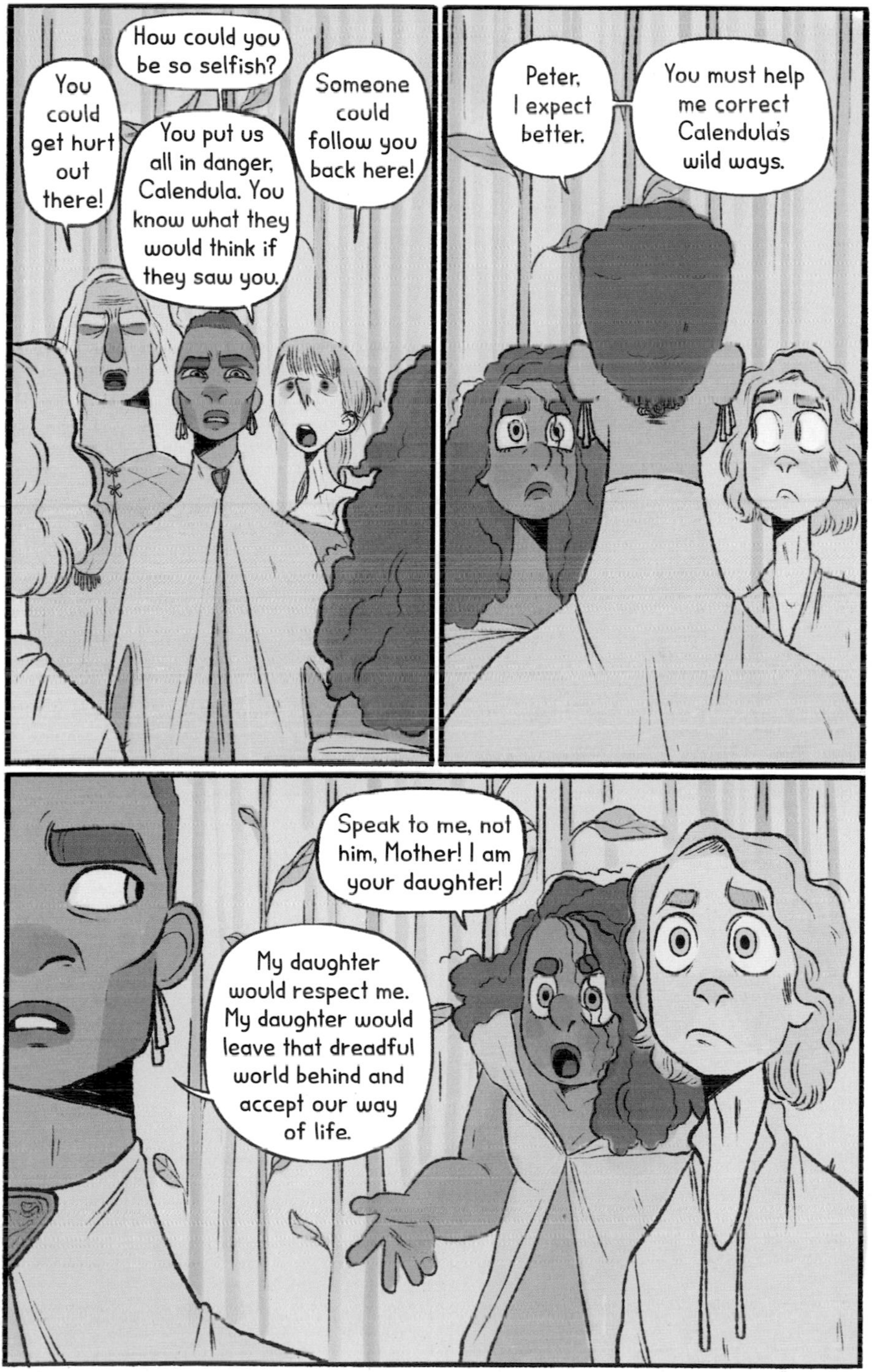

You could get hurt out there!
How could you be so selfish?
You put us all in danger, Calendula. You know what they would think if they saw you.
Someone could follow you back here!
Peter, I expect better.
You must help me correct Calendula's wild ways.
Speak to me, not him, Mother! I am your daughter!
My daughter would respect me. My daughter would leave that dreadful world behind and accept our way of life.

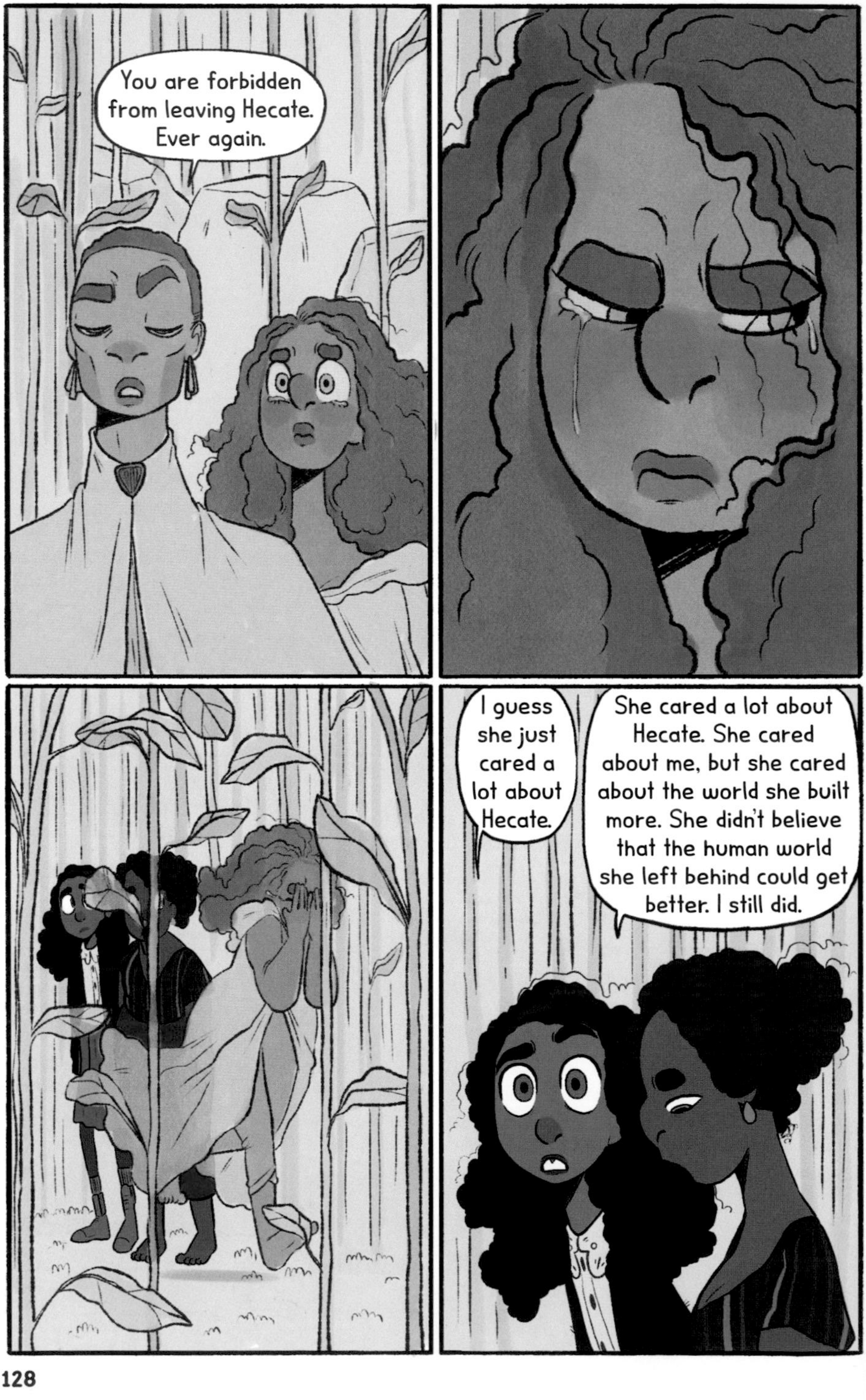
You are forbidden from leaving Hecate. Ever again.
I guess she just cared a lot about Hecate.
She cared a lot about Hecate. She cared about me, but she cared about the world she built more. She didn't believe that the human world she left behind could get better. I still did.

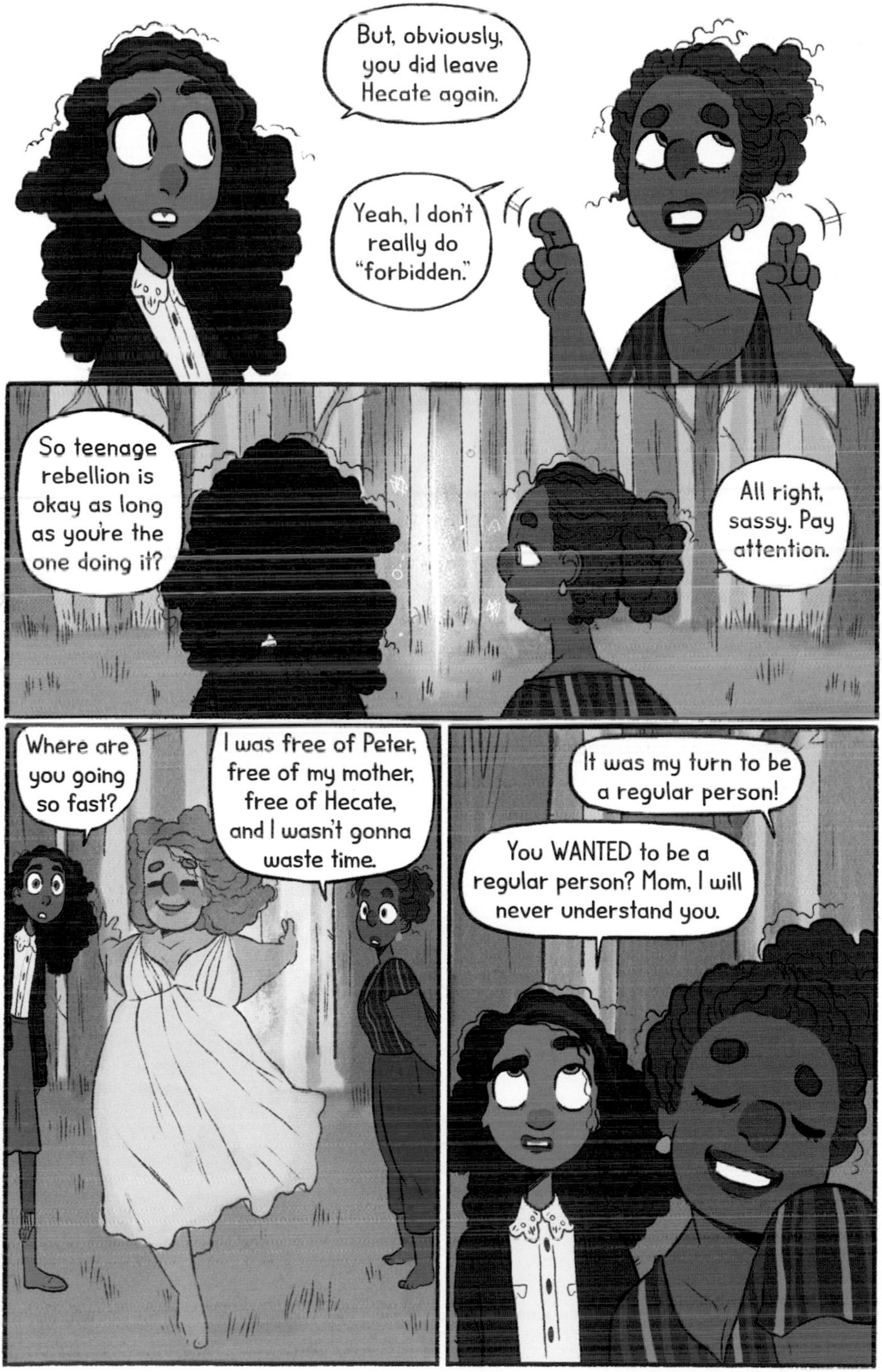
But, obviously, you did leave Hecate again.
Yeah, I don't really do "forbidden."
So teenage rebellion is okay as long as you're the one doing it?
All right, sassy. Pay attention.
Where are you going so fast?
I was free of Peter, free of my mother, free of Hecate, and I wasn't gonna waste time.
It was my turn to be a regular person!
You WANTED to be a regular person? Mom, I will never understand you.

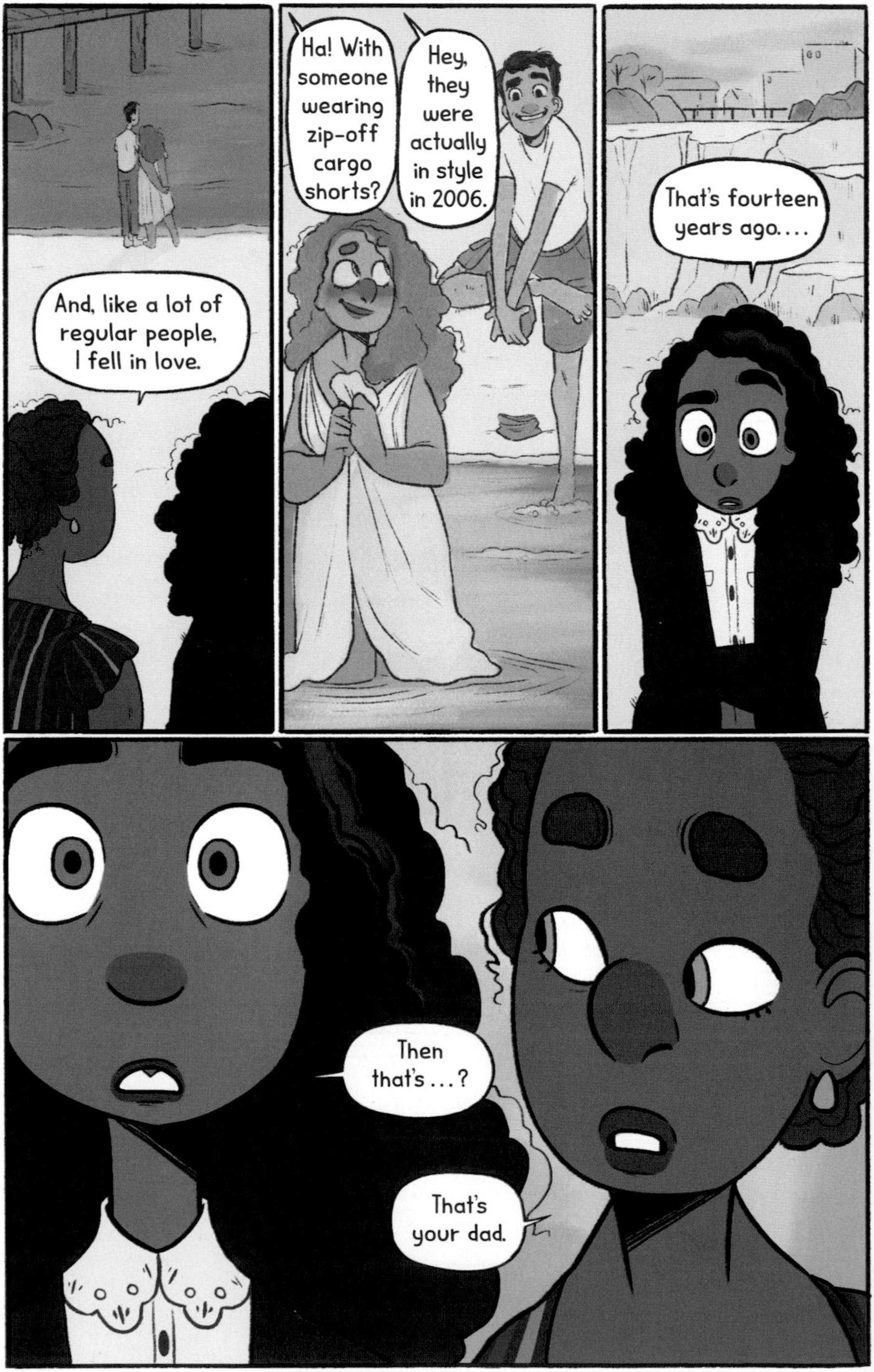
And, like a lot of regular people, I fell in love.
Ha! With someone wearing zip-off cargo shorts?
Hey, they were actually in style in 2006.
That's fourteen years ago....
Then that's...?
That's your dad.

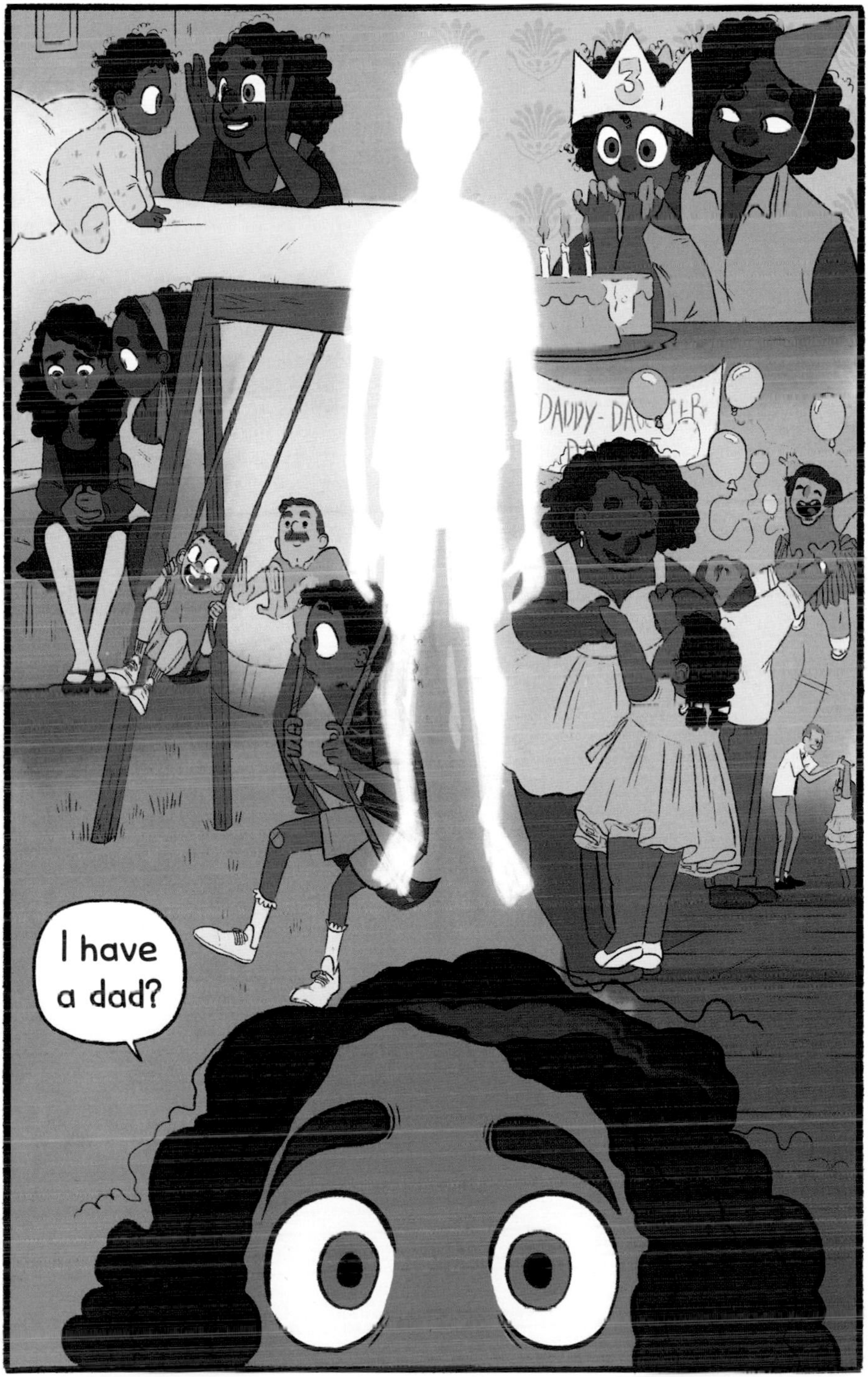
I have a dad?

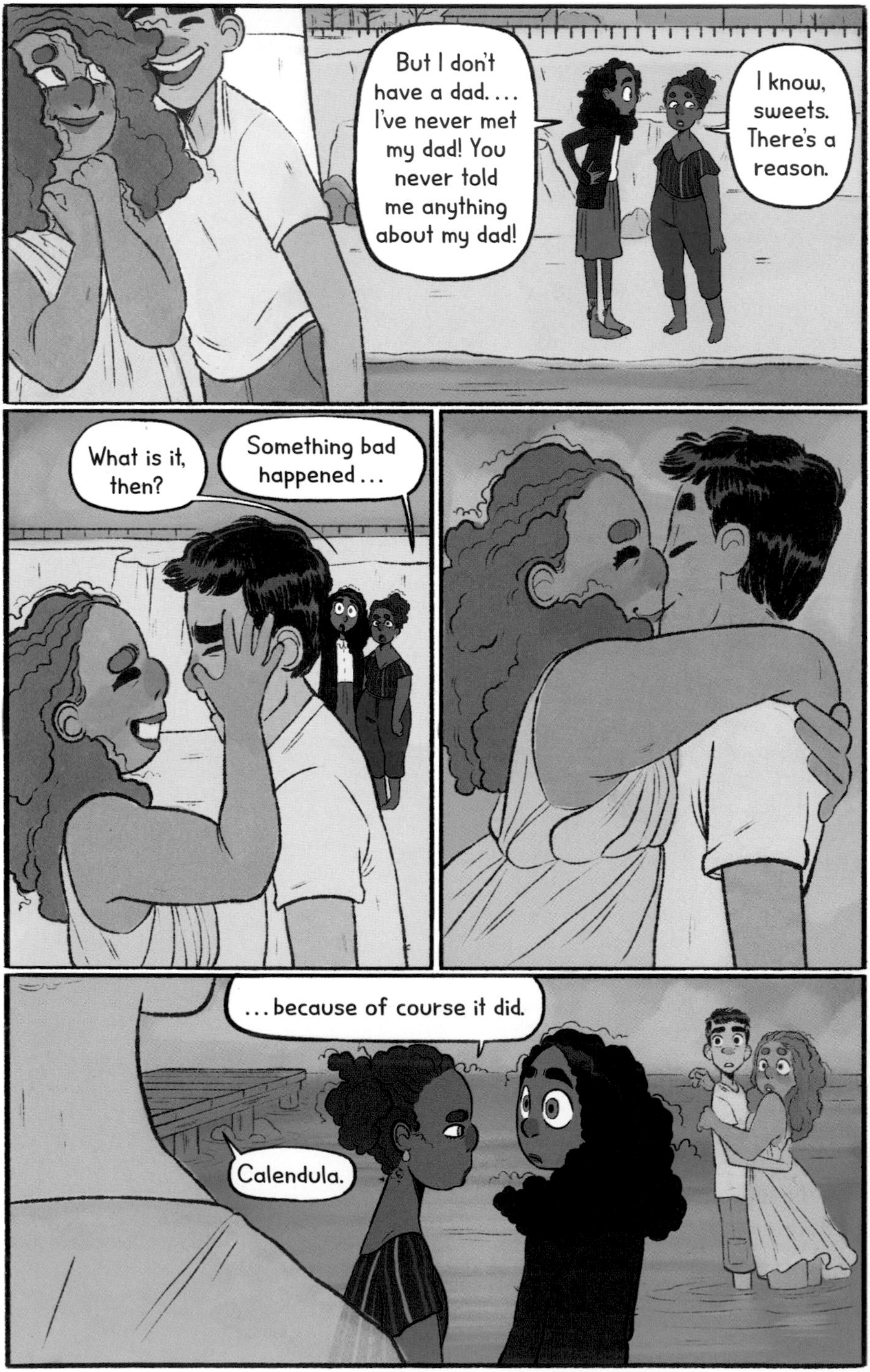
But I don't have a dad. . . . I've never met my dad! You never told me anything about my dad!
I know, sweets. There's a reason.
What is it, then?
Something bad happened . . .
. . . because of course it did.
Calendula.

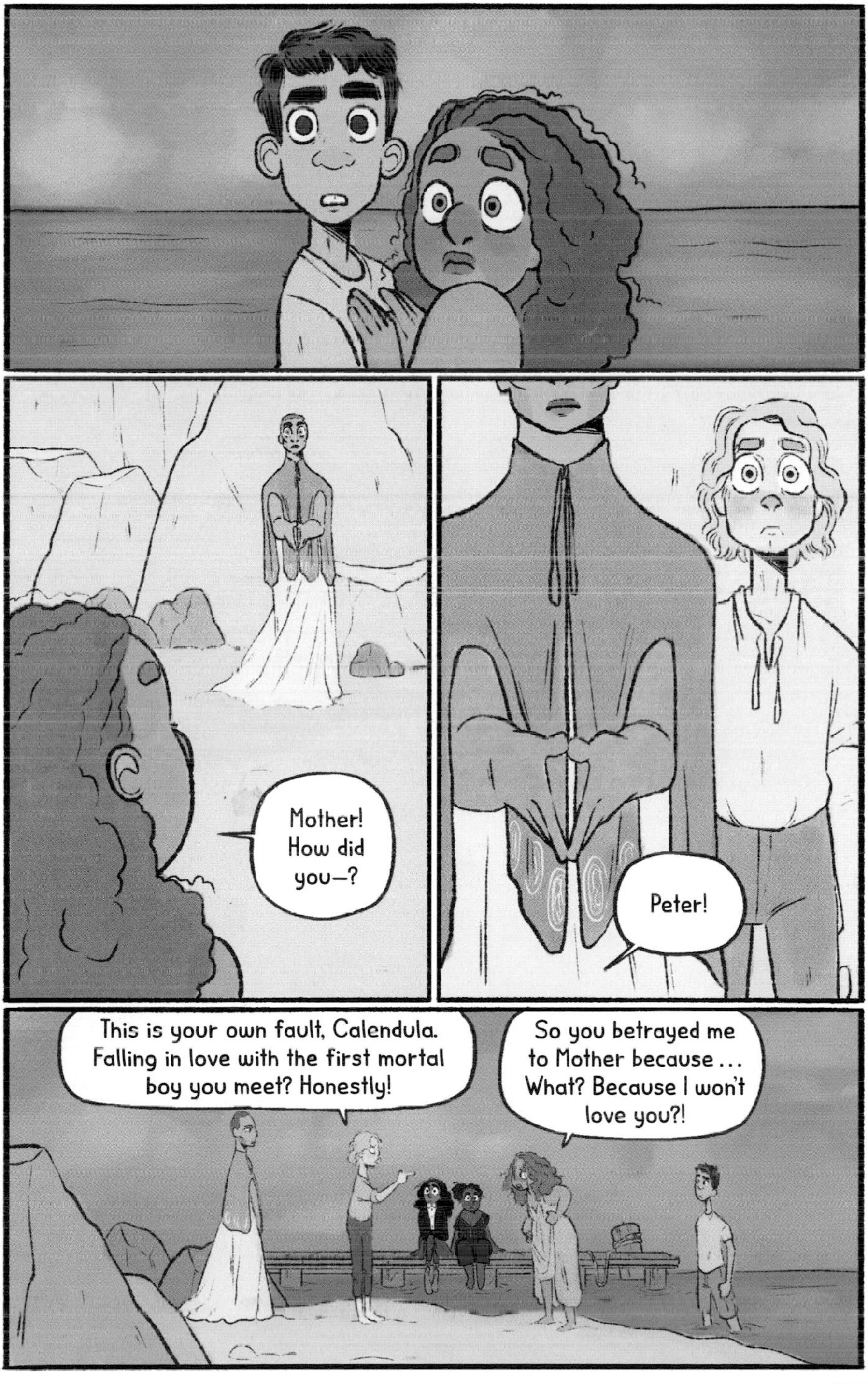
Mother!
How did
you—?
Peter!
This is your own fault, Calendula.
Falling in love with the first mortal
boy you meet? Honestly!
So you betrayed me
to Mother because . . .
What? Because I won't
love you?!

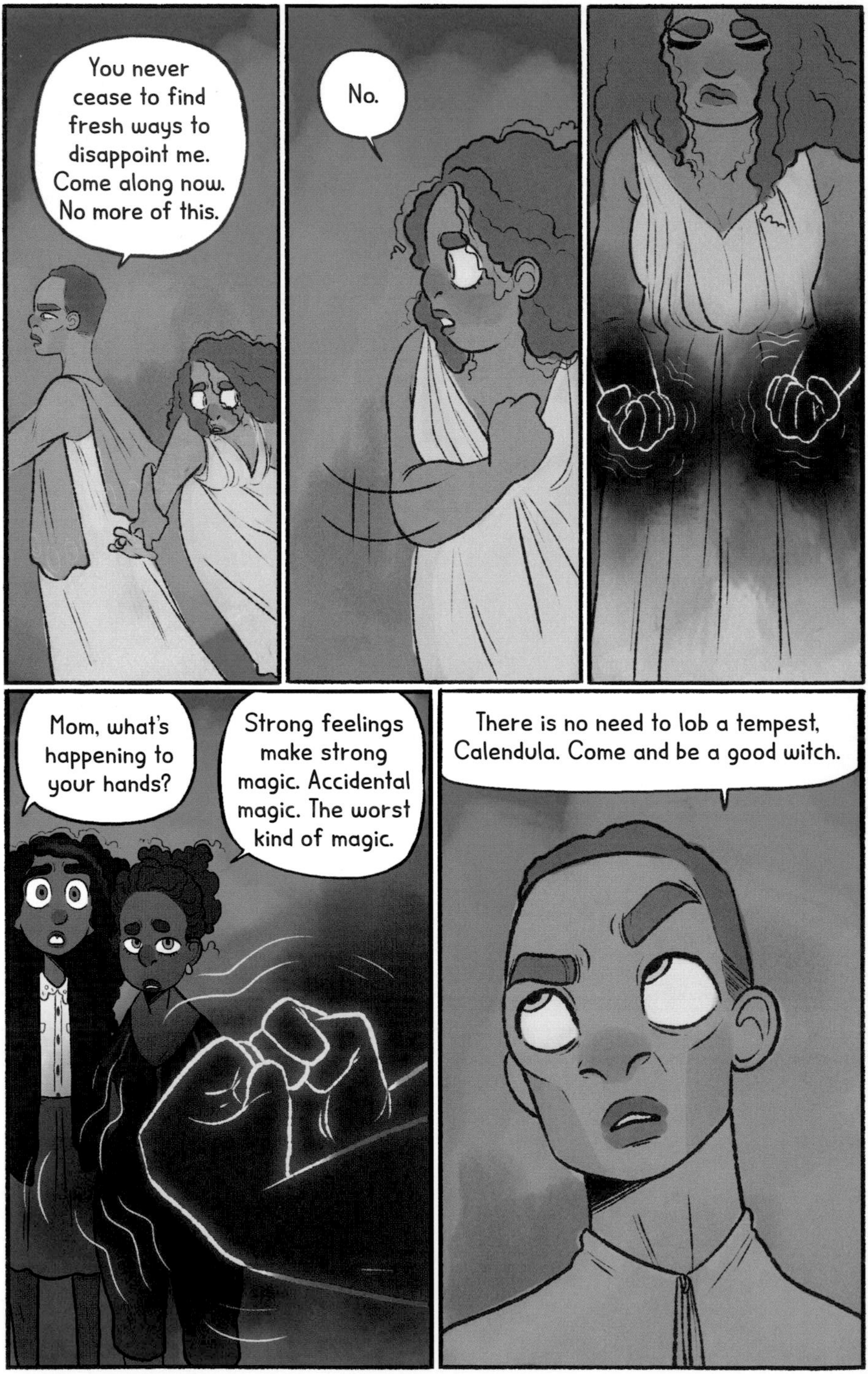

You never cease to find fresh ways to disappoint me. Come along now. No more of this.
No.
Mom, what's happening to your hands?
Strong feelings make strong magic. Accidental magic. The worst kind of magic.
There is no need to lob a tempest, Calendula. Come and be a good witch.

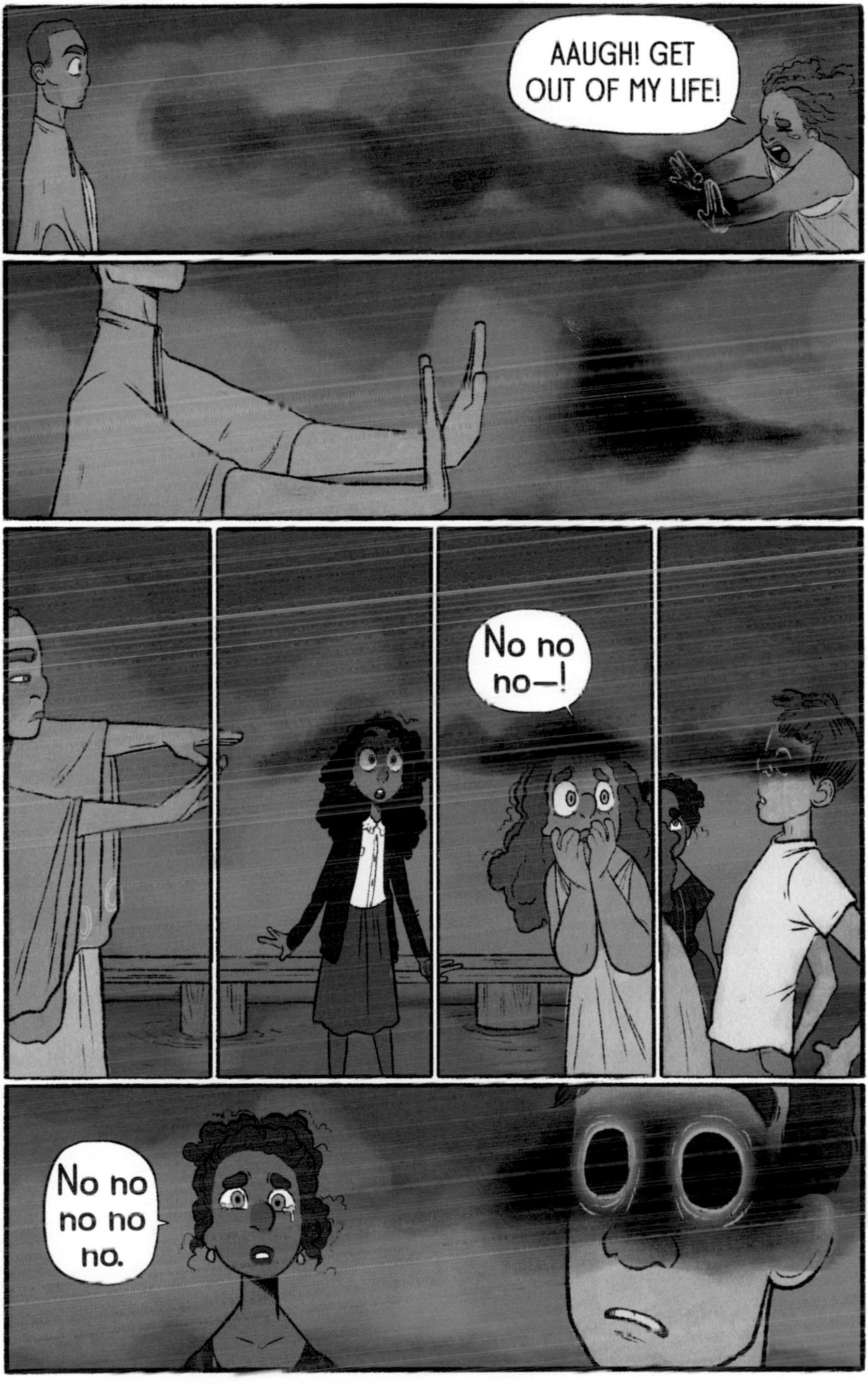
AAUGH! GET OUT OF MY LIFE!
No no no—!
No no no no no.

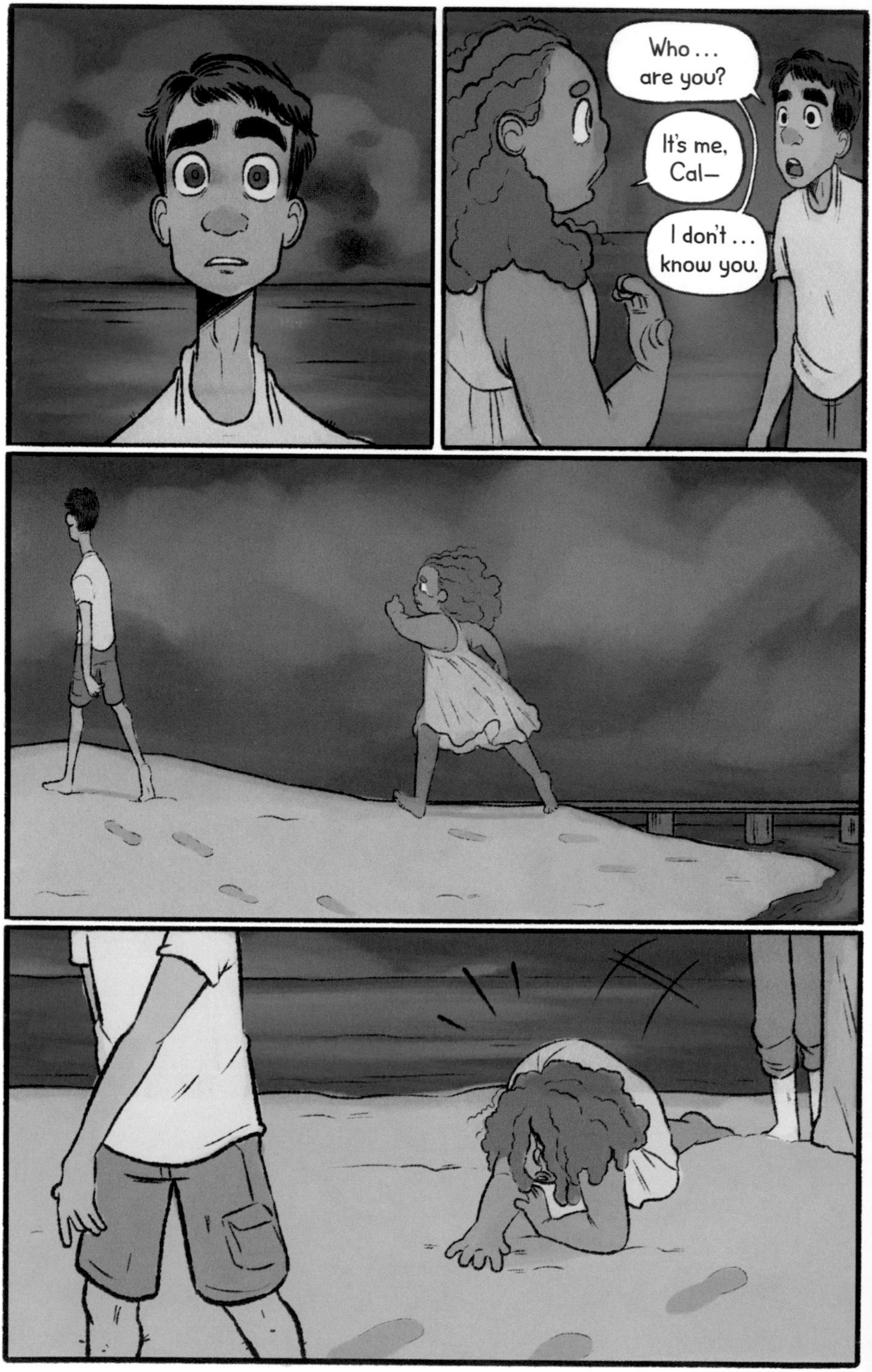
Who . . .
are you?
It's me,
Cal—
I don't . . .
know you.

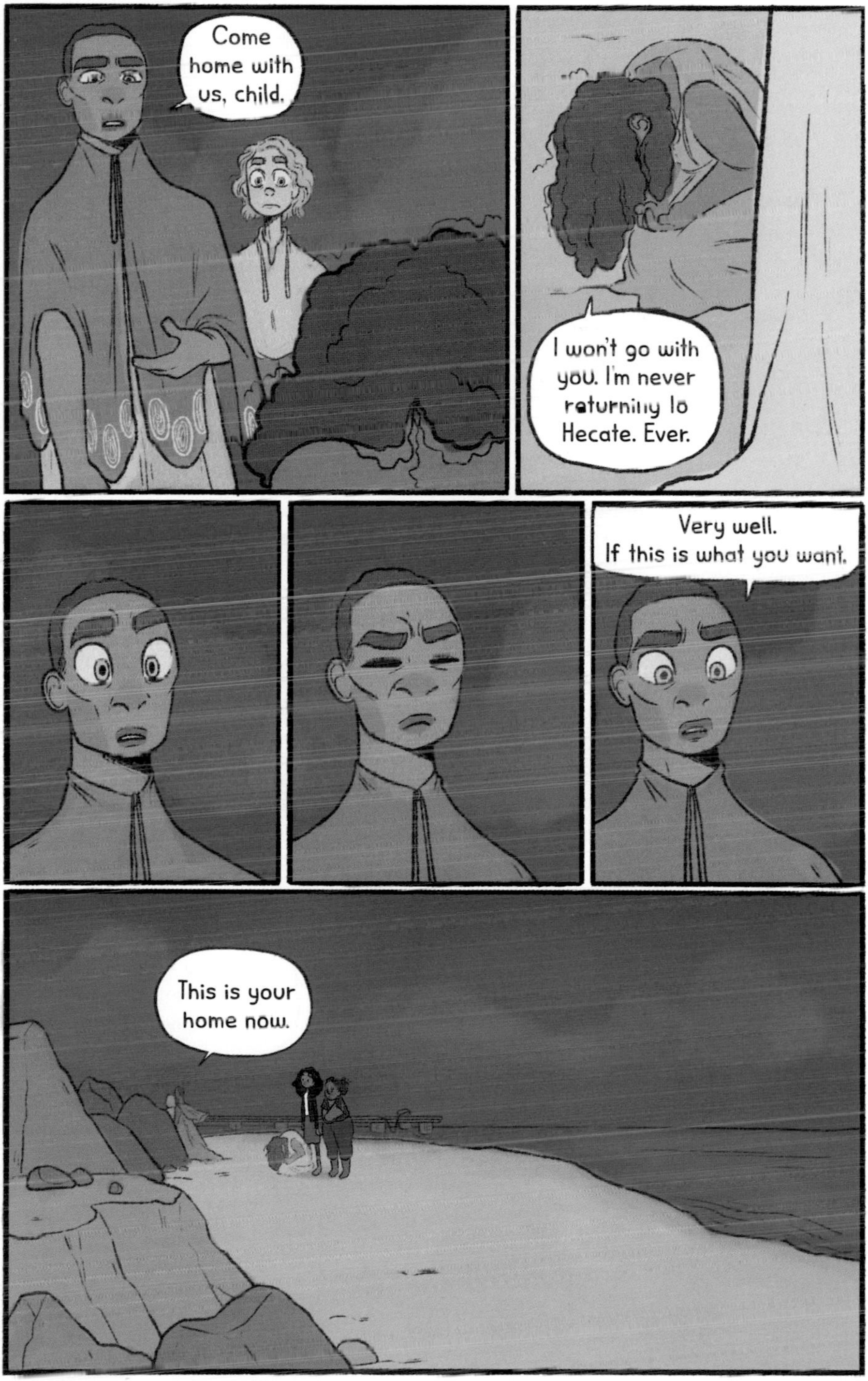
Come home with us, child.
I won't go with you. I'm never returning to Hecate. Ever.
Very well. If this is what you want.
This is your home now.

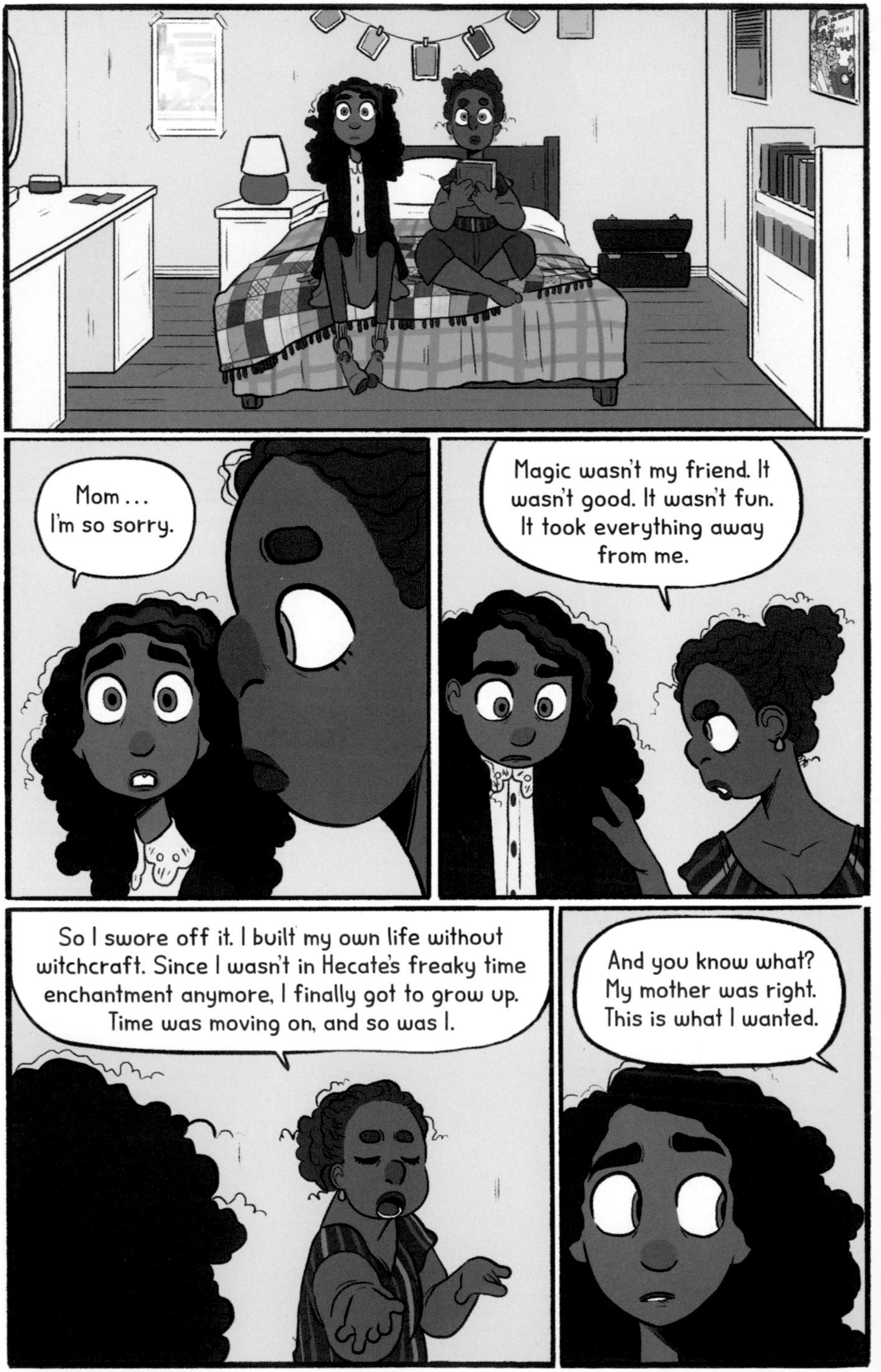
Mom . . .
I'm so sorry.
Magic wasn't my friend. It wasn't good. It wasn't fun. It took everything away from me.
So I swore off it. I built my own life without witchcraft. Since I wasn't in Hecate's freaky time enchantment anymore, I finally got to grow up. Time was moving on, and so was I.
And you know what? My mother was right. This is what I wanted.

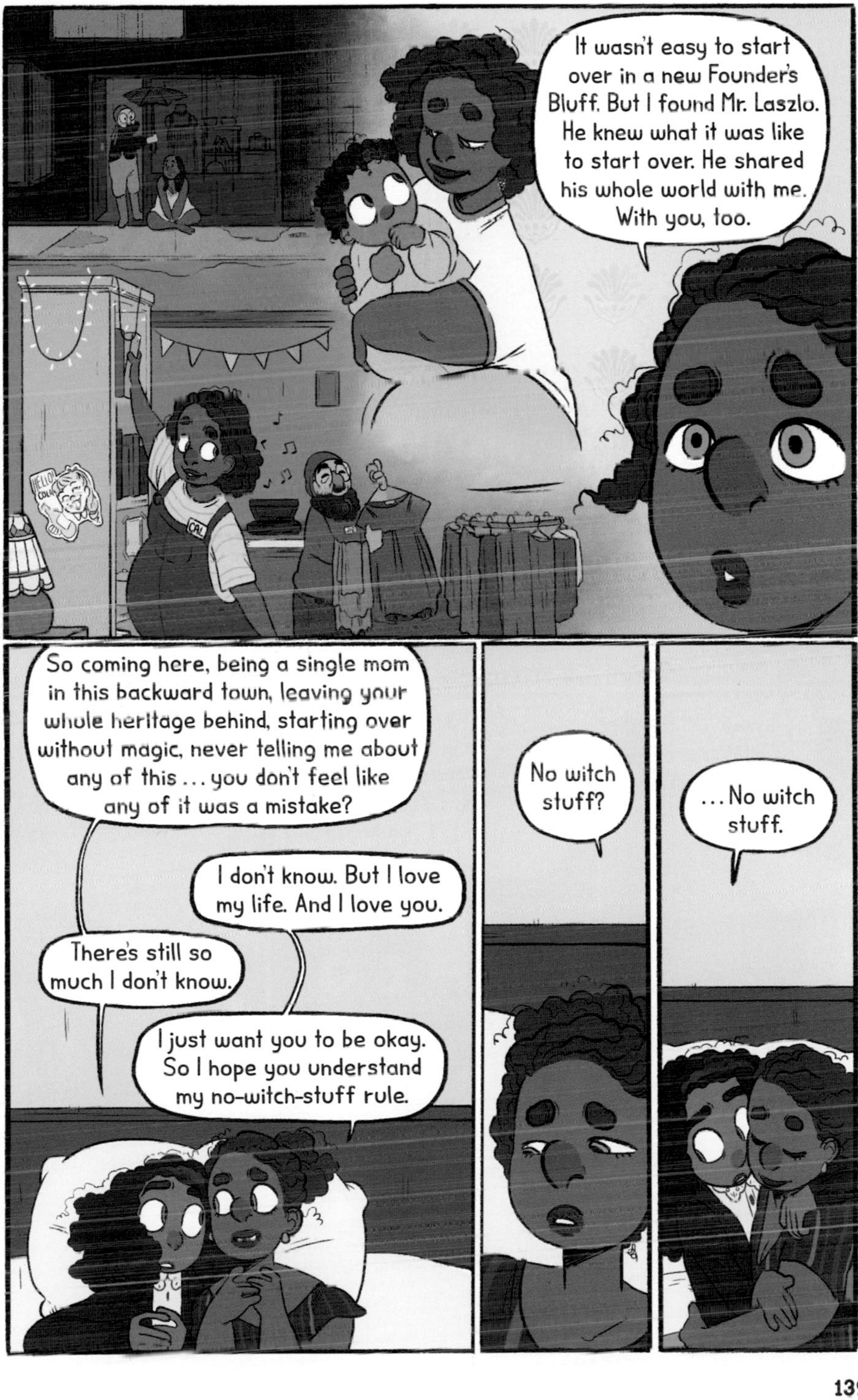
It wasn't easy to start over in a new Founder's Bluff. But I found Mr. Laszlo. He knew what it was like to start over. He shared his whole world with me. With you, too.
HELLO! CAL
CAL
So coming here, being a single mom in this backward town, leaving your whole heritage behind, starting over without magic, never telling me about any of this . . . you don't feel like any of it was a mistake?
There's still so much I don't know.
I don't know. But I love my life. And I love you.
I just want you to be okay. So I hope you understand my no-witch-stuff rule.
No witch stuff?
. . . No witch stuff.

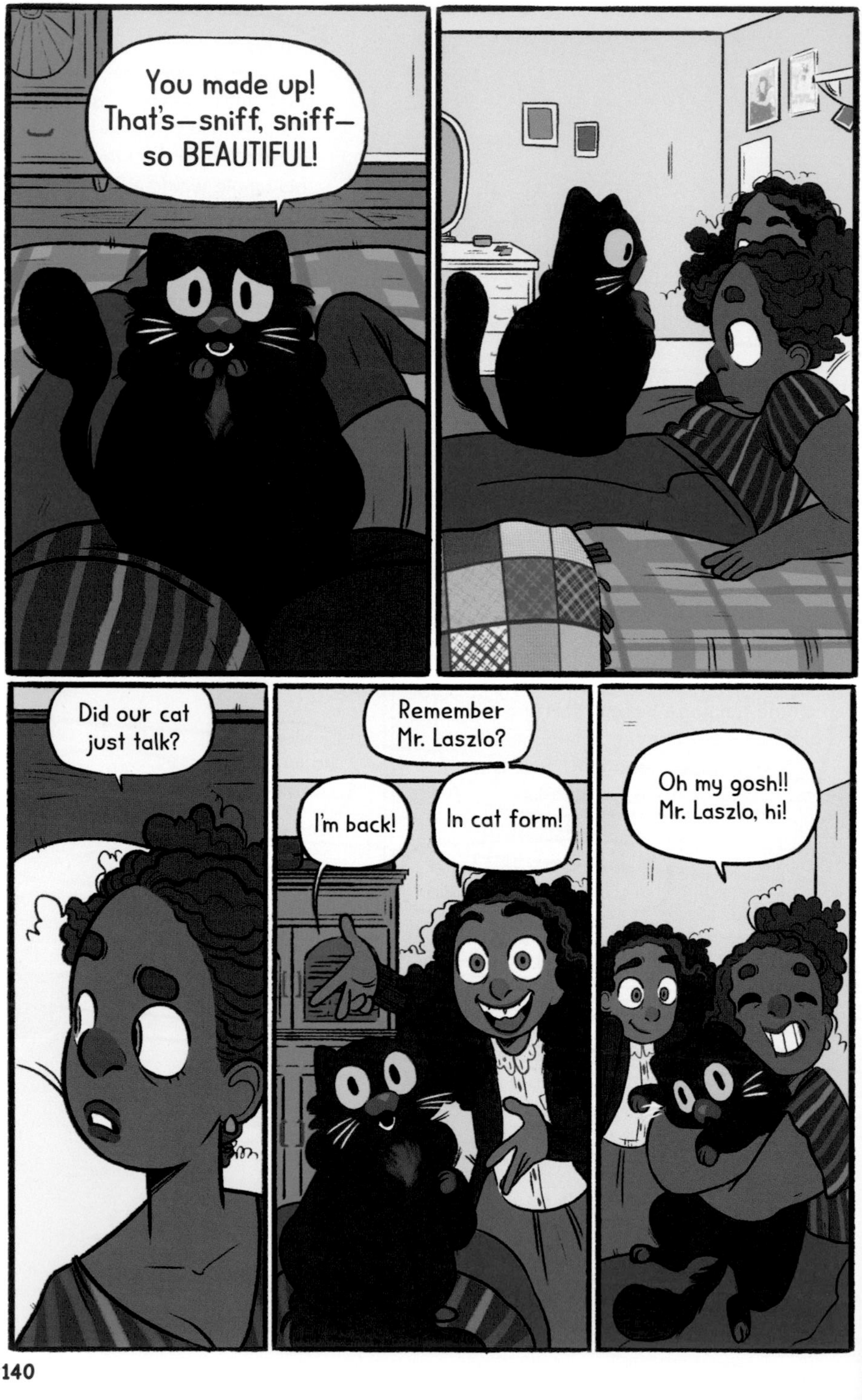
You made up! That's—sniff, sniff—so BEAUTIFUL!
Did our cat just talk?
Remember Mr. Laszlo?
I'm back!
In cat form!
Oh my gosh!! Mr. Laszlo, hi!

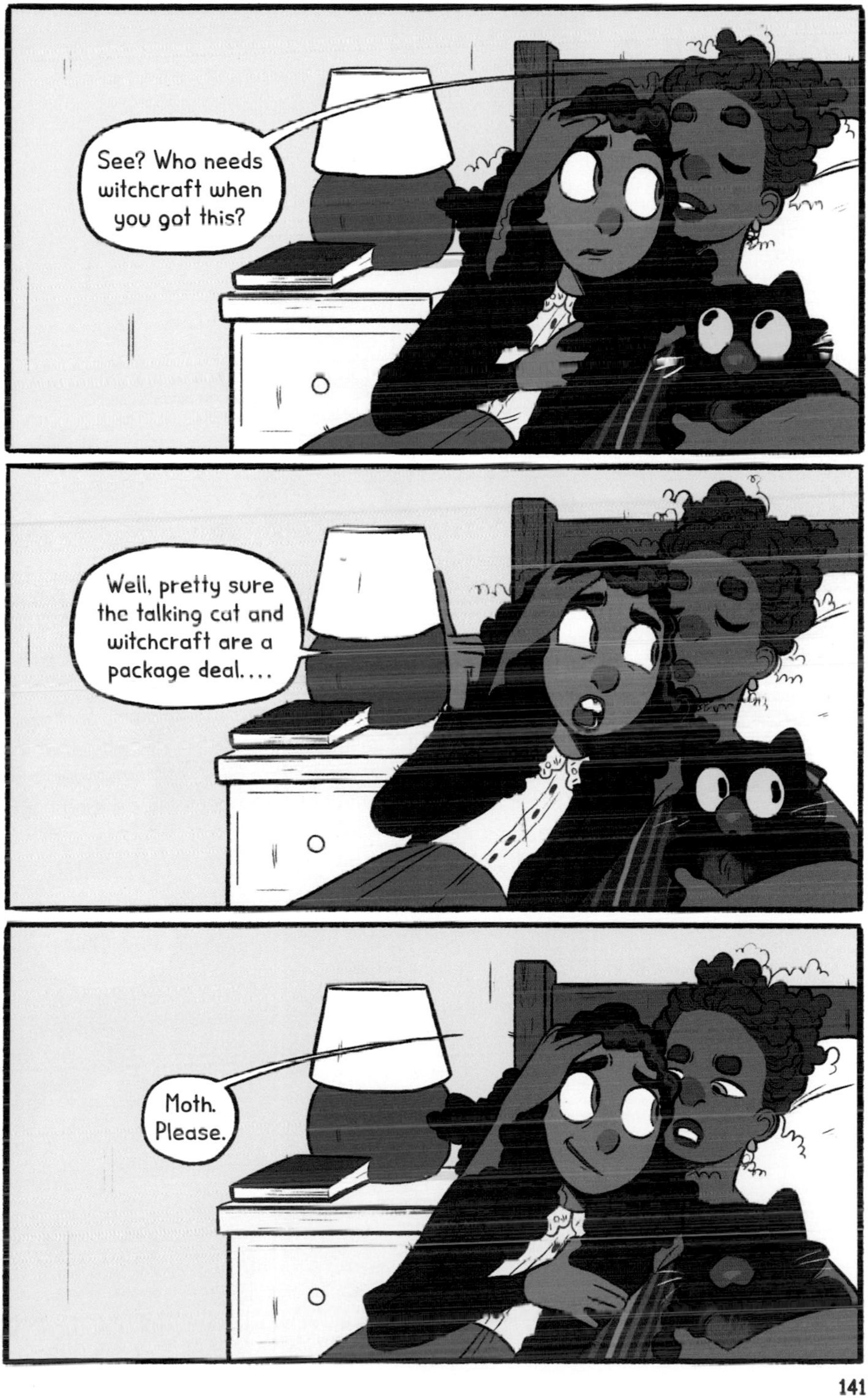
See? Who needs witchcraft when you got this?
Well, pretty sure the talking cat and witchcraft are a package deal....
Moth. Please.

CHAPTER 9
Grandmother Sarah

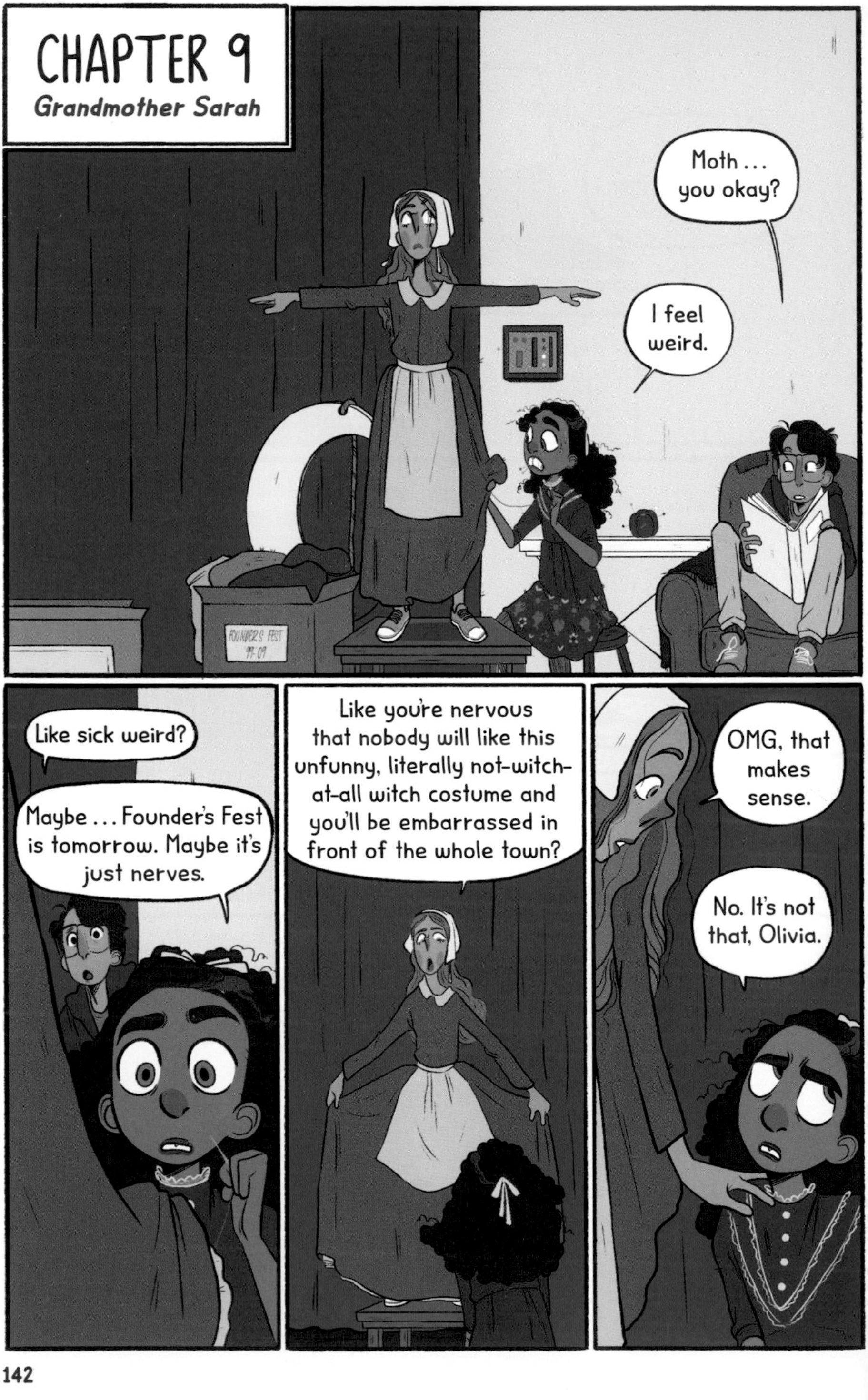

Moth . . .
you okay?
I feel weird.
Like sick weird?
Maybe . . . Founder's Fest is tomorrow. Maybe it's just nerves.
Like you're nervous that nobody will like this unfunny, literally not-witch-at-all witch costume and you'll be embarrassed in front of the whole town?
OMG, that makes sense.
No. It's not that, Olivia.

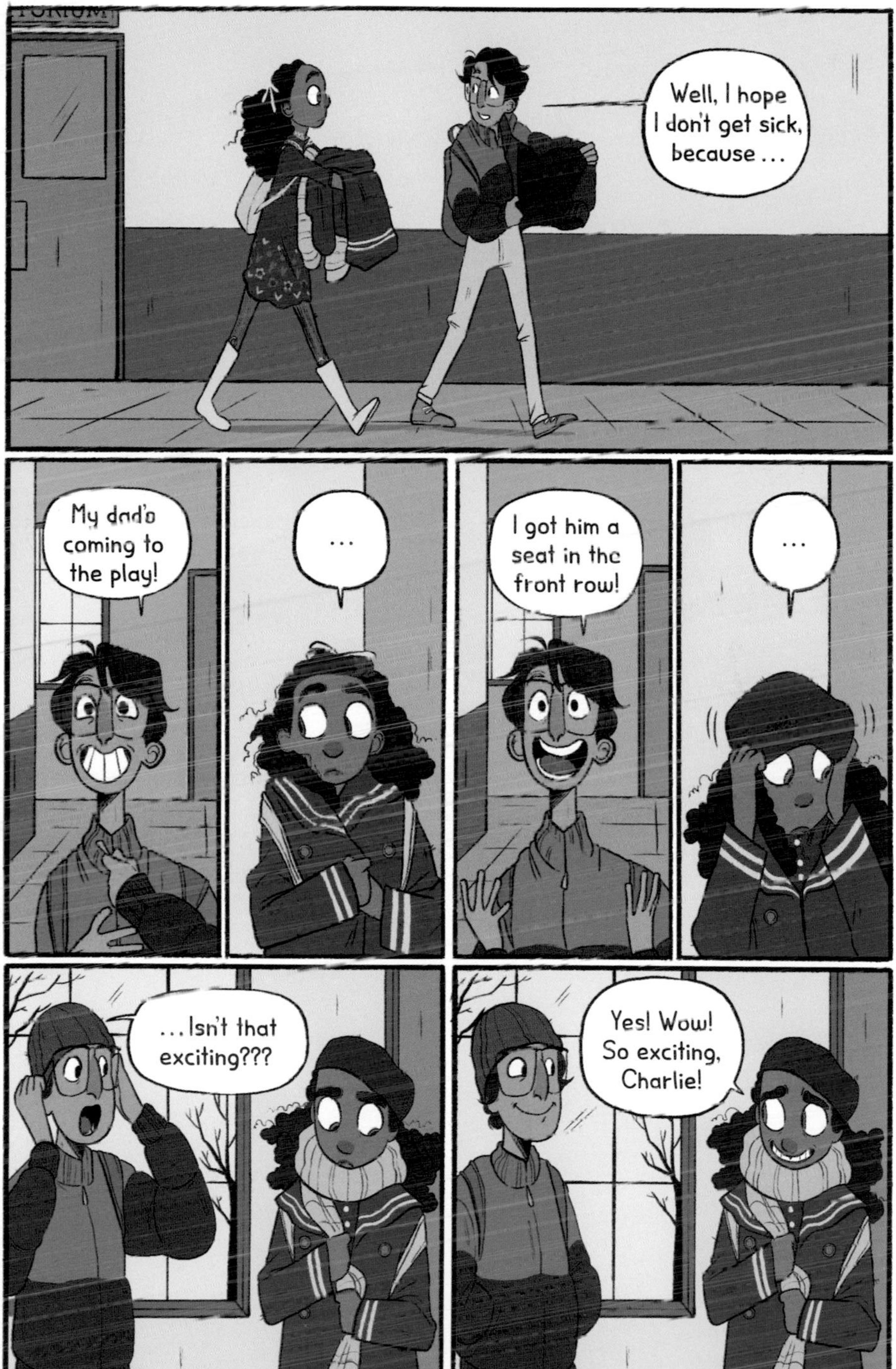
Well, I hope I don't get sick, because . . .
My dad's coming to the play!
. . .
I got him a seat in the front row!
. . .
. . . Isn't that exciting???
Yes! Wow! So exciting, Charlie!

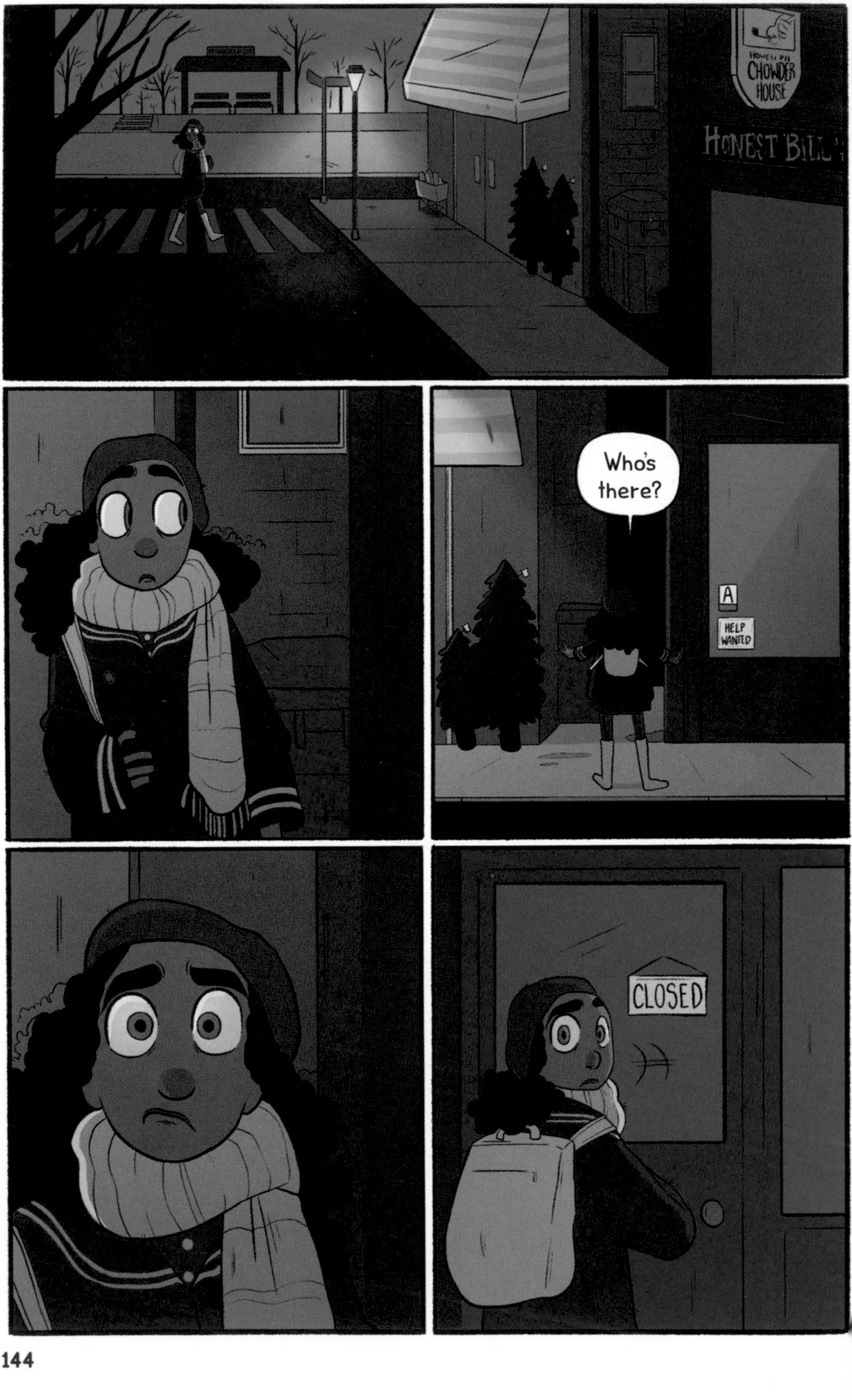
CHOWDER HOUSE
HONEST BILL'
Who's there?
A
HELP WANTED
CLOSED

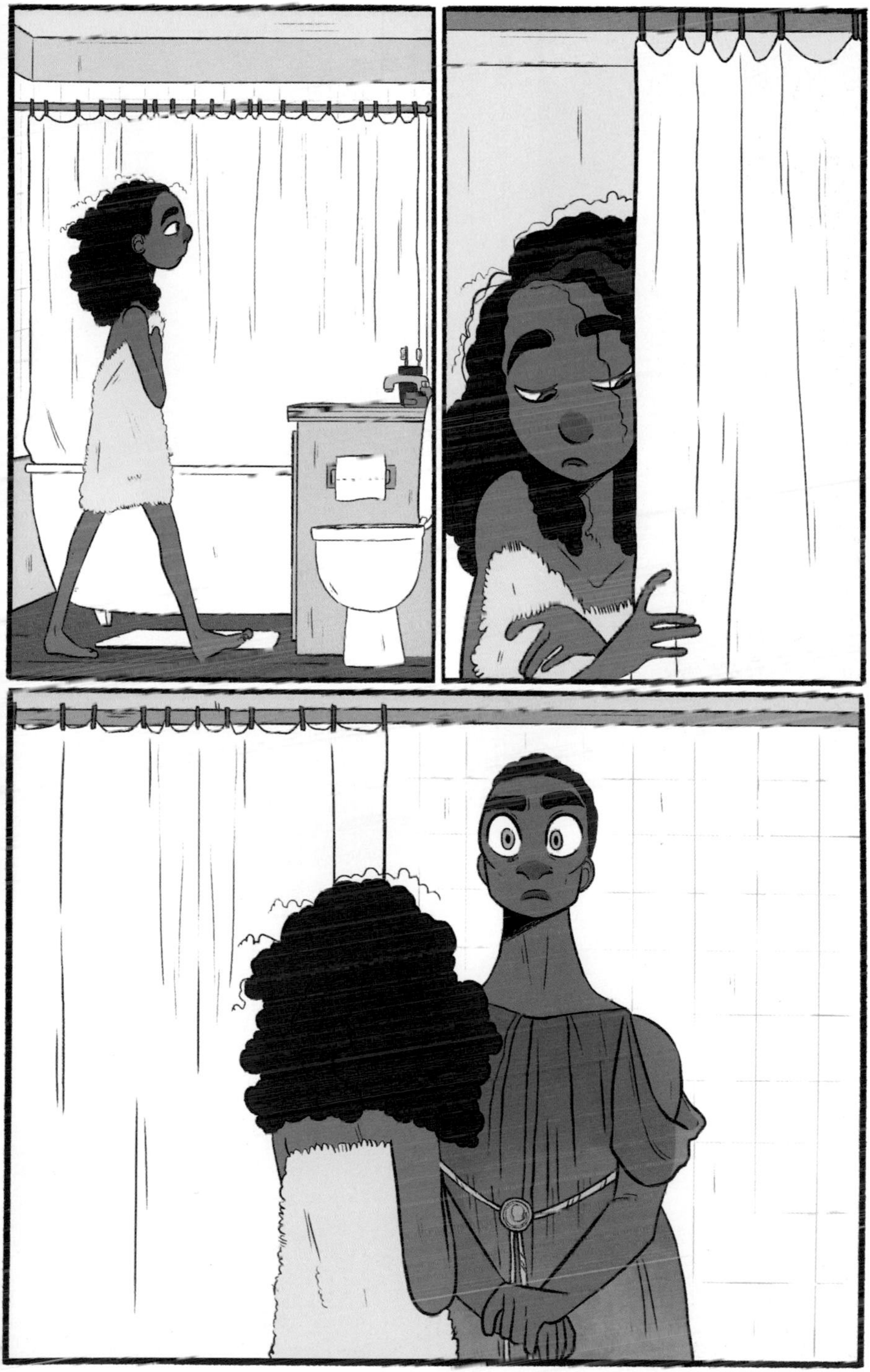

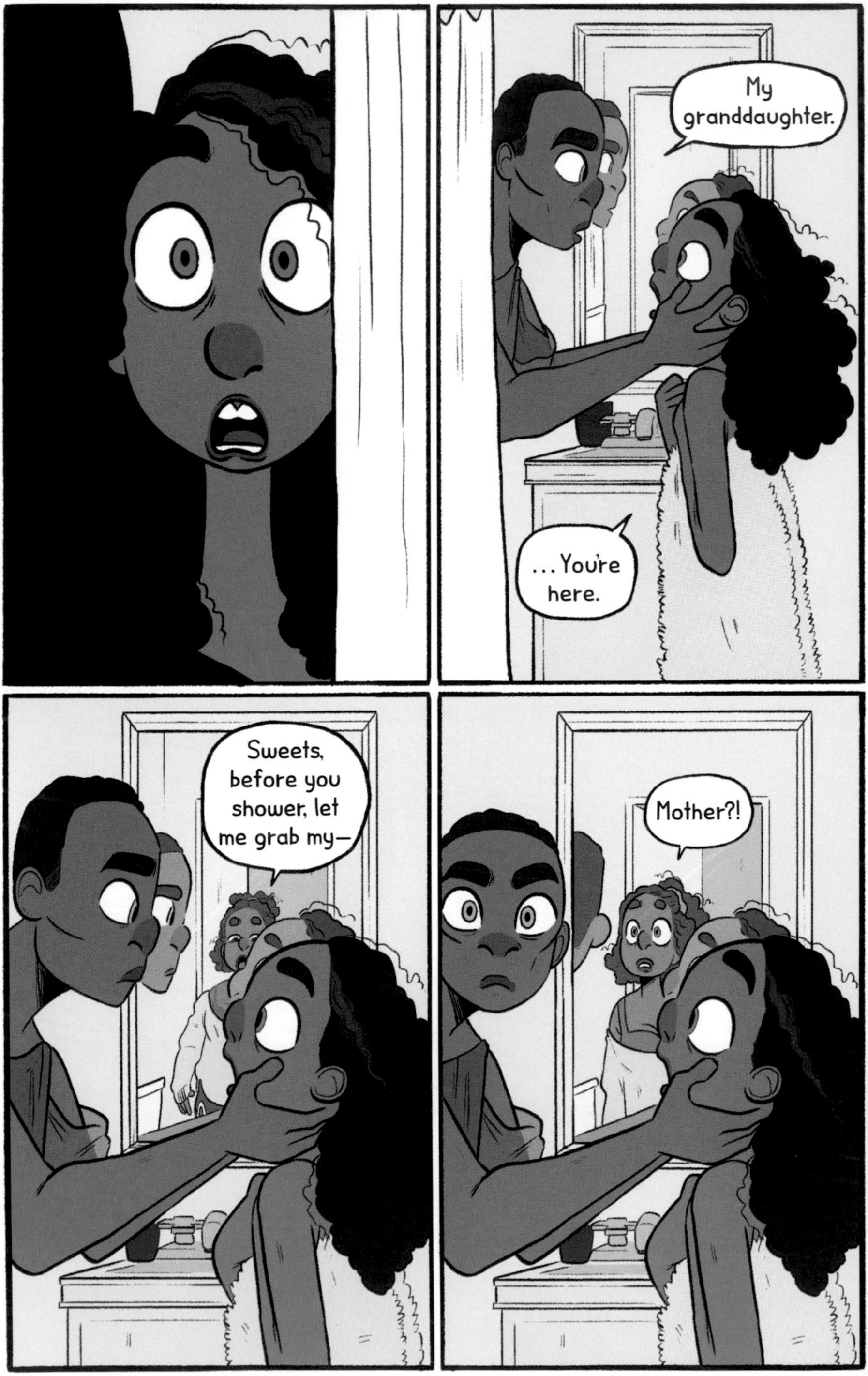
My granddaughter.
...You're here.
Sweets, before you shower, let me grab my—
Mother?!

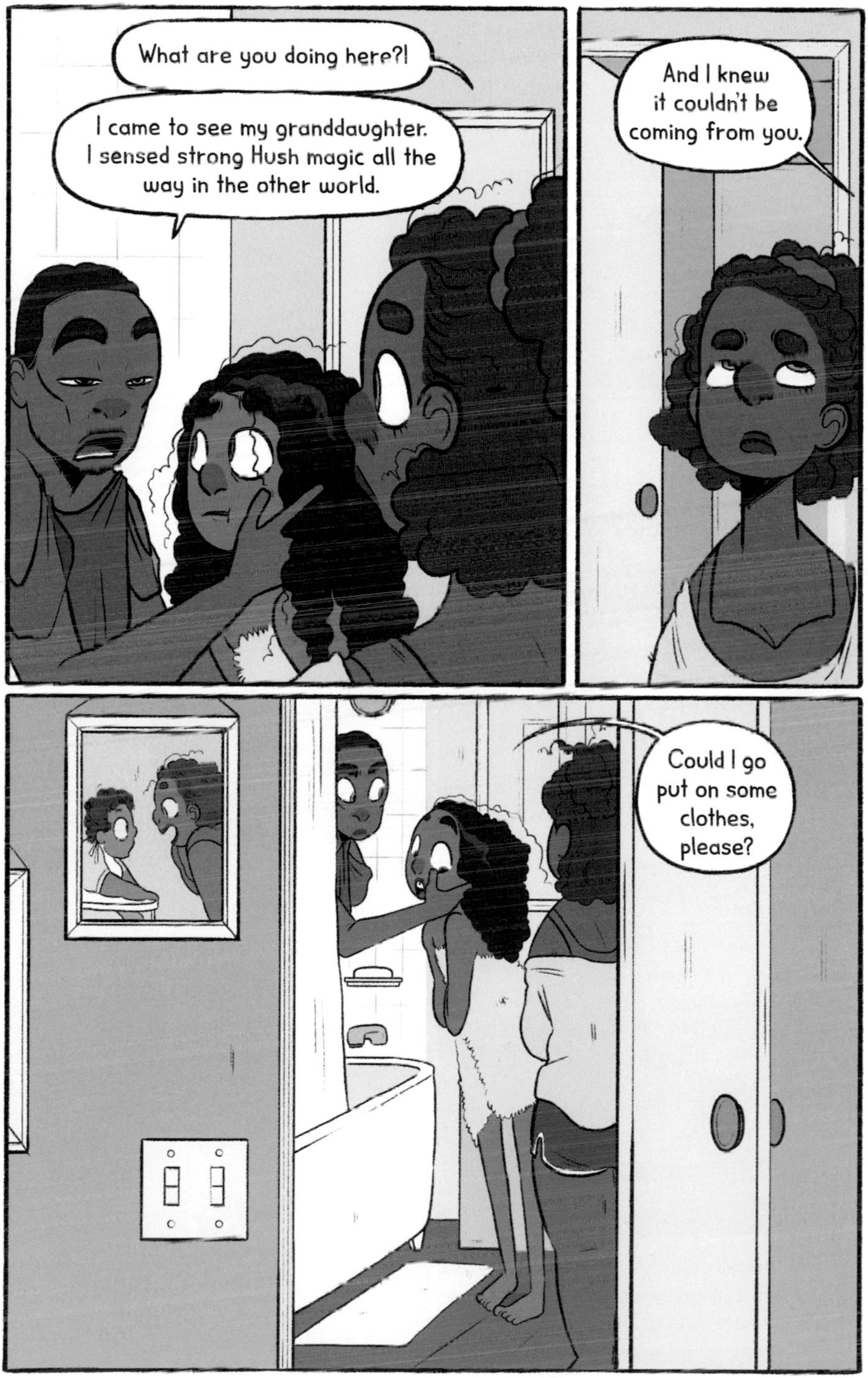
What are you doing here?!
I came to see my granddaughter. I sensed strong Hush magic all the way in the other world.
And I knew it couldn't be coming from you.
Could I go put on some clothes, please?

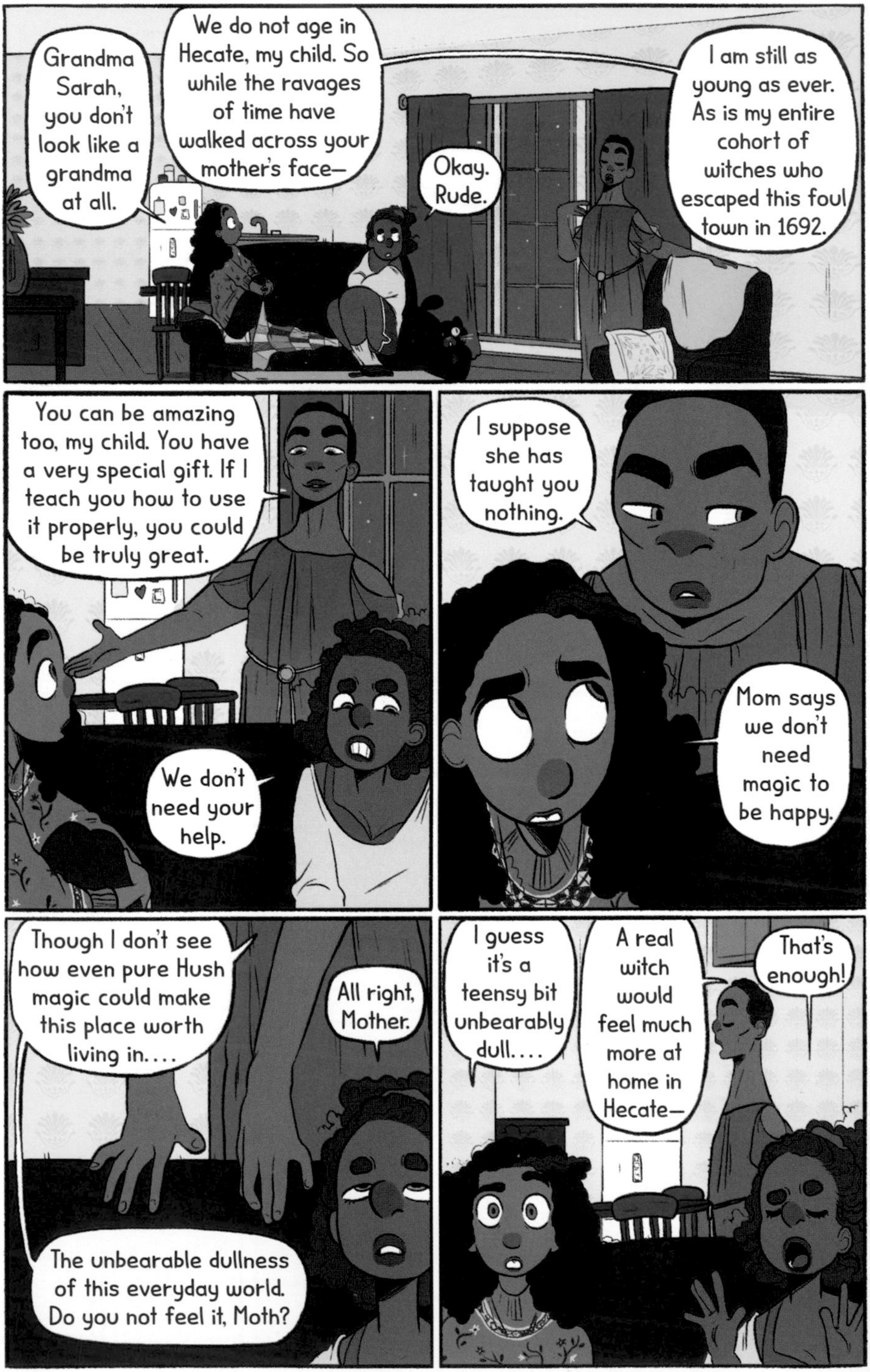

Grandma Sarah, you don't look like a grandma at all.
We do not age in Hecate, my child. So while the ravages of time have walked across your mother's face—
Okay. Rude.
I am still as young as ever. As is my entire cohort of witches who escaped this foul town in 1692.
You can be amazing too, my child. You have a very special gift. If I teach you how to use it properly, you could be truly great.
We don't need your help.
I suppose she has taught you nothing.
Mom says we don't need magic to be happy.
Though I don't see how even pure Hush magic could make this place worth living in....
All right, Mother.
The unbearable dullness of this everyday world. Do you not feel it, Moth?
I guess it's a teensy bit unbearably dull....
A real witch would feel much more at home in Hecate—
That's enough!

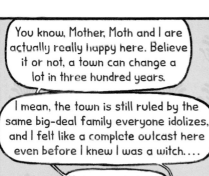

You know, Mother, Moth and I are actually really happy here. Believe it or not, a town can change a lot in three hundred years.

I mean, the town is still ruled by the same big-deal family everyone idolizes, and I felt like a complete outcast here even before I knew I was a witch....

Not super helpful, sweets.

I'm just being honest!

Okay, Founder's Bluff has problems, but... at least there's no more gallows or torturing people by burying them under big rocks.

Ha, I shall believe it when I see it.

You will see it!

You'll come with us to Founder's Fest tomorrow.

Are you sure that's a good idea—?

You'll see the play Moth worked on and how much everything has changed, and then you'll be sorry you were mean.

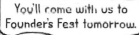

I will never be sorry, and I have never been "mean." I have only ever been right and will continue to be right henceforth.

Yet—any time I can spend with my precious and gifted granddaughter... Very well, I shall come to your fest.

Great! Cool!

Indeed. "Cool."

149

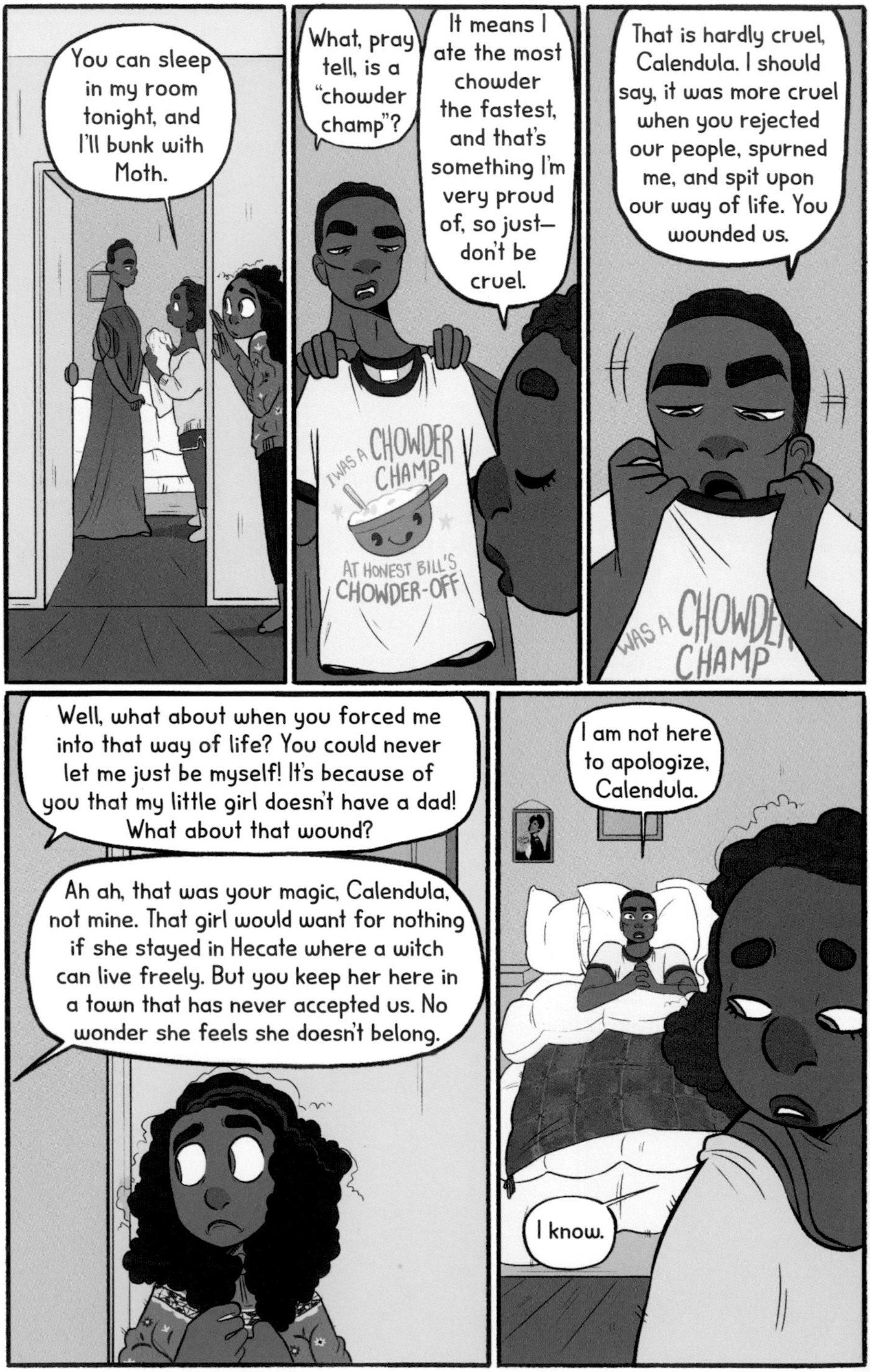
You can sleep in my room tonight, and I'll bunk with Moth.
What, pray tell, is a "chowder champ"?
It means I ate the most chowder the fastest, and that's something I'm very proud of, so just— don't be cruel.
I WAS A CHOWDER CHAMP AT HONEST BILL'S CHOWDER-OFF
That is hardly cruel, Calendula. I should say, it was more cruel when you rejected our people, spurned me, and spit upon our way of life. You wounded us.
WAS A CHOWDE CHAMP
Well, what about when you forced me into that way of life? You could never let me just be myself! It's because of you that my little girl doesn't have a dad! What about that wound?
Ah ah, that was your magic, Calendula, not mine. That girl would want for nothing if she stayed in Hecate where a witch can live freely. But you keep her here in a town that has never accepted us. No wonder she feels she doesn't belong.
I am not here to apologize, Calendula.
I know.

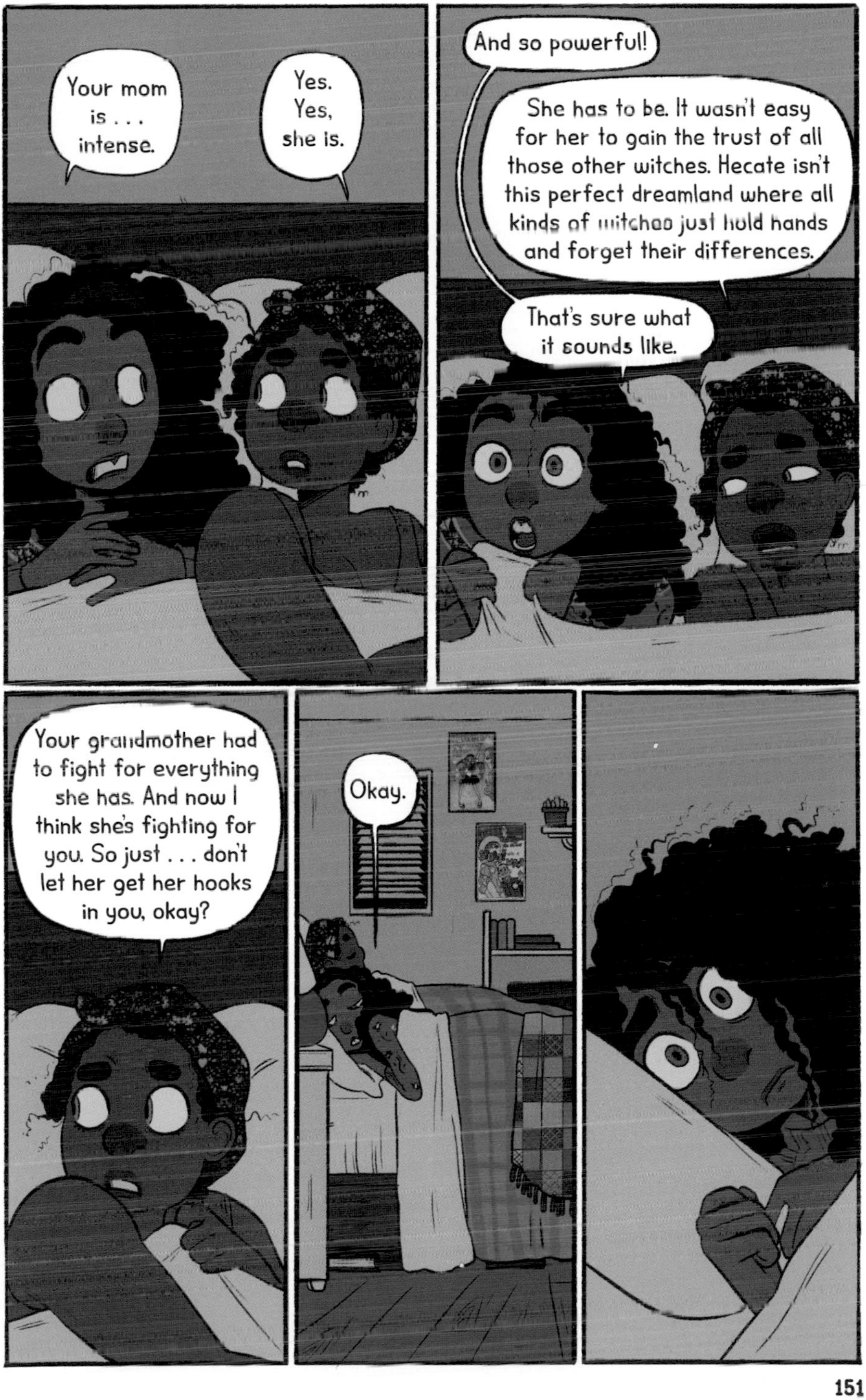
Your mom is . . . intense.
Yes. Yes, she is.
And so powerful!
She has to be. It wasn't easy for her to gain the trust of all those other witches. Hecate isn't this perfect dreamland where all kinds of witches just hold hands and forget their differences.
That's sure what it sounds like.
Your grandmother had to fight for everything she has. And now I think she's fighting for you. So just . . . don't let her get her hooks in you, okay?
Okay.

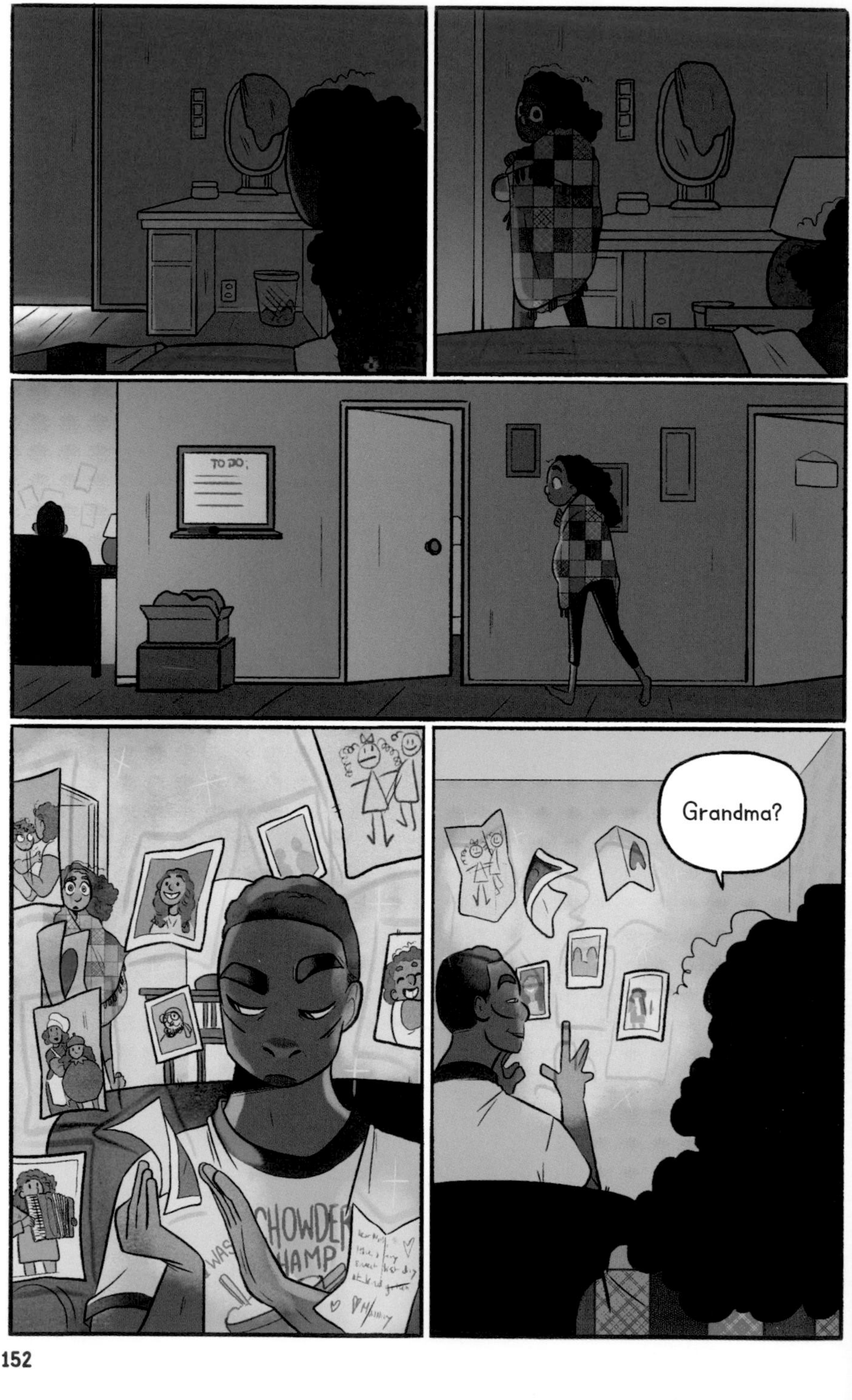
TO DO:
Grandma?

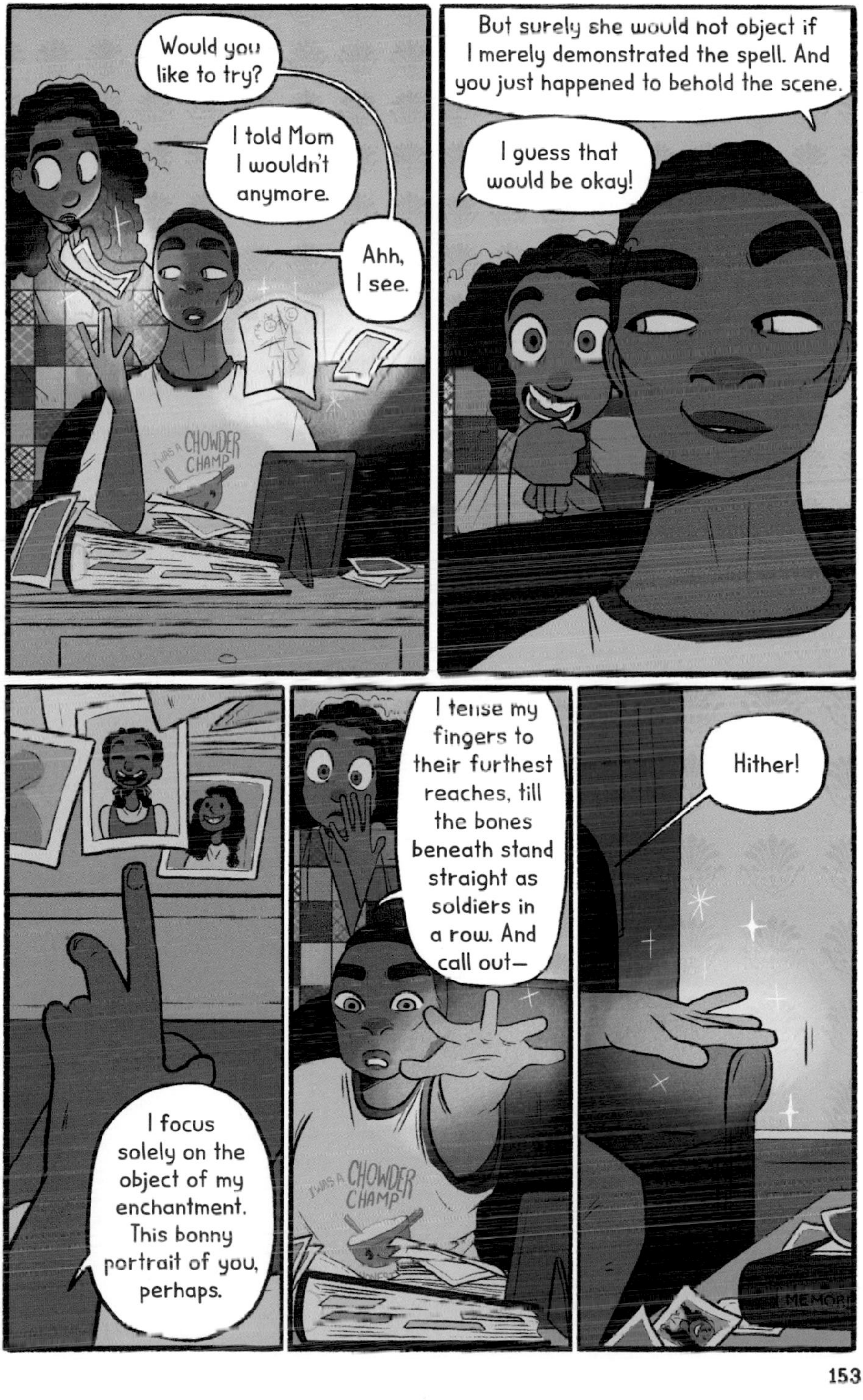
Would you like to try?
I told Mom I wouldn't anymore.
Ahh, I see.
I WAS A CHOWDER CHAMP
But surely she would not object if I merely demonstrated the spell. And you just happened to behold the scene.
I guess that would be okay!
I focus solely on the object of my enchantment. This bonny portrait of you, perhaps.
I tense my fingers to their furthest reaches, till the bones beneath stand straight as soldiers in a row. And call out—
I WAS A CHOWDER CHAMP
Hither!

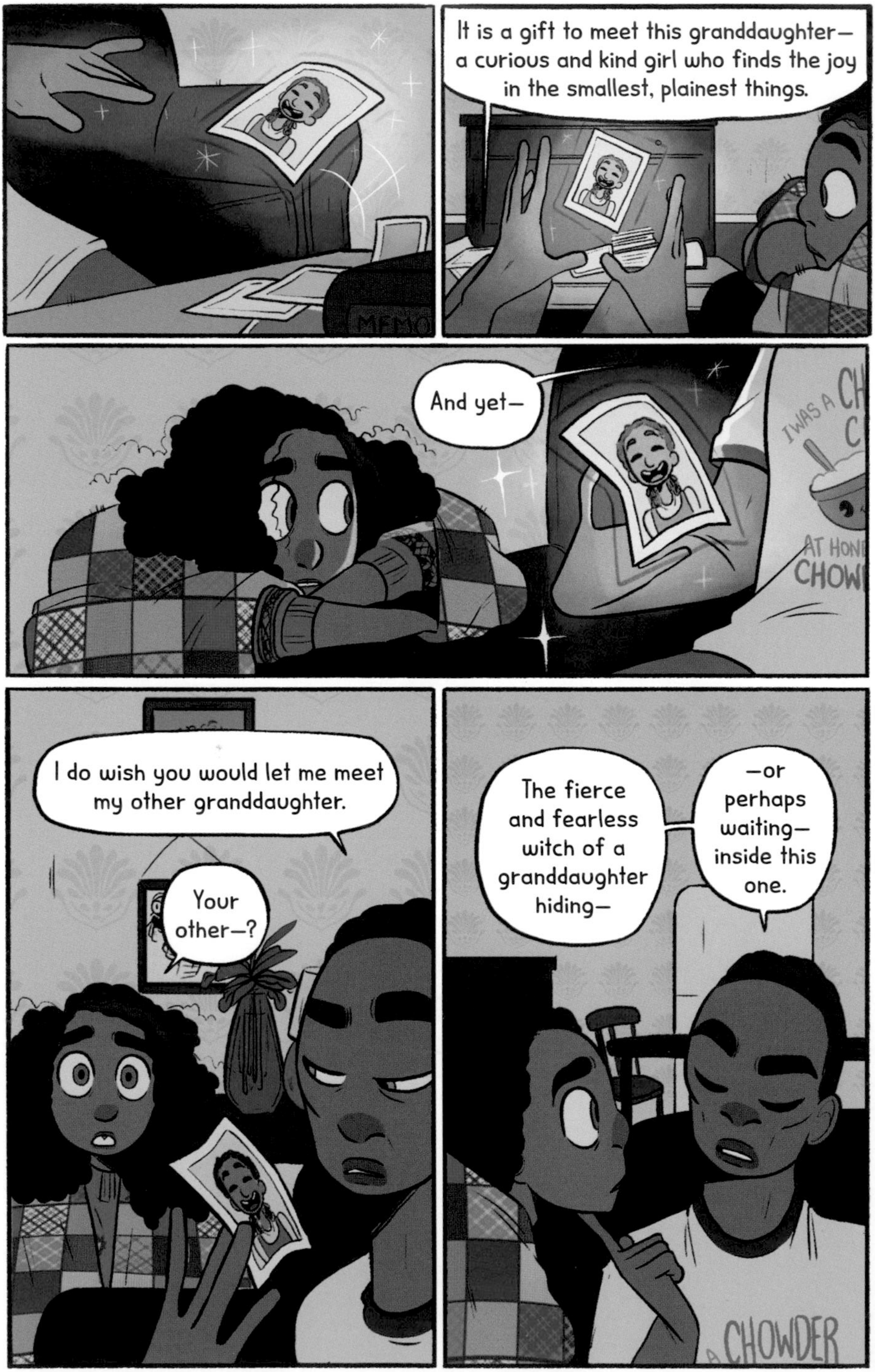

MEMO
It is a gift to meet this granddaughter— a curious and kind girl who finds the joy in the smallest, plainest things.
And yet—
I do wish you would let me meet my other granddaughter.
Your other—?
The fierce and fearless witch of a granddaughter hiding—
—or perhaps waiting— inside this one.
CHOWDER

CHAPTER 10

A Hush Fell over the Crowd

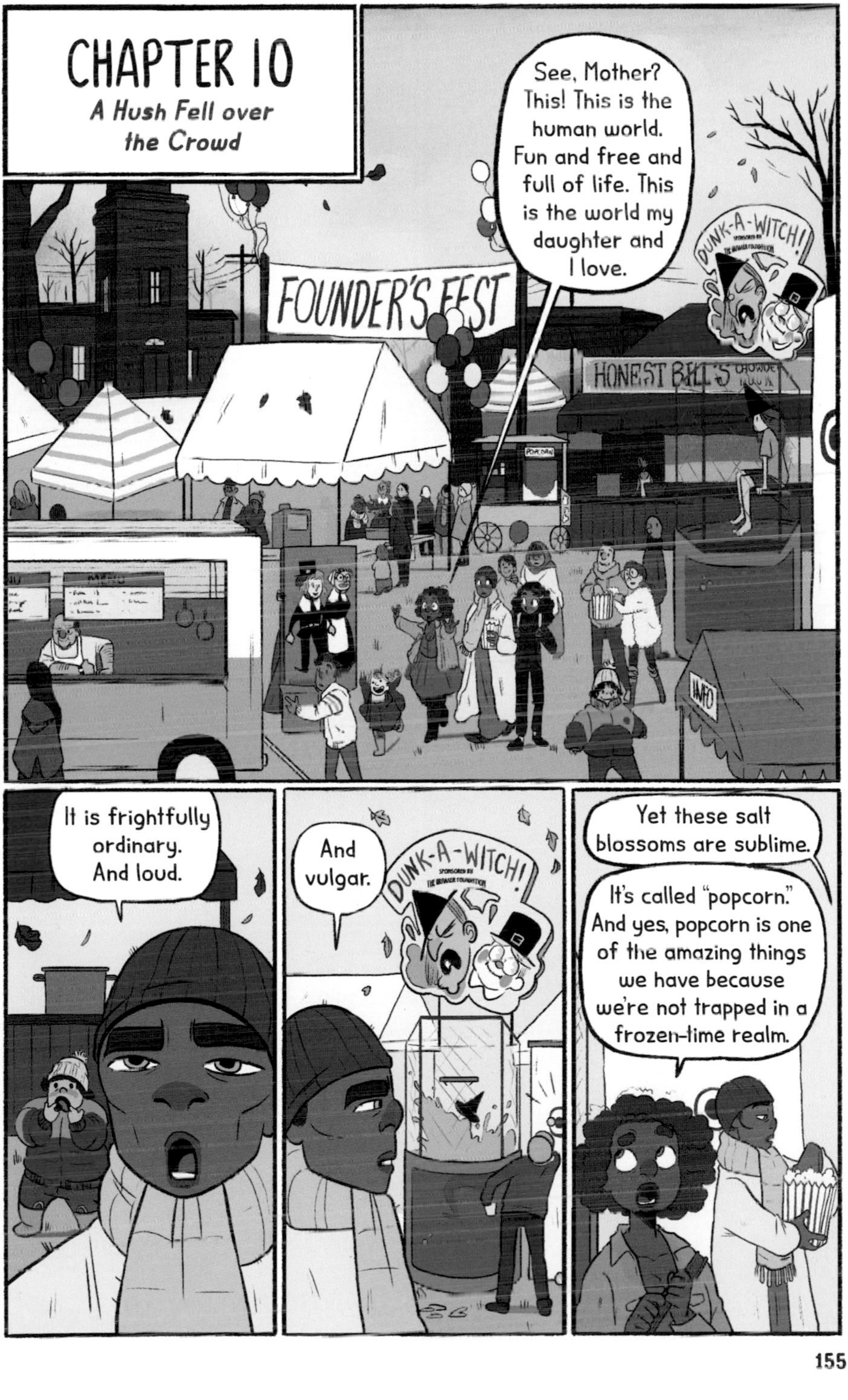

See, Mother? This! This is the human world. Fun and free and full of life. This is the world my daughter and I love.
FOUNDER'S FEST
DUNK-A-WITCH!
HONEST BILL'S
INFO
It is frightfully ordinary. And loud.
And vulgar.
DUNK-A-WITCH!
Yet these salt blossoms are sublime.
It's called "popcorn." And yes, popcorn is one of the amazing things we have because we're not trapped in a frozen-time realm.

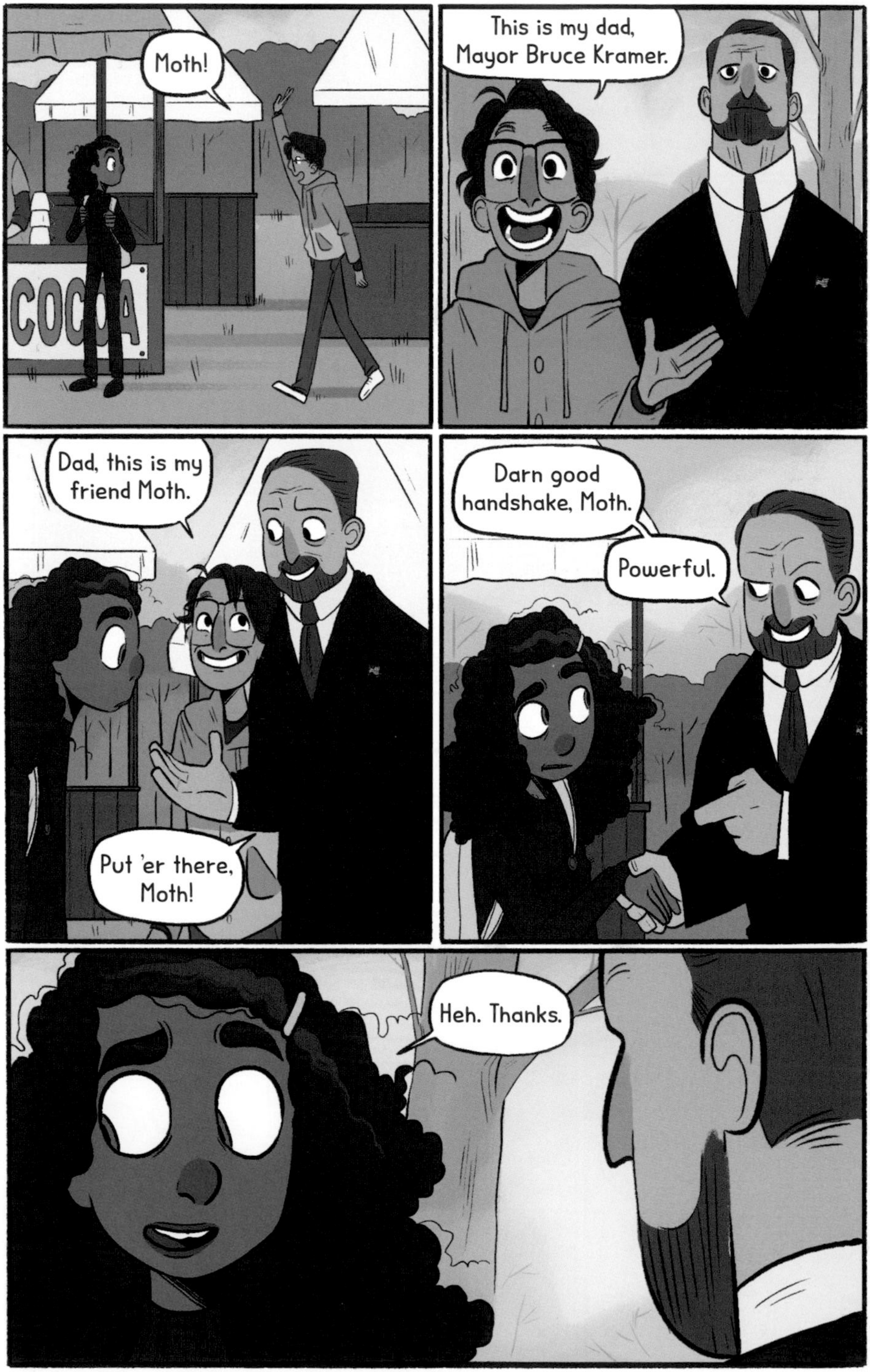
Moth!
This is my dad, Mayor Bruce Kramer.
COCOA
Dad, this is my friend Moth.
Put 'er there, Moth!
Darn good handshake, Moth.
Powerful.
Heh. Thanks.

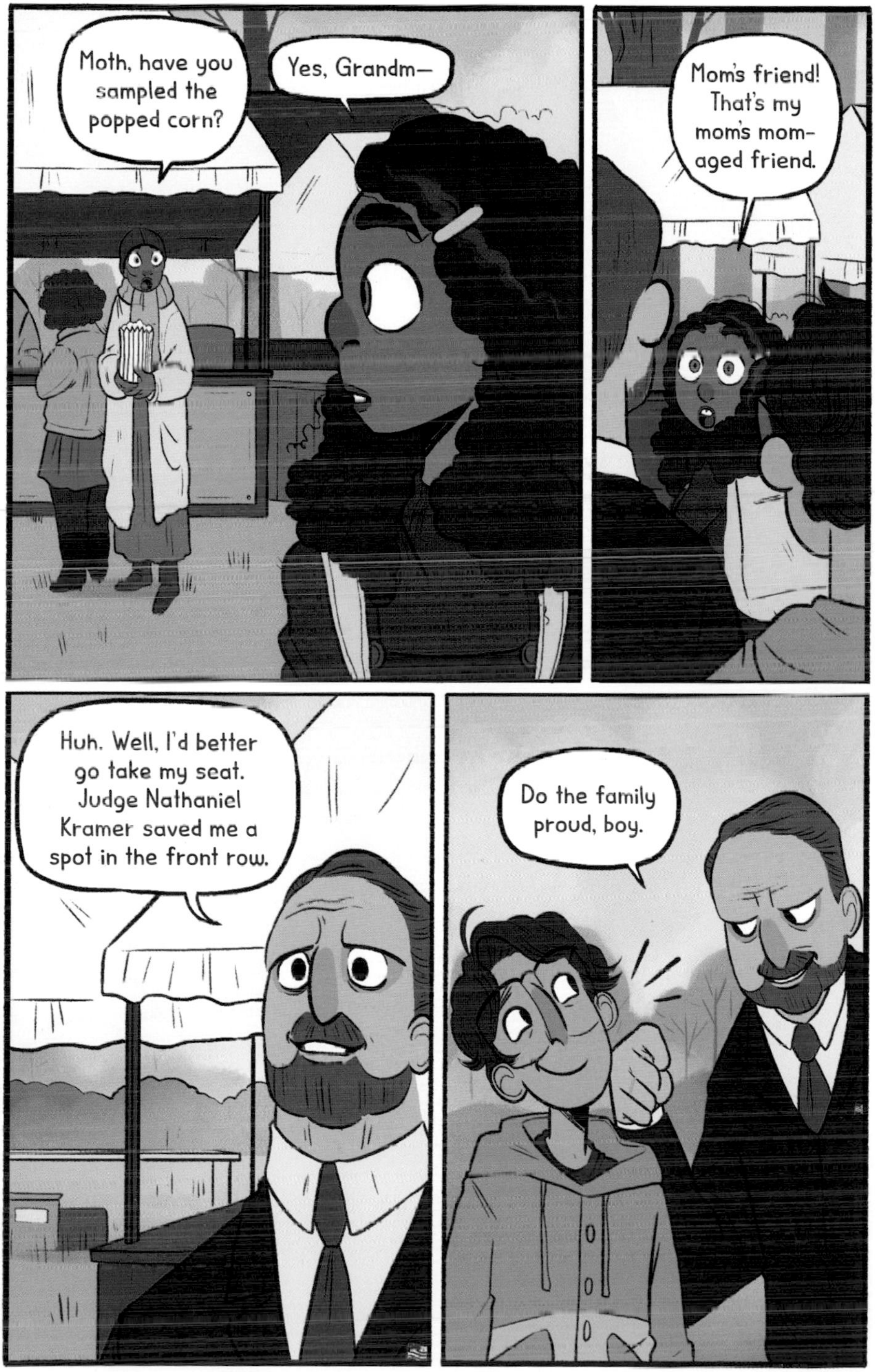
Moth, have you sampled the popped corn?
Yes, Grandm—
Mom's friend! That's my mom's mom-aged friend.
Huh. Well, I'd better go take my seat. Judge Nathaniel Kramer saved me a spot in the front row.
Do the family proud, boy.

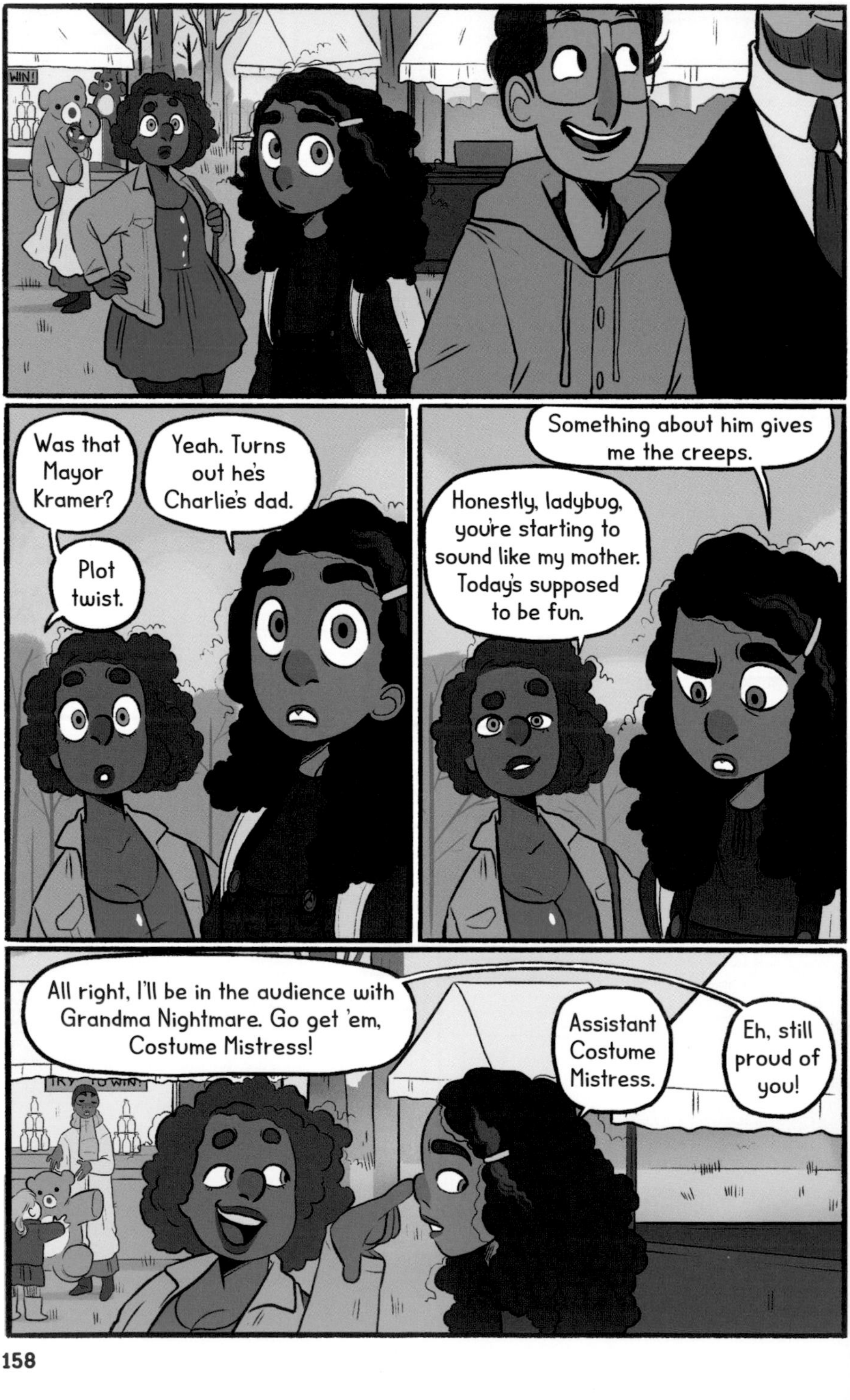
WIN!
Was that Mayor Kramer?
Yeah. Turns out he's Charlie's dad.
Plot twist.
Something about him gives me the creeps.
Honestly, ladybug, you're starting to sound like my mother. Today's supposed to be fun.
All right, I'll be in the audience with Grandma Nightmare. Go get 'em, Costume Mistress!
Assistant Costume Mistress.
Eh, still proud of you!

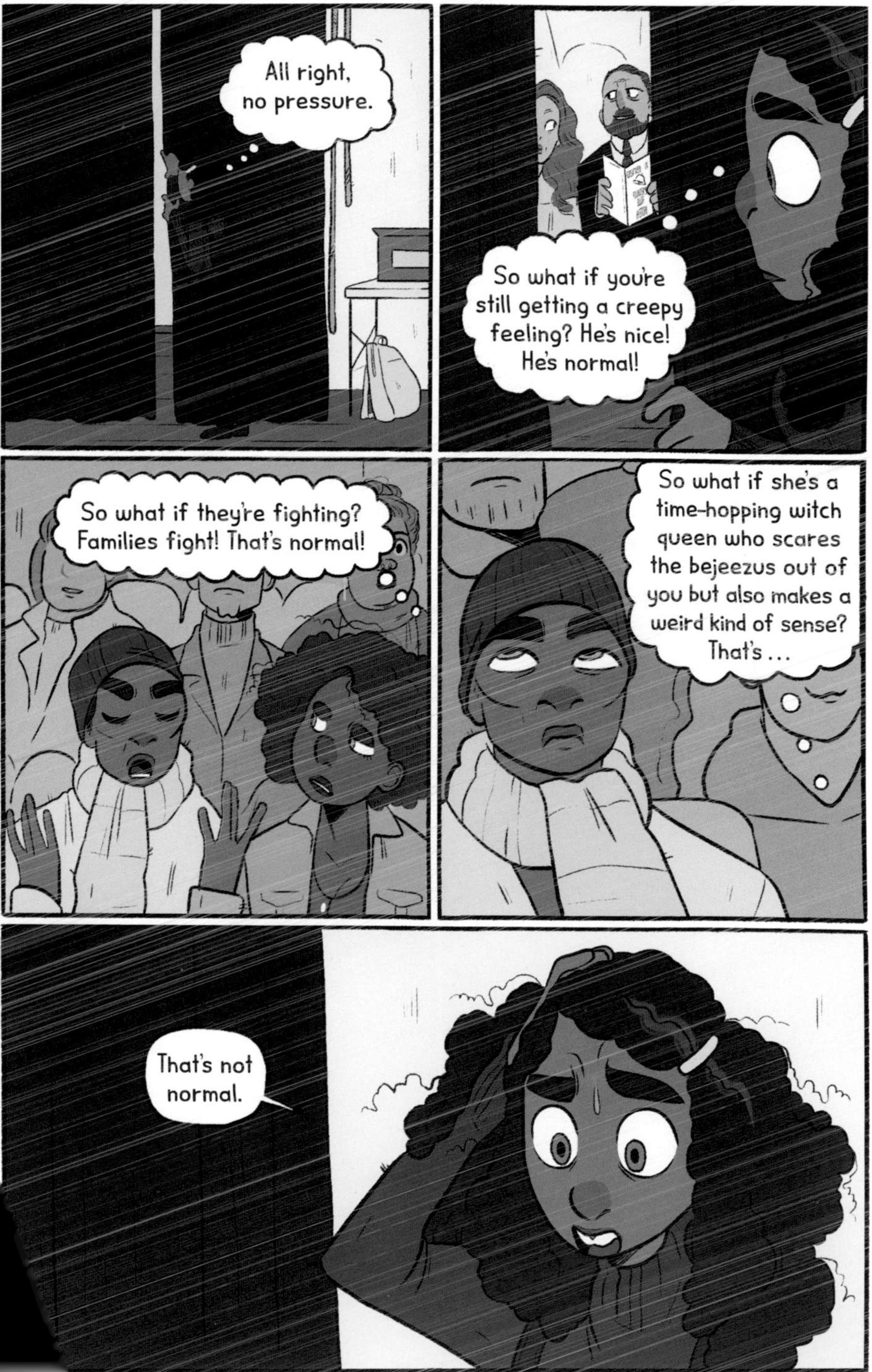
All right, no pressure.
So what if you're still getting a creepy feeling? He's nice! He's normal!
So what if they're fighting? Families fight! That's normal!
So what if she's a time-hopping witch queen who scares the bejeezus out of you but also makes a weird kind of sense? That's . . .
That's not normal.

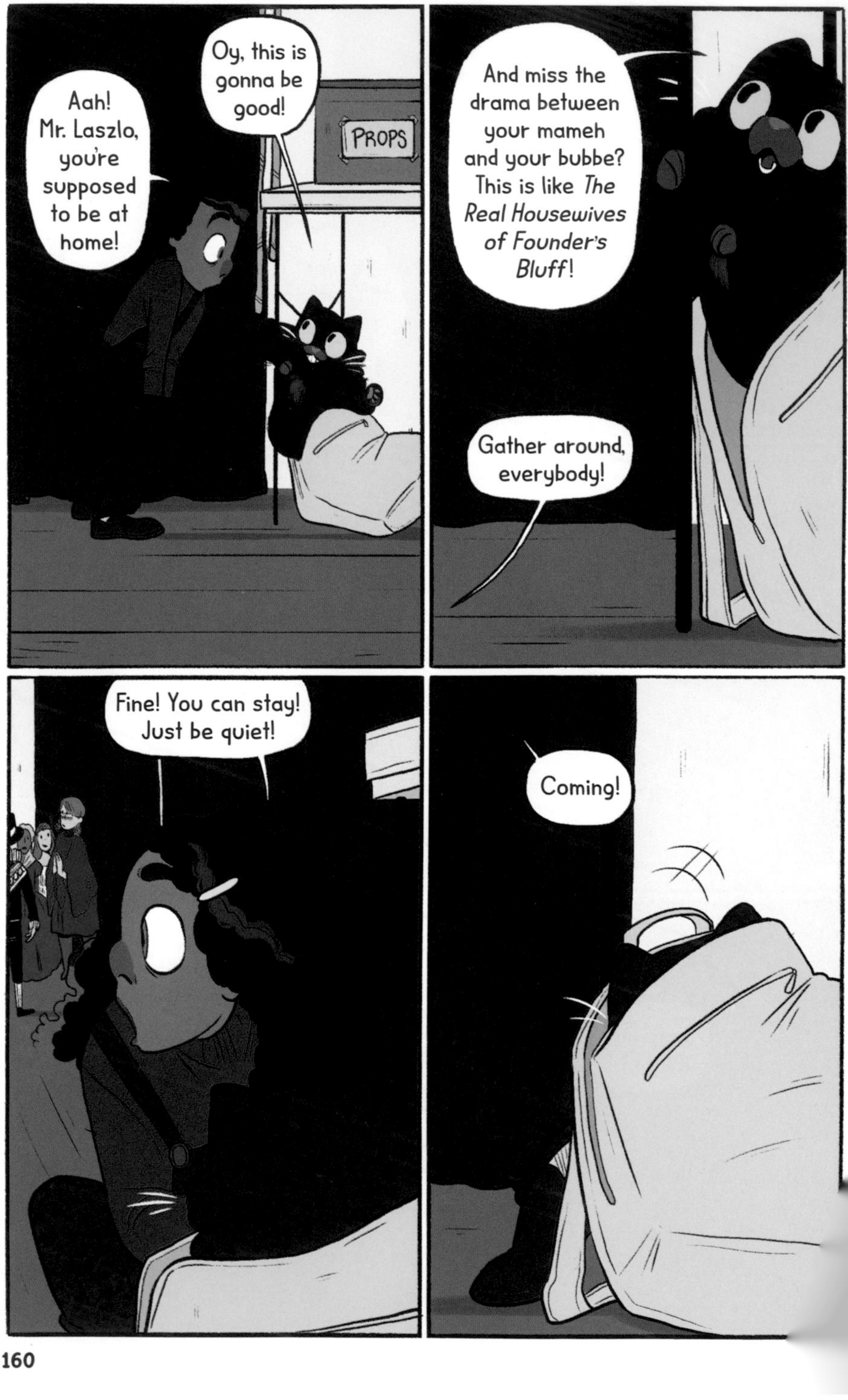
Aah! Mr. Laszlo, you're supposed to be at home!
Oy, this is gonna be good!
PROPS
And miss the drama between your mameh and your bubbe? This is like *The Real Housewives of Founder's Bluff*!
Gather around, everybody!
Fine! You can stay! Just be quiet!
Coming!

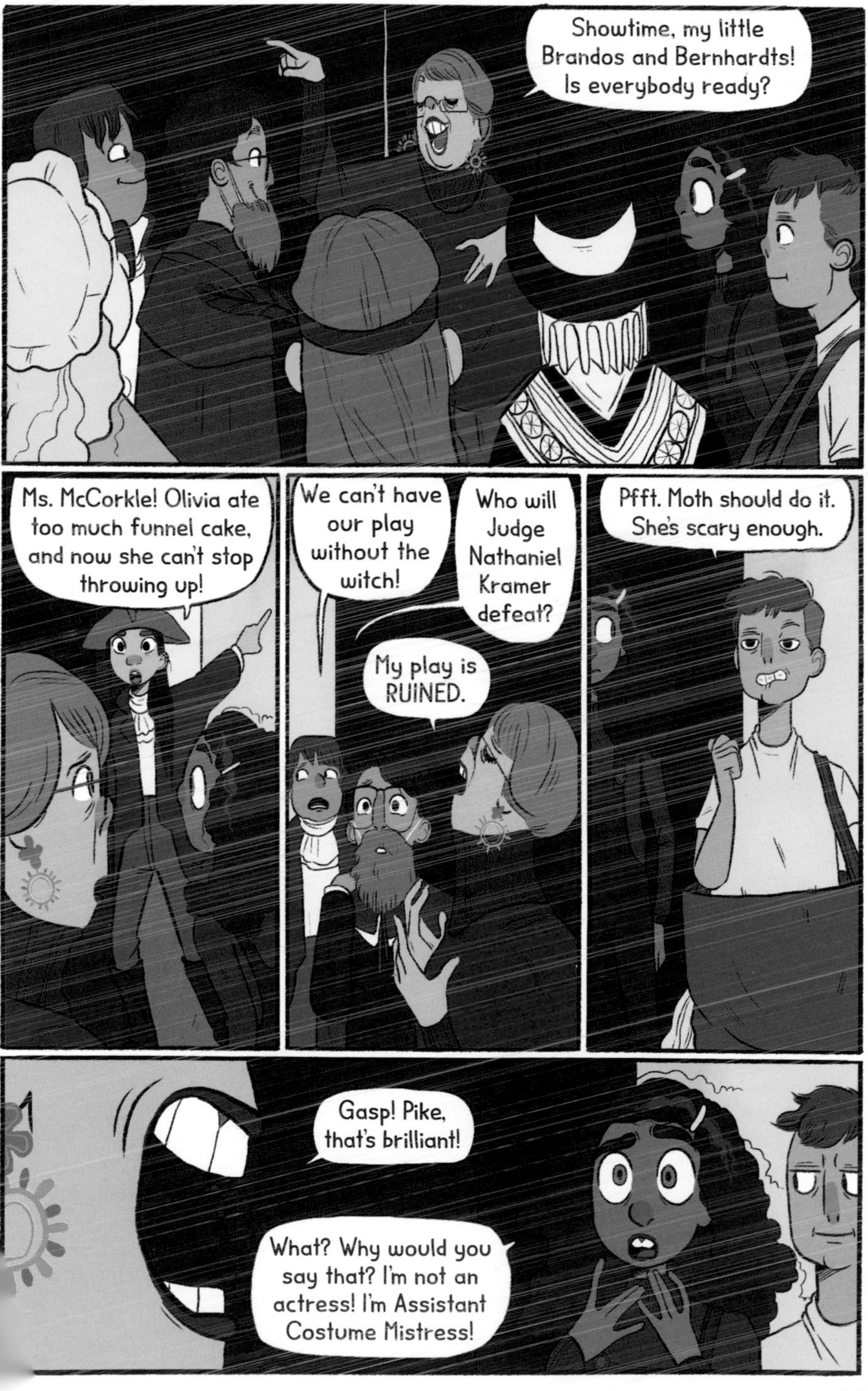
Showtime, my little Brandos and Bernhardts! Is everybody ready?
Ms. McCorkle! Olivia ate too much funnel cake, and now she can't stop throwing up!
We can't have our play without the witch!
Who will Judge Nathaniel Kramer defeat?
My play is RUINED.
Pfft. Moth should do it. She's scary enough.
Gasp! Pike, that's brilliant!
What? Why would you say that? I'm not an actress! I'm Assistant Costume Mistress!

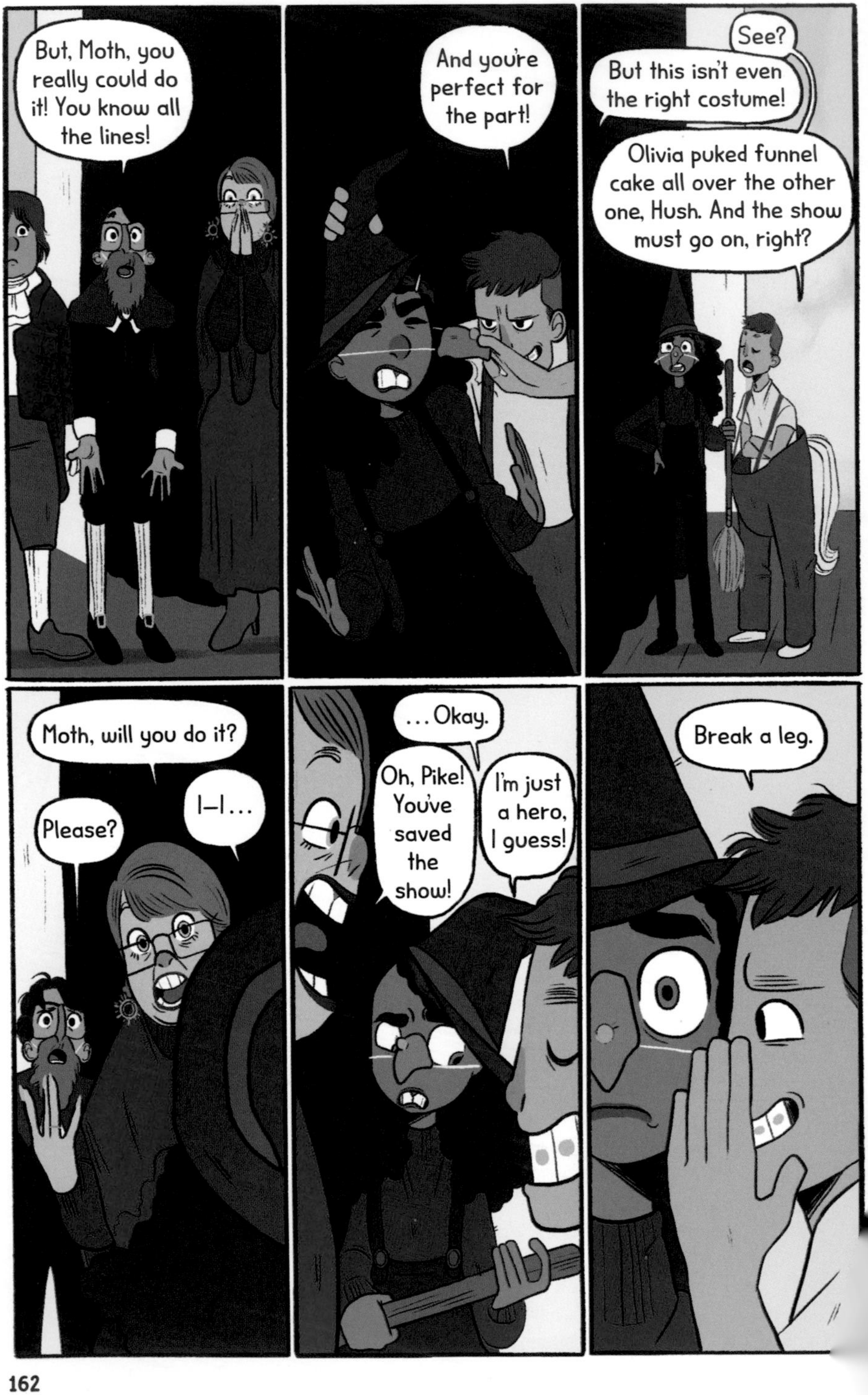
But, Moth, you really could do it! You know all the lines!
And you're perfect for the part!
See?
But this isn't even the right costume!
Olivia puked funnel cake all over the other one, Hush. And the show must go on, right?
Moth, will you do it?
Please?
I–I...
...Okay.
Oh, Pike! You've saved the show!
I'm just a hero, I guess!
Break a leg.

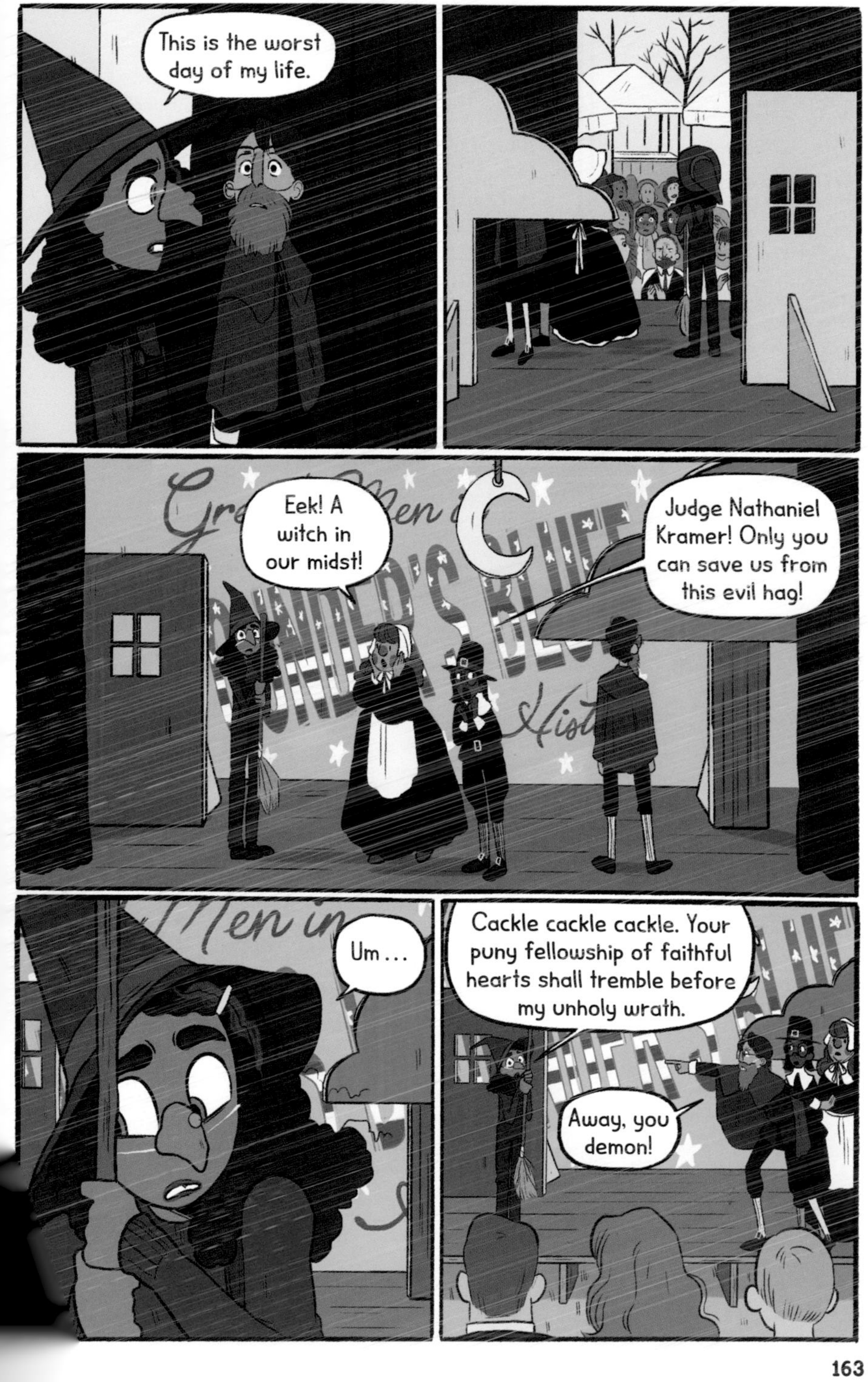
This is the worst day of my life.
Eek! A witch in our midst!
Judge Nathaniel Kramer! Only you can save us from this evil hag!
Um . . .
Cackle cackle cackle. Your puny fellowship of faithful hearts shall tremble before my unholy wrath.
Away, you demon!

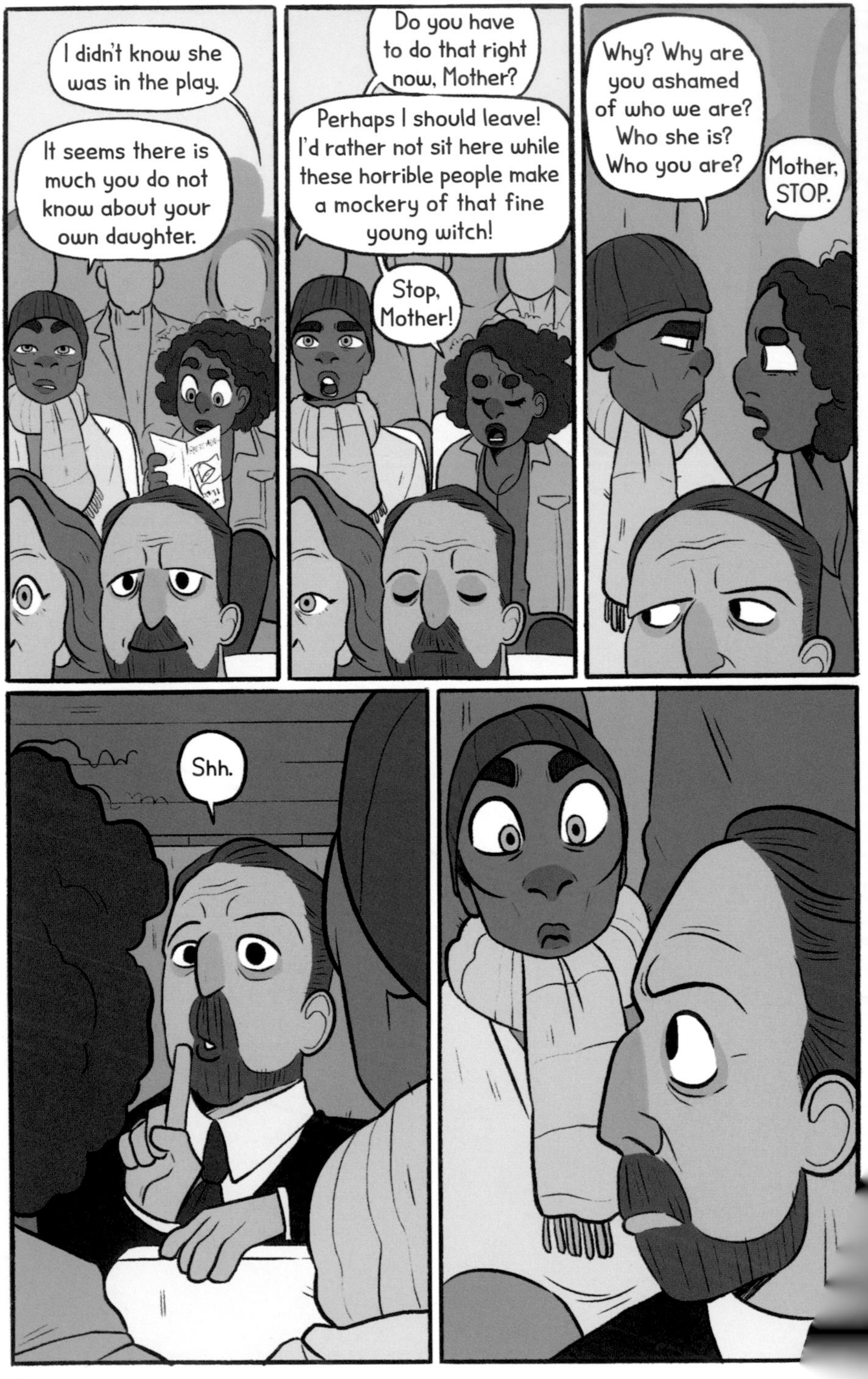
I didn't know she was in the play.
It seems there is much you do not know about your own daughter.
Do you have to do that right now, Mother?
Perhaps I should leave! I'd rather not sit here while these horrible people make a mockery of that fine young witch!
Stop, Mother!
Why? Why are you ashamed of who we are? Who she is? Who you are?
Mother, STOP.
Shh.

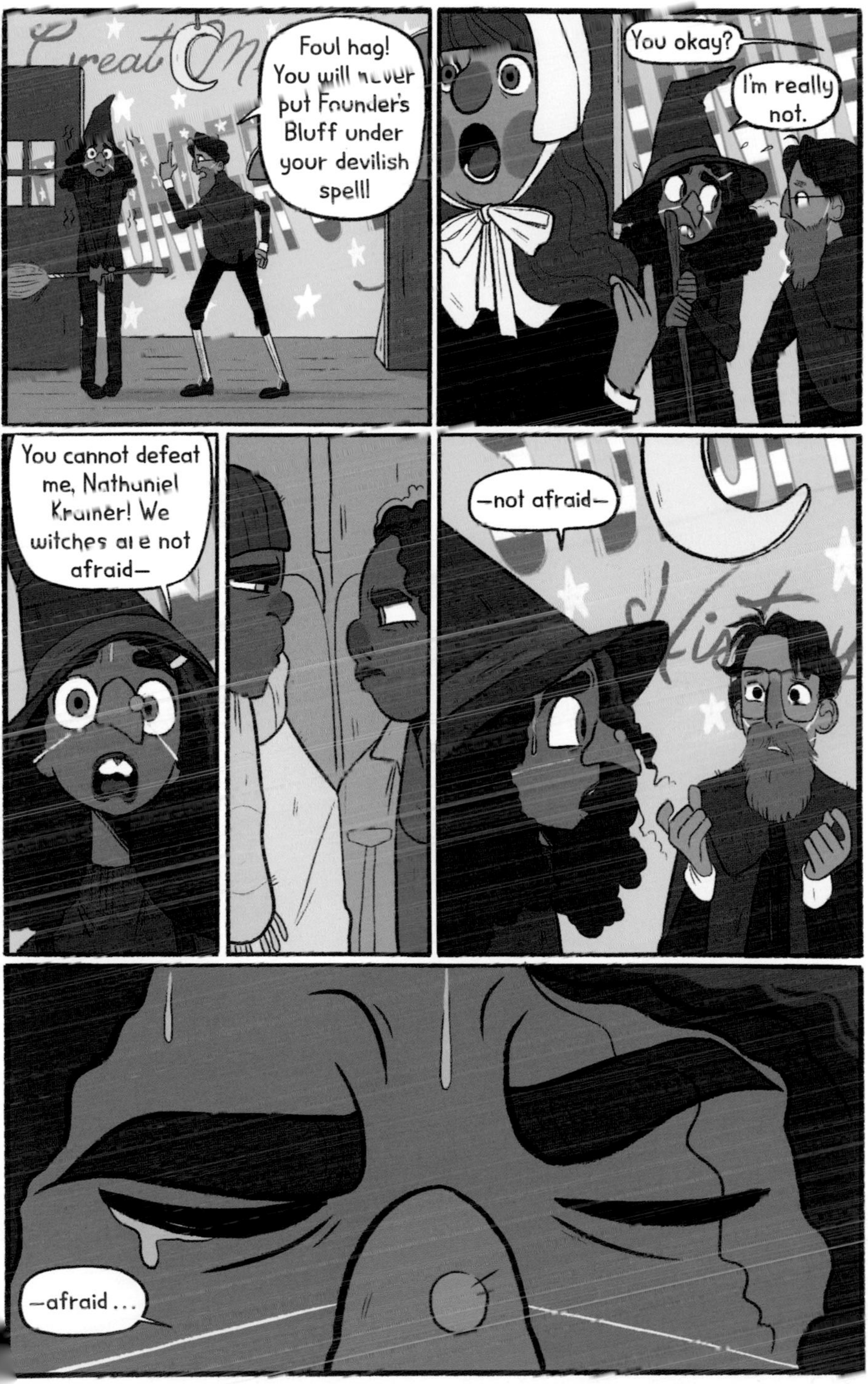
Foul hag! You will never put Founder's Bluff under your devilish spell!
You okay?
I'm really not.
You cannot defeat me, Nathaniel Krainer! We witches are not afraid—
—not afraid—
—afraid...

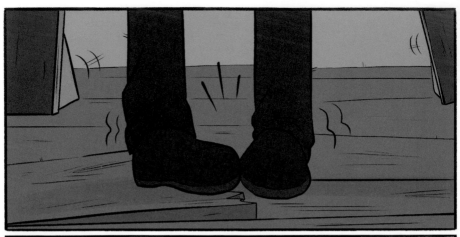

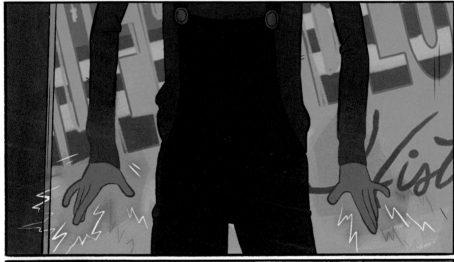

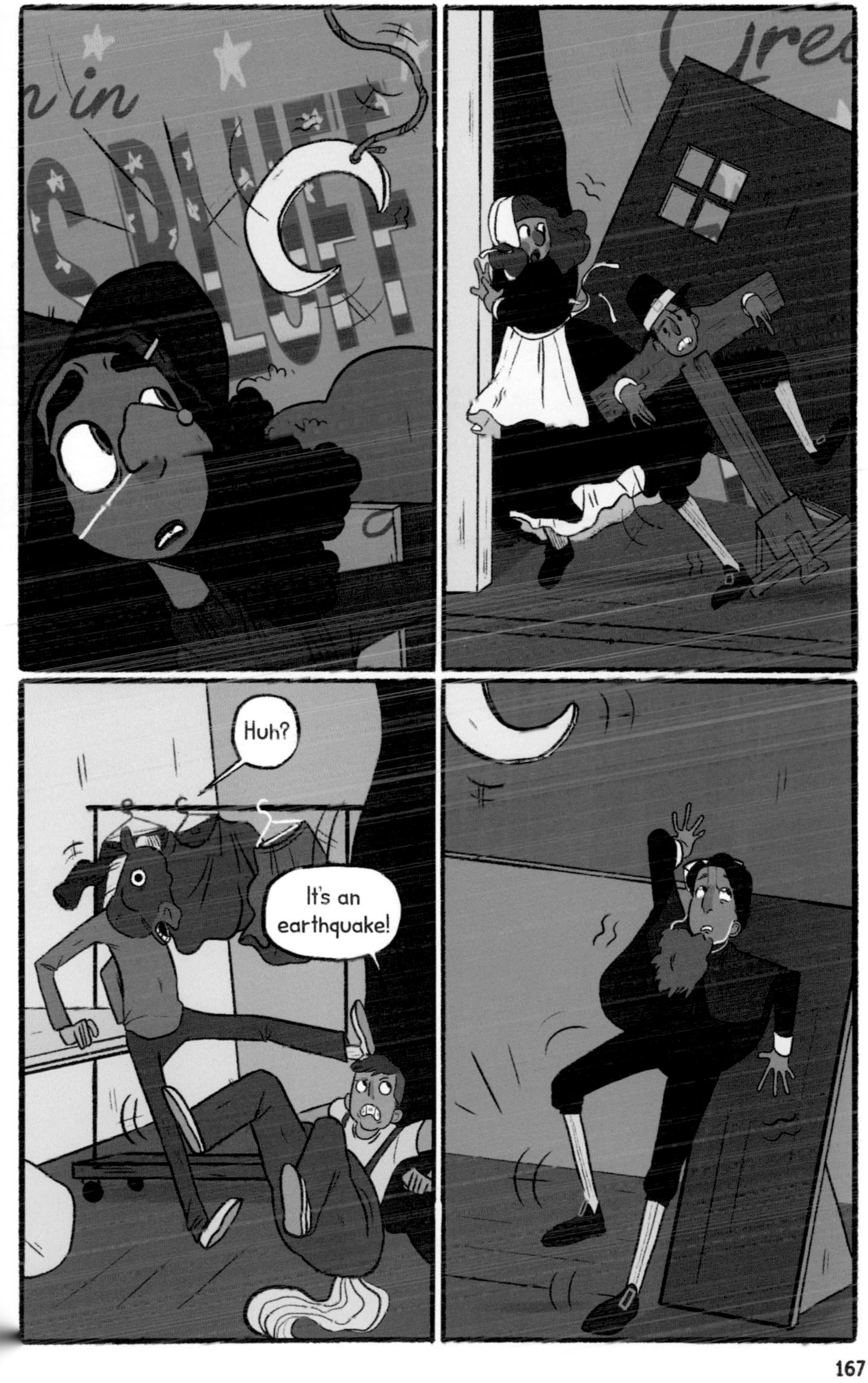
Huh?
It's an earthquake!

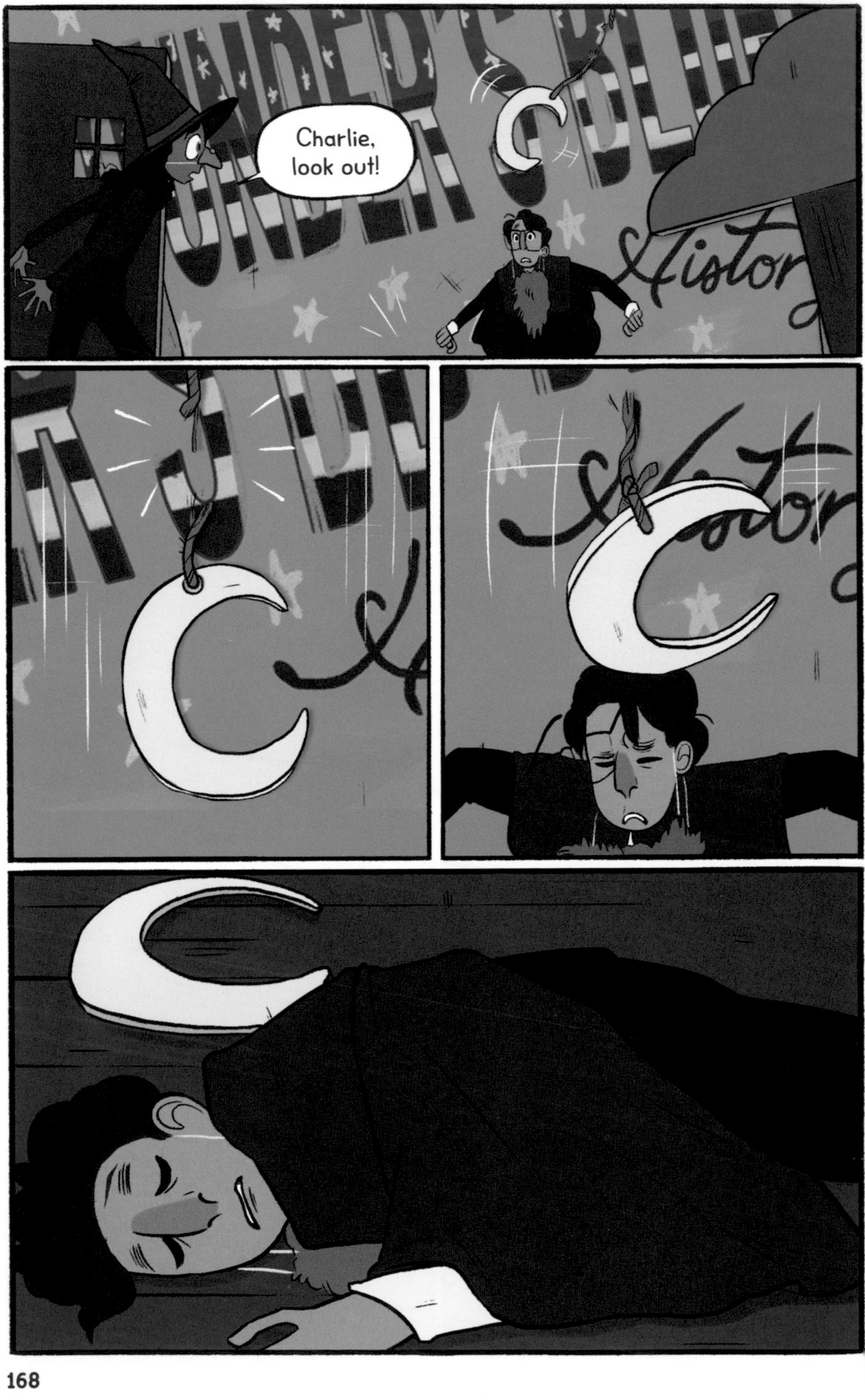
Charlie, look out!

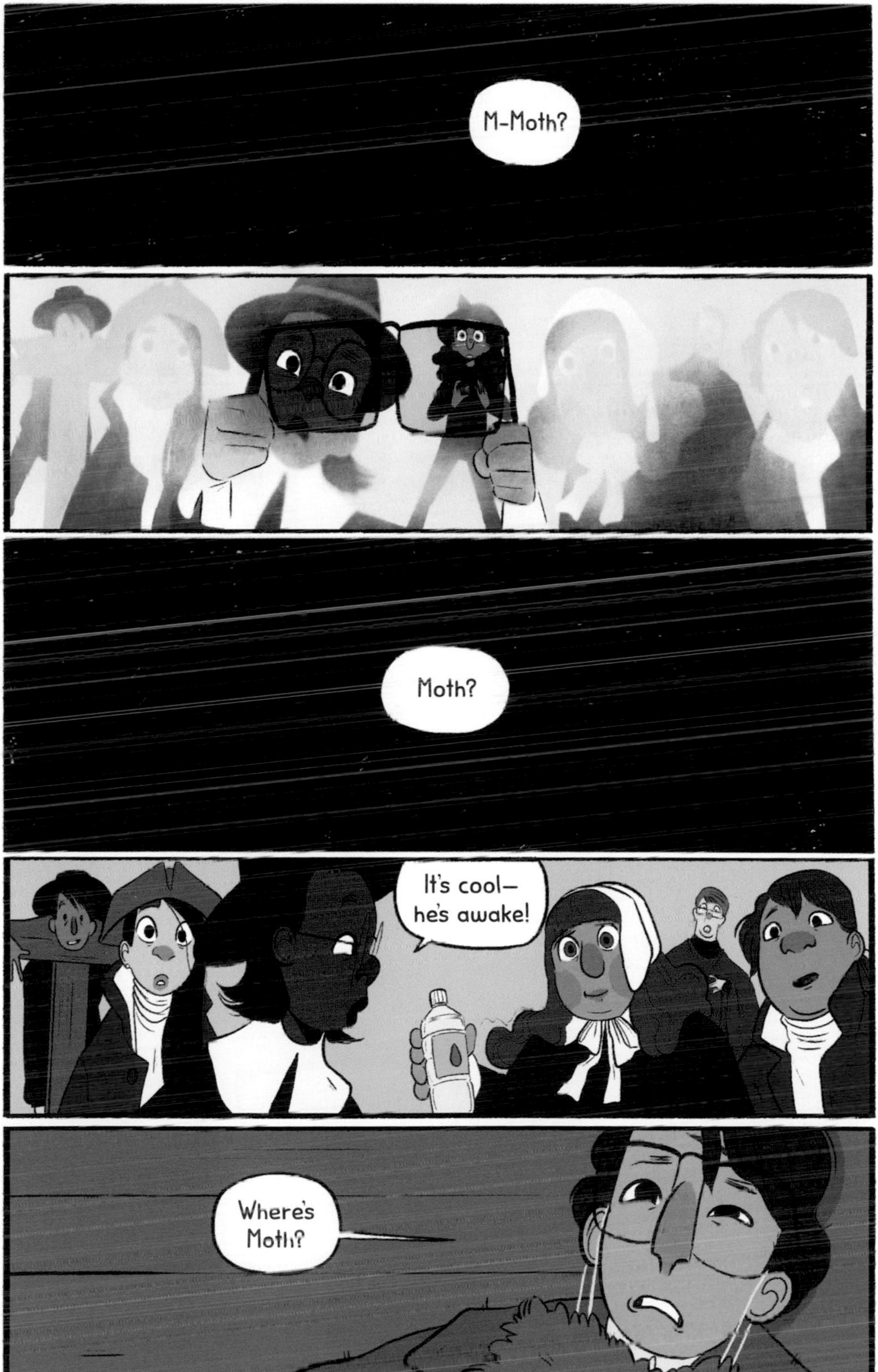
M-Moth?
Moth?
It's cool—
he's awake!
Where's
Moth?

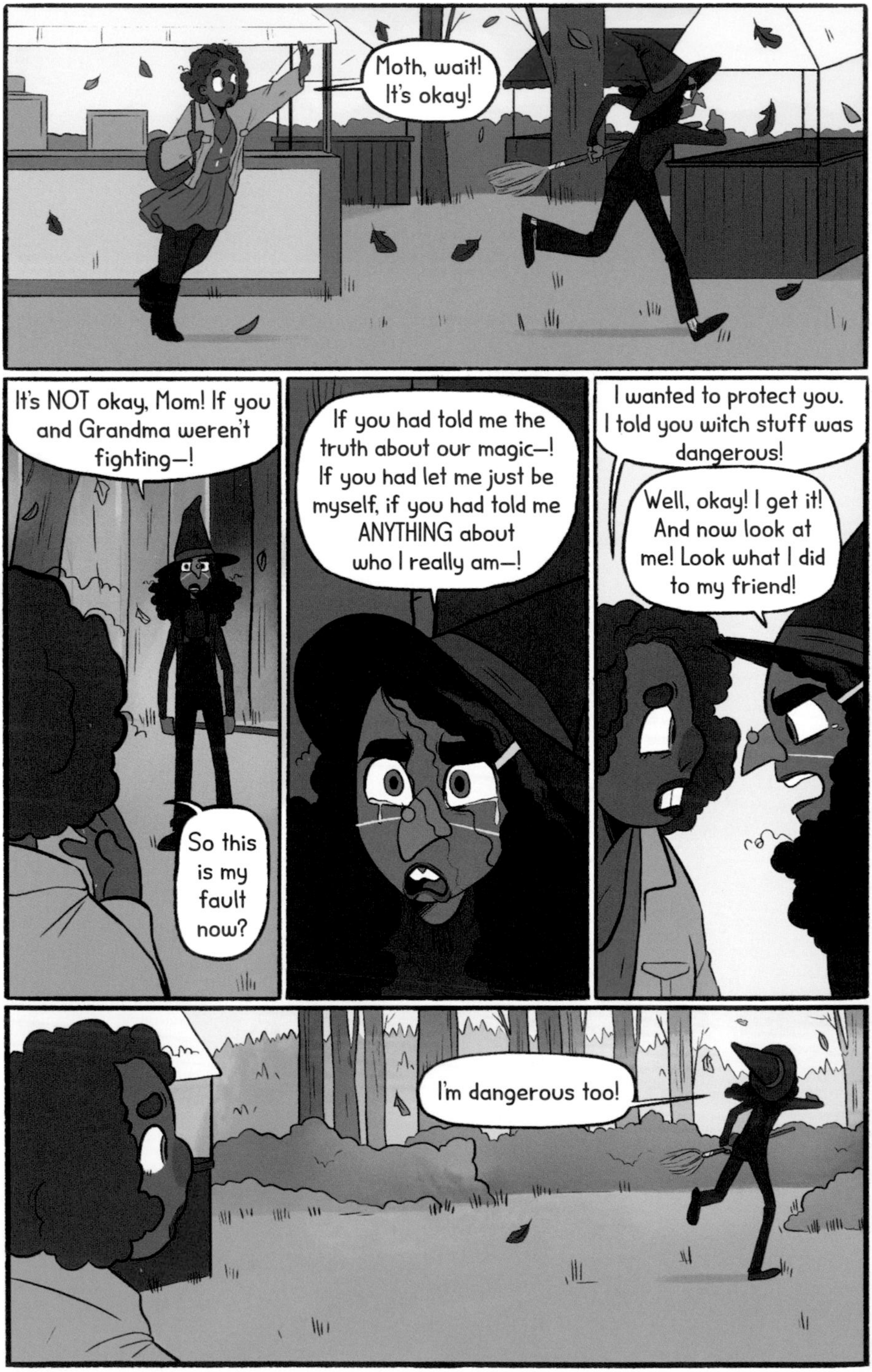
Moth, wait! It's okay!
It's NOT okay, Mom! If you and Grandma weren't fighting—!
So this is my fault now?
If you had told me the truth about our magic—! If you had let me just be myself, if you had told me ANYTHING about who I really am—!
I wanted to protect you. I told you witch stuff was dangerous!
Well, okay! I get it! And now look at me! Look what I did to my friend!
I'm dangerous too!

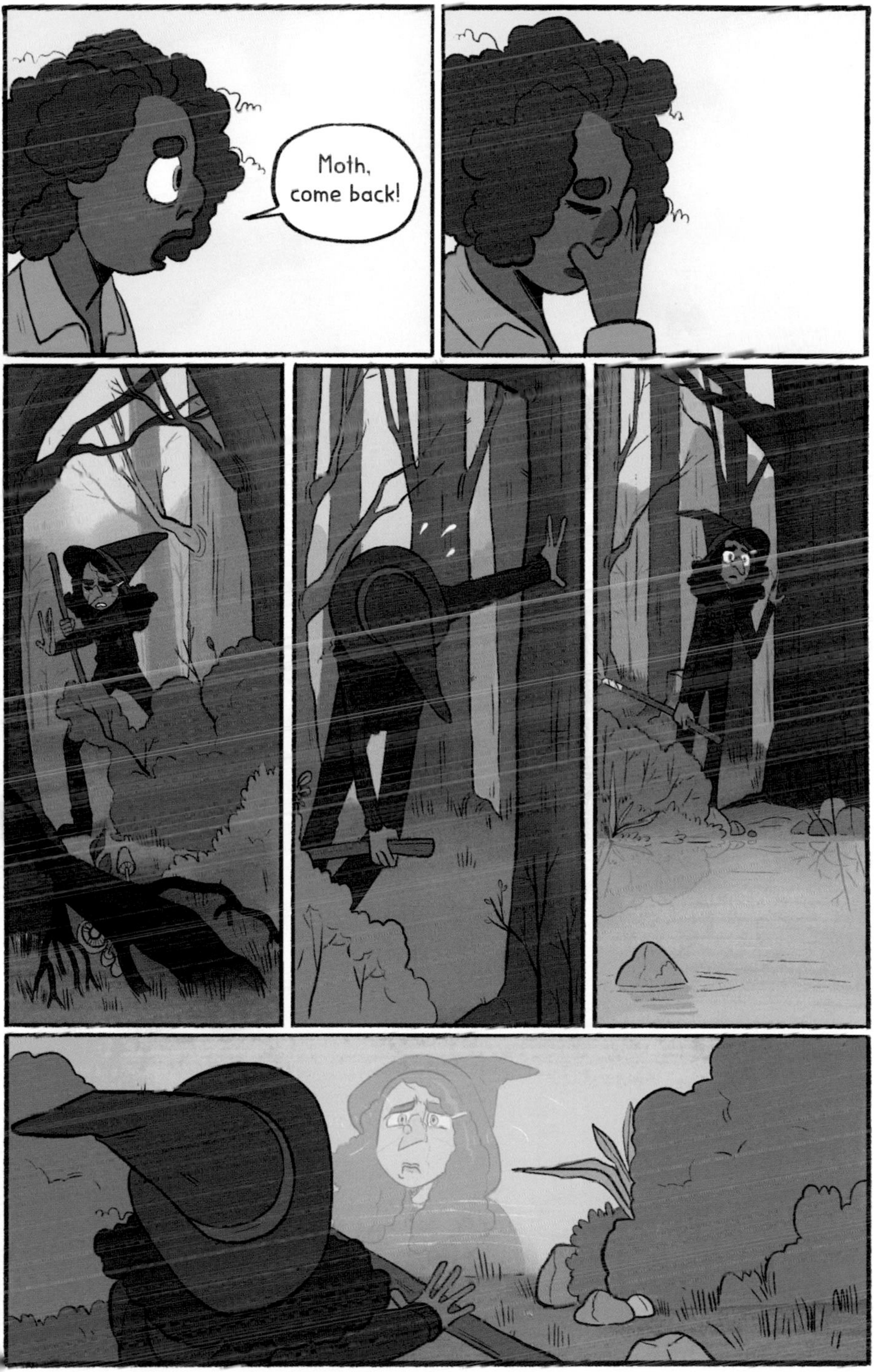
Moth, come back!

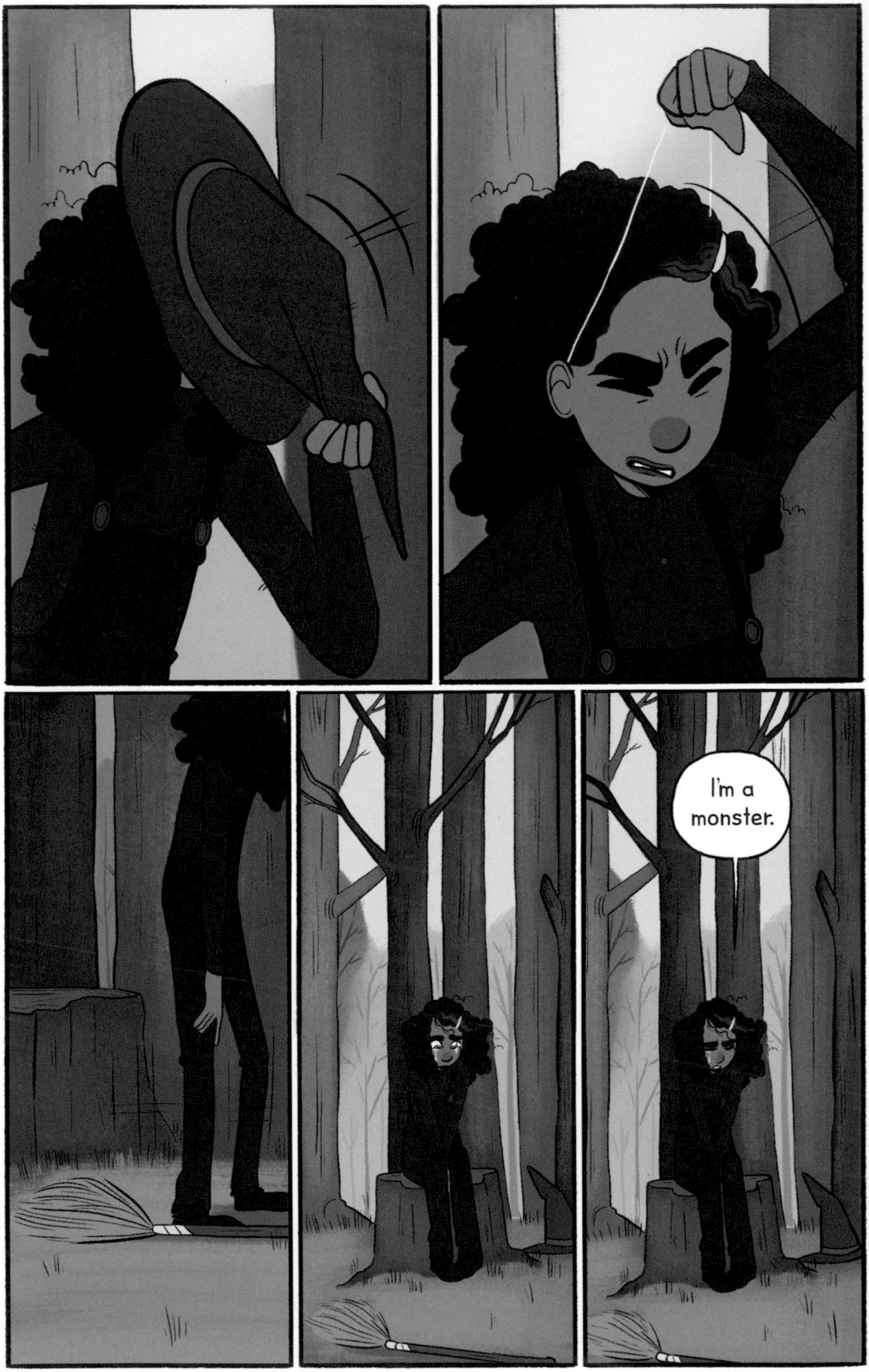
I'm a
monster.

CHAPTER 11
Hecate

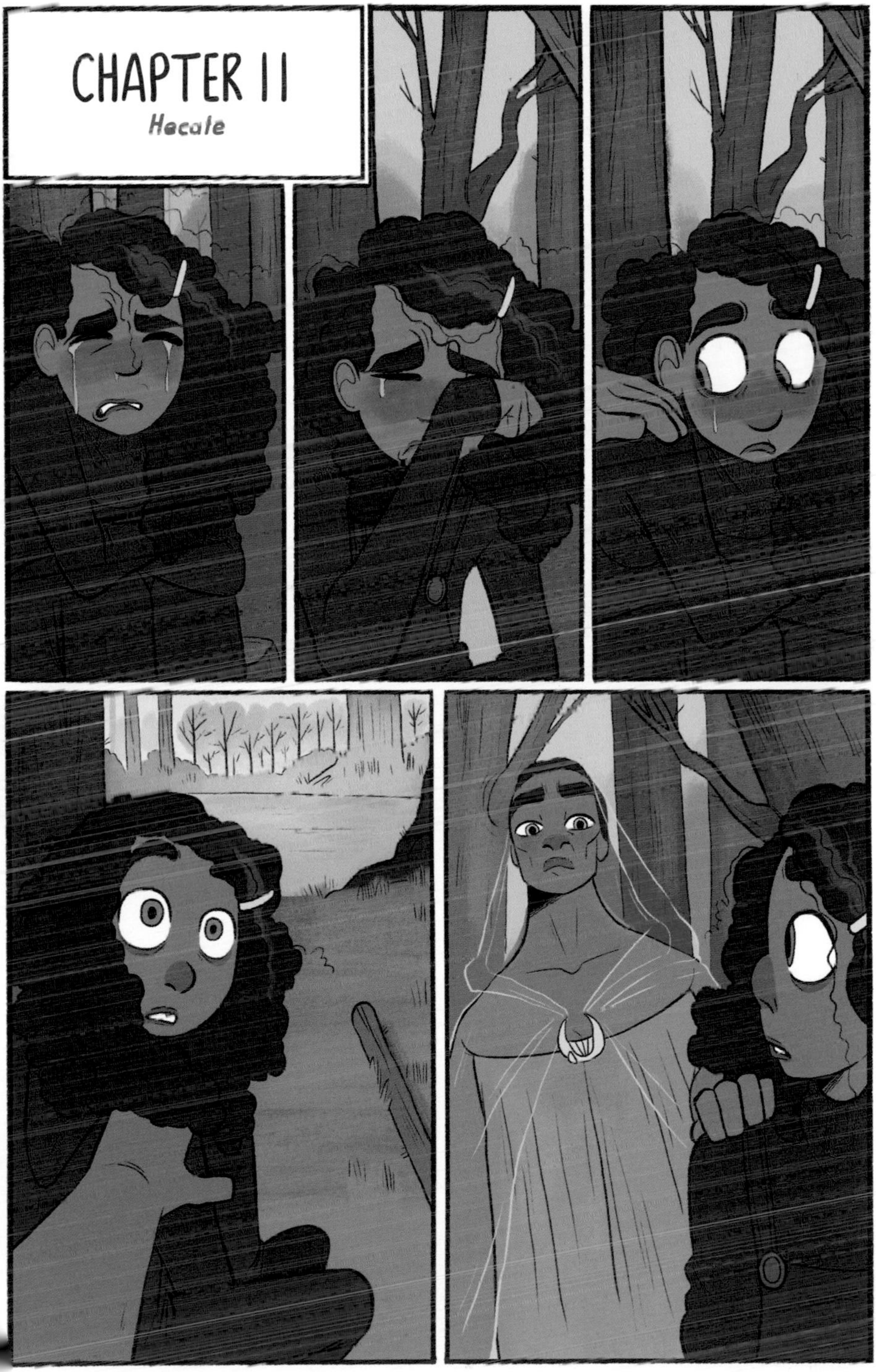

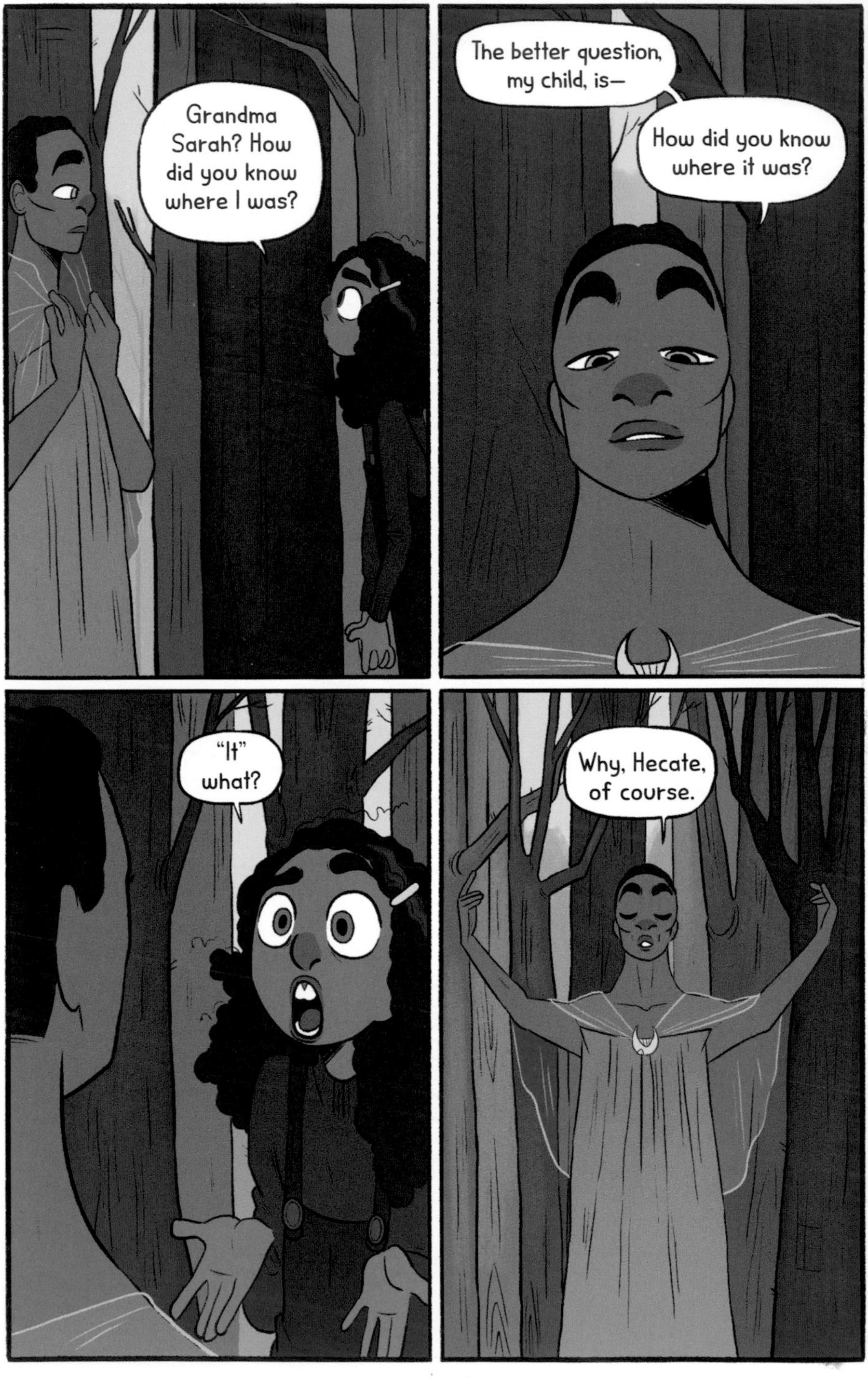
Grandma Sarah? How did you know where I was?
The better question, my child, is—
How did you know where it was?
"It" what?
Why, Hecate, of course.

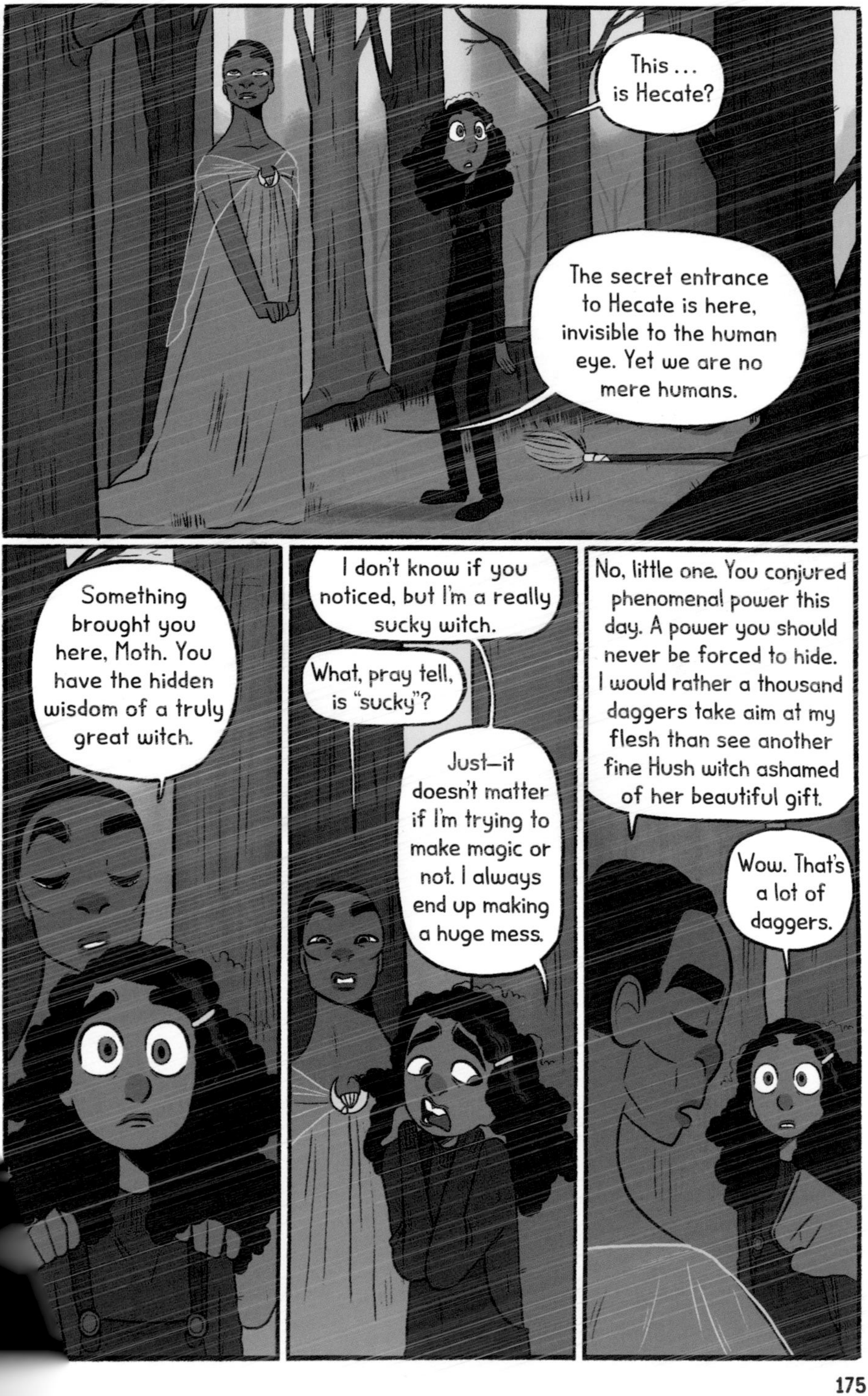
This . . . is Hecate?
The secret entrance to Hecate is here, invisible to the human eye. Yet we are no mere humans.
Something brought you here, Moth. You have the hidden wisdom of a truly great witch.
I don't know if you noticed, but I'm a really sucky witch.
What, pray tell, is "sucky"?
Just—it doesn't matter if I'm trying to make magic or not. I always end up making a huge mess.
No, little one. You conjured phenomenal power this day. A power you should never be forced to hide. I would rather a thousand daggers take aim at my flesh than see another fine Hush witch ashamed of her beautiful gift.
Wow. That's a lot of daggers.

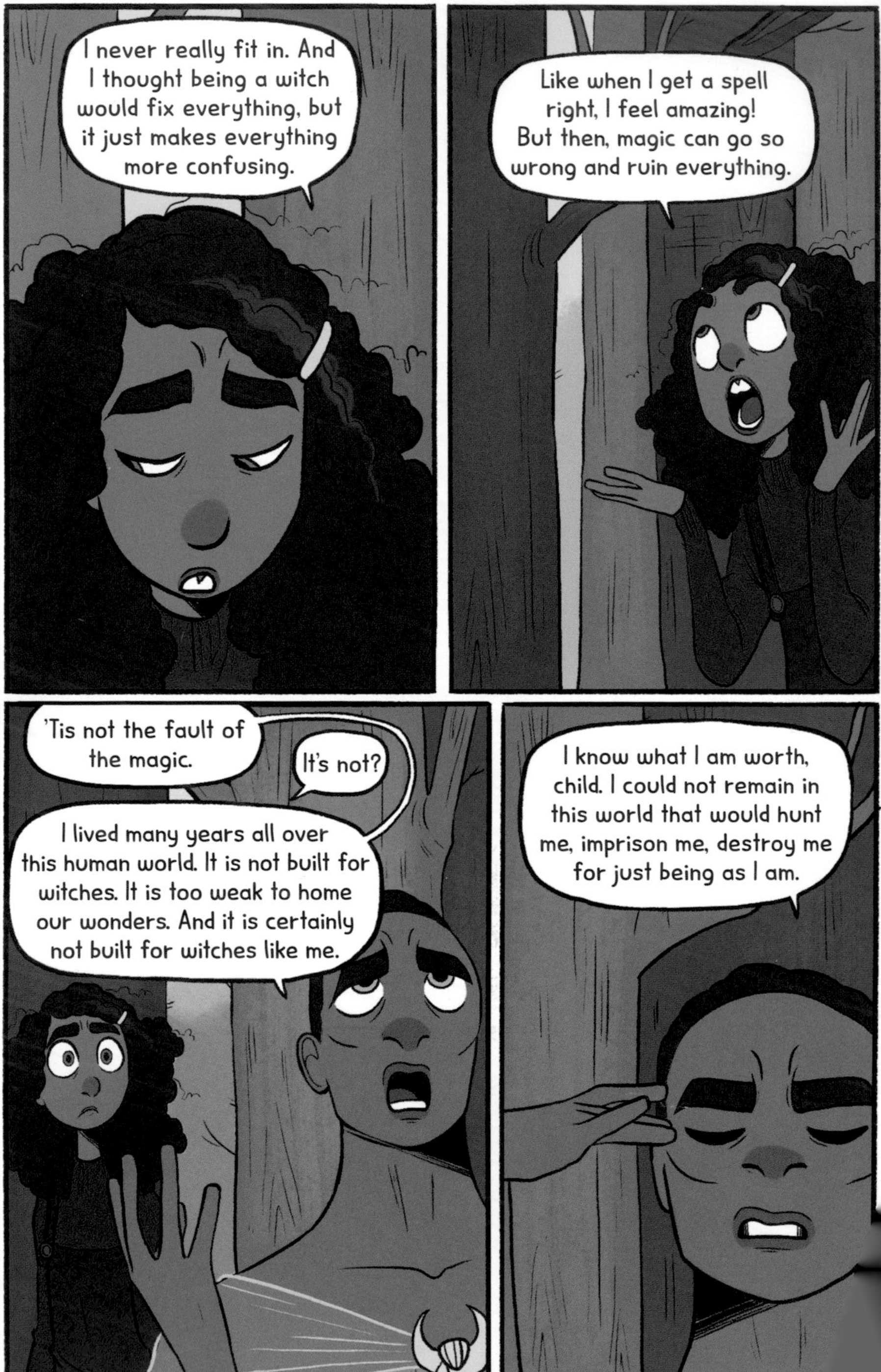
I never really fit in. And I thought being a witch would fix everything, but it just makes everything more confusing.
Like when I get a spell right, I feel amazing! But then, magic can go so wrong and ruin everything.
'Tis not the fault of the magic.
It's not?
I lived many years all over this human world. It is not built for witches. It is too weak to home our wonders. And it is certainly not built for witches like me.
I know what I am worth, child. I could not remain in this world that would hunt me, imprison me, destroy me for just being as I am.

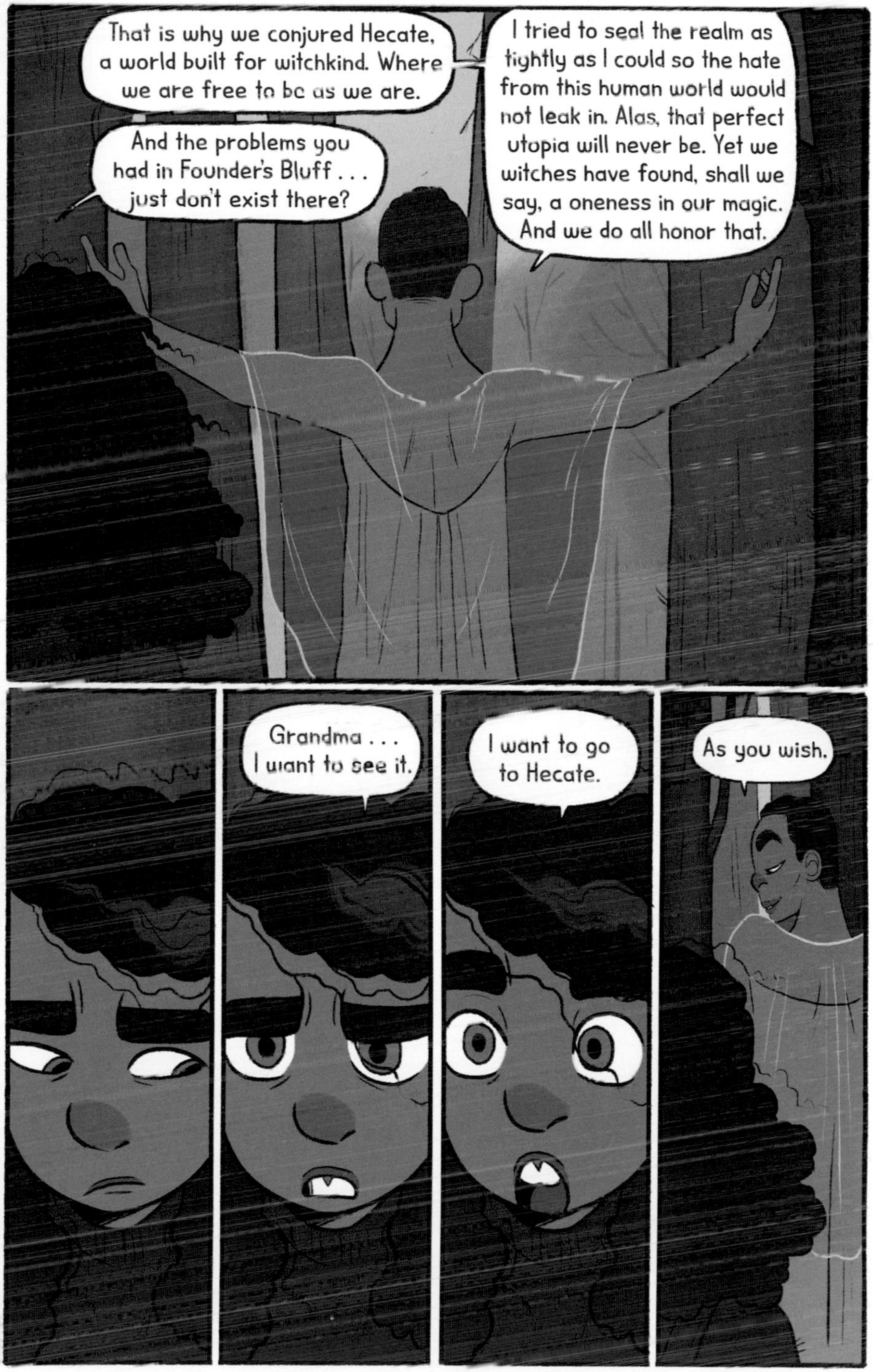
That is why we conjured Hecate, a world built for witchkind. Where we are free to be as we are.
I tried to seal the realm as tightly as I could so the hate from this human world would not leak in. Alas, that perfect utopia will never be. Yet we witches have found, shall we say, a oneness in our magic. And we do all honor that.
And the problems you had in Founder's Bluff . . . just don't exist there?
Grandma . . . I want to see it.
I want to go to Hecate.
As you wish.

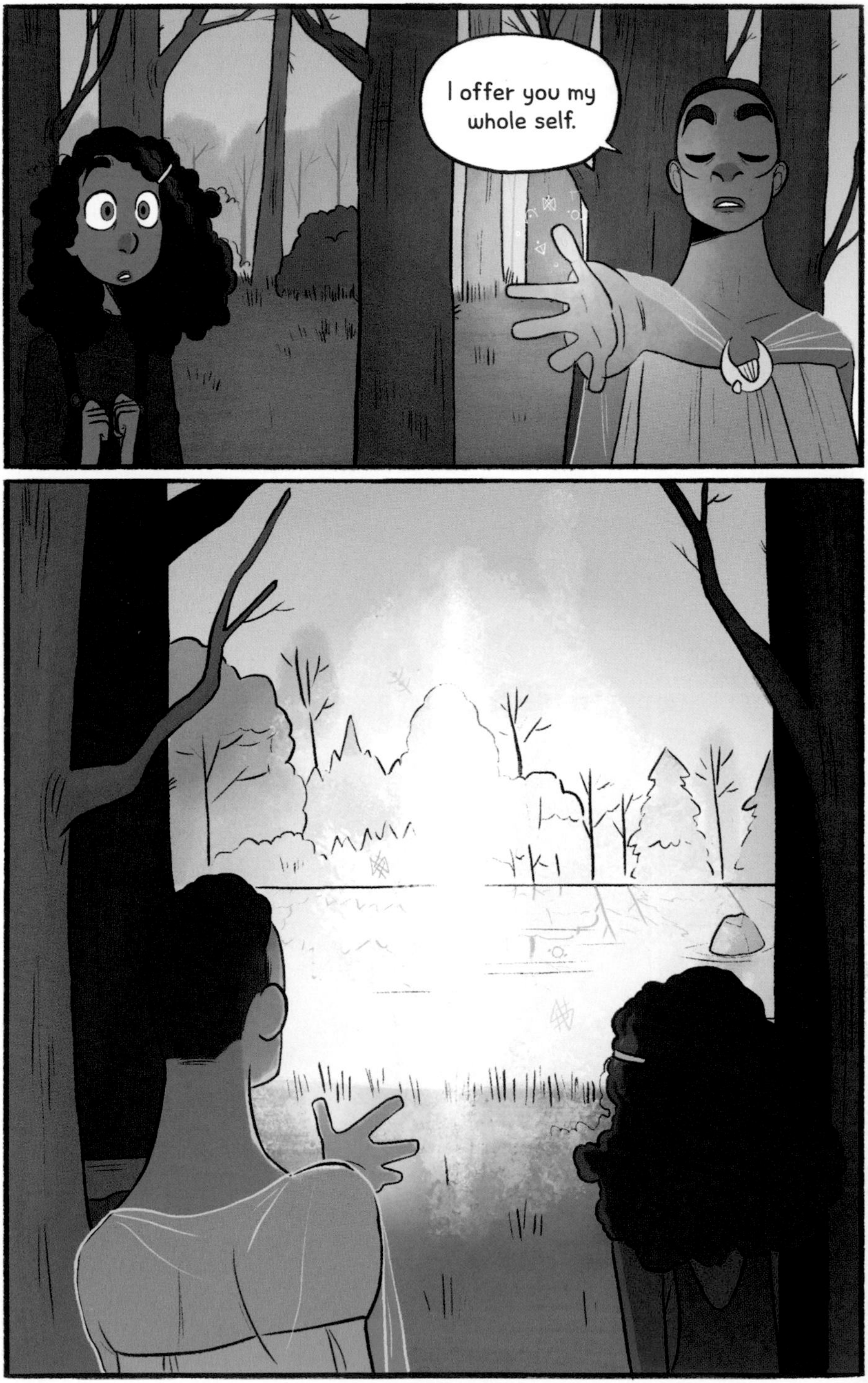
I offer you my whole self.

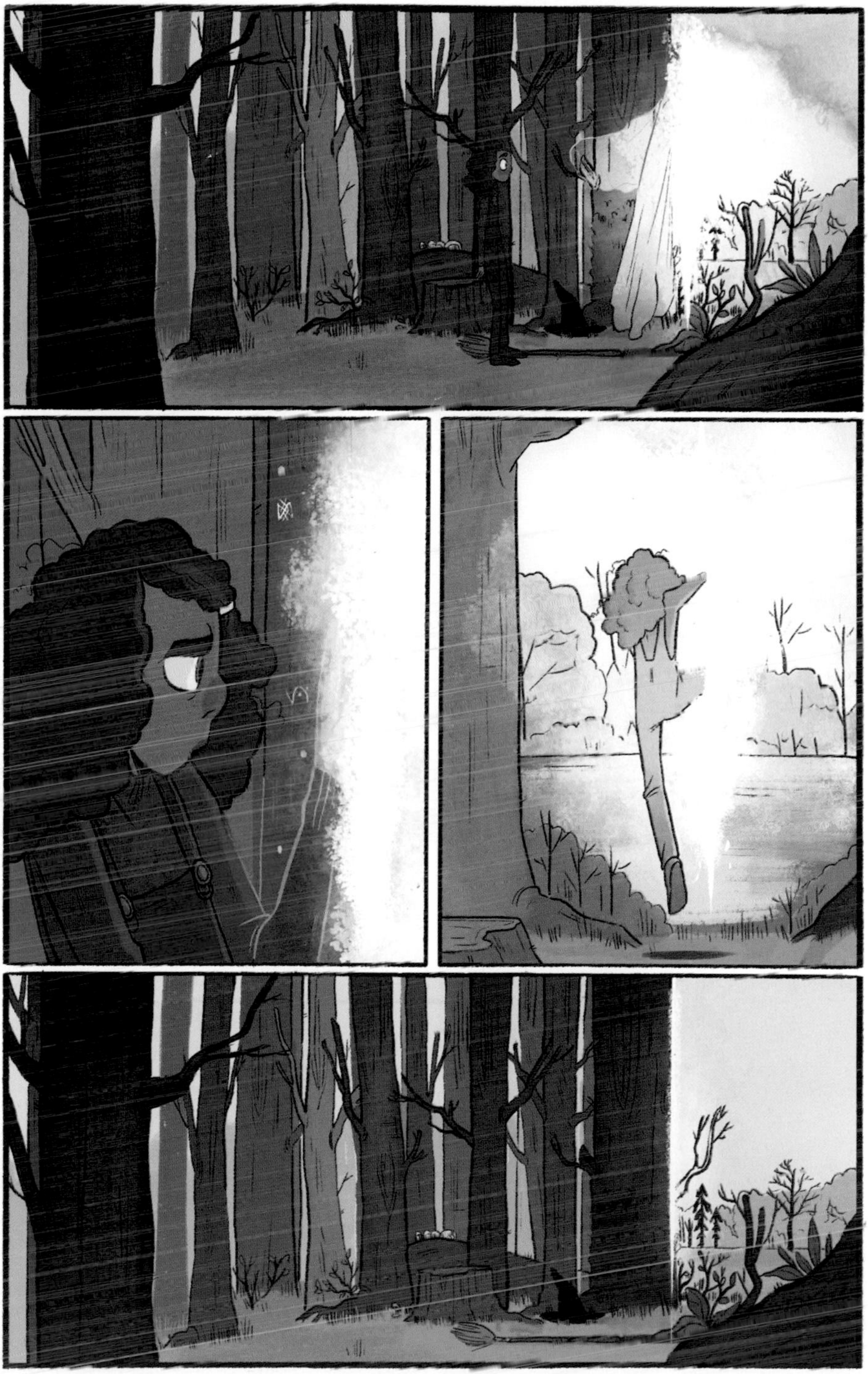

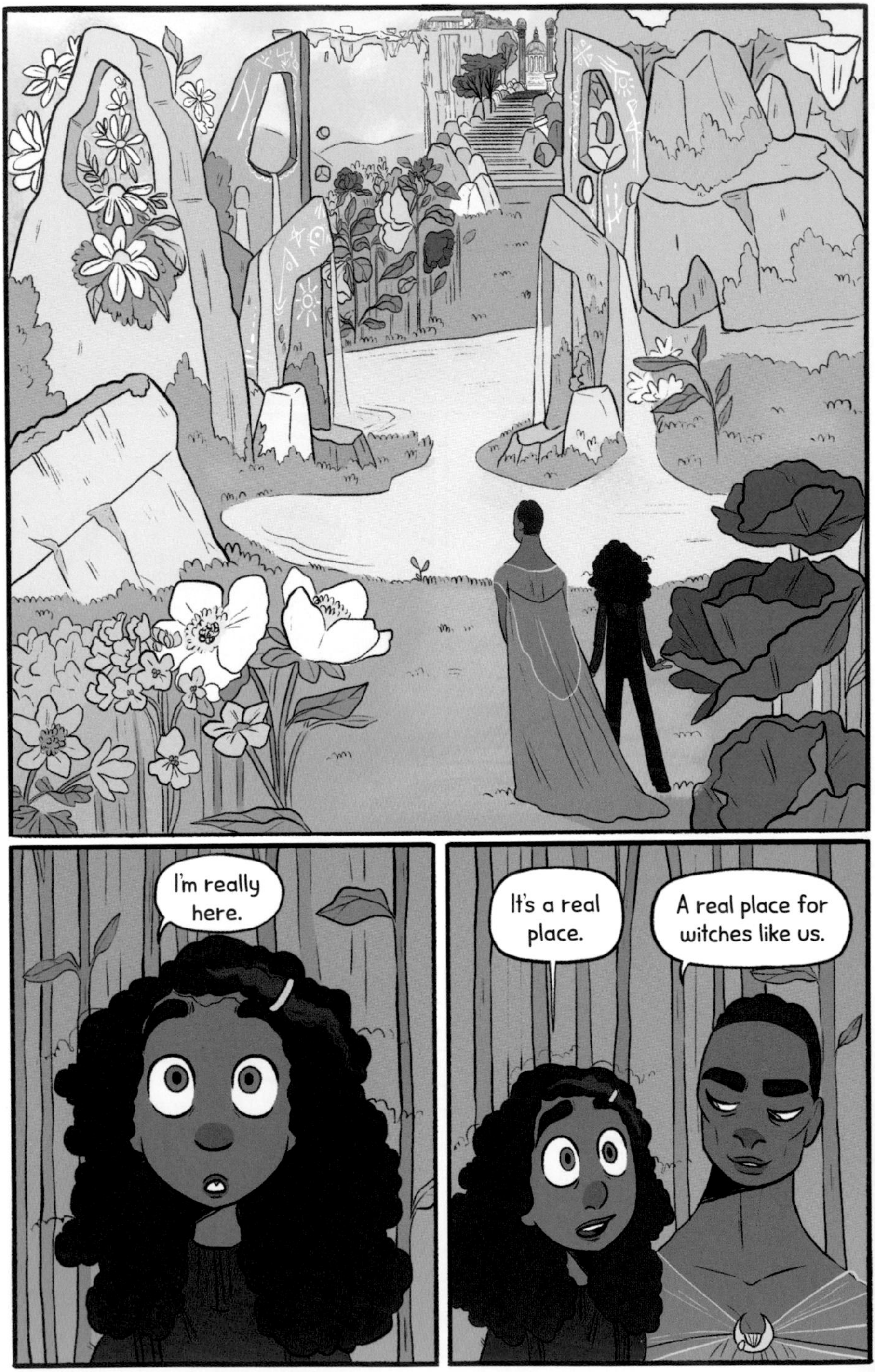
I'm really here.
It's a real place.
A real place for witches like us.

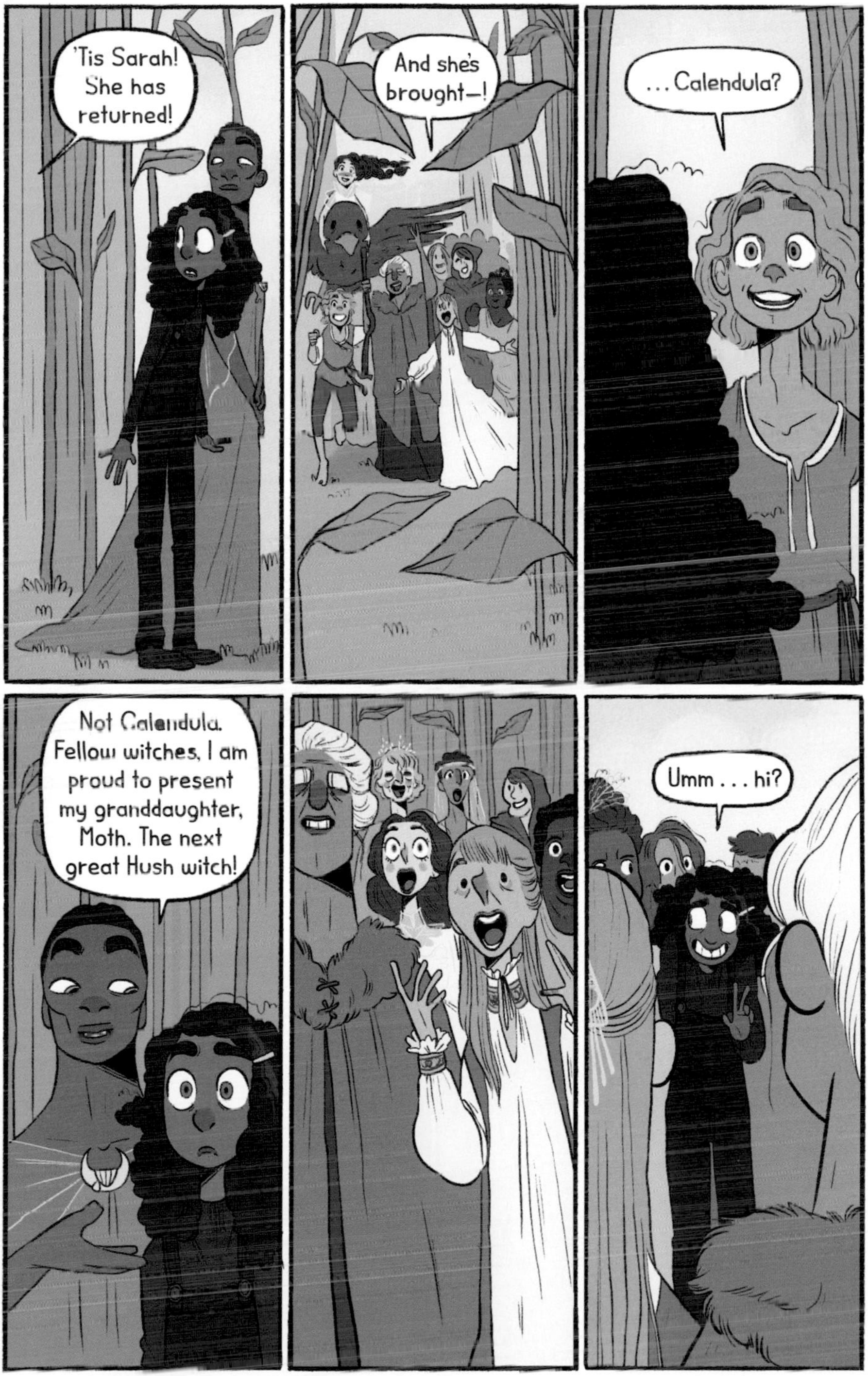
'Tis Sarah! She has returned!
And she's brought—!
. . . Calendula?
Not Calendula. Fellow witches, I am proud to present my granddaughter, Moth. The next great Hush witch!
Umm . . . hi?

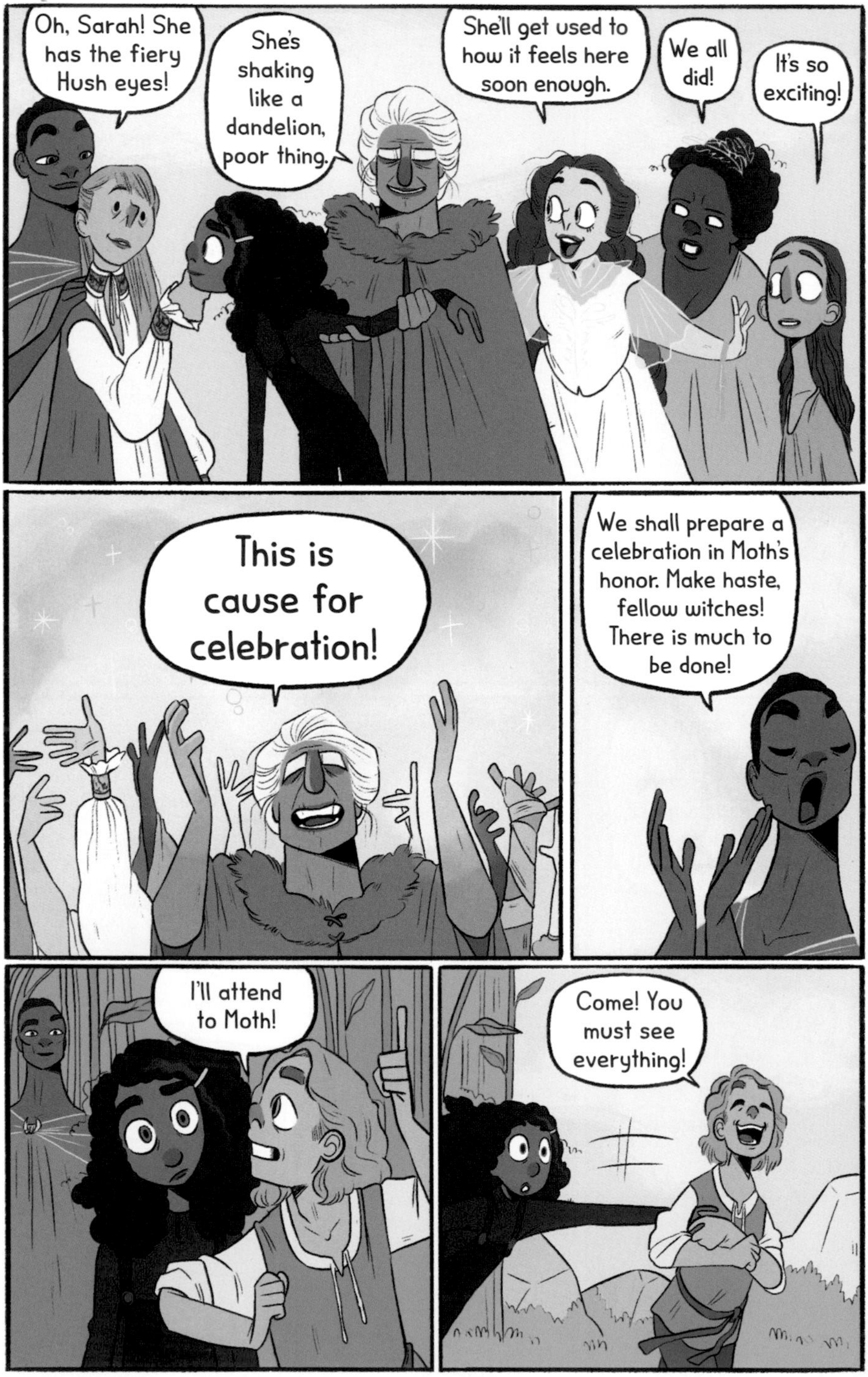
Oh, Sarah! She has the fiery Hush eyes!
She's shaking like a dandelion, poor thing.
She'll get used to how it feels here soon enough.
We all did!
It's so exciting!
This is cause for celebration!
We shall prepare a celebration in Moth's honor. Make haste, fellow witches! There is much to be done!
I'll attend to Moth!
Come! You must see everything!

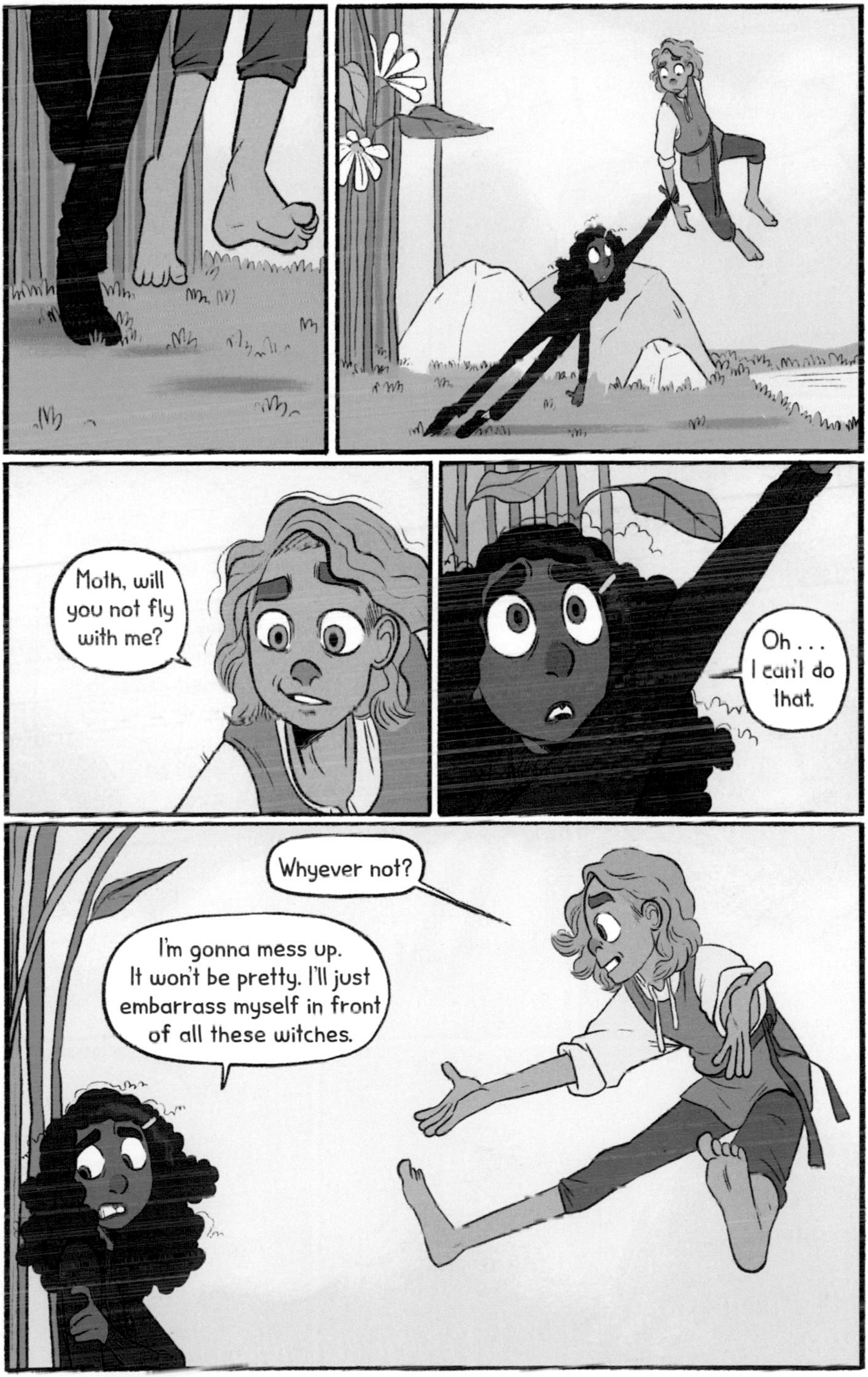
Moth, will you not fly with me?
Oh . . . I can't do that.
Whyever not?
I'm gonna mess up. It won't be pretty. I'll just embarrass myself in front of all these witches.

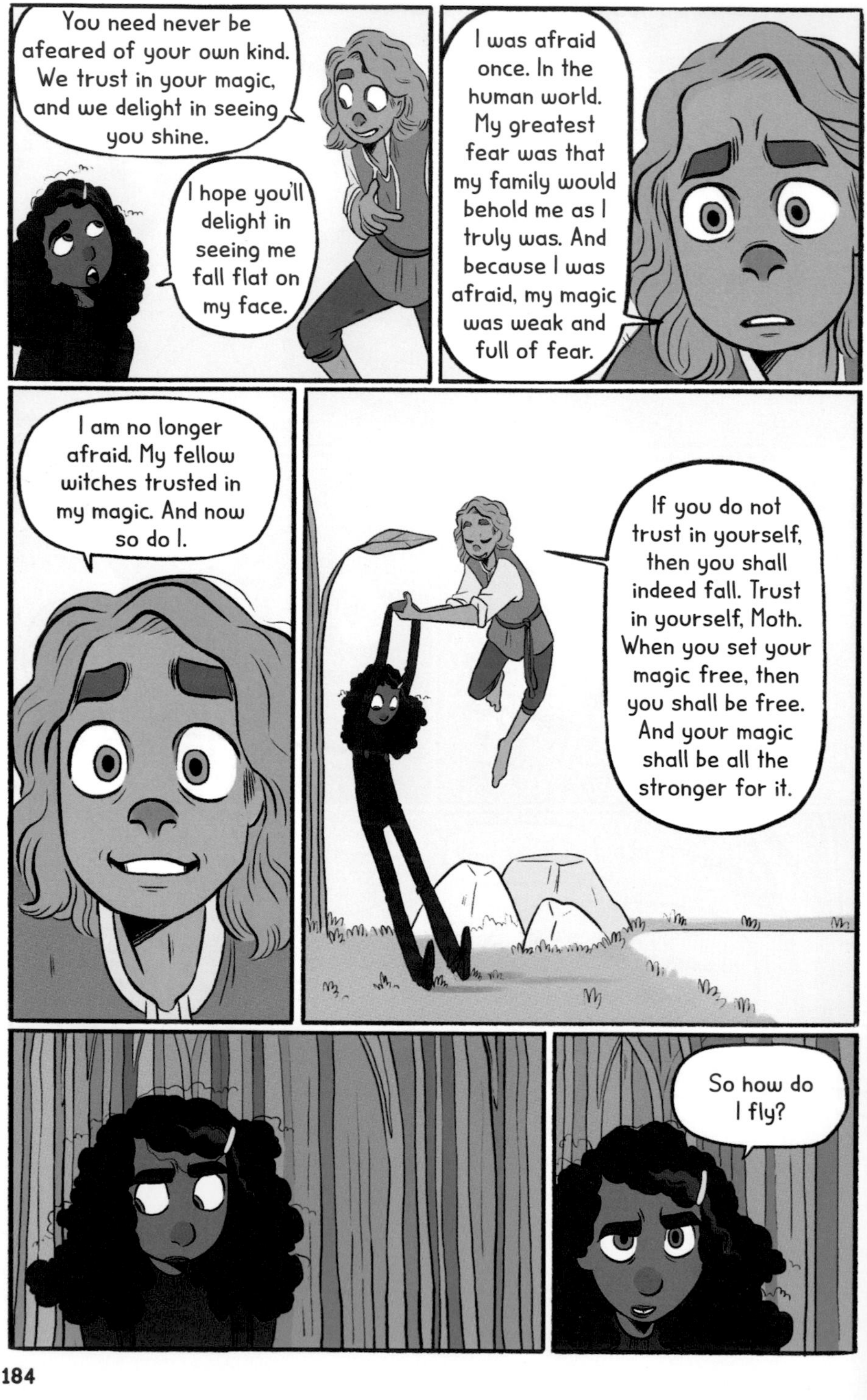
You need never be afeared of your own kind. We trust in your magic, and we delight in seeing you shine.
I hope you'll delight in seeing me fall flat on my face.
I was afraid once. In the human world. My greatest fear was that my family would behold me as I truly was. And because I was afraid, my magic was weak and full of fear.
I am no longer afraid. My fellow witches trusted in my magic. And now so do I.
If you do not trust in yourself, then you shall indeed fall. Trust in yourself, Moth. When you set your magic free, then you shall be free. And your magic shall be all the stronger for it.
So how do I fly?

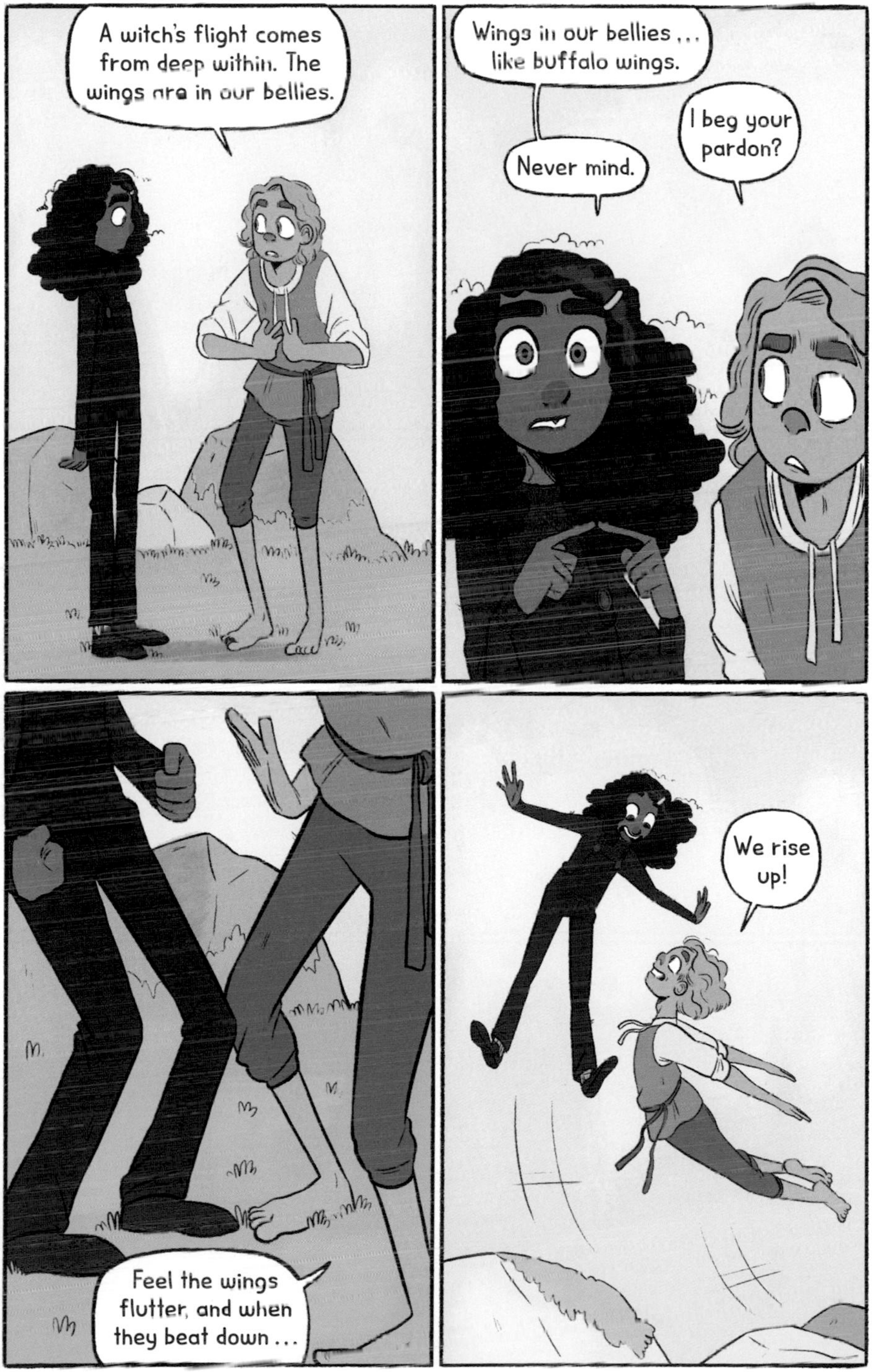
A witch's flight comes from deep within. The wings are in our bellies.
Wings in our bellies . . . like buffalo wings.
I beg your pardon?
Never mind.
Feel the wings flutter, and when they beat down . . .
We rise up!

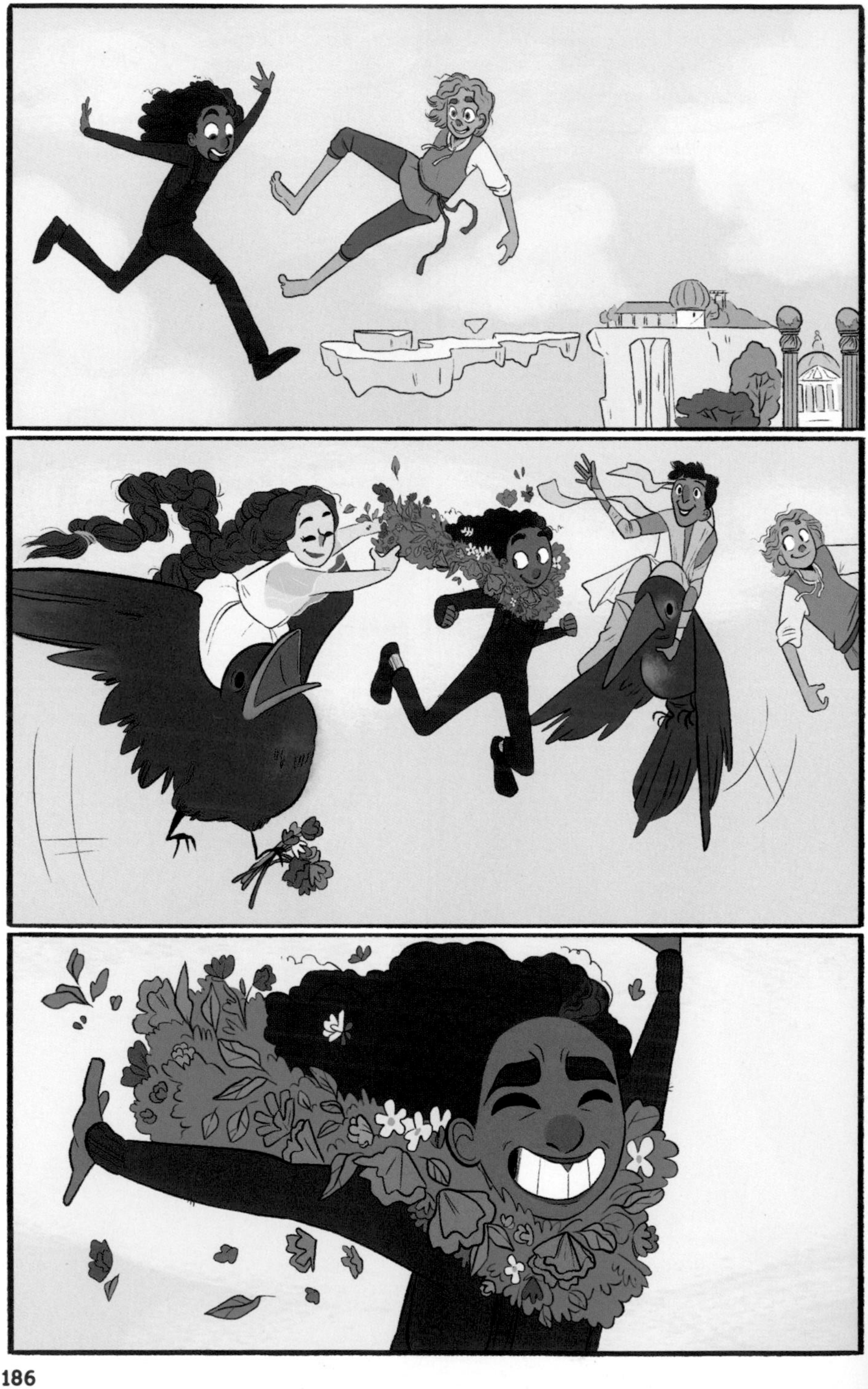

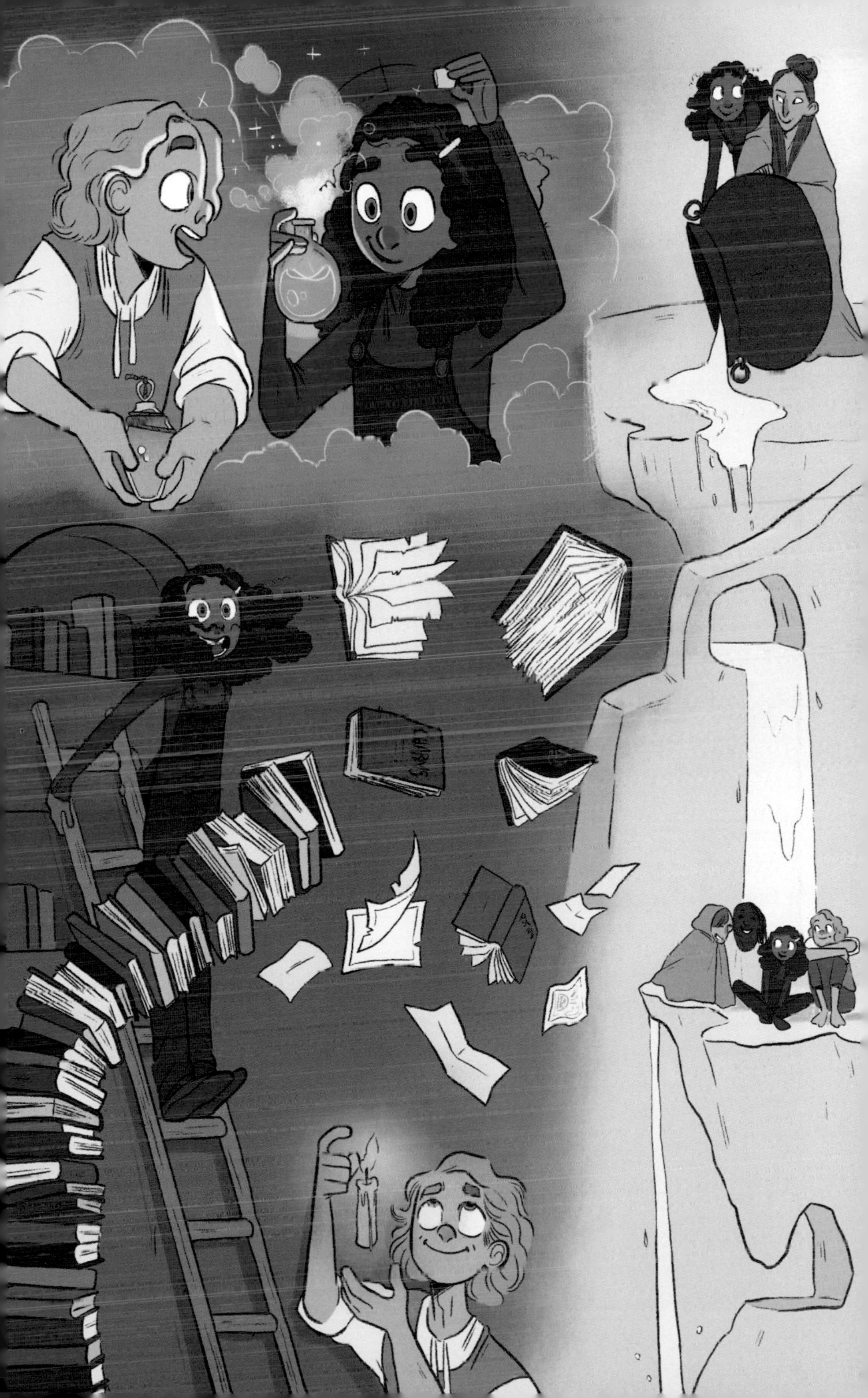

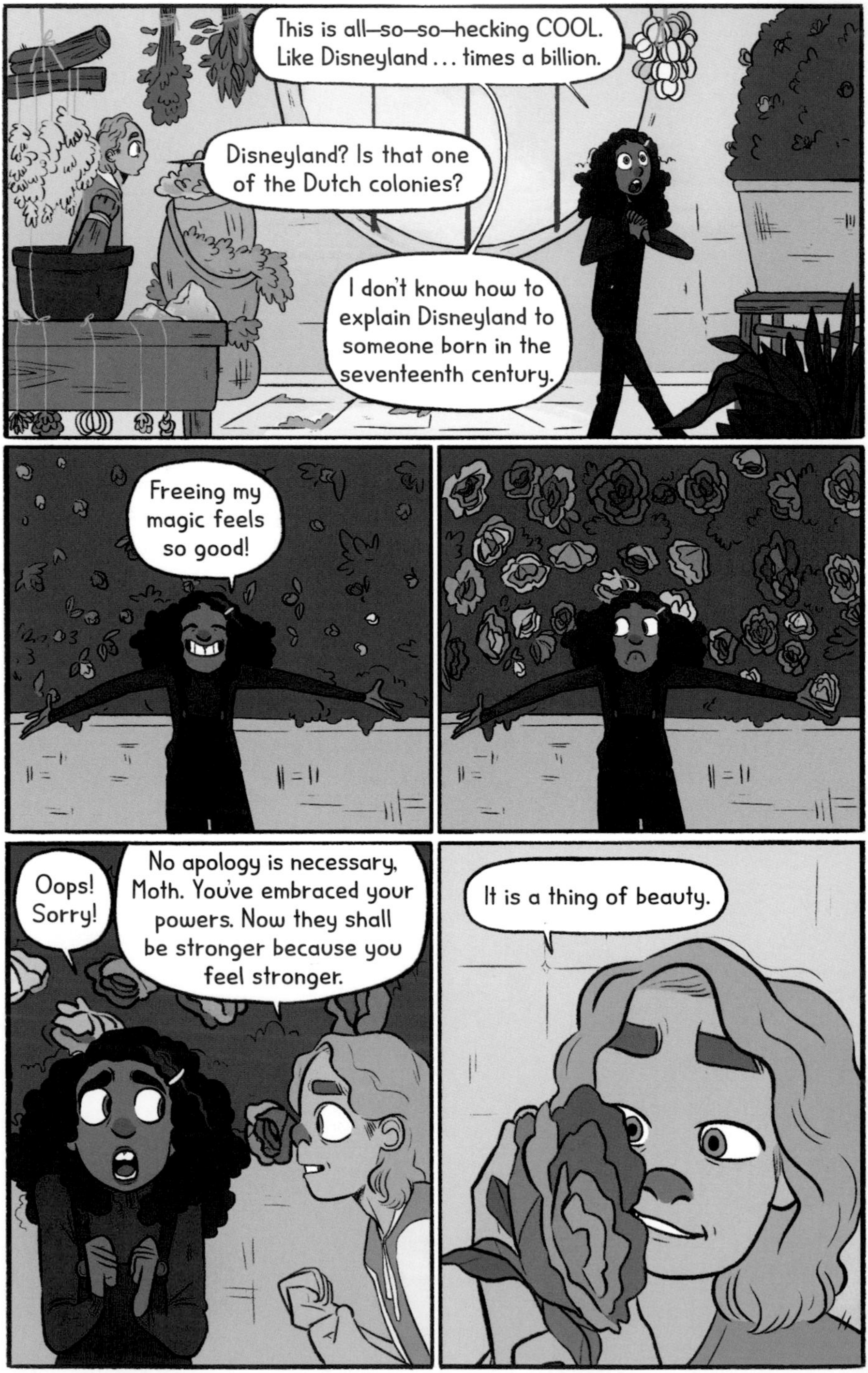
This is all—so—so—hecking COOL. Like Disneyland . . . times a billion.
Disneyland? Is that one of the Dutch colonies?
I don't know how to explain Disneyland to someone born in the seventeenth century.
Freeing my magic feels so good!
Oops! Sorry!
No apology is necessary, Moth. You've embraced your powers. Now they shall be stronger because you feel stronger.
It is a thing of beauty.

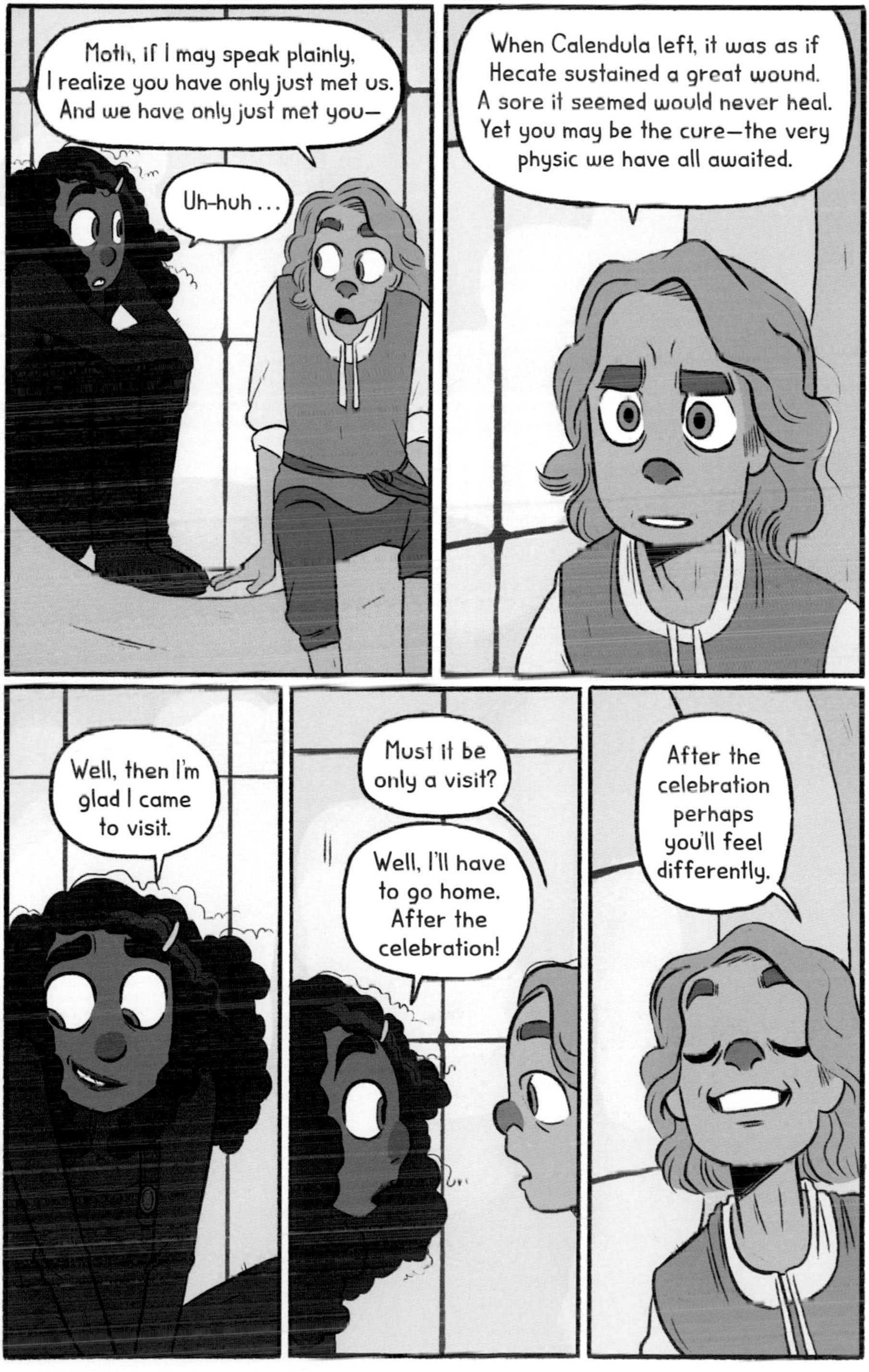
Moth, if I may speak plainly, I realize you have only just met us. And we have only just met you—
Uh-huh . . .
When Calendula left, it was as if Hecate sustained a great wound. A sore it seemed would never heal. Yet you may be the cure—the very physic we have all awaited.
Well, then I'm glad I came to visit.
Must it be only a visit?
Well, I'll have to go home. After the celebration!
After the celebration perhaps you'll feel differently.

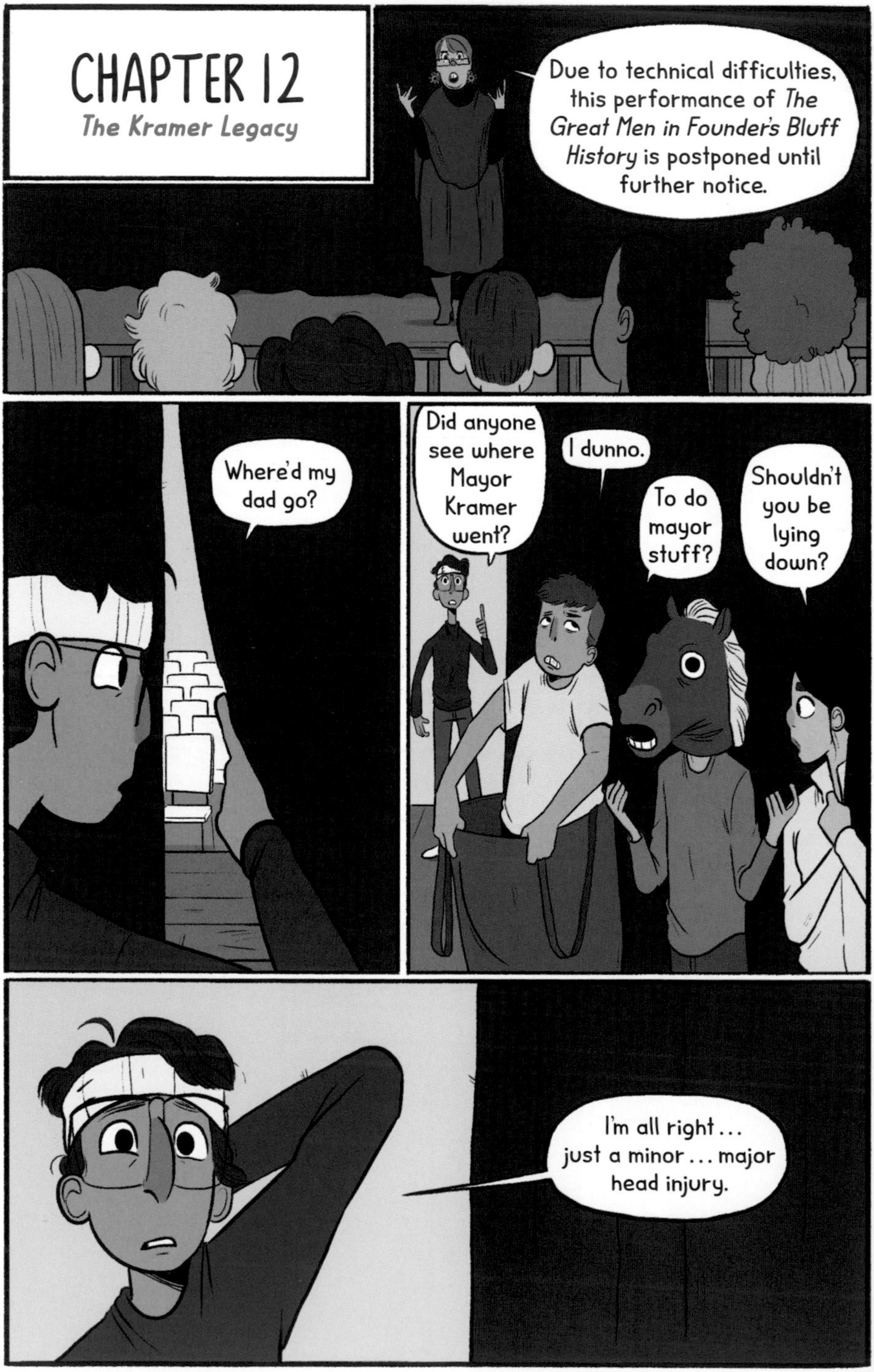
CHAPTER 12
The Kramer Legacy
Due to technical difficulties, this performance of The Great Men in Founder's Bluff History is postponed until further notice.
Where'd my dad go?
Did anyone see where Mayor Kramer went?
I dunno.
To do mayor stuff?
Shouldn't you be lying down?
I'm all right . . . just a minor . . . major head injury.

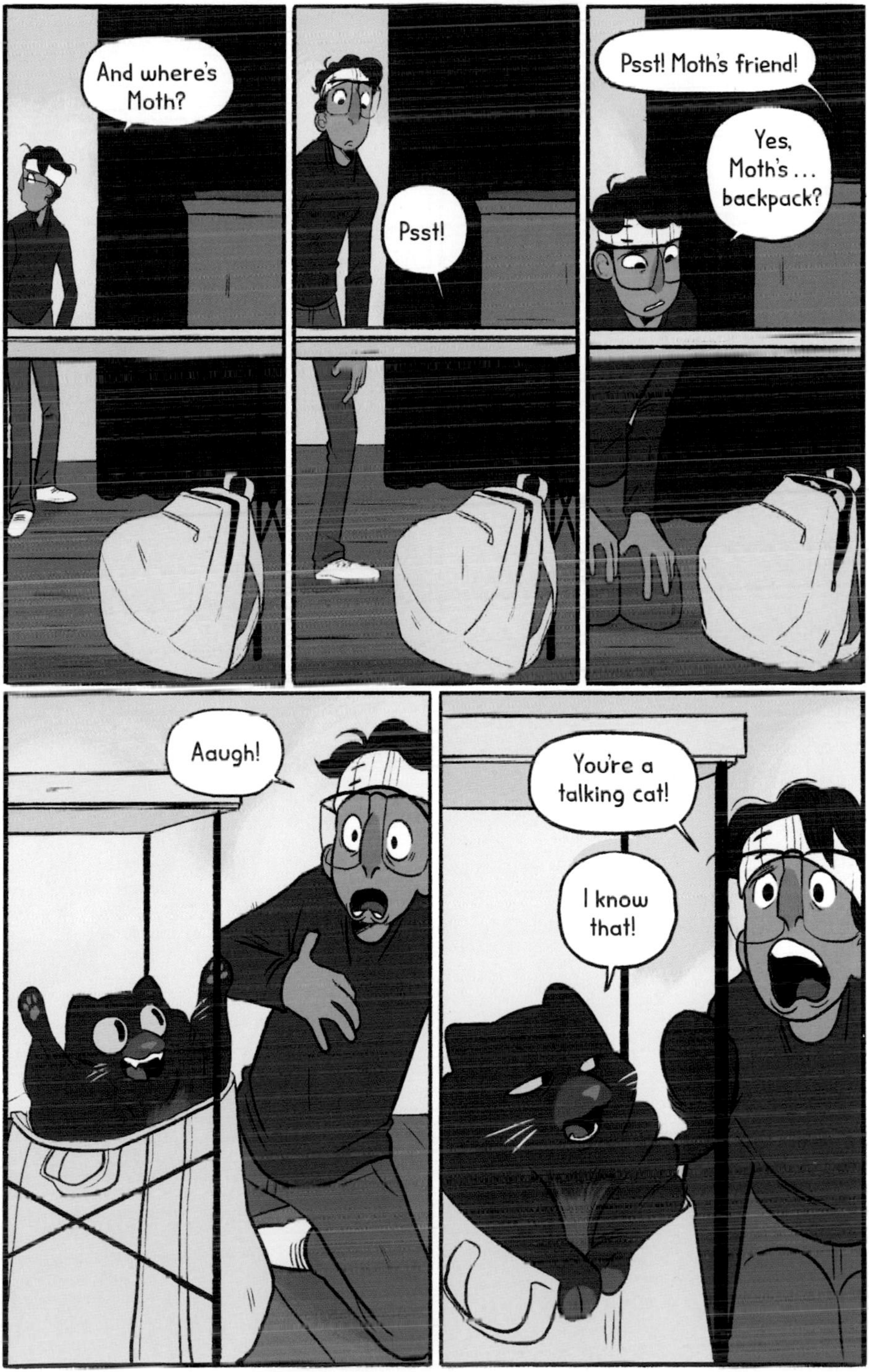
And where's Moth?
Psst!
Psst! Moth's friend!
Yes, Moth's . . . backpack?
Aaugh!
You're a talking cat!
I know that!

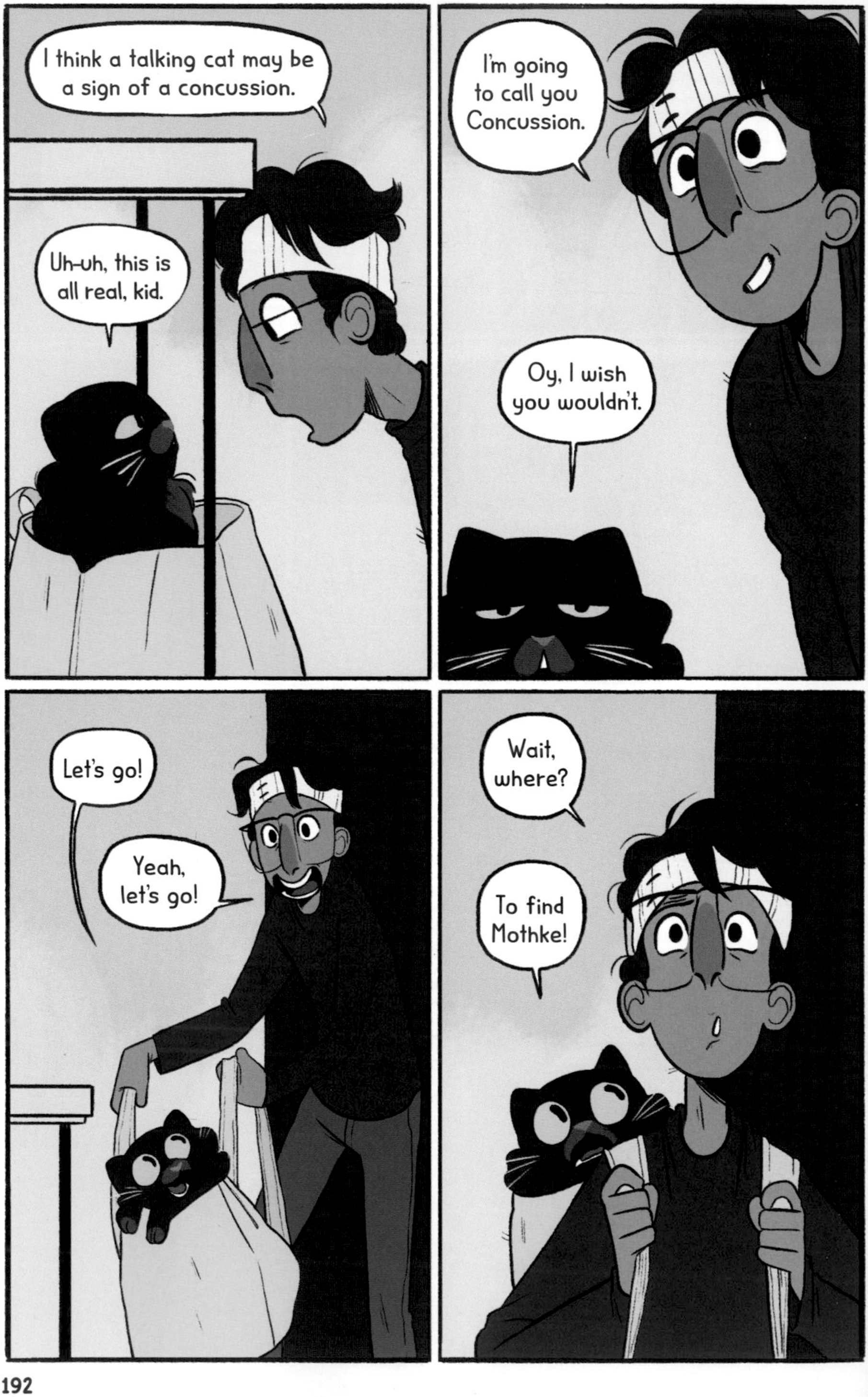
I think a talking cat may be a sign of a concussion.
Uh-uh, this is all real, kid.
I'm going to call you Concussion.
Oy, I wish you wouldn't.
Let's go!
Yeah, let's go!
Wait, where?
To find Mothke!

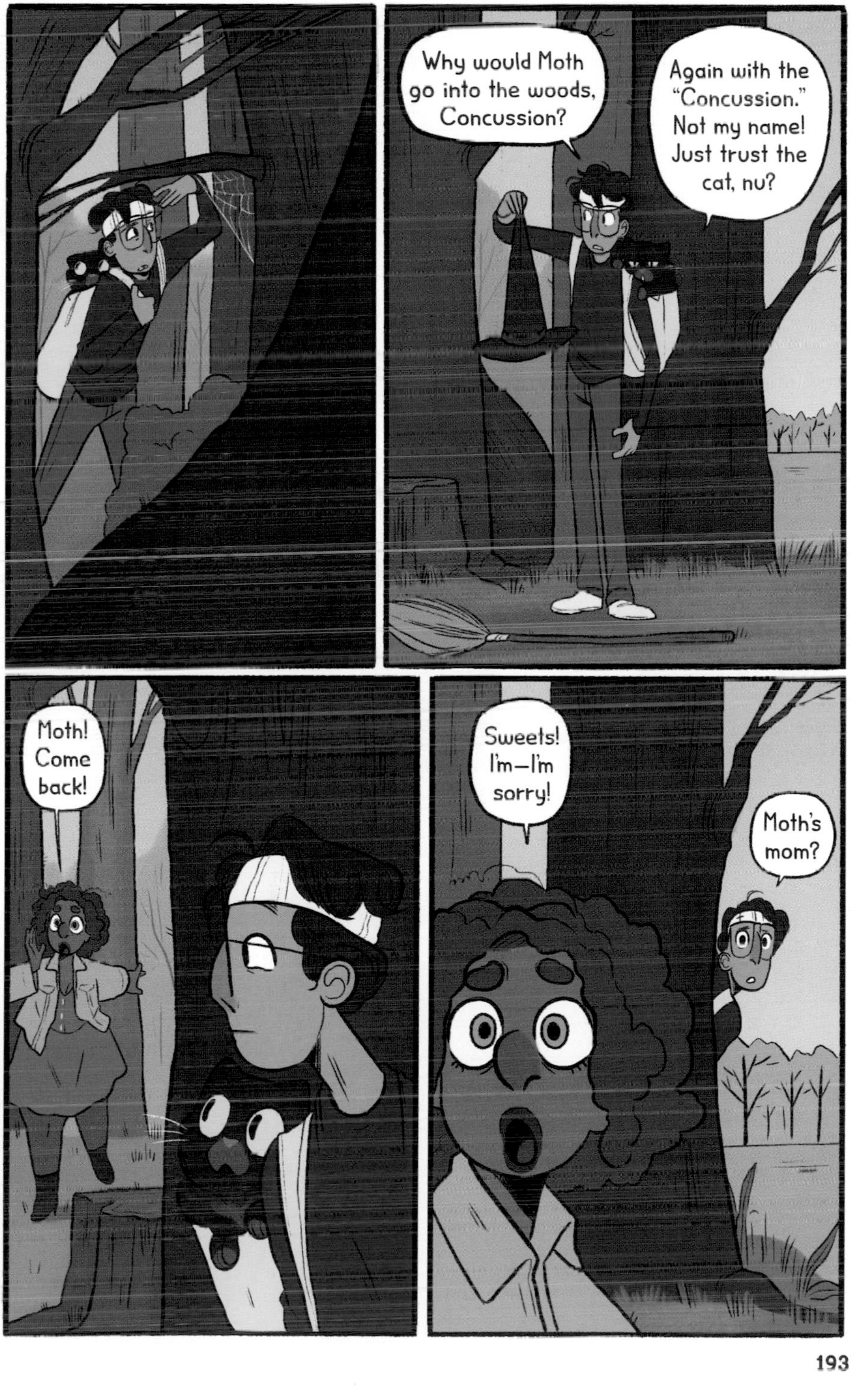
Why would Moth go into the woods, Concussion?
Again with the "Concussion." Not my name! Just trust the cat, nu?
Moth! Come back!
Sweets! I'm—I'm sorry!
Moth's mom?

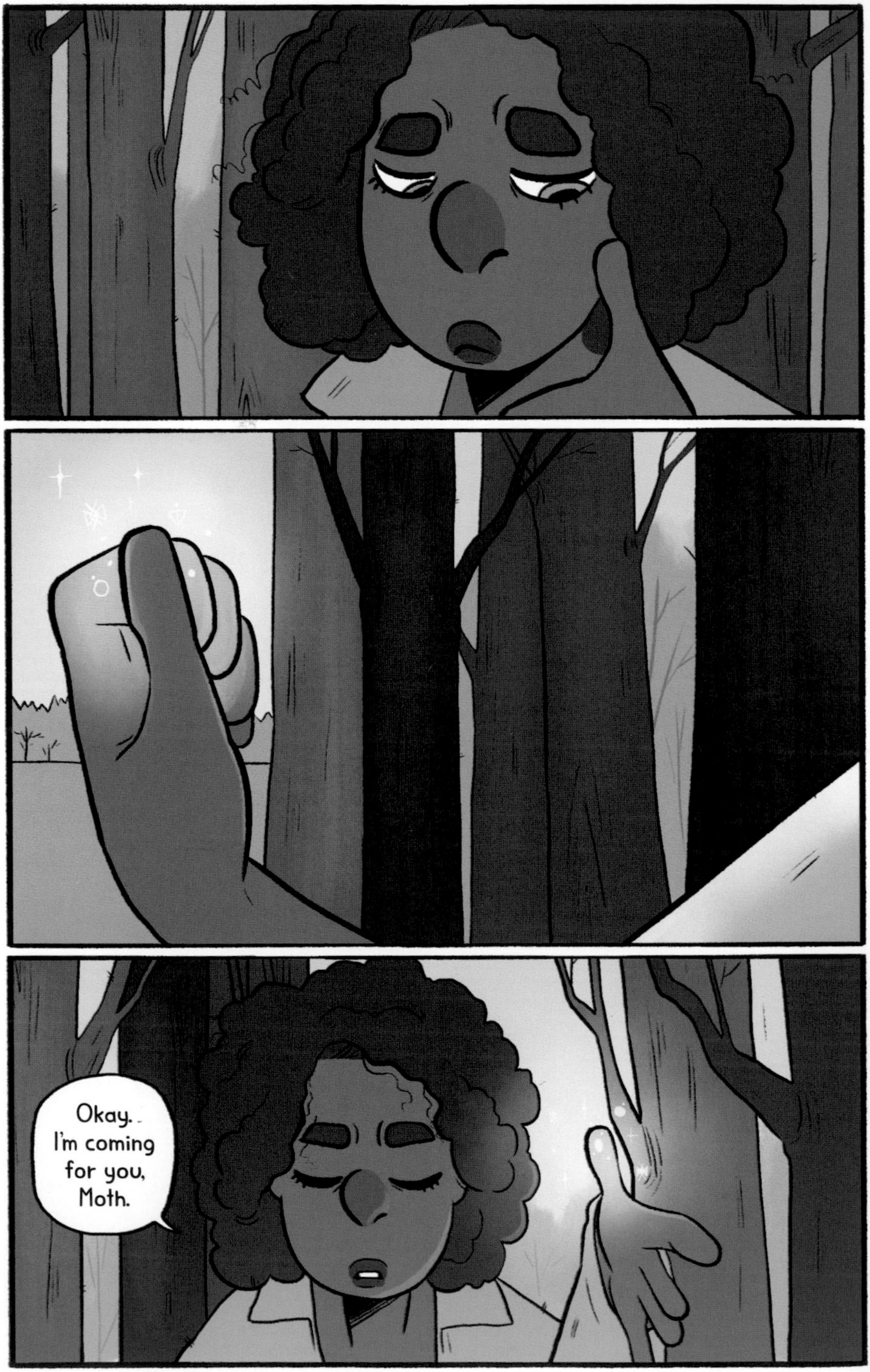
Okay. I'm coming for you, Moth.

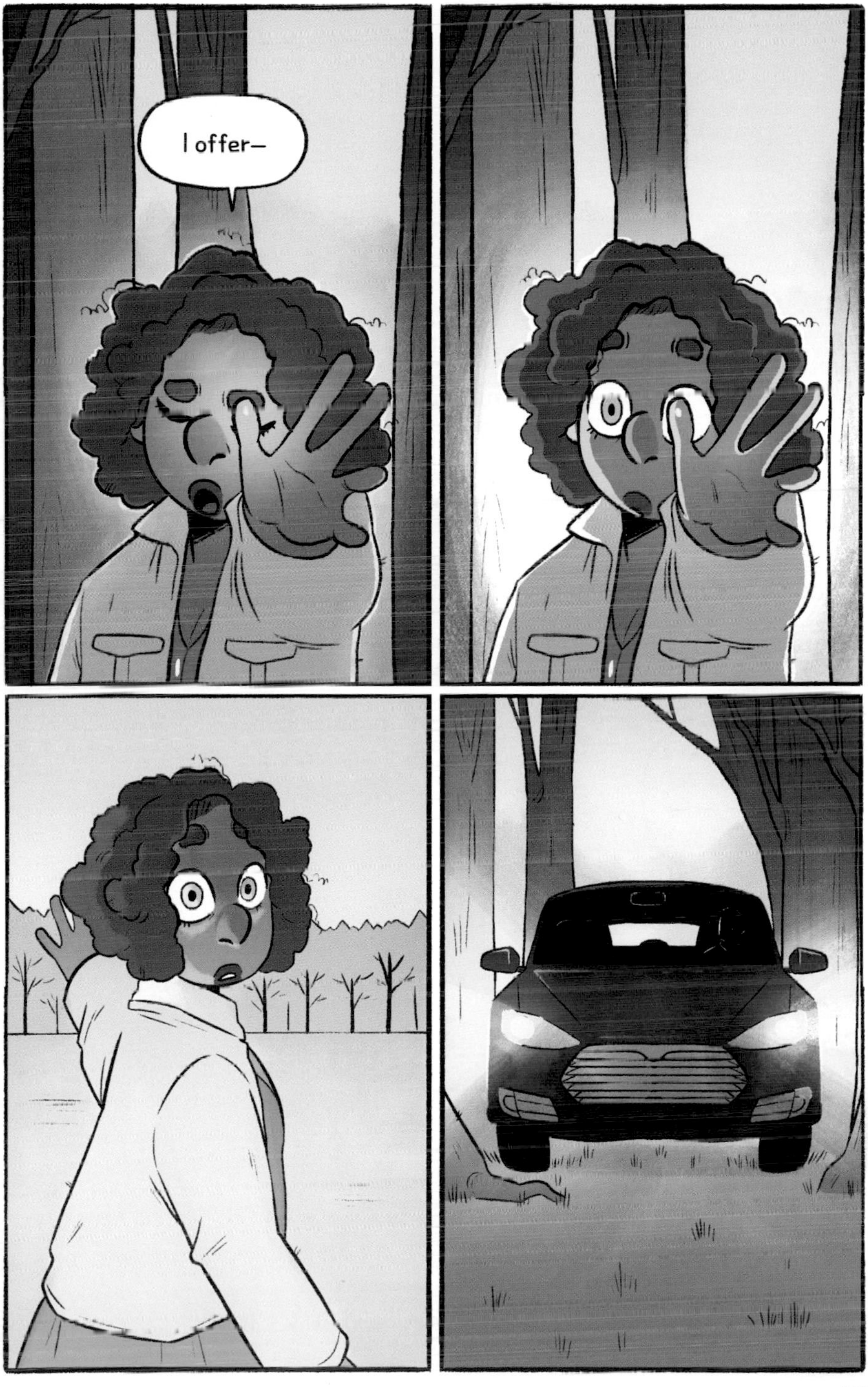
I offer–

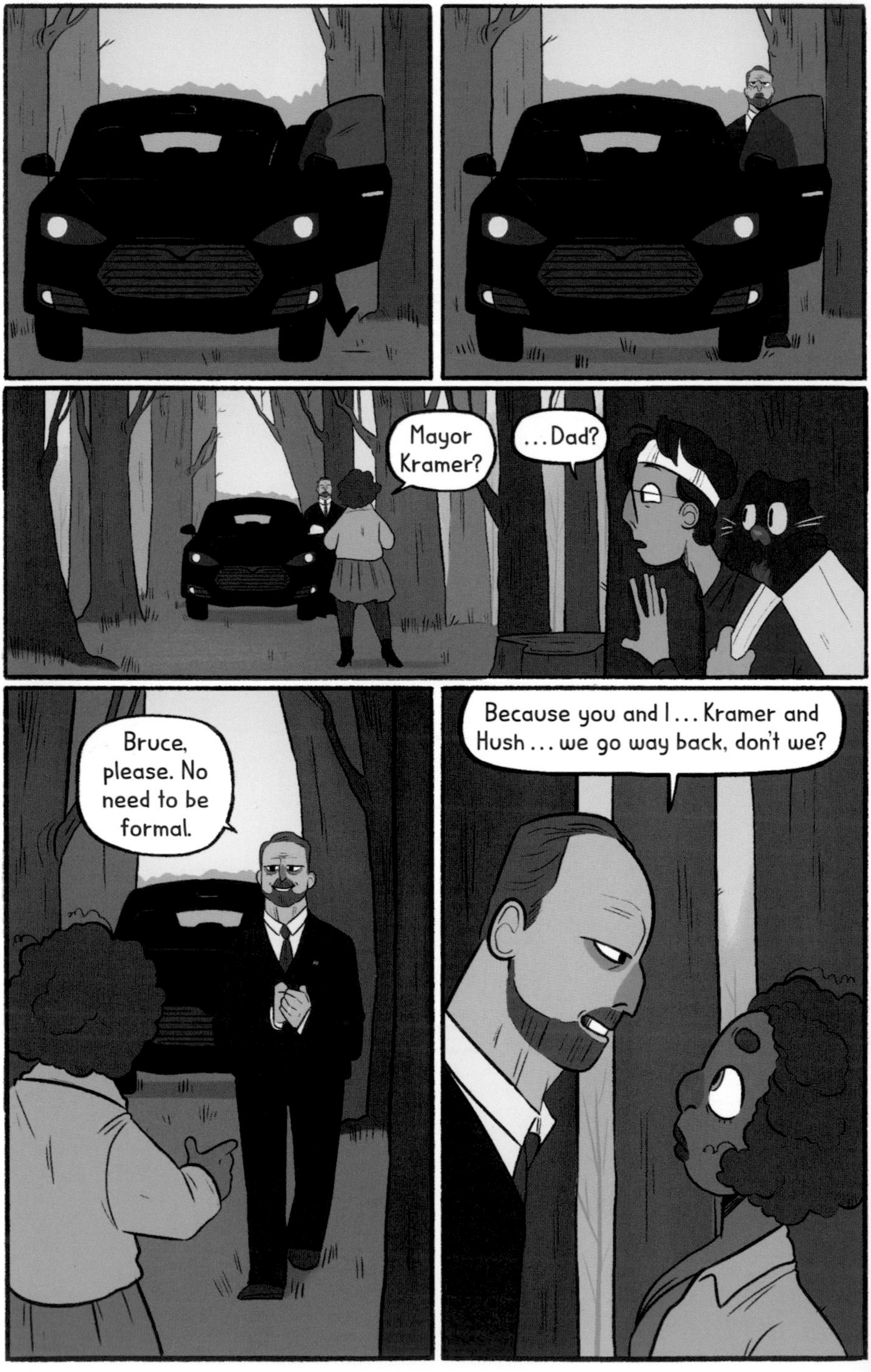
Mayor Kramer?
...Dad?
Bruce, please. No need to be formal.
Because you and I... Kramer and Hush... we go way back, don't we?

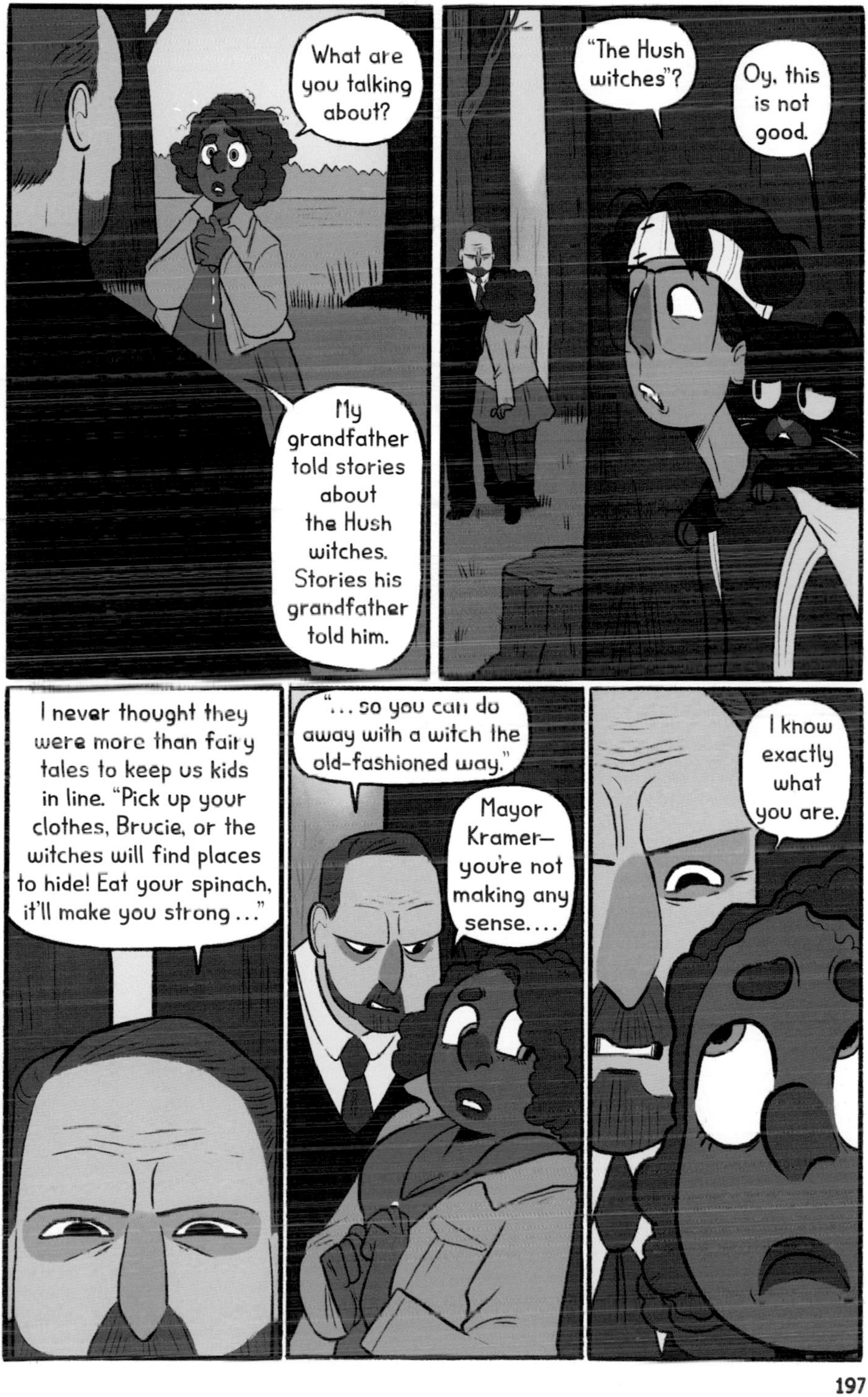
What are you talking about?
My grandfather told stories about the Hush witches. Stories his grandfather told him.
"The Hush witches"?
Oy, this is not good.
I never thought they were more than fairy tales to keep us kids in line. "Pick up your clothes, Brucie, or the witches will find places to hide! Eat your spinach, it'll make you strong . . ."
". . . so you can do away with a witch the old-fashioned way."
Mayor Kramer— you're not making any sense. . . .
I know exactly what you are.

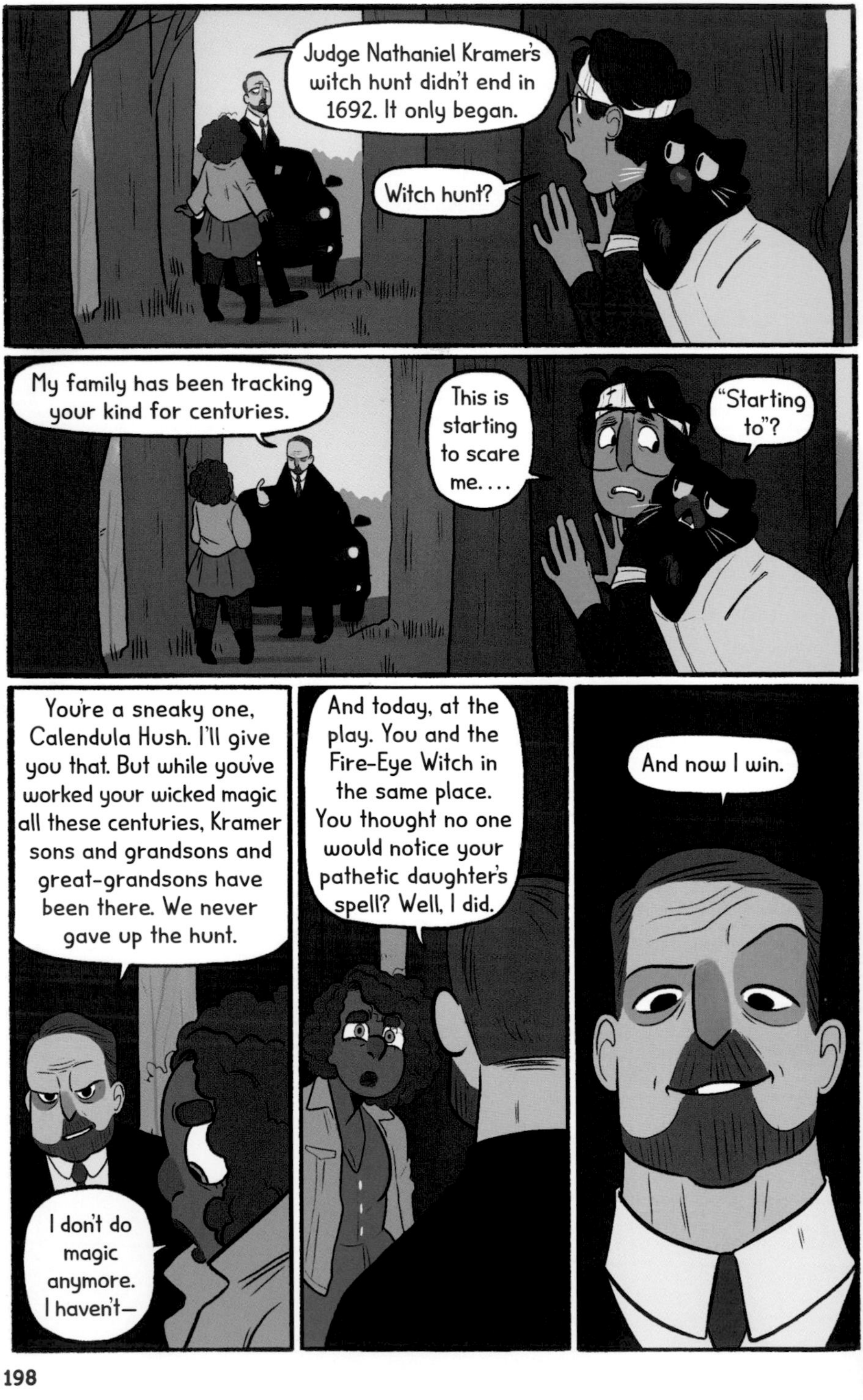
Judge Nathaniel Kramer's witch hunt didn't end in 1692. It only began.
Witch hunt?
My family has been tracking your kind for centuries.
This is starting to scare me. . . .
"Starting to"?
You're a sneaky one, Calendula Hush. I'll give you that. But while you've worked your wicked magic all these centuries, Kramer sons and grandsons and great-grandsons have been there. We never gave up the hunt.
I don't do magic anymore. I haven't—
And today, at the play. You and the Fire-Eye Witch in the same place. You thought no one would notice your pathetic daughter's spell? Well, I did.
And now I win.

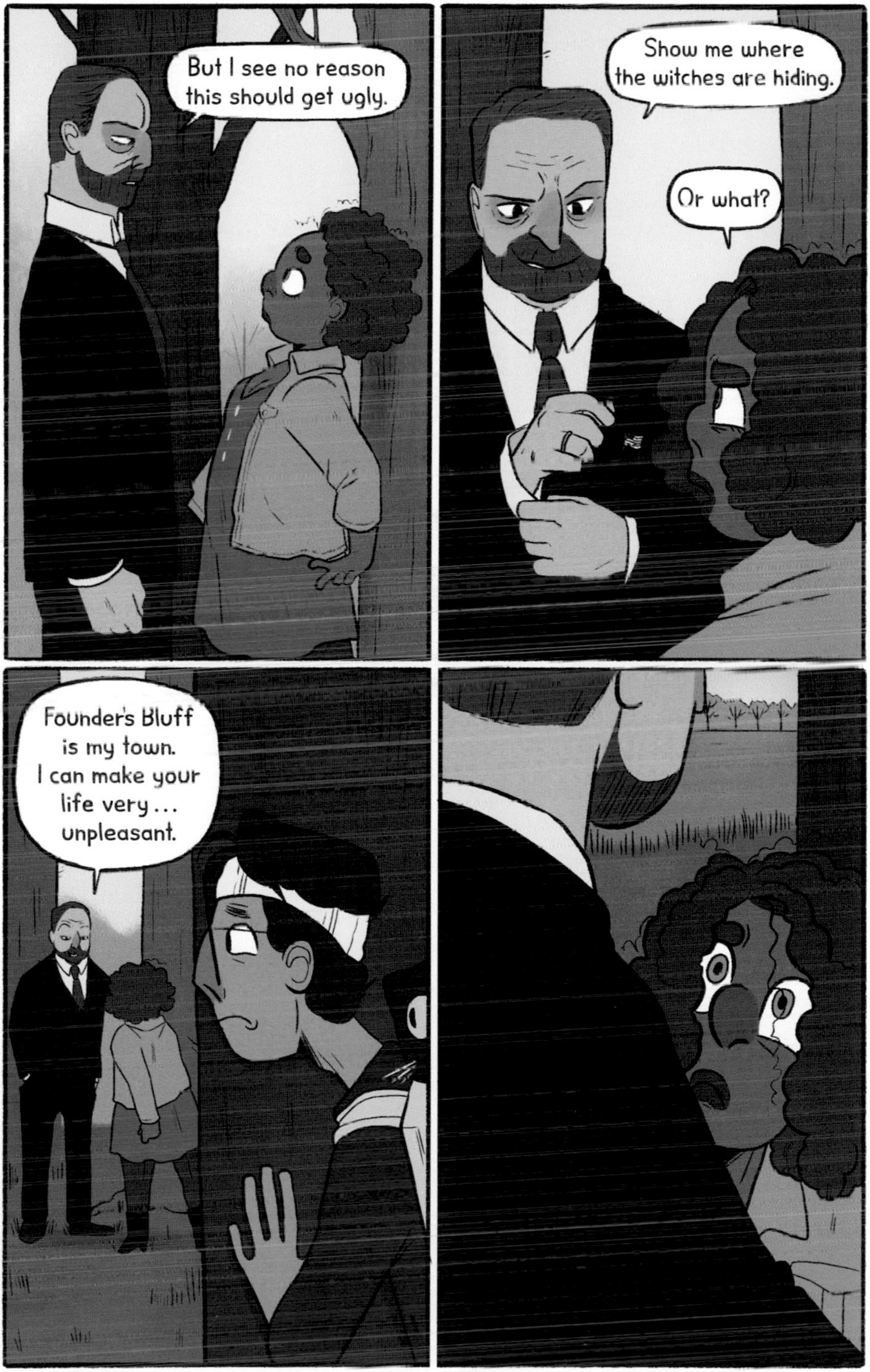
But I see no reason this should get ugly.
Show me where the witches are hiding.
Or what?
Founder's Bluff is my town. I can make your life very . . . unpleasant.

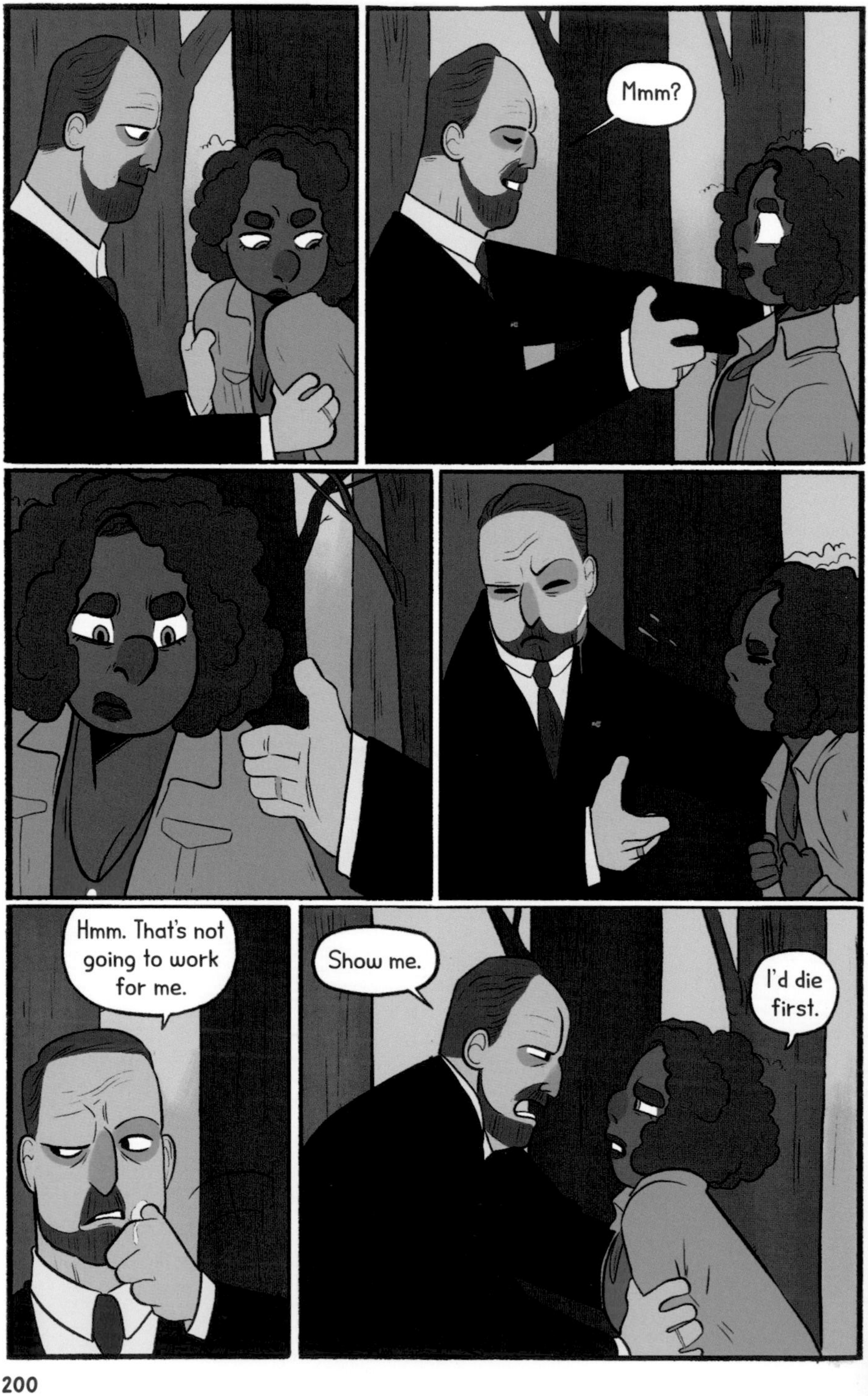
Mmm?
Hmm. That's not going to work for me.
Show me.
I'd die first.

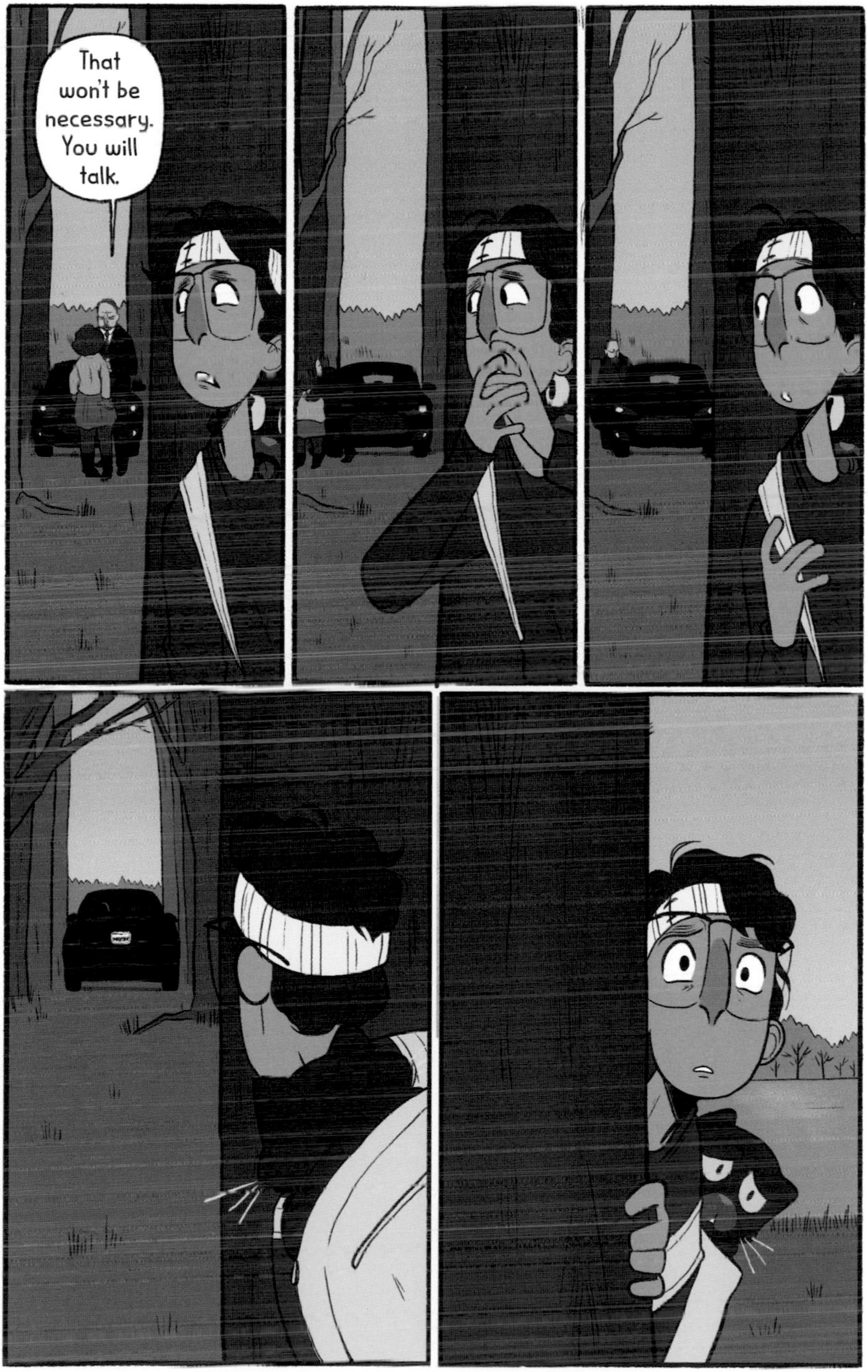
That won't be necessary. You will talk.

CHAPTER 13
Moth's Choice

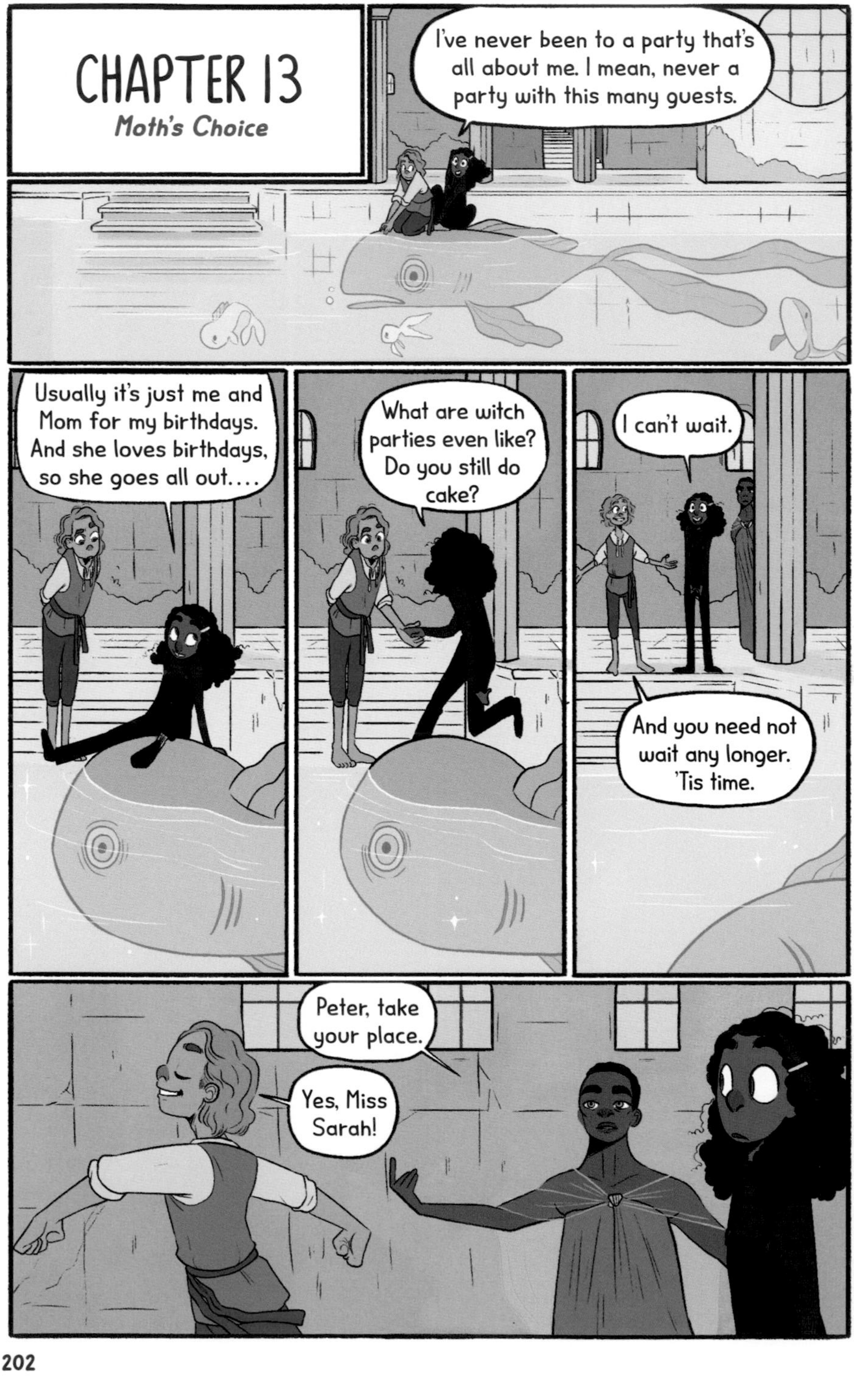

I've never been to a party that's all about me. I mean, never a party with this many guests.
Usually it's just me and Mom for my birthdays. And she loves birthdays, so she goes all out....
What are witch parties even like? Do you still do cake?
I can't wait.
And you need not wait any longer. 'Tis time.
Peter, take your place.
Yes, Miss Sarah!

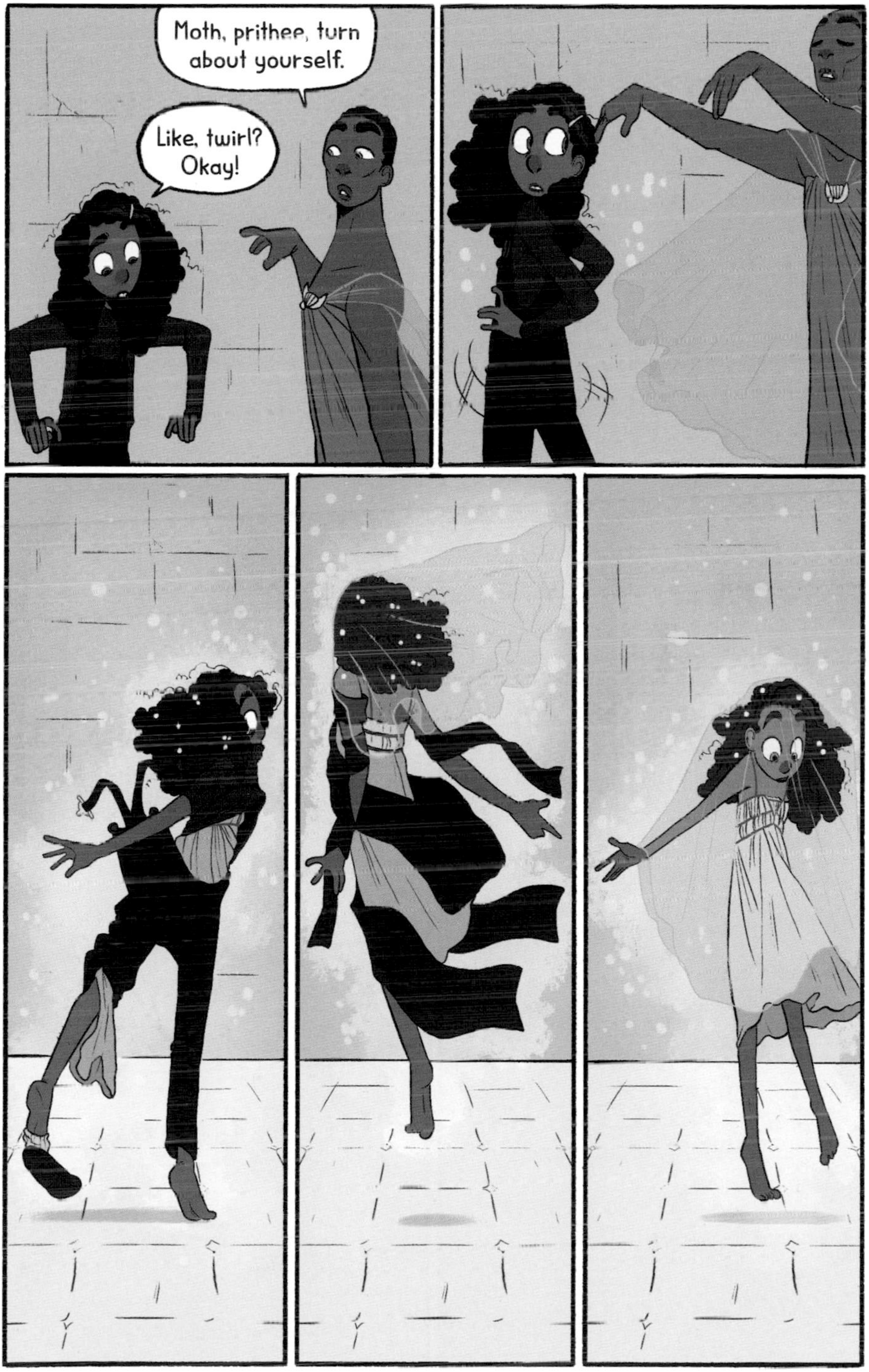
Moth, prithee, turn about yourself.
Like, twirl? Okay!

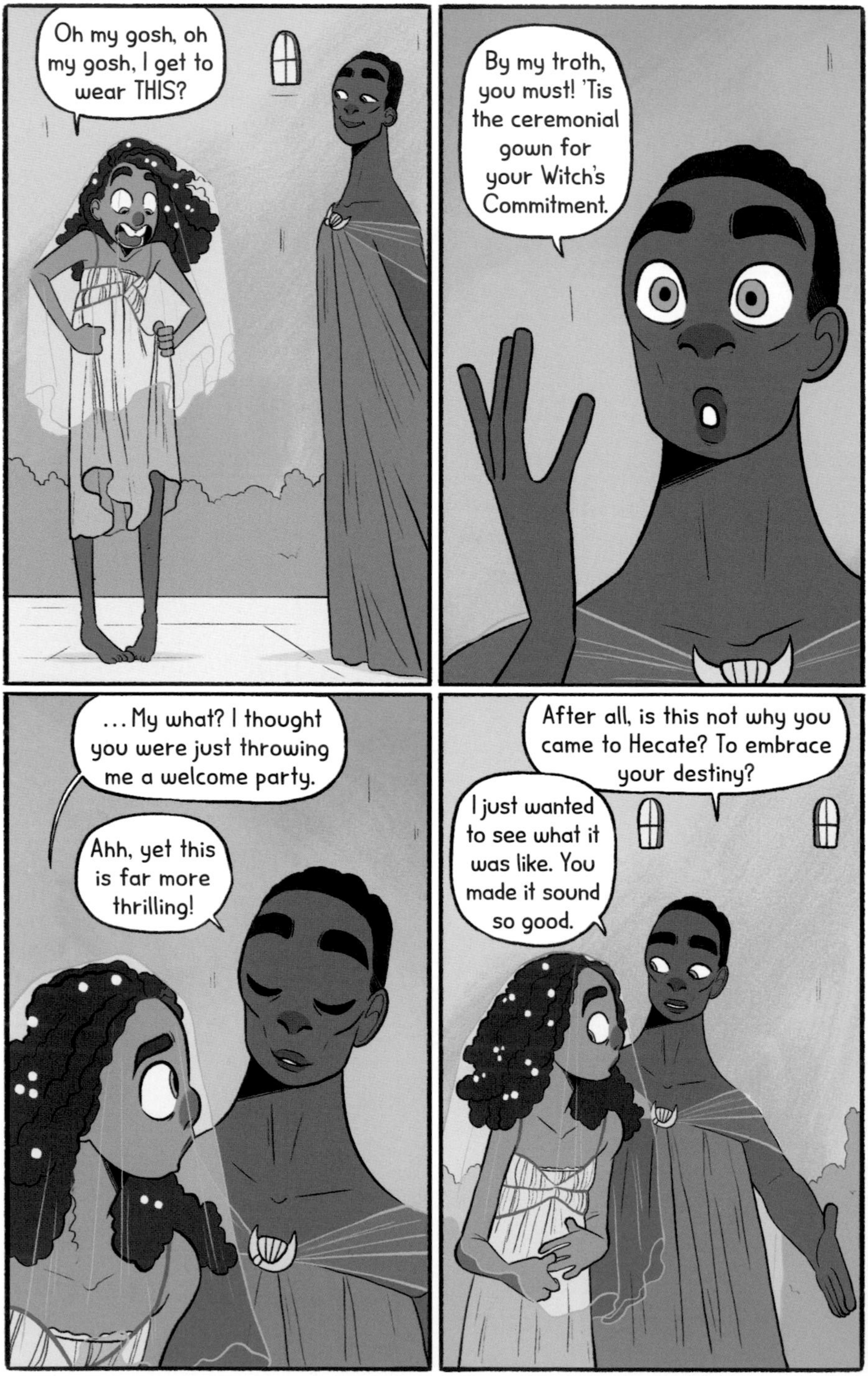
Oh my gosh, oh my gosh, I get to wear THIS?
By my troth, you must! 'Tis the ceremonial gown for your Witch's Commitment.
. . . My what? I thought you were just throwing me a welcome party.
Ahh, yet this is far more thrilling!
After all, is this not why you came to Hecate? To embrace your destiny?
I just wanted to see what it was like. You made it sound so good.

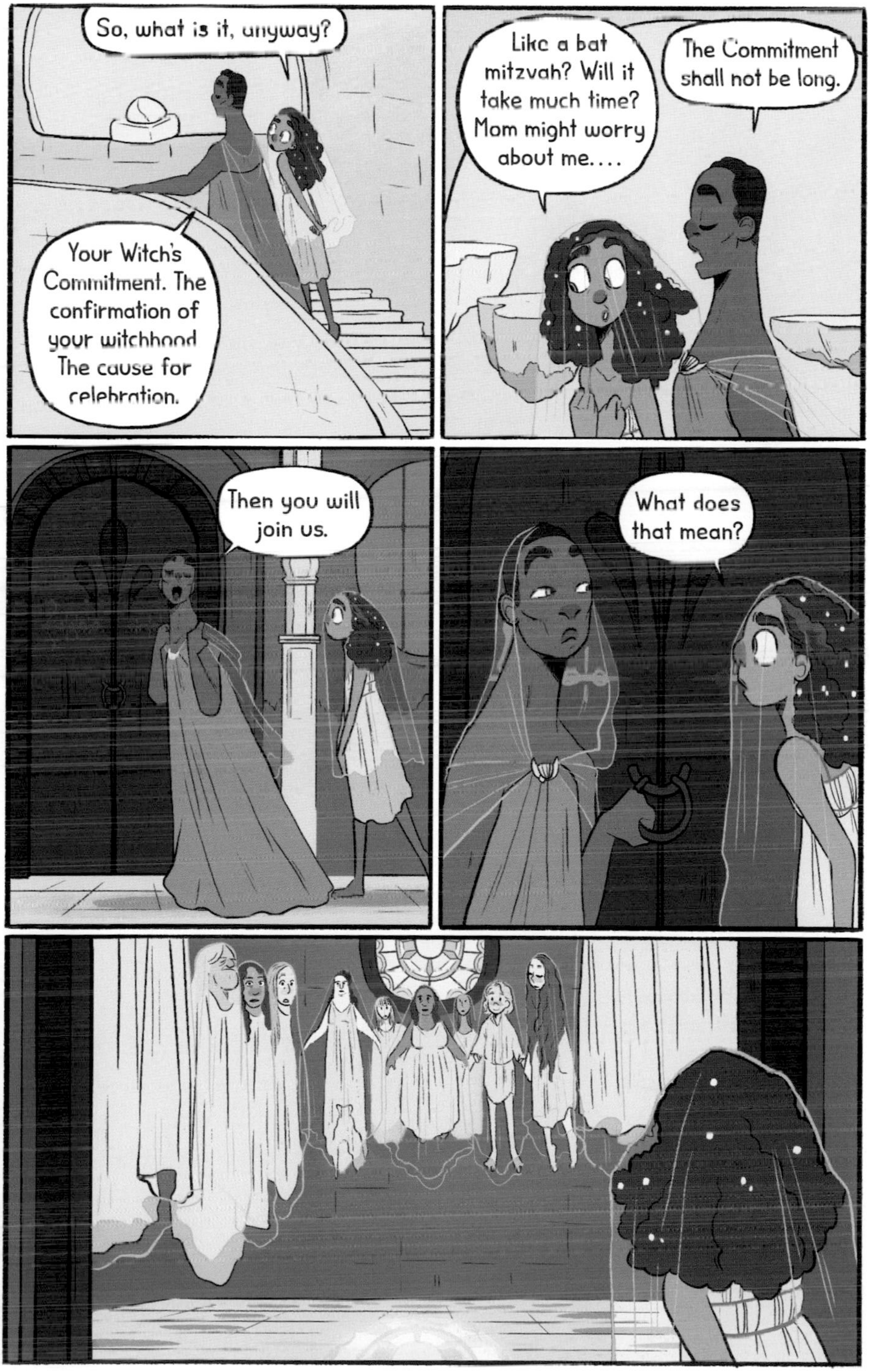
So, what is it, anyway?
Your Witch's Commitment. The confirmation of your witchhood The cause for celebration.
Like a bat mitzvah? Will it take much time? Mom might worry about me....
The Commitment shall not be long.
Then you will join us.
What does that mean?

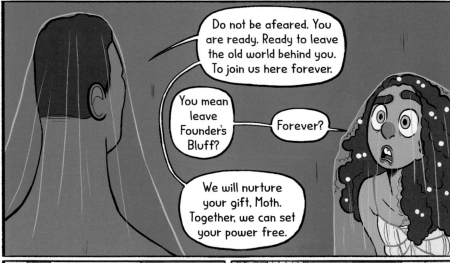

Do not be afeared. You are ready. Ready to leave the old world behind you. To join us here forever.

You mean leave Founder's Bluff?

Forever?

We will nurture your gift, Moth. Together, we can set your power free.

Oh, you look just like your mother at her Commitment...

Only you will be a good witch.

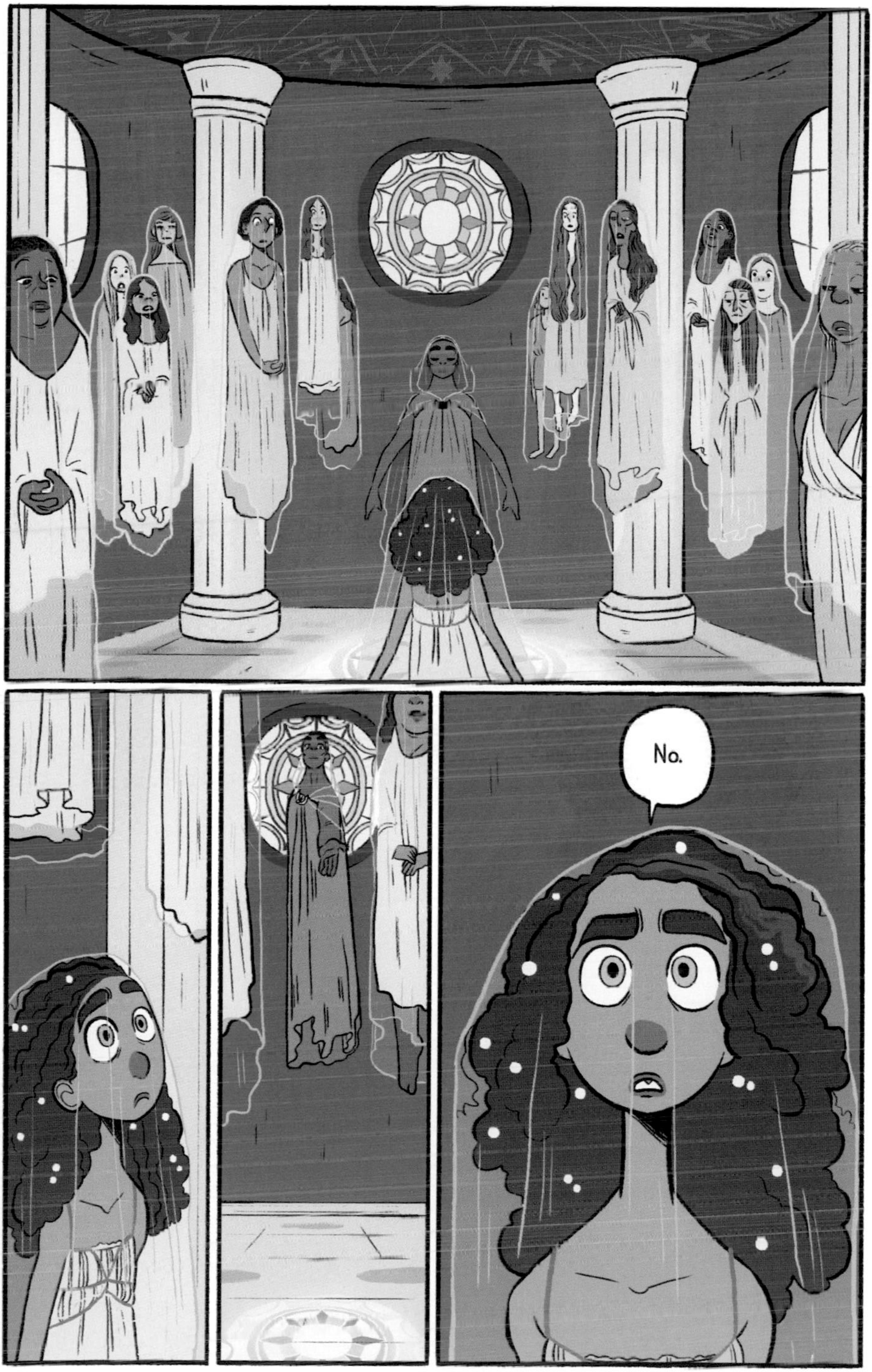
No.

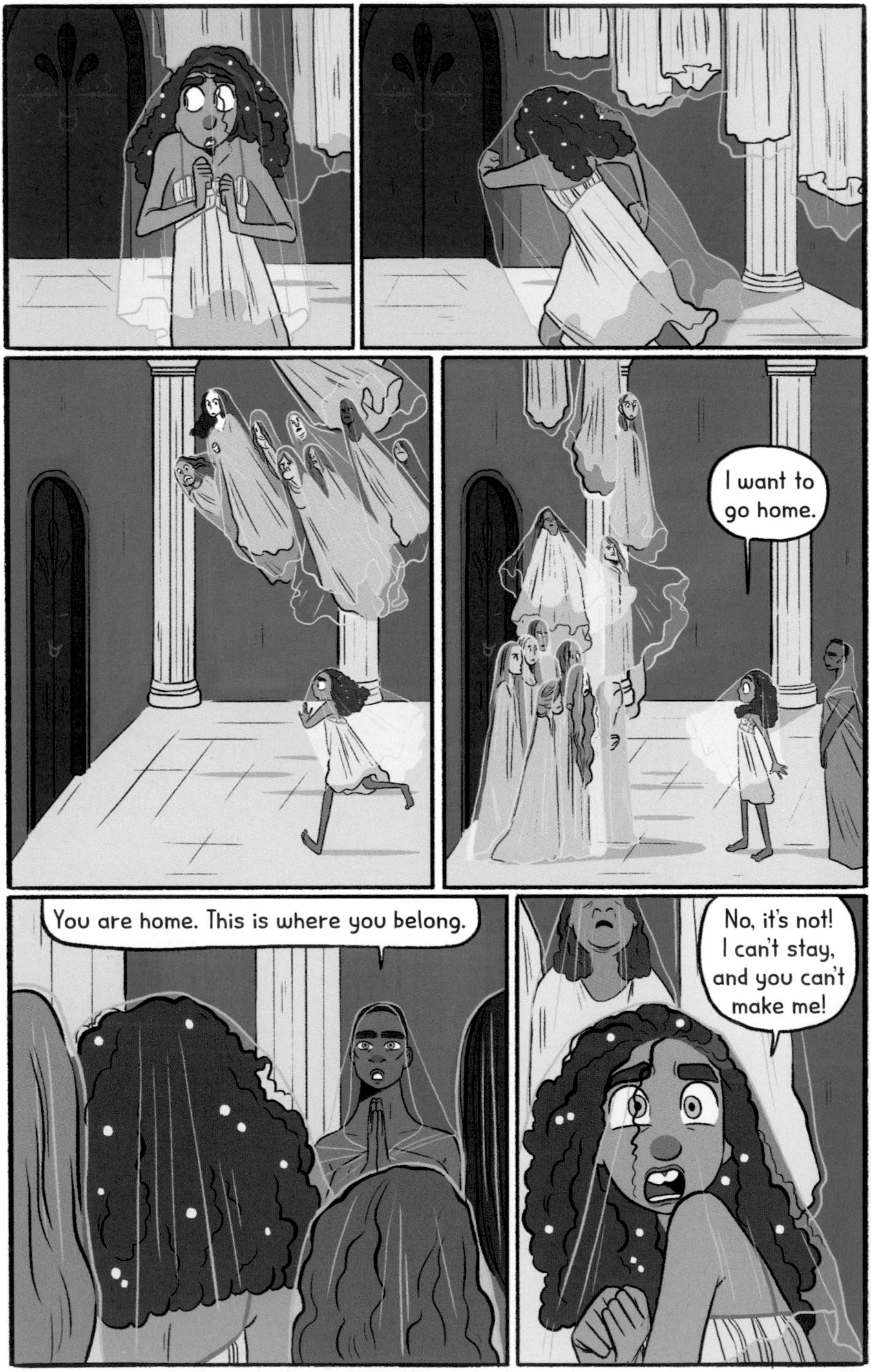
I want to go home.
You are home. This is where you belong.
No, it's not! I can't stay, and you can't make me!

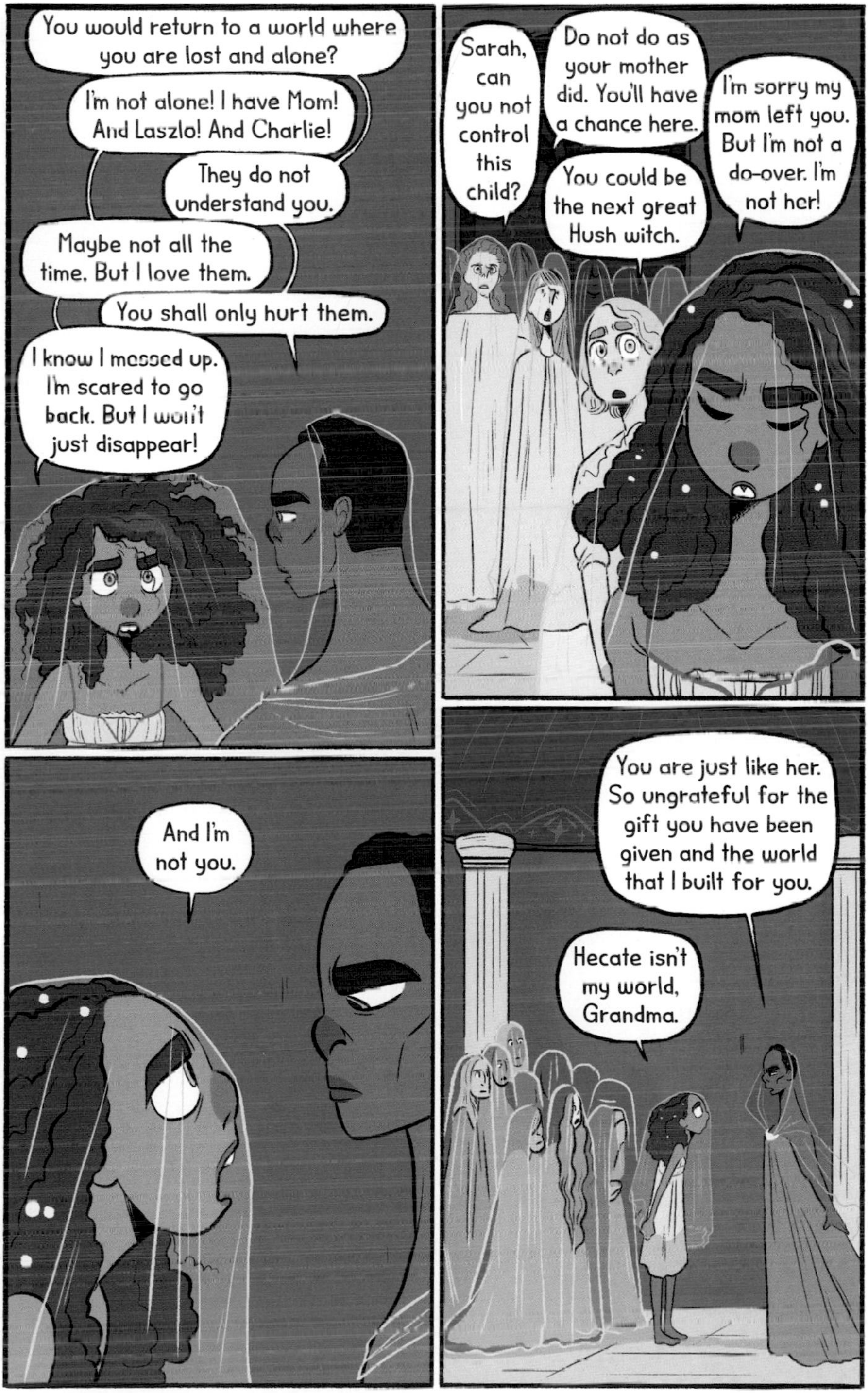
You would return to a world where you are lost and alone?
I'm not alone! I have Mom! And Laszlo! And Charlie!
They do not understand you.
Maybe not all the time. But I love them.
You shall only hurt them.
I know I messed up. I'm scared to go back. But I won't just disappear!
Sarah, can you not control this child?
Do not do as your mother did. You'll have a chance here.
You could be the next great Hush witch.
I'm sorry my mom left you. But I'm not a do-over. I'm not her!
And I'm not you.
You are just like her. So ungrateful for the gift you have been given and the world that I built for you.
Hecate isn't my world, Grandma.

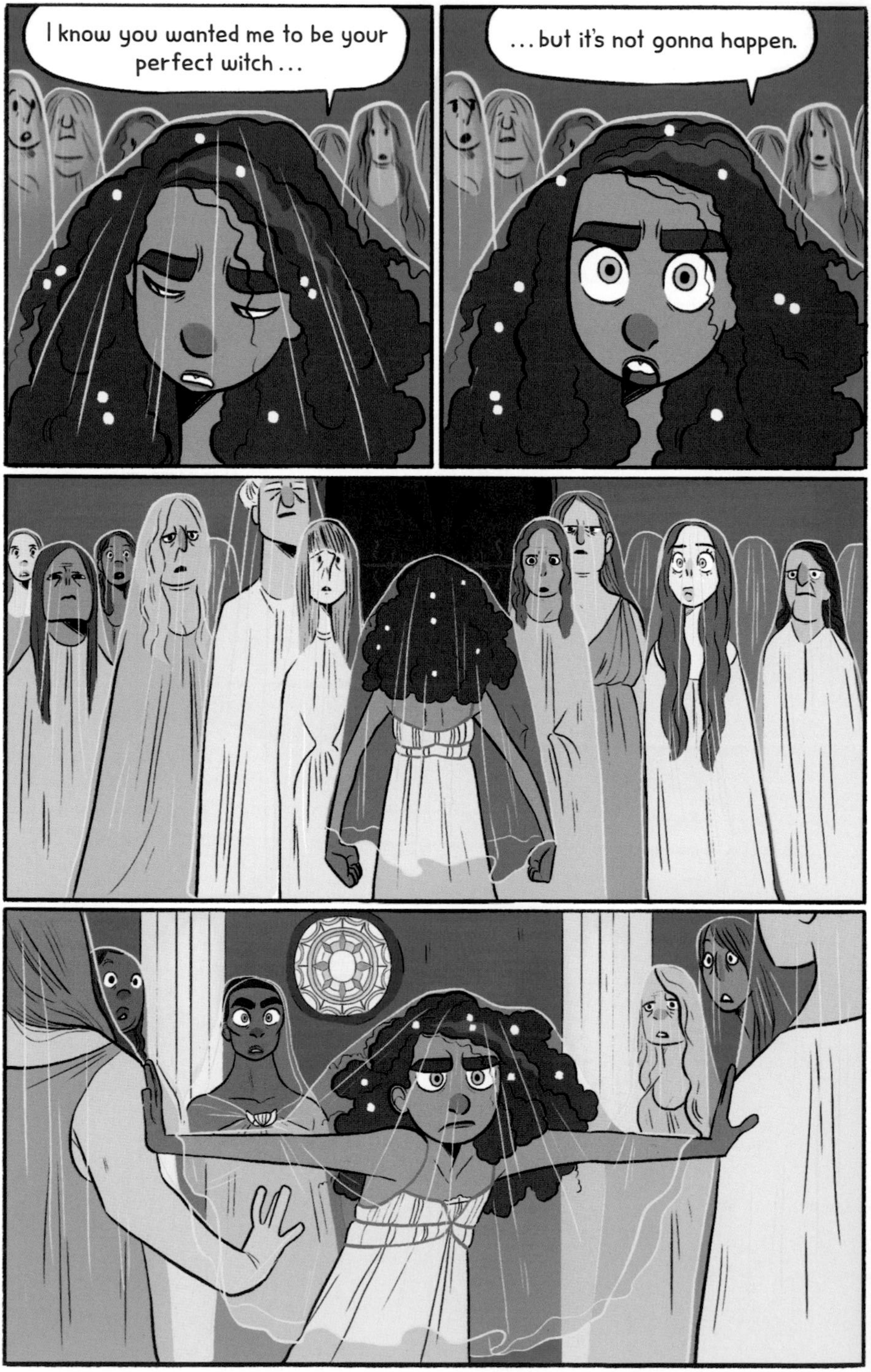
I know you wanted me to be your perfect witch...
...but it's not gonna happen.

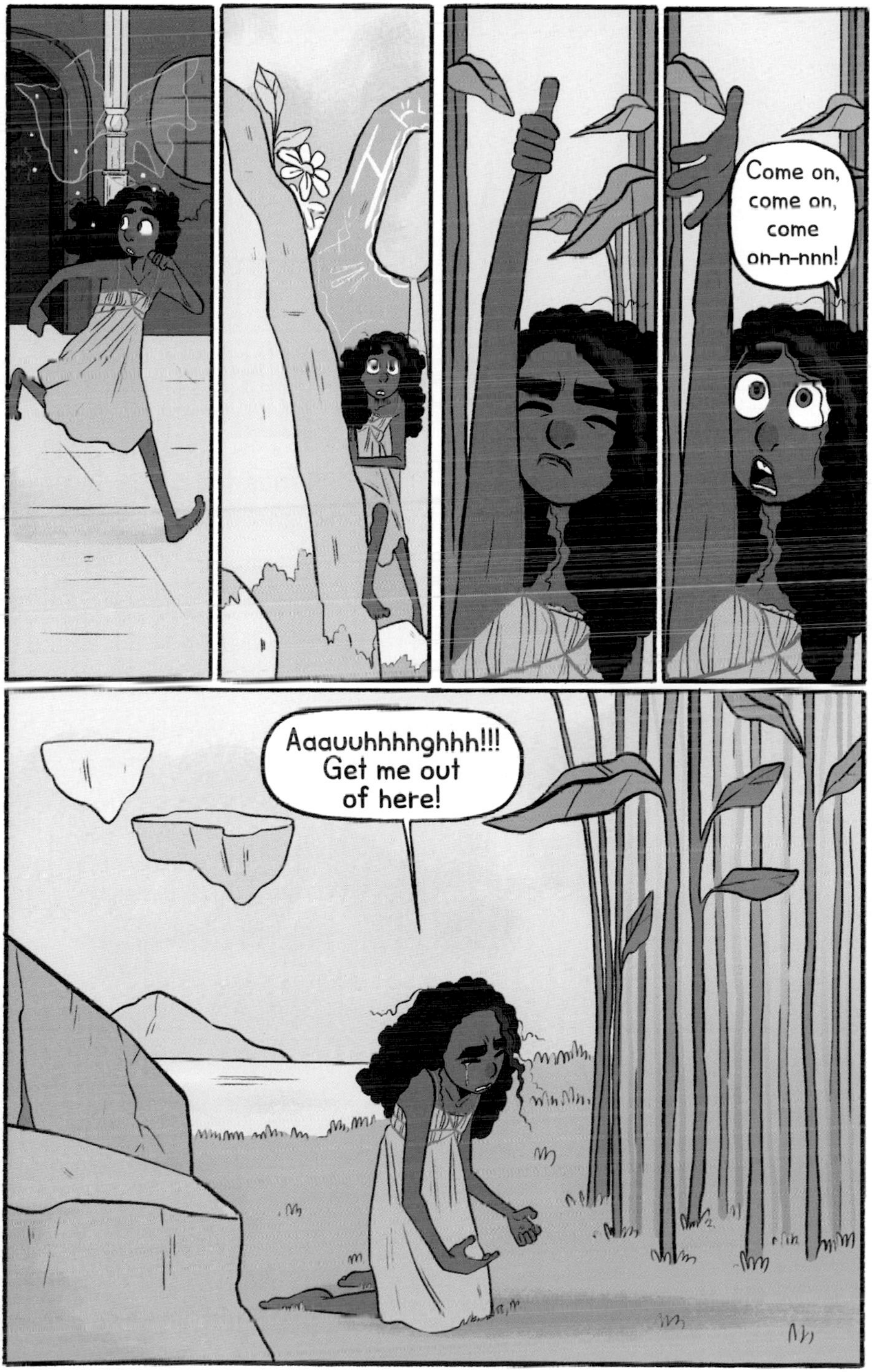
Come on, come on, come on-n-nnn!
Aaauuhhhghhh!!! Get me out of here!

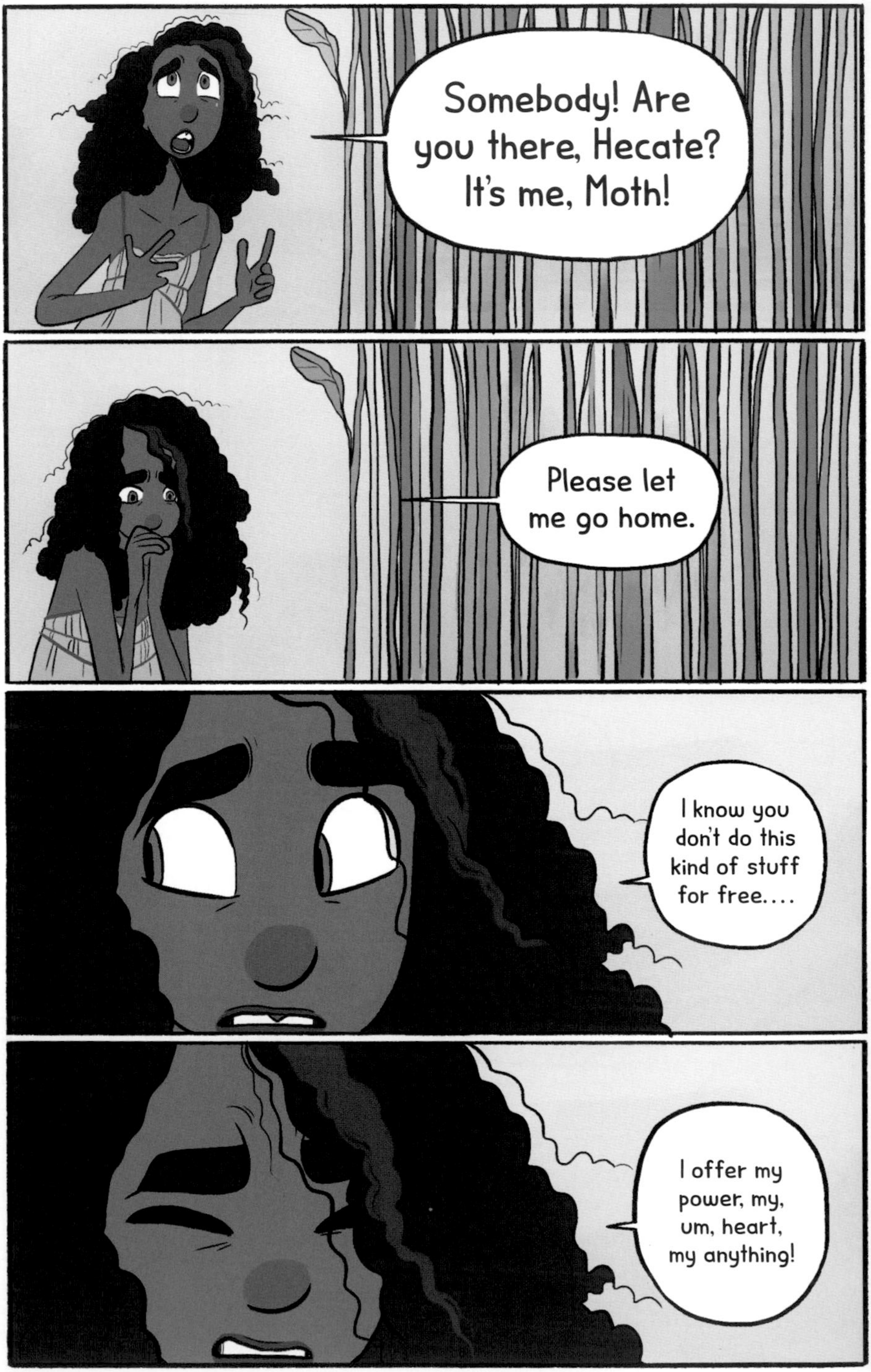
Somebody! Are you there, Hecate? It's me, Moth!
Please let me go home.
I know you don't do this kind of stuff for free....
I offer my power, my, um, heart, my anything!

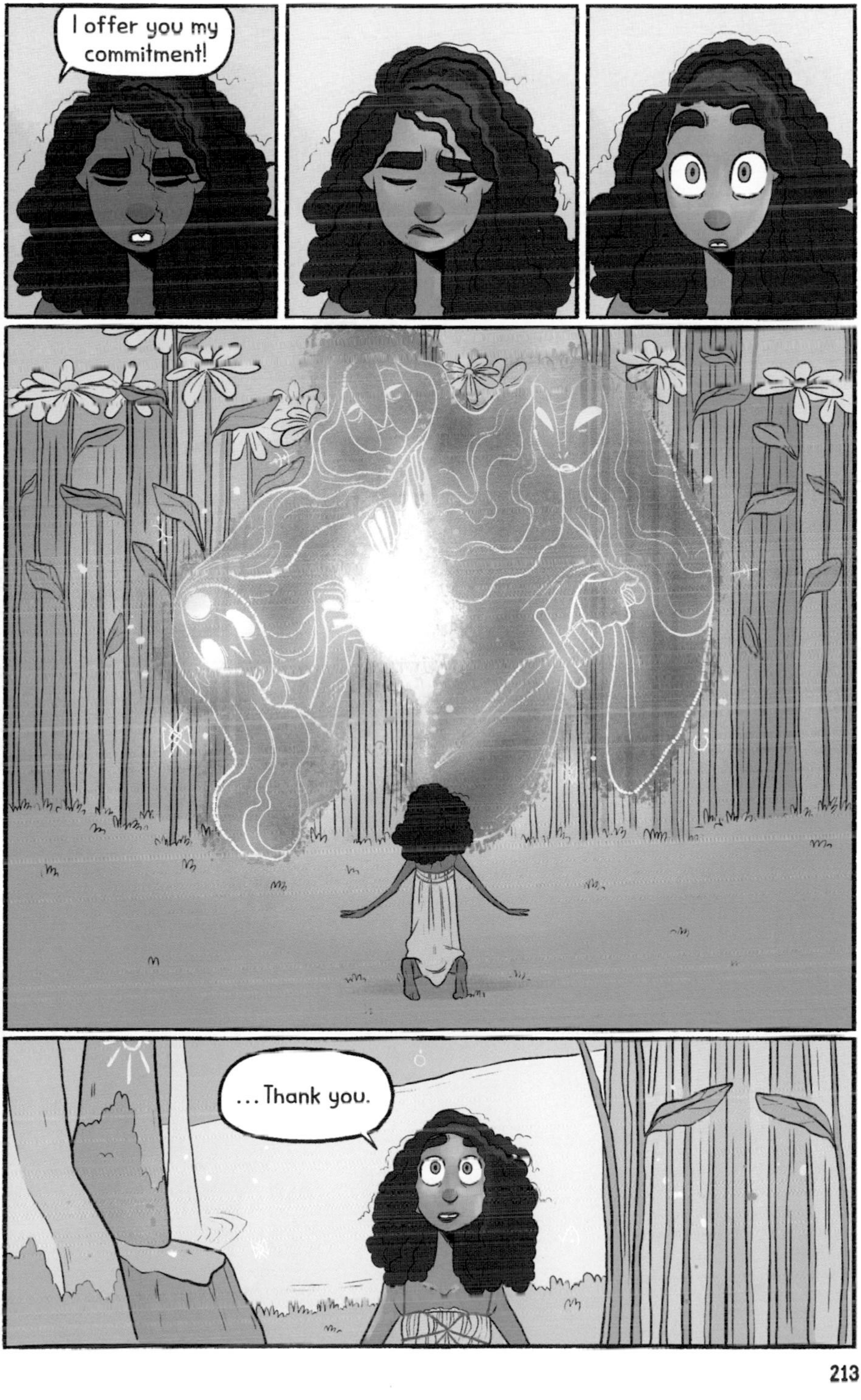
I offer you my commitment!
...Thank you.

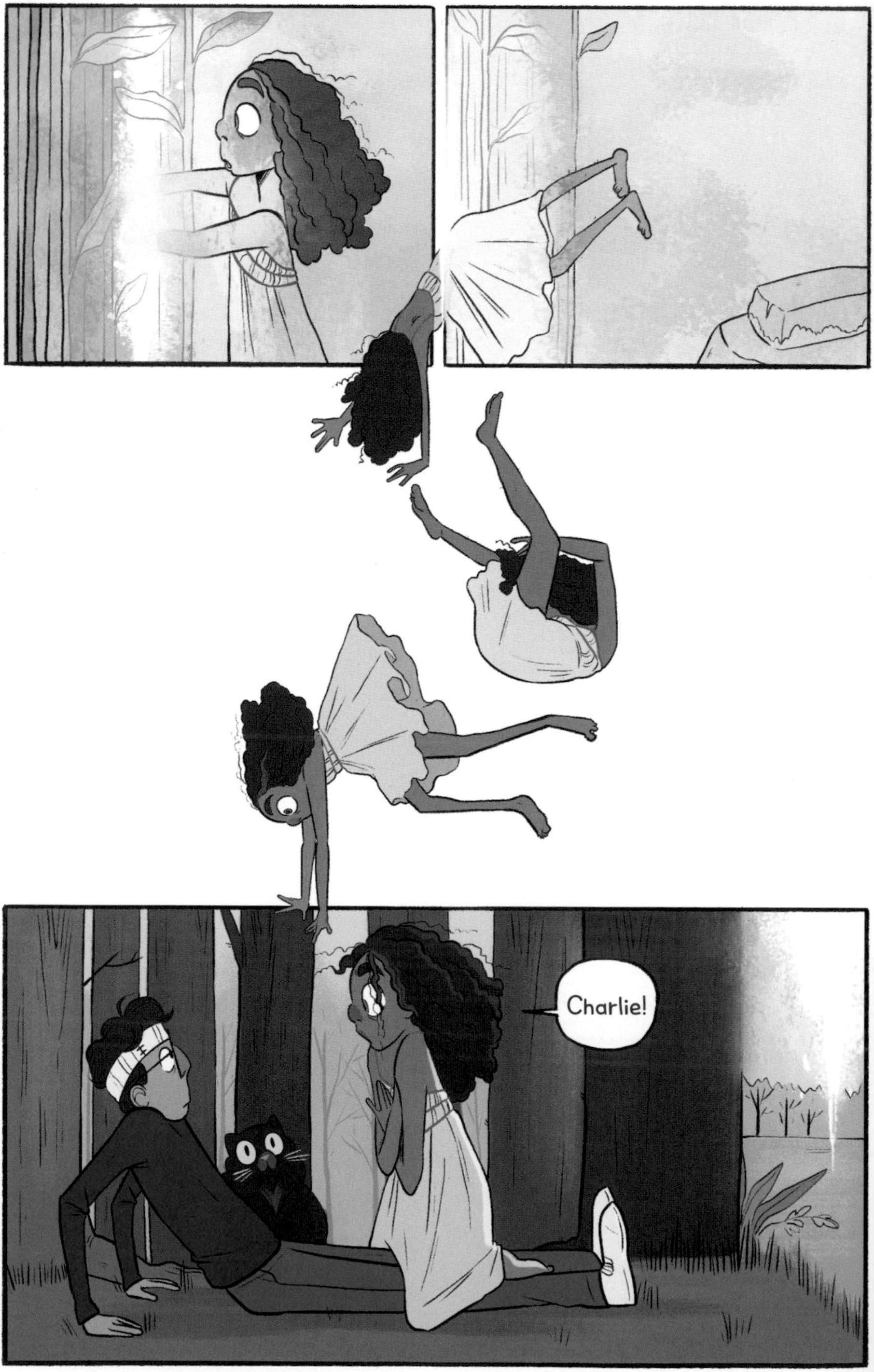
Charlie!

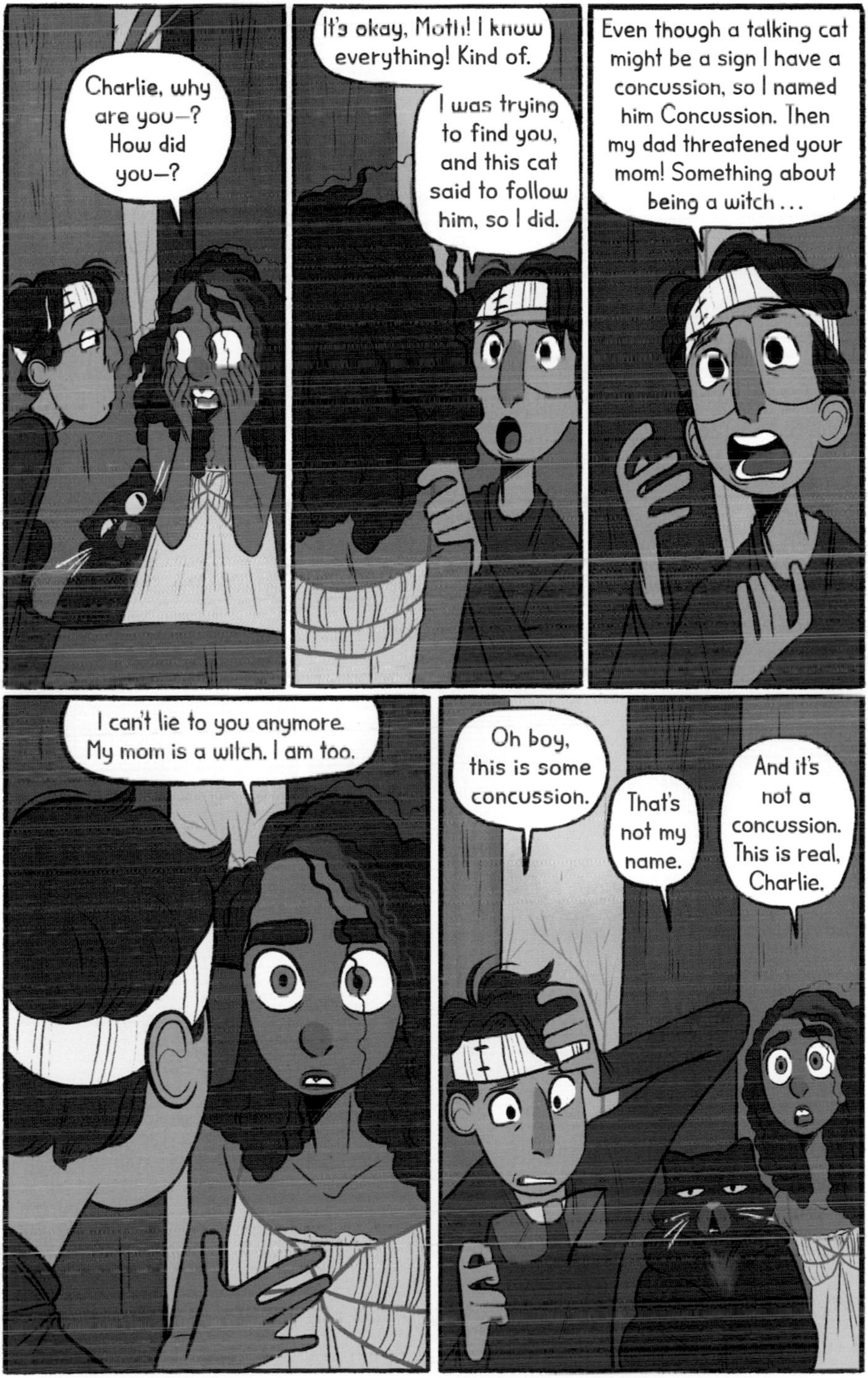
Charlie, why are you—? How did you—?
It's okay, Moth! I know everything! Kind of.
I was trying to find you, and this cat said to follow him, so I did.
Even though a talking cat might be a sign I have a concussion, so I named him Concussion. Then my dad threatened your mom! Something about being a witch . . .
I can't lie to you anymore. My mom is a witch. I am too.
Oh boy, this is some concussion.
That's not my name.
And it's not a concussion. This is real, Charlie.

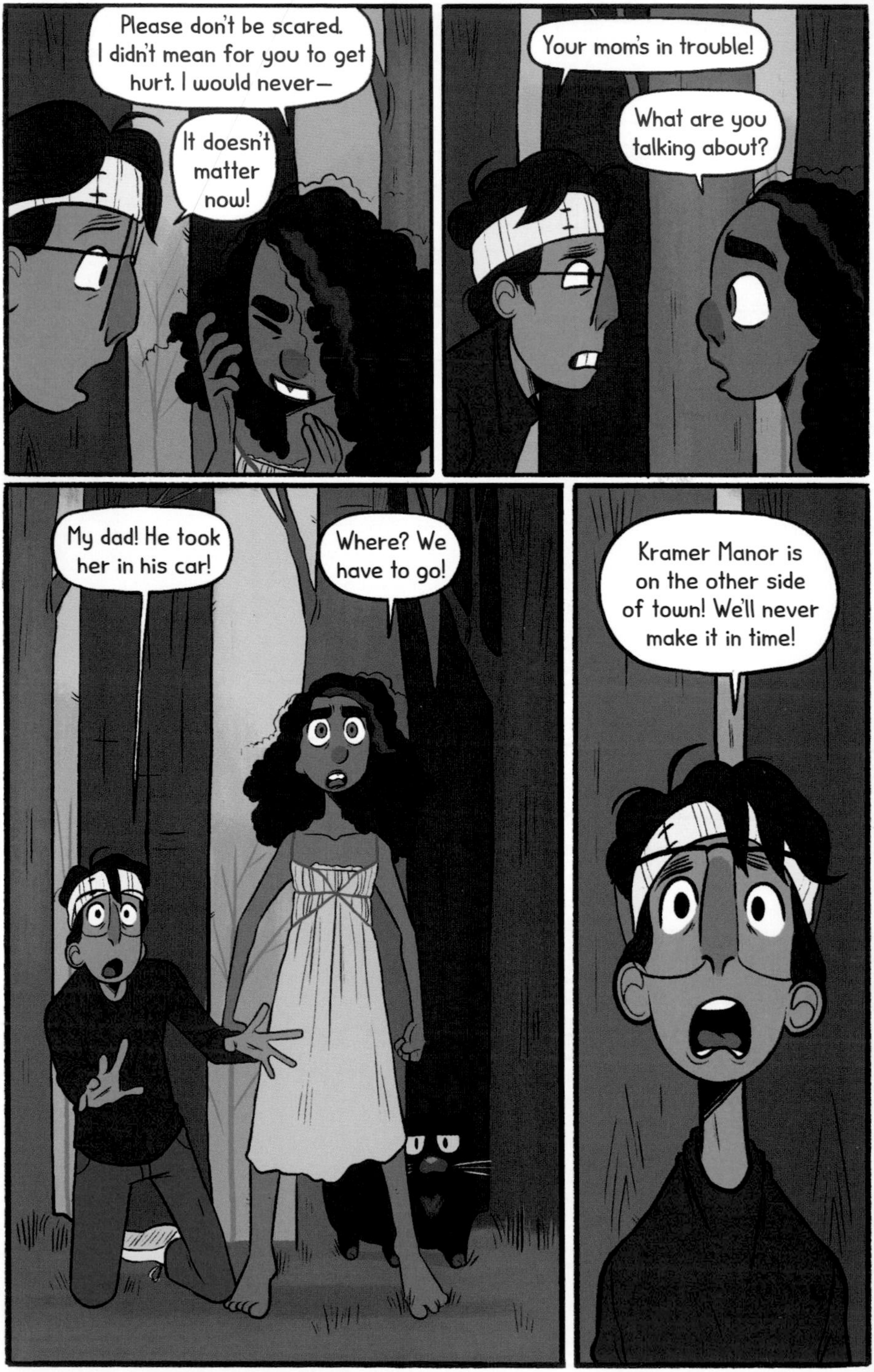
Please don't be scared. I didn't mean for you to get hurt. I would never—
It doesn't matter now!
Your mom's in trouble!
What are you talking about?
My dad! He took her in his car!
Where? We have to go!
Kramer Manor is on the other side of town! We'll never make it in time!

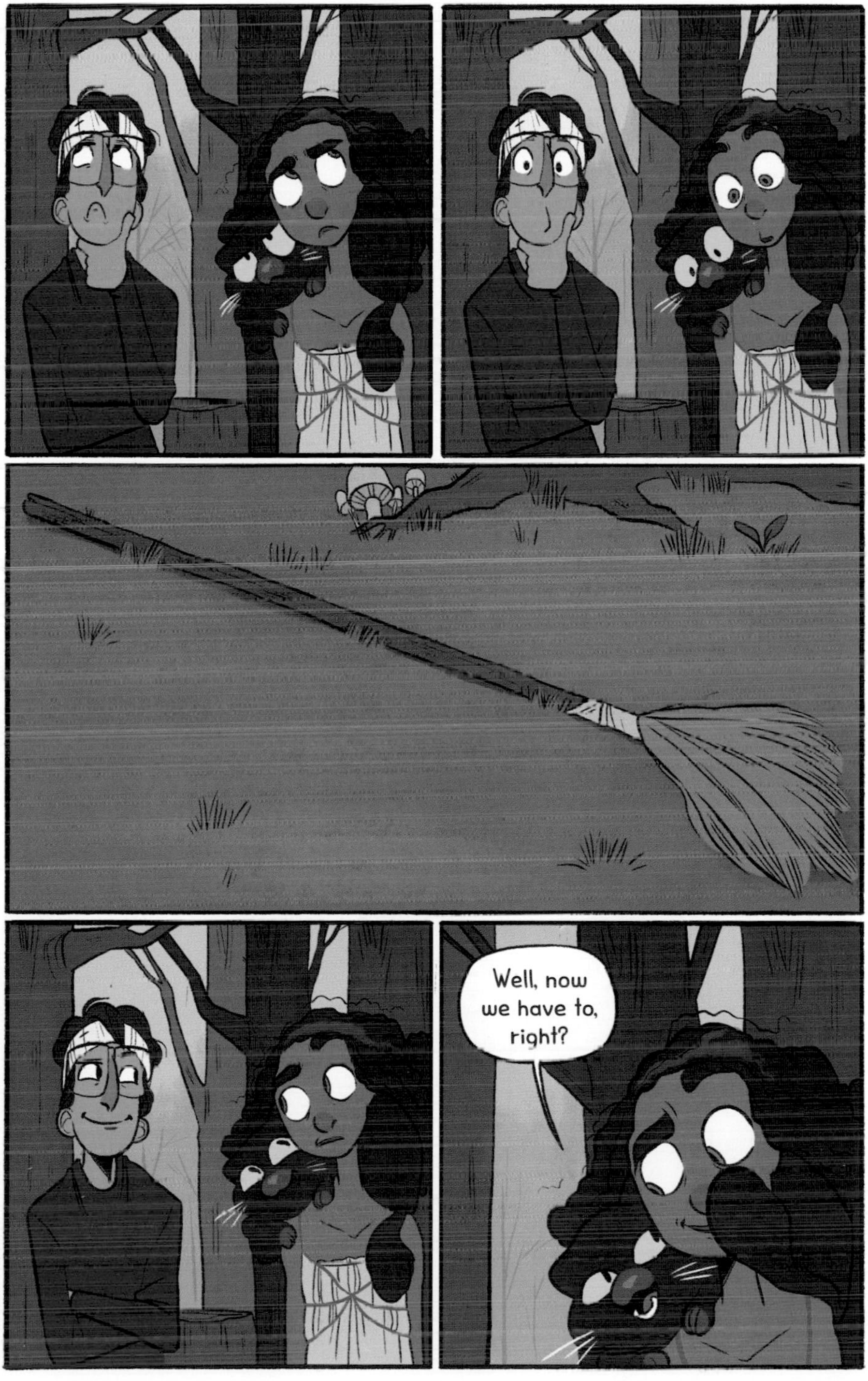
Well, now we have to, right?

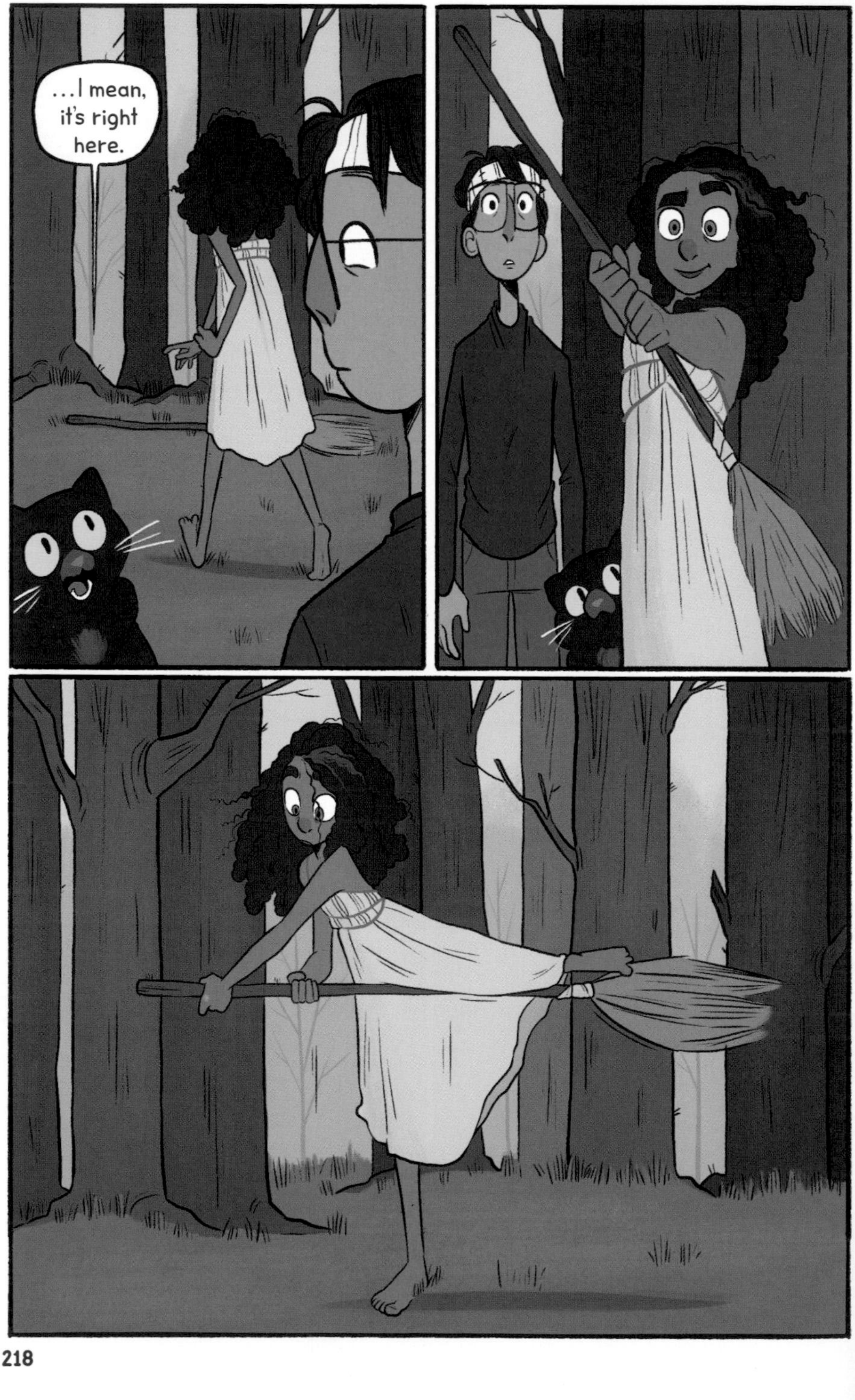
...I mean, it's right here.

So . . . how does this work, exactly?

Ruffalo wings.

Huh?

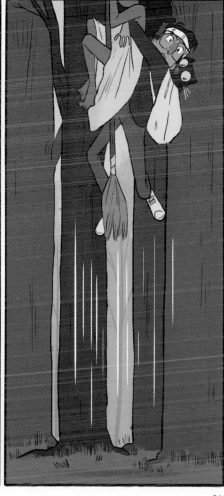

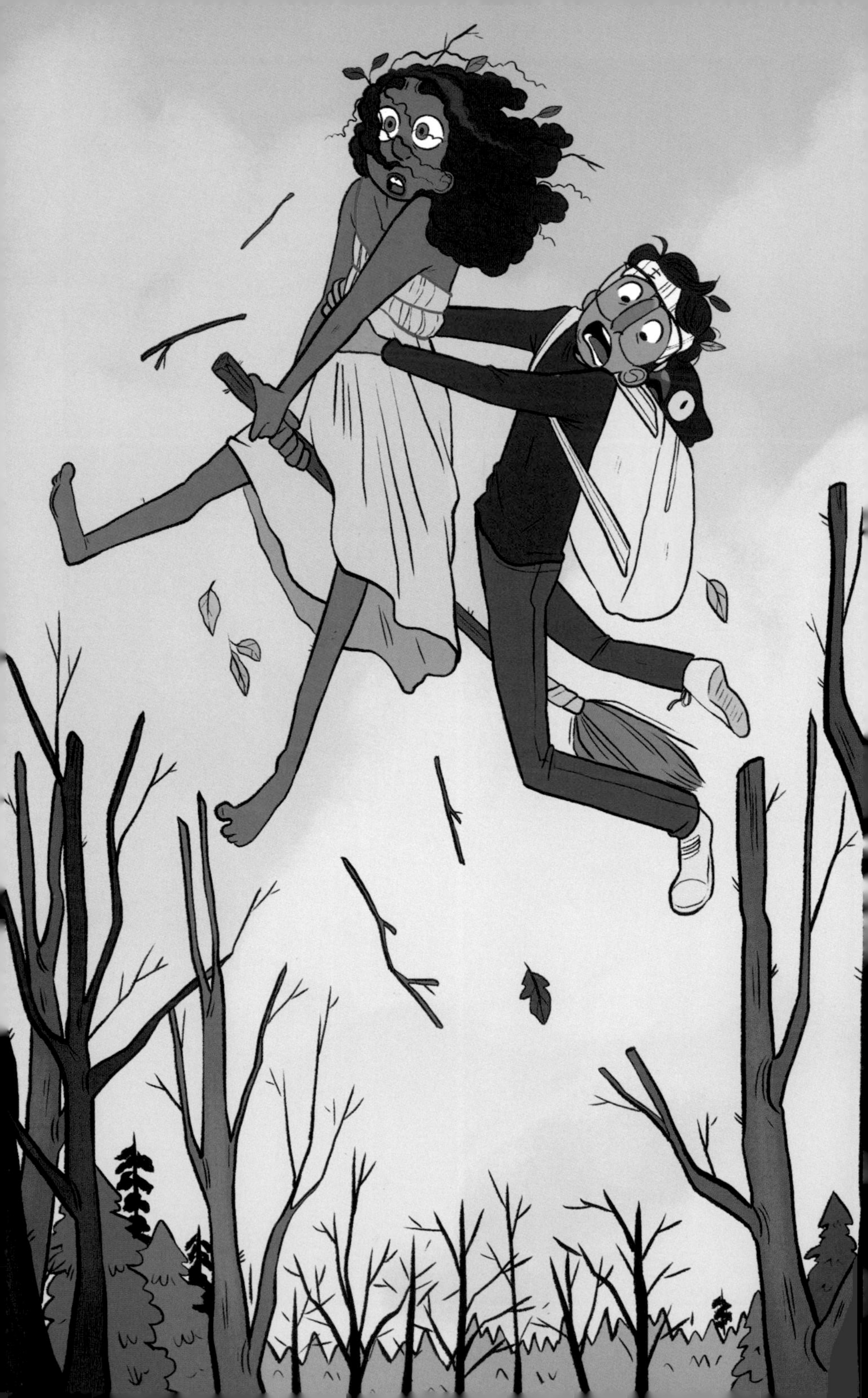

CHAPTER 14
Kramer vs. Hush

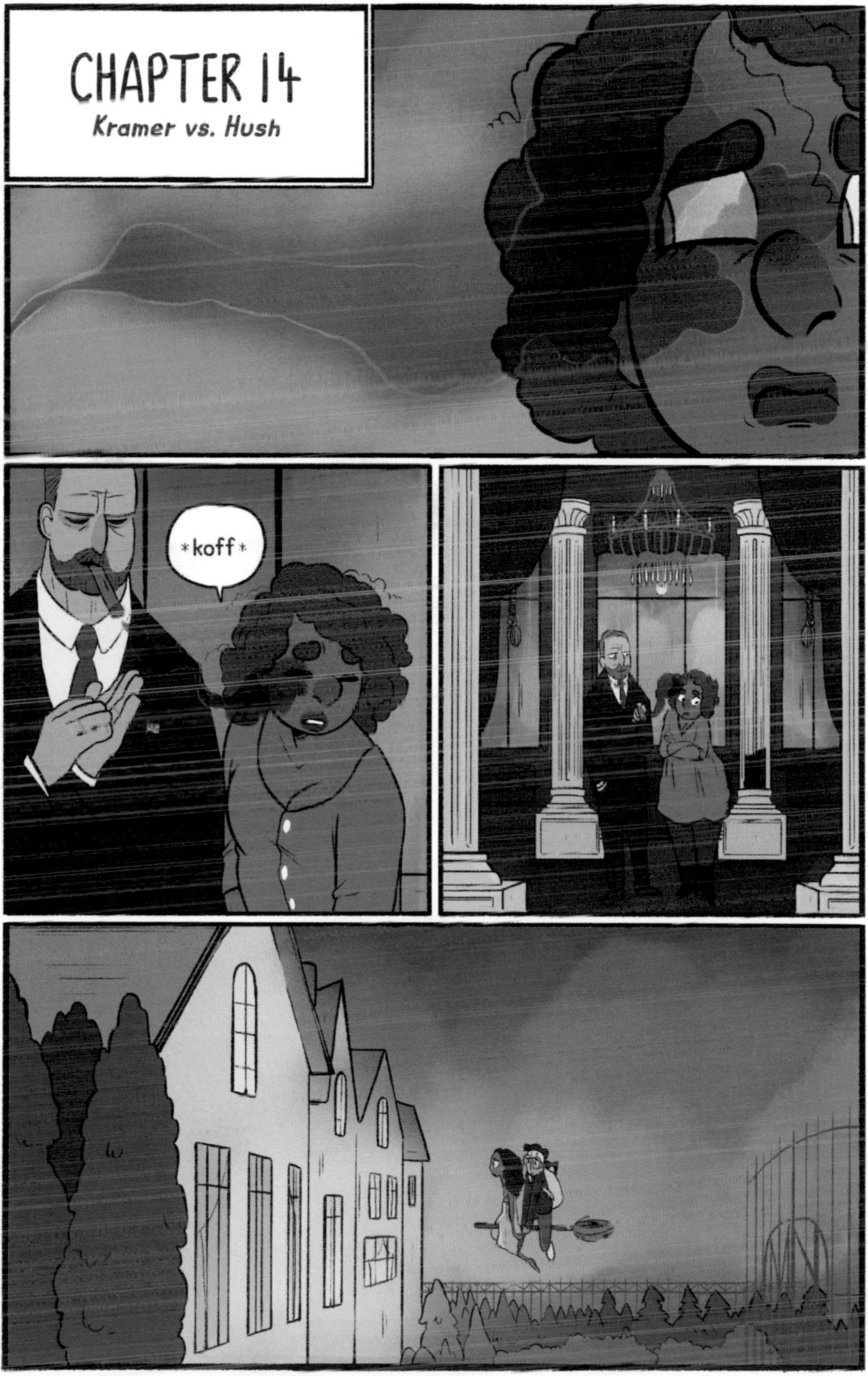
koff

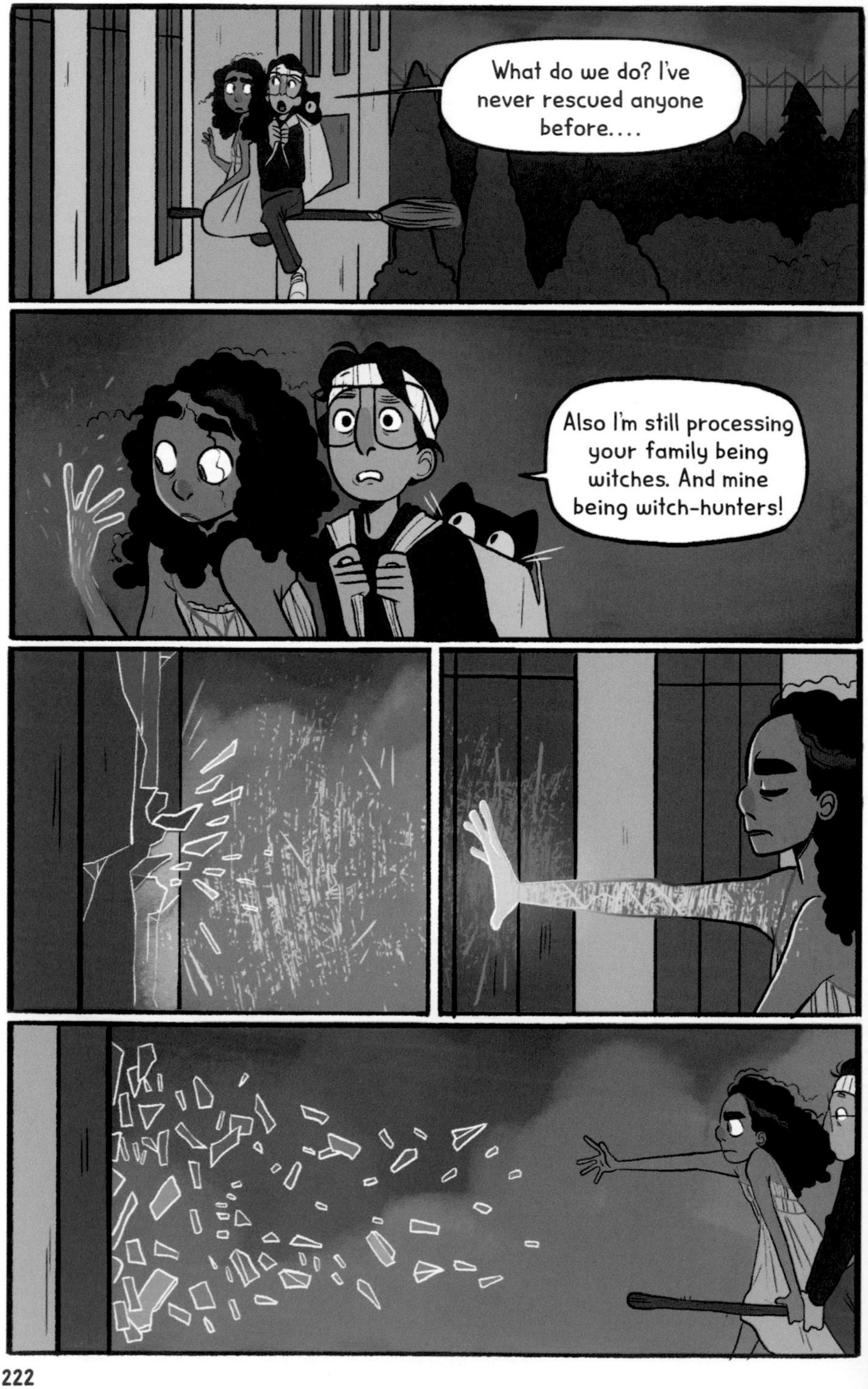
What do we do? I've never rescued anyone before....
Also I'm still processing your family being witches. And mine being witch-hunters!

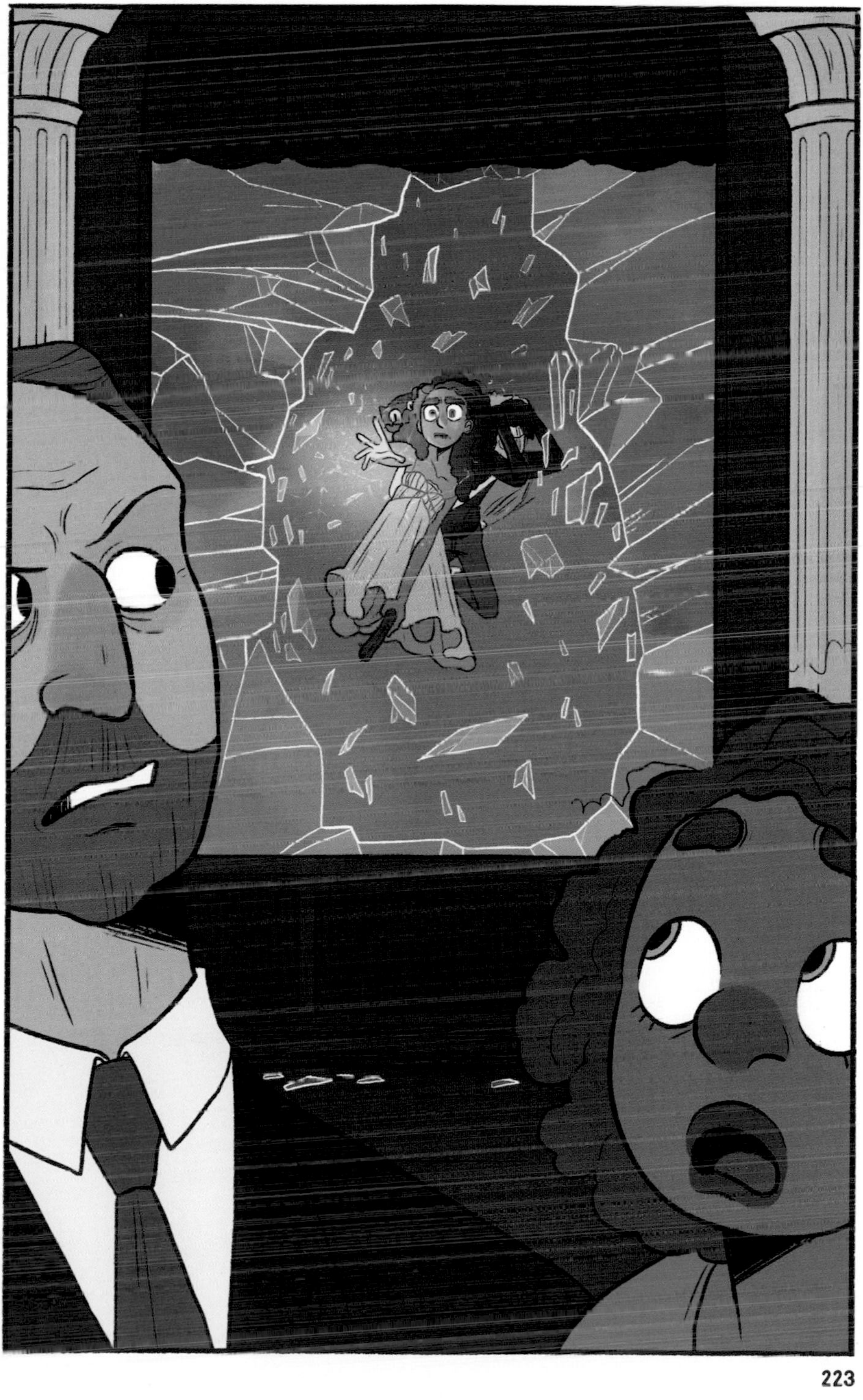

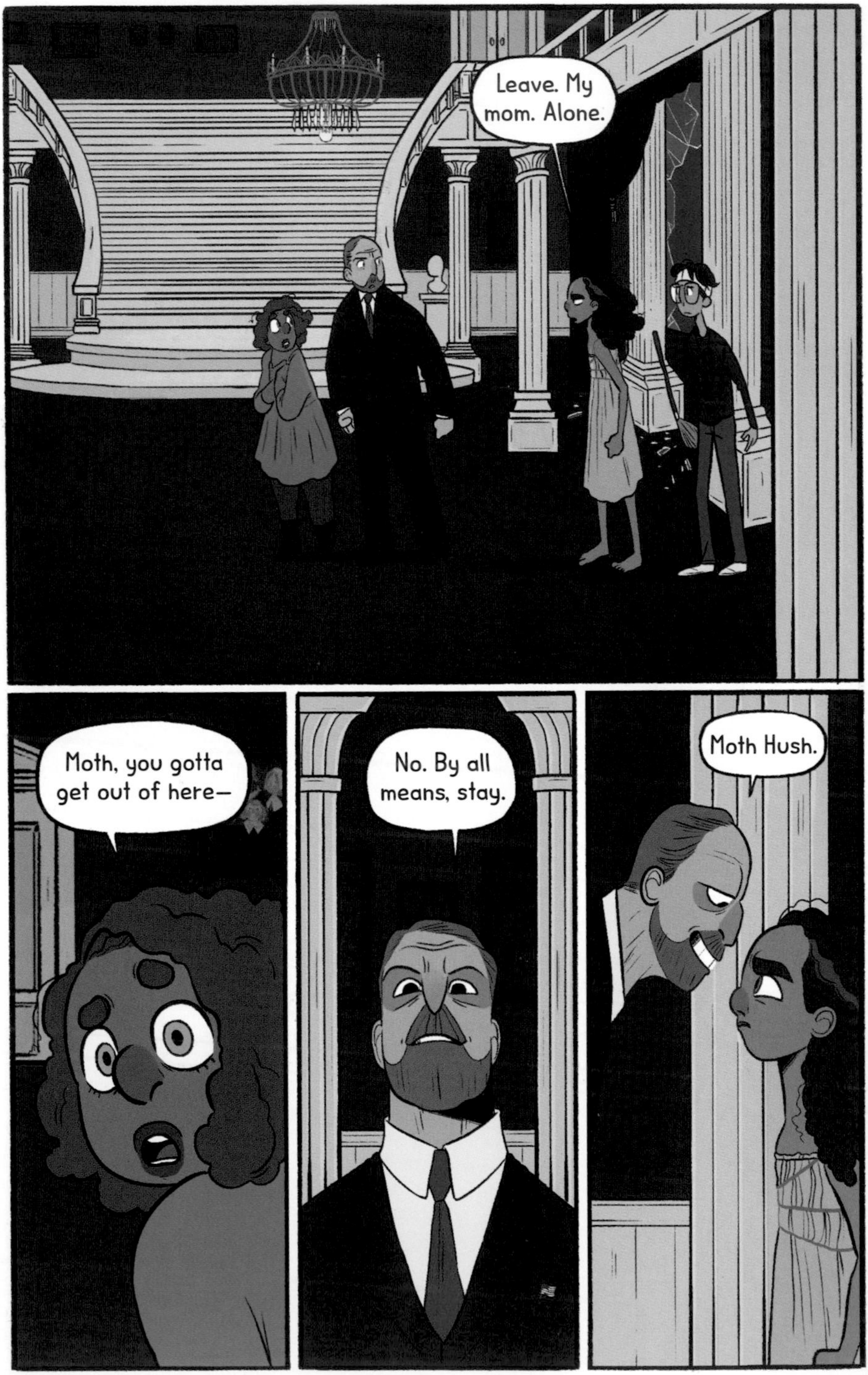
Leave. My mom. Alone.
Moth, you gotta get out of here—
No. By all means, stay.
Moth Hush.

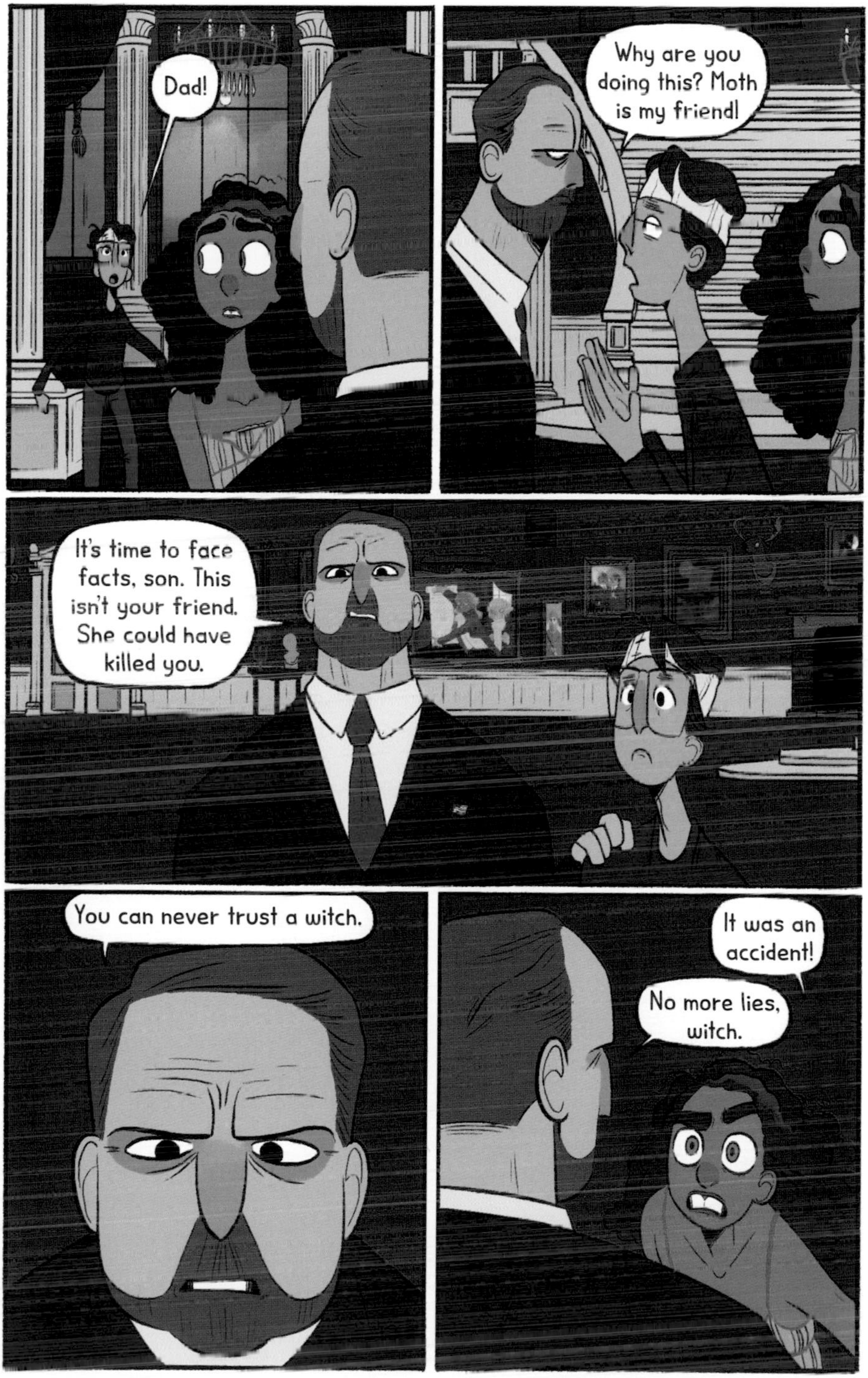
Dad!
Why are you doing this? Moth is my friend!
It's time to face facts, son. This isn't your friend. She could have killed you.
You can never trust a witch.
It was an accident!
No more lies, witch.

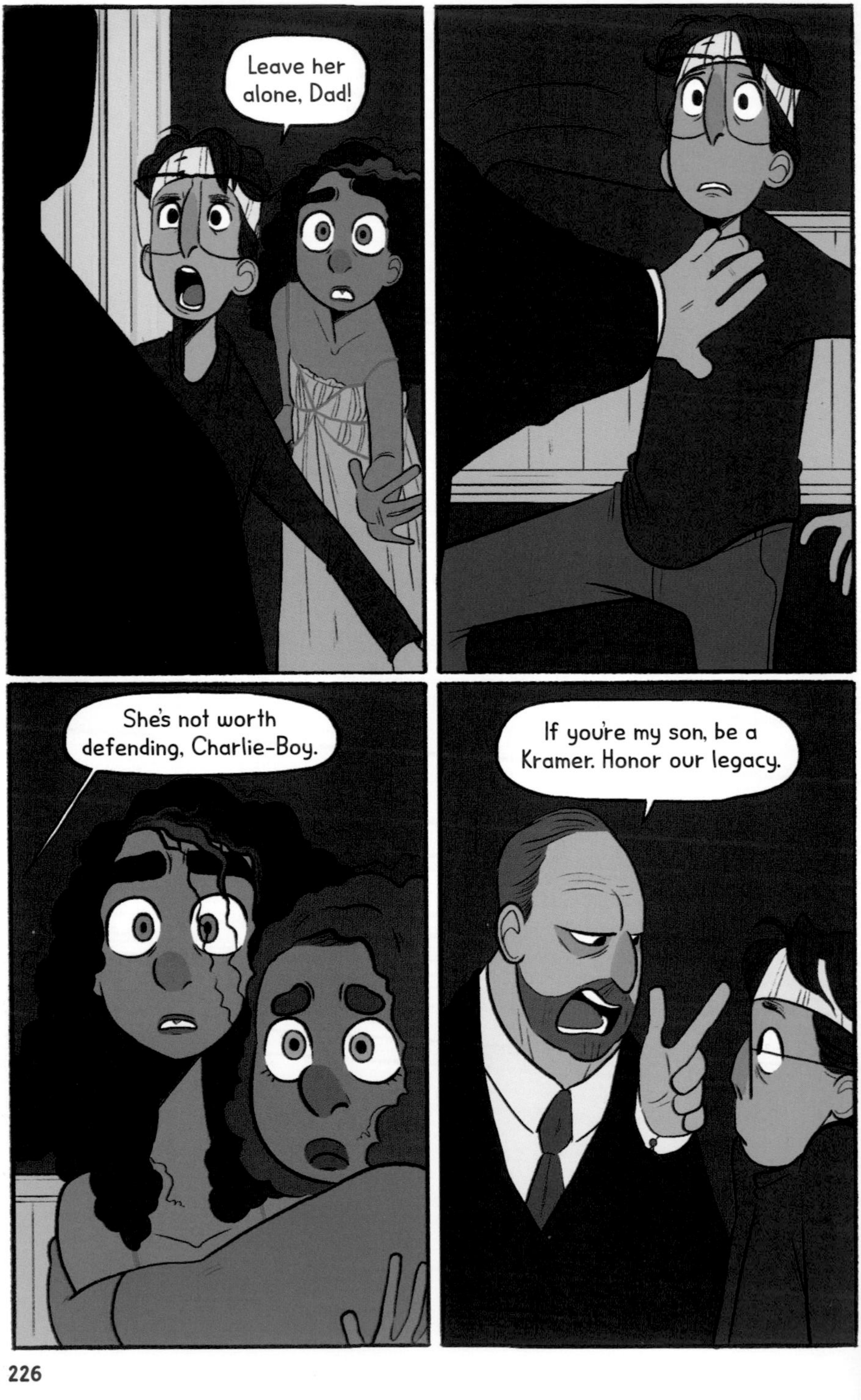
Leave her alone, Dad!
She's not worth defending, Charlie-Boy.
If you're my son, be a Kramer. Honor our legacy.

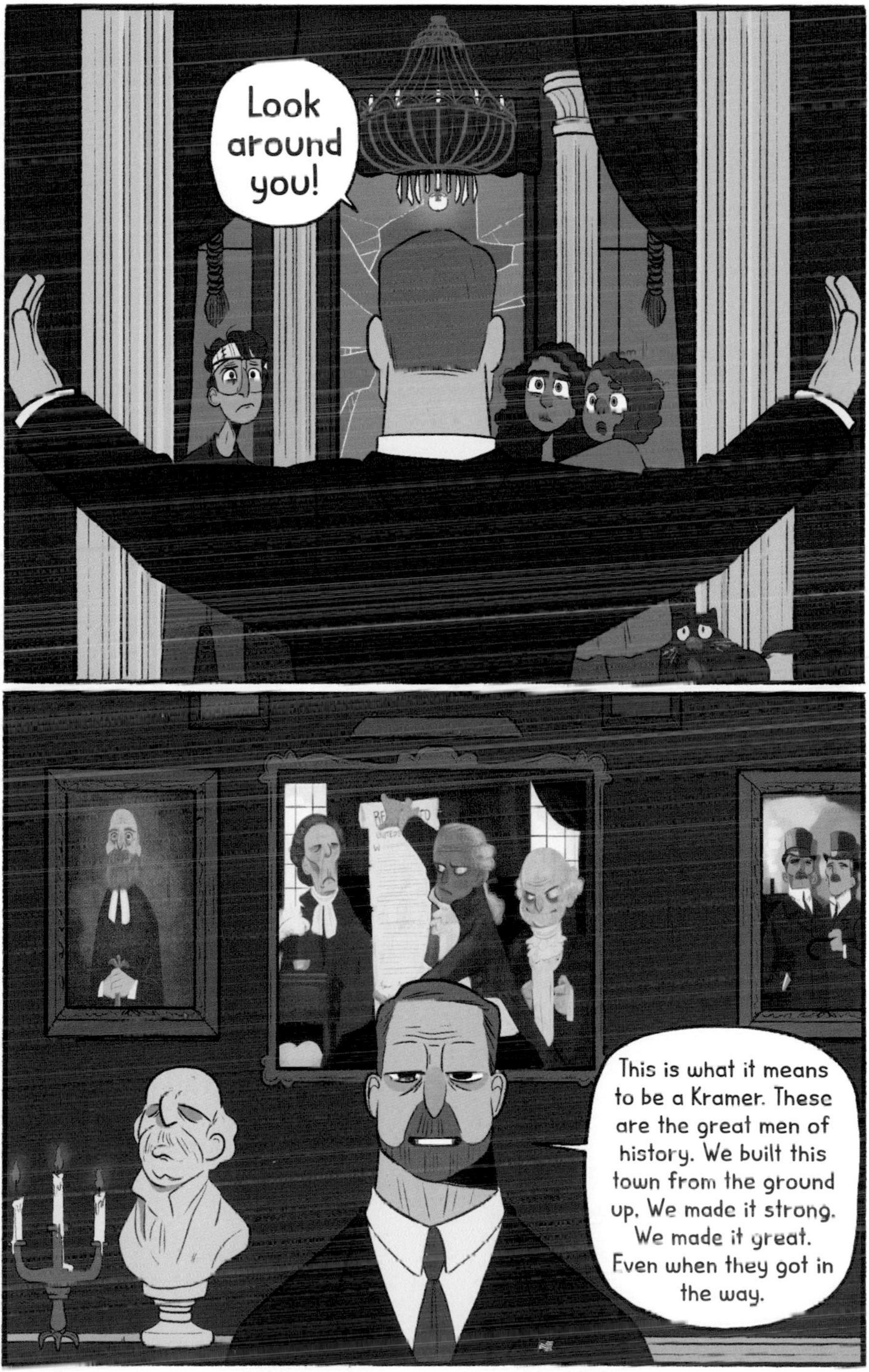
Look around you!
This is what it means to be a Kramer. These are the great men of history. We built this town from the ground up. We made it strong. We made it great. Even when they got in the way.

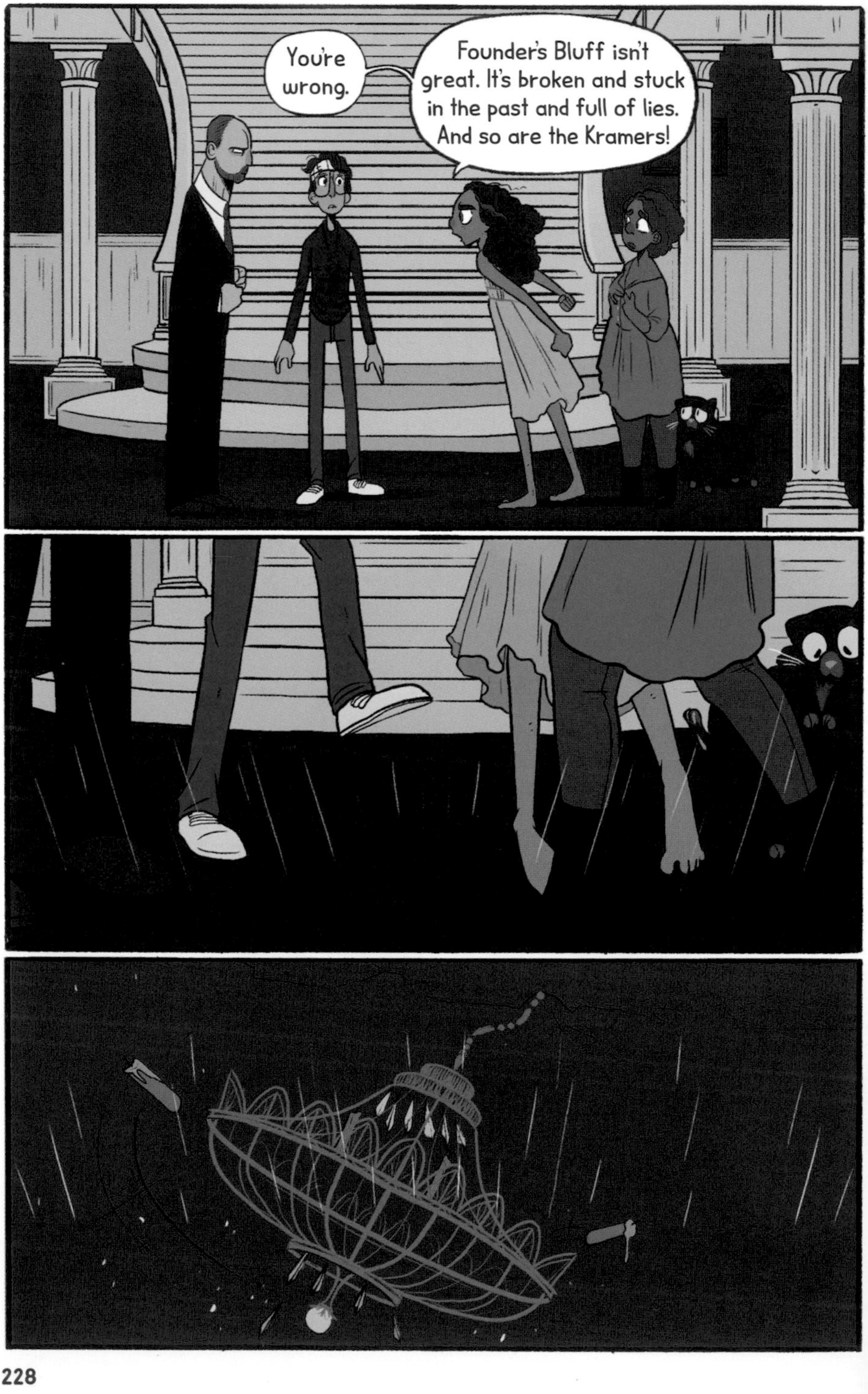
You're wrong.
Founder's Bluff isn't great. It's broken and stuck in the past and full of lies. And so are the Kramers!

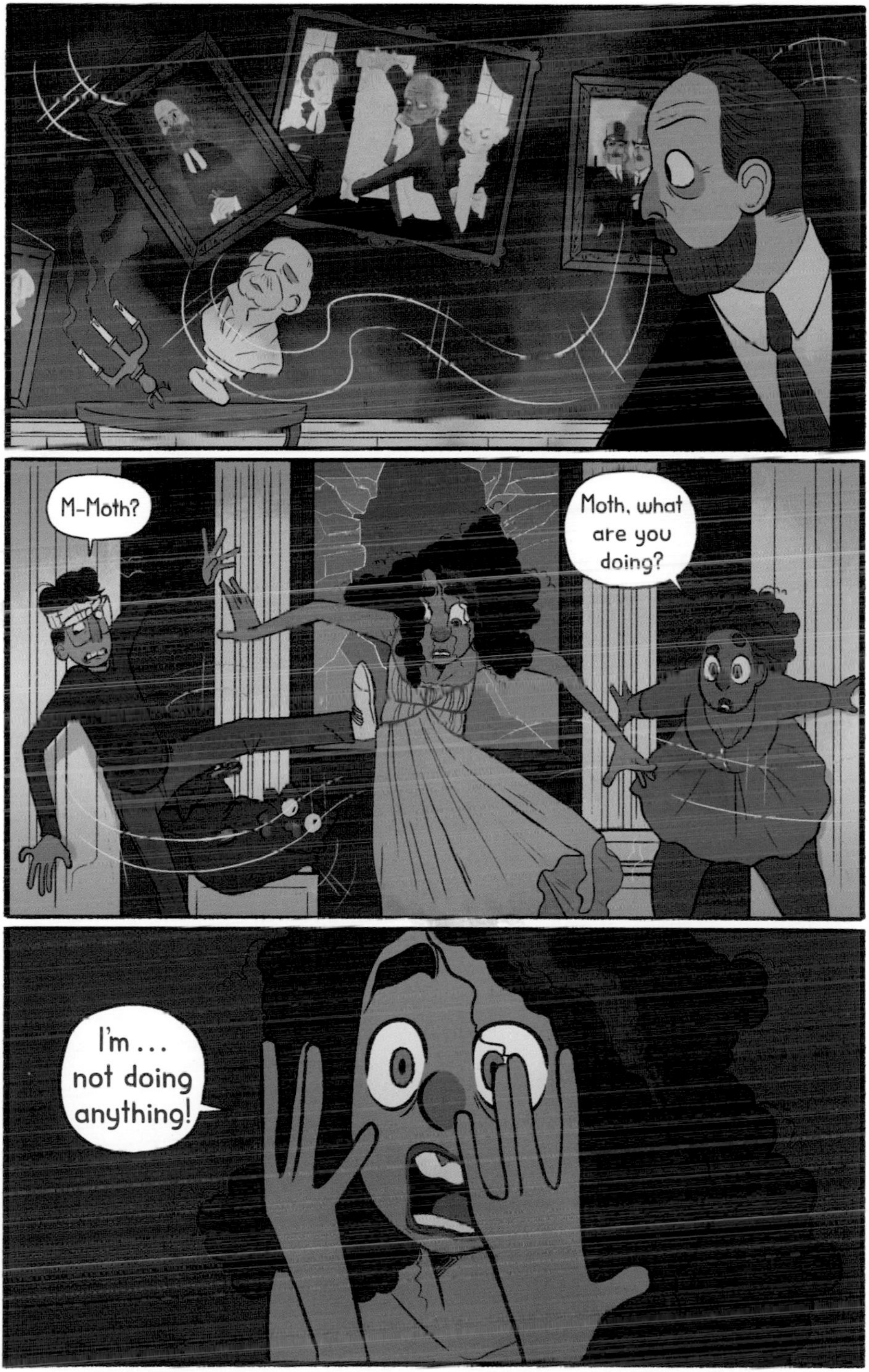

M-Moth?
Moth, what are you doing?
I'm . . . not doing anything!

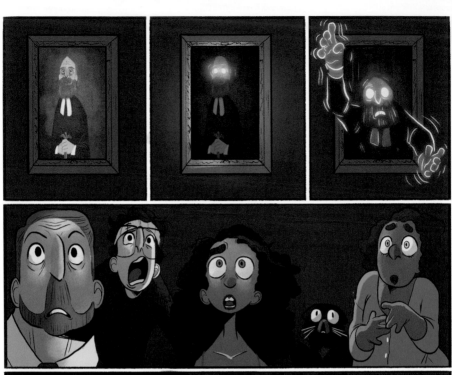

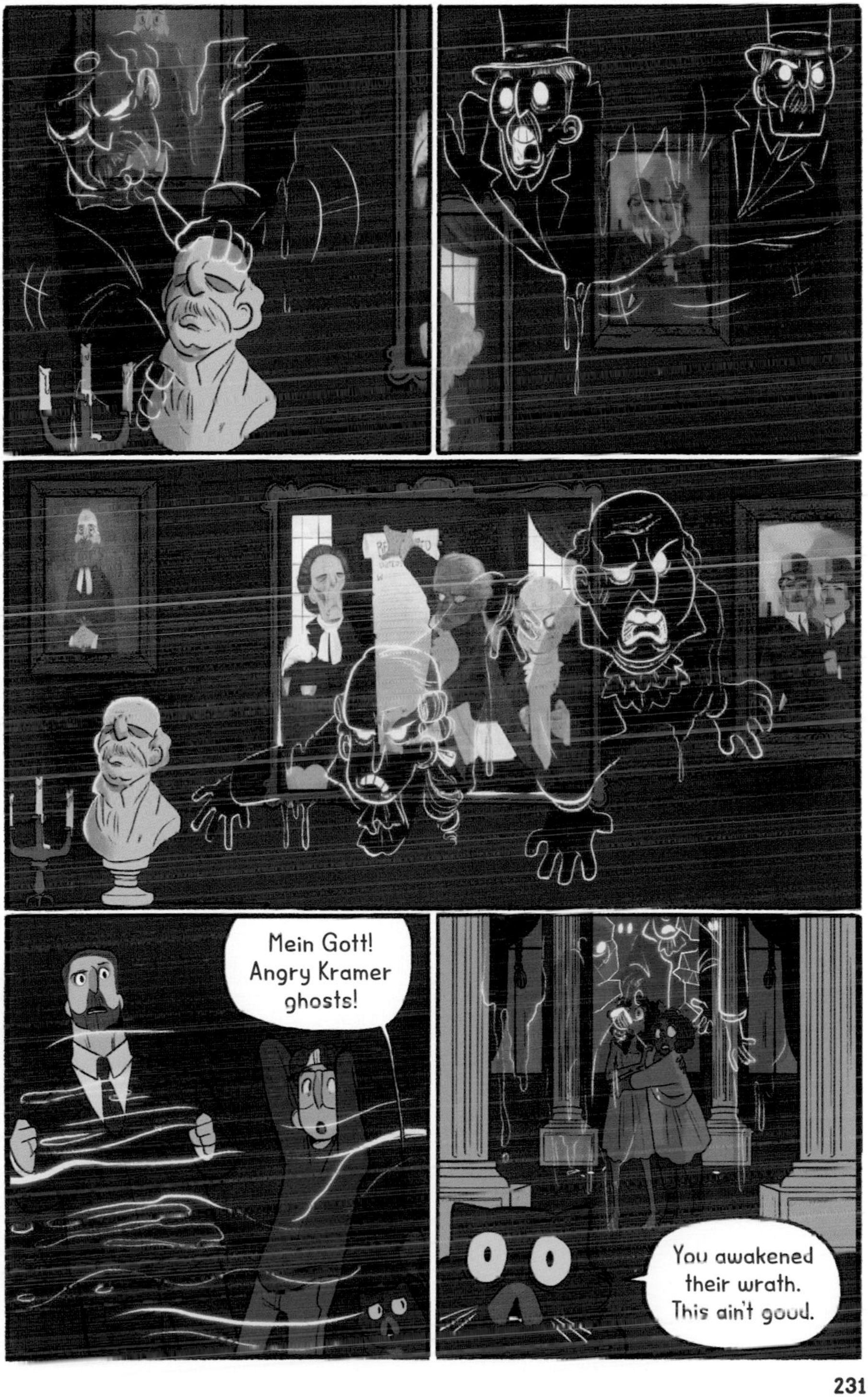
Mein Gott! Angry Kramer ghosts!
You awakened their wrath. This ain't good.

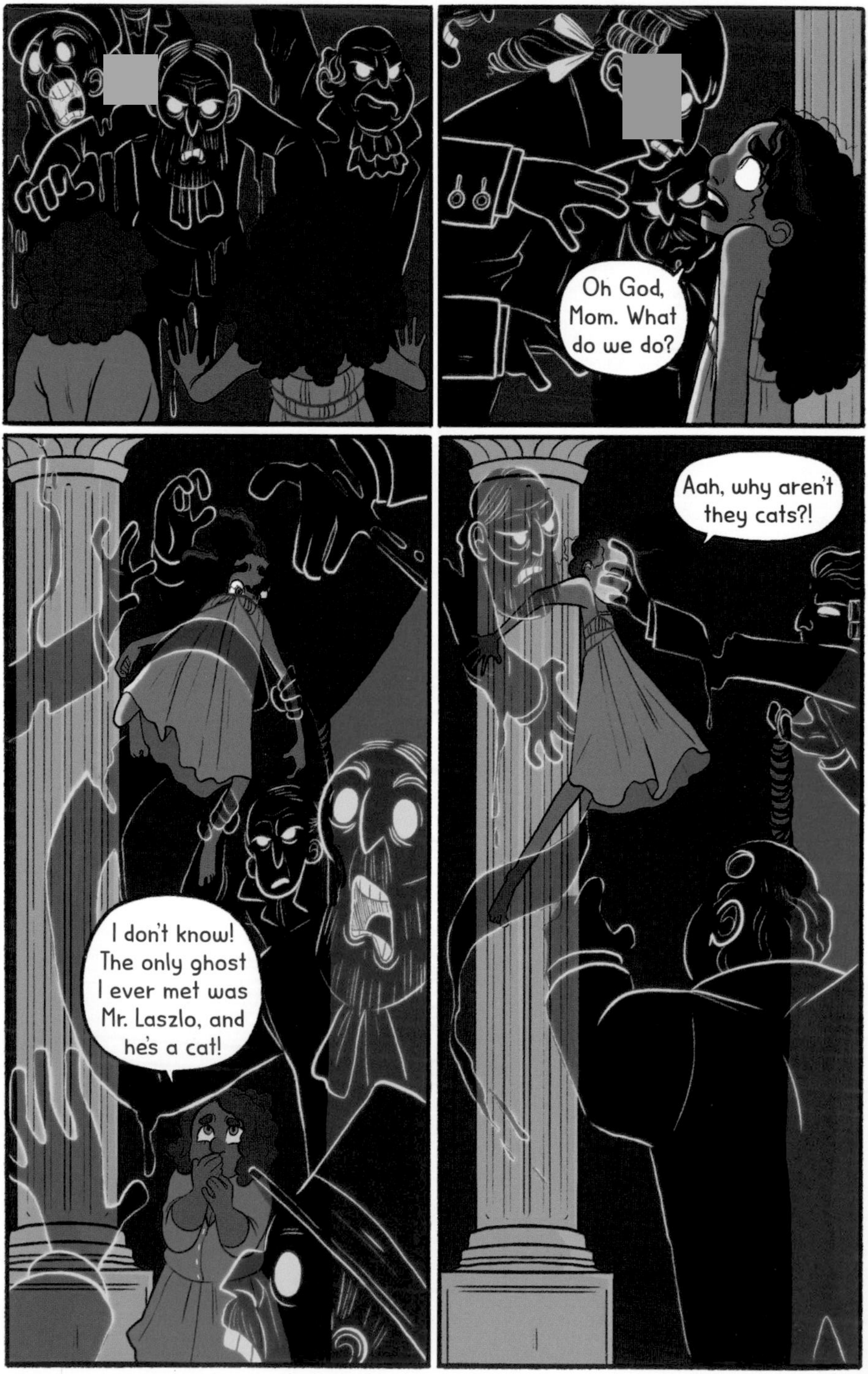

Oh God, Mom. What do we do?
I don't know! The only ghost I ever met was Mr. Laszlo, and he's a cat!
Aah, why aren't they cats?!

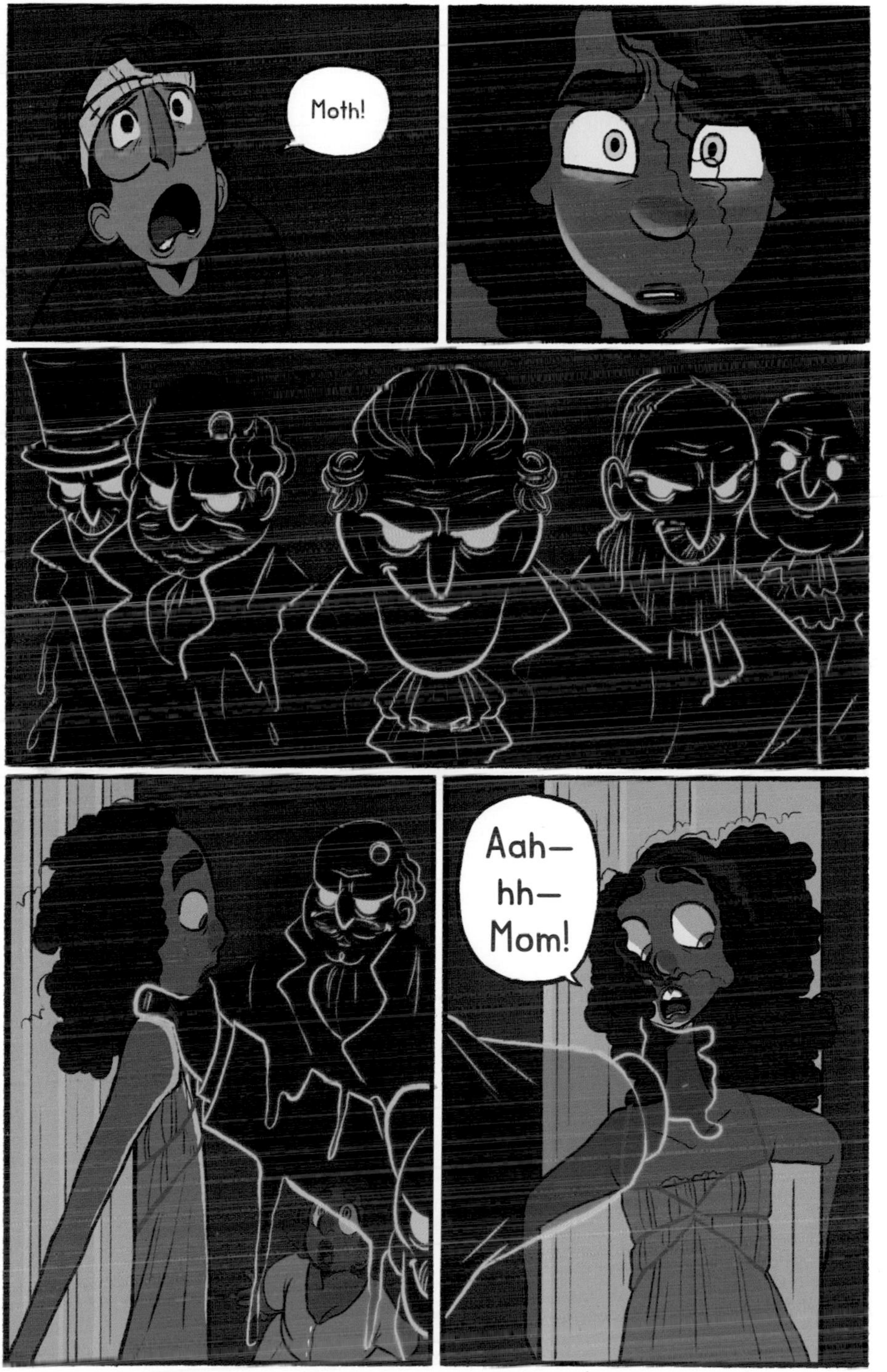
Moth!
Aah—
hh—
Mom!

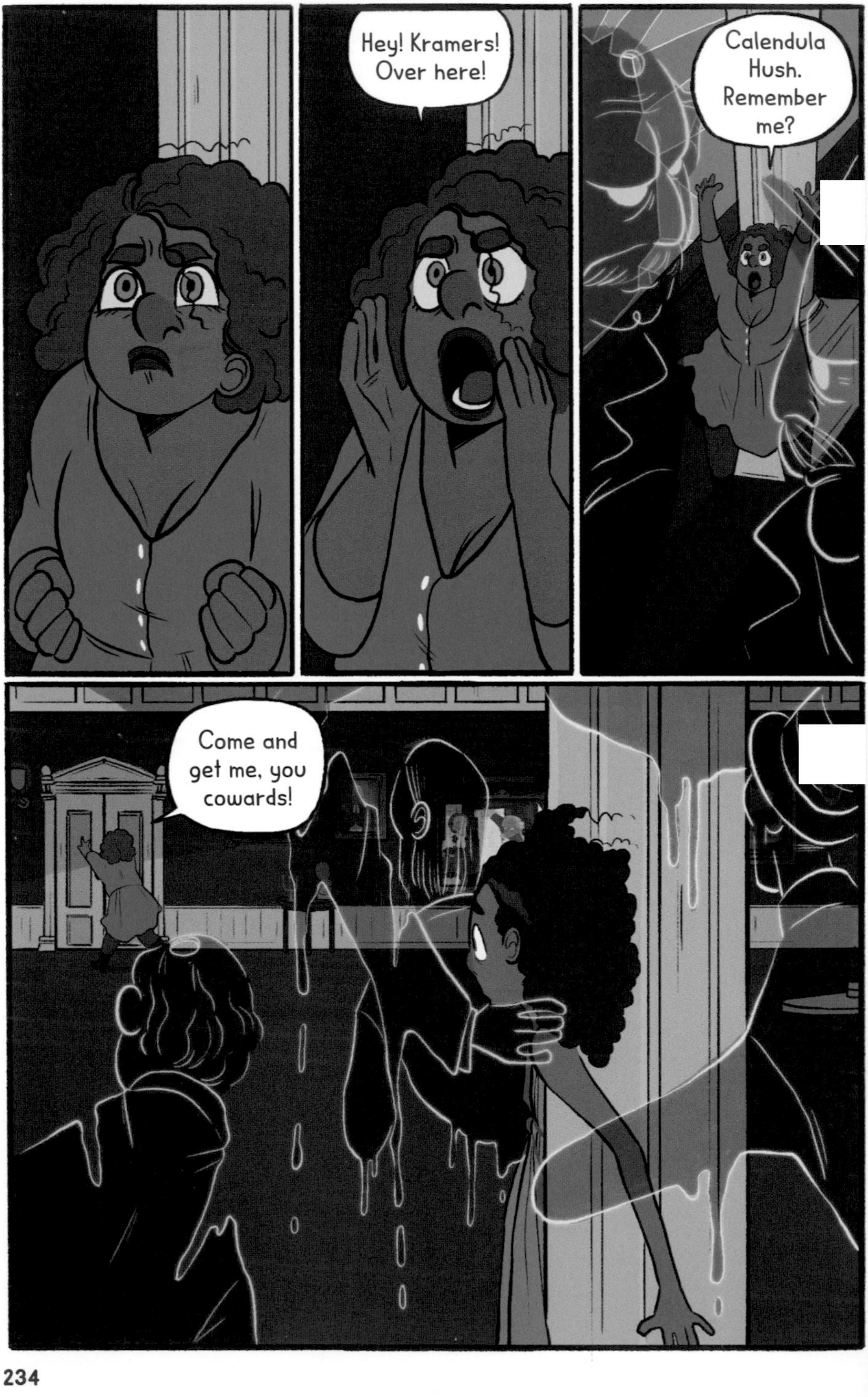
Hey! Kramers! Over here!
Calendula Hush. Remember me?
Come and get me, you cowards!

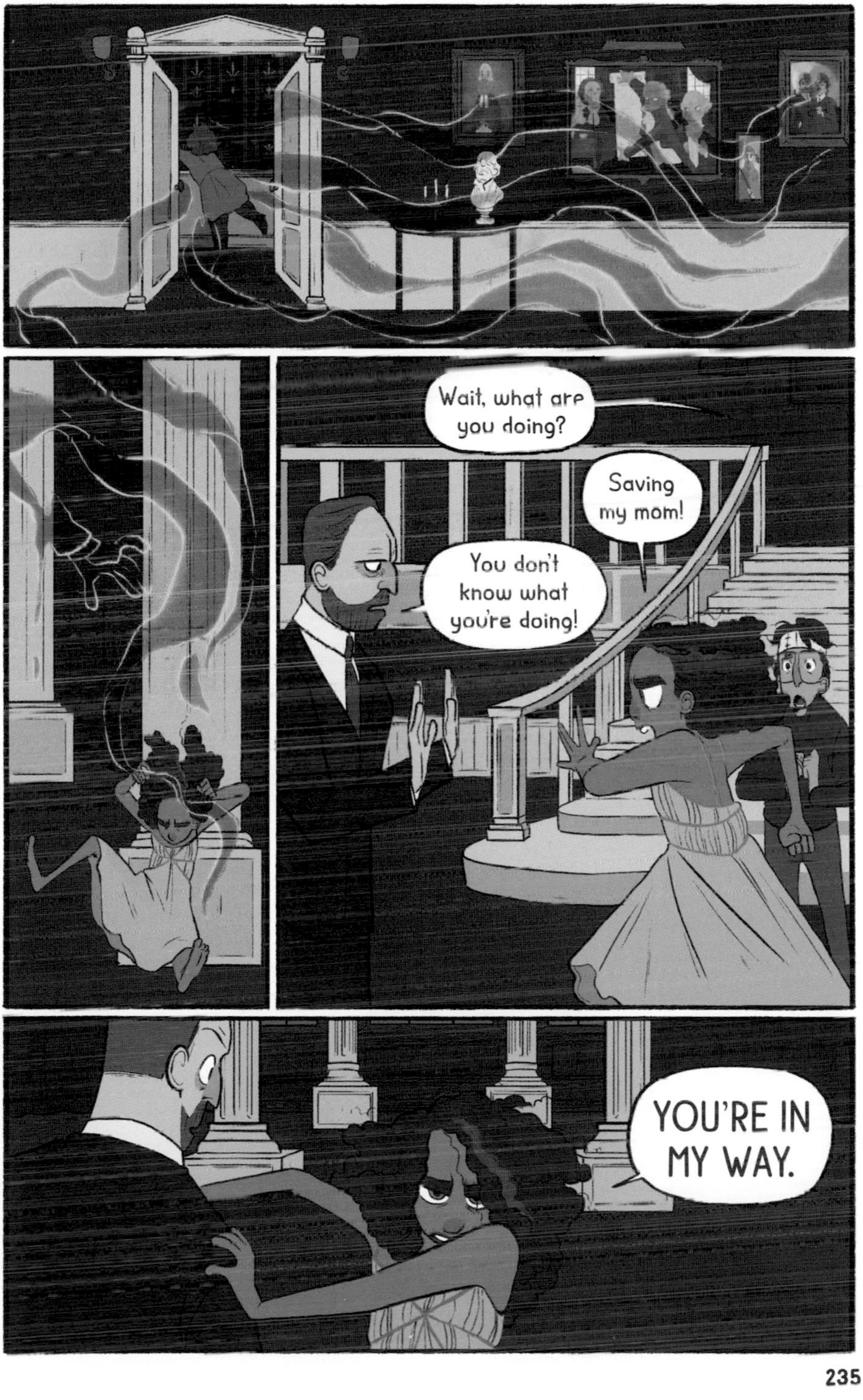
Wait, what are you doing?
Saving my mom!
You don't know what you're doing!
YOU'RE IN MY WAY.

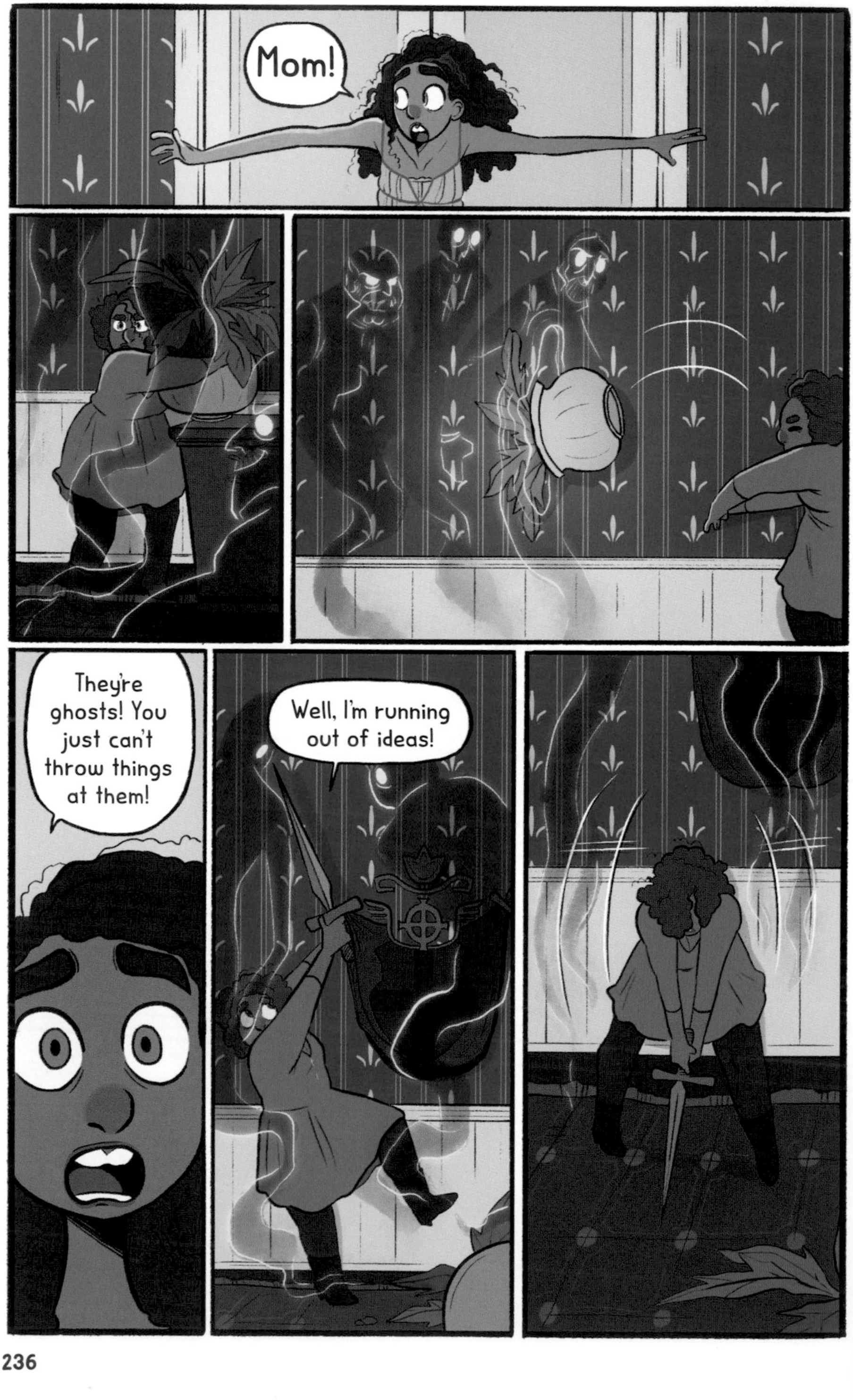
Mom!
They're ghosts! You just can't throw things at them!
Well, I'm running out of ideas!

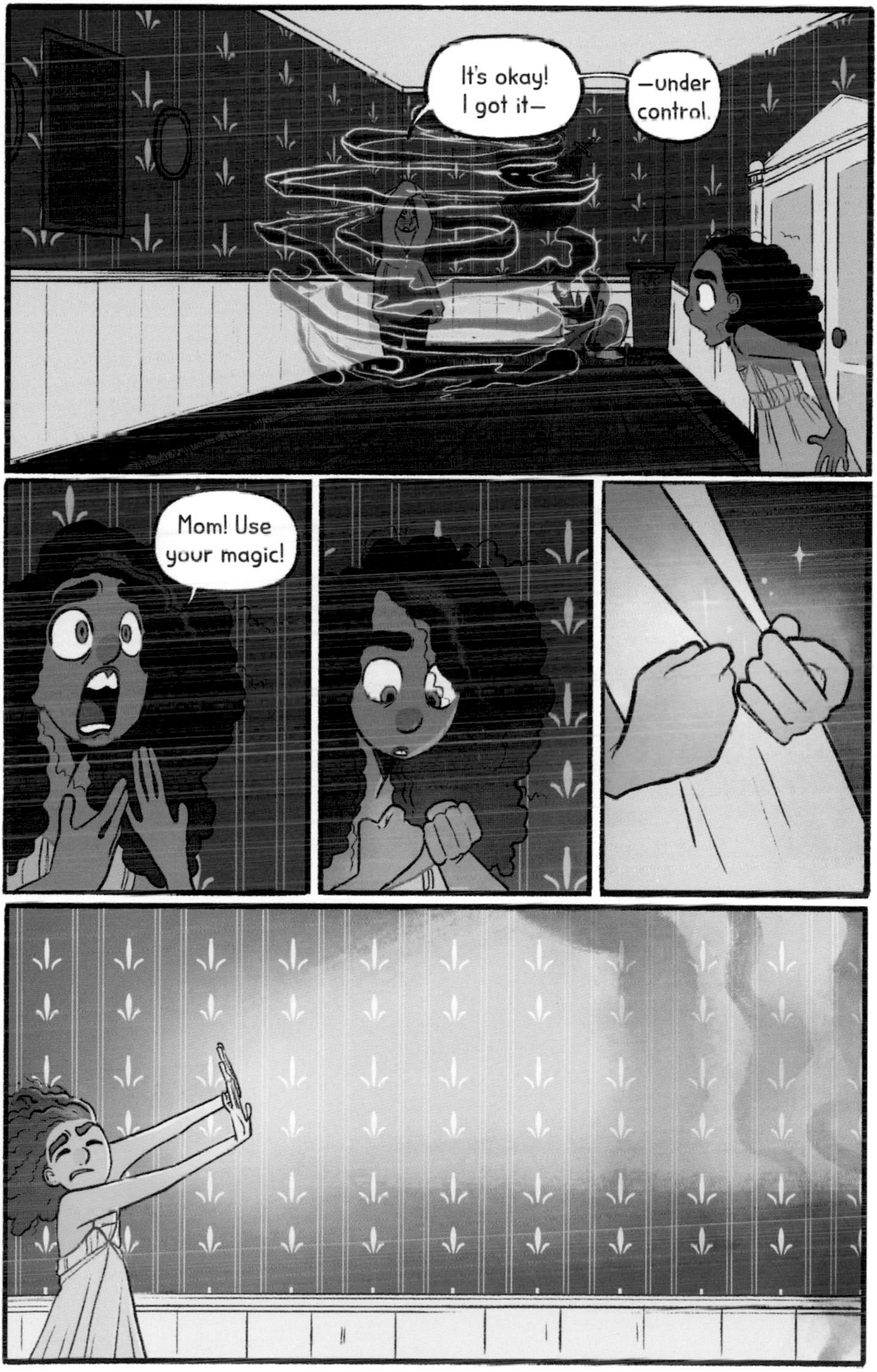
It's okay! I got it—
—under control.
Mom! Use your magic!

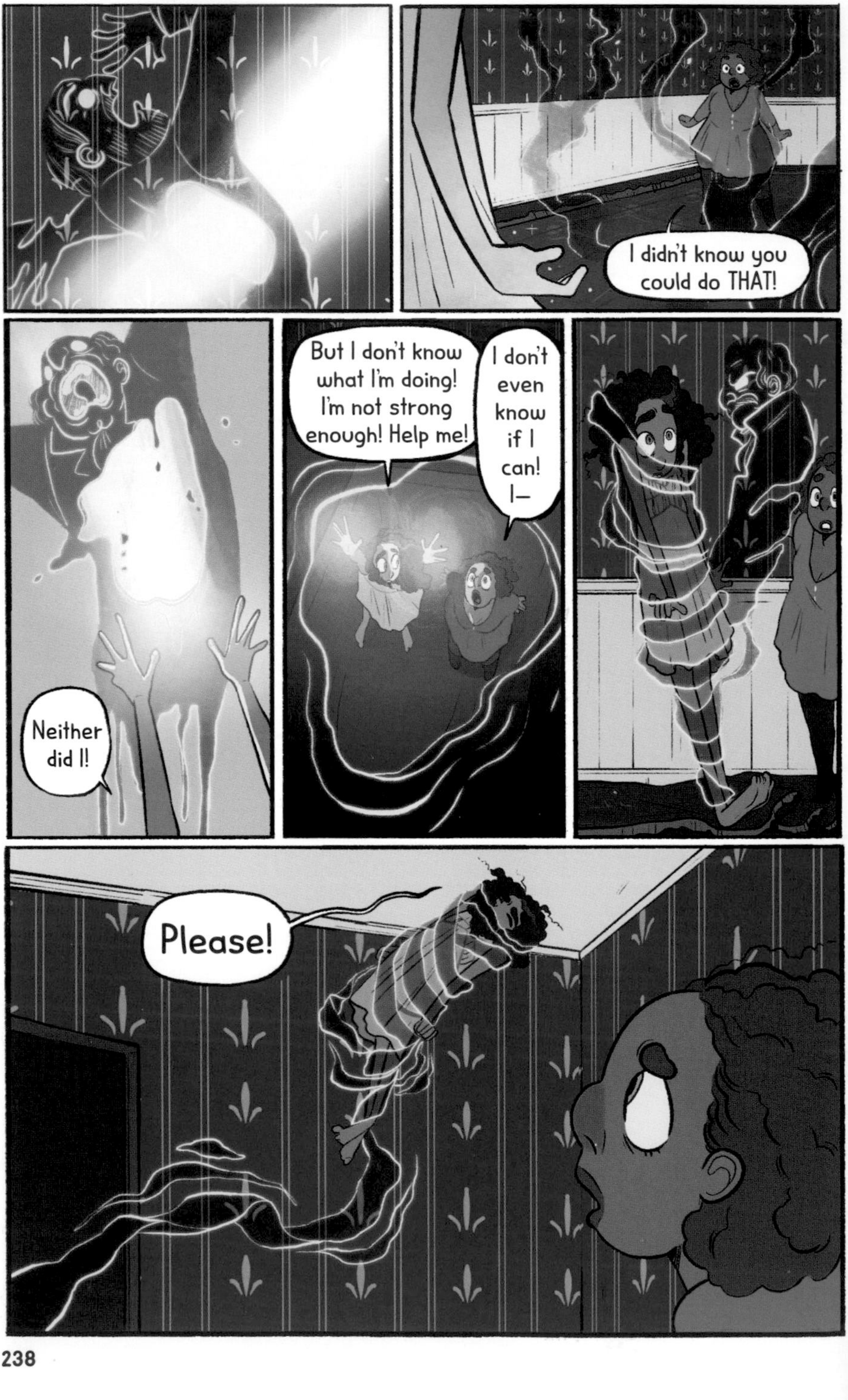
I didn't know you could do THAT!
Neither did I!
But I don't know what I'm doing! I'm not strong enough! Help me!
I don't even know if I can! I—
Please!

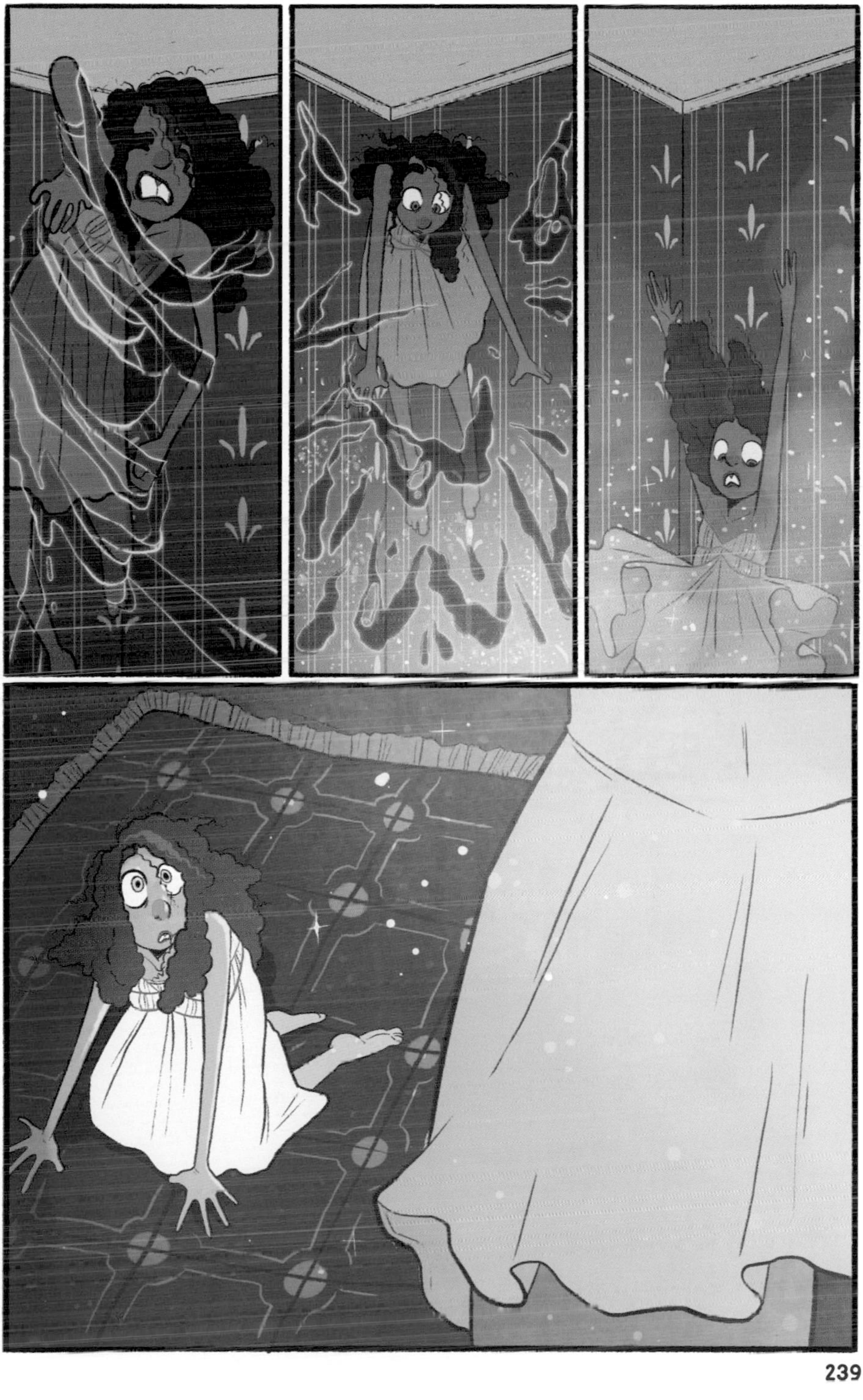

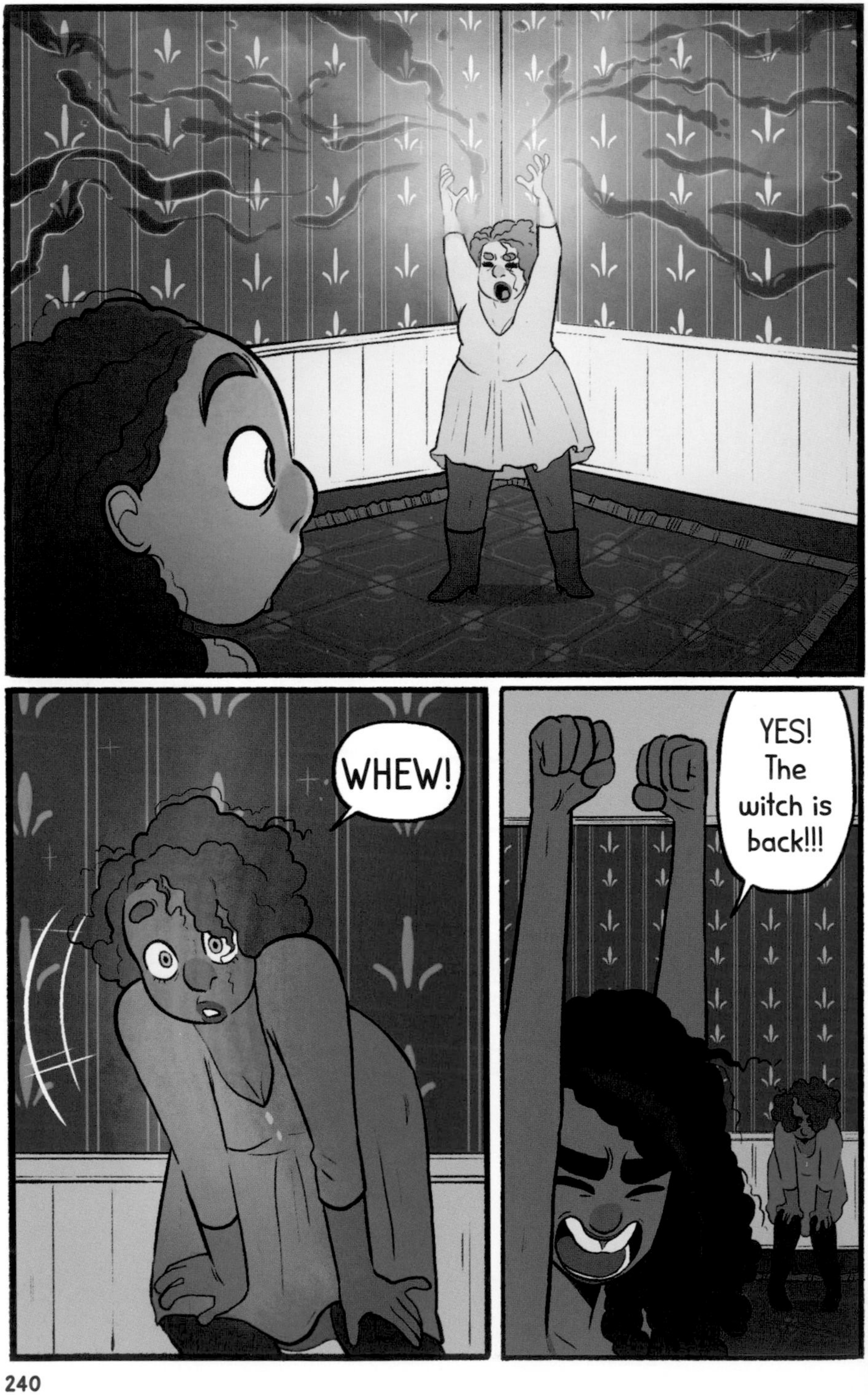
WHEW!
YES! The witch is back!!!

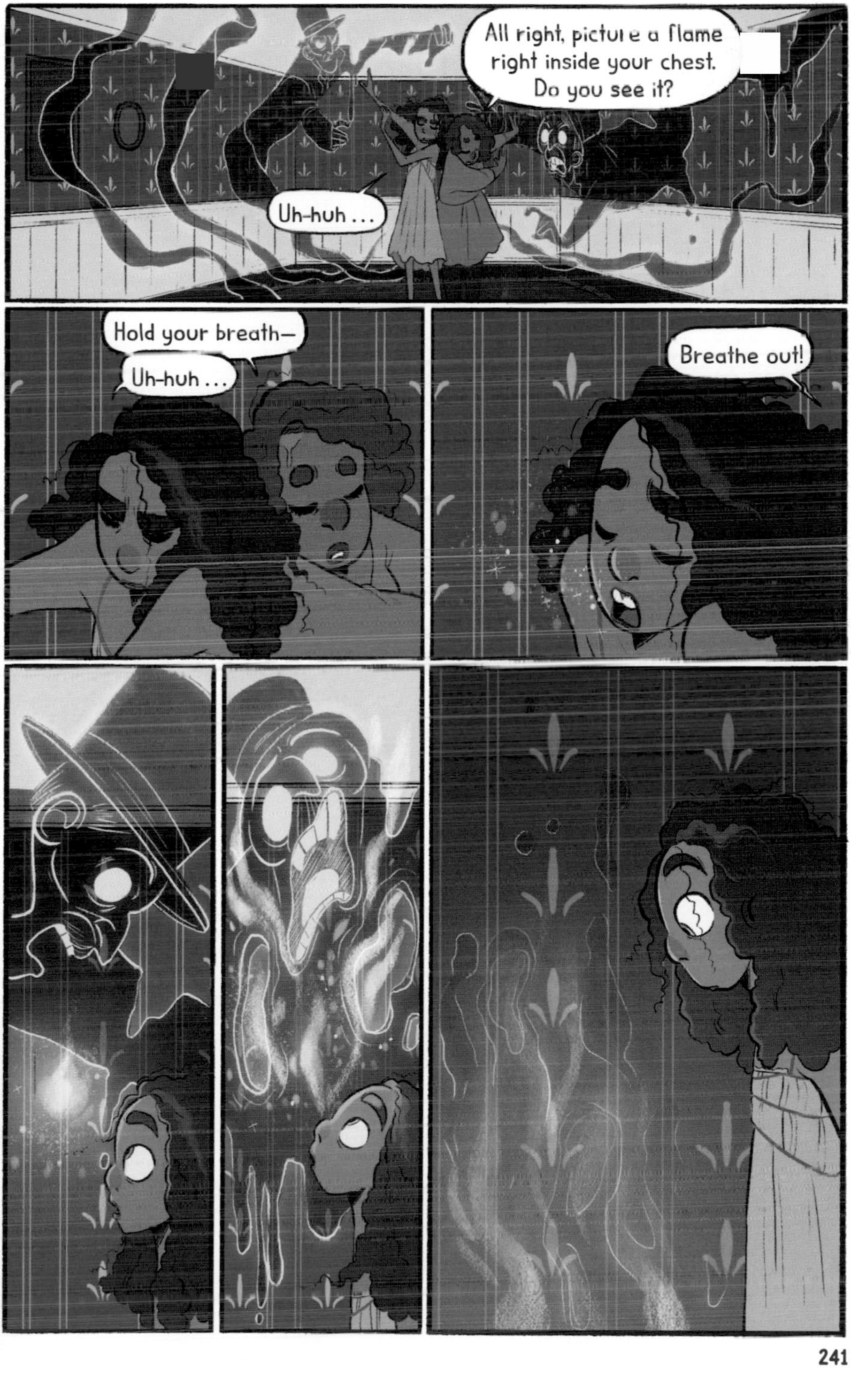
All right, picture a flame right inside your chest. Do you see it?
Uh-huh . . .
Hold your breath—
Uh-huh . . .
Breathe out!

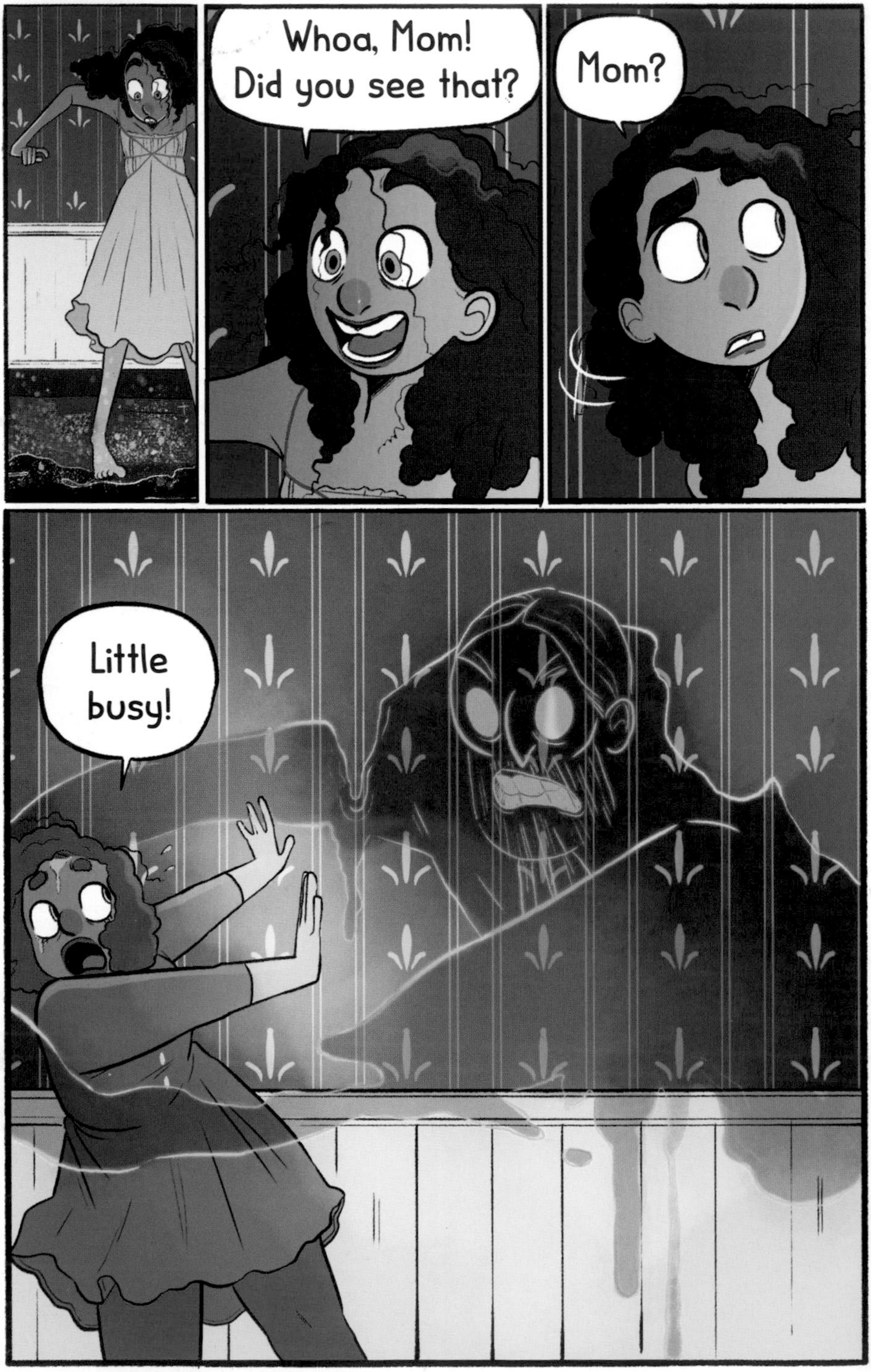
Whoa, Mom!
Did you see that?
Mom?
Little busy!

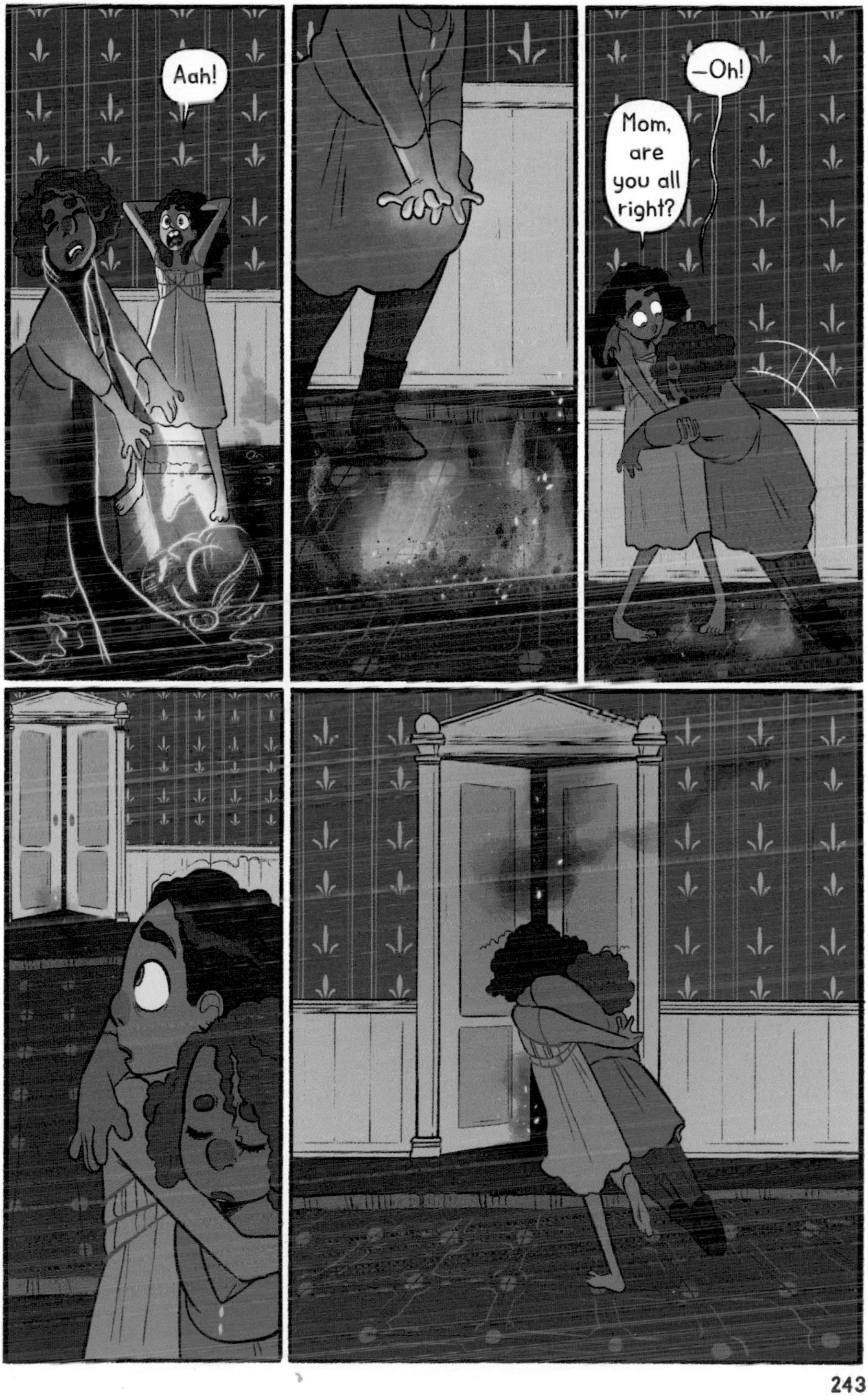
Aah!
—Oh!
Mom, are you all right?

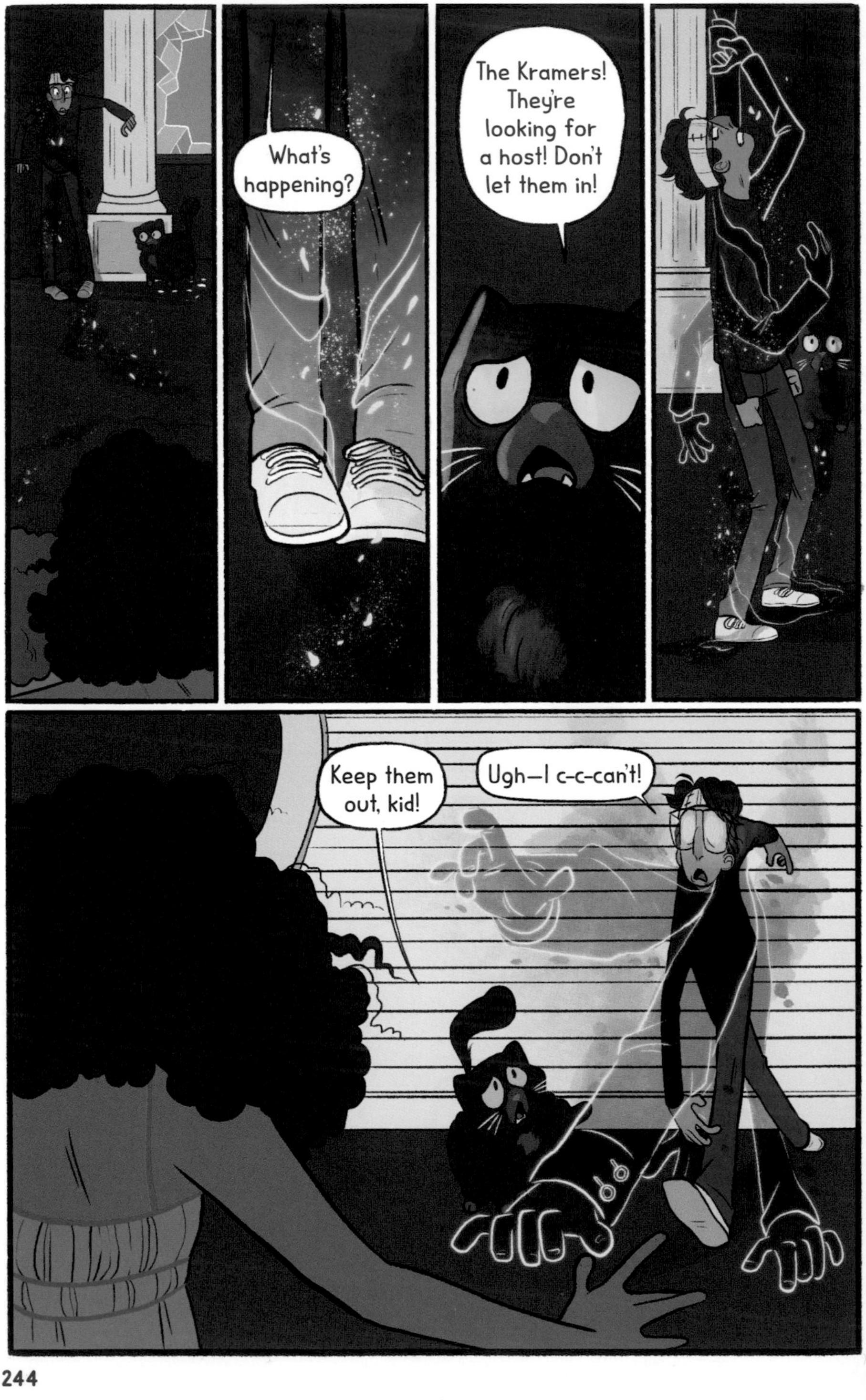
What's happening?
The Kramers! They're looking for a host! Don't let them in!
Keep them out, kid!
Ugh—I c-c-can't!

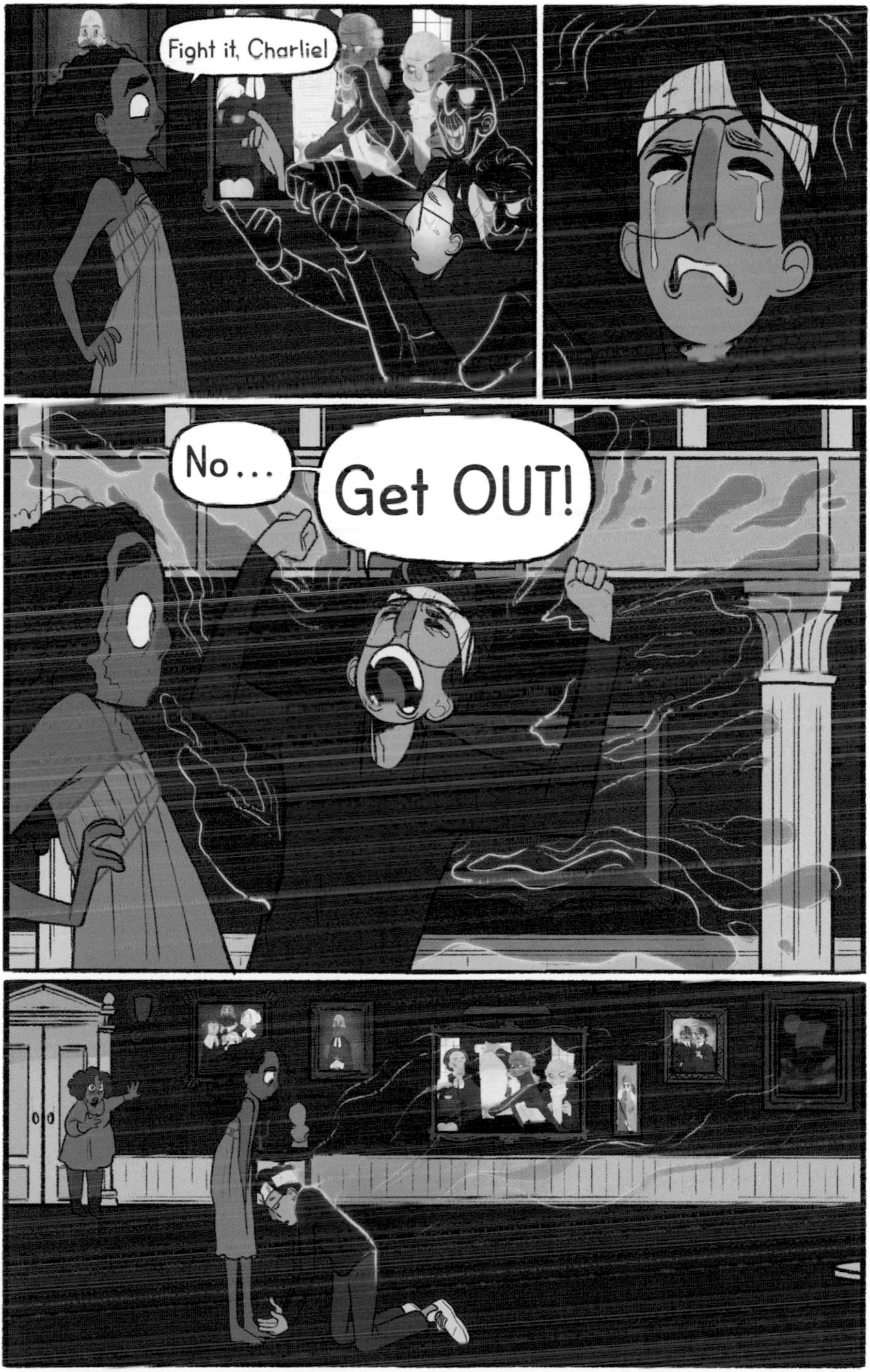
Fight it, Charlie!
No...
Get OUT!

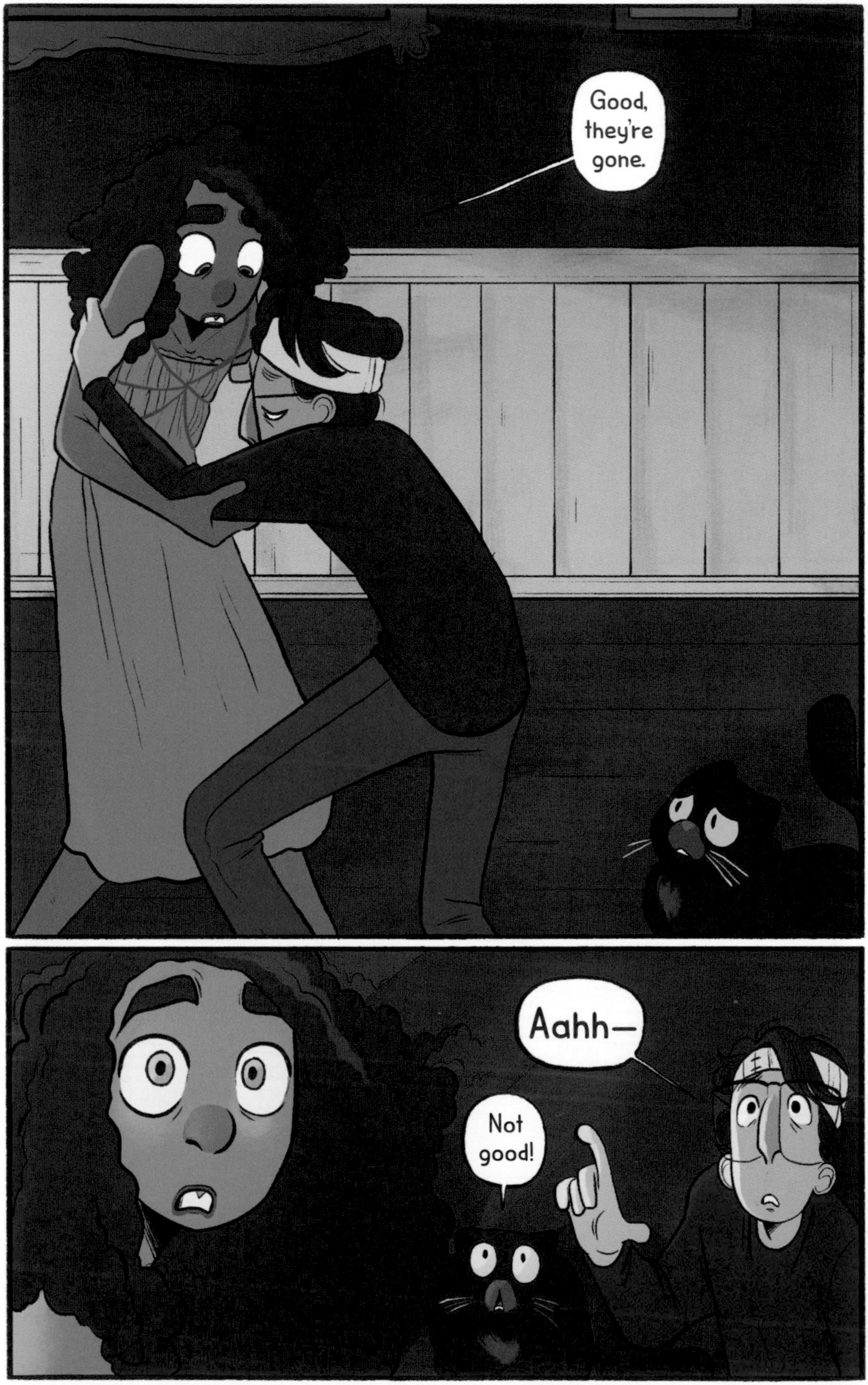
Good, they're gone.
Aahh—
Not good!

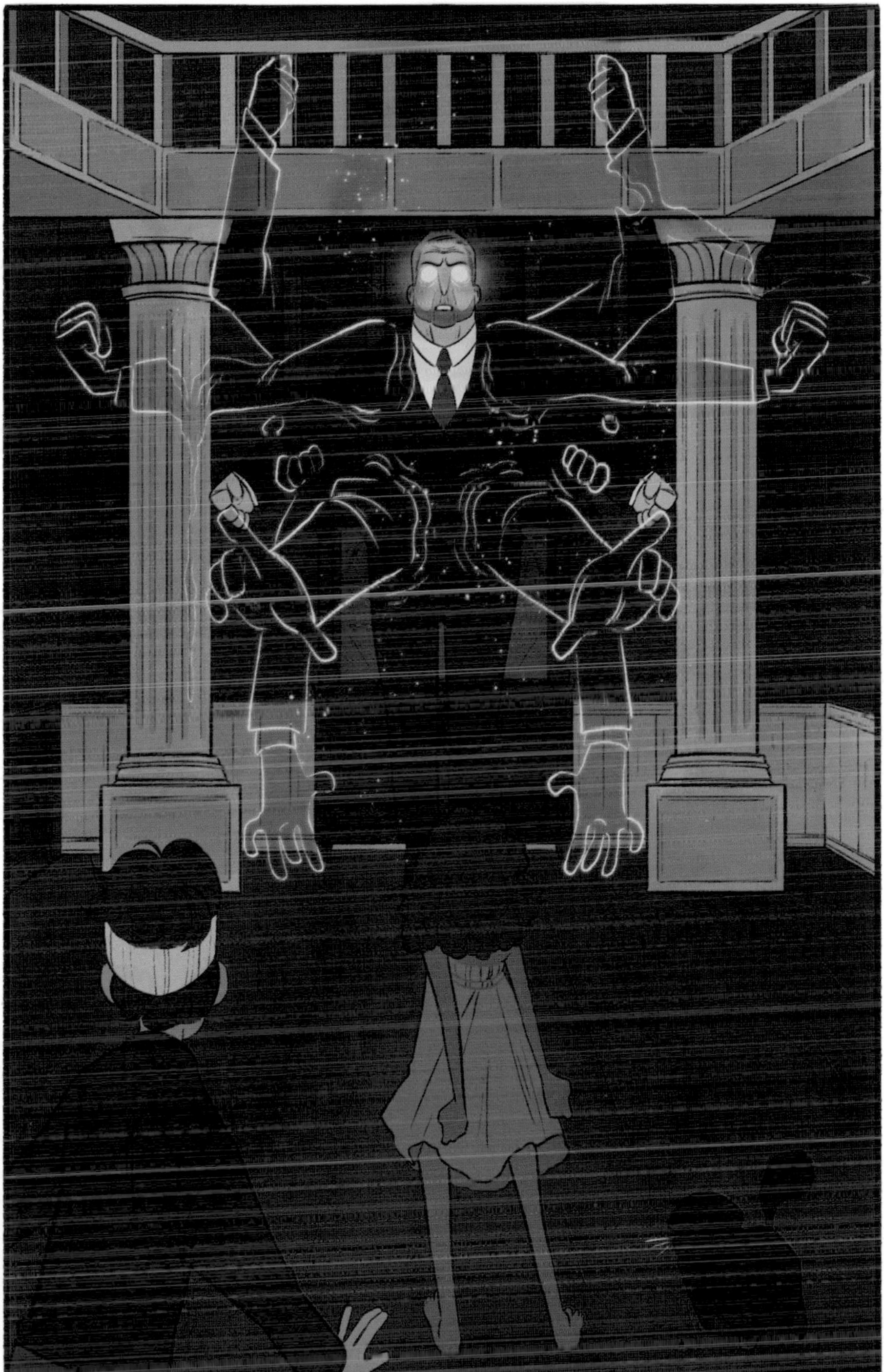

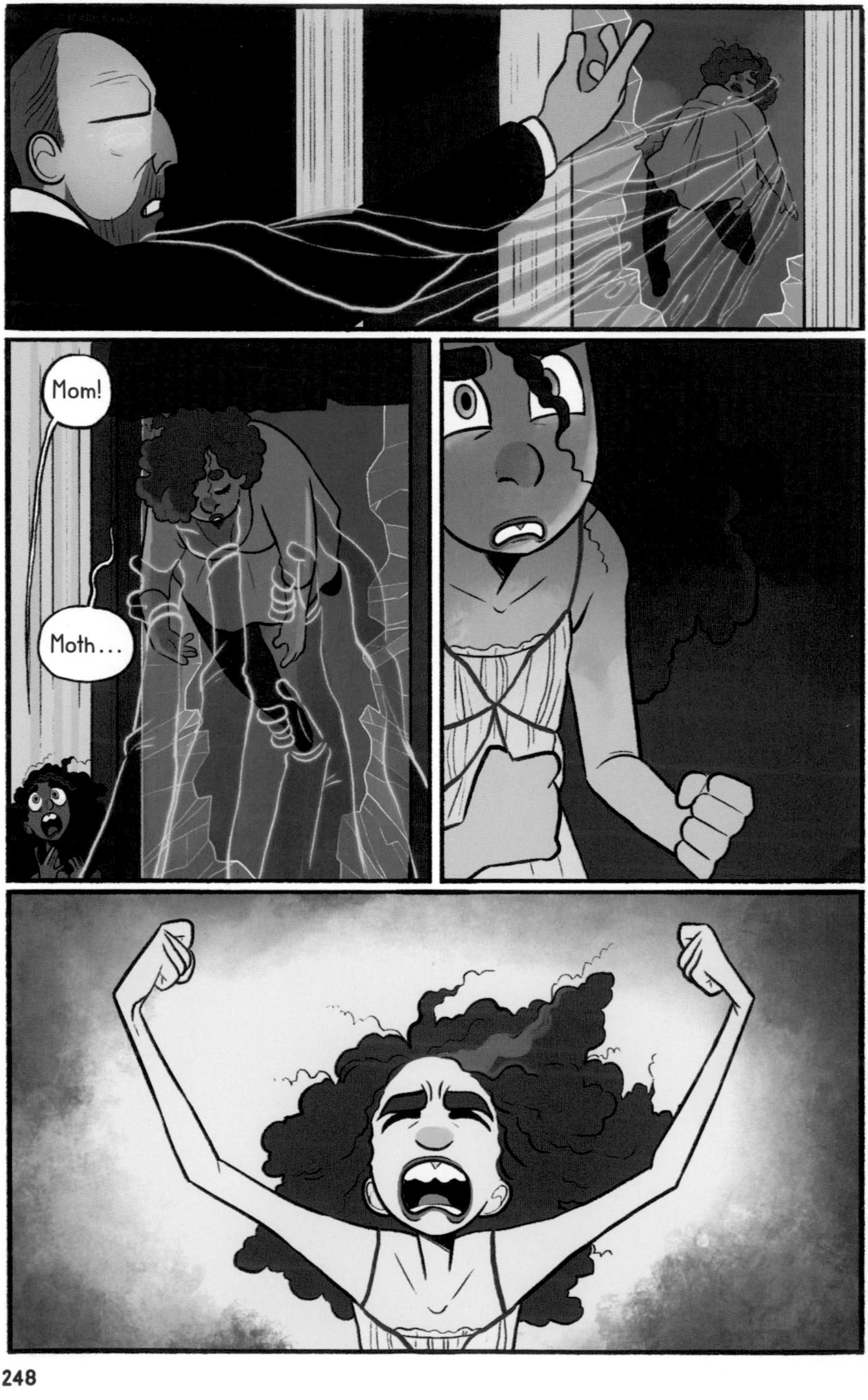
Mom!
Moth...

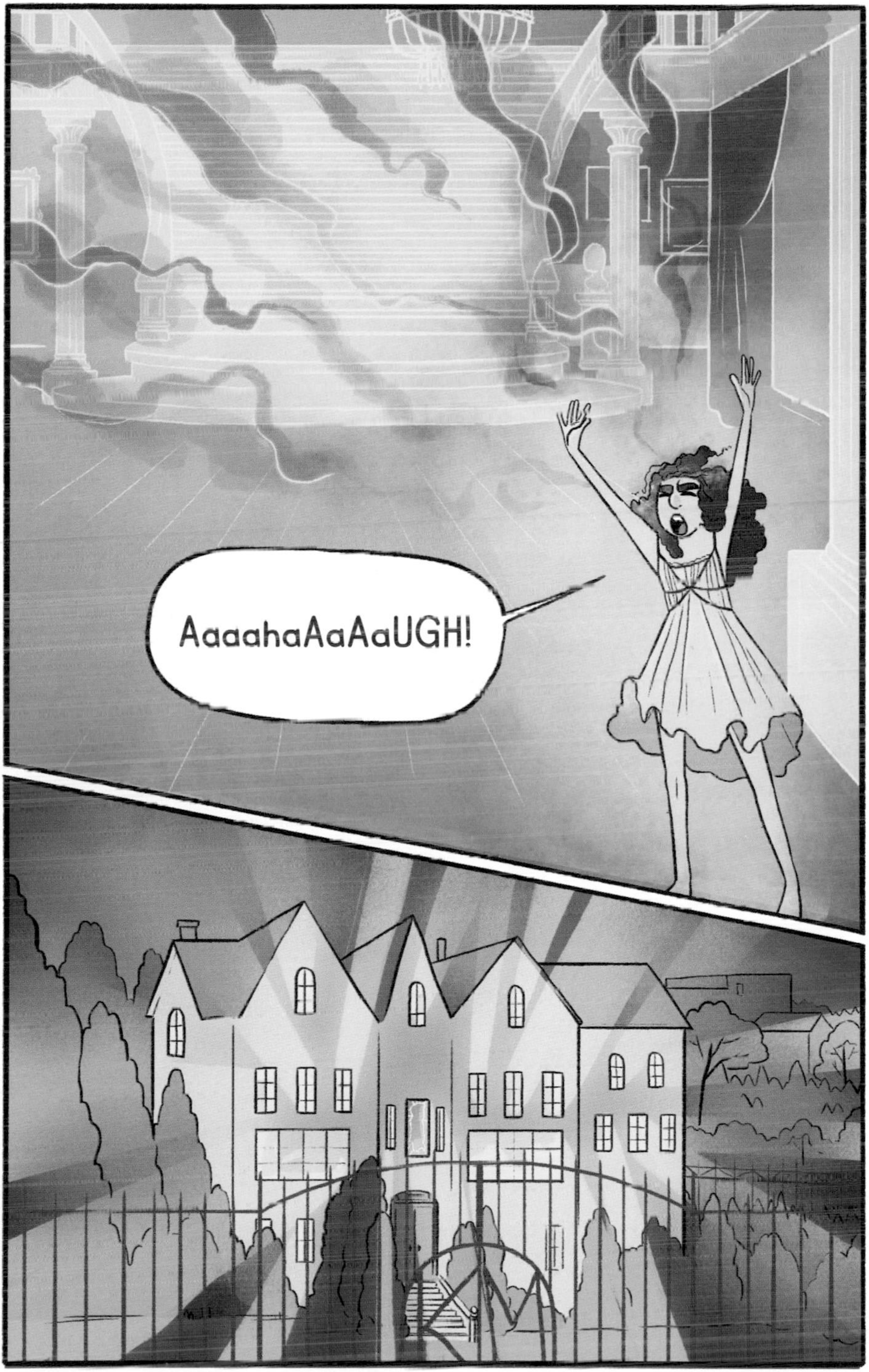
AaaahaAaAaUGH!

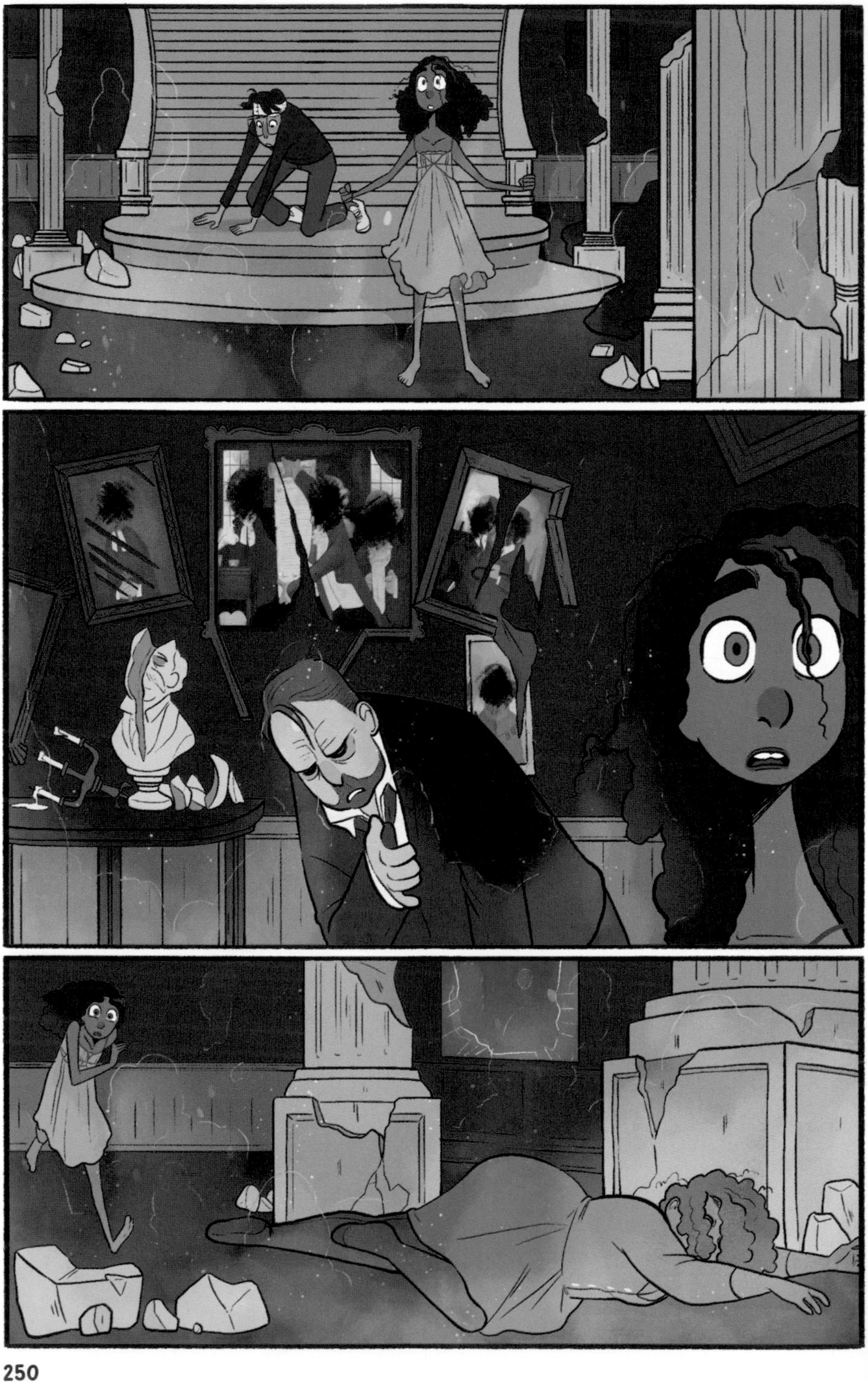

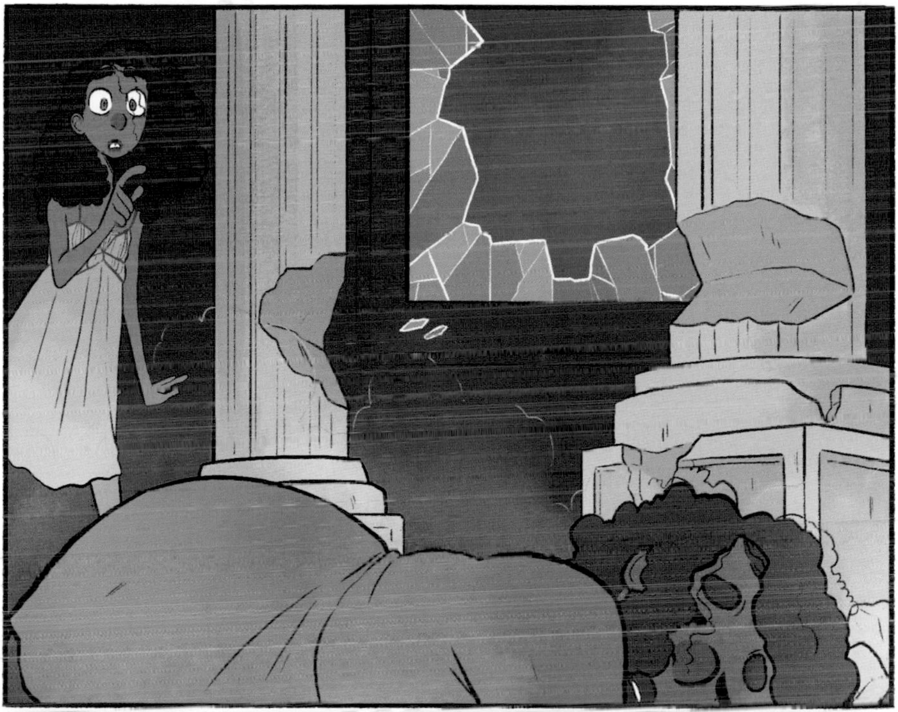

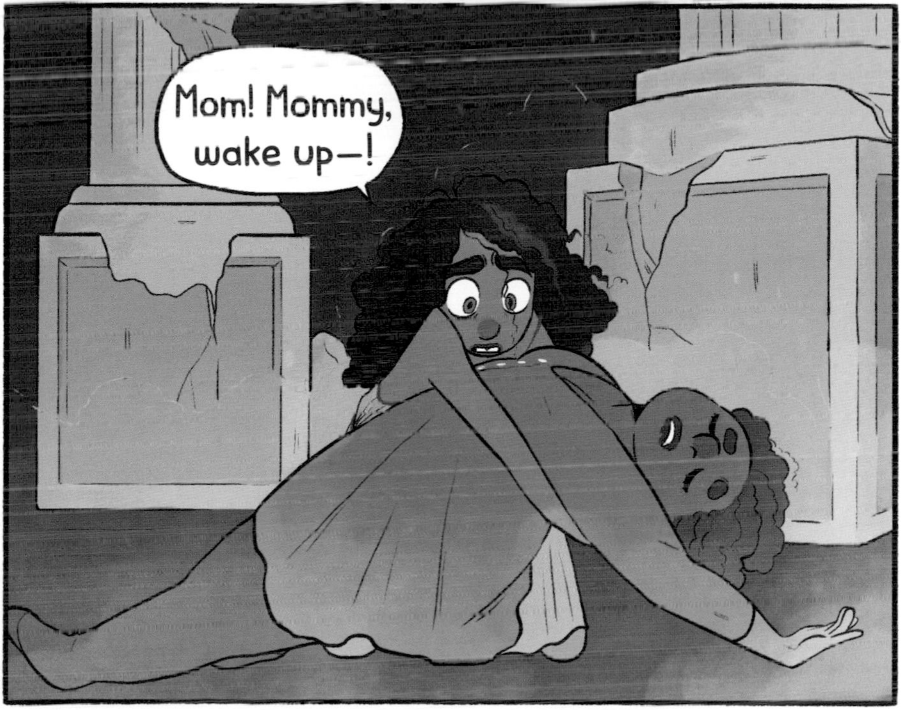
Mom! Mommy, wake up—!

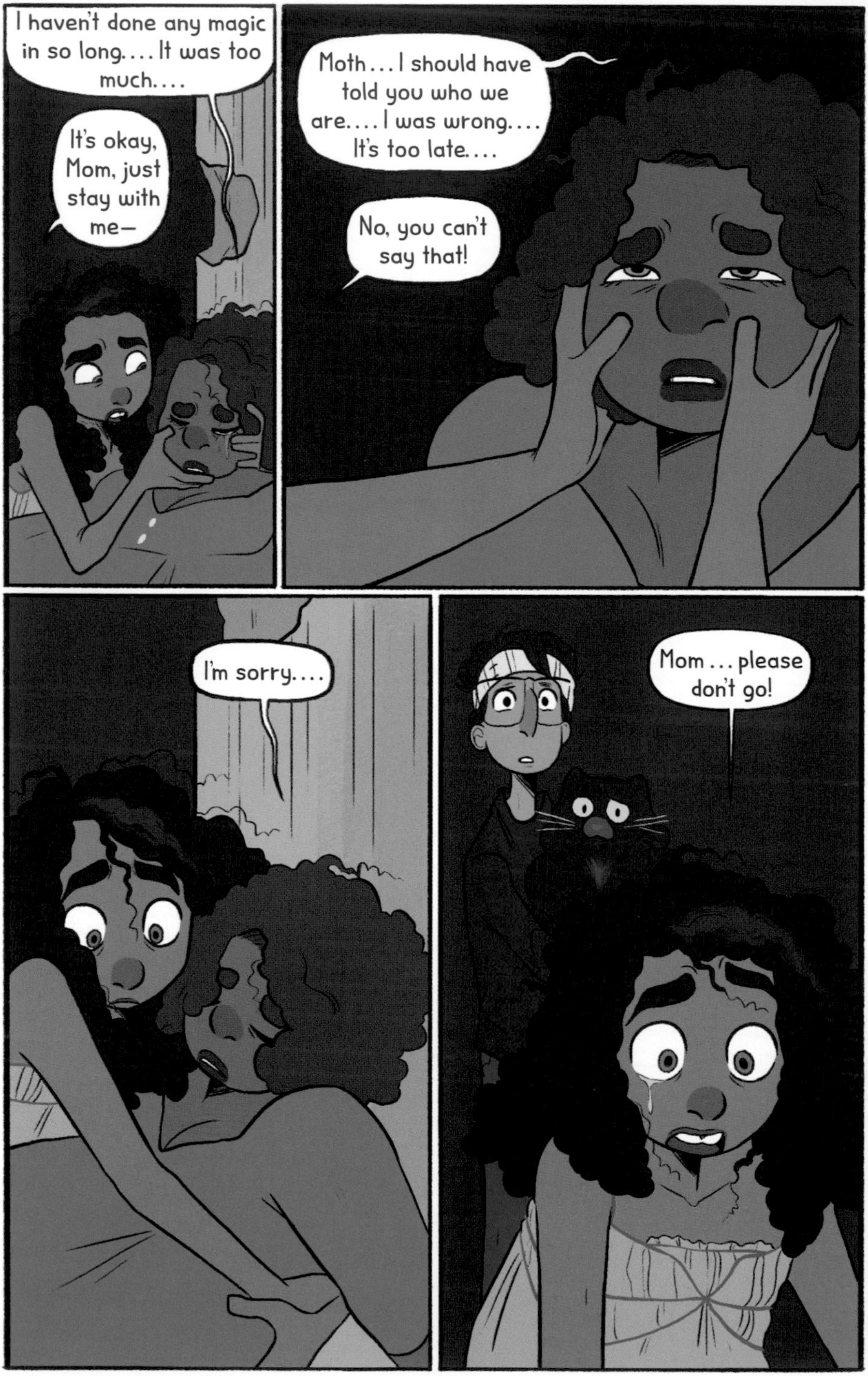
I haven't done any magic in so long.... It was too much....
It's okay, Mom, just stay with me—
Moth... I should have told you who we are.... I was wrong.... It's too late....
No, you can't say that!
I'm sorry....
Mom ... please don't go!

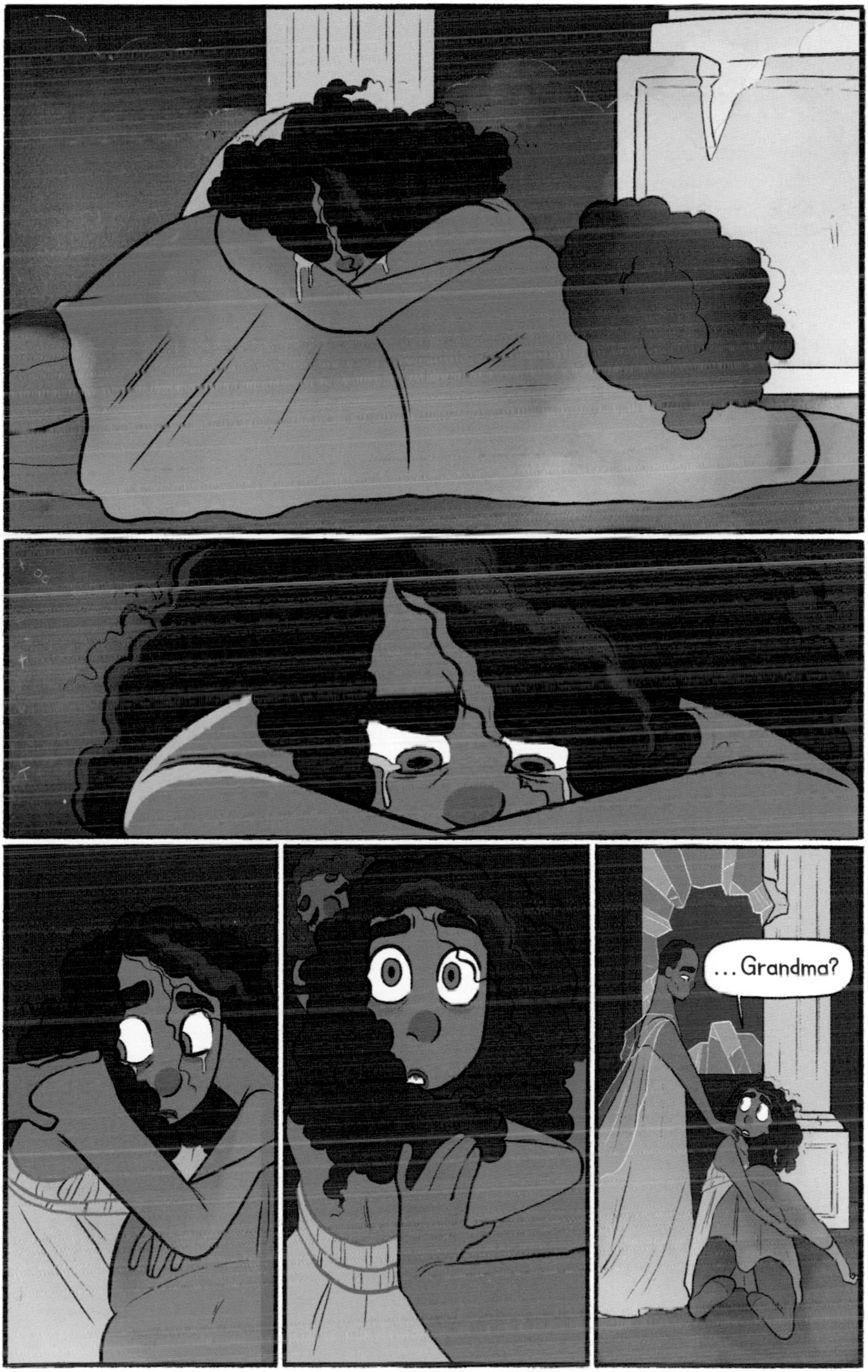
...Grandma?

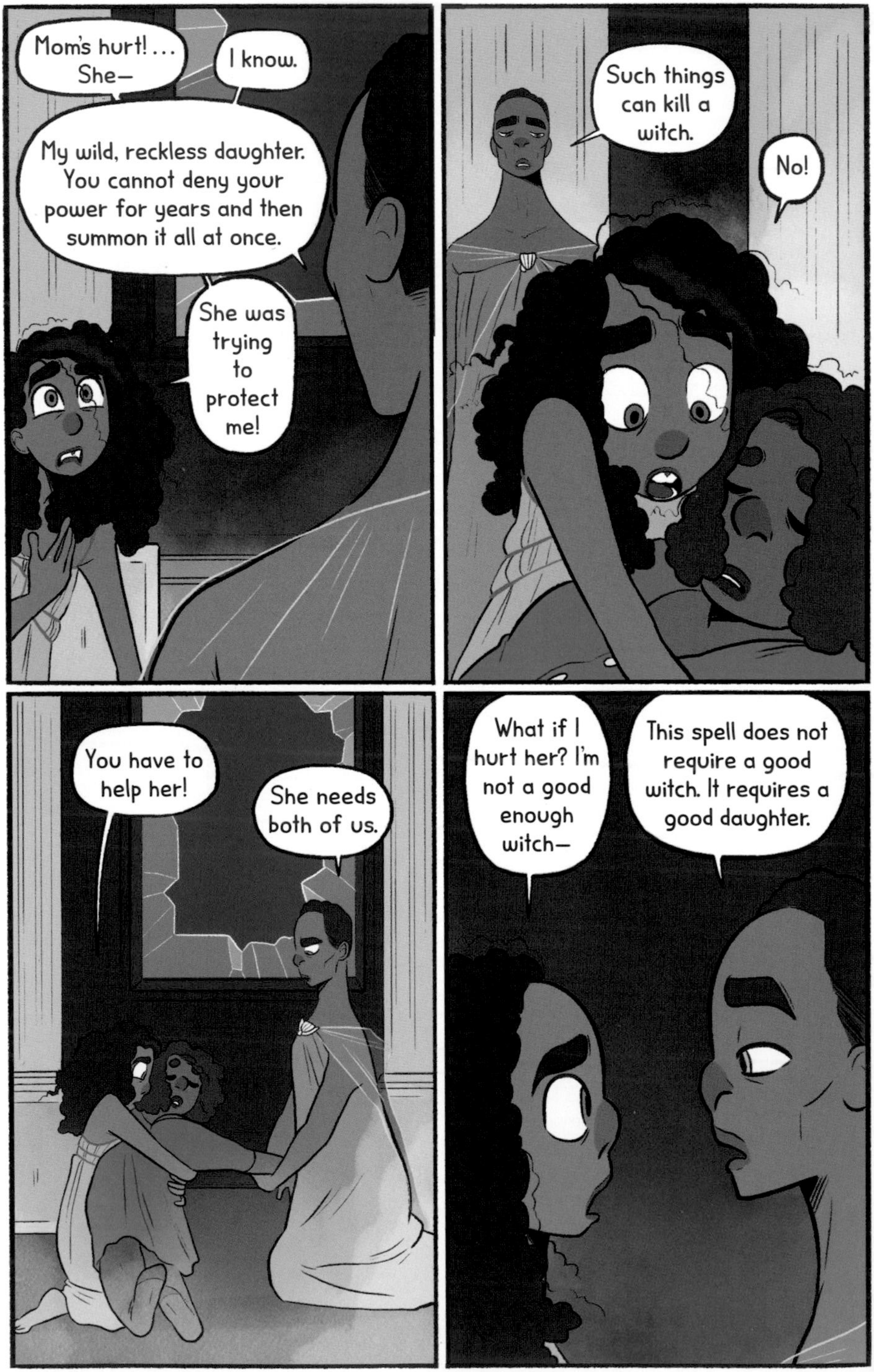
Mom's hurt!...
She—
I know.
My wild, reckless daughter. You cannot deny your power for years and then summon it all at once.
She was trying to protect me!
Such things can kill a witch.
No!
You have to help her!
She needs both of us.
What if I hurt her? I'm not a good enough witch—
This spell does not require a good witch. It requires a good daughter.

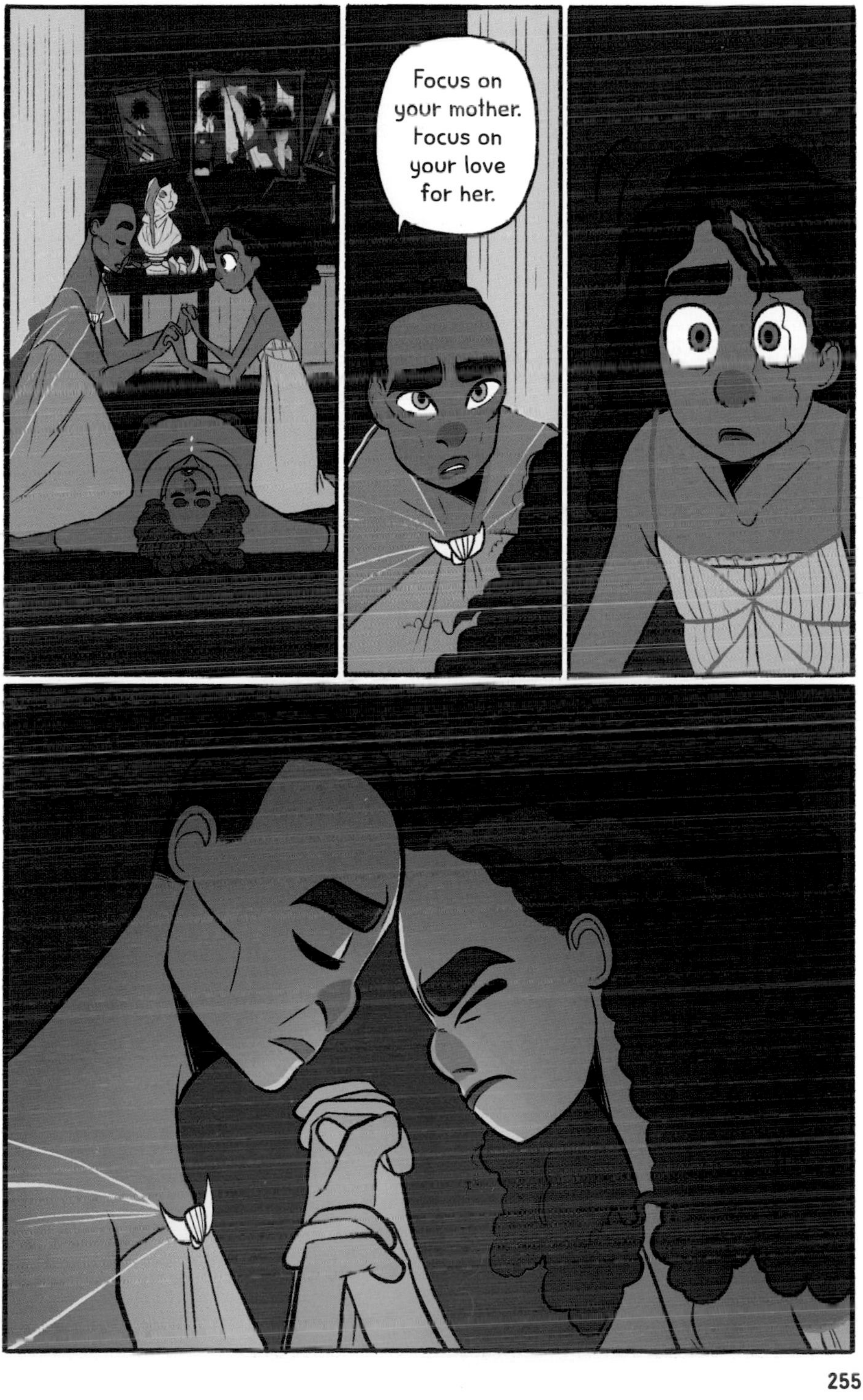
Focus on your mother. Focus on your love for her.

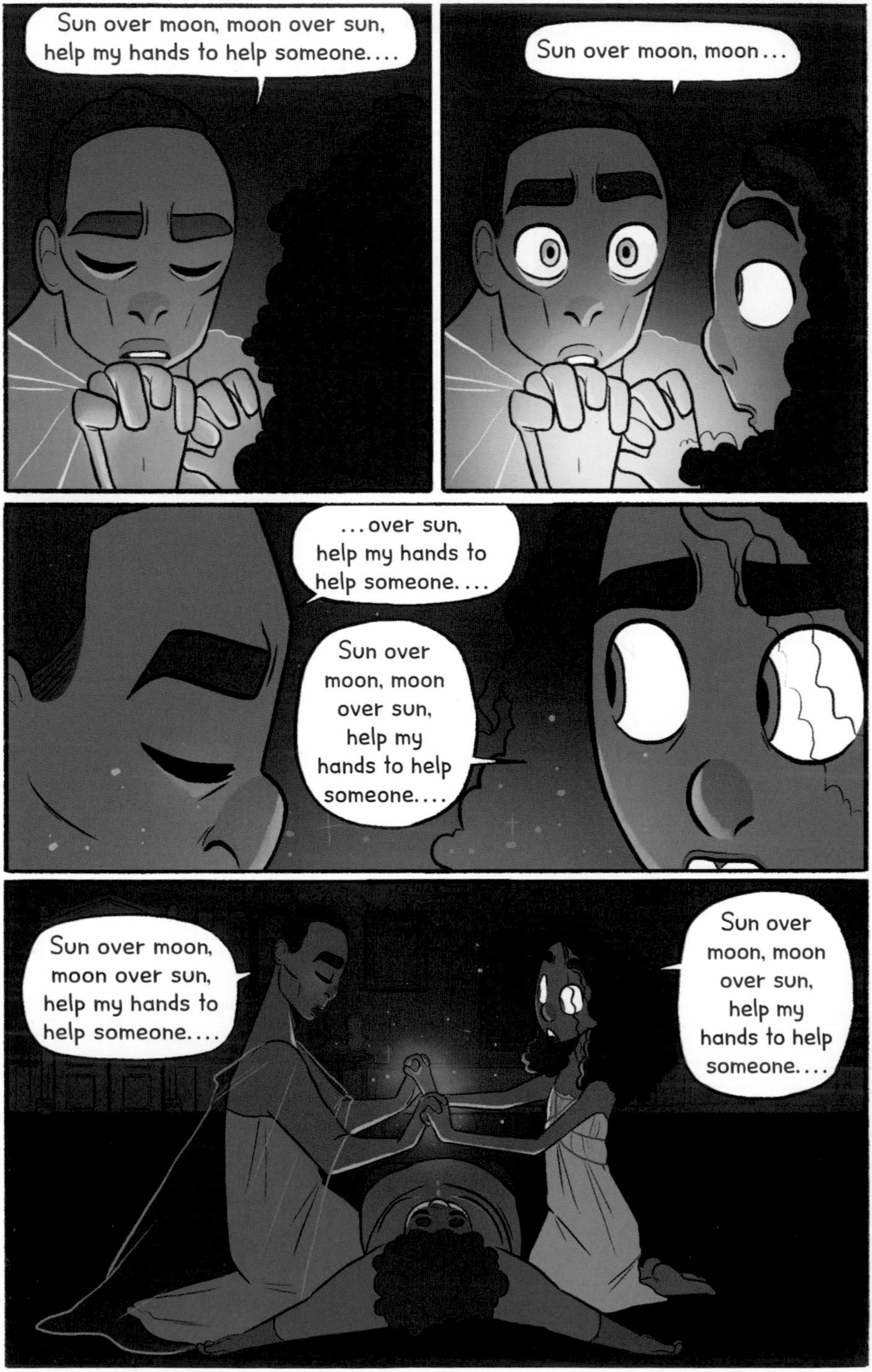
Sun over moon, moon over sun, help my hands to help someone....
Sun over moon, moon...
...over sun, help my hands to help someone....
Sun over moon, moon over sun, help my hands to help someone....
Sun over moon, moon over sun, help my hands to help someone....
Sun over moon, moon over sun, help my hands to help someone....

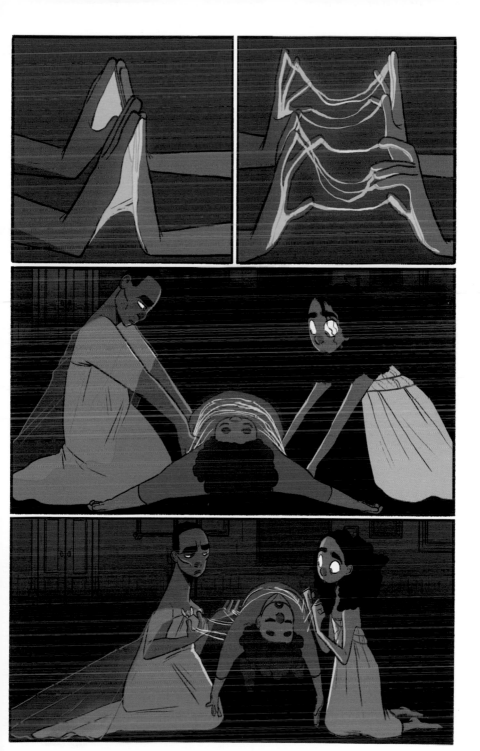

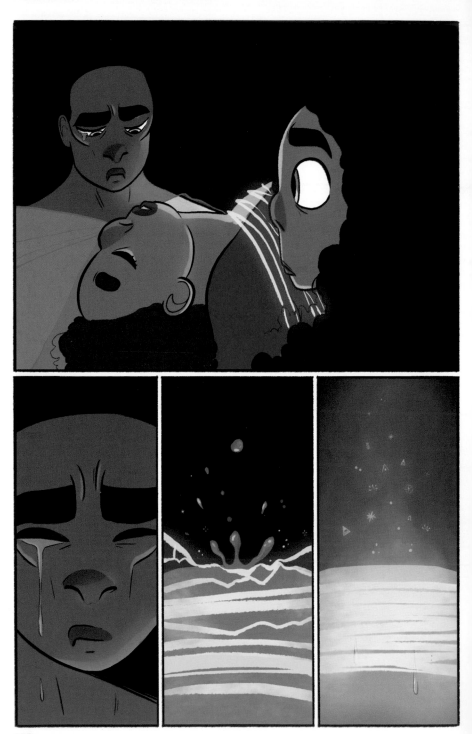

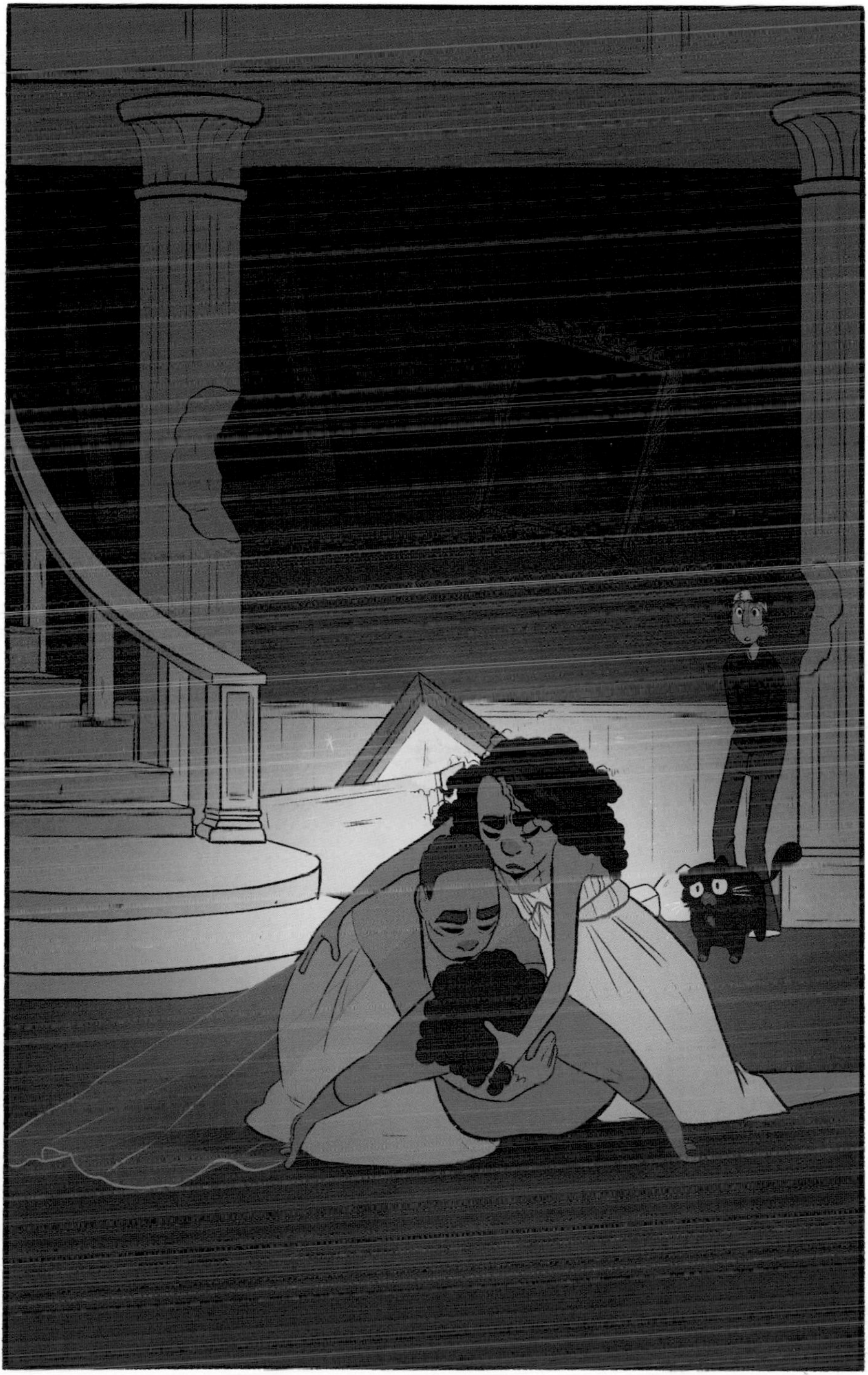

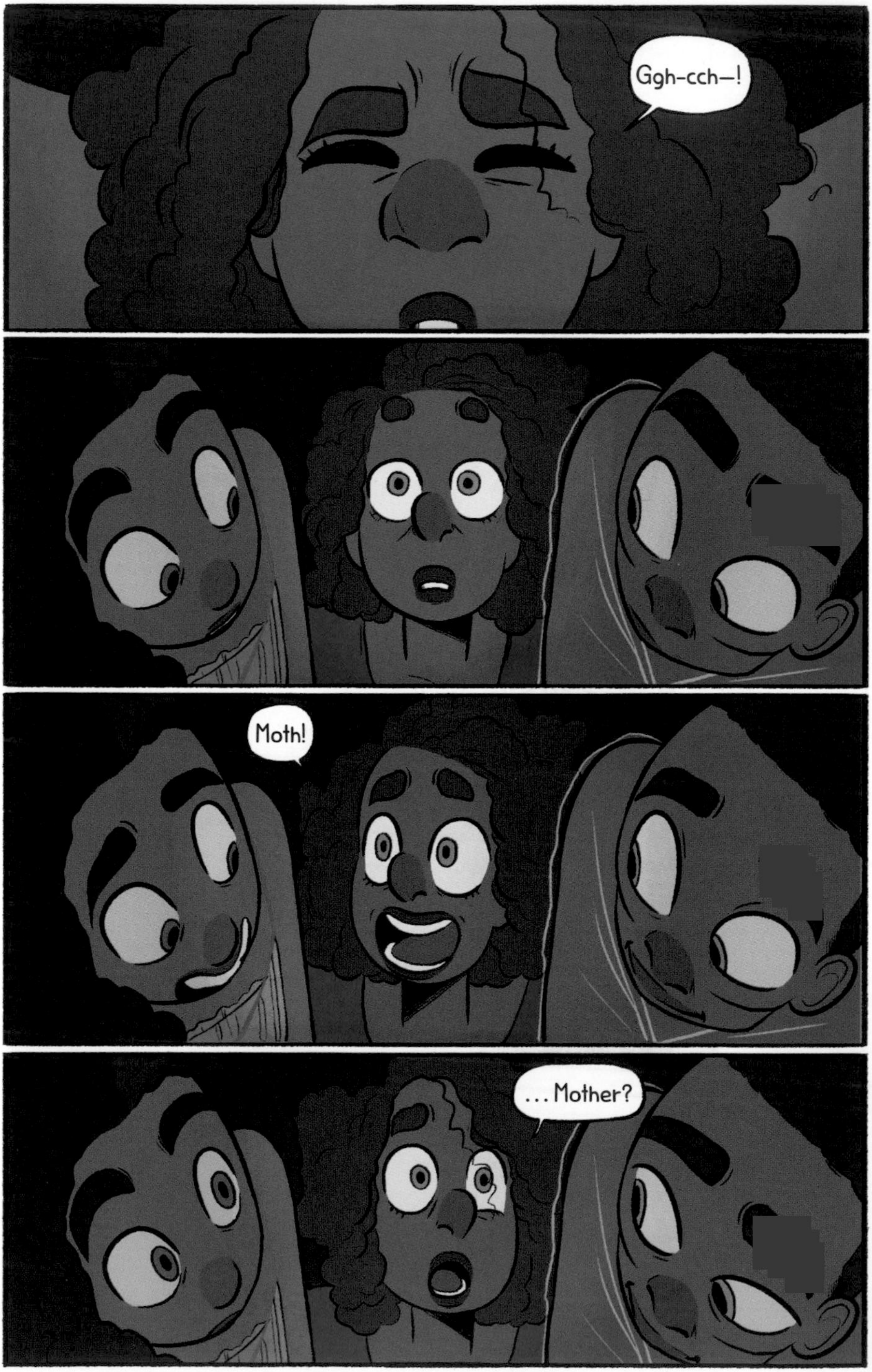
Ggh-cch—!
Moth!
...Mother?

CHAPTER 15
Okay Witch

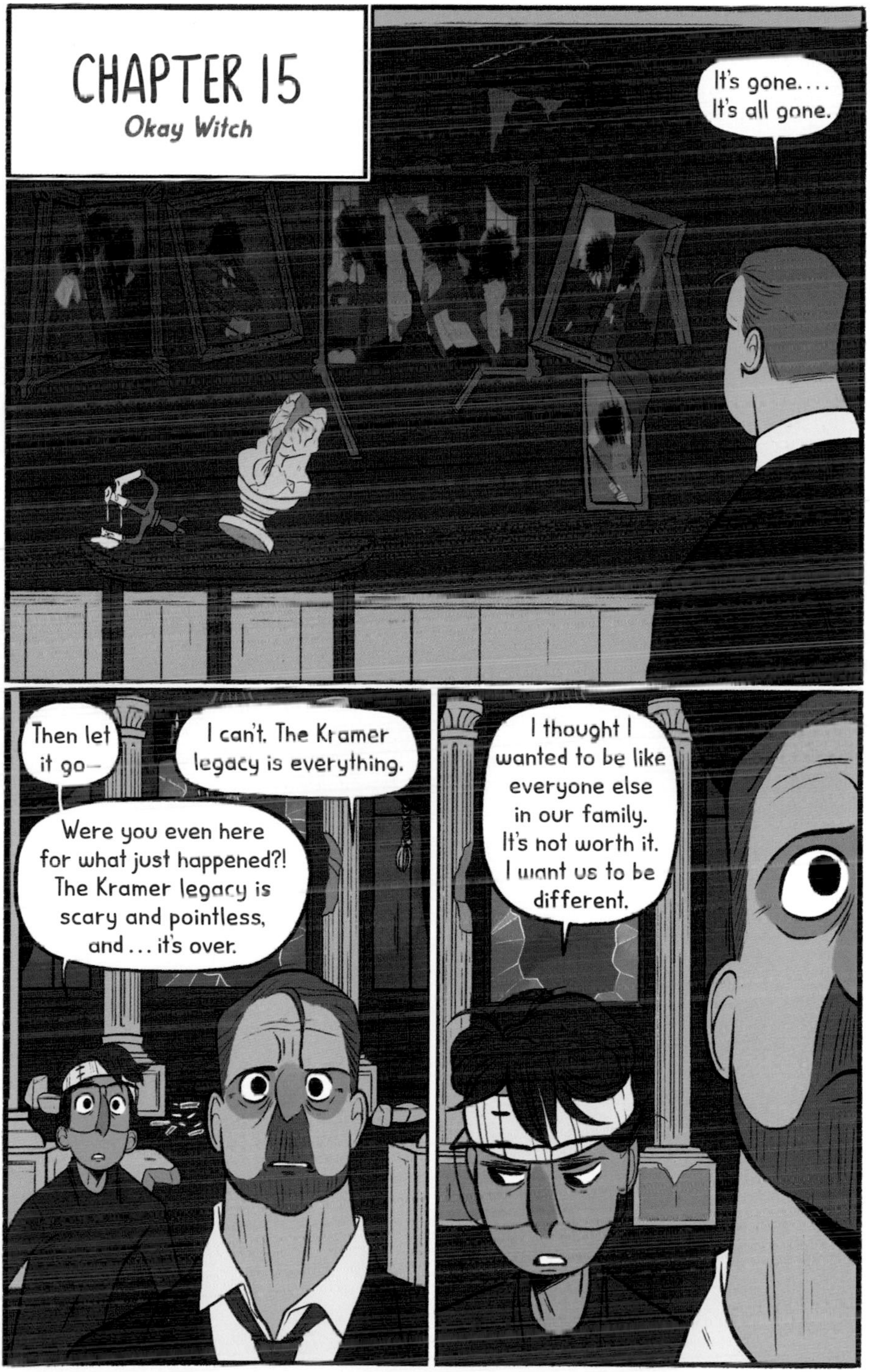

It's gone.... It's all gone.
Then let it go—
I can't. The Kramer legacy is everything.
Were you even here for what just happened?! The Kramer legacy is scary and pointless, and ... it's over.
I thought I wanted to be like everyone else in our family. It's not worth it. I want us to be different.

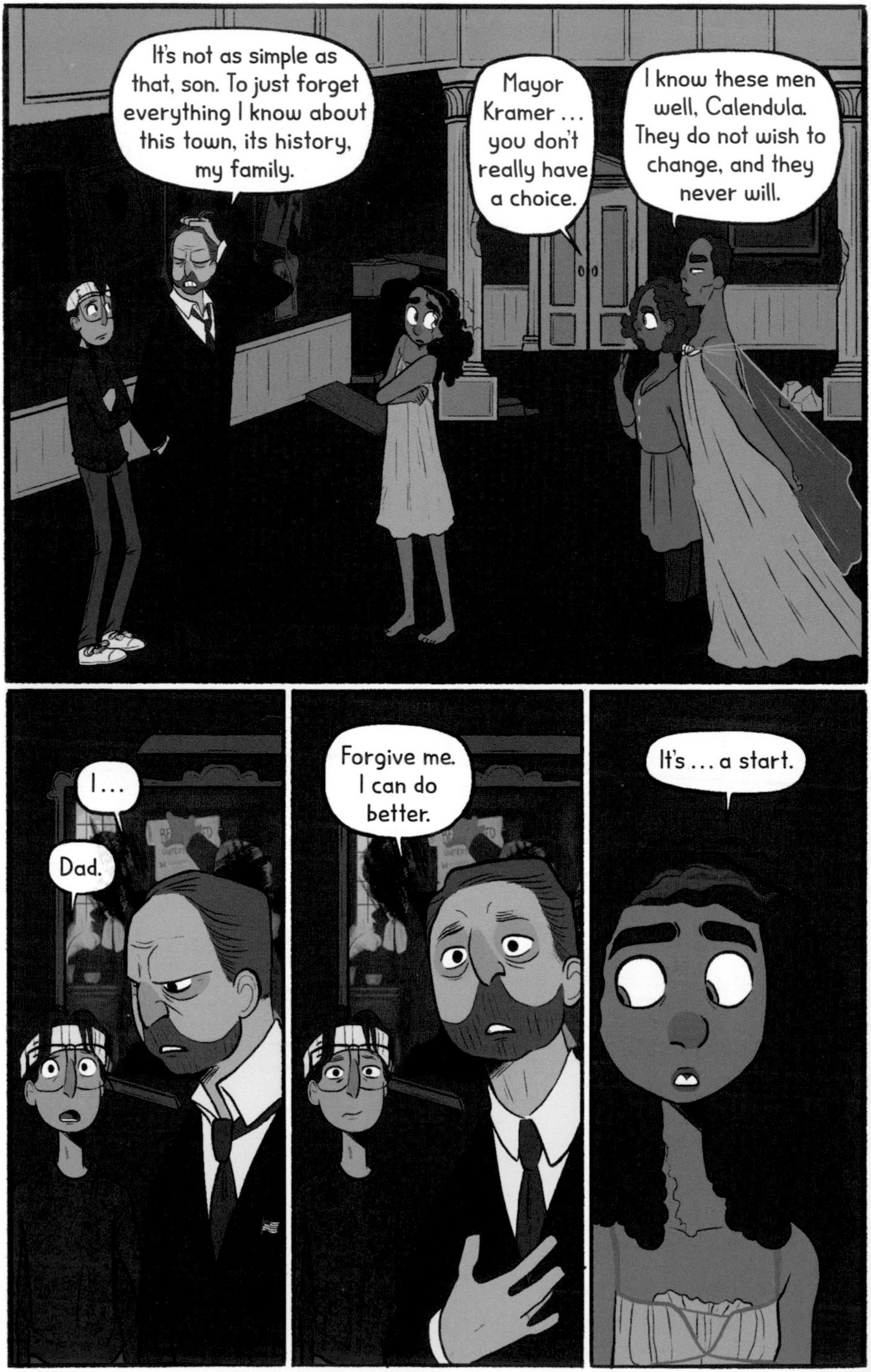
It's not as simple as that, son. To just forget everything I know about this town, its history, my family.
Mayor Kramer . . . you don't really have a choice.
I know these men well, Calendula. They do not wish to change, and they never will.
I . . .
Dad.
Forgive me. I can do better.
It's . . . a start.

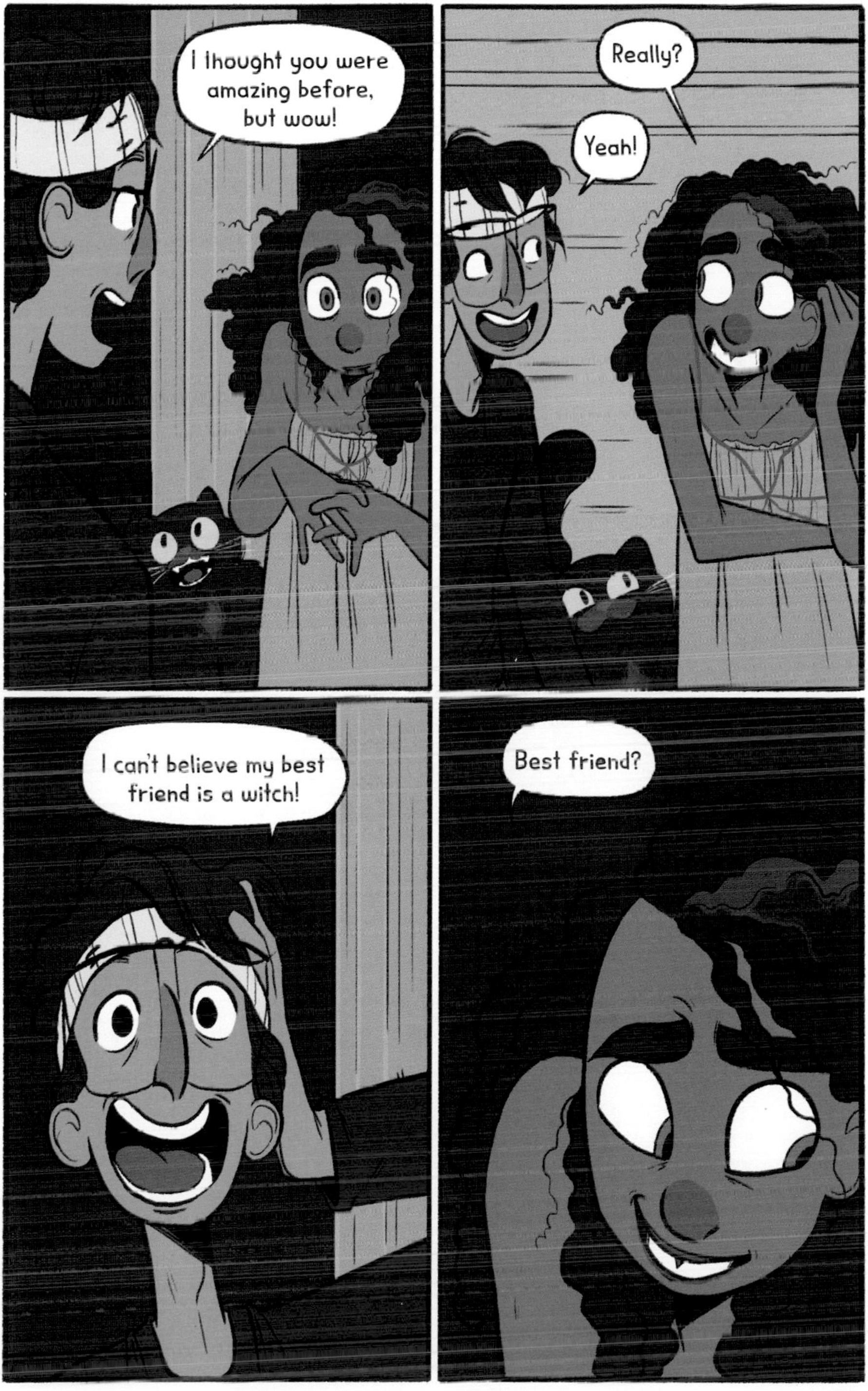
I thought you were amazing before, but wow!
Really?
Yeah!
I can't believe my best friend is a witch!
Best friend?

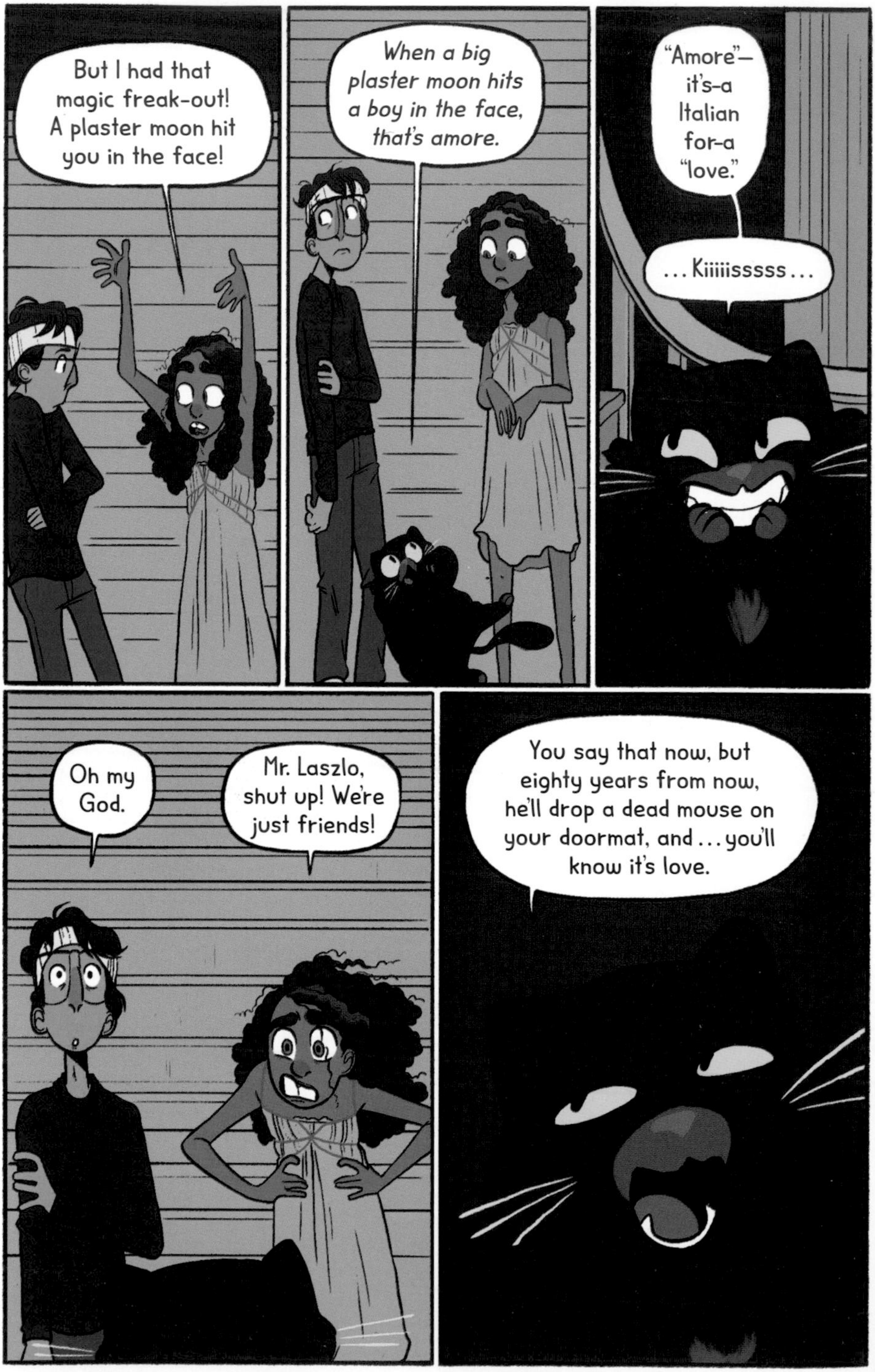
But I had that magic freak-out! A plaster moon hit you in the face!
When a big plaster moon hits a boy in the face, that's amore.
"Amore"— it's-a Italian for-a "love."
... Kiiiiissss ...
Oh my God.
Mr. Laszlo, shut up! We're just friends!
You say that now, but eighty years from now, he'll drop a dead mouse on your doormat, and ... you'll know it's love.

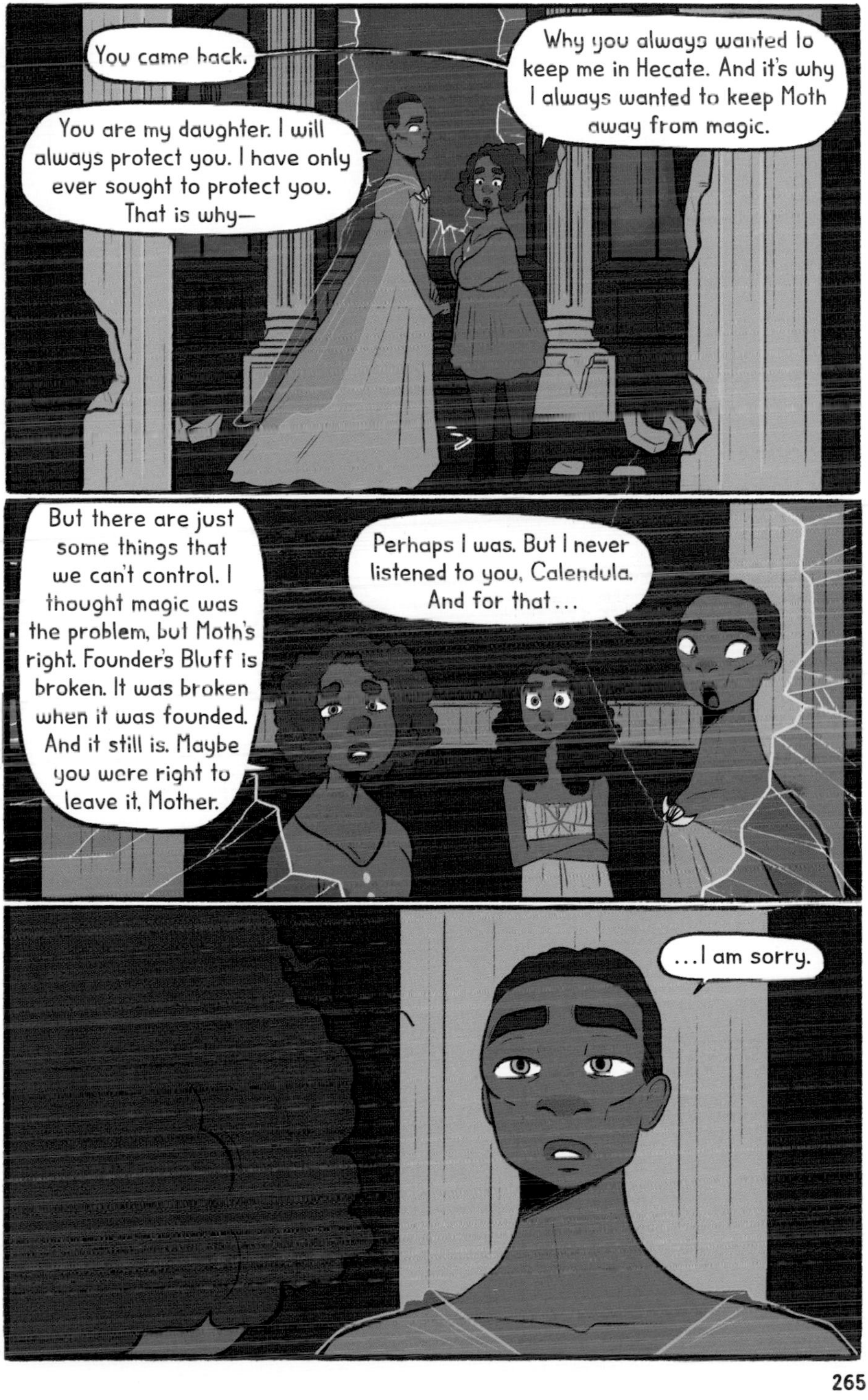
You came back.
Why you always wanted to keep me in Hecate. And it's why I always wanted to keep Moth away from magic.
You are my daughter. I will always protect you. I have only ever sought to protect you. That is why—
But there are just some things that we can't control. I thought magic was the problem, but Moth's right. Founder's Bluff is broken. It was broken when it was founded. And it still is. Maybe you were right to leave it, Mother.
Perhaps I was. But I never listened to you, Calendula. And for that...
...I am sorry.

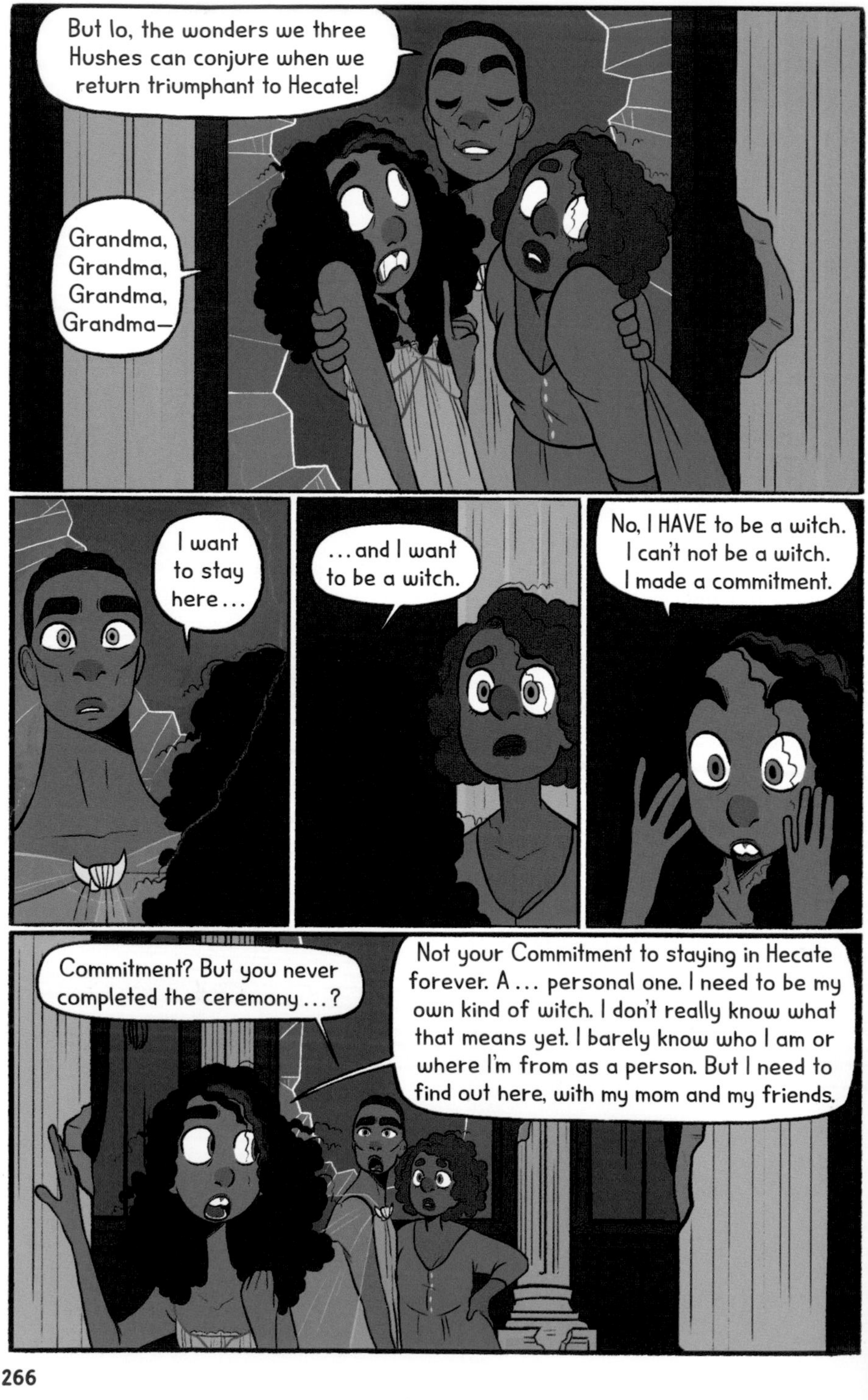

But lo, the wonders we three Hushes can conjure when we return triumphant to Hecate!
Grandma, Grandma, Grandma, Grandma—
I want to stay here...
...and I want to be a witch.
No, I HAVE to be a witch. I can't not be a witch. I made a commitment.
Commitment? But you never completed the ceremony...?
Not your Commitment to staying in Hecate forever. A... personal one. I need to be my own kind of witch. I don't really know what that means yet. I barely know who I am or where I'm from as a person. But I need to find out here, with my mom and my friends.

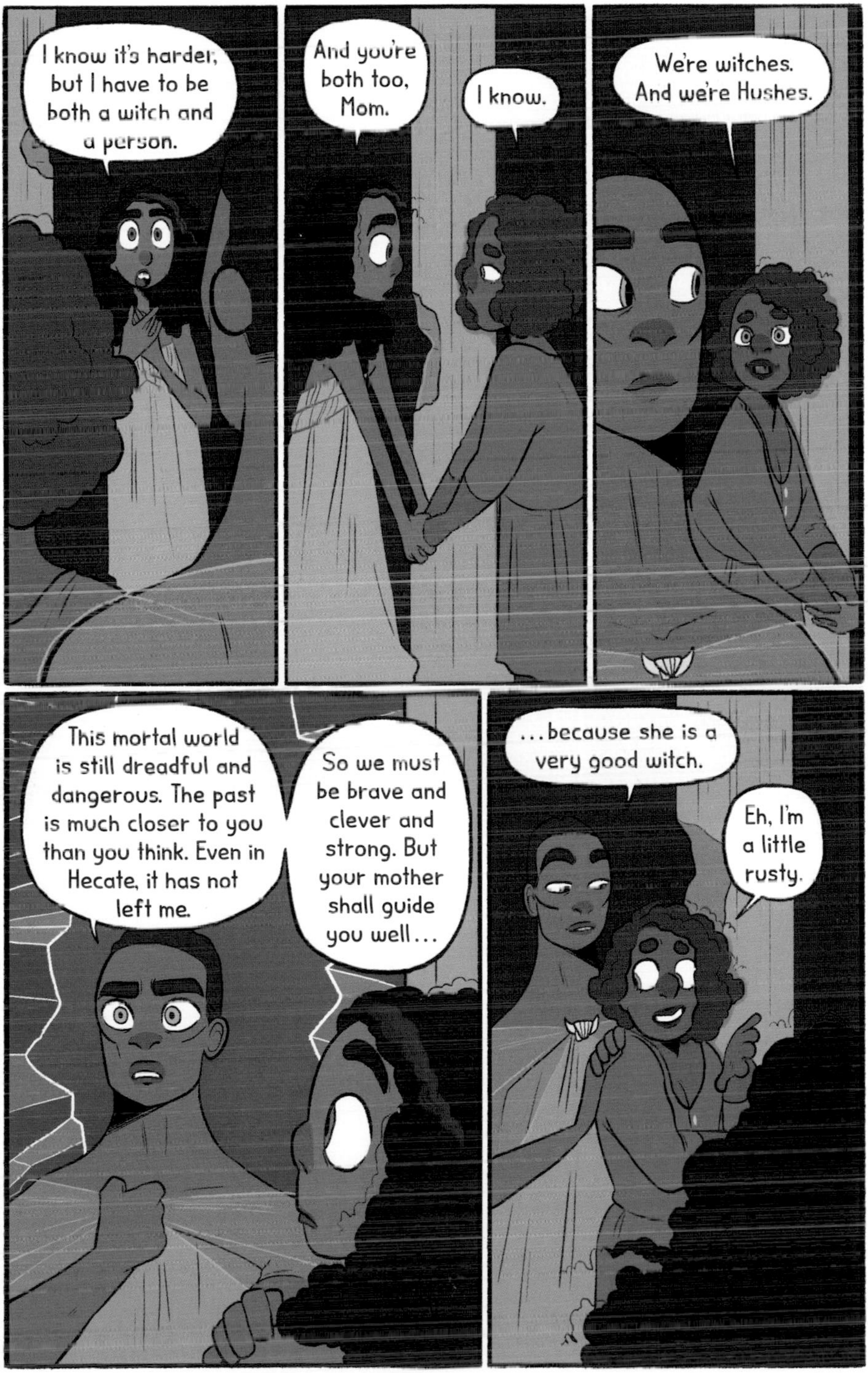
I know it's harder, but I have to be both a witch and a person.
And you're both too, Mom.
I know.
We're witches. And we're Hushes.
This mortal world is still dreadful and dangerous. The past is much closer to you than you think. Even in Hecate, it has not left me.
So we must be brave and clever and strong. But your mother shall guide you well...
...because she is a very good witch.
Eh, I'm a little rusty.

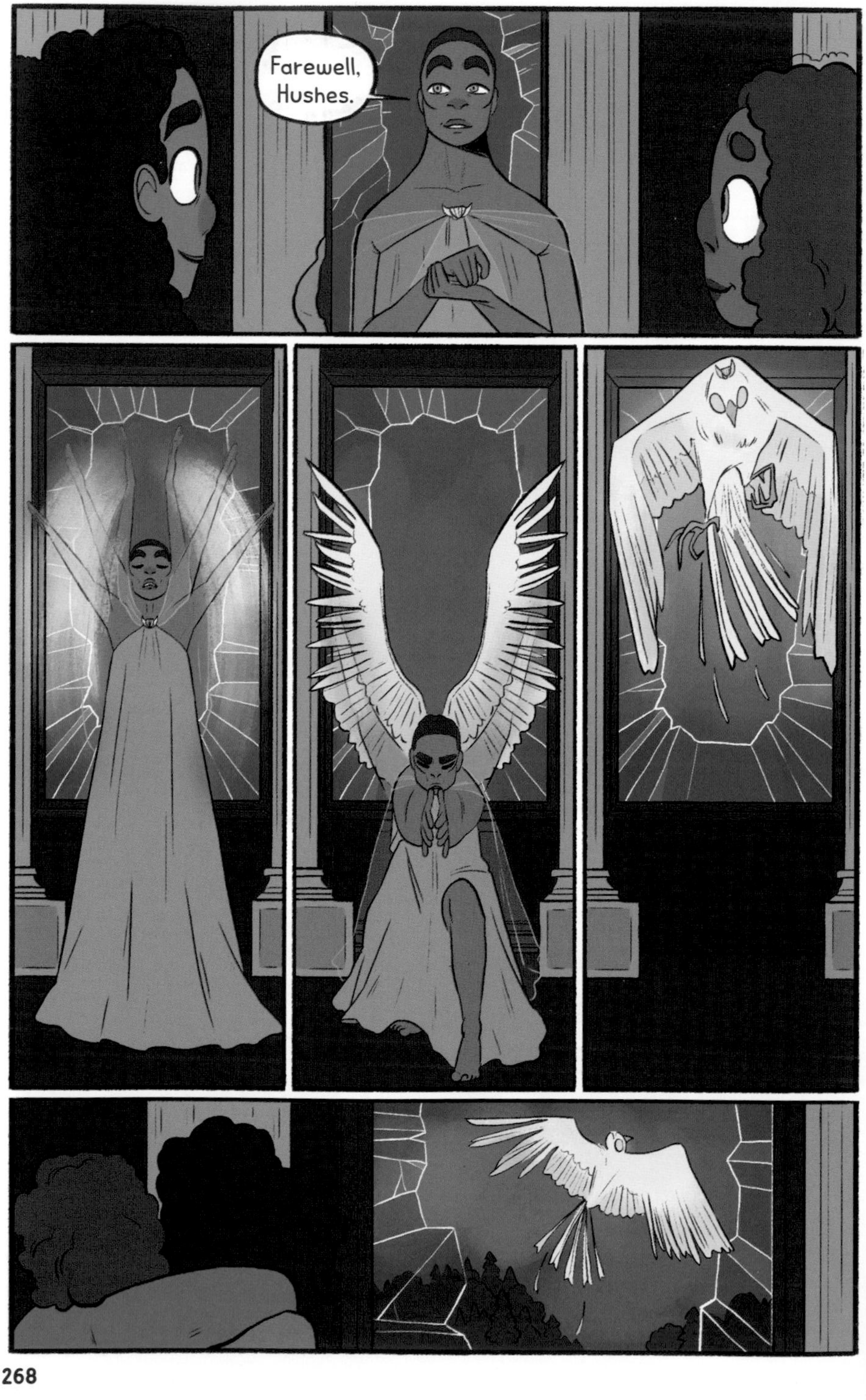
Farewell, Hushes.

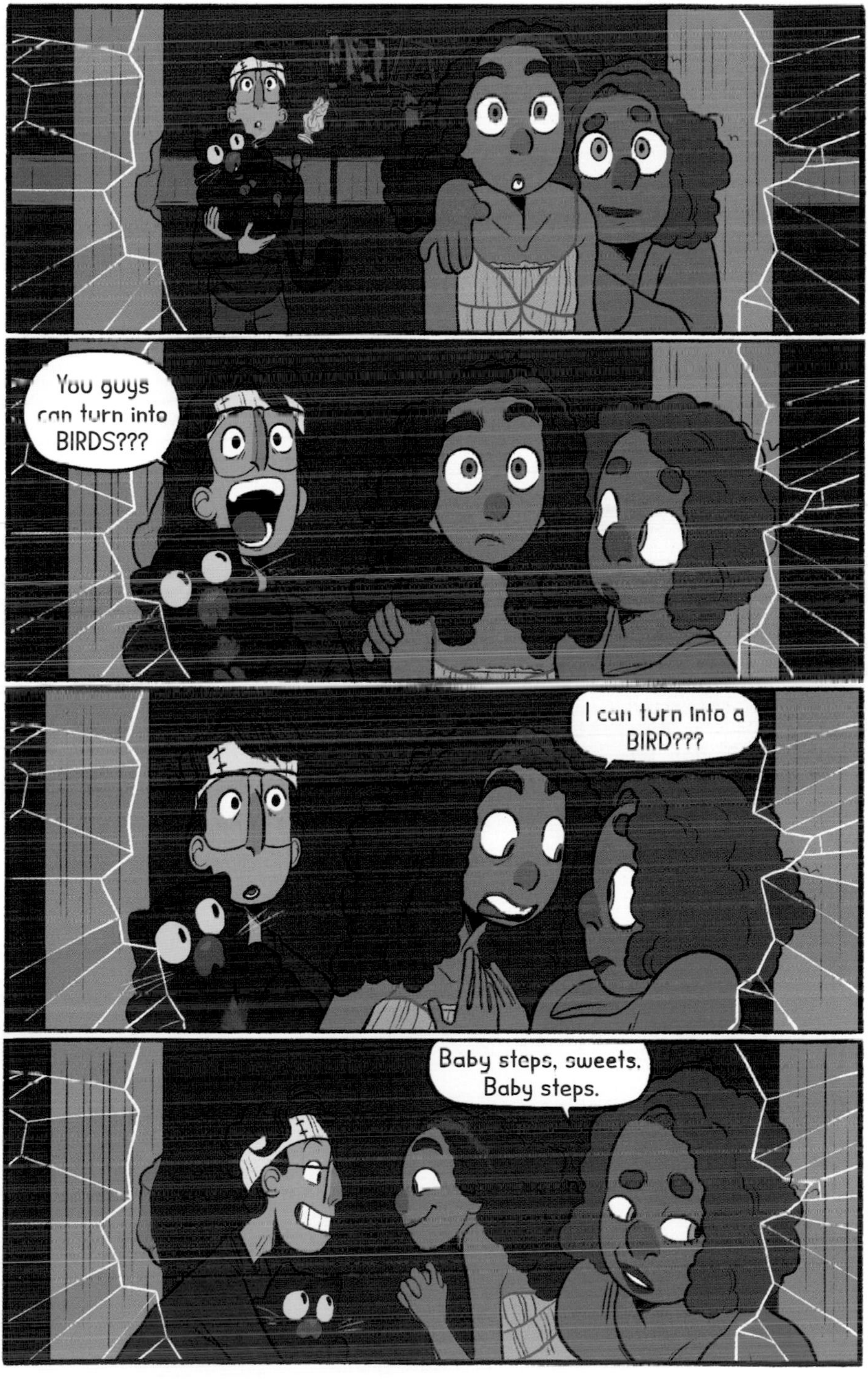
You guys can turn into BIRDS???
I can turn into a BIRD???
Baby steps, sweets. Baby steps.

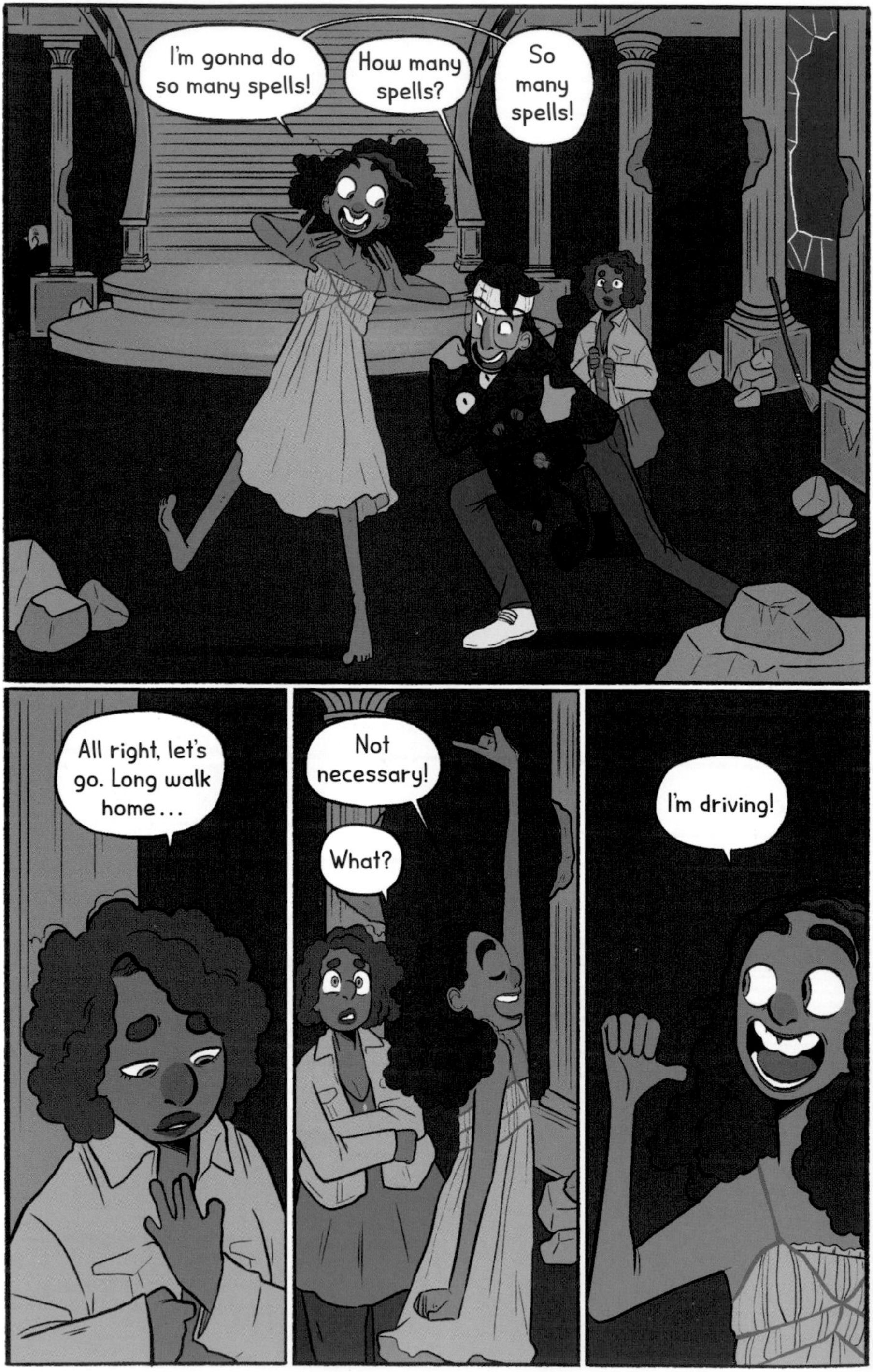
I'm gonna do so many spells!
How many spells?
So many spells!
All right, let's go. Long walk home...
Not necessary!
What?
I'm driving!

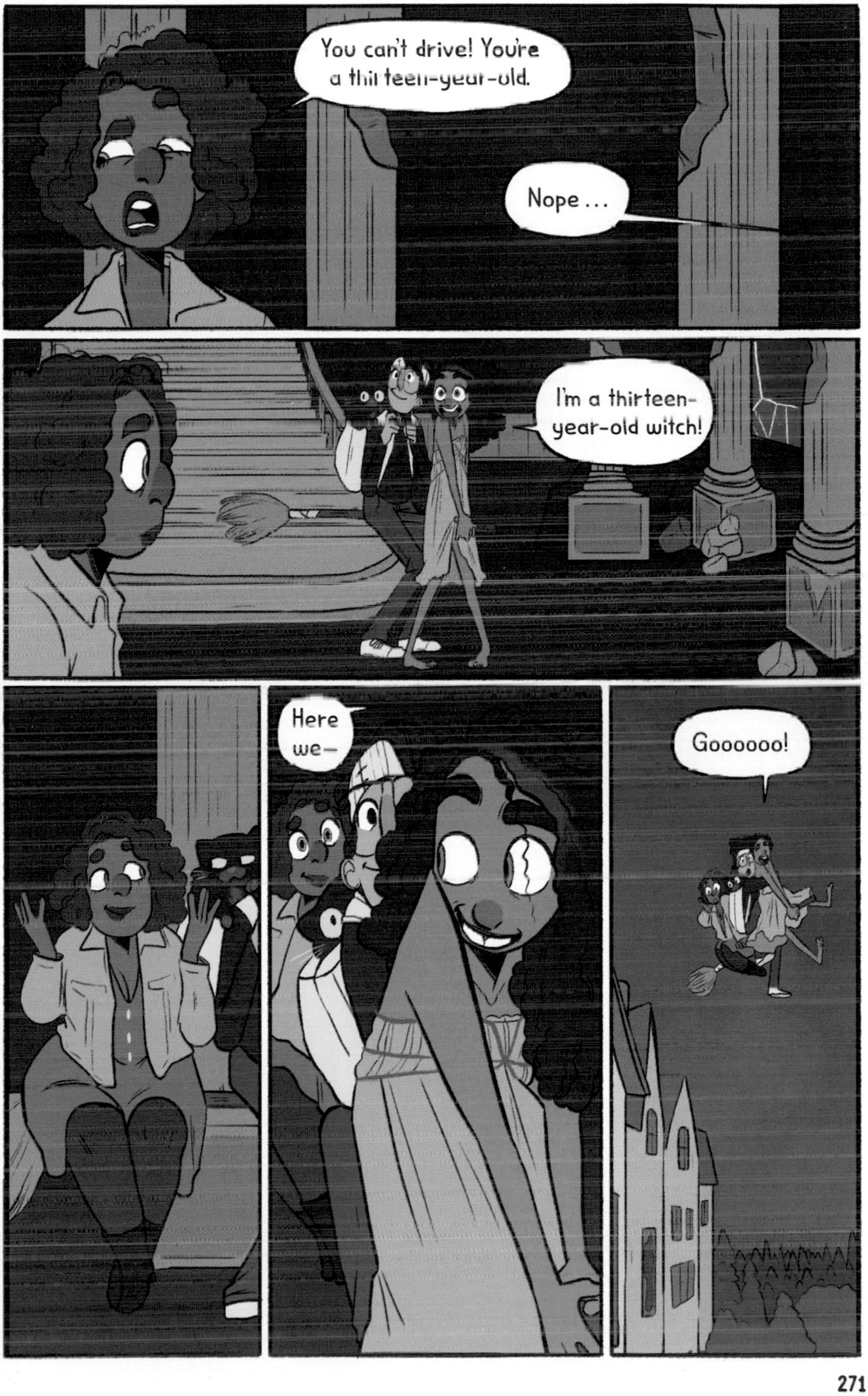
You can't drive! You're a thirteen-year-old.
Nope . . .
I'm a thirteen-year-old witch!
Here we—
Goooooo!

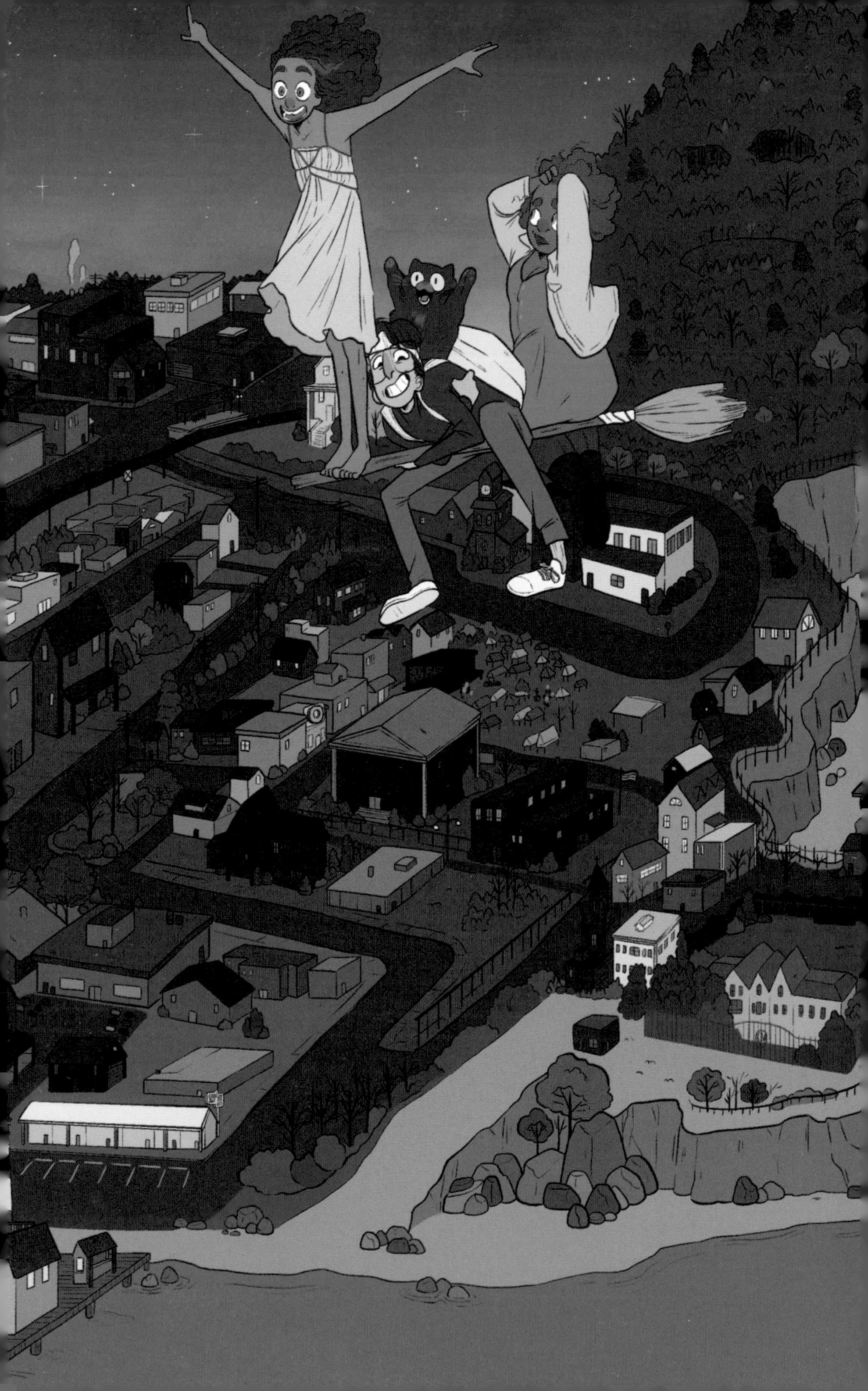